DARKOVER NOVELS IN OMNIBUS EDITIONS

HERITAGE AND EXILE
omnibus:
The Heritage of Hastur / Sharra's Exile

THE AGES OF CHAOS*
omnibus:
Stormqueen! / Hawkmistress!

THE SAGA OF THE RENUNCIATES*
omnibus:
The Shattered Chain / Thendara House / City of Sorcery

HERITAGE AND EXILE

THE HERITAGE OF HASTUR

SHARRA'S EXILE

Marion Zimmer Bradley

DAW BOOKS, INC.
DONALD A. WOLLHEIM, FOUNDER
375 Hudson Street, New York, NY 10014
ELIZABETH R. WOLLHEIM
SHEILA E. GILBERT
PUBLISHERS

Chapter Two of Book One of SHARRA'S EXILE appeared in a slightly different form, as a short story entitiled "Blood Will Tell" in THE KEEPER'S PRICE, edited by Marion Zimmer Bradley, DAW 1980.

Cover Art by Romas

ISBN: 978-0-7394-7706-9
DAW Books are distributed by Penguin Putnam Inc.

PRINTED IN THE U.S.A.

THE HERITAGE OF HASTUR

For Jaqueline Lichtenberg

Who convinced me that this book could and should be written, and kept after me until (and while) I wrote it.

SHARRA'S EXILE

To Walter Breen, whose extensive knowledge of the Darkover Universe is "extensive and peculiar" and to our son Patrick Breen, who read this page by page as it emerged from the typewriter, sometimes actually reading it over my shoulder as I wrote, in his eagerness to find out what happened next.
Thanks!

Storm Heights
Caer Donn
Darriel House
HELLERS
Carthon
RIVER
KILGHARD
GREAT NORTH ROAD
SEA OF DALEREUTH
Neskaya Tower
Serrais (Ridenow)
Edelweiss
CAVES OF CORRESANTI
Syrtis
Lake Mariposa
ARMIDA
Plateau of Armida
Lake of Hali
Old City
LOWLANDS OF VALERON
Lake Dembe
Trade City
THENDARA
Castle Elhalyn
Delta of Valeron
River of
Valeron (Aillards)

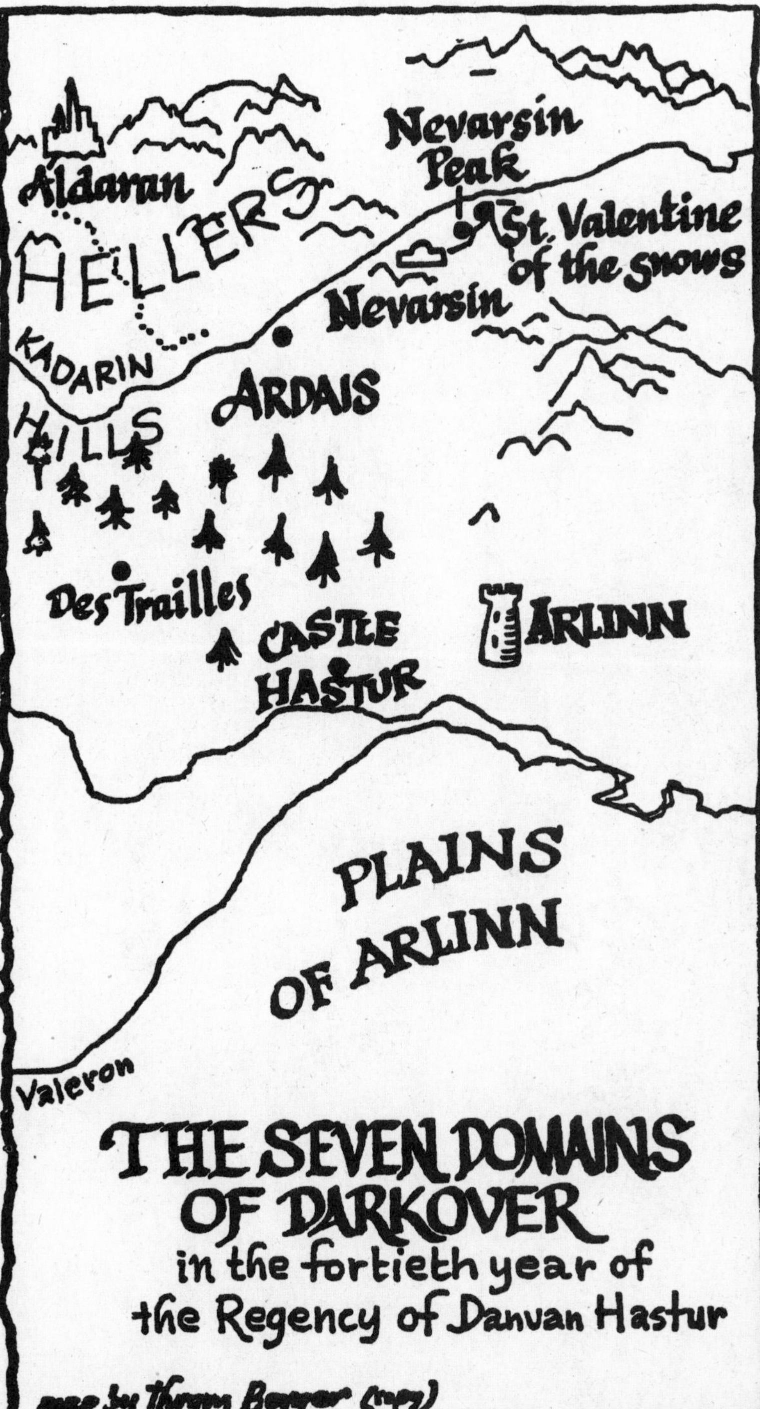

Aldaran
HELLERS
Nevarsin Peak
St. Valentine of the snows
Nevarsin
KADARIN
HILLS
ARDAIS
Des Trailles
CASTLE HASTUR
ARLINN
PLAINS OF ARLINN
Valeron
THE SEVEN DOMAINS OF DARKOVER
in the fortieth year of the Regency of Danvan Hastur

THE HERITAGE OF HASTUR

A Note From The Author

To the faithful followers of the chronicles of Darkover, whose greatest delight seems to be discovering even the most minute inconsistencies from book to book:

This book tells a story which a great many of the friends of Darkover have asked me to tell—the story of the early life of Regis Hastur, and of the Sharra rising, and of Lew Alton's first encounter with Marjorie Scott and the man who called himself Kadarin.

The faithful followers mentioned above will discover a very few minute inconsistencies between the account herein, and the story as Lew Alton told it later. I make no apology for these. The only explanation I can make is that in the years which elapsed between the events in this book, and the later novel dealing with the final destruction of the Sharra matrix, Lew's memories of these events may have altered his perceptions. Or, as I myself believe, the telepaths of the Arilinn Tower may have mercifully blurred his memories, to save his reason.

MARION ZIMMER BRADLEY

CHAPTER ONE

As the riders came up over the pass which led down into Thendara, they could see beyond the old city to the Terran spaceport. Huge and sprawling, ugly and unfamiliar to their eyes, it spread like some strange growth below them. And all around it, ringing it like a scab, were the tightly clustered buildings of the Trade City which had grown between old Thendara and the spaceport.

Regis Hastur, riding slowly between his escorts, thought that it was not as ugly as they had told him in Nevarsin. It had its own beauty, an austere beauty of steel towers and stark white buildings, each for some alien and unknown purpose. It was not a cancer on the face of Darkover, but a strange and not unbeautiful garment.

The central tower of the new headquarters building faced the Comyn Castle, which stood across the valley, with an unfortunate aspect. It appeared to Regis that the tall skyscraper and the old stone castle were squared off and facing one another like two giants armed for combat.

But he knew that was ridiculous. There had been peace between the Terran Empire and the Domains all of his lifetime. The Hasturs made sure of it.

But the thought brought him no comfort. He was not much of a Hastur, he considered, but he was the last. They would make the best of him even though he was a damned poor substitute for his father, and everyone knew it. They'd never let him forget it for a minute.

His father had died fifteen years ago, just a month before Regis had been born. Rafael Hastur had at thirty-five already shown signs of being a strong statesman and leader, deeply loved by his people, respected even by the Terrans. And he had been blown to bits in the Kilghard Hills, killed by contraband weapons smuggled from the Terran Empire. Cut off in the full strength of his youth and promise, he had left only an eleven-year-old daughter and a fragile, pregnant wife. Alanna Elhalyn-Hastur had nearly died of the shock of his death. She had clung fitfully to life only because she knew she was carrying the last of the Hasturs, the longed-for son of Rafael. She had lived, racked with grief, just long enough for Regis to be born alive; then, almost with relief, she had laid her life down.

And after losing his father, after all his mother went through, Regis thought, all they got was him, not the son they would have chosen. He was strong enough physically, even good-looking, but curiously handicapped for a son of the telepathic caste of the Domains, the Comyn. A nontelepath. At fifteen, if he had inherited laran power, he would have shown signs of it.

Behind him, he heard his bodyguards talking in low tones.

"I see they've finished their headquarters building. Hell of a place to put it, within a stone's throw of Comyn Castle."

"Well, they started to build it back in the Hellers, at Caer Donn. It was old Istvan Hastur, in my grandsire's time, who made them move the spaceport to Thendara. He must have had his reasons."

"Should have left it there, away from decent folk!"

"Oh, the Terrans aren't all bad. My brother keeps a shop in the Trade City. Anyway, would you want the *Terranan* back in the hills, where those mountain bandits and the damned Aldarans could deal with them behind our backs?"

"Damned savages," the second man said. "They don't even observe the Compact back there. You see them in the Hellers, wearing their filthy cowards' weapons."

"What would you expect of the Aldarans?" They lowered their voices, and Regis sighed. He was used to it. He put constraint on everyone, just by being what he was: Comyn and Hastur. They probably thought he could read their minds. Most Comyn could.

"Lord Regis," said one of his guards, "there's a party of riders coming down the northward road carrying banners. They must be the party from Armida, with Lord Alton. Shall we wait for them and ride together?"

Regis had no particular desire to join another party of Comyn lords, but it would have been an unthinkable breach of manners to say so. At Council season all the Domains met together at Thendara; Regis was bound by the custom of generations to treat them all as kinsmen and brothers. And the Altons *were* his kinsmen.

They slackened pace and waited for the other riders.

They were still high on the slopes, and he could see past Thendara to the spread-out spaceport itself. A great distant sound, like a faraway waterfall, made the ground vibrate like thunder, even where he stood. A tiny toylike form began to rise far out on the spaceport, slowly at first, then faster and faster. The sound peaked to a faint scream; the shape was a faraway streak, a dot, was gone.

Regis let his breath go. A starship of the Empire, outward bound for distant worlds, distant suns. . . . Regis realized his fists had clenched so tightly on the reins that his horse tossed its head, protesting. He slackened them and gave the horse an absentminded, apologetic pat on the neck. His eyes were still riveted on the spot in the sky where the starship had vanished.

Outward bound, free for the immeasurable immensities of space, the ship was headed to worlds whose wonders he, chained down here, could never guess. His throat felt tight. He wished he were not too old to cry, but the heir to Hastur could not make any display of unmanly emotion in public. He wondered why he was getting so worked up about this, but he knew the answer: that ship was going where he could never go.

The riders from the pass were nearer now; Regis could identify some of them. Next to his bannerman rode Kennard, Lord Alton, a stooped, heavy-set man with red hair going gray. Except for Danvan Hastur, Regent of the Comyn, Kennard was probably the most powerful man in the Seven Domains. Regis had known Kennard all his life; as a child, he had called him uncle. Behind him, among a whole assembly of kinsmen, servants, bodyguards and poor relations, he saw the banner of the Ardais Domain, so Lord Dyan must be with them.

One of Regis' guards said in an undertone, "I see the old buzzard has both his bastards with him. Wonder how he has the face?"

"Old Kennard can face anything, and make Hastur like it," returned the other man in a prison-yard mutter. "Anyway, young Lew's not a bastard; Kennard got him legitimated so he could work in the Arilinn Tower. The younger one—" The guard saw Regis glance his way and he stiffened; the expression slid off his face as if a sponge had wiped it blank.

Damn it, Regis thought irritably, I can't read your mind, man, I've just got good, normal ears. But in any case, he realized, he had overheard an insolent remark about a Comyn lord, and the guard would have been embarrassed about that. There was an old proverb: *The mouse in the walls may look at a cat, but he is wise not to squeak about it.*

Regis, of course, knew the old story. Kennard had done a shocking, even a shameful thing: he had taken, in honorable marriage, a half-Terran woman, kin to the renegade Domain of Aldaran. Comyn Council had never accepted the marriage or the sons. Not even for Kennard's sake.

Kennard rode toward Regis. "Greetings, Lord Regis. Are you riding to Council?"

Regis felt exasperated at the obviousness of the question—where else would he be going, on this road, at this season?—until he realized that the formal words implied recognition as an adult. He replied, with equally formal courtesy, "Yes, kinsman, my grandsire has requested that I attend council this year."

"Have you been all these years in the monastery at Nevarsin, kinsman?"

Kennard knew perfectly well where he had been, Regis reflected; when his grandfather couldn't think of any other way to get Regis off his hands, he packed him away to Saint-Valentine-of-the-Snows. But it would have been a fearful breach of manners to mention this before the assembly so he merely said, "Yes, he entrusted my education to the *cristoforos;* I have been there three years."

"Well, that was a hell of a way to treat the heir to Hastur," said a harsh, musical voice. Regis looked up and recognized Lord Dyan Ardais, a pale, tall, hawk-faced man he had seen making brief visits to the monastery. Regis bowed and greeted him. "Lord Dyan."

Dyan's eyes, keen and almost colorless—there was said to be *chieri* blood in the Ardais—rested on Regis. "I told Hastur that only a fool would send a boy to be brought up in that place. But I gathered that he was much occupied with affairs of state, such as settling all the troubles the *Terranan* have brought to our world. I offered to have you fostered at Ardais; my sister Elorie bore no living child and would have welcomed a kinsman to rear. But your grandsire, I gather, thought me no fit guardian for a boy your age." He gave a faint, sarcastic smile. "Well, you seem to have survived three years at the hands of the *cristoforos*. How was it in Nevarsin, Regis?"

"Cold." Regis hoped that settled that.

"How well I remember," Dyan said, laughing. "I was brought up by the brothers, too, you know. My father still had his wits then—or enough of them to keep me well out of sight of his various excesses. I spent the whole five years shivering."

Kennard lifted a gray eyebrow. "I don't remember that it was so cold."

"But you were warm in the guesthouse," Dyan said with a smile. "They keep fires there all year, and you could have had someone to warm your bed if you chose. The students' dormitory at Nevarsin—I give you my solemn word—is the coldest place on Darkover. Haven't you watched those poor brats shivering their way through the offices? Have they made a *cristoforo* of you, Regis?"

Regis said briefly, "No, I serve the Lord of Light, as is proper for a son of Hastur."

Kennard gestured to two lads in the Alton colors, and they rode forward a little way. "Lord Regis," he said formally, "I ask leave to present my sons: Lewis-Kennard Montray-Alton; Marius Montray-Lanart."

Regis felt briefly at a loss. Kennard's sons were not accepted by Council, but if Regis greeted them as kinsmen and equals, he would give them Hastur recognition. If not, he would affront his kinsman. He was angry at Kennard for making this choice necessary, especially when there was nothing about Comyn etiquette or diplomacy that Kennard did not know.

Lew Alton was a tall, sturdy young man, five or six years older than Regis. He said with a wry smile, "It's all right, Lord Regis, I was legitimated and formally designated heir a couple of years ago. It's quite permissible for you to be polite to me."

Regis felt his face flaming with embarrassment. He said, "Grandfather wrote me the news; I had forgotten. Greetings, cousin, have you been long on the road?"

"A few days," Lew said. "The road is peaceful, although my brother, I think, found it a long ride. He's very young for such a journey. You remember Marius, don't you?"

Regis realized with relief that Marius, called Montray-Lanart instead of Alton because he had not yet been accepted as a legitimate son, was only twelve years old—too young in any case for a formal greeting. The question could be sidestepped by treating him as a child. He said, "You've grown since I last saw you, Marius. I don't suppose you remember me at all. You're old enough now to ride a horse, at least. Do you still have the little gray pony you used to ride at Armida?"

Marius answered politely, "Yes, but he's out at pasture; he's old and lame, too old for such a trip."

Kennard looked annoyed. Diplomacy indeed! His grandfather would be proud of him, Regis considered, even if he was not proud of himself for the art of double tongues. Fortunately, Marius was not old enough to know he'd been snubbed. It occurred to Regis how ridiculous it was for boys their own age to address one another so formally anyway. Lew and he used to be close friends. The years at Armida, before Regis went to the monastery, they were as close as brothers. And now Lew was calling him Lord Regis! It was stupid!

Kennard looked at the sky. "Shall we ride on? It's near sunset and sure to rain. It would be a nuisance to have to stop and pack away the banners. And your grandfather will be eager to see you, Regis."

"My grandfather has been spared my presence for three years," Regis said dryly. "I am sure he can endure another hour or so. But it would be better not to ride in the dark."

Protocol said that Regis should ride beside Kennard and Lord Dyan, but instead he dropped back to ride beside Lew Alton. Marius was riding with a boy about Regis' own age, who looked so familiar that Regis frowned, trying to recall where they'd met.

While the entourage was getting into line, Regis sent his banner-bearer to ride at the head of the column with those of Ardais and Alton. He watched the man ride ahead with the silver-and-blue fir-tree emblem of Hastur and the *casta* slogan, *Permanedál. I shall remain,* he translated wearily, yes, I shall stay here and be a Hastur whether I like it or not.

Then rebellion gripped him again. Kennard hadn't stayed. He was educated on Terra itself, and by the will of the Council. Maybe there was hope for Regis too, Hastur or no.

He felt queerly lonely. Kennard's maneuvering for proper respect for his sons had irritated him, but it had touched him too. If his own father had lived, he wondered, would he have been so solicitous? Would he have schemed and intrigued to keep his son from feeling inferior?

Lew's face was grim, lonely and sullen. Regis couldn't tell if he felt slighted, ill-treated or just lonely, knowing himself different.

Lew said, "Are you coming to take a seat in Council, Lord Regis?"

The formality irritated Regis again. Was it a snub in return for the one he had given Marius? Suddenly he was tired of this. "You used to call me cousin, Lew. Are we too old to be friends?"

A quick smile lighted Lew's face. He was handsome without the sullen, withdrawn look. "Of course not, cousin. But I've had it rubbed into me, in the cadets and elsewhere, that you are Regis-Rafael, Lord Hastur, and I'm . . . well, I'm *nedestro* heir to Alton. They only accepted me because my father has no proper Darkovan sons. I decided that it was up to you whether or not you cared to claim kin."

Regis' mouth stretched in a grimace. He shrugged. "Well, they may have to accept me, but I might as well be a bastard. I haven't inherited *laran*."

Lew looked shocked. "But certainly, you—I was sure—" He broke off. "Just the same, you'll have a seat in Council, cousin. There *is* no other Hastur heir."

"I'm all too well aware of that. I've heard nothing else since the day I was born," Regis said. "Although, since Javanne married Gabriel Lanart, she's having sons like kittens. One of them may very well displace me some day."

"Still, you are in the direct line of male descent. A *laran* gift does skip a generation now and then. All your sons could inherit it."

Regis said with impulsive bitterness, "Do you think that helps—to know that I'm of no value for myself, but only for the sons I may have?"

A thin, fine drizzle of rain was beginning to fall. Lew

drew his hood up over his shoulders and the insignia of the City Guard showed on his cloak. So he's taking the regular duties of a Comyn heir, Regis thought. He may be a bastard, but he's more useful than I am.

Lew said aloud, as if picking up his thoughts, "I expect you'll be going into the cadet corps of the Guard this season, won't you? Or are the Hasturs exempt?"

"It's all planned out for us, isn't it, Lew? Ten years old, fire-watch duty. Thirteen or fourteen, the cadet corps. Take my turn as an officer. Take a seat in Council at the proper time. Marry the right woman, if they can find one from a family that's old enough and important enough and, above all, with *laran*. Father a lot of sons, and a lot of daughters to marry other Comyn sons. They've got our lives all planned, and all we have to do is go through the motions, ride their road whether we want to or not."

Lew looked uneasy, but he didn't answer. Obediently, like a proper prince, Regis drew a little ahead, to ride through the city gates in his proper place beside Kennard and Lord Dyan. His head was getting wet but, he thought sourly, it was his duty to be seen, to be put on display. A little thing like a soaking wasn't supposed to bother a Hastur.

He forced himself to smile and wave graciously at the crowds lining the streets. But far away, through the very ground, he could hear again the dull vibration, like a waterfall. The starships were still there, he told himself, and the stars beyond them. No matter how deep they cut the track, I'll find a way to break loose somehow. Someday.

CHAPTER TWO

(Lewis-Kennard Montray-Alton's narrative)

I hadn't wanted to attend Council this year. To be exact, I never wanted to attend Council at all. That's putting it mildly. I'm not popular with my father's equals in the Seven Domains.

At Armida, nothing bothers me. The house-folk know who I am and the horses don't care. And at Arilinn nobody inquires about your family, your pedigree or your legitimacy. The only thing that matters in a Tower is your ability to manipulate a matrix and key into the energon rings and relay screens. If you're competent, no one cares whether you were born between silk sheets in a great house or in a ditch beside the road; and if you're not competent, you don't come there at all.

You may ask why, if I was good at managing the estate at Armida, and more than adequate in the matrix relays at Arilinn, Father had this flea in his brain about forcing me on the Council. You may ask, but you'll have to ask someone else. I have no idea.

Whatever his reasons, he had managed to force me on the Council as his heir. They hadn't liked it, but they'd had to allow me the legitimate privileges of a Comyn heir and the duties that went with them. Which meant that at fourteen I had gone into the cadets and, after serving as a junior officer, was now a captain in the City Guard. It was a privilege I could have done without. The Council lords might be forced to accept me. But making the younger sons, lesser nobles and so forth who served in the cadets accept me—that was another song!

Bastardy, of course, is no special disgrace. Plenty of Comyn lords have half a dozen. If one of them turns out to have *laran*—which is what every woman who bears a child to a Comyn lord hopes for—nothing is easier than having the child acknowledged and given privileges and duties somewhere in the Domains. But to make one of them the heir-designate to the Domain, *that* was unprecedented, and every unacknowledged son of a minor line made me feel how little I merited this special treatment.

I couldn't help knowing why they felt that way—I had what every one of them wanted, felt he merited as much as I did. But understanding only made things worse. It must be comfortable never to know *why* you're disliked. Maybe then you can believe you don't deserve it.

Just the same, I've made sure none of them could complain about me. I've done a little of everything, as Comyn heirs in the cadets are supposed to: I've supervised street patrols, organizing everything from grain supplies for the pack animals to escorts for Comyn ladies; I've assisted the armsmaster at his job, and made sure that the man who cleaned the barracks knew *his* job. I disliked serving in the cadets and didn't enjoy command duty in the Guard. But what could I do? It was a mountain I could neither cross nor go around. Father needed me and wanted me, and I could not let him stand alone.

As I rode at Regis Hastur's side, I wondered if his choosing to ride beside me had been a mark of friendship or a shrewd attempt to get on the good side of my father. Three years ago I'd have said friendship, certainly. But boys change in three years, and Regis had changed more than most.

He'd spent a few winters at Armida before he went to the monastery, before I went to Arilinn. I'd never thought about him being heir to Hastur. They said his health was frail; old Hastur thought that country living and company would do him good. He'd mostly been left to me to look after. I'd taken him riding and hawking, and he'd gone with me up into the plateaus when the great herds of wild horses were caught and brought down to be broken. I remembered him best as an undersized youngster, following me around, wearing my outgrown breeches and shirts because he kept growing out of his own; playing with the puppies and newborn foals, bending solemnly over the clumsy stitches he was learning to set in hawking-hoods, learning swordplay from Father and practicing with me. During the terrible spring of his twelfth year, when the Kilghard Hills had gone up in forest fires and every able-bodied man between ten and eighty was commandeered into the fire-lines, we'd gone together, working side by side by day, eating from one bowl and sharing blankets at night. We'd been afraid Armida itself would go up in the holocaust; some of the outbuildings were lost in the backfire. We'd been closer than brothers. When he went to Nevarsin, I'd missed him terribly. It was difficult to reconcile my memories of that almost-brother with this self-possessed, solemn young prince. Maybe he'd learned, in the interval, that friendship with Kennard's *nedestro* heir was not quite the thing for a Hastur.

I could have found out, of course, and he'd never have known. But that's not even a temptation for a telepath, after the first few months. You learn not to pry.

But he didn't *feel* unfriendly, and presently asked me outright why I hadn't called him by name; caught off guard by the blunt question, I gave him a straight answer instead of a diplomatic one and then, of course, we were all right again.

Once we were inside the gates, the ride to the castle was not long, just long enough to get thoroughly drenched. I could tell that Father was aching with the damp and cold—he's been lame ever since I could remember, but the last few winters have been worse—and that Marius was wet and wretched. When we came into the lee of the castle it was already dark, and though the nightly rain rarely turns to snow at this season, there were sharp slashes of sleet in it. I slid from my horse and went quickly to help Father dismount, but Lord Dyan had already helped him down and given him his arm.

I withdrew. From my first year in the cadets, I'd made it a habit not to get any closer to Lord Dyan than I could possibly help. Preferably well out of reach.

There's a custom in the Guards for first-year cadets. We're trained in unarmed combat and we're supposed to cultivate a habit of being watchful at all times; so during our first season, in the guardroom and armory, anyone superior to us in the Guards is allowed to take us by surprise, if he can, and throw us. It's good training. After a few weeks of being grabbed unexpectedly from behind and dumped hard on a stone floor, you develop something like eyes in the back of your head. Usually it's fairly good-natured, and although it's a rough game and you collect plenty of bruises, no one really minds.

Dyan, we all agreed, enjoyed it entirely too much. He was an expert wrestler and could have made his point without doing much harm, but he was unbelievably rough and never missed a chance to hurt somebody. Especially me. Once he somehow managed to dislocate my elbow, which I wore in a sling for the rest of that season. He said it was an accident, but I'm a telepath and he didn't even bother to conceal how much he had enjoyed doing it. I wasn't the only cadet who had that experience. During cadet training, there are times when you hate all your officers. But Dyan was the only one we really feared.

I left Father to him and went back to Regis. "Someone's looking for you," I told him, pointing out a man in Hastur livery, sheltering in a doorway and looking wet and miserable, as if he'd been out in the weather, waiting, for some time. Regis turned eagerly to hear the message.

"The Regent's compliments, Lord Regis. He has been urgently called into the city. He asks you to make yourself comfortable and to see him in the morning."

Regis made some formal answer and turned to me with a humorless smile. "So much for the eager welcome of my loving grandsire."

One hell of a welcome, indeed, I thought. No one could expect the Regent of Comyn to stand out in the rain and wait, but he could have sent more than a servant's message! I said quickly, "You'll come to us, of course. Send a message with your grandfather's man and come along for some dry clothing and some supper!"

Regis nodded without speaking. His lips were blue with cold, his hair lying soaked on his forehead. He gave appropriate orders, and I went back to my own task: making sure that all of Father's entourage, servants, bodyguards, Guardsmen, banner-bearers and poor relations, found their way to their appointed places.

Things gradually got themselves sorted out. The Guardsmen went off to their own quarters. The servants mostly knew what to do. Someone had sent word ahead to have fires lighted and the rooms ready for occupancy. The rest of us found our way through the labyrinth of halls and corridors to the quarters reserved, for the last dozen generations, to the Alton lords. Before long no one was left in the main hall of our quarters except Father, Marius and myself, Regis, Lord Dyan, our personal servants and half a dozen others. Regis was standing before the fire warming his hands. I remembered the night when Father had broken the news that he was to leave us and spend the next three years at Nevarsin. He and I had been sitting before the fire in the great hall at Armida, cracking nuts and throwing the shells into the fire; after Father finished speaking he had gone to the fire and stood there just like that, quenched and shivering, his face turned away from us all.

Damn the old man! Was there no friend, no kinswoman, he could send to welcome Regis home?

Father came to the fire. He was limping badly. He looked at Marius' riding companion and said, "Danilo, I had your things sent directly to the cadet barracks. Shall I send a man to show you the way, or do you think you can find it?"

"There's no need to send anyone, Lord Alton." Danilo Syrtis came away from the fire and bowed courteously. He was a slender, bright-eyed boy of fourteen or so, wearing shabby garments which I vaguely recognized as once having been my brother's or mine, long outgrown. That was like Father; he'd make sure that any protégé of his started with the proper outfit for a cadet. Father laid a hand on his shoulder. "You're sure? Well, then, run along, my lad, and good luck go with you."

Danilo, with a polite formula murmured vaguely at all of us, withdrew. Dyan Ardais, warming his hands at the fire, looked after him, eyebrows lifted. "Nice looking youngster. Another of your *nedestro* sons, Kennard?"

"Dani? Zandru's hells, no! I'd be proud enough to claim him, but truly he's none of mine. The family has Comyn blood, a few generations back, but they're poor as miser's mice; old Dom Felix couldn't give him a good start in life, so I got him a cadet commission."

Regis turned away from the fire and said, "Danilo! I knew I should have recognized him; he was at the monastery one year. I truly couldn't remember his name, Uncle. I should have greeted him!"

The word he used for *uncle* was the *casta* term slightly more intimate than *kinsman*: I knew he had been speaking to my father, but Dyan chose to take it as addressed to himself. "You'll see him in the cadets, surely. And I haven't greeted you properly, either." He came and took Regis in a kinsman's embrace, pressing his cheek, to which Regis submitted, a little flustered; then, holding him at arm's length, Dyan looked closely at him. "Does your sister hate you for being the beauty of the family, Regis?"

Regis looked startled and a little embarrassed. He said, laughing nervously, "Not that she ever told me. I suspect Javanne thinks I should be running around in a pinafore."

"Which proves what I have always said, that women are no judge of beauty." My father gave him a black scowl and said, "Damn it, Dyan, don't tease him."

Dyan would have said more—damn the man, was he starting that again, after all the trouble last year—but a servant in Hastur livery came in quickly and said, "Lord Alton, a message from the Regent."

Father tore the letter open, began to swear volubly in three languages. He told the messenger to wait while he got into some dry clothes, disappeared into his room, and then I heard him shouting to Andres. Soon he came out, tucking a dry shirt into dry breeches, and scowling angrily.

"Father, what is it?"

"The usual," he said grimly, "trouble in the city. Hastur's summoned every available Council elder and sending two extra patrols. Evidently a crisis of some sort."

Damn, I thought. After the long ride from Armida and a soaking, to call him out at night . . . "Will you need me, Father?"

He shook his head. "No. Not necessary, son. Don't wait up, I'll probably be out all night." As he went out, Dyan said, "I expect a similar summons awaits me in my own rooms; I had better go and find out. Good night, lads. I envy you your good night's sleep." He added, with a nod to Regis, "These others will never appreciate a proper bed. Only we who have slept on stone know how to do that." He managed to make a deep formal bow to Regis and simultaneously ignore me completely—it wasn't easy when we were standing side by side—and went away.

I looked around to see what remained to be settled. I sent Marius to change out of his drenched clothes—too old for a nanny and too young for an aide-de-camp, he's left to me much of the time. Then I arranged to have a room made ready for Regis. "Have you a man to dress you, Regis? Or shall I have father's body-servant wait on you tonight?"

"I learned to look after myself at Nevarsin," Regis said. He looked warmer now, less tense. "If the Regent is sending for all the Council, I suspect it's really serious and not just that Grandfather has forgotten me again. That makes me feel better."

Now I was free to get out of my own wet things. "When you've changed, Regis, we'll have dinner here in front of the fire. I'm not officially on duty till tomorrow morning."

I went and changed quickly into indoor clothing, slid my feet into fur lined ankle-boots and looked briefly in on Marius; I found him sitting up in bed, eating hot soup and already half asleep. It was a long ride for a boy his age. I wondered again why Father had subjected him to it.

The servants had set up a hot meal before the fire, in front of the old stone seats there. The lights in our part of the castle are the old ones, luminous rock from deep caves which charge with light all day and give off a soft glow all night. Not enough for reading or fine needlework, but plenty for a quiet meal and a comfortable talk by firelight. Regis came back, in dry garments and indoor boots, and I gestured the old steward away. "Go and get your own supper; Lord Regis and I can wait on ourselves."

I took the covers off the dishes. They had sent in a fried fowl and some vegetable stew. I helped him, saying, "Not very festive, but probably the best they could do at short notice."

"It's better than we got on the fire-lines," Regis said and I grinned. "So you remember that too?"

"How could I forget it? Armida was like home to me. Does Kennard still break his own horses, Lew?"

"No, he's far too lame," I said, and wondered again how Father would manage in the coming season. Selfishly, I hoped he would be able to continue in command. It's hereditary to the Altons, and I was next in line for it. They had learned to tolerate me as his deputy, holding captain's rank. As commander, I'd have all those battles to fight again.

We talked for a little while about Armida, about horses

and hawks, while Regis finished the stew in his bowl. He picked up an apple and went to the fireplace, where a pair of antique swords, used only in the sword-dance now, hung over the mantel. He touched the hilt of one and I asked, "Have you forgotten all your fencing in the monastery, Regis?"

"No, there were some of us who weren't to be monks, so Father Master gave us leave to practice an hour every day, and an arms-master came to give us lessons."

Over wine we discussed the state of the roads from Nevarsin.

"Surely you didn't ride in one day from the monastery?"

"Oh, no. I broke my journey at Edelweiss."

That was on Alton lands. When Javanne Hastur married Gabriel Lanart, ten years ago, my father had leased them the estate. "Your sister is well, I hope?"

"Well enough, but extremely pregnant just now," Regis said, "and Javanne's done a ridiculous thing. It made sense to call their first son Rafael, after her father and mine. And the second, of course, is the younger Gabriel. But when she named the third Mikhail, she made the whole thing absurd. I believe she's praying frantically for a girl this time!"

I laughed. By all accounts the "Lanart angels" should be named for the archfiends, not the archangels; and why should a Hastur seek names from *cristoforo* mythology? "Well, she and Gabriel have sons enough."

"True. I am sure my grandfather is annoyed that she should have so many sons, and cannot give them Domain-right in Hastur. And I should have told Kennard; her husband will be here in a few days to take his place in the Guard. He would have ridden with me, but with Javanne so near to her time, he got leave to remain with her till she is delivered."

I nodded; of course he would stay. Gabriel Lanart was a minor noble of the Alton Domain, a kinsman of our own, and a telepath. Of course he would follow the custom of the Domains, that a man shares with his child's mother the ordeal of birth, staying in rapport with her until the child is born and all is well. Well, we could spare him for a few days. A good man, Gabriel.

"Dyan seemed to take it for granted that you would be in the cadets this year," I said.

"I don't know if I'll have a choice. Did you?"

I hadn't, of course. But that the heir to Hastur, of all people, should question it—that made me uneasy.

Regis sat on the stone bench, restlessly scuffing his felt ankle-boots on the floor. "Lew, you're part Terran and yet you're Comyn. Do you feel as if you belonged to us? Or to the Terrans?"

A disturbing question, an outrageous question, and one I had never dared ask myself. I felt angry at him for speaking it, as if taunting me with what I was. Here I was an alien; among the Terrans, a freak, a mutant, a telepath. I said at last, bitterly, "I've never belonged anywhere. Except, perhaps, at Arilinn."

Regis raised his face, and I was startled at the sudden anguish there. "Lew, what does it feel like to have *laran*?"

I stared at him, disconcerted. The question touched off another memory. That summer at Armida, in his twelfth year. Because of his age, and because there was no one else, it had fallen to me to answer certain questions usually left to fathers or elder brothers, to instruct him in certain facts proper to adolescents. He had blurted those questions out, too, with the same kind of half-embarrassed urgency, and I'd found it just as difficult to answer them. There are some things it's almost impossible to discuss with someone who hasn't shared the experience. I said at last, slowly, "I hardly know how to answer. I've had it so long, it would be harder to imagine what it feels like *not* to have *laran*."

"Were you born with it, then?"

"No, no, of course not. But when I was ten, or eleven, I began to be aware of what people were feeling. Or thinking. Later my father found out—proved to them—that I had the Alton gift, and that's rare even—" I set my teeth and said it, "even in legitimate sons. After that, they couldn't deny me Comyn rights."

"Does it always come so early? Ten, eleven?"

"Have you never been tested? I was almost certain . . ." I felt a little confused. At least once during the shared fears of that last season together, on the fire-lines, I had touched his mind, sensed that he had the gift of our caste. But he had been very young then. And the Alton gift is forced rapport, even with non-telepaths.

"Once," said Regis, "about three years ago. The *leronis*

said I had the potential, as far as she could tell, but she could not reach it."

I wondered if that was why the Regent had sent him to Nevarsin: either hoping that discipline, silence and isolation would develop his *laran,* which sometimes happened, or trying to conceal his disappointment in his heir.

"You're a licensed matrix mechanic, aren't you, Lew? What's that like?"

This I could answer. "You know what a matrix is: a jewel stone that amplifies the resonances of the brain and transmutes psi power into energy. For handling major forces, it demands a group of linked minds, usually in a tower circle."

"I know what a matrix is," he said. "They gave me one when I was tested." He showed it to me, hung, as most of us carried them, in a small silk-lined leather bag about his neck. "I've never used it, or even looked at it again. In the old days, I know, they made these mind-links through the Keepers. They don't have Keepers any more, do they?"

"Not in the old sense," I said, "although the woman who works centerpolar in the matrix circles is still called a Keeper. In my father's time they discovered that a Keeper could function, except at the very highest levels, without all the old taboos and terrible training, the sacrifice, isolation, special cloistering. His foster-sister Cleindori was the first to break the tradition, and they don't train Keepers in the old way any more. It's too difficult and dangerous, and it's not fair to ask anyone to give up their whole lives to it any more. Now everyone spends three years or less at Arilinn, and then spends the same amount of time outside, so that they can learn to live normal lives." I was silent, thinking of my circle at Arilinn, now scattered to their homes and estates. I had been happy there, useful, accepted. Competent. Some day I would go back to this work again, in the relays.

"What it's like," I continued, "it's—it's intimate. You're completely open to the members of your circle. Your thoughts, your very feelings affect them, and you're wholly vulnerable to theirs. It's more than the closeness of blood kin. It's not exactly love. It's not sexual desire. It's like—like living with your skin off. Twice as tender to everything. It's not like anything else."

His eyes were rapt. I said harshly, "Don't romanticize it.

It can be wonderful, yes. But it can be sheer hell. Or both at once. You learn to keep your distance, just to survive."

Through the haze of his feelings I could pick up just a fraction of his thoughts. I was trying to keep my awareness of him as low as possible. He was, damn it, too vulnerable. He was feeling forgotten, rejected, alone. I couldn't help picking it up. But a boy his age would think it prying.

"Lew, the Alton gift is the ability to force rapport. If I do have *laran,* could you open it up, make it function?"

I looked at him in dismay. "You fool. Don't you know I could kill you that way?"

"Without *laran,* my life doesn't amount to much." He was as taut as a strung bow. Try as I might, I could not shut out the terrible hunger in him to be part of the only world he knew, not to be so desperately deprived of his heritage.

It was my own hunger. I had felt it, it seemed, since my birth. Yet nine months before my birth, my father had made it impossible for me to belong wholly to his world and mine.

I faced the torture of knowing that, deeply as I loved my father, I hated him, too. Hated him for making me bastard, half-caste, alien, belonging nowhere. I clenched my fists, looking away from Regis. He had what I could never have. He belonged, full Comyn, by blood and law, legitimate—

And yet he was suffering, as much as I was. Would I give up *laran* to be legitimate, accepted, belonging?

"Lew, will you try at least?"

"Regis, if I killed you, I'd be guilty of murder." His face turned white. "Frightened? Good. It's an insane idea. Give it up, Regis. Only a catalyst telepath can ever do it safely and I'm not one. As far as I know, there are no catalyst telepaths alive now. Let well enough alone."

Regis shook his head. He said, forcing the words through a dry mouth. "Lew, when I was twelve years old you called me *bredu.* There is no one else, no one I can ask for this. I don't care if it kills me. I have heard"—he swallowed hard—"that *bredin* have an obligation, one to the other. Was it only an idle word, Lew?"

"It was no idle word, *bredu,*" I muttered, wrung with his pain, "but we were children then. And this is no child's play, Regis, it's your life."

"Do you think I don't know that?" He was stammering. "It *is* my life. At least it can make the difference in what my life will be." His voice broke. "*Bredu* . . ." he said again and was silent, and I knew it was because he could not go on without weeping.

The appeal left me defenseless to him. Try as I might to stay aloof, that helpless, choked "*Bredu* . . ." had broken my last defense. I knew I was going to do what he wanted. "I can't do what was done to me," I told him. "That's a specific test for the Alton gift—forcing rapport—and only a full Alton can live through it. My father tried it, just once, with my full knowledge that it might very well kill me, and only for about thirty seconds. If the gift hadn't bred true, I'd have died. The fact that I didn't die was the only way he could think of to prove to Council that they could not refuse to accept me." My voice wavered. Even after almost ten years, I didn't like thinking about it. "Your blood, or your paternity, isn't in question. You don't need to take that kind of risk."

"*You* were willing to take it."

I had been. Time slid out of focus, and once again I stood before my father, his hands touching my temples, living again that memory of terror, that searing agony. I had been willing because I had shared my father's anguish, the terrible need in him to know I was his true son—the knowledge that if he could not force Council to accept me as his son, life alone was worth nothing. I would rather have died, just then, than live to face the knowledge of failure.

Memory receded. I looked into Regis' eyes.

"I'll do what I can. I can test you, as I was tested at Arilinn. But don't expect too much. I'm not a *leronis,* only a technician."

I drew a long breath. "Show me your matrix."

He fumbled with the strings at the neck, tipped the stone out in his palm, held it out to me. That told me as much as I needed to know. The lights in the small jewel were dim, inactive. If he had worn it for three years and his *laran* was active, he would have rough-keyed it even without knowing it. The first test had failed, then.

As a final test, with excruciating care, I laid a fingertip against the stone; he did not flinch. I signaled to him to put it away, loosened the neck of the case of my own. I laid my matrix, still wrapped in the insulating silk, in the palm of my hand, then bared it carefully.

"Look into this. No, don't touch it," I warned, with a drawn breath. "Never touch a keyed matrix; you could throw me into shock. Just look into it."

Regis bent, focused with motionless intensity on the tiny ribbons of moving light inside the jewel. At last he looked away. Another bad sign. Even a latent telepath should have had enough energon patterns disrupted inside his brain to show *some* reaction: sickness, nausea, causeless euphoria. I asked cautiously, not wanting to suggest anything to him, "How do you feel?"

"I'm not sure," he said uneasily. "It hurt my eyes."

Then he had at least latent *laran*. Arousing it, though, might be a difficult and painful business. Perhaps a catalyst telepath could have roused it. They had been bred for that work, in the days when Comyn did complex and life-shattering work in the higher-level matrices. I'd never known one. Perhaps the set of genes was extinct.

Just the same, as a latent, he deserved further testing. I knew he had the potential. I had known it when he was twelve years old.

"Did the *leronis* test you with *kirian*?" I asked.

"She gave me a little. A few drops."

"What happened?"

"It made me sick," Regis said, "dizzy. Flashing colors in front of my eyes. She said I was probably too young for much reaction, that in some people, *laran* developed later."

I thought that over. *Kirian* is used to lower the resistance against telepathic contact; it's used in treating empaths and other psi technicians who, without much natural telepathic gift, must work directly with other telepaths. It can sometimes ease fear or deliberate resistance to telepathic contact. It can also be used, with great care, to treat threshold sickness—that curious psychic upheaval which often seizes on young telepaths at adolescence.

Well, Regis seemed young for his age. He might simply be developing the gift late. But it rarely came as late as this. Damn it, I'd been positive. Had some event at Nevarsin, some emotional shock, made him block awareness of it?

"I could try that again," I said tentatively. The *kirian*

might actually trigger latent telepathy; or perhaps, under its influence, I could reach his mind, without hurting him too much, and find out if he was deliberately blocking awareness of *laran*. It did happen, sometimes.

I didn't like using *kirian*. But a small dose couldn't do much worse than make him sick, or leave him with a bad hangover. And I had the distinct and not very pleasant feeling that if I cut off his hopes now, he might do something desperate. I didn't like the way he was looking at me, taut as a bowstring, and shaking, not much, but from head to foot. His voice cracked a little as he said, "I'll try." All too clearly, what I heard was, *I'll try anything*.

I went to my room for it, already berating myself for agreeing to this lunatic experiment. It simply meant too much to him. I weighed the possibility of giving him a sedative dose, one that would knock him out or keep him safely drugged and drowsy till morning. But *kirian* is too unpredictable. The dose which puts one person to sleep like a baby at the breast may turn another into a frenzied berserker, raging and hallucinating. Anyway, I'd promised; I wouldn't deceive him now. I'd play it safe though, give him the same cautious minimal dose we used with strange psi technicians at Arilinn. This much *kirian* couldn't hurt him.

I measured him a careful few drops in a wineglass. He swallowed it, grimacing at the taste, and sat down on one of the stone benches. After a minute he covered his eyes. I watched carefully. One of the first signs was the dilation of the pupils of the eyes. After a few minutes he began to tremble, leaning against the back of the seat as if he feared he might fall. His hands were icy cold. I took his wrist lightly in my fingers. Normally I hate touching people; telepaths do, except in close intimacy. At the touch he looked up and whispered, "Why are you angry, Lew?"

Angry? Did he interpret my fear for him as anger? I said, "Not angry, only worried about you. *Kirian* isn't anything to play with. I'm going to try and touch you now. Don't fight me if you can help it."

I gently reached for contact with his mind. I wouldn't use the matrix for this; under *kirian* I might probe too far and damage him. I first sensed sickness and confusion—that was the drug, no more—then a deathly weariness and physical tension, probably from the long ride, and finally an overwhelming sense of desolation and loneliness, which made me want to turn away from his despair. Hesitantly, I risked a somewhat deeper contact.

And met a perfect, locked defense, a blank wall. After a moment, I probed sharply. The Alton gift was forced rapport, even with nontelepaths. He wanted this, and if I could give it to him, then he could probably endure being hurt. He moaned and moved his head as if I was hurting him. Probably I was. The emotions were still blurring everything. Yes, he had *laran* potential. But he'd blocked it. Completely.

I waited a moment and considered. It's not so uncommon; some telepaths live all their lives that way. There's no reason they shouldn't. Telepathy, as I told him, is far from an unmixed blessing. But occasionally it yielded to a slow, patient unraveling. I retreated to the outer layer of his consciousness again and asked, not in words, *What is it you're afraid to know, Regis? Don't block it. Try to remember what it is you couldn't bear to know. There was a time when you could do this knowingly. Try to remember. . . .*

It was the wrong thing. He had received my thought; I felt the response to it—a clamshell snapping rigidly shut, a sensitive plant closing its leaves. He wrenched his hands roughly from mine, covering his eyes again. He muttered, "My head hurts. I'm sick, I'm so sick. . . ."

I had to withdraw. He had effectively shut me out. Possibly a skilled, highly-trained Keeper could have forced her way through the resistance without killing him. But I couldn't force it. I might have battered down the barrier, forced him to face whatever it was he'd buried, but he might very well crack completely, and whether he could ever be put together again was a very doubtful point.

I wondered if he understood that he had done this to himself. Facing that kind of knowledge was a terribly painful process. At the time, building that barrier must have seemed the only way to save his sanity, even if it meant paying the agonizing price of cutting off his entire psi potential with it. My own Keeper had once explained it to me with the example of the creature who, helplessly caught in a trap, gnaws off the trapped foot, choosing maiming to death. Sometimes there were layers and layers of such barricades.

The barrier, or inhibition, might some day dissolve of itself, releasing his potential. Time and maturity could do a lot. It might be that some day, in the deep intimacy of love, he would find himself free of it. Or—I faced this too—it might be that this barrier was genuinely necessary to his life and sanity, in which case it would endure forever, or, if it were somehow broken down, there would not be enough left of him to go on living.

A catalyst telepath probably could have reached him. But in these days, due to inbreeding, indiscriminate marriages with nontelepaths and the disappearance of the old means of stimulating these gifts, the various Comyn psi powers no longer bred true. I was living proof that the Alton gift did sometimes appear in pure form. But as a general thing, no one could sort out the tangle of gifts. The Hastur gift, whatever that was—even at Arilinn they didn't tell me—is just as likely to appear in the Aillard or Elhalyn Domains. Catalyst telepathy was once an Ardais gift. Dyan certainly wasn't one! As far as I knew, there were none left alive.

It seemed a long time later that Regis stirred again, rubbing his forehead; then he opened his eyes, still with that terrible eagerness. The drug was still in his system—it wouldn't wear off completely for hours—but he was beginning to have brief intervals free of it. His unspoken question was perfectly clear. I had to shake my head, regretfully.

"I'm sorry, Regis."

I hope I never again see such despair in a young face. If he had been twelve years old, I would have taken him in my arms and tried to comfort him. But he was not a child now, and neither was I. His taut, desperate face kept me at arm's length.

"Regis, listen to me," I said quietly. "For what it's worth, the *laran* is there. You have the potential, which means, at the very least, you're carrying the gene, your children will have it." I hesitated, not wanting to hurt him further, by telling him straightforwardly that he had made the barrier himself. Why hurt him that way?

I said, "I did my best, *bredu.* But I couldn't reach it, the barriers were too strong. *Bredu,* don't look at me like that," I pleaded, "I can't bear it, to see you looking at me that way."

His voice was almost inaudible. "I know. You did your best."

Had I really? I was struck with doubt. I felt sick with the force of his misery. I tried to take his hands again, forcing myself to meet his pain head-on, not flinch from it. But he pulled away from me, and I let it go.

"Regis, listen to me. It doesn't matter. Perhaps in the days of the Keepers, it was a terrible tragedy for a Hastur to be without *laran*. But the world is changing. The Comyn is changing. You'll find other strengths."

I felt the futility of the words even as I spoke them. What must it be like, to live without *laran*? Like being without sight, hearing . . . but, never having known it, he must not be allowed to suffer its loss.

"Regis, you have so much else to give. To your family, to the Domains, to our world. And your children will have it—" I took his hands again in mine, trying to comfort him, but he cracked.

"Zandru's hells, *stop* it," he said, and wrenched his hands roughly away again. He caught up his cloak, which lay on the stone seat, and ran out of the room.

I stood frozen in the shock of his violence, then, in horror, ran after him. *Gods!* Drugged, sick, desperate, he couldn't be allowed to run off that way! He needed to be watched, cared for, comforted—but I wasn't in time. When I reached the stairs, he had already disappeared into the labyrinthine corridors of that wing, and I lost him.

I called and hunted for hours before, reeling with fatigue since I, too, had been riding for days, I gave up finally and went back to my rooms. I couldn't spend the whole night storming all over Comyn Castle, shouting his name! I couldn't force my way into the Regent's suite and demand to know if he was there! There were limits to what Kennard Alton's bastard son could do. I suspected I'd already exceeded them. I could only hope desperately that the *kirian* would make him sleepy, or wear off with fatigue, and he would come back to rest or make his way to the Hastur apartments and sleep there.

I waited for hours and saw the sun rise, blood-red in the mists hanging over the Terran spaceport, before, cramped and cold, I fell asleep on the stone bench by the fireplace.

But Regis did not return.

CHAPTER THREE

Regis ran down the corridor, dazed and confused, the small points of color still flashing behind his eyes, racked with the interior crawling nausea. One thought was tearing at him:

Failed. I've failed. Even Lew, tower-trained and with all his skill, couldn't help me. There's nothing there. When he said what he did about potential, he was humoring me, comforting a child.

He reeled, feeling sick again, clung momentarily to the wall and ran on.

The Comyn castle was a labyrinth, and Regis had not been inside it in years. Before long, in his wild rush to get away from the scene of his humiliation, he was well and truly lost. His senses, *kirian*-blurred, retained vague memories of stone cul-de-sacs, blind corners, archways, endless stairs up which he toiled and down which he blundered and sometimes fell, courtyards filled with rushing wind and blinding rain, hour after hour. To the end of his life he retained an impression of the Comyn Castle which he could summon at will to overlay his real memories of it: a vast stone maze, a trap through which he wandered alone for centuries, with no human form to be seen. Once, around a corner, he heard Lew calling his name. He flattened himself in a niche and hid for a few thousand years until, long after, the sound was gone.

After an indeterminate time of wandering and stumbling and hallucinating, he became aware that it had been a long time since he had fallen down a flight of stairs; that the corridors were long, but not miles and miles long; and that they were no longer filled with uncanny crawling colors and silent sounds. When he came out at last on to a high balcony at the uppermost level, he knew where he was.

Dawn was breaking over the city below him. Once before, during the night, he had stood against a high parapet like this, thinking that his life was no good to anyone, not to the Hasturs, not to himself, that he should throw himself down and be done with it. This time the thought was remote, nightmarish, like one of those terrible real dreams which wakes you shaking and crying out, but a few seconds later is gone in dissolving fragments.

He drew a long, weary sigh. Now what?

He should go and make himself presentable for his grandfather, who would certainly send for him soon. He should get some food and sleep; *kirian,* he'd been told, expended so much physical and nervous energy that it was essential to compensate with extra food and rest. He should go back and apologize to Lew Alton, who had only very reluctantly done what Regis himself had begged him to do. . . . But he was sick to death of hearing what he should do!

He looked across the city that lay spread out below him. Thendara, the old town, the Trade City, the Terran headquarters and the spaceport. And the great ships, waiting, ready to take off for some unguessable destination. All he really wanted to do now was go to the spaceport and watch, at close range, one of those great ships.

Quickly he hardened his resolve. He was not dressed for out-of-doors at all, still wearing felt-soled indoor boots, but in his present mood it mattered less than nothing. He was unarmed. So what? Terrans carried no sidearms. He went down long flights of stairs, losing his way, but knowing, now that he had his wits about him, that all he had to do was keep going down till he reached ground level. Comyn Castle was no fortress. Built for ceremony rather than defense, the building had many gates, and it was easy to slip out one of them unobserved.

He found himself in a dim, dawnlit street leading downhill through closely packed houses. He was keyed up, having had no sleep after his hard ride yesterday, but the energizing effect of the *kirian* had not worn off yet, and he felt no drowsiness. Hunger was something else, but there were coins in his pockets, and he was sure that soon he would pass some kind of eating-house where workmen ate before their day's business.

The thought excited him with a delicious forbiddenness. He could not remember ever having been completely alone in his entire life. There had always been others ready at hand to look after him, protect him, gratify his every wish:

nurses and nannies when he was small, servants and carefully selected companions when he was older. Later, there were the brothers of the monastery, though they were more likely to thwart his wishes than carry them out. This would be an adventure.

He found a place next to a blacksmith's shop and went in. It was dimly lit with resin-candles, but there was a good smell of food. He was briefly afraid of being recognized, but after all, what could they do to him? He was old enough to be out alone. Besides, if anyone noticed the blue-and-silver cloak with the Hastur badge, they would only think he was a Hastur servant.

The men seated at the table were blacksmiths and stable hands, drinking hot ale or *jaco* or boiled milk, eating foods Regis had never seen or smelled. A woman came to take Regis' order. She did not look at him. He ordered fried nut porridge and hot milk with spices in it. His grandfather, he thought with definite satisfaction, would have a fit.

He paid for the food and ate it slowly, at first feeling the residual queasiness of the drug which wore off as he ate. When he went out, feeling better, the light was spreading, although the sun had not risen. As he went downhill he found himself among unfamiliar houses, built in strange shapes of strange materials. He had obviously crossed the line into the Trade City. He could hear, in the distance, that strange waterfall sound which had excited him so intensely. He must be near the spaceport.

He had been told a little about the spaceport on Darkover. Darkover, which did almost no trading with the Empire, was in a unique location, between the upper and lower spiral arms of the galaxy, unusually well suited as a crossroads stop for much of the interstellar traffic. In spite of the self-chosen isolation of Darkover, therefore, enormous numbers of ships came for rerouting, bearing passengers, personnel and freight bound elsewhere. They also came for repairs and reprovisioning and for rest leaves in the Trade City. Most of the Terrans scrupulously kept the agreement limiting them to their own areas. There had been a few intermarriages, a little trade, some small—very small—importation of Terran machinery and technology. This was strictly limited by the Darkovans, each item studied by Council before permission was given. A few licensed matrix technicians were set up in the cities; a few had even gone out into the Empire. The Terrans, he had heard, were intrigued by Darkovan matrix technology and in the old days had laid intricate plots to uncover some of its secrets. He didn't know details, but Kennard had told him some stories.

He started, realizing that the street directly before him was blocked by two very large men in unfamiliar black leather uniforms. At their belts hung strangely shaped weapons which, Regis realized with a prickle of horror, must be blasters or nerve guns. Such weapons had been outlawed on Darkover since the Ages of Chaos, and Regis had literally never seen one before, except for antiques in a museum. These were no museum pieces. They looked deadly.

One of the men said, "You're violating curfew, sonny. Until the trouble's over, all women and children are supposed to be off the streets from an hour before sunset until an hour after sunrise."

Women and children! Regis' hand strayed to his knife-hilt. "I am no child. Shall I call challenge and prove it?"

"You're in the Terran Zone, son. Save yourself trouble."

"I demand—"

"Oh hell, one of *those,*" said the second man in disgust. "Look here, kiddie, we're not allowed to fight duels, on duty anyhow. You come along and talk to the officer."

Regis was about to make an angry protest—ask a Comyn heir to give an account of himself in Council season?—when it occurred to him that the headquarters building was right on the spaceport, where he was going anyway. With a secret grin he went along.

After they had passed through the spaceport gates, he realized that he had actually had a better view yesterday from the mountainside. Here the ships were invisible behind fences and barricades. The spaceforce patrolmen led him inside a building where a young officer, not in black leather but in ordinary Terran clothing, was dealing with assorted curfew violators. As they came in he was saying, "This man's all right; he was looking for a midwife and took the wrong turn. Send someone to show him back to the town." He looked up at Regis, standing between the officers. "Another one? I'd hoped we'd be through for the night. Well, kid, what's your story?"

Regis threw his head back arrogantly. "Who are you? By what right did you have me brought here?"

"My name's Dan Lawton," the man said. He spoke the same language in which Regis had addressed him, and spoke it well. That wasn't common. He said, "I am an assistant to the Legate and just now I'm handling curfew duty. Which you were violating, young man."

One of the spaceforce men said, "We brought him straight to you, Dan. He wanted to fight a duel with us, for God's sake! Can you handle this one?"

"We don't fight duels in the Terran Zone," Lawton said. "Are you new to Thendara? The curfew regulations are posted everywhere. If you can't read, I suggest you ask someone to read them to you."

Regis retorted, "I recognize no laws but those of the Children of Hastur!"

A strange look passed over Lawton's face. Regis thought for a moment that the young Terran was laughing at him, but face and voice were alike noncommittal. "A praiseworthy objective, sir, but not particularly suitable here. The Hasturs themselves made and recognized those boundaries and agreed to assist us in enforcing our laws within them. Do you refuse to recognize the authority of Comyn Council? Who are you to refuse?"

Regis drew himself to his full height. He knew that between the giant spaceforce men he still looked childishly small.

"I am Regis-Rafael Felix Alar Hastur y Elhalyn," he stated proudly.

Lawton's eyes reflected amazement. "Then what, in the name of all your own gods, are you doing roaming around alone at this hour. Where is your escort? Yes, you look like a Hastur," he said as he pulled an intercom toward him, speaking urgently in Terran Standard. Regis had learned it at Nevarsin. "Have the Comyn Elders left yet?" He listened a moment, then turned back to Regis. "A dozen of your kinfolk left here about half an hour ago. Were you sent with a message for them? If so, you came too late."

"No," Regis confessed, "I came on my own. I simply had a fancy to see the starships take off." It sounded, here in this office, like a childish whim. Lawton looked startled.

"That's easily enough arranged. If you'd sent in a formal request a few days ago, we'd gladly have arranged a tour for any of your kinsmen. At short notice like this, there's nothing spectacular going on, but there's a cargo transport about to take off for Vega in a few minutes, and I'll take you up to one of the viewing platforms. Meanwhile, could I offer you some coffee?" He hesitated, then said, "You couldn't be Lord Hastur; that must be your father?"

"Grandfather. For me the proper address is Lord Regis."

He accepted the proffered Terran drink, finding it bitter but rather pleasant. Dan Lawton led him into a tall shaft which rose upward at alarming speed, opening on a glass-enclosed viewing terrace. Below him an enormous cargo ship was in the final stages of readying for takeoff, with refueling cranes being moved away, scaffoldings and loading platforms being wheeled like toys to a distance. The process was quick and efficient. He heard again the waterfall sound, rising to a roar, a scream. The great ship lifted slowly, then more swiftly and finally was gone . . . out, beyond the stars.

Regis remained motionless, staring at the spot in the sky where the starship had vanished. He knew there were tears in his eyes again but he didn't care. After a little while Lawton guided him down the elevator shaft. Regis went as if sleepwalking. Resolve had suddenly crystallized inside him.

Somewhere in the Empire, somewhere away from the Domains which had no place for him, there must be a world for him. A world where he could be free of the tremendous burden laid on the Comyn, a world where he could be himself, more than simply heir to his Domain, his life laid out in preordained duties from birth to grave. The Domain? Let Javanne's sons have it! He felt almost intoxicated by the smell of freedom. Freedom from a burden he'd been born to—and born unfit to bear!

Lawton had not noticed his preoccupation. He said, "I'll arrange an escort for you back to Comyn Castle, Lord Regis. You can't go alone, put it out of your mind. Impossible."

"I came here alone, and I'm not a child."

"Certainly not," Lawton said, straight-faced, "but with the situation in the city now, anything might happen. And if an accident occurred, I would be personally responsible."

He had used the *casta* phrase implying personal honor.

Regis lifted his eyebrows and congratulated him on his command of the language.

"As a matter of fact, Lord Regis, it is my native tongue. My mother never spoke anything else to me. It was Terran I learned as a foreign language."

"You are Darkovan?"

"My mother was, and kin to Comyn. Lord Ardais is my mother's cousin, though I doubt he'd care to acknowledge the relationship."

Regis thought about that as Lawton arranged his escort. Relatives far more distant than that were often seated in Comyn Council. This Terran officer—half-Terran—might have chosen to be Darkovan. He had as much right to a Comyn seat as Lew Alton, for instance. Lew could have chosen to be Terran, as Regis was about to choose his own future. He spent the uneventful journey across the city thinking how he would break the news to his grandfather.

In the Hastur apartments, a servant told him that Danvan Hastur was awaiting him. As he changed his clothes—the thought of presenting himself before the Regent of Comyn in house clothes and felt slippers was not even to be contemplated—he wondered grimly if Lew had said anything to his grandfather. It occurred to him, hours too late, that if anything had happened to him, Hastur might well have held Lew responsible. A poor return for Lew's friendship!

When he had made himself presentable, in a sky-blue dyed-leather tunic and high boots, he went up to his grandfather's audience room.

Inside he found Danvan Hastur of Hastur, Regent of the Seven Domains, talking to Kennard Alton. As he opened the door, Hastur raised his eyebrows and gestured to him to sit down. "One moment, my lad, I'll talk to you later." He turned back to Kennard and said in a tone of endless patience, "Kennard, my friend, my dear kinsman, what you ask is simply impossible. I let you force Lew on us—"

"Have you regretted it?" Kennard demanded angrily. "They tell me at Arilinn that he is a strong telepath, one of their best. In the Guard he is a competent officer. What right have you to assume Marius would bring disgrace on the Comyn?"

"Who spoke of disgrace, kinsman?" Hastur was standing before his writing table, a strongly built old man, not as tall as Kennard, with hair that had once been silver-gilt and was now nearly all gray. He spoke with a slow, considered mildness. "I let you force Lew on us and I've had no reason to regret it. But there is more to it than that. Lew does not look Comyn, no more than you, but there is no question in anyone's mind that he is Darkovan and your son. But Marius? Impossible."

Kennard's mouth thinned and tightened. "Are you questioning the paternity of an acknowledged Alton son?" Standing quietly in a corner, Regis was glad Kennard's rage was not turned on *him*.

"By no means. But he has his mother's blood, his mother's face, his mother's eyes. My friend, you know what the first year cadets go through in the Guards. . . ."

"He's my son and no coward. Why do you think he would be incompetent to take his place, the place to which he is legally entitled—"

"Legally, no. I won't quibble with you, Ken, but we never recognized your marriage to Elaine. Marius is *legally*, as regards inheritance and Domain-right, entitled to nothing whatever. We *gave* Lew that right. Not by birth entitlement, but by Council action, because he was Alton, telepath, with full *laran*. Marius has received no such rights from Council." He sighed. "How can I make you understand? I'm sure the boy is brave, trustworthy, honest—that he has all the virtues we Comyn demand of our sons. Any lad you reared would have those qualities. Who knows better than I? But Marius *looks* Terran. The other lads would tear him to pieces. I know what Lew went through. I pitied him, even while I admired his courage. They've accepted him, after a fashion. They would never accept Marius. Never. Why put him through that misery for nothing?"

Kennard clenched his fists, striding angrily up and down the room. His voice choked with rage, he said, "You mean that I can get a cadet commission for some poor relation, or my bastard son by a whore or an idiot, sooner than for my own legitimately born son!"

"Kennard, if it were up to me, I'd give the lad his chance. But my hands are tied. There has been enough trouble in Council over citizenship for those of mixed blood. Dyan—"

"I know all too well how Dyan feels. He's made it abundantly clear."

"Dyan has a great deal of support in Council. And Marius' mother was not only Terran but half-Aldaran. If you had hunted over Darkover for a generation, you could not have found a woman less likely to be accepted as the mother of your legitimate sons."

Kennard said in a low voice, "It was your own father who had me sent to Terra, by the will of the Council, when I was fourteen years old. Elaine was reared and schooled on Terra, but she thought of herself as Darkovan. I did not even know of her Terran blood at first. But it made no difference. Even had she been all Terran . . ." He broke off. "Enough of that. It is long past and she is dead. As for me, I think my record and reputation, my years commanding the Guard, my ten years at Arilinn, prove abundantly what I am." He paced the floor, his uneven step and distraught face betraying the emotion he tried to keep out of his voice. "You are not a telepath, Hastur. It was easy for you to do what your caste required of you. The Gods know I tried to love Caitlin. It wasn't her fault. But I did love Elaine, and she *was* mother to my sons."

"Kennard, I'm sorry. I cannot fight the whole Council for Marius, unless—has he *laran*?"

"I have no idea. Does it matter so much?"

"If he had the Alton gift, it might be possible, not easy but possible, to establish some rights for him. There are precedents. With *laran*, even a distant kinsman can be adopted into the Domains. Without it . . . no, Kennard. Don't ask. Lew is accepted now, even respected. Don't ask more."

Kennard said, his head bent, "I didn't want to test Lew for the Alton gift. Even with all my care, it came near to killing him. Hastur, I cannot risk it again! Would you, for your youngest son?"

"My only son is dead." Hastur said and sighed. "If I can do anything else for the boy—"

Kennard answered, "The only thing I want for him is his right, and that is the only thing you will not give. I should have taken them both to Terra. You made me feel I was needed here."

"You are, Ken, and you know it as well as I." Hastur's smile was very sweet and troubled. "Some day, perhaps, you may see why I can't do what you wish." His eyes moved to Regis, fidgeting on the bench. He said, "If you will excuse me, Kennard . . . ?"

It was a courteous but definite dismissal. Kennard withdrew, but his face was grim and he omitted any formal leave-taking. Hastur looked tired. He sighed and said, "Come here, Regis. Where have you been? Haven't I trouble enough without worrying that you've run away like a silly brat, to look at the spaceships or something like that?"

"The last time I gave you too much trouble, Grandfather, you sent me into a monastery. Isn't it too bad you can't do it again, sir?"

"Don't be insolent, you young pup," Hastur growled. "Do you want me to apologize for having no welcome last night? Very well, I apologize. It wasn't my choice." He came and took Regis in his arms, pressing his withered cheeks one after another to the boy's. "I've been up all night, or I'd think of some better way to welcome you now." He held him off at arm's length, blinking with weariness. "You've grown, child. You are very like your father. He would have been proud, I think, to see you coming home a man."

Against his own will, Regis was moved. The old man looked so weary. "What crisis kept you up all night, Grandfather?"

Hastur sank down heavily on the bench. "The usual thing. I expect it's known on every planet where the Empire builds a big spaceport, but we're not used to it here. People coming and going from all corners of the Empire. Travelers, transients, spacemen on leave and the sector which caters to them. Bars, amusement places, gambling halls, houses of . . . er . . ."

"I'm old enough to know what a brothel is, sir."

"At your age? Anyway, drunken men are disorderly, and Terrans on leave carry weapons. By agreement, no weapons can be carried into the old city, but people do stray across the line—there's no way of preventing it, short of building a wall across the city. There have been brawls, duels, knife fights and sometimes even killings, and it isn't always clear whether the City Guard or the Terran space force should properly handle the offenders. Our codes are so different that it's hard to know how to compromise. Last night there was a brawl and a Terran knifed one of the

Guardsmen. The Terran offered as his defense that the Guardsman had made him what he called an indecent proposition. Must I explain?"

"Of course not. But are you trying to tell me, seriously, that this was offered as a legal defense for murder?"

"Seriously. Evidently the Terrans take it even more seriously than the *cristoforos*. He insisted his attack on the Guardsman was justifiable. Now the Guardsman's brother has filed an intent-to-murder on the Terran. The Terrans aren't subject to our laws, so he refused to accept it and instead filed charges against the Guardsman's brother for attempted murder. What a tangle! I never thought I'd see the day when Council had to sit on a knife fight! Damn the Terrans anyhow!"

"So how did you finally settle it?"

Hastur shrugged. "Compromise, as usual. The Terran was deported and the Guardsman's brother was held in the brig until the Terran was off-planet; so nobody gets any peace except the dead man. Unsatisfactory for everyone. But enough of them. Tell me about yourself, Regis."

"Well, I'll have to talk about the Terrans again," Regis said. This wasn't the best time, but his grandfather might not have time to talk with him again for days. "Grandfather, I'm not needed here. You probably know I don't have *laran*, and I found out in Nevarsin that I'm not interested in politics. I've decided what I want to do with my life: I want to go into the Terran Empire Space Service."

Hastur's jaw dropped. He scowled and demanded, "Is this a joke? Or another silly prank?"

"Neither, Grandfather. I mean it, and I'm of age."

"But you can't do that! Certainly they'd never accept you without my consent."

"I hope to have that, sir. But by Darkovan law, which you were quoting at Kennard, I am of legal age to dispose of myself. I can marry, fight a duel, acknowledge a son, stand responsible for a murder—"

"The Terrans wouldn't think so. Kennard was declared of age before he went. But on Terra he was sent to school and required, legally forced, mind you, to obey a stipulated guardian until he was past twenty. You'd hate that."

"No doubt I would. But I learned one thing at Nevarsin, sir—you can live with the things you hate."

"Regis, is this your revenge for my sending you to Nevarsin? Were you so unhappy? What can I say? I wanted you to have the best education possible and I thought it better for you to be properly cared for, there, than neglected at home."

"No, sir," Regis said, not quite sure. "It's simply that I want to go, and I'm not needed here."

"You don't speak Terran languages."

"I understand Terran Standard. I learned to read and write at Nevarsin. As you pointed out, I am excellently well educated. Learning a new language is no great matter."

"You say you are of age," Hastur said coldly, "so let me quote some law back to you. The law provides that before you, who are heir to a Domain, undertake any such risky task as going offworld, you must provide an heir to your Domain. Have you a son, Regis?"

Regis looked sullenly at the floor. Hastur knew, of course, that he had not. "What does that matter? It's been generations since the Hastur gift has appeared full strength in the line. As for ordinary *laran,* that's just as likely to appear at random anywhere in the Domains as it is in the direct male line of descent. Pick any heir at random, he couldn't be less fit for the Domain than I am. I suspect the gene's a recessive, bred out, extinct like the catalyst telepath trait. And Javanne has sons; one of them is as likely to have it as any son of mine, if I had any. Which I don't," he added rebelliously, "or am likely to. Now or ever."

"Where do you get these ideas?" Hastur asked, shocked and bewildered. "You're not, by chance, an *ombredin*?"

"In a *cristoforo* monastery? Not likely. No, sir, not even for pastime. And certainly not as a way of life."

"Then why should you say such a thing?"

"Because," Regis burst out angrily, "I belong to myself, not to the Comyn! Better to let the line die with me than to go on for generations, calling ourselves Hastur, without our gift, without *laran,* political figureheads being used by Terra to keep the people quiet!"

"Is that how you see me, Regis? I took the Regency when Stefan Elhalyn died, because Derik was only five, too young to be crowned even as a puppet king. It's been my ill-fortune to rule over a period of change, but I think I've been more than just a figurehead for Terra."

"I know some Empire history, sir. The Empire will finally take over here too. It always does."

"Don't you think I know that? I've lived with the inevitable for three reigns now. But if I live long enough, it will be a slow change, one our people can live with. As for *laran,* it wakens late in Hastur men. Give yourself time."

"Time!" Regis put all his dissatisfaction into the word.

"I haven't *laran* either, Regis. But even so, I think I've served my people well. Couldn't you resign yourself to that?" He looked into Regis' stubborn face and sighed. "Well, I'll bargain with you. I don't want you to go as a child, subject to a court-appointed guardian under Terran law. That would disgrace all of us. You're the age when a Comyn heir should be serving in the cadet corps. Take your regular turn in the Guards, three cadet seasons. After that, if you still want to go, we'll think of a way to get you offworld without going through all the motions of their bureaucracy. You'd hate it—I've had fifty years of it and I still hate it. But don't walk out on Comyn before you give it a fair try. Three years isn't that long. Will you bargain?"

Three years seemed like an eternity at Nevarsin. But did he have a choice? None, except outright defiance. He could run away, seek aid from the Terrans themselves. But if he was legally a child by their laws, they would simply hand him over again to his guardians. That would indeed be a disgrace.

"Three cadet seasons," he said at last. "But only if you give me your word of honor that if I choose to go, you won't oppose it after that."

"If after three years you still want to go," said Hastur, "I promise to find some honorable way."

Regis listened, weighing the words for diplomatic evasions and half-truths. But the old man's eyes were level and the word of Hastur was proverbial. Even the Terrans knew that.

At last he said, "A bargain. Three years in the cadets, for your word." He added bitterly, "I have no choice, do I?"

"If you wanted a choice," said Hastur, and his blue eyes flashed fire though his voice was as old and weary as ever, "you should have arranged to be born somewhere else, to other parents. I did not choose to be chief councillor to Stefan Elhalyn, nor Regent to Prince Derik. Rafael—sound may he sleep!—did not choose his own life, nor even his death. None of us has ever been free to choose, not in my lifetime." His voice wavered, and Regis realized that the old man was on the edge of exhaustion or collapse.

Against his will, Regis was moved again. He bit his lip, knowing that if he spoke he would break down, beg his grandfather's pardon, promise unconditional obedience. Perhaps it was only the last remnant of the *kirian,* but he knew, suddenly and agonizingly, that his grandfather did not meet his eyes because the Regent of the Seven Domains could not weep, not even before his own grandson, not even for the memory of his only son's terrible and untimely death.

When Hastur finally spoke again his voice was hard and crisp, like a man accustomed to dealing with one unremitting crisis after another. "The first call-over of cadets is later this morning. I have sent word to cadet-master to expect you among them." He rose and embraced Regis again in dismissal. "I shall see you again soon. At least we are not now separated by three days' ride and a range of mountains."

So he'd already sent word to the cadet-master. That was how sure he was, Regis realized. He had been manipulated, neatly mouse-trapped into doing just exactly what was expected of a Hastur. And he had maneuvered himself into promising three years of it!

CHAPTER FOUR

(Lew Alton's narrative)

The room was bright with daylight. I had slept for hours on the stone seat by the fireplace, cold and cramped. Marius, barefoot and in his nightshirt, was shaking me. He said, "I heard something on the stairs. Listen!" He ran toward the door; I followed more slowly, as the door was flung open and a pair of Guards carried my father into the room. One of them caught sight of me and said, "Where can we take him, Captain?"

I said, "Bring him in here," and helped Andres lay him on his own bed. "What happened?" I demanded, staring in dread at his pale, unconscious face.

"He fell down the stone stairs near the Guard hall," one of the men said. "I've been trying to get those stairs fixed all winter; your father could have broken his neck. So could any of us."

Marius came to the bedside, white and terrified. "Is he dead?"

"Nothing like it, sonny," said the Guardsman. "I think the Commander's broken a couple of ribs and done something to his arm and shoulder, but unless he starts vomiting blood later he'll be all right. I wanted Master Raimon to attend to him down there, but he made us carry him up here."

Between anger and relief, I bent over him. What a time for him to be hurt. The very first day of Council season! As if my tumbling thoughts could reach him—and perhaps they could—he groaned and opened his eyes. His mouth contracted in a spasm of pain.

"Lew?"

"I'm here, Father."

"You must take call-over in my place. . . ."

"Father, no. There are a dozen others with better right."

His face hardened. I could see, and feel, that he was struggling against the pain. "Damn you, you'll go! I've fought . . . whole Council . . . for years. You're not going to throw away all my work . . . because I take a damn silly tumble. You have a right to deputize for me and, damn you, you're going to!"

His pain tore at me; I was wide open to it. Through the clawing pain I could feel his emotions, fury and a fierce determination, thrusting his will on me. "You *will*!"

I'm not Alton for nothing. Swiftly I thrust back, fighting his attempt to *force* agreement. "There's no need for that, Father. I'm not your puppet!"

"But you're my son," he said violently, and it was like a storm, as his will pressed hard on me. "My son and my second in command, and no one, *no one* is going to question that!"

His agitation was growing so great, that I realized I could argue no further without harming him seriously.

I had to calm him somehow. I met his enraged eyes squarely and said, "There's no reason to shout at me. I'll do what you like, for now at least. We'll argue it out later."

His eyes fell shut, whether with exhaustion or pain I could not tell. Master Raimon, the hospital-officer of the Guards, came into the room, moving swiftly to his side. I made room for him. Anger, fatigue and loss of sleep made my head pound. Damn him! Father knew perfectly well how I felt! And he didn't give a damn!

Marius was still standing, frozen, watching in horror as Master Raimon began to cut away my father's shirt. I saw great, purple, blood-darkened bruises before I drew Marius firmly away. "There's nothing much wrong with him," I said. "He couldn't shout that loud if he was dying. Go get dressed, and keep out of the way."

The child went obediently and I stood in the outer room, rubbing my fists over my face in dismay and confusion. What time was it? How long had I slept? Where was Regis? Where had he gone? In the state he'd been in when he left me, he could have done something desperate! Conflicting loyalties and obligations held me paralyzed. Andres came out of my father's room and said, "Lew, if you're going to take call-over you'd better get moving," and I realized I'd been standing as if my feet had been frozen to the floor.

My father had laid a task on me. Yet if Regis had run away, in a mood of suicidal despair, shouldn't I go after him, too? In any case I would have been on duty this morning. Now it seemed I was to handle it my own way. There were sure to be those who'd question it. Well, it was Father's right to choose his own deputy, but I was the one who'd have to face the hostility.

I turned to Andres. "Have someone get me something to eat," I said, "and see if you can find where Father put the staff lists and the roll call, but don't disturb him. I should bathe and change. Have I time?"

Andres regarded me calmly. "Don't lose your head. You have what time you need. If you're in command, they can't start till you get there. Take the time to make yourself presentable. You ought to *look* ready to command, even if you don't feel it."

He was right, of course; I knew it even while I resented his tone. Andres has a habit of being right. He had been the *coridom,* chief steward, at Armida since I could remember. He was a Terran and had once been in Spaceforce. I've never known where he met my father, or why he left the Empire. My father's servants had told me the story, that one day he came to Armida and said he was sick of space and Spaceforce, and my father had said, "Throw your blaster away and pledge me to keep the Compact, and I've work for you at Armida as long as you like." At first he had been Father's private secretary, then his personal assistant, finally in charge of his whole household, from my father's horses and dogs to his sons and foster-daughter. There were times when I felt Andres was the only person alive who completely accepted me for what I was. Bastard, half-caste, it made no difference to Andres.

He added now, "Better for discipline to turn up late than to turn up in a mess and not knowing what you're doing. Get yourself in order, Lew, and I don't just mean your uniform. Nothing's to be gained by rushing off in several directions at once."

I went off to bathe, eat a hasty breakfast and dress myself suitably to be stared at by a hundred or more officers and Guardsmen, each one of whom would be ready to find fault. Well, let them.

Andres found the staff lists and Guard roster among my father's belongings; I took them and went down to the Guard hall.

The main Guard hall in Comyn Castle is on one of the lowest levels; behind it lie barracks, stables, armory and parade ground, and before it a barricaded gateway leads down into Thendara. The rest of Comyn Castle leaves me unmoved, but I never looked up at the great fan-lighted windows without a curious swelling in my throat.

I had been fourteen years old, and already aware that because of what I was my life was fragmented and insecure, when my father had first brought me here. Before sending me to my peers, or what he hoped would be my peers—they'd had other ideas—he'd told me of a few of the Altons who had come before us here. For the first and almost the last time, I'd felt a sense of belonging to those old Altons whose names were a roll call of Darkovan history: My grandfather Valdir, who had organized the first fire-beacon system in the Kilghard Hills. Dom Esteban Lanart, who a hundred years ago had driven the catmen from the caves of Corresanti. Rafael Lanart-Alton, who had ruled as Regent when Stefan Hastur the Ninth was crowned in his cradle, in the days before the Elhalyn were kings in Thendara.

The Guard hall was an enormous stone-floored, stone-arched room, cobblestones half worn away by the feet of centuries of Guardsmen. The light came curiously, multicolored and splintered, through windows set in before the art of rolling glass was known.

I drew the lists Andres had given me from a pocket and studied them. On the topmost sheet were names of the first-year cadets. The name of Regis Hastur was at the bottom, evidently added somewhat later than the rest. Damn it, where *was* Regis? I checked the list of second-year cadets. The name of Octavien Vallonde had been dropped from the rolls. I hadn't expected to see his name, but it would have relieved my mind.

On the staff list Father had crossed out his own name as commander and written in mine, evidently with his right hand, and with great difficulty. I wished he had saved himself the trouble. Gabriel Lanart-Hastur, Javanne's husband and my cousin, had replaced me as second-in-command. He should have had the command post. I was no soldier, only a matrix technician, and I fully intended to return to Arilinn at the end of the three-year interval required now by law. Gabriel, though, was a career Guardsman, liked it and was competent. He was Alton too, and seated on Council. Most Comyn felt he should have been designated Kennard's heir. Yet we were friends, after a fashion, and I wished he were here today, instead of at Edelweiss waiting for the birth of Javanne's child.

Father evidently saw no discrepancy. He had been psi technician in Arilinn for over ten years, back in the old days of tower isolation, yet he had been able afterward to return and take command of the Guards without any terrible sense of dissonance. My own inner conflicts evidently were not important, or even comprehensible, to him.

Arms-master again was old Domenic di Asturien, who had been a captain when my father was a cadet of fourteen. He had been my own cadet-master, my first year and was almost the only officer in the Guard who had ever been fair to me.

Cadet-master—I rubbed my eyes and stared at the lists; I must have read it wrong. The words obstinately stayed the same. *Cadet-master: Dyan-Gabriel, Lord Ardais.*

I groaned aloud. Oh, hell, this had to be one of Father's perverse jokes. He's no fool, only a fool would put a man like Dyan in charge of half-grown boys. Not after the scandal last year. We had managed to keep the scandal from reaching Lord Hastur, and I had believed that even Dyan knew he had gone too far.

Let me be clear about one thing: I don't like Dyan and he doesn't approve of me, but he is a brave man and a good soldier, probably the best and most competent officer in the Guards. As for his personal life, no one dares comment on a Comyn lord's private amusements.

I learned, long ago, not to listen to gossip. My own birth had been a major scandal for years. But this had been more than gossip. Personally, I think Father had been unwise to hustle the Vallonde boy away home without question or investigation. Part of what he said was true. Octavien *was* disturbed, unstable, he'd never belonged in the Guards and it was our mistake for ever accepting him as a cadet. But Father had said that the sooner it was hushed up, the quicker the unsavory story would die down. The rumors had never died of course, probably never would.

The room was beginning to fill up with uniformed men. Dyan came to the dais where the officers were collecting, gave me an unfriendly scowl. No doubt *he* had expected to be named as Father's deputy. Even that would have been better than making him cadet-master. Damn it, I *couldn't* go along with that. Father's choice or not.

Dyan's private life was no one's affair but his own and I wouldn't care if he chose to love men, women, or goats. He could have as many concubines as a Dry-Towner, and most people would gossip no more or less. But more scandal in the Guards? Damn it, no! This touched the honor of the Guards, and of the Altons who were in charge of it.

Father had put me in command. This was going to be my first command decision, then.

I signaled for Assembly. One or two late-comers dashed into their places. The seasoned men took their ranks. The cadets, as they had been briefed, stayed in a corner.

Regis wasn't among the cadets. I resented bitterly that I was tied here, but there was no help for it.

I looked them all over and felt them returning the favor. I shut down my telepathic sensitivity as much as I could—it wasn't easy in this crowd—but I was aware of their surprise, curiosity, disgust, annoyance. It all added up, more or less, to *Where the hell is the Commander?* Or, worse, *What's old Kennard's bastard doing up there with the staff?*

Finally I got their attention and told them of Kennard's misfortune. It caused a small flurry of whispers, mutters, comments, most of which I knew it would be unwise to hear. I let them get through most of it, then called them to order again and began the traditional first-day ceremony of call-over.

One by one I read out the name of every Guardsman. Each came forward, repeated a brief formula of loyalty to Comyn and informed me—a serious obligation three hundred years ago, a mere customary formality now—of how many men, trained, armed and outfitted according to custom, he was prepared to put into the field in the event of war. It was a long business. There was a disturbance halfway through it and, escorted by a half dozen in Hastur livery, Regis made an entrance. One of the servants gave me a message from Hastur himself, with some kind of excuse or explanation for his lateness.

I realized that I was blisteringly angry. I'd seen Regis desperate, suicidal, ill, prostrated, suffering some unforeseen aftereffect of *kirian,* even dead—and he walked in casually, upsetting call-over ceremony and discipline. I told him brusquely, "Take your place, cadet," and dismissed the servants.

He could not have resembled less the boy who had sat by my fire last night, eating stew and pouring out his bitterness. He was wearing full Comyn regalia, badges, high boots, a sky-blue tunic of an elaborate cut. He walked to his place among the cadets, his head held stiffly high. I could sense the fear and shyness in him, but I knew the other cadets would regard it as Comyn arrogance, and he would suffer for it. He looked tired, almost ill, behind the façade of arrogant control. What had happened to him last night? Damn him, I recalled myself with a start, why was I worrying about the heir to Hastur? He hadn't worried about me, or the fact that if he'd come to harm, I'd have been in trouble!

I finished the parade of loyalty oaths. Dyan leaned toward me and said, "I was in the city with Council last night. Hastur asked me to explain the situation to the Guards; have I your permission to speak, Captain Montray-Lanart?"

Dyan had never given me my proper title, in or out of the Guard hall. I grimly told myself that the last thing I wanted was his approval. I nodded and he walked to the center of the dais. He looks no more like a typical Comyn lord than I do; his hair is dark, not the traditional red of Comyn, and he is tall, lean, with the six-fingered hands which sometimes turn up in the Ardais and Aillard clans. There is said to be nonhuman blood in the Ardais line. Dyan looks it.

"City Guardsmen of Thendara," he rapped out, "your commander, Lord Alton, has asked me to review the situation." His contemptuous look said more plainly than words that I might play at being in command, but he was the one who could explain what was going on.

There seemed, as nearly as I could tell from Dyan's words, to be a high level of tension in the city, mostly between the Terran Spaceforce and the City Guard. He asked every Guardsman to avoid incidents and to honor the curfew, to remember that the Trade City area had been ceded to the Empire by diplomatic treaty. He reminded us that it was our duty to deal with Darkovan offenders, and to turn Terran ones over to the Empire authorities at once. Well, that was fair enough. Two police forces in one city had to reach some agreements and compromises in living together.

I had to admit Dyan was a good speaker. He managed, however, to convey the impression that the Terrans were so much our natural inferiors, honoring neither the Compact nor the codes of personal honor, that we must take responsibility for them, as all superiors do; that, while we would naturally prefer to treat them with a just contempt, we would be doing Lord Hastur a personal favor by keeping the peace, even against our better judgment. I doubted whether that little speech would really lessen the friction between Terrans and Guardsmen.

I wondered if our opposite numbers in the Trade City, the Legate and his deputies, were laying the law down to Spaceforce this morning. Somehow I doubted it.

Dyan returned to his place and I called the cadets to stand forward. I called the roll of the dozen third-year cadets and the eleven second-year men, wondering if Council meant to fill Octavien Vallonde's empty place. Then I addressed myself to the first-year cadets, calling them into the center of the room. I decided to skip the usual speech about the proud and ancient organization into which it was a pleasure to welcome them. I'm not Dyan's equal as a speaker, and I wasn't going to compete. Father could give them that one when he was well again, or the cadet-master, whoever he was. Not Dyan. Over my dead body.

I confined myself to giving basic facts. After today there would be a full assembly and review every morning after breakfast. The cadets would be kept apart in their own barracks and given instructions until intense drill in basics had made them soldierly enough to take their place in formations and duties. Castle Guard would be set day and night and they would take it in turns from oldest to youngest, recalling that Castle Guard was not menial sentry duty but a privilege claimed by nobles from time out of mind, to guard the Sons of Hastur. And so on.

The final formality—I was glad to reach it, for it was hot in the crowded room by now and the youngest cadets were beginning to fidget—was a formal roll call of first-year cadets. Only Regis and Father's young protégé Danilo were personally known to me, but some were the younger brothers or sons of men I knew in the Guards. The last name I called was Regis-Rafael, cadet Hastur.

There was a confused silence, just too long. Then down the line of cadets there was a small scuffle and an audible whispered "That's *you,* blockhead!" as Danilo poked Regis in the ribs. Regis' confused voice said "Oh—" Another pause. "Here."

Damn Regis anyhow. I had begun to hope that *this* year we would get through call-over without having to play this particular humiliating charade. Some cadet, not always a first-year man, invariably forgot to answer properly to his name at call-over. There was a procedure for such occasions which probably went back three dozen generations. From the way in which the other Guardsmen, from veterans to older cadets, were waiting, expectant snickers breaking out, they'd all been waiting—yes, damn them all, and hoping—for this ritual hazing.

Left to myself, I'd have said harshly, "Next time, answer to your name, cadet," and had a word with him later in private. But if I tried to cheat them all of their fun, they'd probably take it out on Regis anyway. He'd already made himself conspicuous by coming in late and dressed like a prince. I might as well get on with it. Regis would have to get used to worse things than this in the next few weeks.

"Cadet Hastur," I said with a sigh, "suppose you step forward where we can get a good look at you. Then if you forget your name again, we can all be ready to remind you."

Regis stepped forward, staring blankly. "You know my name."

There was a chorus of snickers. Zandru's bells, was he confused enough to make it worse? I kept my voice cold and even. "It's my business to know it, cadet, and yours to answer any question put to you by an officer. What is your name, cadet?"

He said, rapid and furious, "Regis-Rafael Felix Alar Hastur-Elhalyn!"

"Well, Regis-Rafael This-that-and-the-other, your name in the Guard hall is *cadet Hastur,* and I suggest you memorize your name and the proper response to your name, unless you prefer to be addressed as *That's you, blockhead.*" Danilo giggled; I glared at him and he subsided. "Cadet Hastur, nobody's going to call you *Lord Regis* down here. How old are you, cadet Hastur?"

"Fifteen," Regis said. Mentally, I swore again. If he had made the proper response this time—but how could he? No one had warned him—I could have dismissed him. Now I had to play out this farce to the very end. The look of hilarious expectancy on the faces around us infuriated me. But two hundred years of Guardsman tradition were behind it. "Fifteen *what,* cadet?"

"Fifteen *years,*" said Regis, biting on the old bait for the unwary. I sighed. Well, the other cadets had a right to their fun. Generations had conditioned them to demand it, and I gave it to them. I said wearily, "Suppose, men, you all tell cadet Hastur how old he is?"

"Fifteen, *sir,*" they chorused all together, at the top of their voices. The expected uproar of laughter finally broke loose. I signaled Regis to go back to his place. The murderous glance he sent me could have killed. I didn't blame him. For days, in fact, until somebody else did something outstandingly stupid, he'd be the butt of the barracks. I knew. I remembered a day several years ago when the name of the unlucky cadet had been Lewis-Kennard, cadet Montray, and I had, perhaps, a better excuse—never having heard my name in that form before. I haven't heard it since either, because my father had demanded I be allowed to bear his name, Montray-Alton. As usual, he got what he wanted. That was while they were still arguing about my legitimacy. But he used the argument that it was unseemly for a cadet to bear a Terran name in the Guard, even though a bastard legally uses his mother's name.

Finally the ceremony was over. I should turn the cadets over to the cadet-master and let him take command. No, damn it, I couldn't do it. Not until I had urged Father to reconsider. I hadn't wanted to command the Guards, but he had insisted and now, for better or worse, all the Guards, from the youngest cadet to the oldest veteran, were in my care. I was bound to do my best for them and, damn it, my best didn't include Dyan Ardais as cadet-master!

I beckoned to old Domenic di Asturien. He was an experienced officer, completely trustworthy, exactly the sort of man to be in charge of the young. He had retired from active duty years ago—he was certainly in his eighties—but no one could complain of him. His family was so old that the Comyn themselves were upstarts to him. There was a joke, told in whispers, that he had once spoken of the Hasturs as "the new nobility."

"Master, the Commander met with an accident this morning, and he has not yet informed me about his choice for cadet-master." I crushed the staff lists in my hand as if the old man could see Dyan's name written there and give me the lie direct. "I respectfully request you to take charge of them until he makes his wishes known."

As I returned to my place, Dyan started to his feet. "You damned young pup, didn't Kennard tell—" He saw curious eyes on us and dropped his voice. "Why didn't you speak to me privately about this?"

Damn it. He knew. And I recalled that he was said to be a strong telepath, though he had been refused entry to the towers for unknown reasons, so he knew that I knew. I blanked my mind to him. There are few who can read an Alton when he's warned. It was a severe breach of courtesy and Comyn ethics that Dyan had done so uninvited. Or was it meant to convey that he didn't think I deserved Comyn immunity? I said frigidly, trying to be civil, "After I have consulted the Commander, Captain Ardais, I shall make his wishes known to you."

"Damn, you, the Commander has made his wishes known, and you know it," Dyan said, his mouth hardening into a tight line. There was still time. I could pretend to discover his name on the lists. But eat dirt before the filthy he-whore from the Hellers? I turned away and said to di Asturien, "When you please, Master, you may dismiss your charges."

"You insolent bastard, I'll have your hide for this!"

"Bastard I may be," I said, keeping my voice low, "but I consider it no edifying sight for two captains to quarrel in the hearing of cadets, Captain Ardais."

He swallowed that. He was soldier enough to know it was true. As I dismissed the men, I reflected on the powerful enemy I had made. Before this, he had disliked me, but he was my father's friend and anything belonging to a friend he would tolerate, provided it stayed in its place.

Now I had gone a long way beyond his rather narrow concept of that place and he would never forgive it.

Well, I could live without his approval. But I had better lose no time in talking to Father. Dyan wouldn't.

I found him awake and restive, swathed in bandages, his lame leg propped up. He looked haggard and flushed, and I wished I need not trouble him.

"Did the call-over go well?"

"Well enough. Danilo made a good appearance," I said, knowing he'd want to know.

"Regis was added at the last moment. Was he there?"

I nodded, and Father asked, "Did Dyan turn up to take charge? He had a sleepless night too, but said he'd be there."

I stared at him in outrage, finally bursting out, "Father! You can't be serious! I thought it was a joke! Dyan, as cadet-master?"

"I don't joke about the Guards," Father said, his face hard, "and why not Dyan?"

I hesitated, then said, "Must I spell it out for you in full? Have you forgotten last year and the Vallonde youngster?"

"Hysterics," my father said with a shrug. "You took it more seriously than it deserved. When it came to the point, Octavien refused to undergo *laran* interrogation."

"That only proves he was afraid of you," I stormed, "nothing more! I've known grown men, hardened veterans, break down, accept any punishment, rather than face that ordeal! How many mature adults can undergo telepathic examination at the hands of an Alton? Octavien was fifteen!"

"You're missing the point, Lew. The fact is, since he did *not* substantiate the charge, I am not officially required to take notice of it."

"Did you happen to notice that Dyan never denied it either? He didn't have the courage to face an Alton and lie, did he?"

Kennard sighed and tried to hoist himself up in bed. I said, "Let me help you," but he waved me away. "Sit down, Lew, don't stand over me like a statue of an avenging god! What makes you think he would stoop to lie, or that I have any right to ask for any details of his private life? Is your own life so pure and perfect—"

"Father, whatever I may have done for amusement before I was a grown man is completely beside the point," I said. "I have never abused authority—"

He said coldly, "It seems you abused it when you ignored my written orders." His voice hardened. "I told you to sit down! Lew, I don't owe you any explanations, but since you seem to be upset about this, I'll make it clear. The world is made as it's made, not as you or I would like it. Dyan may not be the ideal cadet-master, but he's asked for this post and I'm not going to refuse him."

"Why not?" I was more outraged than ever. "Just because he is Lord Ardais, must he be allowed a free hand for any kind of debauchery, corruption, anything he pleases? I don't care what he does, but does he have to have license to do it in the Guards?" I demanded. "Why?"

"Lew, listen to me. It's easy to use hard words about anyone who's less than perfect. They have one for you, or have you forgotten? I've listened to it for fifteen years, because I needed you. We need Lord Ardais on Council because he's a strong man and a strong supporter of Hastur. Have you become so involved with your private world at Arilinn that you don't remember the real political situation?" I grimaced, but he said, very patient now, "One faction on Council would like to plunge us into war with the Terrans. That's so unthinkable I needn't take it seriously, unless this small faction gains support. Another faction wants us to join the Terrans completely, give up our old ways and traditions, give up the Compact, become an Empire colony. That faction's bigger, and a lot more dangerous to Comyn. I feel that Hastur's solution, slow change, compromise, above all *time,* is the only reasonable answer. Dyan is one of the very few men who are willing to throw their weight behind Hastur. Why should we refuse him a position he wants, in return?"

"Then we're filthy and corrupt," I raged. "Just to get his support for your political ambitions, you're willing to bribe a man like Dyan by putting him in charge of half-grown boys?"

My father's quick rage flared. It had never been turned full on me before. "Do you honestly believe it's my personal ambition I'm furthering? I ask you, which is more important—the personal ethics of the cadet-master or the future of Darkover and the very survival of the Comyn? No, damn it, you sit there and listen to me! When we need Dyan's support so badly in Council do you think I'd quarrel with him over his private behavior?"

I flung back, equally furious, "I wouldn't give a damn if it *was* his private behavior! But if there's another scandal in the Guards, don't you think the Comyn will suffer? I didn't ask to command the Guards. I told you I'd rather not. But you wouldn't listen to my refusal and now you refuse to listen to my best judgment! I tell you, I won't have Dyan as cadetmaster! Not if I'm in command!"

"Oh, yes you will," said my father in a low and vicious voice. "Do you think I am going to let you defy me?"

"Then, damn it, Father, get someone else to command the Guards! Offer Dyan the command—wouldn't *that* satisfy his ambition?"

"But it wouldn't satisfy me," he said harshly. "I've worked for years to put you in this position. If you think I'm going to let you destroy the Domain of Alton by some childish scruples, you're mistaken. I'm still lord of the Domain and you are oath-bound to take my orders without question! The post of cadet-master is powerful enough to satisfy Dyan, but I'm not going to endanger the rights of the Altons to command. I'm doing it for you, Lew."

"I wish you'd save your trouble! I don't want it!"

"You're in no position to know what you want. Now do as I tell you: go and give Dyan his appointment as cadet-master, or"—he struggled again, ignoring the pain—"I'll get out of bed and do it myself."

His anger I could face; his suffering was something else. I struggled between rage and a deadly misgiving. "Father, I have never disobeyed you. But I beg you, I *beg* you," I repeated, "to reconsider. You know that no good will come of this."

He was gentle again. "Lew, you're still very young. Some day you'll learn that we all have compromises to make, and we make them with the best grace we can. You have to do the best you can within a situation. You can't eat nuts without cracking some shells." He stretched out his hand to me. "You're my main support, Lew. Don't force me to fight you too. I need you at my side."

I clasped his hand between my fingers; it felt swollen and

feverish. How could I add to his troubles? He trusted me. What right had I to set up my judgment against his? He was my father, my commander, the lord of my Domain. My only duty was to obey.

Out of his sight, my rage flared again. Who would have believed Father would compromise the honor of the Guards? And how quickly he had maneuvered me again, like a puppet-master pulling strings of love, loyalty, ambition, my own need for his recognition!

I will probably never forget the interview with Dyan Ardais. Oh, he was civil enough. He even commended me on my caution. I kept myself barriered and was scrupulously polite, but I am sure he knew that I felt like a farmer who has just set a wolf to guard the fowl-house.

There was only one grain of comfort in the situation: *I* was no longer a cadet!

CHAPTER FIVE

As the cadets walked toward the barracks, Regis among them, he heard little of their chatter and horseplay. His face was burning. He could cheerfully have murdered Lew Alton.

Then a tardy fairness came back to him. Everybody there obviously knew what was going to happen, so it was evidently something that went on now and then. He was just the one who stumbled into it. It could have been anyone.

Suddenly he felt better. For the first time in his life he was being treated exactly like anybody else. No deference. No special treatment. He brightened and began to listen to what they were saying.

"Where the hell were you brought up, cadet, not to answer to your name?"

"I was educated at Nevarsin," Regis said, provoking more jeers and laughter.

"Hey, we have a monk among us! Were you too busy at your prayers to hear your name?"

"No, it was the hour of Great Silence and the bell hadn't rung for speech!"

Regis listened with an amiable and rather witless grin, which was the best thing he could possibly have done. A third-year cadet, superior and highly polished in his green and black uniform, conveyed them into a barracks room at the far end of the courtyard. "First-year men in here."

"Hey," someone asked, "what happened to the Commander?"

The junior officer in charge said, "Wash your ears next time. He broke some bones in a fall. We all heard."

Someone said, carefully not loud enough for the officer to hear, "Are we going to be stuck with the bastard all season?"

"Shut up," said Julian MacAran, "Lanart-Alton's not a bad sort. He's got a temper if you set him off, but nothing like the old man in a rage. Anyway, it could be worse," he added, with a wary glance at the cadet who was out of range for the moment. "Lew's fair and he keeps his hands to himself, which is more than you can say for *some* people."

Danilo asked, "Who's really going to be cadet-master? Di Asturien's been retired for years. He served with my grandfather!"

Damon MacAnndra said with a careful look at the officer, "I heard it was going to be you-know-who. Captain Ardais."

Julian said, "I hope you're joking. Last night I was down in the armory and . . ." His voice fell to a whisper. Regis was too far away, but the lads crowded around him reacted with nervous, high-pitched giggles. Damon said, "That's nothing. Listen, did you hear about my cousin Octavien Vallonde? Last year—"

"Chill it," a strange cadet said, just loud enough for Regis to hear. "You know what happened to him for gossiping about a Comyn heir. Have you forgotten there's one in the barracks now?"

Silence abruptly fell over the knot of cadets. They separated and began to drift around the barracks room. To Regis it was like a slap in the face. One minute they were laughing and joking, including him in their jokes; suddenly he was an outsider, a threat. It was worse because he had not really caught the drift of what they were saying.

He drifted toward Danilo, who was at least a familiar face. "What happens now?"

"I guess we wait for someone to tell us. I didn't mean to attract attention and get you in trouble, Lord Regis."

"You too, Dani?" That formal *Lord Regis* seemed a symbol of the distance they were all keeping. He managed to laugh. "Didn't you just hear Lew Alton remind me very forcibly that nobody would call me Lord Regis down here?"

Dani gave him a quick, spontaneous grin. "Right." He looked around the barracks room. It was bleak, cold and comfortless. A dozen hard, narrow camp-beds were ranged in two rows along the wall. All but one had been made up. Danilo gestured to the only one still unchosen and said, "Most of us were down here last night and picked beds. I guess that one will have to be yours. It's next to mine, anyhow."

Regis shrugged. "They haven't left me much choice." It was, of course, the least desirable location, in a corner under a high window, which would probably be drafty. Well, it couldn't be worse than the student dormitory at Nevarsin. Or colder.

The third-year cadet said, "Men, you can have the rest of the morning to make up your beds and put away your clothing. No food in barracks at any time; anything left lying on the floor will be confiscated." He glanced around at the boys waiting quietly for his orders. He said, "Uniforms will be given out tomorrow. MacAnndra—"

Damon said, "Sir?"

"Get a haircut from the barber; you're not at a dancing class. Hair below the collarbone is officially out of uniform. Your mother may have loved those curls, but the officers won't."

Damon turned as red as an apple and ducked his head.

Regis examined the bed, which was made of rough planking, with a straw mattress covered with coarse, clean ticking. Folded at the foot were a couple of thick dark gray blankets. They looked scratchy. The other lads were making up the beds with their own sheets. Regis began making a mental list of the things he should fetch from his grandfather's rooms. It began with bed linens and a pillow. At the head of each bed was a narrow wooden shelf on which each cadet had already placed his personal possessions. At the foot of the bed was a rough wooden box, each lid scarred with knife-marks, intertwined initials and hacked or lightly burned-in crests, the marks of generations of restless boys. It struck Regis that years ago his father must have been a cadet in this very room, on a hard bed like this, his possessions reduced, whatever his rank or riches, to what he could keep on a narrow shelf a hand-span wide. Danilo was arranging on his shelf a plain wooden comb, a hairbrush, a battered cup and plate and a small box carved with silver, from which he reverently took the small *cristoforo* statue of the Bearer of Burdens, carrying his weight of the world's sorrows.

Below the shelf were pegs for his sword and dagger. Danilo's looked very old. Heirlooms in his family?

All of them were there because their forefathers had been, Regis thought with the old resentment. He swore he would never walk the trail carved out for a Hastur heir, yet here he was.

The cadet officer was walking along the room, making some kind of final check. At the far end of the room was an open space with a couple of heavy benches and a much-scarred wooden table. There was an open fireplace, but no fire was burning at present. The windows were high and narrow, unglazed, covered with slatted wood shutters, which could be closed in the worst weather at the price of shutting out most of the light. The cadet officer said, "Each of you will be sent for some time today and tested by an arms-master." He saw Regis sitting on the end of his bed and walked down the row of beds to him.

"You came in late. Did anyone give you a copy of the arms-manual?"

"No, sir."

The officer gave him a battered booklet. "I heard you were educated at Nevarsin; I suppose you can read. Any questions?"

"I didn't—my grandfather didn't—no one sent my things down. May I send for them?"

The older lad said, not unkindly, "There's no one to fetch and carry for you down here, cadet. Tomorrow after dinner you'll have some off-duty time and you can go and fetch what you need for yourself. Meanwhile, you'll just have to make out with the clothes on your back." He looked Regis over, and Regis imagined a veiled sneer at the elaborate garments he had put on to present himself to his grandfather this morning. "You're the nameless wonder, aren't you? Remembered your name yet?"

"Cadet Hastur, sir," Regis said, his face burning again, and the officer nodded, said, "Very good, cadet," and went away.

And that was obviously why they did it, Regis thought. Probably nobody ever forgot twice.

Danilo, who had been listening, said, "Didn't anyone tell you to bring down everything you'd need the night before? That's why Lord Alton sent me down early."

"No, no one told me." He wished he had thought to ask Lew, while they could speak together as friends and not as cadet and commander, what he would need in barracks.

Danilo said diffidently, "Those are your best clothes,

aren't they? I could lend you an ordinary shirt to put on; you're about my size."

"Thank you, Dani. I'd be grateful. This outfit isn't very suitable, is it?"

Danilo, who was kneeling in front of his wooden chest, brought out a clean but very shabby linen shirt, much patched around the elbows. Regis pulled off the dyed-leather tunic and the fine frilled shirt under it and slid into the patched one. It was a little large. Danilo apologized. "It's big for me too. It used to belong to Lew—Captain Alton, I mean. Lord Kennard gave me some of his outgrown clothes, so that I'd have a decent outfit for the cadets. He gave me a good horse too. He's been very kind to me."

Regis laughed. "I used to wear Lew's outgrown clothes the years I was there. I kept growing out of mine, and with the fire-watch called every few days, no one had time to make me any new ones or send to town." He laced up the cords at the neck. Danilo said, "It's hard to imagine *you* wearing outgrown clothes."

"I didn't mind wearing Lew's. I hated wearing my sister's outgrown nightgowns, though. Her governess taught her needlework by having her cut them down to size for me. Whenever she was cross about it, she used to pinch or prick me with her pins while she was trying them on. She's never liked sewing." He thought of his sister as he had last seen her, heavy-footed, swollen in pregnancy. Poor Javanne. She was caught too, with nothing ahead of her except bearing children for the house of Hastur.

"Regis, is something wrong?"

Regis was startled at Danilo's look of concern. "Not really. I was thinking of my sister, wondering if her child had been born."

Danilo said gently, "I'm sure they'd have sent word if anything was wrong. The old saying is that good news crawls on its belly; bad news has wings."

Damon MacAnndra came toward them. "Have you been tested yet by the arms-master?"

"No," said Dani, "they didn't get to me yesterday. What happens?"

Damon shrugged. "The arms-master hands you a standard Guardsmen sword and asks you to demonstrate the basic positions for defense. If you don't know which end of it to take hold by, he puts you down for beginner's lessons and you get to practice about three hours a day. In your off-duty time, of course. If you know the basics, he or one of his assistants will test you. When I went up last night, Lord Dyan was there watching. I tell you, I sweat blood! I made a damn fool of myself, my foot slipped and he put me down for lessons every other day. Who could do anything with that one staring at you?"

"Yes," Julian said from the cot beyond, where he was trying to get a spot of rust off his knife. "My brother told me he likes to sit and watch the cadets training. He seems to enjoy seeing them get rattled and do stupid things. He's a mean one."

"I studied swordplay at Nevarsin," Danilo said. "I'm not worried about the arms-master."

"Well, you'd better worry about Lord Dyan. You're just young enough and pretty enough—"

"Shut your mouth," Danilo said. "You shouldn't talk that way about a Comyn lord."

Damon snickered. "I forgot. You're Lord Alton's protégé, aren't you? Strange, I never heard that *he* had any special liking for pretty boys."

Danilo flared, his face burning. "You shut your filthy mouth! You're not fit to wipe Lord Kennard's boots! If you say anything like that again—"

"Well, it seems we have a whole cloister of monks back here." Julian joined in the laughter. "Do you recite the Creed of Chastity when you ride into battle, Dani?"

"It wouldn't hurt any of you dirty-mouths to say something decent," Danilo said and turned his back on them, burying himself in the arms-manual.

Regis had also been shocked by the accusation they had made and by their language. But he realized he could not expect ordinary young men to behave and talk like novice monks, and he knew they would quickly make his life unbearable if he showed any sign of his distaste. He held his peace. That sort of thing must be common enough here to be a joke.

Yet it had touched off a murder and near-riot in the Terran Zone. Could grown men actually take such things seriously enough to kill? Terrans, perhaps. They must have very strange customs, if they were even stricter than the *cristoforos*.

He suddenly recalled, as something that might have taken place years ago, that only this morning he had stood beside young Lawton in the Terran Zone, watching the starship break free from the planet and make its way to the stars. He wondered if Dan Lawton knew which end of a sword to take hold by, and if he cared. He had a strange sense of shuttling, rapidly and painfully, between worlds.

Three years. Three years to study swordplay while the Terran ships came and went less than a bowshot away.

Was this the kind of awareness his grandfather carried night and day, a constant reminder of two worlds rubbing shoulders, with violently opposed histories, habits, manners, moralities? How did Hastur live with the contrast?

The day wore on. He was sent for, and an orderly measured him for his uniform. When the sun was high, a junior officer came to show them the way to the mess hall, where the cadets ate at separate tables. The food was coarse and plain, but Regis had eaten worse at Nevarsin and he made a good meal, though some of the cadets grumbled loudly about the fare.

"It's not so bad," he said in an undertone to Danilo, and the younger boy's eyes glinted with mischief. "Maybe they want to make sure we know they're used to something better! Even if we're not."

Regis, aware of Danilo's patched shirt on his back, remembered how desperately poor the boy's family must be. Yet they had had him well educated at Nevarsin. "I'd thought you were to be a monk, Dani."

"I couldn't be," Dani said. "I'm my father's only son now, and it wouldn't be lawful. My half-brother was killed fifteen years ago, before I was born." As they left the mess hall, he added, "Father had me taught to read and write and keep accounts so that someday I'd be fit to manage his estate. He's growing too old to farm Syrtis alone. He didn't want me to go into the Guards, but when Lord Alton made such a kind offer, he couldn't refuse. I *hate* to hear them gossip about him," he said vehemently. "He's not like that! He's good and kind and decent!"

"I'm sure he doesn't listen," Regis said. "I lived in his house too, you know. And one of his favorite sayings used to be, *if you listen to dogs barking, you'll go deaf without learning much.* Are the Syrtis people under the Alton Domain, Danilo?"

"No, we have always been under Hastur wardship. My father was hawk-master to yours, and my half-brother his paxman."

And something Regis had always known, an old story which had been part of his childhood but which he had never associated with living people, fell into place in his mind. He said excitedly, "Dani! Your brother—was his name Rafael-Felix Syrtis of Syrtis?"

"Yes, that was his name. He was killed before I was born, in the same year Stefan Fourth died—"

"So was my father," said Regis, with a surge of unfamiliar emotion. "All my life I have known the story, known your brother's name. Dani, your brother was my father's personal guard, they were killed at the same instant—he died trying to shield my father with his body. Did you know they are buried side by side, in one grave, on the field of Kilghairlie?"

He remembered, but did not say, what an old servant had told him, that they were blown to bits, buried together where they fell, since no living man could tell which bits were his father's, which Dani's brother's.

"I didn't know," Danilo whispered, his eyes wide. Regis, caught in the grip of a strange emotion, said, "It must be horrible to die like that, but not so horrible if your last thought is to shield someone else. . . ."

Danilo's voice was not entirely steady. "They were both named Rafael and they had sworn to one another, and they fought together and died and were buried in one grave—" As if he hardly knew what he was doing, he reached out to Regis and clasped his hands. He said, "I'd like to die like that. Wouldn't you?"

Regis nodded wordlessly. For an instant it seemed to him that something had reached deep down inside him, an almost painful awareness and emotion. It was almost a physical touch, although Danilo's fingers were only resting lightly in his own. Suddenly, abashed by the intensity of his own feelings, he let go of Danilo's hand, and the surge of emotion receded. One of the cadet officers came up and said, "Dani, the arms-master has sent for you." Danilo caught up his shabby leather tunic, pulled it quickly over his shirt and went.

Regis, remembering that he had been up all night, stretched out on the bare straw ticking of his cot. He was too restless to sleep, but he fell at last into an uneasy doze, mingled with the unfamiliar sounds of the Guard hall the metallic clinking from the armory where someone was mending a shield, men's voices, very different from the muted speech of the monastery. Half asleep, he began to see a nightmarish sequence of faces: Lew Alton looking sad and angry when he told Regis he had no *laran,* Kennard pleading for Marius, his grandfather struggling not to betray exhaustion or grief. As he drifted deeper into the neutral country on the edge of sleep, he remembered Danilo, handling the wooden practice swords at Nevarsin. Someone whose face Regis could not see was standing close behind him; Danilo moved abruptly away, and he heard through the dream a harsh, shrill laugh, raucous as the scream of a hawk. And then he had a sudden mental picture of Danilo, his face turned away, huddled against the wall, sobbing heartbrokenly. And through the dreamlike sobs Regis felt a shocking overtone of fear, disgust and a consuming shame. . . .

Someone laid a careful hand on his shoulder, shook him lightly. The barracks room was filled with the dimness of sunset. Danilo said, "Regis? I'm sorry to wake you, but the cadet-master wants to see you. Do you know the way?"

Regis sat up, still a little dazed by the sharp edges of nightmare. For a moment he thought that Danilo's face, bent over him in the dim light, was actually red and flushed, as if he had been crying, like in the dream. No, that was ridiculous. Dani looked hot and sweaty, as if he'd been running hard or exercising. Probably they'd tested his swordplay. Regis tried to throw off the remnants of dream. He went into the stonefloored washroom and latrine, sluiced his face with the paralyzingly cold water from the pump. Back in the barracks, tugging his leather tunic over Dani's patched shirt, he saw Danilo slumped on his cot, his head in his hands. He must have done badly at his arms-test and he's upset about it, he decided, and left without disturbing his friend.

Inside the armory there was a second-year cadet with

long lists in his hands, another officer writing at a table and Dyan Ardais, seated behind an old worm-eaten desk. Because the afternoon had turned warm, his collar was undone, his coarse dark hair clinging damply around his high forehead. He glanced up, and Regis felt that in one swift feral glance Dyan had learned everything he wanted to know about him.

"Cadet Hastur. Getting along all right so far?"

"Yes, Lord Dyan."

"Just Captain Ardais in the Guard hall, Regis." Dyan looked him over again, a slow evaluating stare that made Regis uncomfortable. "At least they taught you to stand straight at Nevarsin. You should see the way some of the lads stand!" He consulted a long sheet on his desk. "Regis-Rafael Felix Alar Hastur-Elhalyn. You prefer Regis-Rafael?"

"Simply Regis, sir."

"As you wish. Although it seems a great pity to let the name of Rafael Hastur be lost. It is an honored name."

Damn it, Regis thought, I know I'm not my father! He knew he sounded curt and almost impolite as he said, "My sister's son has been named Rafael, Captain. I prefer not to share my father's honor before I have earned it."

"An admirable objective," Dyan said slowly. "I think every man wants a name for himself, rather than resting on the past. I can understand that, Regis." After a moment, with an odd impulsive grin he said, "It must be a pleasant thing to have a father's honor to cherish, a father who did not outlive his moment of glory. You know, I suppose, that *my* father has been mad these twenty years, without wits enough to know his son's face?"

Regis had only heard rumors of old Kyril Ardais, who had not been seen by anyone outside Castle Ardais for so long that most people in the Domains had long forgotten his existence, or that Dyan was not Lord Ardais, but only Lord Dyan. Abruptly, Dyan spoke in an entirely different tone.

"How tall are you?"

"Five feet ten."

The eyebrows went up in amused inquiry. "Already? Yes, I believe you are at that. Do you drink?"

"Only at dinner, sir."

"Well, don't start. There are too many young sots around. Turn up drunk on duty and you'll be booted, no excuses or explanations accepted. You are also forbidden to gamble. I don't mean wagering pennies on card games or dice, of course, but gambling substantial sums is against the rules. Did they give you a manual of arms? Good, read it tonight. After tomorrow you're responsible for everything in it. A few more things. Duels are absolutely forbidden, and drawing your sword or knife on a fellow Guardsman will break you. So keep your temper, whatever happens. You're not married, I suppose. Handfasted?"

"Not that I've heard, sir."

Dyan made an odd derisive sound. "Well, make the best of it; your grandfather will probably have you married off before the year's out. Let me see. What you do in off-duty time is your own affair, but don't get yourself talked about. There's a rule about causing scandalous talk by scandalous behavior. I don't have to tell you that the heir to a Domain is expected to set an example, do I?"

"No, Captain, you don't have to tell me that." Regis had had his nose rubbed in that all his life and he supposed Dyan had too.

Dyan's eyes met his again, amused, sympathetic. "It's unfair, isn't it, kinsman? Not allowed to claim any Comyn privileges, but still expected to set an example because of what we are." With another swift change of mood, he was back to the remote officer. "In general, keep out of the Terran Zone for your . . . amusements."

Regis was thinking of the young Terran officer who, before they parted, had again offered to show him more of the spaceport whenever he wished. "Is it forbidden to go into the Terran Zone at all?"

"By no means. The prohibition doesn't apply to sightseeing, shopping or eating there if you have a taste for exotic foods. But Terran customs differ enough from ours that getting entangled with Terran prostitutes, or making any sexual advances to them, is likely to be a risky business. So keep out of trouble. To put it bluntly—you're supposed to be grown up now—if you have a taste for such adventures, find them on the Darkovan side of the line. Zandru's hells, my boy, aren't you too old to blush? Or hasn't the monastery worn off you yet?" He laughed. "I suppose, brought up at Nevarsin, you don't know a damn thing about arms, either?"

Regis welcomed the change of subject this time. He said he had had lessons, and Dyan's nostrils flared in contempt. "Some broken-down old soldier earning a few coins teaching the basic positions?"

"Kennard Alton taught me when I was a child, sir."

"Well, we'll see." He motioned to one of the junior officers. "Hjalmar, give him a practice sword."

Hjalmar handed Regis one of the wood and leather swords used for training. Regis balanced it in his hand. "Sir, I'm very badly out of practice."

"Never mind," Hjalmar said, bored. "We'll see what kind of training you've had."

Regis raised his sword in salute. He saw Hjalmar lift an eyebrow as he dropped into the defensive stance Kennard had taught him years ago. The moment Hjalmar lowered his weapon Regis noted the weak point in his defense; he feinted, sidestepped and touched Hjalmar almost instantly on the thigh. They reengaged. For a moment there was no sound but the scuffle of feet as they circled one another, then Hjalmar made a swift pass which Regis parried. He disengaged and touched him on the shoulder.

"Enough." Dyan threw off his vest, standing in shirtsleeves. "Give me the sword, Hjalmar."

Regis knew, as soon as Dyan raised the wooden blade, that this was no amateur. Hjalmar, evidently, was used for testing cadets who were shy or completely unskilled, perhaps handling weapons for the first time. Dyan was another matter. Regis felt a tightness in his throat, recalling the gossip of the cadets: Dyan liked to see people get rattled and do something stupid.

He managed to counter the first stroke and the second, but on the third his parry slid awkwardly along Dyan's casually turned blade and he felt the wooden tip thump his ribs hard. Dyan nodded to him to go on, then beat him back step by step, finally touched him again, again, three times in rapid succession. Regis flushed and lowered his sword.

Then he felt the older man's hand gripping his shoulder hard. "So you're out of practice?"

"Very badly, Captain."

"Stop bragging, *chiyu*. You made me sweat, and not even the arms-master can always do that. Kennard taught you well. I'd halfway expected, with that pretty face of yours, you'd have learned nothing but courtly dances. Well, lad, you can be excused from regular lessons, but you'd better turn out for practice every day. If, that is, we can find anyone to match you. If not, I'll have to work out with you myself."

"I would be honored, Captain," Regis said, but hoped Dyan would not hold him to this. Something about the older man's intense stare and teasing compliments made him feel awkward and very young. Dyan's hand on his shoulder was hard, almost a painful grip. He turned Regis gently around to look at him. He said, "Since you already have some skill at swordplay, kinsman, perhaps, if you like the idea, I could ask to have you assigned as my aide. Among other things, it would mean you need not sleep in the barracks."

Regis said quickly, "I'd rather not, sir." He fumbled for an acceptable excuse. "Sir, that is a post for an—an experienced cadet. If I am assigned at once to a post of honor, it will look as if I am taking advantage of my rank, to be excused from what the other cadets have to do. Thank you for the honor, Captain, but I don't think I—I ought to accept."

Dyan threw back his head and laughed, and it seemed to Regis that the raucous laughter sounded a little like the feral cry of a hawk, that there was something nightmarish about it. Regis was caught in the grip of a strange *déjà vu*, feeling that this had happened before.

It vanished as swiftly as it had come. Dyan released his grip on Regis' shoulder.

"I honor you for that decision, kinsman, and I dare say you are right. And in training already to be a statesman, I see. I can find no fault with your answer."

Again the wild, hawklike laugh.

"You can go, cadet. Tell young MacAran I want to see him."

CHAPTER SIX

(Lew Alton's narrative)

Father was bedridden during the first several days of Council season, and I was too busy and beset to have much time for the cadets. I had to attend Council meetings, which at this particular time were mostly concerned with some dreary business of trade agreements with the Dry Towns. One thing I did find time for was having that staircase fixed before someone else broke his leg, or his neck. This was troublesome too: I had to deal with architects and builders, we had stonemasons underfoot for days, the cadets coughed from morning to night with the choking dust and the veterans grumbled constantly about having to go the long way round and use the other stairs.

A long time before I thought he was well enough, Father insisted on returning to his Council seat, which I was glad to be out of. Far too soon after that, he returned to the Guards, his arm still in a sling, looking dreadfully pale and worn. I suspected he shared some of my uneasiness about how well the cadets would fare this season, but he said nothing about it to me. It nagged at me ceaselessly; I resented it as much for my father's sake as my own. If my father had *chosen* to trust Dyan Ardais, I might not have been quite so disturbed. But I felt that he, too, had been *compelled,* and that Dyan had enjoyed having the power to do so.

A few days after that, Gabriel Lanart-Hastur returned from Edelweiss with news that Javanne had borne twin girls, whom she named Ariel and Liriel. With Gabriel at my hand, my father sent me back into the hills on a mission to set up a new system of fire-watch beacons, to inspect the fire-watch stations which had been established in my grandfather's day and to instruct the Rangers in new fire-fighting techniques. This kind of mission demands tact and some Comyn authority, to persuade men separated by family feuds and rivalries, sometimes for generations, to work together peacefully. Fire-truce is the oldest tradition on Darkover but, in districts which have been lucky enough to escape forest fires for centuries, it's hard to persuade anyone that the fire-truce should be extended to the upkeep of the stations and beacons.

I had my father's full authority, though, and that helped. The law of the Comyn transcends, or is supposed to transcend, personal feuds and family rivalries. I had a dozen Guardsmen with me for the physical work, but I had to do the talking, the persuading and the temper-smoothing when old struggles flared out of control. It took a lot of tact and thought; it also demanded knowledge of the various families, their hereditary loyalties, intermarriages and interactions for the last seven or eight generations. It was high summer before I rode back to Thendara, but I felt I'd accomplished a great deal. Every step against the constant menace of forest fire on Darkover impresses me more than all the political accomplishments of the last hundred years. That's something we've actually gained from the presence of the Terran Empire: a great increase in knowledge of fire-control and an exchange of information with other heavily wooded Empire planets about new methods of surveillance and protection.

And back in the hills the Comyn name meant something. Nearer to the Trade Cities, the influence of Terra has eroded the old habit of turning to the Comyn for leadership. But back there, the potency of the very name of Comyn was immense. The people neither knew nor cared that I was a half-Terran bastard. I was the son of Kennard Alton, and that was all that really mattered. For the first time I carried the full authority of a Comyn heir.

I even settled a blood-feud which had run three generations by suggesting that the eldest son of one house marry the only daughter of another and the disputed land be settled on their children. Only a Comyn lord could have suggested this without becoming himself entangled in the feud, but they accepted it. When I thought of the lives it would save, I was glad of the chance.

I rode into Thendara one morning in midsummer. I've heard offworlders say our planet has no summer, but there had been no snow for three days, even in the pre-dawn hours, and that was summer enough for me. The sun was dim and cloud-hidden, but as we rode down from the pass it broke through the layers of fog, throwing deep crimson lights on the city lying below us. Old people and children gathered inside the city gates to watch us, and I found I was grinning to myself. Part of it, of course, was the thought of being able to sleep for two nights in the same bed. But part of it was pure pleasure at knowing I'd done a good job. It seemed, for the first time in my life, that this was *my* city, that I was coming home. I had not chosen this duty—I had been born into it—but I no longer resented it so much.

Riding into the stable court of the Guards, I saw a brace of cadets on watch at the gates and more going out from the mess hall. They seemed a soldierly lot, not the straggle of awkward children they had been that first day. Dyan had done well enough, evidently. Well, it had never been his competence I questioned, but even so, I felt better. I turned my horse over to the grooms and went to make my report to my father.

He was out of bandages now, with his arm free of the sling, but he still looked pale, his lameness more pronounced than ever. He was in Council regalia, not uniform. He waved away my proffered report.

"No time for that now. And I'm sure you did as well as I could have done myself. But there's trouble here. Are you very tired?"

"No, not really. What's wrong, Father? More riots?"

"Not this time. A meeting of Council with the Terran Legate this morning. In the city, at Terran headquarters."

"Why doesn't he wait on you in the Council Chamber?" Comyn lords did not come and go at the bidding of the Terranan!

He caught the thought and shook his head. "It was Hastur himself who requested this meeting. It's more important than you can possibly imagine. That's why I want you to handle this for me. We need an honor guard, and I want you to choose the members very carefully. It would be disastrous if this became a subject of gossip in the Guards—or elsewhere."

"Surely, Father, any Guardsman would be honor-bound—"

"In theory, yes," he said dryly, "but in practice, some of them are more trustworthy than others. You know the younger men better than I do." It was the first time he had ever admitted so much. He had missed me, needed me. I felt warmed and welcomed, even though all he said was, "Choose Guardsmen or cadets who are blood-kin to Comyn if you can, or the trustiest. You know best which of them have tongues that rattle at both ends."

Gabriel Lanart, I thought, as I went down to the Guard hall, an Alton kinsman, married into the Hasturs. Lerrys Ridenow, the younger brother of the lord of his Domain. Old di Asturien, whose loyalty was as firm as the foundations of Comyn Castle itself. I left him to choose the veterans who would escort us through the streets—they would not go into the meeting rooms, so their choice was not so critical—and went off to cadet barracks.

It was the slack time between breakfast and morning drill. The first-year cadets were making their beds, two of them sweeping the floor and cleaning out the fireplaces. Regis was sitting on the corner cot, mending a broken bootlace. Was it meekness or good nature which had let them crowd him into the drafty spot under the window? He sprang up and came to attention as I stopped at the foot of his bed.

I motioned him to relax. "The commander has sent me to choose an honor guard detail," I said. "This is Comyn business; it goes without saying that no word of what you may hear is to go outside Council rooms. Do you understand me, Regis?"

"Yes, Captain." He was formal, but I caught curiosity and excitement in his lifted face. He looked older, not quite so childish, not nearly so shy. Well, as I knew from my own first tormented cadet season, one of two things happened in the first few days. You grew up fast . . . or you crawled back home, beaten, to your family. I've often thought that was why cadets were required to serve a few terms in the Guard. No one could ever tell in advance which ones would survive.

I asked, "How are you getting along?"

He smiled. "Well enough." He started to say something else, but at that moment Danilo Syrtis, covered in dust, crawled out from under his bed. "Got it!" he said. "It evidently slipped down this morning when I—" He saw me, broke off and came to attention.

"Captain."

"Relax, cadet," I said, "but you'd better get that dirt off your knees before you go out to inspection." He was father's protégé, and his family had been Hastur men for generations. "You join the honor guard too, cadet. Did you hear what I said to Regis, Dani?"

He nodded, coloring, and his eyes brightened. He said, with such formality that it sounded stiff, "I am deeply honored, Captain." But through the formal words, I caught the touch of excitement, apprehension, curiosity, unmistakable pleasure at the honor.

Unmistakable. This was not the random sensing of emotions which I pick up in any group, but a definite touch.

Laran. The boy had *laran,* was certainly a telepath, probably had one of the other gifts. Well, it was not much of a surprise. Father had told me they had Comyn blood a few generations back. Regis was kneeling before his chest, searching for the leather tabard of his dress uniform. As Danilo was about to follow suit, I stepped to his side and said, "A word, kinsman. Not now—there is no urgency—but some time, when you are free of other duties, go to my father, or to Lord Dyan if you prefer, and ask to be tested by a *leronis*. They will know what you mean. Say that it was I who told you this." I turned away. "Both of you join the detail at the gates as soon as you can."

The Comyn lords were waiting in the court as the detail of Guards were forming. Lord Hastur, in sky-blue cloak with the silver fir tree badge. My father, giving low-voiced directions to old di Asturien. Prince Derik was not present. Hastur would have had to speak for him as Regent in any case, but Derik at sixteen should certainly have been old enough, and interested enough, to attend such an important meeting.

Edric Ridenow was there, the thickset, red-bearded lord of Serrais. There was also a woman, pale and slender, folded in a thin gray hooded cloak which shielded her from curious eyes. I did not recognize her, but she was evidently *comynara;* she must be an Aillard or an Elhalyn, since only those two Domains give independent Council right to their women. Dyan Ardais, in the crimson and gray of his Domain, strode to his place; he gave a brief glance to the honor guard, stopped briefly beside Danilo and spoke in a low voice. The boy blushed and looked straight ahead. I'd already noticed that he still colored like a child if you spoke to him. I wondered what small fault the cadet-master had found in his appearance and bearing. I had found none, but it's a cadet-master's business to take note of trivialities.

As we moved through the streets of Thendara, we drew surprised glances. Damn the Terrans anyway! It lessened Comyn dignity, that they beckoned and we came at a run!

The Regent seemed conscious of no loss of dignity. He moved between his escort with the energy of a man half his years, his face stern and composed. Just the same I was glad when we reached the spaceport gates. Leaving the escort outside, we were conducted, Comyn lords and honor guard, into the building to a large room on the first floor.

As custom decreed, I stepped inside first, drawn sword in hand. It was small for a council chamber, but contained a large, round table and many seats. A number of Terrans were seated on the far side of the table, mostly in some sort of uniform. Some of them wore a great number of medals, and I surmised they intended to do the Comyn honor.

Some of them showed considerable unease when I stepped inside with my drawn sword, but the gray-haired man at their center—the one with the most medals—said quickly, "It is customary, their honor guard. You come for the Regent of Comyn, officer?"

He had spoken *cahuenga,* the mountain dialect which has become a common tongue all over Darkover, from the Hellers to the Dry Towns. I brought my sword up to salute and replied, "Captain Montray-Alton, at your service, sir." Since I saw no weapons visible anywhere in the room, I forebore any further search and sheathed the sword. I ushered in the rest of the honor guard, placing them around the room, motioning Regis to take a position directly behind the Regent, stationing Gabriel at the doorway, then ushering in the members of the Council and announcing their names one by one.

"Danvan-Valentine, Lord Hastur, Warden of Elhalyn, Regent of the Crown of the Seven Domains."

The gray-haired man—I surmised that he was the Terran

Legate—rose to his feet and bowed. Not deeply enough, but more than I'd expected of a Terran. "We are honored, Lord Regent."

"Kennard-Gwynn Alton, Lord Alton, Commander of the City Guard." He limped heavily to his place.

"Lord Dyan-Gabriel, Regent of Ardais." Whatever my personal feelings about him, I had to admit he looked impressive. "Edric, Lord Serrais. And—" I hesitated a moment as the gray-cloaked woman entered, realized I did not know her name. She smiled almost imperceptibly and murmured under her breath, "For shame, kinsman! Don't you recognize me? I am Callina Aillard."

I felt like an utter fool. Of course I knew her.

"Callina, Lady Aillard—" I hesitated again momentarily; I could not remember in which of the towers she was serving as Keeper. Well, the Terrans would never know the difference. She supplied it telepathically, with an amused smile behind her hood, and I concluded, "*leronis* of Neskaya."

She walked with quiet composure to the remaining seat. She kept the hood of her cloak about her face, as was proper for an unwedded woman among strangers. I saw with some relief that the Legate, at least, had been informed of the polite custom among valley Darkovans and had briefed his men not to look directly at her. I too kept my eyes politely averted; she was my kinswoman, but we were among strangers. I had seen only that she was very slight, with pale solemn features.

When everyone was in his appointed place, I drew my sword again, saluted Hastur and then the Legate and took my place behind my father. One of the Terrans said, "Now that all *that's* over, can we come to business?"

"Just a moment, Meredith," the Legate said, checking his unseemly impatience. "Noble lords, my lady, you lend us grace. Allow me to present myself. My name is Donnell Ramsay; I am privileged to serve the Empire as Legate for Terra. It is my pleasure to welcome you. These"—he indicated the men beside him at the table—"are my personal assistants: Laurens Meredith, Reade Andrusson. If there are any among you, my lords, who do not speak *cahuenga*, our liaison man, Daniel Lawton, will be honored to translate for you into the *casta*. If we may serve you otherwise, you have only to speak of it. And if you wish, Lord Hastur," he added, with a bow, "that this meeting should be conducted according to formal protocol in the *casta* language, we are ready to accede."

I was glad to note that he knew the rudiments of courtesy. Hastur said, "By your leave, sir, we will dispense with the translator, unless some misunderstanding should arise which he can settle. He is, however, most welcome to remain.

Young Lawton bowed. He had flaming red hair and a look of the Comyn about him. I remembered hearing that his mother had been a woman of the Ardais clan. I wondered if Dyan recognized his kinsman and what he thought about it. It was strange to think that young Lawton might well have been standing here among the honor guard. My thoughts were wandering; I commanded them back as Hastur spoke.

"I have come to you, Legate, to draw your attention to a grave breach of the Compact on Darkover. It has been brought to my notice that, back in the mountains near Aldaran, a variety of contraband weapons is being openly bought and sold. Not only within the Trade City boundaries there, where your agreement with us allows your citizens to carry what weapons they will, but in the old city of Caer Donn, where Terrans walk the streets as they wish, carrying pistols and blasters and neural disrupters. I have also been told that it is possible to purchase these weapons in that city, and that they have been sold upon occasion to Darkovan citizens. My informant purchased one without difficulty. It should not be necessary to remind you that this is a very serious breach of Compact."

It took all my self-control to keep the impassive face suitable for an honor guard, whose perfect model is a child's carved toy soldier, neither hearing nor seeing. Would even the Terrans dare to breach the Compact?

I knew now why my father had wanted to be certain no hint of gossip got out. Since the Ages of Chaos, the Darkovan Compact has banned any weapon operating beyond the hand's reach of the man wielding it. This was a fundamental law: the man who would kill must himself come within reach of death. News that the Compact was being violated would shake Darkover to the roots, create public disorder and distrust, damage the confidence of the people in their rulers.

The Legate's face betrayed nothing, yet something, some infinitesimal tightening of his eyes and mouth, told me this was no news to him.

"It is not our business to enforce the Compact on Darkover, Lord Hastur. The policy of the Empire is to maintain a completely neutral posture in regard to local disputes. Our dealings in Caer Donn and the Trade City there are with Lord Kermiac of Aldaran. It was made very clear to us that the Comyn have no jurisdiction in the mountains near Aldaran. Have I been misinformed? Is the territory of Aldaran subject to the laws of Comyn, Lord Hastur?"

Hastur said with a snap of his jaw, "Aldaran has not been a Comyn Domain for many years, Mr. Ramsay. Nevertheless, the Compact can hardly be called a local decision. While Aldaran is not under our law—"

"So I myself believed, sir," the Legate said, "and therefore—"

"Forgive me, Mr. Ramsay, I had not yet finished." Hastur was angry. I tried to keep myself barriered, as any telepath would in a crowd this size, but I couldn't shut out everything. Hastur's calm, stern face did not alter a muscle, but his anger was like the distant glow of a forest fire against the horizon. Not yet a danger, but a faraway menace. He said, "Correct me if I am wrong, Mr. Ramsay, but is it not true that when the Empire negotiated to have Darkover given status as a Class D Closed World"—the technical language sounded strange on his tongue, and he seemed to speak it with distaste—"that one condition of the use and lease of the spaceport and the establishment of the cities of Port Chicago, Caer Donn and Thendara as Trade Cities, was complete enforcement of Compact outside the Trade Cities and control of contraband weapons? Mindful of that agreement, can you truthfully state that it is not your business to enforce the Compact on Darkover, sir?"

Ramsay said, "We did and we do enforce it in the Comyn Domains and under Comyn law, my lord, at considerable trouble and expense to ourselves. Need I remind you that one of our men was threatened with murder, not long ago, because he was unweaponed and defenseless in a society which expects every man to fight and protect himself?"

Dyan Ardais said harshly, "The episode you mention was unnecessary. It is necessary to remind you that the man who was threatened with murder had himself murdered one of our Guardsmen, in a quarrel so trivial that a Darkovan boy of twelve would have been ashamed to make more of it than a joke! Then this Terran murderer hid behind his celebrated *weaponless* status"—even a Terran could not escape that sneer—"to refuse a lawful challenge by the murdered man's brother! If your men choose to go weaponless, sir, they alone are responsible for their acts."

Reade Andrusson said, "They do not *choose* to go weaponless, Lord Ardais. We are forced by the Compact to deprive them of their accustomed weapons."

Dyan said, "They are allowed by our laws to carry whatever ethical weapons they choose. They cannot complain of a defenselessness which is their own choice."

The Legate, turning his eyes consideringly on Dyan, said, "Their defenselessness, Lord Ardais, is in obedience to *our* laws. We have a very distinct bias, which our laws reflect, against carving people up with swords and knives."

Hastur said harshly, "Is it your contention, sir, that a man is somehow less dead if he is shot down from a safe distance without visible bloodshed? Is death cleaner when it comes to you from a killer safely out of reach of his own death?" Even through my own barriers, his pain was so violent, so palpable that it was like a long wail of anguish; I knew he was thinking of his own son, blown to fragments by smuggled contraband weapons, killed by a man whose face he never saw! So intense was that cry of agony that I saw Danilo, impassive behind Lord Edric, flinch and tighten his hands into white-knuckled fists at his sides; my father looked white and shaken; Regis' mouth moved and he blinked rapidly, and I wondered how even the Terrans could be unaware of so much pain. But Hastur's voice was steady, betraying nothing to the aliens. "We banned such coward's weapons to insure that any man who would kill must see his victim's blood flow and come into some danger of losing his own, if not at the hands of his victim, at least at the hands of his victim's family or friends."

The Legate said, "That episode was settled long ago,

Lord Regent, but I remind you we stood ready to prosecute our man for the killing of your Guardsman. We could not, however, expose him to challenges from the dead man's family one after another, especially when it was abundantly clear that the Guardsman had first provoked the quarrel."

"Any man who found provocation in such a trivial occurrence should expect to be challenged," said Dyan, "but your men hide behind your laws and surrender their own personal responsibility! Murder is a private affair and nothing for the laws!"

The Legate surveyed him with what would have been open dislike, had he been a little less controlled. "Our laws are made by agreement and consensus, and whether you approve of them or not, Lord Ardais, they are unlikely to be amended to make murder a matter of private vendetta and individual duels. But this is not the matter at issue."

I admired his control, the firm way in which he cut Dyan off. My own barriers, thinned by the assault of Hastur's anguish, were down almost to nothing; I could feel Dyan's contempt like an audible sneer.

I got my barriers together a little while Hastur silenced Dyan again and reminded him that the incident in question had been settled long since. "Not settled," Dyan half snarled, "hidden from," but Hastur firmly cut him off, insisting that there was a more important matter to be settled. By the time I caught up with the discussion again, the Legate was saying:

"Lord Hastur, this is an ethical question, not a legal one at all. We enforce Comyn laws within the jurisdiction of the Comyn. In Caer Donn and the Hellers, where the laws are made by Lord Aldaran, we enforce what laws *he* requires. If he cannot be bothered to enforce the Compact you value so highly, it is not our business to police it for him—or, my lord, for you."

Callina Aillard said in her quiet clear voice, "Mr. Ramsay, the Compact is not a law, in your sense, at all. I do not believe either of us quite understands what the other means by *law*. The Compact has been the ethical basis of Darkovan culture and history for hundreds of years; neither Kermiac of Aldaran nor any other man on Darkover has any right to disregard or disobey it."

Ramsay said, "You must debate that point with Aldaran

himself, my lady. He is not an Empire subject and I have no authority over him. If you want him to keep the Compact, you'll have to make him keep it."

Edric Ridenow spoke up for the first time. He said, "It is your responsibility, Ramsay, to enforce the substance of your agreement on our world. Are you intending to shirk that duty because of a quibble?"

"I am not shirking any responsibility which comes properly within the scope of my duties, Lord Serrais," he said, "but neither is it my duty to settle your disagreements with Aldaran. It seems to me that would be to infringe upon the responsibility of the Comyn."

Dyan opened his mouth again, but Hastur gestured him to silence. "You need not teach me my responsibilities, Mr. Ramsay. The Empire's agreement with Darkover, and the status of the spaceport, was determined with the Comyn, not with Kermiac of Aldaran. One stipulation of that agreement was enforcement of the Compact; and we intended enforcement, not only in the Domains, but all over Darkover. I dislike using threats, sir, but if you insist upon your right to violate your own agreement, I would be within my authority in closing the spaceport until such time as the agreement is kept in every detail."

The Legate said, "This, sir, is unreasonable. You have said yourself that the Compact is not a law but an ethical preference. I also dislike using threats, but if you take that course, I am certain that my next orders from the Administrative Center would be to negotiate a new agreement with Kermiac of Aldaran and move the Empire headquarters to Caer Donn Trade City, where we need not trouble Comyn scruples."

Hastur said bitterly, "You say you are prohibited from taking sides in local political decisions. Do you realize that this would effectively throw all the force of the Terran Empire against the very existence of the Compact?"

"You leave me no choice, sir."

"You know, don't you, that such a move would mean war? War not of the Comyn's making but, the Compact once abandoned, war would inevitably come. We have had no war here for many years. Small skirmishes, yes. But the enforcement of the Compact has kept such battles within reasonable limits. Do you want the responsibility for letting a different kind of war loose?"

"Of course not," Ramsay said. He was a nontelepath and his emotions were muddy, but I could tell that he was distressed. This distress made me like him just a little more. "Who would?"

"Yet you would hide behind your laws and your orders and your superiors, and let our world be plunged into war again? We had our Ages of Chaos, Ramsay, and the Compact brought them to an end. Does that mean nothing to you?"

The Terran looked straight at Hastur. I had a curious mental picture, a flash picked up from someone in the room, that they were like two massive towers facing one another, as the Comyn Castle and the Terran headquarters faced one another across the valley, gigantic armored figures braced for single combat. The image thinned and vanished and they were just two old men, both powerful, both filled with stubborn integrity, each doing the best for his own side. Ramsay said, "It means a very great deal to me, Lord Hastur. I want to be honest with you. If there was a major war here, it would mean closing and sealing the Trade Cities to be certain of keeping to our law against interference. I don't want to move the spaceport to Caer Donn. It was built there, a good many years ago. When the Comyn offered us this more convenient spot, down here in the plains at Thendara, we were altogether pleased to abandon the operation at Caer Donn, except for trade and certain transport. The Thendara location has been to our mutual advantage. If we are forced to move back to Caer Donn we would be forced to reschedule all our traffic, rebuild our headquarters back in the mountains where the climate is more difficult for Terrans to tolerate and, above all, rely on inadequate roads and inhospitable countryside. I don't want to do that, and we will do anything within reason to avoid it."

Dyan said, "Mr. Ramsay, are you not in command of all the Terrans on Darkover?"

"You have been misinformed, Lord Dyan. I'm a legate, not a dictator. My authority is mostly over spaceport personnel stationed here, and only in matters which for one reason or another supersede that of their individual departments of administration. My major business is to keep order in the Trade City. Furthermore, I have authority from Administration Central to deal with Darkovan citizens through *their* duly constituted and appointed rulers. I have no authority over any individual Darkovan except for a few civilian employees who choose to hire themselves to us, nor over any individual Empire citizen who comes here to do business, beyond determining that his business is a lawful one for a Class D world. Beyond that, if his business disturbs the peace between Darkover and the Empire, I may intervene. But unless someone appeals to me, I have no authority outside the Trade City."

It sounded intolerably complicated. How did the Empire manage to get its business done at all? My father had, as yet, said nothing; now he raised his head and said bluntly, "Well, we're appealing to you. These Empire citizens selling blasters in the marketplace of Caer Donn are *not* doing lawful business for a Class D Closed World, and you know it as well as I do. It's up to you to do something about it, and do it now. That *does* come within your responsibility."

The Legate said, "If the offense were here in Thendara, Lord Alton, I would do so with the greatest pleasure. In Caer Donn I can do nothing unless Lord Kermiac of Aldaran should appeal to me."

My father looked and sounded angry. He *was* angry, with a disrupting anger which could have struck the Legate unconscious if he had not been trying hard to control it. "Always the same old story on Terra, what's your saying, *pass the buck*? You're like children playing that game with hot chestnuts, tossing them from one to another and trying not to get burned! I spent eight years on Terra and I never found even one man who would look me in the eye and say, 'This is my responsibility and I will accept it whatever the consequences.' "

Ramsay sounded harried. "Is it your contention that it is the Empire's business, or mine, to police your ethical systems?"

"I always thought," Callina said in her clear, still voice, "that ethical conduct was the responsibility of every honest man."

Hastur said, "One of our fundamental laws, sir, however law is defined, is that the power to act confers the responsibility to do so. Is it otherwise with you?"

The Legate leaned his chin on his clasped hands. "I can

admire that philosophy, my lord, but I must respectfully refuse to debate it with you. I am concerned at this moment with avoiding great inconvenience for both our societies. I will inquire into this matter and see what can legitimately be done without interfering in your political decisions. And if I may make a respectful suggestion, Lord Hastur, I suggest that you take this matter up directly with Kermiac of Aldaran. Perhaps you can persuade him of the rightness of your view, and he will take it upon himself to stop the traffic in weapons, in those areas where the final legal authority is his."

The suggestion shocked me. Deal, negotiate with that renegade Domain, exiled from Comyn generations ago? But no one seemed inordinately shocked at the idea. Hastur said, "We shall indeed discuss this matter with Lord Aldaran, sir. And it may be that since you refuse to take personal responsibility for enforcing the Empire's agreement with all of Darkover, that I shall myself take the matter directly before the Supreme Tribunal of the Empire. If it is adjudged *there* that the agreement for Darkover does indeed require planetwide enforcement of the Compact, Mr. Ramsay, have I then your assurance that you would enforce it?"

I wondered if the Legate was even conscious of the absolute contempt in Hastur's voice for a man who required orders from a supreme authority to enforce ethical conduct. I felt almost ashamed of my Terran blood. But if Ramsay heard the contempt, he revealed nothing.

"If I receive orders to that effect, Lord Hastur, you may be assured that I will enforce them absolutely. And permit me to say, Lord Hastur, that it would in no way displease me to receive such orders."

A few more words were exchanged, mostly formal courtesies. But the meeting was over, and I had to gather my scattered thoughts and reassemble the honor guard, conduct the Council members formally out of the headquarters building and the spaceport and through the streets of Thendara. I could sense my father's thoughts, as I always could when we were in each other's presence.

He was thinking that no doubt it would be left to him to go to Aldaran. Kermiac would have to receive him, if only as my mother's kinsman. And I felt the utter weariness, like pain, in the thought. That journey into the Hellers was terrible, even in high summer; and summer was fast waning. Father was thinking that he could not shirk it. Hastur was too old. Dyan was no diplomat, he'd want to settle it by challenging Kermiac to a duel. But who else was there? The Ridenow lads were too young. . . .

It seemed to me, as I followed my father through the streets of Thendara, that in fact almost everyone in Comyn was either too old or too young. What was to become of the Domains?

It would have been easier if I could have been wholly convinced that the Terrans were all evil and must be resisted. Yet against my will I had found much that was wise in what Ramsay said. Firm laws, and never too much power concentrated in one pair of hands, seemed to me a strong barrier to the kind of corruption we now faced. And a certain basic law to fall back on when the men could not be trusted. Men, as I had found out when Dyan was placed at the head of the cadets, were all too often fallible, acting from expedience rather than the honor they talked so much about. Ramsay might hesitate to act without orders, but at least he acted on the responsibility of men and laws he could trust to be wiser than himself. And there was a check on his power too, for he knew that if he acted on his own responsibility against the will of wiser heads, he would be removed before he could do too much damage. But who would be a check on Dyan's power? Or my father's? They had the power to act, and therefore the right to do it.

And who could question their motives, or call a halt to their acts?

CHAPTER SEVEN

The day remained clear and cloudless. At sunset Regis stood on the high balcony which looked out over the city and the spaceport. The dying sunlight turned the city at his feet to a gleaming pattern of red walls and faceted windows. Danilo said, "It looks like the magical city in the fairy tale."

"There's nothing much magical about it," Regis said. "We learned that this morning on honor guard. Look, there's the ship that takes off every night about this time. It's too small to be an interstellar ship. I wonder where it's going?"

"Port Chicago, perhaps, or Caer Donn. It must be strange to have to send messages to other people by writing them, instead of by using linked minds as we do through the towers," Danilo said. "And it must feel very, very strange never to know what other people are thinking."

Of course, Regis thought. Dani was a telepath. Suddenly he realized that he'd been in contact with him again and again, and it had seemed so normal that neither had recognized it as telepathy. Today at the Council had been different, terribly different. He must have *laran* after all—but how and when, after Lew had failed?

And then the questions and the doubts came back. There had been so many telepaths there, spreading *laran* everywhere, even a nontelepath might have picked it up. It did not necessarily mean anything. He felt wrung, half desperately hoping that he was not cut off anymore and half fearing.

He went on looking at the city spread out below. This was the hour off-duty, when if a cadet had incurred no demerit or punishment detail, he might go where he chose. Morning and early afternoon were spent in training, swordplay and unarmed combat, the various military and command skills they would need later as Guards in the city and in the field. Later in the afternoon, each cadet was assigned to special duties. Danilo, who wrote the clearest hand among the cadets, had been assigned to assist the supply-officer. Regis had the relatively menial task of walking patrol in the city with a seasoned veteran or two, keeping order in the streets, preventing brawls, discouraging sneak-thieves and footpads. He found that he liked it, liked the very idea of keeping order in the city of Comyn.

Life in the cadet corps was not intolerable, as he had feared. He did not mind the hard beds, the coarse food, the continual demands on his time. He had been even more strictly disciplined at Nevarsin, and life in the barracks was easy by contrast. What troubled him most was always being surrounded by others and yet still being lonely, isolated from the others by a gulf he could not bridge.

From their first day, he and Danilo had drifted together, at first by chance, because their beds were side by side and neither of them had another close friend in the barracks. The officers soon began to pair them off for details needing partners like barrack room cleaning, which the cadets took in turns; and because Regis and Danilo were about the same size and weight, for unarmed-combat training and practice. Within the first-year group they were good-naturedly, if derisively, known as "the cloistered brethren" because, like the Nevarsin brothers, they spoke *casta* by choice, rather than *cahuenga*.

At first they spent much of their free time together too. Presently Regis noticed that Danilo sought his company less, and wondered if he had done something to offend the other boy. Then by chance he heard a second-year cadet jeeringly congratulating Danilo about his cleverness in choosing a friend. Something in Danilo's face told him it was not the first time this taunt had been made. Regis had wanted to reveal himself and do something, defend Danilo, strike the older cadet, anything. On second thought he knew this would embarrass Danilo more and give a completely false impression. No taunt, he realized, could have hurt Danilo more. He was poor, indeed, but the Syrtis were an old and honorable family who had never needed to curry favor or patronage. From that day Regis began to make the overtures himself—not an easy thing to do, as he was diffident and agonizingly afraid of a rebuff. He tried to make it clear, at least to Danilo, that it was he who sought out Dani's company, welcomed it and missed it when it was not offered. Today it was he who had suggested the balcony, high atop Comyn castle, where they could see the city and the spaceport.

The sun was sinking now, and the swift twilight began to race across the sky. Danilo said, "We'd better get back to barracks." Regis was reluctant to leave the silence here, the sense of being at peace, but he knew Danilo was right. On a sudden impulse to confide, he said, "Dani, I want to tell you something. When I've spent my three years in the Guards—I must, I promised—I'm planning to go offworld. Into space. Into the Empire."

Dani stared in surprise and wonder. "Why?"

Regis opened his mouth to pour out his reasons, and found himself suddenly at a loss for words. Why? He hardly knew. Except that it was a strange and different world, with the excitement of the unknown. A world that would not remind him at every turn that he had been born defrauded of his heritage, without *laran*. Yet, after today . . .

The thought was curiously disturbing. If in truth he had *laran,* then he *had* no more reasons. But he still didn't want to give up his dream. He couldn't say it in words, but evidently Danilo did not expect any. He said, "You're Hastur. Will they let you?"

"I have my grandfather's pledge that after three years, if I still want to go, he will not oppose it." He found himself thinking, with a stab of pain, that if he had *laran* they certainly would never let him go. The old breathless excitement of the unknown gripped him again; he shivered as he decided not to let them know.

Danilo smiled shyly and said, "I almost envy you. If my father weren't so old, or if he had another son to look after him, I'd want to come with you. I wish we could go together."

Regis smiled at him. He couldn't find words to answer the warmth that gave him. But Danilo said regretfully, "He does need me, though. I can't leave him while he's alive. And anyway"—he laughed just a little—"from everything I've heard, our world is better than theirs."

"Still, there must be things we can learn from them. Kennard Alton went to Terra and spent years there."

"Yes," Dani said thoughtfully, "but even after that, I

notice, he came back." He glanced at the sun and said, "We're going to be late. I don't want to get any demerits; we'd better hurry!"

It was dim in the stairwell that led down between the towers of the castle and neither of them saw a tall man coming down another staircase at an angle to this one, until they all collided, rather sharply, at its foot. The other man recovered first, reached out and took Regis firmly by the elbow, giving his arm a very faint twist. It was too dark to see, but Regis *felt,* through the touch, the feel and presence of Lew Alton. The experience was such a new thing, such a shock, that he blinked and could not move for a moment.

Lew said good-naturedly, "And now, if we were in the Guard hall, I'd dump you on the floor, just to teach you what to do when you're surprised in the dark. Well, Regis, you do know you're supposed to be alert even when you're off duty, don't you?"

Regis was still too shaken and surprised to speak. Lew let go his arm and said in sudden dismay, "Regis, did I really hurt you?"

"No—it's just—" He found himself almost unable to speak because of his agitation. He had not seen Lew. He had not heard his voice. He had simply touched him, in the dark, and it was clearer than seeing and hearing. For some reason it filled him with an almost intolerable anxiety he did not understand.

Lew evidently sensed the distress he was feeling. He let him go and turned to Danilo, saying amiably, "Well, Dani, are you learning to walk with an eye to being surprised and thrown from behind?"

"Am I ever," Danilo said, laughing. "Gabriel—Captain Lanart-Hastur—caught up with me yesterday. *This* time, though, I managed to block him, so he didn't throw me. He just showed me the hold he'd used."

Lew chuckled. "Gabriel is the best wrestler in the Guards," he said. "I had to learn the hard way. I had bruises everywhere. Every one of the officers had me marked down as the easiest to throw. After my arm had been dislocated by—by accident," he said, but Regis felt he had started to say something else, "Gabriel finally took pity on me and taught me a few of his secrets. Mostly, though, I relied on keeping out of the officers' reach. At fourteen I was smaller than you, Dani."

Regis' distress was subsiding a little. He said, "It's not so easy to keep out of the way, though."

Lew said quietly, "I know. I suppose they have their reasons. It *is* good training, to keep your wits about you and be on the alert all the time; I was grateful for it later when I was on patrol and had to handle hefty drunks and brawlers twice my size. But I didn't enjoy the learning, believe me. I remember Father saying to me once that it was better to be hurt a little by a friend than seriously hurt, some day, by an enemy."

"I don't mind being hurt," said Danilo, and with that new and unendurable *awareness,* Regis realized his voice was trembling as if he was about to cry. "I was bruised all over when I was learning to ride. I can stand the bruises. What I do mind is when—when someone thinks it's funny to see me take a fall. I didn't mind it when Lerrys Ridenow caught me and threw me halfway down the stairs yesterday, because he said that was always the most dangerous place to be attacked and I should always be on guard in such a spot. I don't mind when they're trying to teach me something. That's what I'm here for. But now and then someone seems to—to enjoy hurting me, or frightening me."

They had come away from the stairs now and were walking along an open collonade; Regis could see Lew's face, and it was grim. He said, "I know that happens. I don't understand it either. And I've never understood why some people seem to feel that making a boy into a man seems to mean making him into a brute. If we'd all been in the Guard hall, I'd have felt compelled to throw Regis ten feet, and I don't suppose I'd have been any gentler than any other officer. But I don't like hurting people when there's no need either. I suppose your cadet-master would think me shamefully remiss in my duty. Don't tell him, will you?" He grinned suddenly and his hand fell briefly on Danilo's shoulder, giving him a little shake. "Now you two had better hurry along; you'll be late." He turned a corridor at right angles to their own and strode away.

The two cadets hurried down their own way. Regis was thinking that he had never known Lew felt like that. They must have been hard on him, especially Dyan. But how did he know that?

Danilo said, "I wish all the officers were like Lew. I wish he were the cadet-master, don't you?"

Regis nodded. "I don't think Lew would want to be cadet-master, though. And from what I've heard, Dyan is very serious about honor and responsibility. You heard him speak at Council."

Danilo's mouth twisted. "Anyhow, you don't have to worry. Lord Dyan likes you. Everybody knows *that*!"

"Jealous?" Regis retorted good-naturedly.

"You're Comyn," Danilo said, "you get special treatment."

The words were a sudden painful reminder of the distance between them, a distance Regis had almost ceased to feel. It hurt. He said, "Dani, don't be a fool! You mean the fact that he uses me for a partner at sword practice? That's an honor I'd gladly change with you! If you think it's love-pats I'm getting from him, take a look at me naked some day—you're welcome and more than welcome to Dyan's love-pats!"

He was completely unprepared for the dark crimson flush that flooded Danilo's face, the sudden fierce anger as he swung around to face Regis. "What the hell do you mean by *that* remark?"

Regis stared at him in dismay. "Why, only that sword-practice with Lord Dyan is an honor I'd gladly do without. He's much stricter than the arms-master and he hits harder! Look at my ribs, you'll see that I'm black and blue from shoulder to knee! What did you think I meant?"

Danilo turned away and didn't answer directly. He only said, "We're going to be late. We'd better run."

Regis spent the early evening hours on street-patrol in the city with Hjalmar, the giant young Guardsman who had first tested him for swordplay. They broke up two budding brawls, hauled an obstreperous drunk to the brig, directed half a dozen lost country bumpkins to the inn where they had left their horses and gently reminded a few wandering women that harlots were restricted by law to certain districts in the city. A quiet evening in Thendara. When they returned to the Guard hall to go off duty, they fell in with

Gabriel Lanart and half a dozen officers who were planning to visit a small tavern near the gates. Regis was about to withdraw when Gabriel stopped him.

"Come along with us, brother. You should see more of the city than you can from the barracks window!"

Thus urged, Regis went with the older men. The tavern was small and smoky, filled with off-duty Guardsmen. Regis sat next to Gabriel, who took the trouble to teach him the card game they were playing. It was the first time he had been in the company of older officers. Most of the time he was quiet, listening much more than he talked, but it was good to be one of the company and accepted.

It reminded him, just a little, of the summers he'd spent at Armida. It would never have occurred to Kennard or Lew or old Andres to treat the solemn and precocious boy as a child. That early acceptance among men had put him out of step, probably forever, he realized with a remote sadness, with lads his own age. Now though, and the knowledge felt as if a weight had fallen from him, he knew that he did feel at home among men. He felt as if he was drawing the first really free breaths he had drawn since his grandfather pushed him, with only a few minutes to prepare for it, into the cadets.

"You're quiet, kinsman," Gabriel said as they walked back together. "Have you had too much to drink? You'd better go and get some sleep. You'll be all right tomorrow." He said a good-natured good night and went off to his own quarters.

The night officer patrolling the court said, "You're a few minutes late, cadet. It's your first offense, so I won't put you on report this time. Just don't do it again. Lights are out in the first-year barracks; you'll have to undress in the dark."

Regis made his way, a little unsteadily, into the barracks. Gabriel was right, he thought, surprised and not altogether displeased, he had had too much to drink. He was not used to drinking at all, and tonight he had drunk several cups of wine. He realized, as he hauled off his clothes by the moonlight, that he felt confused and unfocused. It had, he thought with a strange fuzziness, been a meaningful day, but he didn't know yet what it all meant. The Council. The somehow shocking realization that he had reached his grandfather's mind, recognized Lew by touch without seeing or hearing him. The odd half-quarrel with Danilo. It added to the confusion he felt, which was more than just drunkenness. He wondered if they had put *kirian* in his wine, heard himself giggle aloud at the thought, then fell rapidly into an edgy, nightmare-ridden half-sleep.

. . . He was back in Nevarsin, in the cold student dormitory where, in winter, snow drifted through the wooden shutters and lay in heaps on the novices' beds. In his dream, as had actually happened once or twice, two or three of the students had climbed into bed together, sharing blankets and body warmth against the bitter cold, to be discovered in the morning and severely scolded for breaking this inflexible rule. This dream kept recurring; each time, he would discover some strange naked body in his arms and, deeply disturbed, he would wake up with an admixture of fear and guilt. Each time he woke from this repeated dream he was more deeply upset and troubled by it, until he finally escaped into a deeper, darker realm of sleep. Now it seemed that he was his own father, crouched on a bare hillside in darkness, with strange fires exploding around him. He was shuddering with fright as men dropped dead around him, closer and closer, knowing that within moments he too would be blasted into fragments by one of the erupting fires. Then he felt someone close to him in the dark, holding him, sheltering his body with his own. Regis started awake again, shaking. He rubbed his eyes and looked around him at the quiet barracks room, dimly lit with moonlight, seeing the dim forms of the other cadets, snoring or muttering in their sleep. None of it was real, he thought, and slid down again on his hard mattress.

After a while he began to dream again. This time he was wandering in a featureless gray landscape in which there was nothing to see. Someone was crying somewhere in the gray spaces, crying miserably, in long painful sobs. Regis kept turning in another direction, not at first sure whether he was looking for the source of the weeping or trying to get away from the wretched sound. Small shuddering words came through the sobs, *I won't, I don't want to, I can't.* Every time the crying lessened for a moment there was a cruel voice, an almost familiar voice, saying, *Oh, yes you will, you know you cannot fight me,* and at other times, *Hate me as much as you will, I like it better that way.* Regis squirmed with fear. Then he was alone with the weeping, the inarticulate little sobs of protest and pleading. He went on searching in the lonely grayness until a hand touched him in the dark, a rude indecent searching, half painful and half exciting. He cried out "No!" and fled again into deeper sleep.

This time he dreamed he was in the student's court at Nevarsin, practicing with the wooden foils. Regis could hear the sound of his own panting breaths, doubled and multiplied in the great echoing room as a faceless opponent moved before him and kept quickening his movements insistently. Suddenly Regis realized they were both naked, that the blows struck were landing on his bare body. As his faceless opponent moved faster and faster Regis himself grew almost paralyzed, sluggishly unable to lift his sword. And then a great ringing voice forbade them to continue, and Regis dropped his sword and looked up at the dark cowl of the forbidding monk. But it was not the novice-master at Nevarsin monastery, but Dyan Ardais. While Regis stood, frozen with dread, Dyan picked up the dropped sword, no longer a wooden practice sword, but a cruelly sharpened rapier. Dyan, holding it out straight ahead while Regis looked on in dread and horror, plunged it right into Regis' breast. Curiously, it went in without the slightest pain, and Regis looked down in shaking dread at the sight of the sword passing through his entire body. "That's because it didn't touch the heart," Dyan said, and Regis woke with a gasping cry, pulling himself upright in bed. "Zandru," he whispered, wiping sweat from his forehead, "what a nightmare!" He realized that his heart was still pounding, and then that his thighs and his sheets were damp with a clammy stickiness. Now that he was wide awake and knew what had happened, he could almost laugh at the absurdity of the dream, but it still gripped him so that he could not lie down and go to sleep again.

It was quiet in the barrack room, with more than an hour to go before daybreak. He was no longer drunk or fuzzy-headed, but there was a pounding pain behind his eyes.

Slowly he became aware that Danilo was crying in the next bed, crying helplessly, desperately, with a kind of hopeless pain. He remembered the crying in his dream. Had he heard the sound, woven it into nightmare?

Then, in a sort of slow amazement and wonder, he realized that Danilo was not crying.

He could see, by the dimmed moonlight, that Danilo was in fact motionless and deeply asleep. He could hear his breath coming softly, evenly, see his turned-away shoulder moving gently with his breathing. The weeping was not a sound at all, but a sort of intangible pattern of vibrating misery and despair, like the lost little crying in his dream, but soundless.

Regis put his hands over his eyes in the darkness and thought, with rising wonder, that he hadn't heard the crying, but *knew* it just the same.

It was true, then. *Laran*. Not randomly picked up from another telepath, but his.

The shock of that thought drove everything else from his mind. How did it happen? When? And formulating the question brought its own answer: that first day in barracks, when Dani had touched him. He had dreamed about that conversation tonight, dreaming he was his father for a moment. Again he felt that surge of closeness, of emotion so intense that there was a lump in his throat. Danilo slept quietly now, even the telepathic impression of noiseless weeping having died away. Regis worried, troubled and torn with even the backwash of his friend's grief, wondering what was wrong.

Quickly he shut off the curiosity. Lew had said that you learned to keep your distance, in order to survive. It was a strange, sad thought. He could not spy on his friend's privacy, yet he was still near to tears at the awareness of Dani's misery. He had sensed it, earlier that day, when Lew talked to them. Had someone hurt him, ill-treated him?

Or was it simply that Danilo was lonely, homesick, wanting his family? Regis knew so little about him.

He recalled his own early days at Nevarsin. Cold and lonely, heartsick, friendless, hating his family for sending him here, only a fierce remnant of Hastur pride had kept him from crying himself to sleep every night for a long time.

For some reason that thought filled him again with an almost unendurable sense of anxiety, fear, restlessness. He looked across at Danilo and wished he could talk to him about this. Dani had been through it; he would know. Regis knew he would have to tell someone soon. But who should he tell? His grandfather? The sudden realization of his own *laran* had left Regis strangely vulnerable, shaken again and again by waves of emotion; again he was at the edge of tears, this time for his grandfather, reliving that fierce, searing moment of anguish of his only son's terrible death.

And, still vulnerable, he swung from grief to rebellion. He was sure his grandfather would force him to walk the path ready-made for a Hastur heir with *laran*. He would never be free! Again he saw the great ship taking off for the stars, and his whole heart, his body, his mind, strained to follow it outward into the unknown. If he cherished that dream, he could never tell his grandfather at all.

But he could share it with Dani. He literally ached to step across the brief space between their beds, slip into bed beside him, share with him this incredible dual experience of grief and tremendous joy. But he held himself back, recalling with an imperative strange sharpness what Lew had said; it was like living with your skin off. How could he impose this burden of his own emotions on Dani, who was himself so burdened with unknown sorrow, so troubled and nightmare-driven that his unshed tears penetrated even into Regis' dreams as a sound of weeping? If he was to have the telepathic gift, Regis thought sadly, he had to learn to live by the rules of the telepath. He realized that he was cold and cramped, and crawled under his blankets again. He huddled them around him, feeling lonely and sad. He felt curiously unfocused again, drifting in anxious search, but in answer to his questioning mind he saw only flimsy pictures in imagination, men and strange nonhumans fighting along a narrow rock-ledge; the faces of two little children fair and delicate and baby-blurred in sleep, then cold in death with a grief almost too terrible to be borne; dancing figures whirling, whirling like wind-blown leaves in a mad ecstasy; a great towering form, blazing with fire . . .

Exhausted with emotion, he slept again.

CHAPTER EIGHT

(Lew Alton's narrative)

There are two theories about Festival Night, the great midsummer holiday in the Domains. Some say that it is the birthday of the Blessed Cassilda, foremother of the Comyn. Others say that it commemorates the time of year when she found Hastur, Son of Adones, Lord of Light, sleeping on the shores of Hali after his journey from the realms of Light. Since I don't believe that either of them ever existed, I have no emotional preference about either theory.

My father, who in his youth traveled widely in the Empire, told me once that every planet he has ever visited, and most of those he hasn't, have both a midsummer and midwinter holiday. We're no exception. In the Domains there are two traditional celebrations for summer Festival; one is a private family celebration in which the women are given gifts, usually fruit or flowers, in the name of Cassilda.

Early this morning I had taken my foster-sister Linnell Aillard some flowers, in honor of the day, and she had reminded me of the other celebration, the great Festival ball, held every year in the Comyn Castle.

I've never liked these enormous affairs, even when I was too young for the ball and taken to the children's party in the afternoon; I've disliked them ever since my first one, at the age of seven, when Lerrys Ridenow hit me over the head with a wooden horse.

It would be unthinkable to absent myself, however. My father had made it clear that attending was just one of the unavoidable duties of an heir to Comyn. When I told Linnell that I was thinking of developing some illness just severe enough to keep me away, or changing duty with one of the Guard officers, she pouted. "If you're not there, who'll dance with me?" Linnell is too young to dance at these affairs except with kinsmen so, ever since she's been allowed to attend at all, I've been reminded that unless I'm there to dance with her she will find herself watching from the balcony. My father, of course, has the excellent excuse of his lameness.

I resolved to put in an appearance, dance a few dances with Linnell, be polite to a few old ladies and make an unobtrusive exit as early as politeness allowed.

I came late, having been on duty in the Guard hall where I'd heard the cadets gossiping about the affair. I didn't blame them. All Guardsmen, whatever their rank, and all cadets not actually on duty, have the privilege of attending. To youngsters brought up in the outlands, I suppose it's an exciting spectacle. I was more disinclined to go than ever because Marius had come in while I was dressing. He'd been taken to the children's party, had made himself sick with sweets and had skinned knuckles and a black eye from a fight with some supercilious little boy, distantly kin to the Elhalyns, who had called him a Terran bastard. Well, I'd been called worse in my day and told him so, but I really had no comfort for him. I was ready to kick them all in the shins by the time I went down. It was, I reflected, a hell of a good start to the evening.

As was customary, the beginning dances were exhibitions by professionals or gifted amateurs. A troupe of dancers in the costume of the far mountains was doing a traditional dance, with a good deal of skirt-swirling and boot-stamping. I'd seen it danced better, a while since, on my trip into the foothills. Perhaps no professionals can ever give the mountain dances the true gaiety and excitement of the people who dance them for pure pleasure.

I moved slowly around the edges of the room. My father was being polite to elderly dowagers on the sidelines. Old Hastur was doing the same thing with a group of Terrans who had probably been invited for political or ceremonial reasons. The Guardsmen, especially the young cadets, had already discovered the elegant buffet spread out along one wall and kept replenished by a whole troop of servants. So early in the evening, they were almost the only ones there. I grinned reminiscently. I am no longer required to share the men's mess, but I remembered my cadet years vividly enough to know how good the plentiful delicacies would look after what passes for supper in the barracks.

Danilo was there, in dress uniform. A little self-consciously, he wished me a joyous Festival. I returned the greeting. "Where is Regis? I don't see him anywhere."

"He was on duty tonight, sir. I offered to change with him—all his kinsmen are here—but he said he would have years of it, and I should go and enjoy myself."

I wondered which officer, in malice or by way of emphasizing that a Hastur could expect no favors in the cadets, had made certain that Regis Hastur would draw a tour of duty on Festival Night. I only wished I had so good an excuse.

"Well, enjoy yourself by all means, Dani," I told him.

The hidden musicians had struck up a sword dance and Danilo turned eagerly to watch as two Guardsmen came with torches to place the swords. The hall lights were lowered to emphasize the ancient and barbaric quality of this oldest of traditional mountain dances. It is usually danced by one of the greatest dancers in Thendara; to my surprise, it was Dyan Ardais who strode forward, wearing the brilliantly barbaric costume whose history was lost before the Ages of Chaos.

There are not many amateurs, even in the Hellers, who still know all the traditional steps and patterns. I'd seen Dyan dance it when I was a child at Armida, in my father's hall. I thought that it went better there, to the music of a single drone-pipe, by the glare of firelight and a torch or two, than here in the elaborate ballroom, surrounded by ladies in fancy party costumes and bored noblemen and city folk.

Yet even the elaborately garbed ladies and noblemen fell silent, impressed by the strange solemnity of the old dance. And yes—I give him his due—by Dyan's performance. For once he looked grave, stern, free of the flippant cynicism I detested so, wholly caught up in the tense, treading-on-eggs quality of the weaving steps. The dance displays a fierce, almost tigerish masculinity, and Dyan brought a sort of leashed violence to it. As he snatched up the swords in the final figure and held them poised over his head, there was not a sound anywhere in the ballroom. Because I had been impressed against my will, I tried deliberately to break the spell.

I said aloud to Danilo, "I wonder who he's showing off to this time? It's a pity Dyan's indifferent to women; after this he'd have to beat them off with a pitchfork!"

I found myself pitying any woman—or any man, for that matter—who allowed himself to be charmed by Dyan. I hoped for his own sake that Danilo was not one of them. It's natural enough for boys that age to be strongly attracted to any strong character, and a cadet-master is a natural object for such romantic identification. If the older man is an honorable and kindly one, it does no harm and wears off in a short time. I long since grew out of any such childish attachments and, although I've been on the receiving end a time or two, I made sure it went no further than a few exchanged smiles.

Well, I wasn't Dani's guardian, and it had been made clear that Dyan was beyond my reach. Besides, I had enough worries of my own.

Dyan was moving toward the buffet; I saw him stop for a glass of wine, speaking to the Guardsmen there with a show of affability. We came briefly face to face. Resolving that if there was any discourtesy among Comyn I would not be the one to show it, I made some brief polite comment on the dance. He replied with equally meaningless courtesy, his eyes straying past me. I wondered who he was looking for and received in return—my barriers must have been lowered for a moment—a surge of violent anger. *Perhaps after tonight this meddlesome bastard will be busy with his own affairs and have less time for interfering in mine!*

I made the briefest possible bow and moved away for my promised dance with Linnell. The floor was filling quickly with dancers; I took Linnell's fingertips and led her to the floor.

Linnell is a pretty child, with soft bronze-brown hair and blue eyes framed in lashes so long and dark they looked unreal. She was, I thought, considerably prettier than her kinswoman Callina, who had looked so severe and stern at Council yesterday.

The Aillard Domain is the only one in which *laran* and Council-right pass not in the male line, but in the female; males are not allowed to hold full Domain rights in Council. The last *comynara* in the direct line had been Cleindori, the last of the Keepers trained completely in the old, cloistered virginal tradition. While still quite young, she had left the tower, rebelled against the old superstitions surrounding the matrix circles and especially the Keepers and had, in defiance of tradition and belief, taken a consort and borne him a child while continuing to use the powers she had been taught. She had been horribly murdered by fanatics who thought a Keeper's virginity was more important than her competence or her powers. But she had broken the ancient mold, defied the superstitions and created a new scientific approach to what is now called matrix mechanics. For years her very name had been abhorred as a renegade. Now her memory was revered by every psi technician on Darkover.

But she had left no daughters. The old Aillard line had finally died out and Callina Lindir-Aillard, a distant kinswoman of my father's and of the male head of the Aillard domain, had been chosen *comynara,* as nearest female successor. Linnell had come to Armida for my father to foster and had been brought up as my sister.

Linnell was an expert dancer, and I enjoyed dancing with her. I have little interest in feminine fripperies, but Linnell had taught me the courtesies of such things, so I took polite notice of her gown and ornaments. When the dance came to an end, I led Linnell to the sidelines and asked her if she thought I should ask Callina to dance; Callina, too, by Comyn custom for unwed women, was restricted to dancing with kinsmen except at masked balls.

"I don't know if Callina cares to dance," Linnell said, "she's very shy. But you should ask her. I'm sure she'll tell you if she'd rather not. Oh, there is Javanne Hastur! Every time I've seen her in the last nine years, it seems, she's been pregnant. But she's actually pretty, isn't she?"

Javanne was dancing with Gabriel. She had a high color in her cheeks and looked as if she were enjoying herself. I suppose that any young matron would be happy, after four closely spaced pregnancies, to be in society again. Javanne was very tall and excessively thin, a dark girl in an elaborate green-and-golden gown. I did not think her pretty, but she was undeniably handsome.

I conducted Linnell to Callina, but before I could speak to her, my father approached me.

"Come along, Lew," he said, in a tone I had learned to regard, however politely phrased, as a command. "You should pay your respects to Javanne."

I stared. Javanne? She had never liked me, even when

we were going to children's parties. Once we had both been whipped impartially for getting into a kicking-and-scratching fight, at seven or so, and later, when we were about eleven, she rudely refused to dance with me, saying I stepped on her feet. I probably did, but I had already been telepath enough to know that was not her reason. "Father," I said patiently, "I'm quite sure Lady Javanne can dispense with any compliments from me." Had he quite lost his wits?

"And Lew promised to dance with me again," Linnell said sulkily. Father patted her cheek and assured her there would be time enough for that, with a look at me which admitted no further delay unless I wanted to defy him openly and make a scene.

Javanne was standing in a little cluster of younger women, sipping a glass of wine. My father's voice seemed more deliberate than usual, as he presented me.

"I wish you a joyous Festival, kinsman," she said with a courteous bow. Kinsman! Well, Gabriel and I were friendly enough; perhaps she had learned, from husband and brother, that I was not such a scandal after all. At least for once she seemed to speak to me as if I were a human being. She beckoned to one of the young girls in the crowd surrounding her. "I wish to present to you a young kinswoman of your own, Lew, Linnea Storn-Lanart."

Linnea Storn-Lanart was very young, certainly no older than Linnell, with russet hair falling in soft curls around a heart-shaped face. The Storns were old mountain nobility from the region near Aldaran who had intermarried years ago with Lanarts and Leyniers. What was a maiden so young doing alone in Thendara?

Linnea, although she seemed modest enough, raised her eyes with frank curiosity to my face. Mountain girls—I had heard this from my father—did not follow the exaggerated custom of the lowlands, where a direct glance at a strange man is immodest; hence mountain girls are often considered, here in the Domains, to be over-bold. She looked straight at me for a moment, smiling, then caught Javanne's eyes, flushed crimson and looked quickly at the toes of her slippers. I supposed Javanne had given her a lesson in proper manners for the Domains, and she did not wish to be thought countrified.

I was at a loss what to say to her. She was my kinswoman, or had been so presented to me, although the relationship could not be very close. Perhaps that was it—Javanne wished to spend her time dancing, not looking after a kinswoman too young to dance with strangers. I said, "Will you honor me with a dance, *damisela*?"

She glanced quickly at Javanne for permission, then nodded. I led her to the floor. She was a good dancer and seemed to enjoy it, but I kept wondering why my father should go out of his way to make life easy for Javanne. And why had he looked at me so meaningfully as we moved on to the dance floor? And why had he introduced her as a kinswoman, when the relationship must surely be far too distant to notice officially? When the music ended, it was still perplexing me.

I bluntly said, "What is this all about?"

Forgetting her careful briefing in manners, she blurted out, "Didn't they tell you? They told me!" Then her sudden blush flooded her face again. It made her look very pretty, but I was in no mood to appreciate it.

"Tell me *what*?" I demanded.

Her cheeks were like banners of crimson. She stammered. "I was t-told that—that we should look each other over, get to know one another, and that if we l-liked each other, then a—a marriage would be—" My face must have shown what I was thinking, for she broke off, leaving the sentence unfinished.

Damn them! Trying to run my life again!

The girl's gray eyes were wide, her childish mouth trembling. I quickly fought to control my anger, barrier myself. She was obviously very sensitive, at least an empath, perhaps a telepath. I hoped, helplessly, that she wouldn't cry. None of this was her fault. I could just guess how her parents had been bribed or threatened, how she herself had been coaxed and flattered with the lure of a fine marriage to the heir of the Domain.

"Just what did they tell you about me, Linnea?"

She looked confused. "Only that you're Lord Alton's son, that you've served in the Arilinn Tower, that your mother was Terran—"

"And you think you can bear that disgrace?"

"Disgrace?" She looked puzzled. "Many of us in the

Hellers have Terran blood; there are Terrans in my family. Do you think it is a disgrace?"

What could anyone her age know of this kind of court intrigue? I felt revolted, remembering Dyan's gloating look. Busy with his own affairs . . . Evidently he had known this was in the wind.

"*Damisela,* I have no mind to marry, and if I did I would not let Council choose a wife for me." I tried to smile, but I suspect it was grim enough. "Don't look so downcast, *chiya,* a maiden as pretty as you will soon find a husband you'll like better."

"I have no particular wish to marry," she said with composure. "I had intended to apply for admission at one of the towers; my great-granddame was trained as a Keeper, and it seemed to her I was well fitted for it. But I have always obeyed my family and if they had chosen me a husband, I was not ill-content. I am only sorry that I seem not to please you."

She was so calm that I felt trapped, almost frantic. "It is not that you displease me, Linnea. But I would not marry at their bidding." My wrath flared up again; I felt her flinch from its impact. Her hand still rested lightly on my arm, as when we were dancing; she drew it away as if she had been burned. I felt like storming away and actually made a faint move to leave her, when I realized, just in time, that this would be a disgraceful thing to do. To abandon a young girl in the middle of a dance-floor would be a rudeness no man of breeding would ever commit against a gently reared young girl of unquestionable manners and reputation! I couldn't expose her to such gossip for, inevitably, everyone would be wondering what unspeakable thing she could possibly have done to deserve it. I glanced around. Javanne was dancing at the far end of the ballroom so I led Linnea toward the buffet. I offered her a glass of wine; she refused it with a headshake. I got her *shallan* instead, and stood sipping irritably at the wine myself. I didn't like it.

When I was a little calmer I said, "Nothing is irrevocable yet. You can tell whoever put you up to this—my father, old Hastur, whoever—you can tell them you don't like me and that will be the end of it."

She smiled, a faint amused flicker. "But I do like you, Dom Lewis," she said. "I won't lie about it, even if I thought I could. Lord Kennard would know it at once if I tried to lie to him. You're angry and unhappy, but I think if you weren't so angry, you'd be very nice. I would be well content with such a marriage. If you wish to refuse it, Lew, you must do the refusing."

If she had been less young, less naïve, I might have flung at her that she could hardly be expected to give up a marriage into Comyn without protest. Even so, I am sure she caught the thought, for she looked distressed.

I shut out her thoughts and said flatly, "A woman should have the privilege of refusing. I thought to spare you the offense of hearing me say to my father that I did not—" I discovered that I could not simply say that I did not like her. I amended it and said, "That I did not intend to marry at their bidding."

Her composure was disquieting. "No one marries at his own will. Do you really feel that a marriage between us would be unendurable, Lew? It is obvious that they will arrange some marriage or other for you."

For a moment I wavered. She was evidently sensitive and intelligent; she had been considered for tower training, which meant *laran.* My father had evidently gone to some pains to choose a woman who would be maximally acceptable to me, one with Terran blood, one capable of that emotional and mental fusion a telepath must have in any woman he is to know intimately. She was pretty. She was no empty-minded doll, but had wit and poise. For a second I considered. Sooner or later I must marry, I had always known that. A Comyn heir must father children. And, the Gods knew, I was lonely, lonely . . .

And my father, damn him, had counted on just this reaction! My anger flared anew. "*Damisela,* I have told you why I will not be party to any marriage made as this one was made. If you choose to believe that I have rejected you personally, that is your affair." I drank the last in my wineglass and set it down. "Allow me to conduct you to my kinswomen, since Javanne is much occupied."

Javanne was dancing again. Well, let her enjoy herself. She had been married off at fifteen and had spent the last nine years doing her duty to her family. They wouldn't catch me in that trap!

Gabriel had claimed a dance from Linnell—I was glad

to see it—but Callina was standing at the edge of the floor. The crimson draperies she was wearing only accentuated the colorlessness of her bland features. I presented Linnea to her and asked Callina to look after her while I had a word with my father. She looked curious, evidently sensing my anger. I must be broadcasting it right and left.

My rage mounted as I circled the floor, looking for my father. Dyan had known and Hastur had known—how many others had been dragged into this? Had they held a Council meeting to discuss the fate of Lord Alton's bastard heir? How long had it taken them to find a woman who would have me? They'd had to go far afield, I noticed, and get one young enough to obey her father and mother without question! I supposed I ought to feel flattered that they'd pick a nice looking one!

I found myself face to face with the Regent. I gave him a curt greeting and started to pass him by; he laid a hand on my arm to detain me, wishing me the greetings of the season.

"I thank you, my lord. Have you seen my father?"

The old man said mildly, "If you're storming off to complain, Lew, why not come directly to me? It was I who asked my granddaughter to present the girl to you." He turned to the buffet. "Have you had supper? The fruits are exceptional this season. We have ice-melons from Nevarsin; they're not usually obtainable in the market."

"Thank you but I'm not hungry," I said. "Is it permitted to ask why you take such an interest in my marriage, my lord? Or am I to feel flattered that you interest yourself, without asking why?"

"I take it the girl was not to your liking, then."

"What could I possibly have against her? But forgive me, sir, I have certain distaste for airing my personal affairs before half the city of Thendara." I moved my hand to indicate the dancing crowds. He smiled genially.

"Do you really think anyone here is intent on anything but his own affairs?" He was calmly filling his plate for himself with assorted delicacies. Sullenly, I followed suit. He moved toward a couple of reasonably isolated chairs and said, "We can sit here and talk, if you like. What's the matter, Lew? You're just about the proper age to be married."

"Just like that," I said, "and I'm not to be consulted?"

"I thought we were consulting you," Hastur said, taking a forkful of some kind of shredded seafood mixed with greens. "We did not, after all, summon you to the chapel at a few hours' notice, to be married on the spot, as was done only a few years ago. I was given no chance even to see my dear wife's face until a few minutes before the bracelets were locked on our wrists, yet we lived together in harmony for forty years."

My father, speaking of his first years on Terra and being plunged abruptly into their alien customs, had once used a phrase for the way I felt now: *culture shock*. "With all deference, Lord Hastur, times have changed too much for that to be a suitable way of making marriages. Why is there such a hurry?"

Hastur's face suddenly hardened. "Lew, do you really understand that if your father had broken his neck on those damnable stairs, instead of a few ribs and his collarbone, you would now be Lord Alton of Armida, with all that implies? My own son never lived to see his son. With our world in the shape it's in, none of us can afford to take chances with the heirship of a Domain. What is your specific objection to marriage? Are you a lover of men?" He used the very polite *casta* phrase and I, used to the much coarser one customary in the Guards, was not for a moment quite certain what he meant. Then I grinned without amusement. "*That* arrow went wide of the mark, my lord. Even as a boy I had small taste for such games. I may be young, but that young I am not."

"Then what can it possibly be?" He seemed honestly bewildered. "Is it Linnell you wish to marry? We had other marriage-plans for her, but if both of you really wish—"

I said in honest outrage, "Evanda protect us both! Lord Hastur, Linnell is my *sister*!"

"Not blood-kin," he said, "or not so close as to be a grave risk to your children. It might be a suitable match after all."

I took a spoonful of the food on my plate. It tasted revolting and I swallowed and set the plate down. "Sir, I love Linnell dearly. We were children together. If it were only to share my life, I could think of no happier person to spend it with. But," I fumbled to explain, a little embarrassed, "after you've slapped a girl for breaking your toys, taken her into bed with you when she had a nightmare or was crying with a toothache, pinned up her skirts so she could wade in a brook, or dressed her, or brushed her hair—it's almost impossible to think of her as a—a bedmate, Lord Hastur. Forgive this plain speaking."

He waved that away. "No, no. No formalities. I asked you to be honest with me. I can understand that. We married your father very young to a woman the Council thought suitable, and I have been told they lived together in complete harmony and total indifference for many years. But I don't want to wait until you've fixed your desire on someone wholly unsuitable, either. Your father married at the last to please himself and —forgive me, Lew—you and Marius have been suffering for it all your lives. I am sure you would rather spare your own sons that."

"Can't you wait until I *have* sons? Don't you *ever* get tired of arranging other people's lives for them?"

His eyes blazed at me. "I got tired of it thirty years ago but someone has to do it! I'm old enough to sit and think over my past, instead of carrying the burden of the future, but it seems to be left to me! What are *you* doing to arrange your life in the proper way and save me the trouble?" He took another forkful of salad and chewed it wrathfully.

"How much do you know of the history of Comyn, Lew? In far-back days, we were given power and privilege because we *served* our people, not because we ruled them. Then we began to believe we had these powers and privileges because of some innate superiority in ourselves, as if having *laran* made us so much better than other people that we could do exactly as we pleased. Our privileges are used now, not to compensate us for all the things we have given up to serve the people, but to perpetuate our own powers. You're complaining that your life isn't your own, Lew. Well, it isn't and it shouldn't be. You have certain privileges—"

"Privileges!" I said bitterly. "Mostly duties I don't want and responsibilities I can't handle."

"Privileges," he repeated, "which you must earn by serving your people." He reached out and lightly touched the mark of Comyn, deeply blazed in my flesh just above the wrist. His own arm bore its twin, whitened with age. He said, "One of the obligations which goes with that, a sacred obligation, is to make certain your gift does not die out, by fathering sons and daughters to inherit it from you, to serve the people of Darkover in their turn."

Against my will, I was moved by his words. I had felt this way during my journey to the outlands, that my position as heir to Comyn was a serious thing, a sacred thing, that I held an important link in an endless chain of Altons, stretching from prehistory to the future. For a moment I felt that the old man followed my thoughts, as he laid his fingertip again on the mark of Comyn on my wrist. He said, "I know what this cost you, Lew. You won that gift at risk of your life. You have begun well by serving at Arilinn. What little remains of our ancient science is preserved there against the day when it may be fully recovered or rediscovered. Do you think I don't know that you young people there are sacrificing your personal lives, giving up many things a young man, a young woman, holds dear? I never had that option, Lew, I was born with a bare minimum of *laran*. So I do what I can with secular powers, to lighten that burden for you others who bear the heavier ones. So far as I know, you have never misused your powers. Nor are you one of those frivolous young people who want to enjoy the privilege of rank and spend your life in amusements and folly. Why, then, do you shrink from doing this duty to your clan?"

I suddenly wished that I could unburden my fears and misgivings to him. I could not doubt the old man's personal integrity. Yet he was so completely entangled in his single-minded plan for political aims on Darkover that I distrusted him, too. I would not let him manipulate me to serve those aims. I felt confused, half convinced, half more defiant than ever. He was waiting for my answer; I shrank from giving it. Telepaths get used to facing things head-on—you have to, in order to stay even reasonably sane—but you don't learn to put things easily into words. You get used, in a place like Arilinn, to knowing that everyone in your circle can share all your feelings and emotions and desires. There is no reticence there, none of the small evasions and courtesies which outsiders use in speaking of intimate things. But

Hastur could not read my thoughts, and I fumbled at putting it into words that would not embarrass either of us too much.

"Mostly I have never met a woman I wished to spend my life with . . . and, being a telepath, I am not willing to .... to gamble on someone else's choice." No. I wasn't being completely honest. I would have gambled on Linnea willingly, if I had not felt I was being manipulated, used as a helpless pawn. My anger flared again. "Hastur, if you wanted me to marry simply for the sake of perpetuating my gift, of fathering a son for the Domain, you should have had me married off before I was full-grown, before I was old enough to have any feelings about any woman, and would have wanted her just because she *was* a woman and available. Now it's different." I fell silent again.

How could I tell Hastur, who was old enough to be my grandfather, and not even a telepath, that when I took a woman, all her thoughts and feelings were open to me and mine to her, that unless rapport was complete and sympathy almost total, it could quickly unman me? Few women could endure it. And how could I tell him about the paralyzing failures which a lack of sympathy could bring? Did he actually think I could manage to live with a woman whose only interest in me was that I might give her a *laran* son? I know some men in the Comyn manage it. I suppose that almost any two people with healthy bodies can give each other *something* in bed. But not tower-trained telepaths, accustomed to that full sharing. . . . I said, and I knew my voice was shaking uncontrollably, "Even a god cannot be constrained to love on command."

Hastur looked at me with sympathy. That hurt, too. It would have been hard enough to strip myself this way before a man my own age. Finally he said gently, "There's never been any question of compulsion, Lew. But promise me to think about it. The Storn-Lanart girl has applied to Neskaya Tower. We need Keepers and psi technicians. But we also need sensitive women, telepaths, to marry into our families. If you could come to like one another, we would welcome her."

I said, drawing a deep breath, "I'll think about it." Linnea was a telepath. It might be enough. But to put it bluntly, I was afraid. Hastur gestured to a servant to take his emptied plate and my nearly untouched one. "More wine?"

"Thank you, sir, but I have already drunk more than I usually do in a week. And I promised my foster-sister another dance."

Kind as he had been, I was glad to get away from him. The conversation had rubbed me raw-edged, rousing thoughts I had learned to keep firmly below the surface of my mind.

Love—to put it more precisely, sex—is never easy for a telepath. Not even when you're very young and still childishly playing around, discovering your own needs and desires, learning to know your own body and its hungers.

I suppose, from the way other lads talk—and there's plenty of talk in the cadets and the Guards—for most people, at least for a time, anyone of the right sex who is accessible and not completely repulsive will do. But even during those early experiments I had always been too conscious of the other party's motives and reactions, and they would rarely stand up to so close an examination. And after I went to Arilinn and submerged myself in the intense sharing and closeness there, it had changed from merely difficult to impossible.

Well, I had promised Linnell a dance. And what I had told Hastur was true. Linnell was not a woman to me and she would not disturb me emotionally at all.

But Callina was alone, watching a group of classic dancers do a rhythmic dance which mimicked the leaves in a spring storm. Their draperies, gray-green, yellow-green, blue-green, flickered and flowed in the lights like sunshine. Callina had thrown back her hood and, preoccupied in watching the dancers, looked rather forlorn, very small and fragile and solemn. I came and stood beside her. After a moment she turned and said, "You promised Linnell to dance again, didn't you? Well, you can save yourself the trouble, cousin, she and the Storn-Lanart child are in the balcony, watching and chattering to one another about gowns and hair-dressing." She smiled, a small whimsical smile which momentarily lightened her pale stern face. "It's foolish to bring little girls that age to a formal ball, they'd be just as happy at a dancing class!"

I said, letting out my pent-up bitterness, "Oh, they're old enough to be up for auction to the highest bidder. It's how we make fine marriages in the Comyn. Are you for sale too, *damisela*?"

She smiled faintly. "I don't imagine you're making an offer? No, I'm not for sale this year at least. I'm Keeper at Neskaya Tower, and you know what that means."

I knew, of course. The Keepers are no longer required to be cloistered virgins to whom no man dares raise even a careless glance. But while they are working at the center of the energon relays, they are required, by harsh necessity, to remain strictly chaste. They learned not to attract desires they dared not satisfy. Probably they learned not to feel them, either, which is a good trick if you can manage it. I wished I could.

I relaxed. Against Callina, tower-trained and a working Keeper, I need not be on my guard. We shared a deeper kinship than blood, the strong tie of the tower-trained telepath.

I've been a matrix technician long enough to know that the work uses up so much physical and nervous energy that there's not much left over for sex. The will may be there, but not the energy. The Keepers are required, for their physical and emotional safety, to remain celibate. The others in the circle—technicians, mechanics, psi monitors—are usually generous and sensitive about satisfying what little remains. In any case you get too close for playing the elaborate games of flirt and retreat that men and women elsewhere are given to playing. And Callina understood all this without being told, having been part of it.

She was also sensitive enough to be aware of my mood. She said, with a faint tinge of gentle malice, "I have heard Linnea will be sent to Arilinn next year, if you both choose not to marry. You'll have time for second thoughts. Shall I ask them to be sure she is not made Keeper, in case you should change your mind?"

I felt somewhat abashed. That was an outrageous thing to say! But what would have infuriated me from an outsider did not trouble me from her. Within a tower circle such a statement would not have embarrassed me, although I would not have felt constrained to answer, either. She was simply treating me like one of our own kind. In the rapport of the tower circles, we were all very much aware of each other's needs and hungers, eager to keep them from reaching a point of frustration or pain.

But now my circle was scattered, others serving in my place, and somehow I had to cope with a world full of elaborate games and complex relationships. I said, as I would have said to a sister, "They're pressuring me to marry, Callina. What shall I do? It's too soon. I'm still—" I gestured, unable to put it into words.

She nodded gravely. "Perhaps you should take Linnea after all. It would mean they couldn't put any constraint on you for someone less suitable." She was seriously considering my problem, giving it her full attention. "I suppose, mostly, what they want is for you to father a son for Armida. If you could do *that,* they wouldn't care whether you married the girl or not, would they?"

It wouldn't have been difficult to have fathered a child on one of the women in my circle at Arilinn, even though pregnancy makes it too dangerous for a woman to remain in the tower. But the thought of that was like salt in a raw wound. I said at last, and heard my voice crack, "I am a bastard myself. Do you honestly think I would ever inflict that on any son of mine? And Linnea is very young and she was . . . honest with me." This whole conversation troubled me for obscure reasons. "And how do you come to know so much about this? Has my love life become a subject for Council debate, Callina *comynara*?"

She shook her head pityingly. "No, of course not. But Javanne and I played dolls together, and she still tells me things. Not Council gossip, Lew, just women's talk."

I hardly heard her. Like all Altons, I sometimes have a disturbing tendency to see time out of focus, and Callina's image kept wavering and trembling, as if I saw her through running water or through flowing time. For a moment I would lose sight of her as she was now, pale and plain and crimson-draped, as she shimmered in an ice-blue glittering mist. Then she would seem to float, cold and aloof and beautiful, shimmering with a darkness like the midnight sky. I was tormented, struggling with mingled rage and frustration, my whole body aching with it—

I blinked, trying to get the world back in focus.

"Are you ill, kinsman?"

I realized with sheer horror that I had been, for an instant, on the very edge of taking her into my arms. Since she was not now Keeper within the circle, this was only a rudeness, not an unthinkable atrocity. Still, I must be mad! I was actually trembling. This was insane! I was still looking at Callina, reacting to her as if she were a desirable woman, not barred from me by double taboo and oath of a tower technician.

She met my eyes, deeply troubled. There was cool sympathy and kindliness in her glance, but no response to my surge of uncontrollable emotion. Of course not!

"*Damisela,* I apologize profoundly," I said, feeling my breath raw in my throat. "It's this crowd. Plays hell with my . . . barriers."

She nodded, accepting the excuse. "I hate such affairs. I try never to come to them, except when I must. Let's get into the air for a moment, Lew." She led the way out to one of the small balconies where a thin fine rain was falling. I breathed the cold dampness with relief. She was wearing a long, fine, shimmering black veil that spun out behind her like wings, gleaming in the darkness. I could not resist the impulse to seize her in my arms, crush her against me, press her lips against mine—Again I blinked, staring at the cool rainless night, the clear stars, Callina calm in her brilliant drapery. Suddenly I felt sick and faint and clung to the balcony railing. I felt myself falling into infinite distances, a wild nowhere of empty space. . . .

Callina said quietly, "This isn't just the crowd. Have you some *kirian,* Lew?"

I shook my head, fighting to get the world in perspective. I was too old for this, damn it. Most telepaths outgrow these psychic upheavals at puberty. I hadn't had threshold sickness since before I went to Arilinn. I had no idea why it should overcome me just now.

Callina said gently, "I wish I could help you, Lew. You know what's really wrong with you, don't you?" She brushed past me with a feather-light touch and left me. I stood in the cold damp air of the balcony, feeling the sting of the words. Yes, I knew what was wrong and resented it, bitterly, that she should remind me from behind the barricade of her own invulnerability. She did not share my needs, desires; it was a torment from which she, as Keeper, was free. For the moment, in my flaring anger at the girl, I forgot the cruel discipline behind her hard-won immunity.

Yes, I knew what was really wrong with me. At Arilinn I had grown accustomed to women who were sensitive to my needs, who shared them. Now I had been a long time away, a long time alone. I was even barred, being what I am, from the kind of uncomplicated relief which the least of my fellow Guardsmen might find. The few times—very few times—when, in desperation, I had been driven to seek it, it had only made me sick. Sensitive women don't take up that particular profession. Or if they do I've never met them. Leaning my head on the railing, I gave way to envy . . . a bitter envy of a man who could find even temporary solace with any woman with a willing body.

Momentarily, knowing it would make it worse in the end, I let myself think of the girl Linnea. Terran blood. A sensitive, a telepath. Perhaps I had been too hasty.

Rage gripped me again. So Hastur and my father thought they could manipulate me no other way, now they tried to bribe me with sex. They had bribed Dyan by putting him in charge of a barracks-full of half-grown boys, who at the very least would feed his ego by admiring him and flattering him. And however discreetly, he thrived on it.

And they would bribe me, too. Differently, of course, for my needs were different, but essentially still a bribe. They would keep me in control, pliable, by dangling a young, beautiful, sexually exciting girl before me, a half-spoken agreement.

And my own needs, which my telepathic father knew all too well, would do the rest. I felt sick at the knowledge of how nearly I had fallen into their trap.

The festivities inside the ballroom were breaking up. The cadets had long gone back to barracks. A few lingerers were still drinking at the buffet, but servants were moving around, beginning to clear away. I strode through the halls toward the Alton rooms, still alive with rage.

The central hall was deserted, but I saw a light in my father's room and went in without knocking. He was half-dressed, looking weary and off guard.

"I want to talk to you!"

He said mildly, "You didn't have to charge in here like a *cralmac* in rut for that." He reached out briefly and touched my mind. He hasn't done that much since I was grown up, and it made me angry that he should treat me like a child after so many years. He withdrew quickly and said, "Can't it wait till morning, Lew? You're not well."

Even his solicitude added to my wrath. "If I'm not, you know whose fault it is. What in the hell do you mean, trying to marry me off without a word of warning?"

He met my anger head-on. "Because, Lew, you're too proud and too damned stubborn to admit you *need* anything. You're ready, past ready, for marriage. Don't be like the man in the old tale, who when the devil bade him take the road to paradise, set off on the high-road to hell!" He sounded as raw as I felt. "Damn it, do you think I don't *know* how you feel?"

I thought about that for a moment. I've wondered, now and then, if my father has lived alone all these years since my mother died. He'd certainly had no acknowledged mistress. I had never tried to spy on him, or inquire even in thought about his most private life, therefore I was doubly angered that he left me no rag of privacy to cover my nakedness, had forced me to strip myself naked before Hastur and disgrace myself before my cousin Callina.

"It won't work," I flung at him in a fury. "I wouldn't marry the girl now if she was as beautiful as the Blessed Cassilda, and came dowered with all the jewels of Carthon!"

My father shrugged, with a deep sigh. "Of course not," he said wearily. "When did you ever do anything so sensible? Suit yourself. I married to please myself; I told Hastur I would never compel you."

"Do you think you *could*?" I was still raging.

"Since I'm not trying, what does it matter?" My father sounded as weary as I felt. "I think you're a fool, but if it helps you feel independent and virtuous to go around with an ache in your"—to my surprise and shock he used a vulgar phrase from the Guard hall, one I'd never suspected him of knowing—"then be just as damned stubborn as you want. You're my son all right: you have no more sense than I had at your age!" He shrugged in a way that indicated he was through with the subject. "Threshold sickness? I have some *kirian* somewhere, if you need it."

I shook my head, realizing that something, perhaps just

the flooding of my system with violent anger, had dispelled the worst of it.

"I had something to say to you, but it can wait till morning if you're not in shape to listen. Meanwhile, I want another drink." He started to struggle to his feet; I said, "Let me serve you, Father," and brought him a glass of wine, got one for myself and sat beside him to drink it. He sat sipping it slowly. After a time he reached out and laid a hand on my shoulder, a rare gesture of intimacy from childhood. It did not make me angry now.

Finally he said, "You were at the Council. You know what's going on."

"You mean Aldaran." I was glad he had actually changed the subject.

"The worst of it is, I cannot be spared from Thendara, and what's more, I don't think I can make the journey, Lew." His barriers were down, and I could feel his weariness. "I've never admitted, before, that there was anything I could not do. But now," and he gave me his quick, rare smile, "I have a son I can trust to take my place. And since we've both defied Hastur, Thendara might not be too comfortable for you in the next weeks. I'm going to send you to Aldaran as my deputy, Lew."

"Me, Father?"

"Who else? There is no one else I can trust so well. You did as well as I could have done on the fire-beacon business. And you can claim blood-kinship there; old Kermiac of Aldaran is your great-uncle." I had known I was of the Aldaran kin, but I had not known it was so high in the clan, nor so close. "Also, you have Terran blood. You can go and find out, beyond all rumors, what is really happening back there in the mountains."

I felt both elated and uncertain about being sent on this highly sensitive mission, knowing that Father trusted me with it. Hastur had spoken of our duty to serve the Comyn, our world. Now I was ready to take my place among those of our Domain who had done so for more generations than any of us could count. "When do I start?"

"As soon as I can arrange escort and self-conduct for you. There's no time to be lost," he said. "They know you are heir to Comyn. But you are also kinsman to Aldaran; they will welcome you as they would never welcome me."

I was grateful to my father for giving me this mission, then, a new feeling and a good one, I realized that the gratitude need not be all mine. He genuinely needed me. I had a chance to serve him, too, to do something for him better than he could do it himself. I was eager to begin.

CHAPTER NINE

At this season the sun was already up when the rising-bell rang in the barracks. Little runnels of snow were melting in the court as they crossed the cobblestones toward the mess hall. Regis was still sleepy in spite of the icy water he had splashed on his face. He felt that he'd almost rather miss breakfast than get up for it at this hour. But he was proud of his good record; he was the only cadet who had never incurred a punishment detail for sleeping through the bell and stumbling in late and half asleep. Nevarsin had done him some good, after all.

He slid into his assigned seat between Danilo and Gareth Lindir. An orderly slapped battered trays in front of them: thick crockery bowls of porridge mixed with nuts, heavy mugs of the sour country beer Regis hated and never touched. He put a spoon distastefully into the porridge.

"Does the food really get worse every morning, or am I imagining it?" Damon MacAnndra asked.

"It gets worse," said Danilo. "Who's capable of imagining anything at this God-forgotten hour? What's *that*?"

There was a small commotion at the door. Regis jerked up his head and stared. After a brief scuttle a cadet was flung off his feet and went reeling across the room, crashed headfirst into a table and lay still. Dyan Ardais was standing in the doorway waiting for the unfortunate cadet to rise. When he did not stir, Dyan motioned to an orderly to go and pick him up.

Damon said, "Zandru's hells, it's Julian!" He got up from his seat and hurried to his friend's side. Dyan was standing over him, looking grim.

"Back to you seat, cadet. Finish your meal."

"He's my friend. I want to see if he's hurt." Ignoring Dyan's angry glare, Damon knelt beside the fallen cadet; the other cadets, craning their necks, could see the bright smear of blood where Julian's head had struck the table.

"He's bleeding! You've killed him!" Damon said in a shrill, shaking voice.

"Nonsense!" Dyan rapped out. "Dead men don't bleed like that." He knelt, quickly ran his fingertips over the boy's head and motioned to two third-year cadets. "Take him back to the staff offices and ask master Raimon to have a look at him."

As Julian was carried out, Gabriel Vyandal muttered across the table, "It's not fair to pick on us at this hour of the morning when we're all half asleep." It was so quiet in the mess room that his voice carried; Dyan strode across the room and said, looking down at him with a curl of his lip, "Times like this are when you should be most on guard, cadet. Do you think that footpads in the city, or catmen or bandits on the border, will pick an hour of your convenience to attack? This part of your training is to teach you to be on your guard literally every moment, cadets." He turned his back on them and walked out of the room.

Gareth muttered, "He's going to kill one of us some day. I wonder what he'll say then?"

Damon came back to his seat, looking very white. "He wouldn't even let me go with them and hold his head."

Gabriel laid a comforting hand on his arm. He said, "Don't worry, Master Raimon will take good care of him."

Regis had been shocked at the sight of blood, but a sense of scrupulous fairness made him say, "Lord Dyan is right, you know. When we're really in the field, a moment of being off guard can get us killed, not just hurt."

Damon glared at Regis. "It's all right for *you* to talk, Hastur. I notice he never picks on *you*."

Regis, whose ribs were chronically black and blue from Dyan's battering at sword practice, said, "I suppose he thinks I get enough lumps working out with him in armed-combat training." It occurred to him that there was an element of cruelty in this too. Kennard Alton had taught him to handle a sword when he was believed to be the best swordsman in the Domains. Yet in daily practice with either Kennard or Lew for two years, he had collected fewer bruises then he had had from Dyan in a few weeks.

A second-year man said audibly, "What do you expect of the Comyn? They all hang together."

Regis bent his head to the cold porridge. What's the use?

he thought. He couldn't show everybody his bruises—he shouldn't have opened his mouth. Danilo was trying to eat with trembling hands. The sight filled Regis with distress but he did not know what he could say that would not be an intrusion.

In the barracks room, Regis quickly made up his bed, helped Damon fix up Julian's cot and arrange his possessions; when Julian returned, at least he would not have to face demerits for leaving his bed and shelf in disorder. After the other cadets had gone off for arms-drill, he and Danilo remained. It was their turn to sweep the room and clean the fireplace. Regis went meticulously about the work of scraping ashes from the fireplace and cleaning the hearth. You never knew which officer would make inspection and some were stricter than others. He did the work with all the more thoroughness because he detested it, but his thoughts were busy. Had Julian really been hurt? Dyan *had* been too rough.

He was aware that Danilo, shoving the heavy push-broom with scowling determination at the far end of the room, was filled with a kind of sullen misery that overlaid everything else. Regis wondered if there was any way to block *out* other people's emotions, for he was far too sensitive to Danilo's moods. If he knew what Dani was thinking, or why he was so angry and miserable all the time, it might not be so bad, but all Regis got were the raw emotions.

He sensed Lew Alton's presence and looked up to see him coming along the room. "Not finished? Take your time, cadet, I'm a little early."

Regis relaxed. Lew could be strict enough, but he did not go out of his way to look for hidden fragments of dust. He continued his work with the hearth-broom, but after a minute felt Lew bend and touch his arm. "I want a word with you."

Regis rose and followed him to the door of the barracks room, turning to say over his shoulder, "I'll be with you in a minute, Dani, don't try to shift that table until I can help you." Just outside, aware of the touch of Lew's thoughts, he looked up to face his smiling eyes.

"Yes, I knew the other day, in Council," Lew said, "but I had no chance to speak to you then. When did this happen, Regis? And how?"

"I'm not sure," Regis said, "but somehow, I—touched—Danilo, or he touched me, I'm not really sure which it was, and some kind of—of barrier seemed to go down. I don't know how to explain it."

Lew nodded. "I know," he said, "there aren't any words for most of these experiences, and the ones there are, aren't very enlightening. But Danilo? I sensed he had *laran* the other day, but if he could do that, then—" He stopped, his brow furrowed, and Regis followed the thought, *that would mean he's a catalyst telepath! They're rare, I thought there were no functioning ones left.*

"I'll speak to my father before I leave for Aldaran."

"You're going instead of Uncle Kennard? When?"

"A few days before Council season is over, not long now. The trip into the mountains is hard at any season, and impossible after the snows really begin in earnest."

Danilo was standing in the doorway of the barracks room and Regis, recalled abruptly to his work, said, "I'd better get back; Dani will think I'm shirking my share."

Lew took a perfunctory glance inside the room. "Go ahead. It looks all right; I'll sign the inspection report. Finish up at your leisure." He came to Danilo and said, "I'm leaving for Aldaran in a day or two, Dani. I shall be passing Syrtis on my road. Have you any message for Dom Felix?"

"Only that I strive to do my duty among my betters, Captain." His voice was sullen.

"I'll tell him you do us credit, Danilo." The boy did not answer, going off toward the fireplace, dragging the broom. Lew looked after him with curiosity. "What do you think is bothering him?"

Regis was worried about Danilo's moods. His silent weeping had wakened Regis twice more, and again he had been torn between the desire to console his friend and the wish to respect his privacy. He wished he could ask Lew what to do, but they were both on duty and there was no time for personal problems. Anyway, Lew might be required by Guard regulations—he didn't really know—to tell him he should ask his cadet-master about any personal problem. Regis said at last, "I don't know. Homesick, maybe," and left it at that. "How is Julian? *Not dead*?"

Lew looked at him, startled. 'No, no. He'll be all right.

Just a bit of a knock on the head." He smiled again and went out of the barracks.

Danilo leaned the broom against the wall and began to shift the heavy wooden table to get at the littler under it. Regis jumped to catch the other end.

"Here, I *told* you I'd give you a hand; you could hurt your insides trying to lift a heavy thing like that." Danilo looked up, glowering, and Regis said, "I wasn't shirking, I only wanted to say goodbye to my kinsman. You were rude to him, Dani."

"Well, are we going to work or gossip?"

"Work by all means," said Regis, giving his end of the table a heave. "I've nothing to say to you when you're in this mood." He went to fetch the broom. Danilo muttered something under his breath and Regis swung around, demanding, "What did you say?"

"Nothing." Danilo turned his back. It had sounded suspiciously like, "Don't get your hands dirty," and Regis stared.

"What's the matter? Do you think I ought to finish up? I will if you want me to, but I don't think I was away talking *that* long, was I?"

"Oh, I'd never think of imposing on you, Lord Regis! Allow me to serve you!" The sneer was openly apparent in Danilo's voice now and Regis stared in bewilderment.

"Danilo, are you trying to fight with me?"

Danilo looked Regis up and down slowly. "No, I thank you, my lord. Fight, with an heir to Comyn? I may be a fool, but not such a fool as all that." He squared his shoulders and thrust his lip out belligerently. "Run along to your fencing lesson with Lord Ardais and leave the dirty work to me."

Regis' bewilderment gave way to rage. "When did I ever leave any dirty work for you or anyone else around here?" Danilo stared at the floor and did not answer. Regis advanced on him menacingly. "Come on, you started this, answer me! You say I haven't been doing my fair share?" No other accusation could have made him so furious. "And take that look off your face or I'll knock it off!"

"Must I watch the very look on my face, *Lord Hastur*?" The title, as he spoke it, was an open insult, and Regis hit him. Danilo staggered back, sprang up raging and started for him, then stopped short.

"Oh no. You can't get me in trouble *that* way. I told you I'm not going to fight, Lord Hastur."

"Yes you will, damn you. You started this! Now put up your fists, damn you, or I'll use you for a floor-mop!"

"That would be fun, wouldn't it," Danilo muttered, "force me to fight and get me in trouble for fighting? Oh no, Lord Regis, I've had too much of that!"

Regis stepped back. He was now more troubled than angry, wondering what he could possibly have done to upset Dani this way. He reached out to try to touch his friend's mind, met nothing but surging rage that covered everything else. He moved toward Danilo; Dani sprang defensively alert.

"Zandru's hells, what are you two about?" Hjalmar stepped inside the door, took it all in at a glance and collared Regis, not gently. "I heard you shouting halfway across the court! Cadet Syrtis, your lip is bleeding."

He let Regis go, came and took Danilo by the chin, turning his face gently up to look at the wound. Danilo exploded into violence, pushing his hand away, his hand dropping to knife-hilt. Hjalmar grabbed his wrist.

"Zandru's hells! Lad, don't do *that*! Drawing a knife in barracks will break you, and I'd have to report it! What the hell's the matter, boy, I only wanted to see if you were hurt!" He sounded genuinely concerned. Danilo lowered his head and stood trembling.

"What's between you two? You've been close as brothers!"

"It was my fault," said Regis quietly. "I struck him first."

Hjalmar gave Danilo a shove. It looked rude but was, in truth, rather gentle. "Go and put some cold water on your lip, cadet. Hastur can finish doing the barracks alone. It will teach him to keep his big mouth shut." When Danilo had vanished into the washroom he scowled angrily at Regis. "This is a fine example to set for the lads of lower rank!"

Regis did not argue or excuse himself. He stood and accepted the tongue-lashing Hjalmar gave him, and the three days of punishment detail. He felt almost grateful to the young officer for interrupting a nasty situation. Why, *why,* had Danilo exploded that way?

He finished sweeping the barracks, thinking that it was not like Dani to pick a fight.

And he had picked it, Regis thought soberly, throwing the last of the trash, without realizing it, into the newly cleaned fireplace. But why? Had they been tormenting him again about trying to curry favor with a Hastur?

All that day he went about his duties preoccupied and wretched, wondering what had brought his friend to such a point of desperation. He had halfway decided to seek Danilo out in their free time, brave his anger and ask him outright what was wrong. But he was reminded that he was on punishment detail, which turned out to be the distasteful duty of working with the orderlies sweeping the stables. Afterward it took him a long time to get himself clean and free of the stable stink and he had to hurry to be in time for his new assignment, which he found boring beyond words. Mostly it consisted of standing guard at the city gates, checking permits and safe-conducts, questioning travelers who had neither, reminding incoming merchants of the rules covering their trade. After that he and a junior officer were assigned supervision of night guard at the city gates, his first use of authority over any of the Guardsmen. He had known, in theory, that the cadets were in training for officers, but until now he had felt like a menial, a flunky, junior to everyone. Now, after a scant half season, he had a responsible duty of his own. For a time he forgot his preoccupation with his friend's trouble.

He came back to the barracks near midnight, wondering what duty Danilo had been assigned at mid-year rotation. It was strange to walk in and see the night officer simply marking off his name as being on late duty, rather than scolding him for being tardy. He paused to ask the man, "Do you know anything about Julian—cadet MacAran, sir?"

"MacAran? Yes, he has a concussion, they took him to the infirmary, but he'll be all right in a few days. They sent for his friend to come and stay with him there. His wits were wandering, and they were afraid he'd climb out of bed and hurt himself. But he recognized Damon's voice. He didn't seem to hear anyone else but when MacAnndra told him to keep quiet and stay put, they say he went to sleep quiet as a baby. Concussion's like that sometimes."

Regis said he was glad to hear Julian was no worse, and went in to his bed. His end of the dormitory was almost empty, with Damon and Julian in the infirmary. Danilo's bed, too, was empty. He must be on night duty. He felt regretful, having hoped for a word with him, a chance, perhaps, to find out what was troubling him, make friends again.

He was awaked, an hour or two later, by the sounds of heavy rain on the roof and raised voices at the doorway. The night officer was saying, "I'll have you put on report for this," and Danilo answering roughly, "I don't give a damn, what do you think it matters to me now?" A few minutes later he came into the room with blundering steps.

What is the matter with him? Regis wondered. Was he drunk? He decided not to speak to him. If Danilo was drunk enough, or agitated enough, to be rude to the night officer, he might make another scene and find himself in worse trouble yet.

Danilo bumped into Regis' cot, and Regis could feel that Danilo's clothing was soaked through, as if he had been wandering around in the rain. By the dim light left in the washroom at night Regis could see him blundering around, flinging his clothes off every which way, heard the *bump* as he threw his sword down on his clothing chest instead of hanging it on the wall. He stood under the window for a moment, naked, hesitating, and Regis almost said something. He could have spoken in a low voice without attracting attention; with Damon and Julian both out of the barracks, they were a considerable distance from the other cadets. But the old agonizing fear of a rebuff seized him. He could not face the thought of another quarrel. So he remained silent, and after a time Danilo turned away and got into his own bed.

Regis slept lightly, fitfully, and after a long time woke with a start, hearing again the sound of weeping. This time, although the vibration of misery was there, direct to his senses, Danilo was awake and he was really crying, softly, hopelessly, miserably. Regis listened to the sound for some time, wretchedly torn, unwilling to intrude, unable to endure such grief. Finally his sense of friendship drew him out of bed.

He knelt beside Danilo's cot and whispered, "Dani, what's the matter? Are you sick? Have you had bad news from home? Is there anything I can do?"

Danilo muttered drearily, his head still turned away. "No, no, there's nothing anyone can do, it's too late for that. And for that, for that—Holy Bearer of Burdens, what will my father say?"

Regis said, in a whisper that could not be heard three feet away, "Don't talk like that. Nothing's so bad it can't be helped somehow. Would you feel better to tell me about it? Please, Dani."

Danilo turned over, his face only a white blob in the darkness. He said, "I don't know what to do. I think I must be going mad—" Suddenly he drew a long, gasping sob. He said, "I can't see—who—Damon, is that you?"

Regis whispered, "No. Damon's in the infirmary with Julian. And everyone else is asleep. I don't think anyone heard you coming in. I wasn't going to say anything, but you sounded so unhappy . . ." Forgetting their quarrel, forgetting everything except this was his friend in some desperate trouble, he leaned forward and laid his hand on Danilo's bare shoulder, a shy, tentative touch. "Isn't there anything I can—"

He felt the explosion of rage and something else—fear? shame?—running up his arm through his fingers, like an electric shock. He drew his hand away sharply as if it had been burned. With a violent, tigerish movement, Danilo thrust Regis angrily away with both hands. He spoke in a strained whisper.

"Damnable—filthy—*Comyn,* get the hell away from me, get your stinking *hands* off me, you—" He used a word which made Regis, used as he was to Guard Hall coarseness, gasp aloud and draw away, shaking and almost physically sick

"Dani, you're wrong," he protested, dismayed. "I only thought you were sick or in trouble. Look, whatever's gone wrong with you, I haven't done anything to you, have I? You'll really make yourself ill if you go on like this, Dani. Can't you tell me what's happened?"

"Tell *you*? Sharra's chains, I'd soon whisper it to a wolf with his teeth in my throat!" He gave Regis a furious push and said, half aloud, "You come near me again, you filthy *ombredin,* and I'll break your stinking neck!"

Regis rose from his side and silently went back to his own bed. His heart was still pounding with the physical shock of that burst of violent rage which he had felt when he touched Danilo, and he was trembling with the assault on his mind. He lay listening to Danilo's strained breathing, quite simply aghast and almost physically sick under that burst of hatred and his own failure to get through to him. Somehow he had thought that between two people, both with *laran,* this kind of misunderstanding could not possibly arise! He lay listening to Danilo's gasping, heard it finally subside into soft sobbing and at last into a restless, tossing sleep. But Regis himself hardly closed his eyes that night.

CHAPTER TEN

(Lew Alton's narrative)

Heavy rain after midnight had turned to wet snow; the day I was to leave for Aldaran dawned gray and grim, the sun hidden behind clouds still pregnant with unfallen snow. I woke early and lay half asleep, hearing angry voices from my father's room. At first I thought Marius was getting a tongue-lashing for some minor naughtiness, but so early? Then I woke a little further and detected a quality in Father's voice never turned on any of us. All my life I have known him for a harsh, hasty and impatient man, but usually his anger was kept on a leash; the fully-aroused anger of an Alton can kill, but he was tower-disciplined, control normally audible in every syllable he spoke. Hastily I put on a few clothes and went into the central hall.

"Dyan, this isn't worthy of you. Is it so much a matter of personal pride?"

Lord of Light, it happened again! Well, at least, if I knew that note in Father's voice, he wouldn't get off unpunished!

Dyan's voice was a heavy bass, muted to a rumble by the thick walls, but no walls could filter out my father's answering shout; "No, damn it, Dyan, I won't be party to any such monstrous—"

Out in the hall I heard Dyan repeat implacably, "Not personal pride, but the honor of the Comyn and the Guards."

"Honor! You don't know the meaning of—"

"Careful, Kennard, there are some things even you cannot say! As for this—in Zandru's name, Ken, I cannot overlook this. Even if it had been your own son. Or mine, poor lad, had he lived so long. Would you be willing to see a cadet draw steel on an officer and go unpunished? If you cannot accept that I am thinking of the honor of the Guards, what of discipline? Would you have condoned such conduct even in your own bastard?"

"Must you draw Lew into every—"

"I'm trying not to, which is why I came directly to you with this. I do not expect *him* to be sensitive to a point of honor."

My father cut him off again, but they had both lowered their voices. Finally Dyan spoke again, in a tone of inflexible finality. "No, don't speak to me of circumstances. If you let the respect due to the Comyn be eroded away in times like this, in full sight of every insolent little cadet and bastard in Thendara, how can *you* speak of honor?"

The violent rage was gone from my father's voice now, replaced by a heavy bitterness. He said, "Dyan, you use the truth as other men use a lie, to serve your own ends. I've known you since we were boys, and this is the first time I've come close to hating you. Very well, Dyan. You leave me no choice. Since you bring me this complaint officially, as cadet-master to commander, it shall be done. But I find it hard to believe you couldn't have kept it from coming to this."

Dyan thrust the door open and came striding out into the hall. He gave me a brief contemptuous glance, said, "Still spying on your betters?" and went out.

I went to the door he had left open. My father looked up at me blankly, as if he could not remember my name, then sighed and said, "Go and tell the men to gather after breakfast in the main Guard hall. All duty-lists suspended for the morning."

"What . . . ?"

"Disciplinary assembly." He raised his thick, knotted hands, gnarled and stiff from the joint-disease which has ravaged him since I can remember. "You'll have to stand by. I haven't the strength for a sword-breaking any more and I'm damned if I'll leave it to Dyan."

"Father, what happened?"

"You'll have to know," Kennard said. "One of the cadets drew his sword on Dyan."

I felt my face whiten with dismay. That was indeed something which could not be overlooked. Of course I wondered—who wouldn't?—what provocation Dyan had given. In my own cadet year, he had dislocated my arm, but even then I had known better than that. Even if two cadets in some childish squabble drew their pocketknives, it would have been sufficient to have them both expelled in disgrace.

I was amazed that my father had even tried to interfere. It seemed that for once I had misjudged Dyan.

Even so, I made a quick guess at what had happened. If the MacAran boy had died of his concussion and Damon held Dyan responsible—three different officers had told me of the event and all of them agreed Dyan had been inexcusably rough—then Damon would have held himself honor-bound to avenge his friend. Both boys were mountain-bred and friendship went deep in the Kilghard hills. I did not blame the boy, but I was angry with Dyan. A kinder man would have understood; Dyan, being what he was, might well have shown understanding of the love between them.

Father reminded me that I would need full-dress uniform. I hurried with my tunic-laces, wanting to reach the mess hall while the men were still at breakfast.

The sun had broken through the cloud cover; the melting snow lay in puddles all over the cobblestone court, but it was still gray and threatening to the north. I'd hoped to leave the city shortly after daybreak. If it started snowing again later, I'd have a soggy journey.

Inside the mess room there were sausages for breakfast, their rich spicy smell reminding me that I had not eaten yet. I was tempted to ask the orderly for a plate of them, but remembered I was in full-dress uniform. I came to the center of the crowded tables and called for attention.

As I announced the assembly, I glanced at the table where the cadets were seated. To my surprise, Julian MacAran was there, his head heavily bandaged, but there and looking only a little pale. So much for my theory about what had happened! Regis was there, looking so white and sick that for a moment, in dismay, I wondered if he were the disgraced cadet. But no, he would have been under arrest somewhere.

My way back led me past the first-year barracks room and I heard voices there, so I stopped to see if I should repeat my message to anyone. As I approached I heard the voice of old Domenic. He should have been cadet-master, I thought bitterly.

"No, son, there's no need for that. Your sword is an

heirloom in your family. Spare your father that, at least. Take this plain one."

I had often thought during my own cadet years that old Dominic was the kindest man I had ever known. Any sword would do for breaking. The answer was soft, indistinguishable, blurred by a pain which, even at this distance, clamped around me like an iron band gripping my forehead.

Hjalmar's deep voice rebuked gently, "None of that now, my lad. I'll not hear a word against Comyn. I warned you once that your temper would get you into trouble."

I glanced in, then wished I hadn't. Danilo was sitting on his cot, hunched over in misery, and the arms-master and Hjalmar were helping him gather his possessions. *Danilo!* What in all of Zandru's nine hells could have happened? No wonder Father had been willing to plead with Dyan! Could any sane man make a point of honor against such a child? Well, if he was old enough to be a cadet, he was old enough to bear the consequences of a rash act.

I hardened my conscience and went on without speaking. I too had had such provocation—for some time, while my arm was still in a sling, I'd put myself to sleep nights thinking up ways to kill him—but I had kept my hands off my sword. If Danilo was not capable of self-restraint, the cadet corps was no place for him.

By the time I came back to the Guard hall the men were gathering. Disciplinary assemblies were not common since minor offenses and punishments were handled by the officers or the cadet-master in private, so there was a good deal of whispered curiosity and muttered questions. I had never seen a cadet formally expelled. Sometimes a cadet dropped out because of illness or family trouble, or was quietly persuaded to resign because he was unable physically or emotionally, to handle the duties or the discipline. Octavien Vallonde's case had been hushed up that way. Damn him, that was Dyan's doing too!

Dyan was already in place, looking stern and self-righteous. My father came in, limping worse than I had ever seen him. Di Asturien brought in Danilo. He was as white as the plastered wall, his face taut and controlled, but his hands were shaking. There was an audible murmur of surprise and dismay. I tried to barrier myself against it. Any way you looked at it, this was tragedy, and worse.

My father came forward. He looked as bad as Danilo. He took out a long and formal document—I wondered if Dyan had brought it already drawn up—and unfolded it.

"Danilo-Felix Kennard Lindir-Syrtis, stand forth," he said wearily. Danilo looked so pale I thought he would faint and I was glad di Asturien was standing close to him. So he was my father's namesake, as well?

Father began to read the document. It was written in *casta*. Like most hillsmen, I had been brought up speaking *cahuenga* and I followed the legal language only with difficulty, concentrating on every word. The gist of it I knew already. Danilo Syrtis, cadet, in defiance of all order and discipline and against any and all regulations of the cadet corps, had willfully drawn bared steel against a superior office, his cadet-master, Dyan-Gabriel, Regent of Ardais. He was therefore dismissed, disgraced, stripped of all honor and privilege and so forth and so on, two or three times over in different phraseology, until I suspected that reading the indictment had taken longer than the offense.

I was trembling myself with the accumulated leakage of emotion I could not entirely barracade in this crowd. Danilo's misery was almost physical pain. Regis looked ready to collapse. Get it over, I thought in anguish, listening to the interminable legal phrases, hearing the words now only through their agonized reverberations in Danilo's mind. Get it over before the poor lad breaks down and has hysterics, or do you want to see that humiliation, too?

". . . and shall therefore be stripped of honorable rank and returned to his home in disgrace . . . in token of which . . . his sword to be broken before his eyes and in the sight of all the Guardsmen together assembled. . . ."

This was my part of the dirty work. Hating it, I went and unfastened his sword. It was a plain Guardsman's sword, and I blessed the kind old man for that much mercy. And besides, I thought sourly, those heirloom swords are of such fine temper you'd need the forge-folk and Sharra's fires to make any impression on one!

I had to touch Danilo's arm. I tried to give him a kindly thought of reassurance, that this wasn't the end of the world, but I knew it wasn't getting through to him. He flinched from my gauntleted hand as if it had been a red-hot branding iron. This would have been a frightful ordeal for any boy who was not a complete clod; for one with *laran,* possibly a catalyst telepath, I knew it was torture. Could he come through it at all without a complete breakdown? He stood motionless, staring straight forward, eyes half closed, but he kept blinking as if to avoid breaking into anguished tears. His hands were clenched into tight fists at his side.

I took Danilo's sword and walked back to the dais. I gripped it between my heavily gauntleted hands and bent it across my knee. It was heavy and harder to bend than I'd realized, and I had time to wonder what I'd do if the damned thing didn't break or if I lost my grip and it went flying across the room. There was a little nervous coughing deep in the room. I strained at the blade, thinking, Break, damn you, break, let's get this filthy business over before we all start screaming!

It broke, shattered with a sound shockingly like breaking glass. If anything, I'd expected a noisy metallic resonance. One half slithered away to the floor; I let it lie.

Straightening my back I saw Regis' eyes full of tears. I looked across at Dyan.

Dyan. . . .

For an instant his barriers were down. He was not looking at me, or at the sword. He was staring at Danilo with a hateful, intense, mocking, *satiated* look. A look of horrid, satisfied lust. There was simply no other word for it.

And all at once I knew—I should have known all along—exactly how and why Danilo had been persecuted, until in a moment of helpless desperation he had been goaded into drawing a knife against his persecutor . . . or possibly against himself.

Either way, the moment the knife was loose from the sheath, Dyan had him exactly where he wanted him. Or the next best thing.

I don't think I'll ever know how I got through the rest of the ceremony. My mind retains only shaken vignettes: Danilo's face as white as his shirt after the full-dress uniform tabard had been cut away. How shabby he looked. And how young! Dyan taking the sword from my hand, smirking. By the time my brain fully cleared again, I was out of the Guard hall and on the stairs to the Alton rooms.

My father was wearily taking off his dress-uniform. He

looked drawn and exhausted. He was really ill, I thought, and no wonder. This would make anyone sick. He looked up, saying tiredly, "I have all your safe-conducts arranged. There is an escort ready for you, with pack animals. You can get away before midday, unless you think the snow's likely to be too heavy before nightfall."

He handed me a packet of folded papers. It looked very official, hung with seals and things. For a minute I could hardly remember what he was talking about. The trip to Aldaran had receded very far. I put the papers into my pocket without looking at them.

"Father," I said, "you *cannot* do this. You cannot ruin a boy's life through Dyan's spite, not again."

"I tried to talk him out of it, Lew. He could have condoned it or handled it privately. But since he made it official, I couldn't pass it over. Even if it had been you, or the Hastur boy."

"And what of Dyan? Is it soldierly to provoke a child?"

"Leave Dyan out of it, son. A cadet must learn to control himself under any and all conditions. He will have the life and death of dozens, of hundreds, of men in his hands some day. If he cannot control his personal feelings . . ." My father reached out, laying his hand on my wrist in a rare caress. "My son, do you think I never knew how hard he tried to provoke you to the same thing? But I trusted you, and I was right. I'm disappointed in Dani."

But there was a difference. Though he was perhaps harsher than most people thought an officer should be, Dyan had done nothing to me that was not permitted by the regulations of the cadet corps. I said so, adding, "Do the regulations require that the cadets must endure *that* from an officer too? Cruelty, even sadistic discipline, is bad enough. But persecution of this kind, the threat of sexual attack—"

"What proof have you of that?"

It was like a deluge of ice water. Proof. I had none. Only the satisfied, triumphant look on Dyan's face, the sickness of shame in Danilo, a telepathic awareness I had had no right to read. Moral certainty, yes, but no proof. I just *knew*.

"Lew, you're too sensitive. I'm sorry for Dani, too. But if he had reason to complain of Dyan's treatment of him, there is a formal process of appeal—"

"Against the Comyn? He would have heard what happened to the *last* cadet to try that," I said bitterly. Again, against all reason, Father was standing with the Comyn, with Dyan. I looked at him almost in disbelief. Even now I could not believe he would not right this wrong.

Always. *Always* I had trusted him utterly, implicitly, certain that he would somehow see justice done. Harsh, yes, demanding, but he was always fair. Now Dyan had done—*again!*—what I had always known Dyan would do, and my father was prepared to gloss it over, let this monstrous injustice remain, let Dyan's corrupt and vicious revenge or whatever prevail against all honor and reason.

And I had trusted him! Trusted him literally with my life. I had known that if he failed in testing me for the Alton gift, I would die a very quick, very painful death. I felt I would burst into a flood of tears that would unman me. Once again time slid out of focus and again, eleven years old, terrified but wholly trusting, I stood trembling before him, awaiting the touch that would bring me into full Comyn birthright . . . or kill me! I felt the solemnity of that moment, horribly afraid, yet eager to justify his faith in me, his faith that I was his true-born son who had inherited his gift and his power. . . .

Power! Something inside me exploded into anguish, an anguish I must have been feeling through all the years since that day, which I had never dared let myself feel.

He had been willing to kill me! Why had I never seen this before? Cold-blooded, he had been willing to risk my death, against the hope that he would have a tool to power. Power! Like Dyan, he didn't care what torture he inflicted to get it! I could still remember the exploding agony of that first contact. I had been so deathly ill for a long time afterward that, in his attentive love and concern, I had forgotten—more accurately, had buried—the knowledge that he had been willing to risk my death.

Why? Because if I had proved *not* to have the gift, why, then . . . why, then, my life was of small concern to him, my death no worse than the death of a pet puppy!

He was looking up at me, appalled. He whispered, "No. No, my son, no. Oh, my boy, my boy, it wasn't like that!" But I slammed my mind shut, for the first time deaf to the loving words.

Loving words merely to force his will on me again! And his pain now was for seeing his plans all go awry, when his puppet, his blind tool, his creature, turned in his hand!

He was no better than Dyan, then. Honor, justice, reason—all these could be swept aside in the ruthless hunger for power! Did he even *know* that Danilo was a catalyst telepath, that most sensitive and powerful of talents, that talent thought to be almost extinct?

For a moment it seemed that would be the last argument to move him. Danilo was no ordinary cadet, expendable to salve Dyan's bruised pride. He must be saved for the Comyn at all costs!

With the very words on my lips, I stopped. No. If I told Father that, he would find some way to use Danilo too, as a tool in his driving quest for more power! Danilo was well freed of the Comyn and lucky to be beyond our reach!

My father drew back his extended hands. He said coldly, "Well, it's a long road to Aldaran; maybe you'll calm down and see sense before you get there."

I felt like saying Aldaran, hell! Go do your own dirty work this time, I'm still sick from the last job! I don't give a fart in a high wind for all your power politics! Go to Aldaran yourself and be damned to you!

But I didn't. I recalled that I, too, was Aldaran, and Terran. I'd had it flung in my face often enough. They all took it for granted that I would feel enough shame at the disgrace of my origins to do anything, *anything,* to be accepted as Comyn and my father's heir. He'd kept me subservient, unquestioning, all my life, that way.

But Terran blood, so Linnea had said, was no disgrace in the mountains. It had amazed her that I thought it so. And the Aldarans, too, were kinsmen.

My father had allowed me to think the Terrans and the Aldarans were evil. It had suited his purposes to let me think so.

And maybe that was another lie, a step on his road to power.

I bowed with ironic submissiveness. "I am entirely at your command, Lord Alton," I said and turned my back, leaving him without a farewell embrace or a word.

And sealed my own doom.

CHAPTER ELEVEN

Since Danilo's departure the cadet barracks had been silent, hostile, astir with little eddies of gossip from which Regis was coldly excluded. He was not surprised. Danilo had been a favorite and they identified Regis with the Comyn who had brought about his expulsion.

His own suffering, his loneliness—all the worse because for a time it had been breached—was nothing, he knew, to what his friend must have been feeling. Dani had turned on him that night, he realized, because he was no longer just Regis, he was another persecutor. Another Comyn. But what could have made him so desperate?

He went over it again and again in his mind, without reaching any conclusions at all. He wished he could talk it over with Lew, who had been just as shocked and horrified by it. Regis had felt it in him. But Lew had gone to Aldaran, and Regis had no idea when he would be back.

The day before the cadets were dismissed to their homes, to return next summer in Council season, Regis was scheduled for his regular practice session with Dyan Ardais. He went with the usual blend of excitement and apprehension. He enjoyed his reputation among the cadets as a swordsman too expert for ordinary teaching and the sessions with Dyan challenged him to the utmost, but at the same time he knew these sessions alienated him further from the other cadets. Besides he emerged from them battered, bruised and completely exhausted.

Cadets were readying for practice in the little dressing room off the armory, strapping on the padded surcoats which were worn to protect against the worst blows. The heavy wood and leather practice swords could not kill, but they could inflict substantial injury and pain and even break bones. Regis flung off his cloak and tunic, pulling the padded coat over his head and flinching as he twisted his body to fasten the straps. His ribs were always sore these days.

As he fastened the last buckle, Dyan strode in, threw his

jerkin on a bench and got quickly into his own practice outfit. Behind the thick fencing-mask he looked like some giant insect. Impatiently he gestured Regis toward the practice room. In his haste to obey Regis forgot to pick up his gauntlets, and the older man said harshly, "After all these months? Look here—" He thrust out his own clenched fist, pointed to the lump on the tendons on the back of the hand. "I got that when I was about your age. I ought to make you try it one day without gloves; forget again and I will do just that. I promise you'd never forget another time!"

Feeling like a slapped child, Regis went back hastily and snatched up the heavily padded gauntlets. He hurried back. At the far end, one of the arms-master's aides was giving young Gareth Lindir a lesson, patiently positioning and repositioning his arms and legs, shoulders and hands, after every separate stroke. Regis could not see their faces behind the masks, but they both moved as if they were bored with the business. Bruises were better than that, Regis thought as he hurried to join Dyan.

The bout was brief today. Dyan moved more slowly than usual, almost awkwardly. Regis found himself recalling, with a faint embarrassment, a dream he had had some time ago, about fencing with Dyan. He couldn't remember the details, but for some unremembered reason it filled him with anxiety. He touched Dyan at last and waited for the older man to regain his stance. Instead Dyan flung the wooden sword aside.

"You will have to excuse me for today," he said. "I am somewhat—" He paused. "Somewhat—disinclined to go on." Regis had the impression that he had intended to plead illness. "If you want to continue, I can find someone to practice with you."

"As you wish, Captain."

"Enough, then." He pulled off his mask and went back into the dressing room. Regis followed slowly. Dyan was breathing hard, his face dripping with sweat. He took up a towel and plunged his head into it. Regis, unbuckling his padding, turned away. Like most young people, he felt embarrassed at witnessing the weakness of an elder. Under the thick surcoat his own shirt was dripping wet; he pulled it off and went to his locker for the spare one he had learned to keep there. Dyan put aside the towel and came up behind him. He stood looking at Regis' naked upper body, darkened with new and healing bruises, and finally said, "You should have told me. I had no idea I'd been so heavy-handed." But he was smiling. He reached out and ran both his hands, firmly and thoroughly, over Regis' ribs. Regis flinched from the touch and laughed nervously. Dyan shrugged, laughing in return. "No bones broken," he said, running his fingers along the lowest ribs, "so no harm done."

Regis hurriedly drew on his clean shirt and tunic, thinking that Dyan knew precisely to the inch every time he hit an old bruise—or made a fresh one!

Dyan sat on the bench, lacing up his boots. He threw his fencing-slippers into his locker. "I want to talk to you," he said, "and you're not on duty for another hour. Walk down to the tavern with me. You must be thirsty too."

"Thank you." Regis picked up his cloak and they went down the hill to the inn near the military stables, not the big one where the common soldiers went to drink, but the small wineshop where the officers and cadets spent their leisure time. At this hour the place was not crowded. Dyan slid into an empty booth. "We can go into the back room if you'd rather."

"No, this will do very well."

"You're wise," said Dyan impersonally. "The other cadets would resent it if you kept away from their common haunts and amusements. What will you drink?"

"Cider, sir."

"Nothing stronger? Please yourself." Dyan called the waiter and gave his order, commanding wine for himself. He said, "I think that's why so many cadets take to heavy drinking: the beer they serve in the mess is so near undrinkable they take to wine instead! Perhaps we should improve the beer they're given as a way of keeping them sober!"

He sounded so droll that Regis could not help laughing. At that moment half a dozen cadets came in, started to sit at the next table, then, seeing the two Comyn seated there and laughing together, went back and crowded at a smaller table near the door. Dyan had his back turned to them. Several of them were Regis' barracks-mates; he nodded politely to them, but they pretended not to see.

"Well, tomorrow your first cadet season will be over," Dyan said. "Have you decided to come back for a second?"

"I'd expected to, Captain."

Dyan nodded. "If you survive the first year, everything else is easy. It's that first year which separates the soldiers from the spoiled children. I spoke to the arms-master and suggested he try you as one of his aides next year. Do you think you can teach the brats some of the things I've been trying to pound into you?"

"I can try, sir."

"Just don't be too gentle with them. A few bruises at the right time can save their lives later on." He grinned suddenly. "I seem to have done better by you than I thought, kinsman, judging by the look of your ribs!"

The grin was infectious. Regis laughed and said, "Well, you haven't spared the bruises. No doubt I'll be properly grateful for them, some day."

Dyan shrugged. "At least you haven't complained," he said. "I admire that in someone your age." He held Regis' eyes for a split second longer than Regis felt comfortable, then took a long drink from his mug. "I would have been proud of such behavior from my own son."

"I didn't know you had a son, sir."

Dyan poured himself more wine and said, not looking up, "I *had* a son." His tone did not alter even a fraction, but Regis felt the genuine pain behind Dyan's carefully steady voice. "He was killed in a rockslide at Nevarsin a few years ago."

"I am sorry, kinsman. I had never been told."

"He came to Thendara only once, when I had him legitimated. He was in his mother's care so, I saw him very seldom. We never really got to know one another."

The silence stretched. Regis could not barricade the sharp sense of regret, of loss, he could feel in Dyan. He had to say something.

"Lord Dyan, you are not yet an old man. You could have many sons."

Dyan's smile was a mere mechanical stretching of his mouth. "More likely I shall adopt one of my father's bastards," he said. "He strewed them all about the countryside from the Hellers to the Plains of Valeron. It should be easy enough to find one with *laran,* which is all the Council cares about. I have never been a man for women, nor ever made any secret of it. I forced myself to do my duty by my clan. Once. That was enough." To Regis' awakened sensitivity he sounded immeasurably bitter. "I refuse to think of myself as a very special sort of stud animal whose fees are paid to Comyn. I am sure that you"—he raised his eyes and met Regis', again prolonging the glance with intensity—"can understand what I mean."

Dyan's words struck home, yet his intent look, the feeling he was apparently trying to create, that there was a special rapport between them, suddenly embarrassed the boy. He lowered his eyes and said, "I'm not sure just what you mean, kinsman."

Dyan shrugged and the sudden intensity was gone as quickly as it had come. "Why, just that, being heir to Hastur, they've already begun placing you under pressure to marry, just as they did with me when I was your age. Your grandsire has a reputation in Council as a most persistent and tenacious matchmaker. Do you mean he let Festival Night pass without parading a dozen suitable maidens in front of you, in the hope you'd develop an intolerable itch for one of them?"

Regis said stiffly, "Indeed he did not, sir. I was on duty Festival Night."

"Truly?" Dyan raised an expressive eyebrow. "There were a dozen high-born maidens there, all pretty, and I thought they were all intended for you! I'm surprised he allowed you to stay away."

"I've never asked to be excused from duty, sir. I'm sure Grandfather would not have asked it for me."

"A most commendable attitude," Dyan said, "and one I might have expected from your father's son. But how disappointed the old man must have been! I've accused him to his face of being a disgraceful old procurer!" Dyan was grinning again. "But he assured me that he is always careful to have the wedding properly in order before the bedding."

Regis could not help laughing, although he knew he should be ashamed to join in making fun of his grandfather. "No, Lord Dyan, he hasn't spoken of marriage. Not yet. He only said that I should have an heir as young as possible."

"Why, I'm ashamed of him!" Dyan said and laughed

again. "He had Rafael married off by the time he was your age!"

Regis had resented the memory of his father, whose death had robbed him of so much; now he felt an almost wistful longing to know what kind of man he had been. "Kinsman, am I so like my father as they say? Did you know him well?"

"Not as well as I could have wished," Dyan said, "He married young, while I was in Nevarsin where my father's . . . debaucheries . . . could not contaminate me. Yes, I suppose you are like him." He looked attentively at Regis. "Although you are handsomer than Rafael, handsomer by far."

He was silent, staring down at the swirl in his wineglass. Regis picked up the mug of cider and sipped at it, not looking up. He had grown sensitive to the far-too-frequent comments on his good looks at Nevarsin and in the barracks. From Dyan they seemed somehow more pointed. He gave a mental shrug, recalling what else they said in the barracks, that Lord Dyan had an eye for pretty boys.

Dyan looked up suddenly from his glass. "Where do you intend to spend the winter, kinsman? Will you return to Castle Hastur?"

"I think not. Grandfather is needed here, and I think he would rather have me close at hand. The estate is in good hands, so I'm not needed there."

"True. He lost so much of Rafael's life, I suspect it's a mistake he doesn't want to repeat. I imagine I'll be here too, with crisis on crisis in the city and Kennard ill much of the time. Well, Thendara is an interesting place to spend the winter. There are concerts enough to satisfy any music-lover. And there are fashionable restaurants, balls and dances, all manner of amusements. And, for a young man your age, one should not omit the houses of pleasure. Are you familiar with the House of Lanterns, cousin?"

In contrast to the other flashes of intensity, this was almost too casual. The House of Lanterns was a discreet brothel, one of the very few which were not specifically forbidden to the cadets and officers. Regis knew that some of the older cadets visited the place occasionally but although he shared the curiosity of the other first-year cadets, curiosity had not yet overcome his distaste for the idea. He shook his head. "Only by reputation."

"I find the place tiresome," Dyan said offhandedly. "The Golden Cage is rather more to my liking. It's at the edge of the Terran Zone, and one can find various exotic entertainments there, even aliens and nonhumans, as well as all kinds of women. Or," he added, again in that carefully casual tone, "all kinds of men or boys."

Regis blushed hard and tired to hide it by coughing as if he'd choked on his cider.

Dyan had seen the blush, and grinned. "I had forgotten how conventional young people can be. Perhaps a taste for . . . exotic entertainments . . . needs to be cultivated, like a taste for fine wine instead of cider. And three years in a monastery hardly cultivates the taste for *any* of the finer amusements and luxuries which help a young man to make the most of his life." As Regis only blushed more furiously, he reached out and laid a hand on his arm. "Cousin, the monastery is behind you; have you truly realized that you are no longer bound by all its rules?"

Dyan was watching him carefully. When Regis said nothing, he continued, "Kinsman, one can waste years, precious years of youth, trying to cultivate tastes which turn out to be mistaken. You can miss too much that way. Learn what you want and what you are while you're young enough to enjoy it. I wish someone had given me such advice at your age. My own son never lived to need it. And your father is not here to give it . . . and your grandfather, I have no doubt, is more concerned with teaching you your duty to family and Comyn than with helping you enjoy your youth!"

Dyan's intensity did not embarrass him now. Regis realized that for a long time he had felt starved for just such an opportunity to talk about these things with a man of his own caste, one who understood the world he must live in. He set down his mug and said, "Kinsman, I wonder if that isn't why Grandfather insisted I should serve in the cadets."

Dyan nodded. "Probably so," he said. "It was I who advised him to send you into the cadets, instead of letting you spend your time in idleness and amusements. There's a time for that, of course. But it's true I felt that time spent in the cadets would teach you, more quickly, the things you'd failed to learn before."

Regis looked at him eagerly. "I didn't want to go in the cadets. I hated it at first."

Dyan laid a light hand on his shoulder again and said affectionately, "Everyone does. If you hadn't, I'd be disturbed; it would mean you'd hardened too young."

"But now I think I know why Comyn heirs have to serve in the cadets," Regis said. "Not just the discipline. I got plenty of that in Nevarsin. But learning how to be one of the people, doing the same work they do, sharing their lives and their problems, so we—" He bit his lip, searching carefully for words. "So we'll know what our people are."

Dyan said softly, "That was eloquent, lad. As your cadet-master, I'm content. As your kinsman, too. I wish more boys your age had that kind of understanding. I've been accused of being ruthless. But whatever I've done, I've done it out of allegiance to Comyn. Can you understand that, Regis?"

Regis said, "I think so." He felt warmed, somehow less lonely, by having someone care how he felt or what he thought.

Dyan said, "Do you also understand what I said about how the other cadets would take it ill if you shunned their common amusements."

Regis bit his lip. He said, "I know what you mean. I do, really. Just the same, I feel very strange about—" He was suddenly embarrassed again. "About places like the House of Lanterns. Maybe it will wear off as I get older. But I'm a . . . a telepath—" How strange it felt to say it! How strange that Dyan should be the first one he told! "And it feels . . . wrong," he said, stumbling from phrase to phrase.

Dyan lifted his glass and drank the last in it before he answered. "Maybe you're right. Life can be complicated enough for a telepath, without that, too. Some day you'll know what you want, and then will be the time to trust your instincts and your needs." He fell silent, brooding, and Regis found himself wondering what bitter memories lay behind the pensive look. Finally Dyan said, "You'd probably do well, then, to keep clear of such places and wait until, if the Gods are good to you, someone you can love helps you discover that part of your life." He sighed heavily and said, "If you can. You may discover needs even more imperative than those instincts. It's always a difficult balance for a telepath. There are physical needs. And there are needs which can be even stronger. Emotional needs.

And that's a balance which can tear any of us to pieces." Regis had the curious feeling that Dyan was not really talking to him at all, but to himself.

Abruptly, Dyan set down his empty wineglass and rose. He said, "But one pleasure which has no danger attached is to watch young people grow in wisdom, cousin. I hope to see much of that growth in you this winter, and I'll watch with interest. Meanwhile, keep this in mind: I know the city well and it would be a pleasure to show you anything you wish to see." He laughed aloud suddenly and said, "And believe me, cousin, such instruction would at least leave no bruises."

He strode quickly away. Regis, collecting his cloak from the seat, felt more puzzled than ever, feeling there was something else Dyan had wanted to say.

He had to pass the table crowded with cadets, lounging over cider or beer; he noticed that they were staring at him in no friendly fashion. None of them offered him even the bare civility of a formal greeting. He set his chin and turned his back on them. He heard one say in a low tone, "Catamite!"

Regis felt a flood of intense anger washing over him. He wanted to turn on the boy and beat him to a crimson pulp. Then he set his jaw, disciplining himself to walk away and pretend he had not heard. *If you listen to dogs barking, you'll go deaf and never learn much.*

He remembered various insults he had pretended not to hear, mostly to the intent that the Comyn hung together, that he had had special favors because he was a Comyn heir. But this one was new. He recalled the taunt Danilo had flung at him the night before his expulsion. Dani was a *cristoforo* and to him it was more than an insult.

He knew Dyan would have nothing but scorn for such gossip. He never made any secret of his tastes. Yet Regis felt oddly protective toward his kinsman, having sensed his bitterness. He felt a strange wish to defend him.

It occurred to him again, with frustration too new for him to realize it was a commonplace among telepaths, that there were times when *laran* was absolutely no help at all in personal relationships.

The season ended. The cadets were dismissed to their homes and Regis moved into the Hastur apartments in

Comyn Castle. He appreciated the peace and quiet and felt a certain pleasure in being able to sleep as late as he pleased in the morning. And the Hastur cooks were certainly better than those in the Guards mess. The prolonged austerity, though, first in Nevarsin, then in the barracks, had made him almost guilty about this kind of luxury. He couldn't appreciate it as he wanted to.

One morning he was at breakfast with his grandfather when Lord Hastur said abruptly, "You're not looking like yourself. Is something wrong?"

Regis thought that his grandfather had seen so little of him that he would have no idea what he usually looked like. He was too polite to say it, of course, so answered, "Bored, maybe. Not getting enough exercise."

It disturbed him that he could not help picking up his grandfather's thoughts: *It's wrong to keep the boy hanging about here when I've so little time to spend with him.*

Hastur said aloud, "I'm afraid I've been too busy to notice, my boy. I'm very sorry. Would you like to return to Castle Hastur, or go somewhere else?"

"I wasn't complaining, sir. But I feel I'm no use to you. When you asked me to stay for the winter, I thought there was something I could do to help you."

"I wish you could. Unfortunately, you haven't the experience to be a great deal of help yet," Hastur said, but could not conceal a faint flicker of satisfaction. *He's beginning to be interested.* "Some time this winter you might attend a few sessions of the *Cortes* and find out about the problems we're facing. I'll get you a pass. Or you could ride to Edelweiss, spend a few days with Javanne."

Regis shrugged. He found Edelweiss dull. There was no hunting except for rabbits and squirrels, the rain kept them indoors much of the time, and he and Javanne were too far apart in age and too unlike in personality to find much pleasure in each other's company.

"I know it's not very exciting there either," Hastur said, almost apologizing, "but she is your sister, and we do not have so many kinfolk that we can neglect one another. If you want hunting, you know, you are free to go to Armida at any time. Lew is away and Kennard too ill to travel, but you can go there and take a friend."

But the only friend he'd made in the cadets, Regis

thought, was sent home in disgrace. "Kennard is ill, sir? What's wrong?"

Danvan sighed. "This climate doesn't agree with him. He grows more crippled every year. He'll be better when the rains—" He broke off as a servant came in with a message. "Already? Yes, I have to go and talk with a trade delegation from the Dry Towns," he said with weary resignation, laying down his napkin. He excused himself to Regis, adding, "Let me know your plans, lad, and I'll arrange for escort."

Left alone, Regis poured himself another cup of Terran coffee, one of the few luxuries the austere old man allowed himself, and thought it over. The duty visit to Javanne could not, of course be avoided. A visit to Armida could await Lew's return; he could hardly be intending to spend the winter at Aldaran.

If Kennard was ill, courtesy demanded that Regis pay him a visit in his suite, but for some unknown reason he was unwilling to face the Alton lord. He did not know why. Kennard had always been kind to him. After a time he focused it down to resentment: he stood by and watched Danilo's disgrace and didn't say a word. Lew wanted to interfere, but he couldn't. Kennard didn't care.

And Kennard was one of the most powerful telepaths in Comyn. Regis, feeling this much resentment, was reluctant to face him. Kennard would know immediately how he felt.

He knew, rationally, that he should go to Kennard at once, if only to tell him about his newly developing *laran*. There were training techniques to help him master and control his new facilities. But in the cadets it had not seemed to matter, and the proper time to speak to Lew about it had never come till too late. Dyan had seemed to take it for granted that he already had what training he needed. Kennard was the obvious one to tell. He admonished himself sternly that he should go at once, now, today.

But he was still reluctant to face him. He decided to go to Javanne for a few days first. By that time perhaps Lew would be back.

A few days later he rode north, the weight of it still on his mind. Syrtis lay half a mile from the northward road and, on an impulse, he told his escort to wait in a nearby village. He rode alone to Syrtis.

It lay at the far end of a long valley, leading downward to the lake country around Mariposa. It was a clear autumn day, with ripening fruit trees hanging low under their thick harvest and small animals making scurrying noises in the dry brushwood at the side of the road. The sounds and smells made Regis feel content as he rode along, but as he came down toward the farm his spirits sank. He had been thinking Danilo well off, to be coming home to this pleasant country, but he had not realized how poor the place was. The main house was small, one wing falling into such disrepair that it could hardly have been safe for human habitation. The sparse outbuildings showed how few men must live on the place. The old moat had been drained, ditched and put to kitchen-gardens with neat rows of vegetables and pot-herbs. An old, bent servant told him, touching his breast in rustic courtesy, that the master was just returning from the hunt. Regis suspected that in a place like this rabbit would be more plentiful on the table than butcher's meat.

A tall, aging man in a once-fine threadbare cloak rode slowly toward him. He was moustached and bearded, and sat his horse with the erect competence of an old soldier. A fine hawk sat, hooded, on his saddle.

"Greetings," he said in a deep voice. "We see few travelers at Syrtis. How may I serve you?"

Regis alighted from his horse, making him a courteous bow. "Dom Felix Syrtis? Regis-Rafael Hastur, *para servirte.*"

"My house and I are at your service, Lord Regis. Let me see to your mount. Old Mauris is half blind; I'd not trust him with such a fine animal. Will you come with me?"

Leading the horse, Regis followed the old man toward a stone barn in better repair than most of the outbuildings, being weathertight and newly roofed. At the far end was a screened-off enclosure; nearer were open box stalls, and Regis tethered his horse in the closest while Dom Felix took a cluster of small birds from the hook at his saddle and unsaddled his mount. Regis saw Danilo's beautiful black gelding in another stall, the old bony hunter Dom Felix had been riding and two good, but aging mares. The other stalls were empty, except for a couple of clumsy plowhorses and a milk animal or two. This was abysmal poverty indeed for a family of noble blood and Regis was ashamed to witness it. He remembered that Danilo had hardly had a whole shirt to his back when he joined the cadets.

Dom Felix was looking at Regis' black mare with the kind of love that men of his type bestowed openly only on their horses and hawks. "A fine mount, *vai dom.* Armida-bred, no doubt? I know that pedigree."

"True. A birthday gift from Lord Kennard, before I went to Nevarsin."

"Might I ask her name, Lord Regis?"

"Melisande," Regis told him, and the old man stroked the velvet muzzle tenderly. Regis nodded to Danilo's fine black. "And there is another of the same breed; they might well be foals of the same dam."

"Aye," said Dom Felix curtly, "Lord Alton does not withdraw a gift, however unworthy given." He shut his mouth with a snap and Regis' heart sank; it promised ill for his mission. Dom Felix turned away to see to the hawk, and Regis asked politely, "Had you good hunting, sir?"

"Indifferent," said Dom Felix shortly, taking the hawk from his saddle and carrying her to the enclosure at the far end. "No, my lord, you will frighten a haggard I have here. Be pleased to remain where you are."

Rebuked, Regis kept his distance. When the old man returned, he complimented him on a well-trained bird.

"It is my life's work, Lord Regis. I was hawk-master to your grandsire, when your father was a lad."

Regis raised a mental eyebrow, but in these disturbed days it was not unusual to find a former courtier out of favor.

"How is it that you honor my house, Dom Regis?"

"I came to see your son Danilo."

The old man's tight-pressed lips almost disappeared between moustache and chin. Finally he said, "My lord, by your uniform you know of my son's disgrace. I beg you, leave him in peace. Whatever his crime, he has paid more than you can know."

Regis said, in shock, "No! I am his friend!"

Now the pent-up hostility exploded.

"The friendship of a Comyn lord is as the sweetness of a beehive: it bears a deadly sting! I have lost one son already to the love of a Hastur lord; must I lose the last child of my old age as well?"

Regis spoke gently. "All my life, Dom Felix, I have heard nothing but good of the man who gave his life in a vain attempt to shield my father. Do you think me evil enough to wish harm on the house of such a man? Whatever your grudge against my forefathers, sir, you have no quarrel with me. If Danilo has, he must tell me himself. I had not known your son was so young he must seek a parent's leave to welcome a guest."

A faint, unlovely flush spread slowly over the bearded face. Regis realized too late that he had been impertinent. It came as no surprise that Danilo should be under his father's displeasure, yet he had spoken the truth: by the law of the Domains, Danilo was a responsible adult.

"My son is in the orchard, Dom Regis. May I send to summon him? We have but few servants to bear messages."

"I'll walk down, if I may."

"Forgive me, then, if I do not accompany you, since you say your business is with my son. I must take these birds to my kitchen folk. The path will lead you to the orchard."

Regis walked down the narrow lane the old man pointed out. At its end the path opened out to an orchard of apple and pear trees. The fruit, fully ripe, hung glistening among the darkening leaves. Danilo was there at the far end of the grove, his back to Regis, stooping to rake up some mulch around the tree roots. He was stripped to the waist, his feet thrust into wooden clogs. A damp sweat-rag was tied around his forehead, his dark hair in disorder above it.

The smell of apples was sweet and winy. Danilo slowly straightened his back, picked up a windfall and thoughtfully bit into it. Regis stood watching him, unseen, for a moment. He looked tired, preoccupied and, if not content, at least lulled by hard physical work and the warm sun into a momentary peace.

"Dani?" Regis said at last, and the boy, startled, dropped the apple and stumbled over his rake as he turned. Regis wondered what to say.

Danilo took a step toward him. "What do *you* want?"

"I was on the road to my sister's house; I stopped to pay my respects to your father and to see how you did."

He saw Danilo visibly struggling between the impulse to

fling the polite gesture back into his face—what more had he to lose?—and the lifelong habit of hospitality. At last he said, "My house and I are at your service, Lord Regis." His politeness was exaggerated almost to a caricature. "What is my lord's will?"

Regis said, "I want to talk to you."

"As you can see, my lord, I am very much occupied. But I am entirely at your bidding."

Regis ignored the irony and took him at his word.

"Come here, then, and sit down," he said, taking his seat on a fallen log, felled so long ago that it was covered with gray lichen. Silently Danilo obeyed, keeping as far away as the dimensions of the log allowed.

Regis said after a moment, "I want you to know one thing: I have no idea why you were thrown out of the Guards, or rather, I only know what I heard that day. But from the way everyone acted, you'd think I left you to take the blame for something I myself did. Why? What did I do?"

"You know—" Danilo broke off, kicking a windfall apple with the point of his clog. It broke with a rotten, slushy *clunk*. "It's over. Whatever I did to offend you, I've paid."

Then for a moment the rapport, the awareness Danilo had wakened in him, flared again between them. He could feel Danilo's despair and grief as if it were his own. He said, harsh with the pain of it, "Danilo Syrtis, speak your grudge and let me avow or deny it! I tried not to think ill of you even in disgrace! But you called me foul names when I meant you nothing but kindness, and if you have spread lies about me or my kinsmen, then you deserve everything they have done to you, and you still have a score to settle with me!" Without realizing it, he had sprung to his feet, his hand going to the hilt of his sword.

Danilo stood defiant. His eyes gray, gleaming like molten metal beneath dark brows, blazed with anger and sorrow. "*Dom* Regis, I beg you, leave me in peace! Isn't it enough that I am here, my hopes gone, my father shamed forever—I might as well be dead!" he cried out desperately, his words tumbling over themselves. "Grudge, Regis? No, no, none against you, you showed me nothing but kindness, but you were one of them, one of those, those—" He stopped again, his voice tight with the effort not to cry. At last he cried out passionately, "Regis Hastur, as the Gods live, my conscience is clear and your Lord of Light and the God of the *cristoforos* may judge between the Sons of Hastur and me!"

Almost without volition, Regis drew his sword. Danilo, startled, took a step backward in fear; then he straightened and stiffened his mouth. "Do you punish blasphemy so quickly, lord? I am unarmed, but if my offense merits death, then kill me now where I stand! My life is no good to me!"

Shocked, Regis lowered the point of the sword. "Kill you, Dani?" he said in horror. "God forbid! It never crossed my mind! I wished . . .Dani, lay your hand on the hilt of my sword."

Confused, startled into obedience, Danilo put a tentative hand on the hilt. Regis gripped hand and hilt together in his own fingers.

"Son of Hastur who is the Son of Aldones who is the Lord of Light! May this hand and this sword pierce my heart and my honor, Danilo, if I had part or knowledge in your disgrace, or if anything you say now shall be used to work you harm!" Again, from the hand-touch, he felt that odd little shock running up his arm, blurring his own thoughts, felt Danilo's sobs tight in his own throat.

Danilo said on a drawn breath, "No Hastur would forswear that oath!"

"No Hastur would forswear his naked word," Regis retorted proudly, "but if it took an oath to convince you, an oath you have." He sheathed the sword.

"Now tell me what happened, Dani. Was the charge a lie, then?"

Danilo was still visibly dazed. "The night I came in—it had been raining. You woke, you *knew*—"

"I knew only that you were in pain, Dani. No more. I asked if I could help, but you drove me away." The pain and shock he had felt that night returned to him in full force and he felt his heart pounding again with the agony of it, as he had done when Danilo thrust him away.

Danilo said, "You are a telepath. I thought—"

"A very rudimentary one, Danilo," said Regis, trying to steady his voice. "I sensed only that you were unhappy, in pain. I didn't know why and you would not tell me."

"Why should you care?"

Regis put out his hand, slowly closed it around Danilo's wrist. "I am Hastur and Comyn. It touches the honor of my clan and my caste that anyone should have cause to speak ill of us. With false slanders we can deal, but with truth, we can only try to right the wrong. We Comyn can be mistaken." Dimly, at the back of his mind, he realized he had said "We Comyn" for the first time. "More," he said, and smiled fleetingly, "I like your father, Dani. He was willing to anger a Hastur in order to have you left in peace."

Danilo stood nervously locking and unlocking his hands. He said, "The charge is true. I drew my dagger on Lord Dyan. I only wish I had cut his throat while I was about it; whatever they did to me, the world would be a cleaner place."

Regis stared, disbelieving. "*Zandru!* Dani—"

"I know, in days past, the men who touched Comyn lord in irreverence would have been torn on hooks. In those days, perhaps, Comyn were worth reverence—"

"Leave that," Regis said sharply. "Dani, I am heir to Hastur, but even I could not draw steel on an officer without disgrace. Even if the officer I struck were no Comyn lord but young Hjalmar, whose mother is a harlot of the streets."

Danilo stood fighting for control. "If I struck young Hjalmar, Regis, then I would have deserved my punishment; he is an honorable man. It was not as my officer I drew on Lord Dyan. He had forfeited all claim to obedience or respect."

"Is that for you to judge?"

"In those circumstances . . ." Danilo swallowed. "Could I respect and obey a man who has so far forgotten himself as to try to make me his—" He used a *cahuenga* word Regis did not know, only that it was unspeakably obscene. But he was still in rapport with Danilo, so there was no scrap of doubt about his meaning. Regis went white. He literally could not speak under the shock of it.

"At first I thought he was joking," Danilo said, almost stammering. "I do not like such jests—I am a *cristoforo*—but I gave him some similar joke for an answer and thought that was the end of it, for if he meant the jest in seriousness, then I had given him his answer without offense. Then he made himself clearer and grew angry when I answered him no, and swore he could force me to it. I don't know what he did to me, Regis, he did something with his mind, so that wherever I was, alone or with others, I *felt* him touching me, heard his . . . his foul whispers, that awful, mocking laugh of his. He pursued me, he seemed to be inside my mind all the time. All the time. I thought he meant to drive me out of my mind! I had thought . . . a telepath could not inflict pain. . . . I can't stand it even to be *around* anyone who's really unhappy, but he took some awful, hateful kind of pleasure in it." Danilo sobbed suddenly. "I went to him, then, I begged him to let me be! Regis, I am no gutter-brat, my family has served the Hasturs honorably for years, but if I were a whore's foundling and he the king on his throne, he would have had no right to use me so shamefully!" Danilo broke down again and sobbed. "And then . . . and then he said I knew perfectly well how I could be free of him. He *laughed* at me, that awful, hideous laugh. And then I had my dagger out, I hardly know how I came to draw it, or what I meant to do with it, kill myself maybe . . ." Danilo put his hands over his face. "You know the rest," he said through them.

Regis could hardly draw breath. "Zandru send him scorpion whips! Dani, why didn't you lay charge and claim immunity? He is subject to the laws of Comyn too, and a telepath who misuses his *laran* that way . . ."

Danilo gave a weary little shrug. It said more than words.

Regis felt wholly numbed by the revelation. How could he ever face Dyan again, knowing this?

I knew it wasn't true what they said of you, Regis. But you were Comyn too, and Dyan showed you so much favor, and that last night, when you touched me, I was afraid . . .

Regis looked up, outraged, then realized Danilo had not spoken at all. They were deeply in rapport; he felt the other boy's thoughts. He sat back down on the log, feeling that his legs were unable to hold him upright.

"I touched you . . . only to quiet you." he said at last.

"I know that now. What good would it do to say I am sorry for that, Regis? It was a shameful thing to say."

"It is no wonder you cannot believe in honor or decency from my kin. But it is for us to prove it to you. All the more since you are one of us. Danilo, how long have you had *laran*?"

"I? *Laran?* I, Lord Regis?"

"Didn't you know? How long have you been able to read thoughts?"

"That? Why, all my life, it seems. Since I was twelve or so. Is *that* . . ."

"Don't you know what it means, if you have one of the Comyn gifts? You do, you know. Telepaths aren't uncommon, but you opened up my own gift, even after Lew Alton failed." With a flood of emotion, he thought, *you brought me my heritage.* "I think you're what they call a catalyst telepath. That's very rare and a precious gift." He forebore to say it was an Ardais gift. He doubted if Danilo would appreciate that information just now. "Have you told anyone else?"

"How could I, when I didn't know myself? I thought everyone could read thoughts."

"No, it's rarer than that. It means you too are Comyn, Dani."

"Are you saying my parentage is—"

"Zandru's hells, no! But your family is noble, it may well be that your mother had Comyn kinsmen, Comyn blood, even generations ago. With full *laran,* though, it means you yourself are eligible for Comyn Council, that you should be trained to use these gifts, sealed to Comyn." He saw revulsion on Danilo's face and said quickly, "Think. It means you are Lord Dyan's equal. He can be held accountable for having misused you."

Regis blessed the impulse that had brought him here. Alone, his mind burdened with the brooding, hypersensitive nature of the untrained telepath, under his father's grim displeasure . . . Danilo might have killed himself after all.

"I won't, though," Danilo said aloud. Regis realized they had slid into rapport again. He reached out to touch Danilo, remembered and didn't. To conceal the move he bent and picked up a windfall apple. Danilo got to his feet and began putting on his shirt. Regis finished the apple and dropped the core into a pile of mulch.

"Dani, I am expected to sleep tonight at my sister's house. But I give my word: you shall be vindicated. Meanwhile, is there anything else I can do for you?"

"Yes, Regis! Yes! Tell my father the disgrace and dishonor were not mine! He asked no questions and spoke no word of reproach, but no man in our family has ever been dishonored. I can bear anything but his belief that I lied to him!"

"I promise you he shall know the full—no." Regis broke off suddenly. "Isn't that why you dared not tell him yourself? He would kill—" He saw that he had, in truth, reached the heart of Danilo's fear.

"He would challenge Dyan," Danilo said haltingly, "and though he looks strong he is an old man and his heart is far from sound. If he knew the truth—I *wanted* to tell him everything, but I would rather have him . . . despise me . . . than ruin himself."

"Well, I shall try to clear your name with your father without endangering him. But for yourself, Dani? We owe you something for the injury."

"You owe me nothing, Regis. If my name is clean before my kinsmen, I am content."

"Still, the honor of Comyn demands we right this injustice. If there is rot at our heart, well, it must be cleansed." At this moment, filled with righteous anger, he was ready to fling himself against a whole regiment of unjust men who abused their powers. If the older men in Comyn were corrupt or power-mad, and the younger ones idle, then boys would have to set it right!

Danilo dropped to one knee. He held out his hands, his voice breaking. "There is a life between us. My brother died to shield your father. As for me, I ask no more than to give my life in the service of Hastur. Take my sword and my oath, Lord Regis. By the hand I place on your sword, I pledge my life."

Startled, deeply moved, Regis drew his sword again, held out the hilt to Danilo. Their hands met on the hilt again as Regis, stumbling on the ritual words, trying to recall them one by one, said, "Danilo-Felix Syrtis, be from this day paxman and shield-arm to me . . . and this sword strike me if I be not just lord and shield to you. . . ." He bit his lip, fighting to remember what came next. Finally he said, "The Gods witness it, and the holy things at Hali." It seemed there was something else, but at least their intention was clear, he thought. He slid the sword back into its sheath, raised Danilo to his feet and shyly kissed him on either cheek. He saw tears on Danilo's eyelids and knew that his own were not wholly dry.

He said, trying to lighten the moment, "Now you've only had formally what we both knew all along, *bredu.*" He heard himself say the word with a little shock of amazement, but knew he meant it as he had never meant anything before.

Danilo said, trying to steady his voice, "I should have . . . offered you my sword. I'm not wearing one, but here—"

That was what had been missing in the ritual. Regis started to say that it did not matter, but without it there was something wanting. He looked at the dagger Danilo held out hilt-first to him. Regis drew his own, laid it hilt-to-blade along the other before giving it to Danilo, saying quietly. "Bear this, then, in my service."

Danilo laid his lips to the blade for a moment, saying, "In your service alone I bear it," and put it into his own sheath.

Regis thrust Danilo's knife into the scabbard at his waist. It did not quite fit, but it would do. He said, "You must remain here until I send for you. It will not be long, I promise, but I have to think what to do."

He did not say goodbye. It was not necessary. He turned and walked back along the lane. As he went into the barn to untie his horse, Dom Felix came slowly toward him.

"Lord Regis, may I offer you some refreshment?"

Regis said pleasantly, "I thank you, but grudged hospitality has a bitter taste. Yet it is my pleasure to assure you, on the word of a Hastur"—he touched his hand briefly to swordhilt—"you may be proud of your son, Dom Felix. His dishonor should be your pride."

The old man frowned. "You speak riddles, *vai dom.*"

"Sir, you were hawk-master to my grandsire, yet I have not seen you at court in my lifetime. To Danilo a choice even more bitter was given: to win favor by dishonorable means, or to keep his own honor at the price of apparent disgrace. In brief, sir, your son offended the pride of a man who has power but none of the honor which gives power its dignity. And this man revenged himself."

The old man's brow furrowed as he slowly puzzled out what Regis was saying. "If the charge was unjust, an act of private revenge, why did my son not tell me?"

"Because, Dom Felix, Dani feared you would ruin yourself to avenge him." He added quickly, seeing a thousand questions forming in the old man's eyes, "I promised Danilo I would tell you no more than this. But will you accept the word of a Hastur that he is blameless?"

Light broke in the troubled face. "I bless you for coming and I beg you to pardon my rough words, Lord Regis. I am no courtier. But I am grateful."

"And loyal to your son," Regis said. "Have no doubt, Dom Felix, he is worthy of it."

"Will you not honor my house, Lord Regis?" This time the offer was heartfelt, and Regis smiled. "I regret that I cannot, sir, I am expected elsewhere. Danilo has shown me your hospitality; you grow the finest apples I have tasted in a long time. And I give you my word that one day it shall be my pleasure to show honor to the father of my friend. Meanwhile, I beg you to be reconciled to your son."

"You may be sure of it, Lord Regis." He stood staring after Regis as the boy mounted and rode away, and Regis could sense his confusion and gratitude. As he rode slowly down the hill to rejoin his bodyguard, he realized what he had, in substance, pledged himself to do: to restore Danilo's good name and make certain that Dyan could not again misuse power this way. What it meant was that he, who had once sworn to renounce the Comyn, now had to reform it from inside out, single-handedly, before he could enjoy his own freedom.

CHAPTER TWELVE

(Lew Alton's narrative)

The hills rise beyond the Kadarin, leading away into the mountains, into the unknown country where the law of the Comyn does not run. In my present state, as soon as I had forded the Kadarin I felt that a weight had been lifted from my shoulders.

In this part of the world, five days' ride north of Thendara, my safe-conducts meant nothing. We slept at night in tents, with a watch set. It was a barren country, long deserted. Only perhaps three or four times in a day's ride did we see some small village, half a dozen poor houses clustered in a clearing, or some small-holding where a hardy farmer wrested a bare living from the stony and perpendicular forest. There were so few travelers here that the children came out to watch us as we passed.

The roads got worse and worse as we went further into the hills, degenerating at times into mere goat-tracks and trails. There are not many good roads on Darkover. My father, who lived on Terra for many years, has told me about the good roads there, but added that there was no way to bring that system here. For roads you needed slave labor or immense numbers of men willing to work for the barest subsistence, or else heavy machinery. And there have never been slaves on Darkover, not even slaves to machinery.

It was, I thought, small wonder that the Terrans were reluctant to move their spaceport into these hills again.

I was the more surprised when, on the ninth day of traveling, we came on to a wide road, well-surfaced and capable of handling wheeled carts and several men riding abreast. My father had also told me that when he last visited the hills near Aldaran, Caer Donn had been little more than a substantial village. Reports had reached him that it was now a good-sized city. But this did not diminish my astonishment when, coming to the top of one of the higher hills, we saw it spread out below us in the valley and along the lower slopes of the next mountain.

It was a clear day, and we could see a long distance. Deep in the lowest part of the valley, where the ground was most even, there was a great fenced-in area, abnormally smooth-surfaced, and even from here I could see the runways and the landing strips. This, I thought, must be the old Terran spaceport, now converted to a landing field for their aircraft and the small rockets which brought messages from Thendara and Port Chicago. There was a similar small landing field near Arilinn. Beyond the airfield lay the city, and as my escort drew to a halt behind me, I heard the men murmuring about it.

"There was no city here when I was a lad! How could it grow so fast?"

"It's like the city which grew up overnight in the old fairy tale!"

I told them a little of what Father had said, about prefabricated construction. Such cities were not built to stand for ages, but could be quickly constructed. They scowled skeptically and one of them said, "I'd hate to be rude about the Commander, sir, but he must have been telling you fairy tales. Even on Terra human hands can't build so quick."

I laughed. "He also told me of a hot planet where the natives did not believe there was such a thing as snow, and accused him of tale-telling when he spoke of mountains which bore ice all year."

Another pointed. "Castle Aldaran?"

There was nothing else it could have been, unless we were unimaginably astray: an ancient keep, a fortress of craggy weathered stone. This was the stronghold of the renegade Domain, exiled centuries ago from Comyn—no man alive now knew why. Yet they were the ancient Seventh Domain, of the ancient kin of Hastur and Cassilda.

I felt curiously mingled eagerness and reluctance, as if taking some irrevocable step. Once again the curiously unfocused time-sense of the Altons thrust fingers of dread at me. What was waiting for me in that old stone fortress lying at the far end of the valley of Caer Donn?

With a scowl I brought myself back to the present. It

needed no great precognition to sense that in a completely strange part of the world I might meet strangers and that some of them would have a lasting effect on my life. I told myself that crossing that valley, stepping through the gates of Castle Aldaran, was *not* some great and irrevocable division in my life which would cut me off from my past and all my kindred. I was here at my father's bidding, an obedient son, disloyal only in thought and will.

I struggled to get myself back in focus. "Well, we might as well try to reach it while we still have some daylight," I said, and started down the excellent road.

The ride across Caer Donn was in a strange way dreamlike. I had chosen to travel simply, without the complicated escort of an ambassador, treating this as the family visit it purported to be, and I attracted no particular attention. In a way the city was like myself, I thought, outwardly all Darkovan, but with a subliminal difference somewhere, something that did not quite belong. For all these years I had been content to accept myself as Darkovan; now, looking at the old Terran port as I had never looked at the familiar one at Thendara, I thought that this too was my heritage . . . if I had courage to take it.

I was in a curious mood, feeling a trifle fey, as if, without knowing what shape or form it would take, I could smell a wind that bore my fate.

There were guards at the gates of Aldaran, mountain men, and for the first time I gave my full name, not the one I bore as my father's *nedestro* heir, but the name given before either father or mother had cause to suspect anyone could doubt my legitimacy. "I am Lewis-Kennard Lanart-Montray Alton y Aldaran, son of Kennard, Lord Alton, and Elaine Montray-Aldaran. I have come as envoy of my father, and I ask a kinsman's welcome of Kermiac, Lord Aldaran."

The guards bowed and one of them, some kind of majordomo or steward, said, "Enter, *dom,* you are welcome and you honor the house of Aldaran. In his name I extend you welcome, until you hear it from his own lips." My escort was taken away to be housed elsewhere while I was led to a spacious room high in one of the far wings of the castle; my saddle bags were brought and servants sent to me when they found I traveled with no valet. In general they established me in luxury. After a while the steward returned.

"My lord, Kermiac of Aldaran is at dinner and asks, if you are not too weary from travel, that you join him in the hall. If you are trail-wearied, he bids you dine here and rest well, but he bade me say he was eager to welcome his sister's grandson."

I said I would join him with pleasure. At that moment I was not capable of feeling fatigue; the fey mood of excitement was still on me. I washed off the dust of travel and dressed in my best, a fine tunic of crimson-dyed leather with breeches to match, low velvet boots, a dress cape lined with fur—not vanity, this, but to show honor to my unknown kinsman.

Dusk was falling when the servant returned to conduct me to the great dining hall. Expecting dim torchlight, I was struck amazed by the daylight flood of brilliance. Arc-light, I thought, blinking, arc-light such as the Terrans use in their Trade City. It seemed strange to go at night into a room flooded by such noonday brilliance, strange and disorienting, yet I was glad, for it allowed me to see clearly the faces in the great hall. Evidently, despite his use of the newfangled lights, Kermiac kept to the old ways, for the lower part of his hall was crammed with a motley conglomeration of faces, Guardsmen, servants, mountain people, rich and poor, even some Terrans and a *cristoforo* monk or two in their drab robes.

The servant led me toward the high table at the far end where the nobles sat. At first they were only a blur of faces: a tall man, lean and wolfish, with a great shock of fair hair; a pretty, red-haired girl in a blue dress; a small boy about Marius' age; and at their center, an aging man with a dark reddish beard, old to decrepitude but still straight-backed and keen-eyed. He bent his eyes on me, studying my face intently. This, I knew, must be Kermiac, Lord Aldaran, my kinsman. He wore plain clothes, of a simple cut like those the Terrans wore, and I felt briefly ashamed of my barbarian finery.

He rose and came down from the dais to greet me. His voice, thinned with age, was still strong.

"Welcome, kinsman." He held out his arms and gave me a kinsman's embrace, his thin dry lips pressing each of my cheeks in turn. He held my shoulders between his hands for a moment. "It warms my heart to see your face at last,

Elaine's son. We hear tidings in the Hellers here, even of the *Hali'imyn.*" He used the ancient mountain word, but without offense. "Come, you must be weary and hungry after this long journey. I am glad you felt able to join us. Come and sit beside me, nephew."

He led me to a place of honor at his side. Servants brought us food. In the Domains the choicest food is served a guest without asking his preference, so that he need not in courtesy choose the simplest; here they made much of asking whether I would have meat, game-bird or fish, whether I would drink the white mountain wine or the red wine of the valleys. It was all cooked well and served to perfection, and I did it justice after days of trail food.

"So, nephew," he said at last, when I had appeased my hunger and was sipping a glass of white wine and nibbling at some strange and delicious sweets, "I have heard you are tower-trained, a telepath. Here in the mountains it's believed that men tower-trained are half eunuch, but I can see you are a man; you have the look of a soldier. Are you one of their Guardsmen?"

"I have been a captain for three years."

He nodded. "There is peace in the mountains now, although the Dry-Towners get ideas now and then. Yet I can respect a soldier; in my youth I had to keep Caer Donn by force of arms."

I said, "In the Domains it is not known that Caer Donn is so great a city."

He shrugged. "Largely of Terran building. They are good neighbors, or we find them so. Is it otherwise in Thendara?"

I was not yet ready to discuss my feelings about the Terrans, but to my relief he did not pursue that topic. He was studying my face in profile.

"You are not much like your father, nephew. Yet I see nothing of Elaine in you, either."

"It is my brother Marius who is said to have my mother's face and her eyes."

"I have never seen him. I last saw your father twelve years ago, when he brought Elaine's body here to rest among her kin. I asked then for the privilege of fostering her sons, but Kennard chose to rear you in his own house."

I had never known that. I had been told nothing of my

mother's people. I was not even sure what degree of kin I was to the old man. I said something of this to him, and he nodded.

"Kennard has had no easy life," Kermiac said. "I cannot blame him that he never wanted to look back. But if he chose to tell you nothing of your mother's kin, he cannot take offense that I tell you now in my own fashion. Years ago, when the Terrans were mostly stationed at Caer Donn and the ground had just been broken for the fine building at Thendara—I hear it has been finished in this winter past—years ago, then, when I was not much more than a boy, my sister Mariel chose to marry a Terran, Wade Montray. She dwelt with him many years on Terra. I have heard the marriage was not a happy one and they separated, after she had borne him two children. Mariel chose to remain with her daughter Elaine on Terra; Wade Montray came with his son Larry, whom we called Lerrys, back to Darkover. And now you may see how the hand of fate works, for Larry Montray and your father, Kennard, met as boys and swore friendship. I am no great believer in predestination or a fate foretold, but so it came about that Larry Montray remained on Darkover to be fostered at Armida and your father was sent back to Terra, to be fostered as Wade Montray's son, in the hope that these two lads would build again the old bridge between Terra and Darkover. And there, of course, your father met Montray's daughter, who was also the daughter of my sister Mariel. Well, to make a long tale short, Kennard returned to Darkover, was given in marriage to a woman of the Domains, who bore him no child, served in Arilinn Tower—some of this you must have been told. But he bore the memory of Elaine, it seems, ever in his heart, and at last sought her in marriage. As her nearest kinsman, it was I who gave consent. I have always felt such marriages are fortunate, and children of mixed blood the closest road to friendship between people of different worlds. I had no idea, then, that your Comyn kinsmen would not bless the marriage as I had done, and rejoice in it."

All the more wrong of the Comyn, I thought, since it was by their doing that my father had first gone to Terra. Well, it was all of a piece with their doings since. And another score I bore against them.

Yet my father stood with them!

Kermiac concluded, "When it was clear they would not accept you, I offered to Kennard that you should be fostered here, honored at least as Elaine's son if not as his. He was certain he could force them, at last, to accept you. He must have succeeded, then?"

"After a fashion," I said slowly. "I am his heir." I did not want to discuss the costs of that with him. Not yet.

The steward had been trying to attract Lord Kermiac's attention; he saw it and gave a signal for the tables to be cleared. As the great crowd who dined at his table began to disperse, he led me into a small sitting room, dimly lighted, a pleasant room with an open fireplace. He said, "I am old, and old men tire quickly, nephew. But before I go to rest, I want you to know your kinsmen. Nephew, your cousin, my son Beltran."

To this day, even after all that came later, I still remember how I felt when I first looked on my cousin. I knew at last what blood had shaped me such a changeling among the Comyn. In face and feature we might have been brothers; I have known twins who were less like. Beltran held out his hand, drew it back and said, "Sorry, I have heard that telepaths don't like touching strangers."

"I won't refuse a kinsman my hand," I said, and returned the clasp lightly. In the strange mood I was in the touch gave me a swift pattern of impressions: curiosity, enthusiasm, a disarming friendliness. Kermiac smiled at us as we stood close together and said, "I leave your cousin to you, Beltran. Lew, believe me, you are at home." He said good night and left us, and Beltran drew me toward the others. He said, "My father's foster-children and wards, cousin, and my friends. Come and meet them. So you're tower-trained? Are you a natural telepath as well?"

I nodded and he said, "Marjorie is our telepath." He drew forward the pretty, red-haired girl in blue whom I had noticed at the table. She smiled, looking directly into my eyes in the way mountain girls have. She said, "I am a telepath, yes, but untrained; so many of the old things have been forgotten here in the mountains. Perhaps you can tell us what you were taught at Arilinn, kinsman."

Her eyes were a strange color, a tint I had never seen before: gold-flecked amber, like some unknown animal.

Her hair was almost red enough for the valley Comyn. I gave her my hand, as I had done with Beltran. It reminded me a little of the way the women at Arilinn had accepted me, simply as a human being, without fuss or flirtatiousness. I felt strangely reluctant to let her fingers go. I asked, "Are you a kinswoman?"

Beltran said, "Marjorie Scott, and her sister and brother, too, are my father's wards. It's a long story, he may tell you some day if he will. Their mother was my own mother's foster-sister, so I call them, all three, sister and brother." He drew the others forward and presented them. Rafe Scott was a boy of eleven or twelve, not unlike my own brother Marius, with the same gold-flecked eyes. He looked at me shyly and did not speak. Thyra was a few years older than Marjorie, a slight, restless, sharp-featured woman, with the family eyes but a look of old Kermiac, too. She met my eyes but did not offer her hand. "This is a long and weary journey for a lowlander, kinsman."

"I had good weather and skilled escort for the mountains," I said, bowing to her as I would have done to a lady of the Domains. Her dark features looked amused, but she was friendly enough, and for a little we talked of weather and the mountain roads. After a time Beltran drew the conversation back.

"My father was greatly skilled in his youth and has taught all of us some of the skills of a matrix technician. Yet I am said to have but little natural talent for it. You have had the training, Lew, so tell me, which is the most important, talent or skill?"

I told him what I had been told myself. "Talent and skill are the right hand and the left; it is the will that rules both, and the will must be disciplined. Without talent, little skill can be learned; but talent alone is worth little without training."

"I am said to have the talent," said the girl Marjorie. "Uncle told me so, yet I have no skill, for by the time I was old enough to learn, he was old past teaching. And I am half-Terran. Could a Terran learn those skills, do you think?"

I smiled and said, "I too am part-Terran, yet I served at Arilinn—Marjorie?" I tried to speak her Terran name and she smiled at my stumbling formation of the syllables.

"*Marguerida,* if you like that better," she said softly in *cahuenga.* I shook my head. "As you speak it, it is rare and strange . . . and precious," I said, wanting to add, "like you."

Beltran curled his lip disdainfully and said, "So the Comyn actually let you, with your Terran blood, into their sacred towers? How very condescending of them! I'd have laughed in their faces and told them what they could do with their tower!"

"No, cousin, it wasn't like that," I said. "It was only in the towers that no one took thought of my Terran blood. Among the Comyn I was *nedestro,* bastard. In Arilinn, no one cared what I was, only what I could do."

"You're wasting your time, Beltran," said a quiet voice from near the fire. "I am sure he knows no more of history than any of the *Hali'imyn,* and his Terran blood has done him little good." I looked across to the bench at the other side of the fire and saw a tall thin man, silver-gilt hair standing awry all around his forehead. His face was shadowed, but it seemed to me for a moment that his eyes came glinting out of the darkness like a cat's eyes by torchlight. "No doubt he believes, like most of the valley-bred, that the Comyn fell straight from the arms of the Lord of Light, and has come to believe all their pretty romances and fairy tales. Lew, shall I teach you your own history?"

"Bob," said Marjorie, "no one questions your knowledge. But your manners are terrible!"

The man gave a short laugh. I could see his features now by firelight, narrow and hawklike, and as he gestured I could see that he had six fingers on either hand, like the Ardais and Aillard men. There was something terribly strange about his eyes, too. He unfolded his long legs, stood up and made me an ironic bow.

"Must I respect the chastity of your mind, *via dom,* as you respect that of your deluded sorceresses? Or have I leave to ravish you with some truths, in hope that they may bring forth the fruits of wisdom?"

I scowled at the mockery. "Who in hell are you?"

"In hell, I am no one at all," he said lightly. "On Darkover, I call myself Robert Raymon Kadarin, *s'dei par servu.*" On his lips the elegant *casta* words became a mockery. "I regret I cannot follow your custom and add a long string of names detailing my parentage for generations. I know no more of my parentage than you Comyn know of yours but, unlike you, I have not yet learned to make up the deficiency with a long string of make-believe gods and legendary figures!"

"Are you Terran?" I asked. His clothing looked it.

He shrugged. "I was never told. However, it's a true saying: only a race-horse or a Comyn lord is judged by his pedigree. I spent ten years in Terran Empire intelligence, though they wouldn't admit it now; they've put a price on my head because, like all governments who buy brains, they like to limit what the brains are used for. I found out, for instance," he added deliberately, "just what kind of game the Empire's been playing on Darkover and how the Comyn have been playing along with them. No, Beltran," he said, swinging around to face my cousin, "I'm going to tell him. He's the one we've been waiting for."

The harsh, disconnected way he spoke made me wonder if he was raving or drunk. "Just what do you mean, a game the Terrans are playing, with the Comyn to help?"

I had come here to find out if Aldaran was dangerously allied with Terra, to the danger of Comyn. Now this man Kadarin accused the Comyn of playing Terra's games. I said, "I don't know what in the hell you're talking about. It sounds like rubbish."

"Well, start with this," Kadarin said. "Do you know who the Darkovans are, where we came from? Did anyone ever tell you that we're the first and oldest of the Terran colonies? No, I thought you didn't know that. By rights we should be equal to any of the planetary governments that sit in the Empire Council, doing our part to make the laws of the Empire, as other colonies do. We should be part of the galactic civilization we live in. Instead, we're treated like a backward, uncivilized world, poor relations to be content with what crumbs of knowledge they're willing to dole out to us drop by drop, kept carefully apart from the mainstream of the Empire, allowed to go on living as barbarians!"

"Why? If this is true, why?"

"Because the Comyn want it that way," Kadarin said. "It suits their purposes. Don't you even *know* Darkover is a Terran colony? You said they mocked your Terran blood.

Damn them, what do they think *they* are? Terrans, all of them."

"You're stark raving mad!"

"You'd like to think so. So would they. More flattering, isn't it, to think of your father's precious caste as being descended from gods and divinely appointed to rule all Darkover. Too bad! They're just Terrans, like all the rest of the Empire colonies!" He stopped pacing and stood, staring down at us from his great height, he was a full head taller than I am, and I am not small. "I tell you, I've seen the records on Terra, and in the Administrative Archives on the Coronis colony. The facts are buried there, or supposed to be buried, but anybody with a security clearance can get them quickly enough."

I demanded, "Where did you get all this *stuff*?" I could have used a much ruder word; out of deference to the women I used one meaning, literally, stable-sweepings.

He said, "Remarkable fertile stuff, stable-sweepings. Grows good crops. The facts are there. I have a gift for languages, like all telepaths—oh, yes, I am one, Dom Lewis. By the way, do you know you have a Terran name?"

"Surely not," I said. Lewis had been a given name among the Altons for centuries.

"I have stood on the island of Lewis on Terra itself," said the man Kadarin.

"Coincidence," I said. "Human tongues evolve the same syllables, having the same vocal mechanism."

"Your ignorance, Dom Lewis, is appalling," said Kadarin coldly. "Some day, if you want a lesson in linguistics, you should travel in the Empire and hear for yourself what strange syllables the human tongue evolves for itself when there is no common language transmitted in culture." I felt a sudden twinge of dread, like a cold wind. He went on. "Meanwhile, don't make ignorant statements which only show what an untraveled boy you are. Virtually every given name ever recorded on Darkover is a name known on Terra, and in a very small part of Terra at that. The drone-pipe, oldest of Darkovan instruments, was known once on Terra, but they survive only in museums, the art of playing them lost; musicians came here to relearn the art and found music that survived from a very small geographical area, the British or Brictish Islands. Linguists studying your language found traces of three Terran languages. Spanish is your *casta;* English and Gaelic in your *cahuenga,* and the Dry-Town languages. The language spoken in the Hellers is a form of pure Gaelic which is no longer spoken on Terra but survives in old manuscripts. Well, to make a long tale short, as the old wife said when she cropped her cow's brush, they soon found the record of a single ship, sent out before the Terran colonies had bound themselves together into the Empire, which vanished without trace and was believed crashed or lost. And they found the crewlist of that ship."

"I don't believe a word of it."

"Your belief wouldn't make it true; your doubt won't make it false," Kadarin said. "The very name of this world, Darkover, is a Terran word meaning," he considered a minute, translated, " 'color of night overhead.' On that crewlist there were di Asturiens and MacArans and these are, you would say, good old Darkovan names. There was a ship's officer named Camilla Del Rey. Camilla is a rare name among Terrans now, but it is the most common name for girl-children in the Kilghard Hills; you have even given it to one of your Comyn demi-goddesses. There was a priest of Saint Christopher of Centaurus, a Father Valentine Neville, and how many of the Comyn's sons have been taught in the *cristoforo* monastery of Saint-Valentine-of-the-Snows? I brought Marjorie, who is a *cristoforo,* a little religious medal from Terra itself; its twin is enshrined in Nevarsin. Must I go on with such examples, which I assure you I could quote all night without tiring? Have your Comyn forefathers ever told you so much?"

My head was reeling. It sounded infernally convincing.

"The Comyn cannot know this. If the knowledge was lost—"

"They know, all right," Beltran said with contempt. "Kennard knows certainly. He has lived on Terra."

My father knew this and had never told me?

Kadarin and Beltran were still telling me their tale of a "lost ship" but I had ceased to listen. I could sense Marjorie's soft eyes on me in the dying firelight, though I could no longer see them. I felt that she was following my thoughts, not intruding on them but rather responding to me so completely that there were no longer any barriers between us. This had never happened before. Even at Arilinn, I had never felt so wholly attuned to any human being. I felt she knew how distressed and weary all this had made me.

On the cushioned bench she stretched out her hand to me and I could feel her indignation running up from her small fingers into my hand and arm and all along my body. She said, "Bob, what are you trying to *do* to him? He comes here weary from long travel, a kinsman and a guest; is this our mountain hospitality?"

Kadarin laughed. "Set a mouse to guard a lion!" he said. I felt those unfathomably strange eyes piercing the darkness to see our hands clasped. "I have my reasons, child. I don't know what fate sent him here, but when I see a man who has lived by a lie, I try to tell him the truth if I feel he's worth hearing it. A man who must make a choice must make it on facts, not fuzzy loyalties and half-truths and old lies. The tides of fate are moving—"

I said rudely, "Is fate one of your facts? You called *me* superstitious."

He nodded. He looked very serious. "You're a telepath, an Alton; you know what precognition is."

Beltran said, "You're going too fast. We don't even know why he's come here, and he *is* heir to a Domain. He may even have been sent to carry tales back to the old graybeard in Thendara and all his deluded yes-men."

Beltran swung around to face me. "Why *did* you come here?" he demanded. "After all these years, Kennard cannot be all that eager for you to know your mother's kin, otherwise you would have been my foster-brother, as Father wished."

I thought of that with a certain regret. I would willingly have had this kinsman for foster-brother. Instead I had never known of his existence till now, and it had been our mutual loss. He demanded again, "Why have you come, cousin, after so long?"

"It's true I came at my father's will," I said at last, slowly. "Hastur heard reports that the Compact was being violated in Caer Donn; my father was too ill to travel and sent me in his place." I felt strangely pulled this way and that. Had Father sent me to spy on kinsfolk? The idea filled me with revulsion. Or had he, in truth, wished me to know my mother's kin? I did not know, and not knowing made me uncertain, wretched.

"You see," said the woman Thyra, from her place in Kadarin's shadow, "it's useless to talk to him. He's one of the Comyn puppets."

Anger flared through me. "I am no man's puppet. Not Hastur's. Not my father's. Nor will I be yours, cousin or no. I came at my free will, because if Compact is broken it touches all our lives. And more than that, whatever my father said, I wished to know for myself whether what they had told me of Aldaran and Terra was true."

"Spoken honestly," Beltran said. "But let me ask you this, cousin. Is your loyalty to Comyn . . . or to Darkover?"

Asked that question at almost any other time, I would have said, without hesitation, that to be loyal to Comyn *was* to be loyal to Darkover. Since leaving Thendara I was no longer so sure. Even those I wholly trusted, like Hastur, had no power, or perhaps no wish, to check the corruption of the others. I said, "To Darkover. No question, to Darkover."

He said vehemently, "Then you should be one of us! You were sent to us at this moment, I think, because we needed you, because we couldn't go on without someone like you!"

"To do what?" I wanted no part in any Aldaran plots.

"Only this, kinsman, to give Darkover her rightful place, as a world belonging to our own time, not a barbarian backwater! We deserve the place on the Empire Council which we should have had, centuries ago, if the Empire had been honest with us. And we are going to have it!"

"A noble dream," I said, "if you can manage it. Just how are you going to bring this about?"

"It won't be easy," Beltran said. "It's suited the Empire, and the Comyn, to perpetuate their idea of our world: backward, feudal, ignorant. And we have become many of these things."

"Yet," Thyra said from the shadows, "we have one thing which is wholly Darkovan and unique. Our psi powers." She leaned forward to put a log on the fire and I saw her features briefly, lit by flame, dark, vital, glowing. I said, "If they are unique to Darkover, what of your theory that we are all Terrans?"

"Oh, yes," she said, "these powers are all recorded and remembered on Terra. But Terra neglected the powers of the mind, concentrating on material things, metal and machinery and computers. So their psi powers were forgotten and bred out. Instead we developed them, deliberately bred for them—that much of the Comyn legend is true. And we had the matrix jewels which convert energy. Isolation, genetic drift and selective breeding did the rest. Darkover is a reservoir of psi power and, as far as I know, is the only planet in the galaxy which turned to psi instead of technology."

"Even with matrix amplification, these powers are dangerous," I said. "Darkovan technology has to be used with caution, and sparsely. The price, in human terms, is usually too high."

The woman shrugged. "You cannot take hawks without climbing cliffs," she said.

"Just what is it you intend to do?"

"Make the Terrans take us seriously!"

"You don't mean war?" That sounded like suicidal nonsense and I said so. "Fight the Terrans, weapons against weapons?"

"No. Or only if they need to be shown that we are neither ignorant nor helpless," Kadarin said. "A high-level matrix, I understand, is a weapon to make even the Terrans tremble. But I hope and trust it will never come to that. The Terran Empire prides itself on the fact that they don't conquer, that planets *ask* to be admitted to the Empire. Instead, the Comyn committed Darkover to withdrawal, barbarianism, a search for yesterday, not tomorrow. We have something to give the Empire in return for what they give us, our matrix technology. We can join as equals, not suppliants. I have heard that in the old days there were matrix-powered aircraft in Arilinn—"

"True," I said, "as recently as in my father's time."

"And why not now?" He did not wait for me to answer. "Also, we could have a really effective communications technique—"

"We have that now."

"But the towers work only under Comyn domination, not for the entire population of the world."

"The risks—"

"Only the Comyn seem to know anything about those risks," Beltran said. "I'm tired of letting the Comyn decide for everyone else what risks we may take. I want us to be accepted as equals by the Terrans. I want us to be part of Terran trade, not just the trickle which comes in and out by the spaceports under elaborate permits signed and countersigned by their alien culture specialists to make certain it won't disturb our primitive culture! I want good roads and manufacturing and transportation and some control over the God-forgotten weather on this world! I want our students in the Empire universities, and theirs coming here! Other planets have these things! And above all I want star-travel. Not as a rich man's toy, as with the Ridenow lads spending a season now and then on some faraway pleasure world and bringing back new toys and new debaucheries, but free trade, with Darkovan ships coming and going at our will, not the Empire's!"

"Daydreams," I said flatly. "There's not enough metal on Darkover for a spaceship's hulk, let alone fuel to power it!"

"We can trade for metal," Beltran said. "Do you think matrices, manned by psi power, won't power a spaceship? And wouldn't that make most of the other power sources in the Galaxy obsolete overnight?"

I stood motionless for a moment, gripped by the force of his dream. Starships for Darkover . . . matrix-powered! By all the Gods, what a dream! And Darkovans comrades, competitors, not forgotten stepchildren of the Empire. . . .

"It can't be possible," I said, "or the matrix circles would have done it in the old days."

"It *was* done," Kadarin said. "The Comyn stopped it. It would have diluted their power on this world. We turned our back on a Galactic civilization because that crew of old women in Thendara decided they liked our world the way it was, with the Comyn up there with the Gods and everyone else running around bowing and scraping to them! They even disarmed us all. Their precious Compact sounds very civilized, but what it's done, in effect, is to make it impossible to organize any kind of armed rebellion that could endanger the Comyn's power!"

This went along, all too uncomfortably, with some of my own thoughts. Even Hastur spoke noble words about the Comyn devoting themselves to the service of Darkover, but what it came to was that he knew what was best for Darkover, and wanted no independent ideas challenging his power to enforce that "best."

"It's a noble dream. I said that before. But what have I to do with it?"

It was Marjorie who answered, squeezing my hand eagerly. "Cousin, you're tower-trained. You know the skills and techniques, and how they can be used even by latent telepaths. So much of the old knowledge has been lost, outside the towers. We can only experiment, work in the dark. We don't have the skills, the disciplines with which we could experiment further. Those of us who are telepaths have no chance to develop our natural gifts; those who are not have no way to learn the mechanics of matrix work. We need someone—someone like you, cousin!"

"I don't know . . . I have only worked within the towers. I have been taught it is not safe . . ."

"Of course," Kadarin said contemptuously. "Would they risk any trained man experimenting on his own and perhaps learning more than the little they allow? Kermiac was training matrix technicians here in the Hellers when you people in the Domains were still working in guarded circles, looked on as sorceresses and warlocks! But he is very old and he cannot guide us now." He smiled, a brief, bleak smile. "We need someone who is young and skilled and above all fearless. I think you have the strength for it. Have you the will?"

I found myself recalling the fey sense of destiny which had gripped me as I rode here. Was this the destiny I had foreseen, to break the hold of a corrupt clan on Darkover, to overthrow their grip at our throats, set Darkover in its rightful place among the equals of the Empire?

It was almost too much to grasp. I was suddenly very tired. Marjorie, still stroking my hand gently in her small fingers, said without looking up, "Enough, Beltran, give him time. He's weary from traveling and you've been jumping at him till he's confused. If it's right for him, he'll decide."

She was thinking of me. Everyone else was thinking of how well I could fit into their plans.

Beltran said with a rueful, friendly smile, "Cousin, my apologies! Marjorie is right, enough for now! After that long journey, you're more in need of a quiet drink and a soft bed than a lecture on Darkovan history and politics! Well, the drink for now and the bed soon, I promise!" He called for wine and a sweet fruit-flavored cordial not unlike the *shallan* we drank in the valley. He raised his glass to me. "To our better acquaintance, cousin, and to a pleasant stay among us."

I was glad to drink to that. Marjorie's eyes met mine over the rim of her glass. I wanted to take her hand again. Why did she appeal to me so? She looked young and shy, with an endearing awkwardness, but in the classic sense, she was not beautiful. I saw Thyra sitting within the curve of Kadarin's arm, drinking from his cup. Among valley folk that would have proclaimed them admitted lovers. I didn't know what, if anything, it meant here. I wished I were free to hold Marjorie like that.

I turned my attention to what Beltran was saying, about Terran methods used in the rapid building of Caer Donn, of the way in which trained telepaths could be used for weather forecasting and control. "Every planet in the Empire would send people here to be trained by us, and pay well for the privilege."

It was all true, but I was tired, and Beltran's plans were so exciting I feared I would not sleep. Besides, my nerves were raw-edged with trying to keep my awareness of Marjorie under control. I felt I would rather be beaten into bleeding pulp than intrude, even marginally, on her sensitivities. But I kept wanting to reach out to her, test her awareness of me, see if she shared my feelings or if her kindness was the courtesy of a kinswoman to a wearied guest. . . .

"Beltran," I said at last, cutting off the flow of enthusiastic ideas, "there's one serious flaw in your plans. There just aren't enough telepaths. We haven't enough trained men and women even to keep all nine of the towers operating. For such a galactic plan as you're contemplating, we'd need dozens, hundreds."

"But even a latent telepath can learn matrix mechanics," he said. "And many who have inherited the gifts never develop them. I believed the tower-trained could awaken latent *laran*."

I frowned. "The Alton gift is to force rapport. I learned

to use it in the towers to awaken latents if they weren't too barricaded. I can't always do it. That demands a catalyst telepath. Which I'm not."

Thyra said sharply, "I told you so, Bob. *That* gene's extinct."

Something in her tone made me want to contradict her. "No, Thyra," I said, "I know of one. He's only a boy, and untrained, but definitely a catalyst telepath. He awakened *laran* in a latent, even after I failed."

"Much good that does us," Beltran said in disgust. "Comyn Council has probably bound him so tight, with favors and patronage, that he'll never see beyond their will! They usually do, with telepaths. I'm surprised they haven't already bribed and bound *you* that way."

I thought, but did not say, that they had tried.

"No," I said, "they have not. Dani has no reason at all to love the Comyn . . . and reason enough to hate."

I smiled at Marjorie and began to tell them about Danilo and the cadets.

CHAPTER THIRTEEN

Regis lay in the guest chamber at Edelweiss, tired to exhaustion, but unable to sleep. He had come to Edelweiss through a late-afternoon fall of snow, still too stunned and sickened to talk, or to eat the supper Javanne had had prepared for him. His head throbbed and his eyes flickered with little dots of light which remained even when his eyes were shut, crawling, forming odd visual traceries behind the eyelids.

Dyan, he kept thinking. In charge of cadets, misusing power like that, and no one knew, or cared, or interfered.

Oh, they knew, he realized. They must have known. He would never believe Dyan could have deceived Kennard!

He remembered that curious unsatisfactory talk in the tavern with Dyan and his head throbbed harder, as if the very violence of his emotions would burst it asunder. He felt all the worse because he had, in truth, liked Dyan, had admired him and been flattered by his attention. He had welcomed the chance to talk to a kinsman as an equal . . . like a stupid, silly child! Now he knew what Dyan was trying to find out, so subtle it was never even an invitation.

It was not the nature of Dyan's desires that troubled him so greatly. It was not considered anything so shameful to be an *ombredin,* a lover of men. Among boys too young for marriage, rigidly kept apart by custom from any women except their own sisters or cousins, it was considered rather more suitable to seek companionship and even love from their friends than to consort with such women as were common to all. It was eccentric, perhaps, in a man of Dyan's years, but certainly not shameful.

What sickened Regis was the *kind* and *type* of pressure used against Danilo, the deliberate, sadistic cruelty of it, the particularly subtle revenge Dyan had taken for the wound to his pride.

Petty harrassment would have been cruel but understandable. But to use *laran* against him! To force himself on

Danilo's mind, to torment him that way! Regis felt physically ill with disgust.

Besides, he thought, still tossing restlessly, there were enough men or young lads who would have welcomed Dyan's interest. Some, perhaps, only because Dyan was a Comyn lord, rich and able to give presents and privileges to his friends, but others, certainly, would find Dyan a charming, pleasing and sophisticated companion. He could have had a dozen minions or lovers and no one would have thought of criticizing him. But some perverse cruelty made him seek the one boy in the cadets who would have none of him. A *cristoforo*.

He turned on his side, thrust a pillow over his face to shut out the light of the single candle he was too weary to get up and extinguish, and tried to sleep. But his mind kept going back to the frightening, disturbingly sexual nightmares which had preceded the wakening of his own *laran*. He knew now how Dyan had pursued Danilo even in sleep, enjoying the boy's fright and shame. And he knew now the ultimate corruption of power: to make another person a toy to do your will.

Was Dyan mad, then? Regis considered. No, he was very sane, to choose a poor boy, one without powerful friends or patrons. He played with Dani as a cat plays with a captive bird, torturing where he could not kill. Regis felt sick again. Pleasure in pain. Did it give Dyan that kind of pleasure to batter him black and blue at swordplay? With the vivid tactile memory of a telepath he relived that moment when Dyan had run his hands over his bruised body, the deliberate sensual quality of the touch. He felt physically used, contaminated, shamed. If Dyan had been physically present then, Regis would have struck him and dared the consequences himself.

And Dani was a catalyst telepath. That terrible force, that loathsome compulsion, against the rarest and most sensitive of telepaths!

Again and again, compulsively, he returned to that night in the barracks when he had tried—and failed—to reach out to Danilo and comfort him. He felt again and again the pain, the physical and mental shock of that wild rejection, the flood of guilt, terror, shame which had flooded him from that brief and innocent touch on Danilo's bare shoulder. Cassilda, blessed Mother of the Comyn! Regis thought in scalding shame, I touched him! Is it any wonder he thought me no better than Dyan!

He turned over on his back and lay staring at the vaulted ceiling, feeling his body ice over with dread. Dyan was a member of Council. They could not be so corrupt that they would know what Dyan had done, and say nothing. But who could tell them?

The single candle near his bed wavered, flickered in and out of focus; colors looped and spun across his visual field and the room swelled up, receded and shrank until it seemed to lie far away, then loom enormously around him in great echoing space.

He recognized the feeling from when Lew gave him *kirian,* but he was not drugged now!

He clutched at the bedclothes, squeezing his eyes shut. He could still see the candleflame, a dark fire printed inside his eyelids, the room around him lit with blazing brilliance, reversed afterimages, dark to bright and bright to dark, and a roaring in his ears like the distant roaring of a forest fire . . .

. . . The fire-lines at Armida! For an instant it seemed that he saw Lew's face again, crimson, gazing into a great fire, drawn with terror and wonder, then the face of a woman, shining, ecstatic, crowned with fire, burning, burning alive in the flames . . . Sharra, golden-chained Forge-Goddess. The room was alive with the fire and he burrowed beneath the blankets, sunk, battered, swirled. The room was dissolving around him, tilting . . . every thread in the smooth fine linen of the blankets seemed to cut into him, hard and rough, the twisted fibers of blanket trying to curl and frizzle and dig painfully into his skin, like cutting edges. He heard someone moan aloud and wondered who was there moaning and crying like that. The very air seemed to separate itself and come apart against his skin as if he had to sort it out into little droplets before he could breathe. His own breath hissed and whistled and moaned as it went in and out, like searing fire, to be quenched by the separate droplets of water in his lungs. . . .

Pain crashed through his head. He felt his skull smashing, shattering into little splinters; another blow sent him flying high, falling into darkness.

"Regis!" Again the crashing, reeling sickness of the blow and the long spin into space. The sound was only meaningless vibration but he tried to focus on it, make it mean something. *"Regis!"* Who was Regis? The roaring candle-flame died to a glimmer and Regis heard himself gasp aloud. Someone was standing over him, calling his name, slapping him hard and repeatedly. Suddenly, noiselessly, the room fell into focus.

"Regis, wake up! Get up and walk around, don't drift with it!"

"Javanne . . ." he said, struggling fuzzily upright to catch her hand as it was descending for another blow. "Don't, sister . . ."

He was surprised at how weak and faraway his voice sounded. She gave a faint cry of relief. She was standing beside his bed, a white shawl slipping from her shoulders above her long nightgown. "I thought one of the children cried out, then heard you. Why didn't you tell me you were likely to have threshold sickness?"

Regis blinked and dropped her hand. Even without the touch he could feel her fear. The room was still not quite solid around him. "Threshold sickness?" He thought about it a moment. He'd heard of it, of course, born into a Comyn family: a physical and psychic upheaval of awakening telepaths in adolescence, the inability of the brain to cope with sudden overloads of sensory and extrasensory data, resulting in perceptual distortions of sight, sound, touch. . . . "I never had it before. I didn't know what it was. Things seemed to thin out and disappear, I couldn't see properly, or feel . . ."

"I know. Get up now and walk around a little."

The room was still tilting around him; he clung to the bed-frame. "If I do, I'll fall. . . ."

"And if you don't, your balance centers will start drifting out of focus again. Here," she said with a faint laugh, tossing the white shawl to him, looking courteously away as he wrapped it around his body and struggled to his feet. "Regis, did no one warn you of this when your *laran* wakened?"

"Didn't *who* warn me? I don't think anyone knew," he said, taking a hesitant step and then another. She was right; under the concentrated effort of getting up and moving, the room settled into solidity again. He shuddered and went toward the candle. The little lights still danced and jiggled behind his eyes, but it was candle-sized again. How had it grown to a raging forest fire out of childhood? He picked it up, was amazed to see how his hand shook. Javanne said sharply, "Don't touch the candle when your hand's not steady, you'll set something afire! Regis, you frightened me!"

"With the candle?" He set it down.

"No, the way you were moaning. I spent half a year at Neskaya when I was thirteen, I saw one of the girls go into convulsions in crisis once."

Regis looked at his sister as if for the first time. He could sense, now, the emotion behind her cross, brisk manner, real fear, a tenderness he had never guessed. He put his arm around her shoulders and said, wonderingly, "Were you really afraid?" The barriers were wholly down between them and what she heard was, *Would you really care if something happened to me?* She reacted to the wondering amazement of that unspoken question with real dismay.

"How can you doubt it? You are my only kinsman!"

"You have Gabriel, and five children."

"But you are my father's son and my mother's," she said, giving him a short, hard hug. "You seem to be all right now. Get back into that bed before you take a chill and I must nurse you like one of the babies!"

But he knew now what the sharpness of her voice concealed and it did not trouble him. Obediently he got under the covers. She sat on the bed.

"You should spend some time in one of the towers, Regis, just to learn control. Grandfather can send you to Neskaya or Arilinn. An untrained telepath is a menace to himself and everyone around him, they told me so when I was your age."

Regis thought of Danilo. Had anyone thought to warn him?

Javanne drew the covers up under his chin. He recalled now that she had done this when he was very small, before he knew the difference between elder sister and a never-known mother. She was only a child herself, but she had tried to mother him. Why had he forgotten that?

She kissed him gently on the forehead and Regis, feeling

safe and protected for the moment, toppled over the edge of a vast gulf of sleep.

The next day he felt ill and dazed, but although Javanne told him to keep to his bed, he was too restless to stay there.

"I must return at once to Thendara," he insisted. "I've learned something which makes it necessary to talk to Grandfather. You said, yourself, I should arrange to go to one of the towers. What can happen to me with three Guardsmen for escort?"

"You know perfectly well you're not able to travel! I should spank you and put you to bed as I'd do with Rafael if he were so unreasonable," she said crossly.

His new insight into her made him speak with gentleness. "I'd like to be young enough for your cosseting, sister, even if it meant a spanking. But I know what I must do, Javanne, and I've outgrown a woman's rule. Please don't treat me like a child."

His seriousness sobered her, too. Still unwilling, she sent for his escort and horses.

All that long day's ride, he seemed to move through torturing memories, repeating themselves over and over, and a growing unease and uncertainty: would they believe him, would they even listen? Danilo was out of Dyan's reach, now; there was time enough to speak if he endangered another. Yet Regis knew that if he was silent, he connived at what Dyan had done.

In midafternoon, still miles from Thendara, wet snow and sleet began to fall again, but Regis ignored the suggestions of his escort that he should seek shelter and hospitality somewhere. Every moment between him and Thendara now was a torture; he yearned to be there, to have this frightening confrontation over. As the long miles dragged by, and he grew more and more soggy and wretched, he drew his soaked cape around him, huddling inside it like a protective cocoon. He knew his guards were talking about him, but he shut them firmly away from his consciousness, withdrawing further and further into his own misery.

As they came over the top of the pass he heard the distant vibration from the spaceport, carried thick and reverberating in the heavy, moist air. He thought with wild longing of the ships taking off, invisible behind the wall of rain and sleet, symbols of the freedom he wished he had now.

He let the thickening storm batter him, uncaring. He welcomed the icy wind, the sleet freezing in layers on his heavy riding-cloak, on his eyelashes and hair. It kept him from sliding back into that strange, hypersensitive, hallucinatory awareness.

What shall I say to Grandfather?

How did you face the Regent of Comyn and tell him his most trusted counselor was corrupt, a sadistic pervert using his telepathic powers to meddle with a mind placed in his charge?

How do you tell the Commander of the Guard, your own commanding officer, that his most trusted friend, holding the most trusted and responsible of posts, has ill-treated and shamefully misused a boy in his care. How do you accuse your own uncle, the strongest telepath in Comyn, of standing by, indifferent, watching the rarest and most sensitive of telepaths being falsely accused, his mind battered and bruised and dishonored, while he, a tower-trained psi technician, did nothing?

The stone walls of the Castle closed about them, cutting off the biting wind. Regis heard his escort swearing as they led their horses away. He knew he should apologize to them for subjecting them to this cold, wearying ride in such weather. It was a totally irresponsible thing to do to loyal men and the fact that they would never question his motives made it worse. He gave them brief formal thanks and admonished them to go quickly for supper and rest, knowing that if he offered them any reward they would be offended beyond measuring.

The long steps to the Hastur apartments seemed to loom over him, shrinking and expanding. His grandfather's aged valet rushed at him, blurred and out of focus, clucking and shaking his head with the privilege of long service. "Lord Regis, you're soaked through, you'll be ill, let me fetch you some wine, dry clothes—"

"Nothing, thank you." Regis blinked away the drops of ice melting on his eyelashes. "Ask the Lord Regent if he"—he tensed to keep his teeth from chattering—"if he can receive me."

"He's at supper, Lord Regis. Go in and join him."

A small table had been laid before the fire in his grandfather's private sitting room, and Danvan Hastur looked up, dismayed, almost comically echoing the elderly servant's dismay.

"My boy! At this hour, so wet and dripping? Marton, take his cloak, dry it at the fire! Child, you were to be with Javanne some days, what has happened?"

"Necessary—" Regis discovered his teeth were chattering so hard he could not speak; he clenched them to get control. "To return at once—"

The Regent shook his head skeptically. "Through a blizzard? Sit down there by the fire." He picked up the jug on his table, tilted a thick stream of steaming soup into a stoneware mug and held it out to Regis. "Here. Drink this and warm yourself before you say anything."

Regis started to say he did not want it, but he had to take it to keep it from falling from the old man's hand. The hot fragrant steam was so enticing that he began to sip it, slowly. He felt enraged at his own weakness and angrier at his grandfather for seeing it. His barriers were down and he had a flash of Hastur as a young man, a commander in the field, knowing his men, judging each one's strengths and weaknesses, knowing what each one needed and precisely how and when to get it to him. As the hot soup began to spread warmth through his shivering body he relaxed and began to breathe freely. The heat of the stoneware mug comforted his fingers, which were blue with cold, and even when he had finished the soup he held it between his hands, enjoying the warmth.

"Grandfather, I must talk to you."

"Well, I'm listening, child. Not even Council would call me out in such weather."

Regis glanced at the servants moving around the room. "Alone, sir. This concerns the honor of the Hasturs."

A startled look crossed the old man's face and he waved them from the room. "You're not going to tell me Javanne has managed to disgrace herself!"

Even the thought of his staid and fastidious sister playing the wanton would have made Regis laugh, if he could have laughed. "Indeed not, sir, all at Edelweiss is well and the babies thriving." He was not cold now, but felt an inner trembling he did not even recognize as fear. He put down the empty mug which had grown chill in his hands, shook his head at the offer of a refill.

"Grandfather. Do you remember Danilo Syrtis?"

"Syrtis. The Syrtis people are old Hastur folk, your father's paxman and bodyguard bore that name, old Dom Felix was my hawk-master. Wait, was there not some shameful thing in the Guards this year, a disgraced cadet, a sword-breaking? What has this to do with the honor of Hastur, Regis?"

Regis knew he must be very calm now, must keep his voice steady. He said, "The Syrtis men are our wards and paxmen, sir. From their years of duty to us, is it not our duty to safeguard them from being attacked and abused, even by Comyn? I have learned . . . Danilo Syrtis was wrongfully attacked and disgraced, sir, and it's worse than that. Danilo is a . . . a catalyst telepath, and Lord Dyan ill-used him, contrived his disgrace for revenge—"

Regis' voice broke. That searing moment of contact with Danilo flooded him again. Hastur looked at him in deep distress.

"Regis, this cannot possibly be true!"

He doesn't believe me! Regis heard his voice crack and break again. "Grandfather, I swear—"

"Child, child, I know you are not lying, I know you better than that!"

"You don't know me at all!" Regis flung at him, almost hysterical.

Hastur rose and came to him, laying a concerned hand on his forehead. "You are ill, Regis, feverish, perhaps delirious."

Regis shook the hand off. "I know perfectly well what I am saying. I had an attack of threshold sickness at Edelweiss, it's better now."

The old man looked at him with startled skepticism. "Regis, threshold sickness is nothing to take lightly. One of the symptoms is delusion, hallucination. I cannot accuse Lord Dyan of the wild ravings of a sick child. Let me send for Kennard Alton; he is tower-trained and can deal with this kind of illness."

"Send to Kennard indeed," Regis demanded, his voice wavering, "he is the one man in Thendara who will know for a fact that I am neither lying nor raving! This was by his contrivance, too; he stood by and watched Danilo disgraced and the cadet corps shamed!"

Hastur looked deeply troubled. He said, "Can it not wait—" He looked at Regis sharply and said, "No. If you rode through a blizzard at this hour to bring me such news, it certainly cannot wait. But Kennard is very ill, too. Can you possibly manage to go to him, child?"

Regis cut off another angry outburst and only said, with tight control, "I am not ill. I can go to him."

His grandfather looked at him steadily. "If you are not ill you will soon be so, if you stand there shivering and dripping. Go to your room and change your clothes while I send word to Kennard."

He was angry at being sent like a child to change his clothes but he obeyed. It seemed the best way to convince his grandfather of his rationality. When he returned, dry-clad and feeling better, his grandfather said shortly, "Kennard is willing to talk to you. Come with me."

As they went through the long corridors, Regis was aware of his grandfather's bristling disapproval. In the Alton rooms, Kennard was seated in the main hall, before the fire. He rose and took one step toward them and Regis saw with deep compunction that the older man looked terribly ill, his gaunt face flushed, his hands looking hugely swollen and shapeless. But he smiled at Regis with heartfelt welcome and held out the misshapen hand. "My lad, I'm glad to see you."

Regis touched the swollen fingers with awkward carefulness, unable to blur out Kennard's pain and exhaustion. He felt raw-edged, hypersensitive. Kennard could hardly stand!

"Lord Hastur, you honor me. How may I serve you?"

"My grandson has come to me with a strange and disturbing story. It's his tale, I'll leave him to tell it."

Regis felt consuming relief. He had feared to be treated like a sick child dragged unwilling to a doctor. For once he was being treated like a man. He felt grateful, a little disarmed.

Kennard said, "I cannot stand like this long. You there—" He gestured to a servant. "An armchair for the Regent. Sit beside me, Regis, tell me what's troubling you."

"My lord Alton—"

Kennard said kindly, "Am I no longer Uncle, my boy?"

Regis knew if he did not resist that fatherly warmth with all his strength, he would sob out his story like a beaten child. He said stiffly, "My lord, this is a serious matter concerning the honor of the Guardsmen. I have visited Danilo Syrtis at his home—"

"That was a kindly thought, nephew. Between ourselves, that was a bad business. I tried to talk Dyan out of it, but he chose to make an example of Dani and the law is the law. I couldn't have done anything if Dani had been my own son."

"Commander," Regis said, using the most formal of Kennard's military titles, "on my most solemn word as a cadet and a Hastur, there has been a terrible injustice done. Danilo was, I swear, wrongly accused, and Lord Dyan guilty of something so shameful I hardly dare name it. Is a cadet forced to submit—"

"Now you wait a minute," Kennard said, turning blazing eyes on him. "I had this already from Lew. I don't know what those three years among the *cristoforos* did to you, but if you're going to come whining to me about the fact that Dyan likes young lads for lovers, and accuse—"

"Uncle!" Regis protested in shock. "What kind of ninny do you think me? No, Commander. If that had been all—" He stopped, hunting for words, in confusion.

He said, "Commander, he would not accept refusal. He persecuted him day and night, invaded his mind, used *laran* against him. . . ."

Kennard's eyes sharpened. "Lord Hastur, what do you know of this wild tale? The boy looks ill. Is he raving?"

Regis stood up with a surge of violent anger that matched Kennard's own. "Kennard Alton, I am a Hastur *and I do not lie*! Send for Lord Dyan if you will, and question me in his presence!"

Kennard met his eyes, not angry now, but very serious. He said, "Dyan is not in the city tonight. Regis, tell me, how do you know this?"

"From Danilo's own lips, and from rapport with his mind," Regis said quietly. "You of all men know there is no way to lie to the mind."

Kennard did not release his eyes. "I did not know you had *laran*."

Regis held out his hand to Kennard, palm upward, a gesture he had never seen before, yet instinct guided him to it. He said, "*You* have. You will know. See for yourself, sir."

He saw dawning respect in the older man's gaunt, feverish face in the instant before he felt, with a thrill of fear, the touch on his mind. He heard Lew saying in Kennard's memory, *I've known grown men who dared not face that test.* Then he felt Kennard's touch, the shock of rapport . . . the moment he had stood before Danilo in the orchard, reeling with the shock of Danilo's anger and shame . . . his own liking for Dyan, the moment of half-shamed response to him . . . Kennard's own memories of Dyan blurring his own, a younger Dyan, a slender, eager boy, to be loved and protected and cherished . . . Danilo's sick, stunned terror, the flood of nightmarish dreams and cruelties he had shared with Danilo, the weeping in the dark, the harsh hawklike laughter. . . .

The blur of memories and impressions was gone. Kennard had covered his eyes with his hands. His eyes were dry and blazing, but just the same Regis got the impression that the older man was weeping in dismay. He said in a whisper, "Zandru's hells, *Dyan*!" Regis could feel the knifing anguish in the words. Kennard sank down on the bench again and Regis knew that he would have fallen if he had not, but for the first time Regis felt the iron strength and control with which a tower-trained telepath can control himself when he must. He had a frightening flash of agony, as if Kennard were holding his hand steadily in a fire, but Kennard only drew a deep breath and said, "So Danilo has *laran*. Lew did not tell me, nor did he tell me Dani had awakened you." A long silence. "That is a crime, and a terrible one—to use *laran* to force the will. I trusted Dyan; I never thought to question him. We were *bredin*. It is my responsibility and I will bear the guilt."

He looked shattered, dazed. "Aldones, Son of Light! I trusted him with *my* cadets! And Lew tried to warn me and I would not hear. I sent my own son from me in wrath because he tried to make me hear. . . . Hastur, what shall we do?"

Hastur looked grieved. "All the Ardais are unstable," he said. "Dom Kyril has been mad these twenty years. But you know the law as well as I do. You forced us to name Lew your heir with that same law. There must be one in the direct line, male and healthy, to represent every Domain, and Dyan has appointed no heir. We cannot even dismiss him from Comyn Council, as we did with Kyril when he began to rave. I do not know how we can send him from Council even long enough to heal his mind, if he is truly mad. Is he sane enough even to choose an heir?"

Regis felt angry and bruised. They seemed to care only about Dyan. Dani was nothing to them, no more than he was to Dyan. He said aggressively, "What of Danilo? What of his disgrace and his suffering? He has the rarest of the Comyn gifts, and the way he has been treated dishonors us all!"

Both men turned to look at him as if they had forgotten him. He felt like a noisy rude child intruding on the counsels of his elders, but he stood his ground, watching the torchlight make flickering patterns on the antique swords over the fire, saw Dyan, the sharp foil in hand, plunging it into his breast. . . .

"Amends shall be made," Hastur said quietly, "but you must leave it to us."

"I'll leave Dyan to you. But Dani is *my* responsibility! I pledged him my sworn word. I am a Hastur, and the heir to a Domain, and I demand—"

"You demand, do you?" said his grandfather, swinging around to face him. "I deny your right to demand anything! You have told me you wish to renounce that right, to go offworld. It took all I had even to extract your promise to give the minimum duty to the cadets! You have refused, even as Dyan refused, to give an heir to your Domain. By what right do you dare criticize him? You have renounced your heirship to Hastur; by what right do you stand here in front of us and make demands? Sit down and behave yourself or go back to your room and leave these things to your betters!"

"Don't you treat me like a child!"

"You are a child," said Hastur, his lips pressed tightly together, "a sick, silly child."

The room was flickering in and out of focus with the firelight. Regis clenched his fists, fighting for words. "An injury to anyone with *laran* . . . dishonors us all." He turned to Kennard, pleading. "For the honor of the Guards . . . for your own honor . . ."

Kennard's crippled hands touched him gently; Regis could feel pain ripping through those swollen hands as he wrenched them away. He felt himself sliding in and out of his body, unable to bear the jangle and confusion of all their thoughts. He thought with wild longing of being aboard a starship outward bound, *free,* leaving this little world behind with all its intrigue. He stood for a moment in Kennard's memory on the faraway surface of Terra, struggling with the pull of honor and duty against all he longed for, back to the heritage laid out for him before he was born, a path he must walk whether he would or not . . . felt his grandfather's anguish, *Rafael, Rafael, you would not have deserted me like this* . . . heard Dyan's slow cynical voice, *a very special stud animal whose fees are paid to Comyn* . . .

It forced him physically to his knees with the weight of it. Past, present, future spun together, whirling, he saw Dani's hand meet his on the hilt of a gleaming sword, felt it rip his mind open, overshadowing him. *Son of Hastur who is the Son of Light!* He was crying like a child. He whispered, "To the House of Hastur . . . I swear . . ."

Kennard's hands, hot and swollen, touched his temples; he felt for an instant that Kennard was holding him upright. Gradually the seething flood of emotion, foreknowledge, memory, receded. He heard Kennard say, "Threshold sickness. Not crisis, but he's pretty sick. Speak to him, sir."

"Regis . . ."

Regis struggled, whispered, "Grandfather, Lord Hastur . . . I swear, I will swear . . ."

His grandfather's arms enfolded him gently. "Regis, Regis, I know. But I cannot accept any pledge from you now. Not in your present state. The Gods know I want to, but I cannot. You must leave this to us. You *must,* child. We will deal with Dyan. You have done all you need to do. Just now your task is to go, as Kennard says, to Neskaya, to teach yourself to control your gift."

He tried again to fight his way upright . . . kneeling on cold stones, crystal lights around him. Words came slowly, painfully, yet he could not escape them: *I pledge my life and honor . . . to Hastur, forever* . . . and terrible pain, knowing he spoke into a closing door, he gave away his life and his freedom. He could not get a word out, not a syllable, and he felt his body and brain would explode with the words bursting in him. He whispered and knew no one could hear him, as his senses slipped away, ". . . swear . . . honor . . ."

His grandfather's eyes met his briefly, a momentary anchor over a swaying darkness where he hung. He heard his grandfather's voice, deep and compassionate, saying firmly, "The honor of the Comyn has been safe in my hands for ninety years, Regis. You can leave it to me now."

Regis let them lay him, nearly senseless, on the stone bench.

He let himself slip away into unconsciousness like a little death.

CHAPTER FOURTEEN

(Lew Alton's narrative)

For three days a blizzard had raged in the Hellers. On the fourth day I woke to sunshine and the peaks behind Castle Aldaran gleaming under their burden of snow. I dressed and went down into the gardens behind the castle, standing atop the terraces and looking down on the spaceport below where great machines were already moving about, as tiny at this distance as creeping bugs, to shift the heavy layers of snow. No wonder the Terrans didn't want to move their main port here!

Yet, unlike Thendara, here spaceport and castle seemed part of a single conjoined whole, not warring giants, striding toward battle.

"You're out early, cousin," said a light voice behind me. I turned to see Marjorie Scott, warmly wrapped in a hooded cloak with fur framing her face. I made her a formal bow.

"Damisela."

She smiled and stretched her hand to me. "I like to be out early when the sun's shining. It was so dark during the storm!"

As we walked down the terraces she grasped my cold hand and drew it under her cloak. I had to tell myself that this freedom did not imply what it would mean in the lowlands, but was innocent and unaware. It was hard to remember that with my hand lying between her warm breasts. But damn it, the girl was a telepath, she had to know.

As we went along the path, she pointed out the hardy winter flowers, already thrusting their stalks up through the snow, seeking the sun, and the sheltered fruits casting their snow-pods. We came to a marble-railed space where a waterfall tumbled, storm-swollen, away into the valley.

"This stream carries water from the highest peaks down

into Caer Donn, for their drinking water. The dam above here, which makes the waterfall, serves to generate power for the lights, here and down in the spaceport, too."

"Indeed, *damisela*? We have nothing like this in Thendara." I found it hard to keep my attention on the stream. Suddenly she turned to face me, swift as a cat, her eyes flashing gold. Her cheeks were flushed and she snatched her hand away from mine. She said, with a stiffness that concealed anger, "Forgive me, Dom Lewis. I presumed on our kinship," and turned to go. My hand, in the cold again, felt as chilled and icy as my heart at her sudden wrath.

Without thinking, I reached out and clasped her wrist. "Lady, how have I offended you? Please don't go!"

She stood quite still with my hand clasping her wrist. She said in a small voice, "Are all you valley men so queer and formal? I am not used to being called *damisela,* except by servants. Do you . . . dislike me . . . Lew?"

Our hands were still clasped. Suddenly she colored and tried to withdraw her wrist from my fingers. I tightened them, saying, "I feared to be burned . . . too near the fire. I am very ignorant of your mountain ways. How should I address you, cousin?"

"Would a woman of your valley lands be thought too bold if she called you by name, Lew?"

"Marjorie," I said, caressing the name with my voice. "Marjorie." Her small fingers felt fragile and live, like some small quivering animal that had taken refuge with me. Never, not even at Arilinn, had I known such warmth, such acceptance. She said my hands were cold and drew them under her cloak again. All she was telling me seemed wonderful. I knew something of electric power generators—in the Kilghard Hills great windmills harnessed the steady winds—but her voice made it all new to me, and I pretended less knowledge so she would go on speaking.

She said, "At one time matrix-powered generators provided lights for the castle. That technique is lost."

"It is known at Arilinn," I said, "but we rarely use it; the cost is high in human terms and there is some danger." Just the same, I thought, in the mountains they must need more energy against the crueler climate. Easy enough to give up a luxury, but here it might make the difference between civilized life and a brutal struggle for existence.

"Have you been taught to use a matrix, Marjorie?"

"Only a little. Kermiac is too old to show us the techniques. Thyra is stronger than I because she and Kadarin can link together a little, but not for long. The techniques of making the links are what we do not know."

"That is simple enough," I said, hesitating because I did not like to think of working in linked circles outside the safety of the tower force-fields. "Marjorie, who is Kadarin, where does he come from?"

"I know no more than he told you," she said. "He has traveled on many worlds. There are times when he speaks as if he were older than my guardian, yet he seems no older than Thyra. Even she knows not much more than I, yet they have been together for a long time. He is a strange man, Lew, but I love him and I want you to love him too."

I had warmed to Kadarin, sensing the sincerity behind his angry intensity. Here was a man who met life without self-deception, without the lies and compromises I had lived with so long. I had not seen him for days; he had gone away before the blizzard on unexplained business.

I glanced at the strengthening sun. "The morning's well on. Will anyone be expecting us?"

"I'm usually expected at breakfast, but Thyra likes to sleep late and no one else will care." She looked shyly up into my face and said, "I'd rather stay with you."

I said, with a leaping joy, "Who needs breakfast?"

"We could walk into Caer Donn and find something at a food-stall. The food will not be as good as at my guardian's table. . . ."

She led the way down a side path, going by a flight of steep steps that were roofed against the spray from the waterfall. There was frost underfoot, but the roofing had kept the stairway free of ice. The roaring of the waterfall made so much noise that we left off trying to talk and let our clasped hands speak for us. At last the steps came out on a lower terrace leading gently downslope to the city. I looked up and said, "I don't relish the thought of climbing back!"

"Well, we can go around by the horse-path," she said. "You came up that way with your escort. Or there's a lift on the far side of the waterfall; the Terrans built it for us, with chains and pulleys, in return for the use of our water power."

A little way inside the city gates Marjorie led the way to a food-stall. We ate freshly baked bread and drank hot spiced cider, while I pondered what she had said about matrices for generating power. Yes, they had been used in the past, and misused, too, so that now it was illegal to construct them. Most of them had been destroyed, not all. If Kadarin wanted to try reviving one there was, in theory at least, no limit to what he could do with it.

If, that was, he wasn't afraid of the risks. Fear seemed to have no part in that curious enigmatic personality. But ordinary prudence?

"You're lost somewhere again, Lew. What is it?"

"If Kadarin wants to do these things he must know of a matrix capable of handling that kind of power. What and where?"

"I can only tell you that it's not on any of the monitor screens in the towers. It was used in the old days by the forge-folk to bring their metals from the ground. Then it was kept at Aldaran for centuries, until one of Kermiac's wards, trained by him, used it to break the siege of Storn Castle."

I whistled. The matrix had been outlawed as a weapon centuries ago. The Compact had not been made to keep us away from such simple toys as the guns and blasters of the Terrans, but against the terrifying weapons devised in our Ages of Chaos. I wasn't happy about trying to key a group of inexperienced telepaths into a really large matrix, either. Some could be harnessed and used safely and easily. Others had darker histories, and the name of Sharra, Goddess of the forge-folk, was linked in old tales with more than one matrix. This one might, or might not, be possible to bring under control.

She said, looking incredulous, "Are you afraid?"

"Damn right," I said. "I thought most of the talismans of Sharra-worship had been destroyed before the time of Regis Fourth. I *know* some of them were destroyed."

"This one was hidden by the forge-folk and given back for their worship after the siege of Storn." Her lip curled. "I have no patience with that kind of superstition."

"Just the same, a matrix is no toy for the ignorant." I stretched my hand out, palm upward over the table, to show her the coin-sized white scar, the puckered seam running up my wrist. "In my first year of training at Arilinn I lost control for a split second. Three of us had burns like this. I'm not joking when I speak of risks."

For a moment her face contracted as she touched the puckered scar tissue with a delicate fingertip. Then she lifted her firm little chin and said, "All the same, what one human mind can build, another human mind can master. And a matrix is no use to anyone lying on an altar for ignorant folk to worship." She pushed aside the cold remnants of the bread and said, "Let me show you the city."

Our hands came irresistibly together again as we walked, side by side, through the streets. Caer Donn was a beautiful city. Even now, when it lies beneath tons of rubble and I can never go back, it stands in my memory as a city in a dream, a city that for a little while *was* a dream. A dream we shared.

The houses were laid out along wide, spacious streets and squares, each with plots of fruit trees and its own small glass-roofed greenhouse for vegetables and herbs seldom seen in the hills because of the short growing season and weakened sunlight. There were solar collectors on the roofs to collect and focus the dim winter sun on the indoor gardens.

"Do these work even in winter?"

"Yes, by a Terran trick, prisms to concentrate and reflect more sunlight from the snow."

I thought of the darkness at Armida during the snow-season. There was so much we could learn from the Terrans!

Marjorie said, "Every time I see what the Terrans have made of Caer Donn I am proud to be Terran. I suppose Thendara is even more advanced."

I shook my head. "You'd be disappointed. Part of it is all Terran, part of it all Darkovan. Caer Donn . . . Caer Donn is like you, Marjorie, the best of each world, blended into a single harmonious whole . . ."

This was what our world could be. Should be. This was Beltran's dream. And I felt, with my hands locked tight in Marjorie's, in a closeness deeper than a kiss, that I would risk anything to bring that dream alive and spread it over the face of Darkover.

I said something about how I felt as we climbed together

upward again. We had elected to take the longer way, reluctant to end this magical interlude. We must have known even then that nothing to match this morning would ever come again, when we shared a dream and saw it all bright and new-edged and too beautiful to be real.

"I feel as if I were drugged with *kirian*!"

She laughed, a silvery peal. "But the *kireseth* no longer blooms in these hills, Lew. It's all real. Or it can be."

I began as I had promised later that day. Kadarin had not returned, but the rest of us gathered in the small sitting room.

I felt nervous, somehow reluctant. It was always nerve-racking to work with a strange groups of telepaths. Even at Arilinn, when the circle was changed every year, there was the same anxious tension. I felt naked, raw-edged. How much did they know. What skills, potentials, lay hidden in these strangers? Two women, a man and a boy. Not a large circle. But large enough to make me quiver inside.

Each of them had a matrix. That didn't really surprise me since tradition has it that the matrix jewels were first found in these mountains. None of them had his or her matrix what I would call properly safeguarded. That didn't surprise me either. At Arilinn we're very strict in the old traditional ways. Like most trained technicians, I kept mine on a leather thong around my neck, silk-wrapped and inside a small leather bag, lest some accidental stimulus cause it to resonate.

Beltran's was wrapped in a scrap of soft leather and thrust into a pocket. Marjorie's was wrapped in a scrap of silk and thrust into her gown between her breasts, where my hand had lain! Rafe's was small and still dim; he had it in a small cloth bag on a woven cord around his neck. Thyra kept hers in a copper locket, which I considered criminally dangerous. Maybe my first act should be to teach them proper shielding.

I looked at the blue stones lying in their hands. Marjorie's was the brightest, gleaming with a fiery inner luminescence, giving the lie to her modest statement that Thyra was the stronger telepath. Thyra's was bright enough, though. My nerves were jangling. A "wild telepath," one who has taught himself by trial and error, extremely difficult to work with. In a tower the contact would first be made by a Keeper, not the old carefully-shielded *leronis* of my father's day, but a woman highly trained, her strength safeguarded and disciplined. Here we had none. It was up to me.

It was harder than taking my clothes off before such an assembly, yet somehow I had to manage it. I sighed and looked from one to the other.

"I take it you all know there's nothing magical about a matrix," I said. "It's simply a crystal which can resonate with, and amplify, the energy-currents of your brain."

"Yes, I know that," said Thyra with amused contempt. "I didn't expect anyone trained by Comyn to know it, though."

I tried to discipline my spontaneous flare of anger. Was she going to make this as hard for me as she could?

"It was the first thing they taught me at Arilinn, kinswoman, I am glad you know it already." I concentrated on Rafe. He was the youngest and would have least to unlearn. "How old are you, little brother?"

"Thirteen this winter, kinsman," he said, and I frowned slightly. I had no experience with children—fifteen is the lowest age limit for the Towers—but I would try. There was light in his matrix, which meant that he had keyed it after a fashion.

"Can you control it?" We had none of the regular test materials; I would have to improvise. I made brief contact. *The fireplace. Make the fire flame up twice and die down.*

The stone reflected blue glimmer on his childish features as he bent, his forehead wrinkling up with the effort of concentration. The light grew; the fire flamed high, sank, flared again, sank down, down . . .

"Careful," I said, "don't put it out. It's cold in here." At least he could receive my thoughts; though the test was elementary, it qualified him as part of the circle. He looked up, delighted with himself, and smiled.

Marjorie's eyes met mine. I looked quickly away. Damn it, it's never easy to make contact with a woman you're attracted to. I'd learned at Arilinn to take it for granted, for psi work used up all the physical and nervous energy available. But Marjorie hadn't learned that, and I felt shy. The thought of trying to explain it to her made me squirm.

In the safe quiet of Arilinn, chaperoned by nine or ten centuries of tradition, it was easy to keep a cool and clinical detachment. Here we must devise other ways of protecting ourselves.

Thyra's eyes were cool and amused. Well, *she* knew. If she and Kadarin had been working together, no doubt she'd found it out already. I didn't like her and I sensed she didn't like me either, but thus far, at least, we could touch one another with easy detachment; her physical presence did not embarrass me. Where, working alone, had she picked up that cool, knife-like precision? Was I glad or sorry that Marjorie showed no sign of it?

"Beltran," I said, "what can you do?"

"Children's tricks," he said, "little talent, less skill. Rafe's trick with the fire." He repeated it, more slowly, with somewhat better control. He reached an unlighted taper from a side table and bent over it with intense concentration. A narrow flame leaped from the fireplace to the tip of the taper, where it burst into flame.

A child's trick, of course, one of the simplest tests we used at Arilinn. "Can you call the fire without the matrix?" I asked.

"I don't try," he said. "In this area it's too great a danger to set something on fire. I'd rather learn to put fires *out*. Do your tower telepaths do that, perhaps, in forest-fire country?"

"No, though we do call clouds and make rain sometimes. Fire is too dangerous an element, except for baby tricks like these. Can you call the overlight?"

He shook his head, not understanding. I held out my hand and focused the matrix. A small green flame flickered, grew in the palm of my hand. Marjorie gasped. Thyra held out her own hand; cold white light grew, pale around her fingers, lighting up the room, flaring up like jagged lightning. "Very good," I said, "but you must control it. The strongest or brightest light is not always the best. Marjorie?"

She bent over the blue shimmer of her matrix. Before her face, floating in the air, a small blue-white ball of fire appeared, grew gradually larger, then floated to each of us in turn. Rafe could make only flickers of light; when he tried to shape them or move them, they flared up and vanished. Beltran could make no light at all. I hadn't expected it. Fire, the easiest of the elements to call forth, was still the hardest to control.

"Try this." The room was very damp; I condensed the moist air into a small splashing fountain of water-drops, each sizzling a moment in the fire as it vanished. Both of the women proved able to do this easily; Rafe mastered it with little trouble. He needed practice, but had excellent potential.

Beltran grimaced. "I told you I had small talent and less skill."

"Well, some things I can teach you without talent, kinsman," I said. "Not all mechanics are natural telepaths. Do you read thoughts at all?"

"Only a little. Mostly I sense emotions," he said.

Not good. If he could not link minds with us, he would be no use in the matrix circle. There were other things he could do, but we were too few for a circle, except for the very smallest matrices.

I reached out to touch his mind. Sometimes a telepath who has never learned the touching technique can be *shown,* when all else fails. I met slammed, locked resistance. Like many who grow up with minimal *laran,* untrained, he had built defenses against the use of his gift. He was cooperative, letting me try again and again to force down the barrier, and we were both white and sweating with pain by the time I finally gave up. I had used a force on him far harder than I had used on Regis, to no avail.

"No use," I said at last. "Much more of this will kill both of us. I'm sorry, Beltran. I'll teach you what I can outside the circle, but without a catalyst telepath this is as far as you can go." He looked miserably downcast, but he took it better than I had hoped.

"So the women and children can succeed where I fail. Well, if you've done the best you can, what can I say?"

It was, on the contrary, easy to make contact with Rafe. He had built no serious defense against contact, and I gathered, from the ease and confidence with which he dropped into rapport with me, that he must have had a singularly happy and trusting childhood, with no haunting fears. Thyra sensed what we had done; I felt her reach out, and made the telepathic overture which is the equivalent of an extended hand across a gulf. She met it quickly, dropping into contact without fumbling, and . . .

A savage animal, dark, sinuous, prowling an unexplored jungle. A smell of musk . . . claws at my throat . . .

Was this her idea of a joke? I broke the budding rapport, saying tersely, "This is no game, Thyra. I hope you never find that out the hard way."

She looked bewildered. Unconscious, then. It was just the inner image she projected. Somehow I'd have to learn to live with it. I had no idea how she perceived *me.* That's one thing you can never know. You try, of course, at first. One girl in my Arilinn circle had simply said I felt "steady." Another tried, confusedly, to explain how I "felt" to her mind and wound up saying I felt like the smell of saddle-leather. You're trying, after all, to put into words an experience that has nothing to do with verbal ideas.

I reached out for Marjorie and sensed her in the fragmentary circle . . . a falling swirl of golden snowflakes, silk rustling, like her hand on my cheek. I didn't need to look at her. I broke the tentative four-way contact and said, "Basically, that's it. Once we learn to match resonances."

"If it's so simple, why could we never do it before?" Thyra demanded.

I tried to explain that the art of making a link with more than one other mind, more than one other matrix, is the most difficult of the basic skills taught at Arilinn. I felt her fumbling to reach out, to make contact, and I dropped my barriers and allowed her to touch me. *Again the dark beast, the sense of claws* . . . Rafe gasped and cried out in pain and I reached out to knock Thyra loose. "Not until you know how," I said. "I'll try to teach you, but you have to learn the precise knack of matching resonance *before* you reach out. Promise me not to try it on your own, Thyra, and I'll promise to teach you. Agreed?"

She promised, badly shaken by the failure. I felt depressed. Four of us, then, and Rafe only a child. Beltran unable to make rapport at all, and Kadarin an unknown quality. Not enough for Beltran's plans. Not nearly enough.

We needed a catalyst telepath. Otherwise, that was as far as I could go.

Rafe's attempts to lower the fire and our experiments with water-drops had made the hearth smolder; Marjorie began to cough. Any of us could have brought it back to brightness, but I welcomed the chance to get out of the room. I said, "Let's go into the garden."

The afternoon sunshine was brilliant, melting the snow. The plants which had just this morning been thrusting up spikes through snow were already budding. I asked, "Will Kermiac be angry if we destroy a few of his flowers?"

"Flowers? No, take what you need, but what will you do with them?"

"Flowers are ideal test and practice material," I said. "It would be dangerous to experiment with most living tissue; with flowers you can learn a very delicate control, and they live such a short time that you are not interfering with the balance of nature very much. For instance." Cupping matrix in hand, I focused my attention on a bud full-formed but not yet opened, exerting the faintest of mental pressures. Slowly, while I held my breath, the bud uncurled, thrusting forth slender stamens. The petals unfolded, one by one, until it stood full-blown before us. Marjorie drew a soft breath of excitement and surprise.

"But you didn't destroy it!"

"In a way I did; the bud isn't fully mature and may never mature enough to be pollinated. I didn't try; maturing a plant like that takes deep intercellular control. I simply manipulated the petals." I made contact with Marjorie. *Try it with me. Try first to see deep into the cell structure of the flower, to see exactly how each layer of petals is folded. . . .*

The first time she lost control and the petals crushed into an amorphous, colorless mass. The second time she did it almost as perfectly as I had done. Thyra, too, quickly mastered the trick, and Rafe, after a few tries. Beltran had to struggle to achieve the delicate control it demanded, but he did it. Perhaps he would make a psi monitor. Nontelepaths sometimes made good ones.

I saw Thyra by the waterfall, gazing into her matrix. I did not speak to her, curious to see what she could do unaided. It was growing late—we had spent considerable time with the flowers—and dusk was falling, lights appearing here and there in the city below us. Thyra stood so still she hardly appeared to breathe. Suddenly the raging, foaming torrent next to her appeared to freeze motionless, arrested in midair, only one or two of the furthest droplets floating downward. The rest hung completely stopped, poised, frozen as if time itself and motion had stopped. Then, deliberately, the water began to flow uphill.

Beneath us, one after another, the lights of Caer Donn blinked and went out.

Rafe gasped aloud; in the eerie stillness the small sound brought me back to reality. I said sharply, "Thyra!" she started, her concentration broken, and the whole raging torrent plunged downward with a crash.

Thyra turned angry eyes on me. I took her by the shoulder and drew her back from the edge, to where we could hear ourselves speak above the torrent.

"Who gave you leave to meddle—!"

I deliberately smothered my flare of anger. I had assumed responsibility for all of them now, and Thyra's ability to make me angry was something I must learn to control. I said, "I am sorry, Thyra, had you never been told that this is dangerous?"

"Danger, always danger! Are you such a coward, Lew?"

I shook my head. "I'm past the point where I have to prove my courage, child." Thyra was older than I, but I spoke as to a rash, foolhardy little girl. "It was an astonishing display, but there are wiser ways to prove your skill." I gestured. "Look, you have put their lights out; it will take repair crews some time to restore their power relays. That was thoughtless and silly. Second, it is unwise to disturb the forces of nature without great need, and for some good reason. Remember, rain in one place, even to drown a forest fire, may mean drought elsewhere, and balance disturbed. Until you can judge on planet-wide terms, Thyra, don't presume to meddle with a natural force, and never, *never,* for your pride! Remember, I asked Beltran's leave even to destroy a few flowers!"

She lowered her long lashes. Her cheeks were flaming, like a small girl lectured for some naughtiness. I regretted the need to lay down the law so harshly, but the incident had disturbed me deeply, rousing all my own misgivings. Wild telepaths were dangerous! How far could I trust any of them?

Marjorie came up to us; I could tell that she shared Thyra's humiliation, but she made no protest. I turned and slipped my arm around her waist, which would have proclaimed us acknowledged lovers in the valley. Thyra sent me a sardonic smile of amusement beneath her meekly dropped lashes, but all she said was, "We are all at your orders, Dom Lewis."

"I've no wish to give orders, cousin," I said, "but your guardian would have small cause to love me if I disregarded the simplest rules of safety in your training!"

"Leave him alone, Thyra," Marjorie flared. "He knows what he's doing! Lew, show her your hand!" She seized the palm, turned it over, showing the white ridged scars. "He has learned to follow rules, and learned it with pain! Do you want to learn like that?"

Thyra flinched visibly, averting her eyes from the scar as if it sickened her. I would not have thought her squeamish. She said, visibly shaken, "I had never thought . . . I did not know. I'll do what you say, Lew. Forgive me."

"Nothing to forgive, kinswoman," I said, laying my free hand on her wrist. "Learn caution to match your skill and you will be a strong *leronis* some day." She smiled at the word which, taken literally, meant *sorceress.*

"Matrix technician, if you like. Some day, perhaps, there will be new words for new skills. In the towers we are too busy mastering skills to worry about words for them, Thyra. Call it what you like."

Thin fog was beginning to move down from the peaks behind the castle. Marjorie shivered in her light dress and Thyra said, "We'd better go in, it will be dark soon." With one bleak look at the darkened city below, she walked quickly toward the castle. Marjorie and I walked with our arms laced, Rafe tagging close to us.

"Why do we need the kind of control we practiced with the flowers, Lew?"

"Well, if someone in the circle gets so involved in what he's doing that he forgets to breathe, the monitor outside has to start him breathing again without hurting him. A well-trained empath can stop bleeding even from an artery, or heal wounds." I touched the scar. "This would have been worse, except that the Keeper of the circle worked with it, to heal the worst damage." Janna Lindir had been Keeper at Arilinn for two of my three years. At seventeen, I had been in love with her. I had never touched her, never so much as kissed her fingertips. Of course.

I looked at Marjorie. *No. No, I have never loved before, never. . . . The other women I have known have been nothing. . . .*

She looked at me and whispered, half laughing. "Have you loved so many?"

"Never like this. I swear it—"

Unexpectedly she threw her arms around me, pressed herself close. "I love you," she whispered quickly, pulled away and ran ahead of me along the path into the hall.

Thyra smiled knowingly at me as we came in, but I didn't care. You had to learn to take that kind of thing for granted. She swung around toward the window, looking into the gathering darkness and mist. We were still close enough that I followed her thoughts. *Kadarin, where was he, how did he fare on his mission?* I began to draw them together again, Marjorie's delicate touch. Rafe alert and quick like some small frisking animal, Thyra with the strange sense of a dark beast prowling.

Kadarin. The interlinked circle formed itself and I discovered to my surprise, and momentary dismay, that Thyra was at the center, weaving us about her mind. But she seemed to work with a sure, deft touch, so I let her keep that place. Suddenly I *saw* Kadarin, and heard his voice speaking in the middle of a phrase;

". . . refuse me then, Lady Storn?"

We could even see the room where he was standing, a high-arched old hall with the blue glass windows of almost unbelievable antiquity. Directly before his eyes was a tall old woman, proudly erect, with gray eyes and dazzling white hair. She sounded deeply troubled.

"Refuse you, *dom*? I have no authority to give or refuse. The Sharra matrix was given into the keeping of the forge-folk after the siege of Storn. It had been taken from them without authority, generations ago, and now it is safe in their keeping, not mine. It is theirs to give."

Kadarin's deep exasperation could be felt by all of us—*stubborn, superstitious old beldame!*—as he said, "It is Kermiac of Aldaran who bids me remind you that you took Sharra's matrix from Aldaran without leave—"

"I do not recognize his right."

"Desideria," he said, "let's not quarrel or quibble. Kermiac sent me to bring the Sharra matrix back to Aldaran; Aldaran is liege-lord to Storn and there's an end to it."

"Kermiac does not know what I know, sir. The Sharra matrix is well where it is; let it lie there. There are no Keepers today powerful enough to handle it. I myself called it up only with the aid of a hundred of the forge-folk, and it would be ill done of me to deprive them of their goddess. I beg you say to Kermiac that by my best judgment, which he trusted always, it should stay where it is."

"I am sick of this superstitious talk of goddesses and talismans, lady. A matrix is a machine, no more."

"Is it? So I thought when I was a maiden," the old woman said. "I knew more of the art of a matrix at fifteen, sir, than you know now, and I know how old you really are." I felt the man flinch from her sharp, steady gaze. "I know *this* matrix, you do not. Be advised by me. You could not handle it. Nor could Kermiac. Nor could I, at my age. Let it lie, man! Don't wake it! If you do not like the talk of goddesses, call it a force basically beyond human control in these days, and evil."

Kadarin paced the floor and I paced with him, sharing a restlessness so strong it was pain. "Lady, a matrix can be no more good or evil in itself than the mind of the man who wields it. Do you think me evil, then?"

She waved that away with an impatient gesture. "I think you honest, but you will not believe there are some powers so strong, so far from ordinary human purpose, that they warp all things to evil. Or to evil in ordinary human terms, at least. And what would you know of that? Let it be, Kadarin."

"I cannot. There is no other force strong enough for my purposes, and these are honest. I have safeguarded all, and I have a circle ready to my hand."

"You do not mean to use it alone, then, or with the Darriell woman?"

"*That* foolhardy I am not. I tell you, I have safeguarded all. I have won a Comyn telepath to aid me. He is cautious and skilled," Kadarin said persuasively, "and trained at Arilinn."

"Arilinn," said Desideria at last. "I know how they were trained at Arilinn. I did not believe that knowledge still survived. That should be safe, then. Promise me, Kadarin, to place it in his hands and leave all things to his judgment, and I will give you the matrix."

"I promise you," Kadarin said. We were so deeply in rapport that it seemed it was I myself, Lew Alton, who bowed before the old Keeper, feeling her gray eyes search *my* very soul rather than his.

It is in the memory of that moment that I will swear, even after all the nightmare that came later, that Kadarin was honest, that he meant no evil. . . .

Desideria said, "Be it so, then, I will entrust it to you." Again the sharp gray eyes met his. "But I tell you, Robert Kadarin, or whatever you call yourself now, *beware*! If you have any flaw, it will expose it brutally; if you seek only power, it will turn your purposes to such ruin as you cannot even guess; and if you kindle its fires recklessly, they will turn on you, and consume you and all you love! I *know*, Kadarin! I have stood in Sharra's flame and though I emerged unburnt, I was not unscarred. I have long put aside my power, I am old, but this much I can still say—*beware*!"

And suddenly the identity swirled and dissolved. Thyra sighed, the circle dropped like strands of cobweb and we stood, staring at one another dazed, in the darkening hallway. Thyra was white with exhaustion and I felt Marjorie's hands trembling on mine.

"Enough," I said firmly, knowing that until it was certain who was to take the centerpolar place, until we knew which of us was Keeper, it was my responsibility to safeguard them all. I motioned to the others to separate, draw apart physically, to break the last clinging strands of rapport. I let Marjorie's hands go with regret. "Enough. We all need rest and food. You must learn never to overtax your physical strength." I spoke deliberately, in a firm, didactic manner, to minimize any emotional contact or concern. "Self-discipline is just as important as talent, and far more important than skill."

But I was not nearly as detached as I sounded, and I suspected they knew it.

Three days later, at dinner in the great lighted hall, I spoke of my original mission to Kermiac. Beltran, I knew, felt that I had wholly turned my back on Comyn. It was true that I no longer felt bound to my father's will. He had lied to me, used me ruthlessly. Kadarin had spoken of Compact as just another Comyn plot to disarm Darkover, to keep the Council's rule intact. Now I wondered how my elderly kinsman felt about it. He had ruled many years in the mountains, with the Terrans ever at hand. It was reasonable he should see everything differently from the Comyn lords. I had heard their side; I had never been given opportunity to know the other view.

When I spoke to him of Hastur's disquiet about the violations of Compact and told him I had been sent to find out the truth, he nodded and frowned, thinking deeply. At last he said, "Danvan Hastur and I have crossed words over this before. I doubt we will ever really agree. I have a good bit of respect for that man: down there between the Dry Towns and the Terrans he has no bed of roses, and all things considered he's managed well. But his choices aren't mine, and fortunately I'm not oath-bound to abide by them. Myself, I believe the Compact has outlived its usefulness, if it ever had any, which I'm no longer sure of."

I had known he felt this way, yet I felt shocked. From childhood I had been taught to think of Compact as the first ethical code of civilized men.

"Stop and think," he said. "Do you realize that we are a part of a great galactic civilization? The days when any single planet could live in isolation are over forever. Swords and shields belong to that day and must be abandoned with it. Do you realize what an anachronism we are?"

"No, I don't realize that, sir. I don't know that much about any world but this one."

"And not too much even about this one, it seems. Let me ask you this, Lew, when did you learn the use of weapons?"

"At seven or eight, more or less." I had always been proud that I need fear no swordsman in the Domains—or out of them.

"I, too," said the old man. "And when I came to rule in my father's high seat, I took it for granted that I would have bodyguards following me everywhere but my marriage-bed! Halfway through my life I realized I was living inside a dead past, gone for centuries. I sent my bodyguards home to their farms, except for a few old men who had no other skills and no livelihood. I let *them* walk around looking important, more for their own usefulness than mine, and yet I sit here, untroubled and free in my own house, my rule unquestioned."

I felt horrified. "At the mercy of any malcontent—"

He shrugged. "I am here, alive and well. By and large, those who give allegiance to Aldaran *want* me here. If they did not, I would persuade them peacefully or step aside and let them try to rule better. Do you honestly believe Hastur keeps authority over the Domains only because he has a bigger and better bodyguard than his rivals?"

"Of course not. I never heard him seriously challenged."

"So. My people too are content with my rule, I need no private army to enforce it."

"But still . . . some malcontent, some madman—"

"Some slip on a broken stair, some lightning-bolt, some misstep by a frightened or half-broken horse, some blunder by my cook with a deadly mushroom for a wholesome one . . . Lew, every man alive is divided from death by that narrow a line. That's as true at your age as mine. If I put down rebellion with armed men, does it prove me the better man, or only the man who can pay the better swordsmen or build the bigger weapons? The long reign of Compact has meant only that every man is expected to settle his affairs with his sword instead of his brains or the rightness of his cause."

"Just the same, it has kept peace in the Domains for generations."

"Flummery!" the old man said rudely. "You have peace in the Domains because, by and large, most of you down there are content to obey Comyn law and no longer put every little matter to the sword. Your celebrated Castle Guard is a police force keeping drunks off the streets! I'm not insulting it, I think that's what it should be. When did *you* last draw your sword in earnest, son?"

I had to stop and think. "Four years ago bandits in the Kilghard hills broke into Armida, stealing horses. We chased them back across the hills and hanged a few of them."

"When did you last fight a duel?"

"Why, never."

"And you last drew your sword against common horse-thieves. No rebellions, wars, invasions from nonhumans?"

"Not in my time." I began to see what he was driving at.

"Then," he said, "why risk law-abiding men, good men and loyal, against horse-thieves, bandits, rabble who have no right to the protection given men of honor? Why not develop really effective protection against the lawless and let your sons learn something more useful than the arts of the sword? I am a peaceful man and Beltran will, I think, have no reason to force himself on my people by armed force. The law in the Hellers states that no man given to breach of the peace may own any weapon, even a sword, and there are laws about how long a pocketknife he may carry. As for the men who keep my laws, they are welcome to any weapon they can get. An honest man is less threat to our world with a Terran's nerve-blaster than a lawless one with my cook's paring knife or a stonemason's hammer. I don't believe in matching good honest men against rogues, both armed with the same weapons. When I left off fairy tales I left off believing that an honest man must always be a better swordsman than a horse-thief or a bandit. The Compact, which allows unlimited handweapons and training in their use to good men and criminals alike, has simply meant that honest men must struggle day and night to make themselves stronger than brutes."

There was certainly some truth in what he said. Now that my father was so lame, Dyan was certainly the best swordsman in the Domains. Did that mean if Dyan fought a duel, and won, that his cause was therefore just? If the horse-thieves had been better swordsmen than ours at Armida, would they have had a right to our horses? Yet there was a flaw in his logic too. Perhaps there was no flawless logic anywhere.

"What you say is true, Uncle, as far as it goes. Yet ever since the Ages of Chaos, it's been known that if an unjust man gets a weapon he can do great damage. With the Compact, and such a weapon as he can get under the Compact, he can do only one man's worth of damage."

Kermiac nodded, acknowledging the truth of what I said. "True. Yet if weapons are outlawed, soon only outlaws can get them—and they always do. Old Hastur's heir so died. The Compact is only workable as long as everybody is willing to keep it. In today's world, with Darkover on the very edge of becoming part of the Empire, it's unenforceable. Completely unenforceable. And if you try to make an unworkable law work and fail, it encourages other men to break laws. I have no love for futile gestures, so I enforce only such laws as I can. I suspect the only answer is the one that Hastur, even though he pays lip service to Compact, is trying to spread in the Domains: make the land so safe that no man seriously needs to defend himself, and let weapons become toys of honor and tokens of manhood."

Uneasily I touched the hilt of the sword I had worn every day of my adult life.

Kermiac patted my wrist affectionately. "Don't trouble yourself, nephew. The world will go as it will, not as you or I would have it. Leave tomorrow's troubles for tomorrow's men to solve. I'll leave Beltran the best world I can, but if he wants a better one he can always build it himself. I'd like to think that some day Beltran and the heir to Hastur could sit down together and build a better world, instead of spitting venom at one another between Thendara and Caer Donn. And I'd like to think that when that day comes you'll be there to help, whether you're standing behind Beltran or young Hastur. Just that you'll be *there*."

He picked up a nut and cracked it with his strong old teeth. I wondered what he knew of Beltran's plans, wondered too how much of what he said was straightforward, how much meant to reach Hastur's ears. I was beginning to love the old man, yet unease nagged at my mind. Most of the crowd at dinner had dispersed; Thyra and Marjorie were gathered with Beltran and Rafe near one of the windows. Kermiac saw the direction of my eyes and laughed.

"Don't sit here among the old men, nephew, take yourself along to the young folk."

"A moment," I said. "Beltran calls them foster-sisters; are they your kinswomen too?"

"Thyra and Marguerida? That's an odd story," Kermiac said. "Some years ago I had a bodyguard in my house, a Terran named Zeb Scott, while I still indulged in such foolishness, and I gave him Felicia Darriell to wife—Does this long tale weary you, Lew?"

"By no means." I was eager to know all I could about Marjorie's parentage.

"Well, then. The Darriells are an old, old family in these hills, and the last of them, old Rakhal—Rafe's true name is Rakhal, you know, but my Terrans find that hard to say—old Rakhal Darriell dwelt as a hermit, half mad and all drunk, in his family mansion, which was falling to ruins even then. And now and then, when he was maddened with wine or when the Ghost Wind blew—the *kireseth* still grows in some of the far valleys—he would wander crazed in the forests. He'd tell strange tales, afterward, of women astray in the forests, dancing naked in the winds and taking him to their arms—such a tale as any madman might tell. But a long time ago, a very long time now, old Rakhal, they say, came to Storn Castle bearing a girl-child in his arms, saying he had found her like this, naked in the snow at his doorway. He told them the babe was his child by one of the forest-folk, cast out to die by her kin. So the lady of Storn took her in for, whatever the babe was, human or of the forest-folk, old Rakhal could not rear her. She fostered her with her own daughters. And many years after, when I was married to Lauretta Storn-Lanart, Felicia Darriell, as she was called, came with Lauretta among her ladies and companions. Felicia's oldest child—Thyra there—may well be my daughter. When Lauretta was heavy with child it was Felicia, by her wish, that I took to my bed. Lauretta's first child was stillborn and she took Thyra as a fosterling. I have always treated her as Beltran's sister, although nothing is certain. Later, Felicia married Zeb Scott, and these two, Rafe and Marguerida, are half-Terran and none of your kin. But Thyra may well be your cousin."

He added, musing, "Old Rakhal's tale may well have been true. Felicia was a strange woman; her eyes were very strange. I always thought such tales mere drunken babble. Yet, having known Felicia . . ." He was silent, lost in memories of time long past. I looked at Marjorie, wondering. I had never believed such tales, either. Yet those eyes . . .

Kermiac laughed and dismissed me. "Nephew, since your eyes and heart are over there with Marguerida, take the rest of yourself along over there too!"

Thyra was gazing intently out into the storm; I could feel the questing tendrils of her thought and knew she was searching, through the gathering darkness, for her lover. Now Thyra, I could well believe, was not all human.

But Marjorie? She reached her hands to me and I caught them in one of mine, circled her waist with my free arm. Beltran said, joining us, "He'll be here soon. What then, Lew?"

"It's your plan," I said, "and Kadarin is certainly enough

of a telepath to fit into a circle. You know what we want to do, though there are limits to what can be done with a group this size. There are certainly technologies we can demonstrate. Road-building and surfacing, for instance. It should convince the Terrans we are worth watching. Powered aircraft may be more difficult. There may be records of that at Arilinn. But it won't be fast or easy."

"You still feel I'm not fit to take a place in the matrix circle."

"There's no question of fitness, you're not *able*. I'm sorry, Beltran. Some powers may develop. But without a catalyst . . ."

He set his mouth and for a moment he looked ugly. Then he laughed. "Maybe some day we can persuade the young one at Syrtis to join us, since you say he does not love the Comyn."

There had been no sound I could hear, but Thyra turned from the window and went out of the hall. A few moments later she came back with Kadarin. He held in his arms a long, heavily wrapped bundle, waving away the servants who would have taken it.

Kermiac had risen to leave the table; he waited for Kadarin at the edge of the dais while the other people in the hall were leaving. Kadarin said, "I have it, kinsman, and a fine struggle I had with the old lady, too. Desideria sends you her compliments." He made a wry face. Kermiac said, with a bleak smile, "Aye, Desideria ever had a mind of her own. You didn't have to use strong persuasion?"

There was sarcasm in Kadarin's grin. "You know Lady Storn better than I. Do you really think it would have availed much? Fortunately, it was not needed. I have small talent for bullying womenfolk."

Kermiac held out his hand to take it, but Kadarin shook his head. "No, I made her a pledge and I must keep it, kinsman, to place it only in the hands of the Arilinn telepath and be guided by his judgment."

Kermiac nodded and said, "Her judgment is good; honor your pledge, then, Bob."

Kadarin laid the long bundle on the bench while he began removing his snow-crusted outer wear. I said, "You look as if you'd been out in the worst weather in the Hellers, Bob. Was it as bad as that?"

He nodded. "I didn't want to linger or be stormbound on the way, carrying *this*." He nodded at the bundle, accepted the hot drink Marjorie brought him and gulped it thirstily. "Season's coming in early; another bad storm on the way. What have you done while I was away?"

Thyra met his eyes and I felt, like a small palpable shock, the quick touch and link as he came into the circle. It was easier than long explanations. He set down the empty cup and said, "Well done, children."

"Nothing's done," I said, "only begun."

Thyra knelt and began to unfasten the knots in the long bundle. Kadarin caught her wrist. "No," he said, "I made a pledge. Take it, Lew."

"We know," said Thyra, "we heard you." She sounded impatient.

"Then will you set my word at nothing, wild-bird?" His hand holding hers motionless was large, brown, heavy-knuckled. Like the Ardais and the Aillards, he had six fingers on his hand. I could easily believe nonhuman blood there, too. Thyra smiled at him and he drew her against him, saying, "Lew, it's for you to take this."

I knelt beside the bundle and began to unfasten the heavy wrappings. It was longer than my arm and narrow, and had been bundled into layer on layer of heavy canvas cloth, the layers bound and knotted with embroidered straps. Marjorie and Beltran came to look over my shoulder as I struggled with the knots. Inside the last layer of heavy canvas was a layer of raw colorless silk, like the insulation of a matrix. When I finally got it unrolled, I saw that it was a ceremonial or ornamental sword, forged of pure silver. An atavistic little prickle went down to the ends of my spine. I had never set eyes on this before. But I knew what it was.

My hands almost refused to take it, despite the thing of beauty the forge-folk had made to cover and guard it. Then I forced myself back to sanity. Was I as superstitious as Thyra thought me? I took the hilt in my hand, sensing the pulsing life within. I seized the sword in both hands and gave the hilt a hard twist.

It came off in my hand. Inside lay the matrix itself, a great blue stone, with an inner glimmer of curling fires which, trained as I was, made my head reel and my vision blur.

I heard Thyra gasp aloud. Beltran had quickly turned away. If it made me, after three seasons in Arilinn, fight for control, I could imagine what it had done to him. I quickly wadded it up in the silk, then took it gingerly between my fingers. I was immensely reluctant to look, even for a moment, into those endlessly *live* depths. Finally I bent my eyes to it. Space wrenched, tore at me. For a moment I felt myself falling, saw the face of a young girl shrouded in flame, crimson and orange and scarlet. It was a face I *knew* somehow—*Desideria*! The old woman I had seen in Kadarin's mind! Then the face shifted, shrouded, was no more a woman but a looming, towering form of fire, a woman's form, chained in gold, rising, flaming, striking, walls crumbling like dust. . . .

I wrapped it in the silk again and said, "Do you know what this is?"

Kadarin said, "It was used of old by the forge-folk to bring metals from the deeps of the ground to their fires."

"I'm not so sure," I said. "Some of the Sharra matrices were used that way. Others were . . . less innocent. I'm not sure this is a monitored matrix."

"All the better. We want no Comyn eyes spying on what we do."

"But that means it's essentially uncontrollable," I said. "A monitored matrix has a safety factor: if it gets out of hand the monitor takes over and breaks the circle. Which is why I still have a right hand." I held out the ugly scar. He flinched slightly and said, "Are you afraid?"

"Of this happening again? No. I know what precautions to take. But of this matrix? Yes, I am."

"You Comyn are superstitious cowards! All my life I've heard about the powers of the Arilinn-trained telepaths and mechanics. Now you are afraid—"

Anger surged through me. Comyn, was I? And cowardly? It seemed that the anger pulsed, beat within me, surging up my arm from the matrix in my fist. I thrust it back into the sword, sealing it there. Thyra said, "Nothing's gained by calling names. Lew, *can* this be used for what Beltran has in mind?"

I found I had an incomprehensible desire to take the sword in my hand again. The matrix seemed to call me, demanding that I take it out, master it. . . . It was almost a sensual hunger. Could it really be dangerous, then? I put the canvas wrappings around it and gave Thyra's question some thought.

Finally I said, "Given a fully trained circle, one I can trust, yes, probably. A tower circle is usually seven or eight mechanics and a Keeper, and we seldom handle more than fourth- or fifth-level matrices. I know this one is stronger than that. And we have no trained Keeper."

"Thyra can do that work," Kadarin said.

I considered it for a moment. She had, after all, drawn us all around her, taking the central position with swift precision. But finally I shook my head.

"I won't risk it. She's worked wild too long. She's self-taught and her training could come apart under stress." I thought of the prowling beast I had sensed when the circle formed. I felt Thyra's eyes on me and was painfully embarrassed, but I had been disciplined to rigid honesty within a circle. You can't hide from one another, it's disaster to try.

"I can control her," Kadarin said.

"I'm sorry, Bob. That's no answer. She herself must be in control or she'll be killed, and it's not a nice way to die. I could control her myself, but the essence of a Keeper is that she does the controlling. I trust her powers, Bob, but not her judgment under stress. If I'm to work with her, I must trust her implicitly. And I can't. Not as Keeper. I think Marjorie can do it—if she will."

Kadarin was regarding Marjorie with a curious wry smile. He said, "You're rationalizing. Do you think I don't know you're in love with her, and want her to have this post of honor?"

"You're mad," I said. "Damn it, yes, I'm in love with her! But it's clear you know nothing about matrix circles. Do you think I *want* her to be Keeper in this circle? Don't you know that will make it impossible for me to touch her? As long as she's a functioning Keeper, none of us may touch her, and I least of all, because I love her and want her. Didn't you know that?" I drew my fingers slowly away from Marjorie's. My hand felt cold and alone.

"Comyn superstition," Beltran said scornfully, "driveling nonsense about virgins and purity! Do you really believe all that rubbish?"

"Belief has nothing to do with it," I said, "and no, Keepers don't have to be sheltered virgins in this day and age. But while they're working in the circles they stay strictly chaste. That's a physical fact. It has to do with nerve currents. It's no more superstition than what every midwife knows, that a pregnant woman must not ride too fast or hard, nor wear tight lacing in her dresses. And even so, it's dangerous. Terribly dangerous. If you think I *want* Marjorie to be our Keeper, you are more ignorant than I thought!"

Kadarin looked at me steadily, and I saw that he was weighing what he said. "I believe you," he said at last. "But you believe Marjorie can do it?"

I nodded, wishing I could lie and be done with it. A telepath's love life is always infernally complicated. And Marjorie and I had just found each other. We had had so very little, so very little. . . .

"She can, if she will," I said at last, "but she must consent. No woman can be made Keeper unwilling. It is too strong a weight to carry, except by free will."

Kadarin looked at us both then and said, "So it all hangs on Marjorie, then. What about it, Margie? Will you be Keeper for us?"

She looked at me and, biting her lip, she stretched out her hands to mine. She said, "Lew, I don't know . . ."

She was afraid, and small wonder. And then, like a compelling, magical dream, I remembered the morning when we had walked together through Caer Donn and shared our dreams for this world. Wasn't this worth a little danger, a little waiting for our happiness? A world where we need not feel shame but pride for our dual heritage, Darkovan and Terran? I felt Marjorie catch the dream, too, as without a word, she slowly loosed her hand from mine and we drew apart. From this moment until our work was ended and the circle dissolved, Marjorie would stand inviolate, set apart, alone. The Keeper.

No words were necessary, but Marjorie spoke the simple words as if they were an oath sealed in fire.

"I agree. If you will help me, I will do what I can."

CHAPTER FIFTEEN

For ten days the storm had raged, sweeping down from the Hellers through the Kilghard Hills and falling on Thendara with fury almost unabated. Now the weather was clear and fine, but Regis rode with his head down, ignoring the bright day.

He'd failed, he felt, having made a pledge and then doing nothing. Now he was being packed off to Neskaya in Gabriel's care, like a sick child with a nanny! But he raised his head in surprise as they made the sharp turn that led down the valley toward Syrtis.

"Why are we taking this road?"

"I have a message for Dom Felix," Gabriel said. "Will the few extra miles weary you? I can send you on to Edelweiss with the Guards. . . ."

Gabriel's careful solicitude set him on edge. As if a few extra miles could matter! He said so, irritably.

His black mare, sure-footed, picked her way down the path. Despite his disclaimer to Gabriel, he felt sick and faint, as he had felt most of the time since his collapse in Kennard's rooms. For a day or two, delirious and kept drugged, he had had no awareness of what was going on, and even now much of what he remembered from the last few days was illusion. Danilo was there, crying out in wild protest, being roughly handled, afraid, in pain. It seemed that Lew was there sometimes too, looking cold and stern and angry with him, demanding again and again, *What is it that you're afraid to know?* He knew, because they told him afterward, that for a day or two he had been so dangerously ill that his grandfather never left his side, and when, waking once between sick intervals of fragmented hallucinations, he had seen his grandfather's face and asked, "Why are you not at Council?" the old man had said violently, "Damn the Council!" Or was that another dream? He knew that once Dyan had come into the room, but Regis had hidden his face in the bedclothes and refused to speak to him, gently though Dyan spoke. Or was *that* a dream, too? And then, for what seemed like years, he had been on the fire-lines at Armida, when they had lived day and night with terror; during the day the hard manual work kept it at bay, but at night he would wake, sobbing and crying out with fear. . . . *That* night, his grandfather told him, his half-conscious cries had grown so terrified, so insistent, that Kennard Alton, himself seriously ill, had come and stayed with him till morning, trying to quiet him with touch and rapport. But he kept crying out for Lew and Kennard couldn't reach him.

Regis, ashamed of this childish behavior, had finally agreed to go to Neskaya. The blur of memory and thought-images embarrassed him, and he didn't try to sort out the truth from the drugged fantasies. Just the same, he knew that at least once Lew *had* been there, holding him in his arms like the frightened child he had been. When he told Kennard so, Kennard nodded soberly and said, "It's very likely. Perhaps you were astray in time; or perhaps from where he is, Lew sensed that you had need for him, and reached you as a telepath can. I had never known you were so close to him." Regis felt helpless, vulnerable, so when he was well enough to ride, he had meekly agreed to go to Neskaya Tower. It was intolerable to live like this. . . .

Gabriel's voice roused him now, saying in dismay, "Look! What's this? Dom Felix—"

The old man was riding up the valley toward them, astride Danilo's black horse, the Armida-bred gelding which was the only really good horse at Syrtis. He was coming at what was, for a man his age, a breakneck pace. For a few minutes it seemed he would ride full tilt into the party on the path, but just a few paces away he pulled up the black and the animal stood stiff-legged, breathing hard, its sides heaving.

Dom Felix glared straight at Regis. "Where is my son? What have you thieving murderers done with him?"

The old man's fury and grief were like a blow. Regis said in confusion, "Your son? Danilo, sir? Why do you ask *me*?"

"What have you vicious, detestable tyrants done with him? How dare you show your faces on my land, after stealing from me my youngest—"

Regis tried to interrupt and quell the torrent of words. "Dom Felix, I do not understand. I parted from Danilo some days ago, in your own orchard. I have not laid eyes on him since; I have been ill—" The memory of his drugged dream tormented him, of Danilo being roughly handled, afraid, in pain. . . .

"Liar!" Dom Felix shouted, his face red and ugly with rage and pain. "Who but you—"

"That's enough, sir," said Gabriel, breaking in with firm authority. "No one speaks like that to the heir to Hastur. I give you my word—"

"The word of a Hastur lickspittle and toady! *I* dare speak against these filthy tyrants! Did you take my son for your—" He flung a word at Regis next to which "catamite" was a courtly compliment. Regis paled against the old man's rage.

"Dom Felix—if you will hear me—"

"Hear you! My son heard you, sir, all your fine words!"

Two Guardsmen rode close to the enraged old man, grasping the reins of his horse, holding him motionless.

"Let him go," Gabriel said quietly. "Dom Felix, we know nothing of your son. I came to you with a message from Kennard Alton concerning him. May I deliver it?"

Dom Felix quieted himself with an effort that made his eyes bulge. "Speak, then, Captain Lanart, and the Gods deal with you as you Comyn dealt with my son."

"The Gods do so to me and more also, if I or mine harmed him," Gabriel said. "Hear the message of Kennard, Lord Alton, Commander of the Guard: 'Say to Dom Felix of Syrtis that it is known to me what a grave miscarriage of justice was done in the Guards this year, of which his son Danilo-Felix, cadet, may have been an innocent victim; and ask that he send his son Danilo-Felix to Thendara under any escort of his own choosing, to stand witness in a full investigation against men in high places, even within Comyn, who may have misused their powers.' " Gabriel paused, then added, "I was also authorized to say to you, Dom Felix, that ten days from now, when I have escorted my brother-in-law, who is in poor health at this moment, to Neskaya Tower, that I shall myself return and escort your son to Thendara, and that you are yourself welcome to accompany him as his protector, or to name any guardian or relative of your own choosing, and that Kennard

Alton will stand personally responsible for his safety and honor."

Dom Felix said unsteadily, "I have never had reason to doubt Lord Alton's honor or goodwill. Then Danilo is not in Thendara?"

One of the Guards, a grizzled veteran, said, "You know me, sir, I served with Rafael in the war, sixteen years gone. I kept an eye on young Dani for his sake. I give you my word, sir, Dani isn't there, with Comyn conniving or without it."

The old man's face gradually paled to its normal hue. He said, "Then Danilo did not run away to join you, Lord Regis?"

"On my honor, sir, he did not. I saw him last when we parted in your own orchard. Tell me, how did he go, did he leave no word?"

The old man's face was clay-colored. "I saw nothing. Dani had been hunting; I was not well and had kept my bed. I said to him I had a fancy for some birds for supper, the Gods forgive me, and he took a hawk and went for them, such a good obedient son—" His voice broke. "It grew late and he did not return. I had begun to wonder if his horse had gone lame, or he'd gone on some boy's prank, and then old Mauris and the kitchen-folk came running into my chamber and told me, they saw him meet with riders on the path and saw him struck down and carried away. . . ."

Gabriel looked puzzled and dismayed. "On my word, Dom Felix, none of us had art, part or knowledge of it. What hour was this? Yesterday? The day before?"

"The day before, Captain. I swooned away at the news. But as soon as my old bones would bear me I took horse to come and hold . . . someone to account. . . ." His voice faded again. Regis drew his own horse close to Dom Felix and took his arm. He said impulsively, "Uncle," using the same word he used to Kennard Alton, "you are father to my friend; I owe you a son's duty as well. Gabriel, take the Guards, go and look, question the house-folk." He turned back to Dom Felix, saying gently, "I swear I will do all I can to bring Danilo safely back. But you are not well enough to ride. Come with me." Taking the other's reins in his own hands, he turned the old man's mount and led him down the path into the cobbled courtyard. Dismounting quickly, he helped Dom Felix down and guided his tottering steps. He led him into the hall, saying to the old half-blind servant there, "Your master is ill, fetch him some wine."

When it had been brought and Dom Felix had drunk a little, Regis sat beside him, near the cold hearth.

"Lord Regis, your pardon . . ."

"None needed. You have been sorely tried, sir."

"Rafael . . ."

"Sir, as my father held your elder son dear, I tell you Danilo's safety and honor are as dear to me as my own." He looked up as the Guardsmen came into the hall. "What news, Gabriel?"

"We looked over the ground where he was taken. The ground was trampled and he had laid about him with his dagger."

"Hawking, he had no other weapon."

"They cut off sheath and all." Gabriel handed Dom Felix the weapon. He drew it forth a little way, saw the Hastur crest on it. He said, "Dom Regis—"

"We swore an oath," said Regis, drawing Danilo's dagger from his own sheath where he wore it, "and exchanged blades, in token of it." He took the dagger with the Hastur crest, saying, "I will bear this to restore to him. Did you see anything else, Gabriel?"

One of the Guardsmen said, "I found this on the ground, torn off in the fight. He must have fought valiantly for a young lad outnumbered." He held out a long, heavy cloak of thick colorless wool, bound with leather buckles and straps. It was much cut and slashed. Dom Felix sat up a little and said, "That fashion of cloak has not been worn in the Domains in my lifetime; I believe they wear them still in the Hellers. And it is lined with marl-fur; it came from somewhere beyond the river. Mountain bandits wore such cloaks. But why Dani? We are not rich enough to ransom him, nor important enough to make him valuable as a hostage."

Regis thought grimly that Dyan's men came from the Hellers. Aloud he said only, "Mountain men act for whoever pays them well. Have you enemies, Dom Felix?"

"No. I have dwelt in peace, farming my acres, for fifteen

years." The old man sounded stunned. He looked at Regis and said, "My lord, if you are sick—"

"No matter," Regis said. "Dom Felix, I pledge you by the oath no Hastur may break that I shall find out who has done this to you, and restore Dani to you, or my own life stand for it." He laid his hand over the old man's for a moment. Then he straightened and said, "One of the Guardsmen shall remain here, to look after your lands in your son's absence. Gabriel, you ride back with the escort to Thendara and carry this news to Kennard Alton. And show him this cloak; he may know where in the Hellers it was woven."

"Regis, I have orders to take you to Neskaya."

"In good time. This must come first," Regis said. "You are a Hastur, Gabriel, if only by marriage-right, and your sons are Hastur heirs. The honor of Hastur is your honor, too, and Danilo is my sworn man."

His brother-in-law looked at him, visibly wavering. There were good things about being heir to a Domain, Regis decided like having your orders obeyed without question. He said impatiently, "I shall remain here to bear my friend's father company, or wait at Edelweiss."

"You cannot stay here unguarded," Gabriel said at last. "Unlike Dani, you *are* rich enough for ransom, and important enough for a hostage." He stood near enough to Comyn to be undecided. "I should send a Guardsmen with you to Edelweiss," he said. Regis protested angrily. "I am not a child! Must I have a nanny trotting at my heels to ride three miles?"

Gabriel's own older sons were beginning to chafe at the necessity of being guarded night and day. Finally Gabriel said, "Regis, look at me. You were placed in my care. Pledge me your word of honor to ride directly to Edelweiss, without turning aside from your road unless you meet armed men, and you may ride alone."

Regis promised and, taking his leave of Dom Felix, rode away. As he rode toward Edelweiss, he thought, a little triumphantly, that he had actually outwitted Gabriel. A more experienced officer would have allowed him, perhaps, to ride to Edelweiss on his promise to go directly . . . but he would also have made Regis give his pledge not to depart from there without leave!

His triumph was short-lived. The knowledge of what he must do was tormenting him. He had to find out where—and how—Danilo was taken. And there was only one way to do that: his matrix. He had never touched the jewel since the ill-fated experiment with *kirian*. It was still in the insulated bag around his neck. The memory of that twisting sickness when he looked into Lew's matrix was still alive in him, and he was horribly afraid.

Surprisingly for these peaceful times, the gates of Edelweiss were shut and barred, and he wondered what alarm had sealed them. Fortunately most of Javanne's servants knew his voice, and after a moment Javanne came running down from the house, a servant-woman puffing at her heels. "Regis! We had word that armed men had been seen in the hills! Where is Gabriel?"

He took her hands. "Gabriel is well, and on his way to Thendara. Yes, armed men were seen at Syrtis, but I think it was a private feud, not war, little sister."

She said shakily, "I remember so well the day Father rode to war! I was a child then, and you not born. And then word came that he was dead, with so many men, and the shock killed Mother. . . ."

Javanne's two older sons came racing toward them, Gabriel and Rafael, nine years old and seven, dark-haired, well-grown boys. They stopped short at the sight of Regis and Rafael said, "I thought you were sick and going to Neskaya. What are you doing here, kinsman?"

Gabriel said, "Mother said there would be war. Is there going to be war, Regis?"

"No, as far as I know, there is no war here or anywhere, and you be thankful for it," Regis said. "Go away now, I must talk with your mother."

"May I ride Melisande down to the stables?" Gabriel begged, and Regis lifted the child into the saddle and went up to the house with Javanne.

"You have been ill; you are thinner," Javanne said. "I had word from Grandfather you were on your way to Neskaya. Why are you here instead?"

He glanced at the darkening sky. "Later, sister, when the boys are abed and we can talk privately. I've been riding all the day; let me rest a little and think. I'll tell you everything then."

Left alone, he paced his room for a long time, trying to steel himself to what he knew he must do.

He touched the small bag around his neck, started to draw it out, then thrust it back, unopened. Not yet.

He found Javanne before the fire in her small sitting room; she had just finished nursing the smaller of the twins and was ready for dinner. "Take the baby to the nursery, Shani," she told the nurse, "and tell the women I'm not to be disturbed for any reason. My brother and I will dine privately."

"*Su serva, domma,*" the woman said, took the baby and went away. Javanne came and served Regis herself. "Now tell me, brother. What happened?"

"Armed men have taken Danilo Syrtis from his home."

She looked puzzled. "Why? And why should you disturb yourself about it?"

"He is my paxman; we have sworn the oath of *bredin,*" Regis said, "and it may well be private revenge. This is what I must find out." He gave her such an edited version of the affair in the cadet corps as he thought fit for a woman's ears. She looked sick and shocked. "I have heard of Dyan's . . . preferences, who has not? At one time there was talk he should marry me. I was glad when he refused, although I, of course, was offered no choice in the matter. He seems to me a sinister man, even cruel, but I had not thought him criminal as well. He is Comyn, and oath-bound never to meddle with the integrity of a mind. You think *he* took Dani, to silence him?"

"I cannot accuse him without proof," Regis said. "Javanne, you spent time in a tower. How much training have you?"

"I spent one season there," she said. "I can use a matrix, but they said I had no great talent for it, and Grandfather said I must marry young."

He drew out his own matrix and said, "Can you show me how to use it?"

"Yes, no great skill is needed for that. But not as safely as they can at Neskaya, and you are not yet wholly well. I would rather not."

"I must know now, at once, what has come to Danilo. The honor of our house is engaged, sister." He explained why. She sat with her plate pushed aside, twirling a fork. At last she said "Wait" and turned away from him, fumbling at the throat of her gown. When she turned back there was something silk-wrapped in her hands. She spoke slowly, the troubled frown still on her features. "I have never seen Danilo. But when I was a little maiden, and old Dom Felix was the hawk-master, I knew Dom Rafael well; he was Father's bodyguard and they went everywhere together. He used to call me pet names and take me up on his saddle and give me rides. . . . I was in love with him, as a little girl can be with any handsome man who is kind and gentle to her. Oh, I was not yet ten years old, but when word came that he had been killed, I think I wept more for him than I did for Father. I remember once I asked him why he had no wife and he kissed my cheek and said he was waiting for me to grow up to be a woman." Her cheeks were flushed, her eyes far away. At last she sighed and said, "Have you any token of Danilo, Regis?"

Regis took the dagger with the Hastur crest. He said, "We both swore on this, and it was cut from his belt when he was taken."

"Then it should resonate to him," she said, taking it in her hands and laying it lightly against her cheekbone. Then, the dagger resting in her palm, she uncovered the matrix. Regis averted his eyes, but not before he got a glimpse of a blinding blue flash that wrenched at his gut. Javanne was silent for a moment, then said in a faraway voice, "Yes, on the hillside path, four men—strange cloaks—an emblem, two eagles—cut away his dagger, sheath and all—*Regis*! He was taken away in a Terran helicopter!" She raised her eyes from the matrix and looked at him in amazement.

Regis' heart felt as if a fist were squeezing it. He said, "Not to Thendara; the Terrans there would have no use for him. Aldaran?"

Her voice was shaking. "Yes. The ensign of Aldaran is an eagle, doubled . . . and they would find it easy to beg or borrow Terran aircraft—Grandfather has done it here in urgency. But why?"

The answer was clear enough. Danilo was a catalyst telepath. There had been a time when Kermiac of Aldaran trained Keepers in his mountains, and no doubt there were ways he could still use a catalyst.

Regis said in a low voice, "He has already borne more

than any untrained telepath was meant to bear. If further strain or coercion is put on him his mind may snap. I should have brought him back with me to Thendara instead of leaving him there unguarded. This is my fault."

Bleakly, struggling against a horrible fear, he raised his head. "I must rescue him. I am sworn. Javanne, you must help me key into the matrix. I have no time to go to Neskaya."

"Regis, is there no other way?"

"None. Grandfather, Kennard, the council—Dani is nothing to them. If it had been Dyan they might have exerted themselves. If Aldaran's men had kidnapped *me,* they'd have an army on the road! But Danilo? What do *you* think?"

Javanne said, "That *nedestro* heir of Kennard's. He was sent to Aldaran and he's kin to them. I wonder if he had a hand in this."

"Lew? He wouldn't."

Javanne looked skeptical. "In your eyes he can do no wrong. As a little boy you were in love with him as I with Dom Rafael; I have no child's passion for him, to blind me to what he is. Kennard forced him on Council with ugly tricks."

"You have no right to say so, Javanne. He is sealed to Comyn and tower-trained!"

She refused to argue. "In any case, I can see why you feel you must go, but you have no training, and it is dangerous. Is there such need for haste?" She looked into his eyes and said after a moment, "As you will. Show me your matrix."

His teeth clenched, Regis unwrapped the stone. He drew breath, astonished: faint light glimmered in the depths of the matrix. She nodded. "I can help you key it, then. Without that light, you would not be ready. I'll stay in touch with you. It won't do much good, but if you . . . go out and can't get back to your body, it could help me reach you." She drew a deep breath. For an instant then he felt her touch. She had not moved, her head was lowered over the blue jewel so that he saw only the parting in her smooth dark hair, but it seemed to Regis that she bent over him, a slim childish girl still much taller than he. She swung him up, as if he were a tiny child, astride her hip, holding him loosely on her arm. He had not thought of this in years, how she had done this when he was very little. She walked back and forth, back and forth, along the high-arched hall with the blue windows, singing to him in her husky low voice. . . . He shook his head to clear it of the illusion. She still sat with her head bent over the matrix, an adult again, but her touch was still on him, close, protective, sheltering. For a moment he felt that he would cry and cling to her as he had done then.

Javanne said gently, "Look into the matrix. Don't be afraid, this one isn't keyed to anyone else; mine hurt you because you're out of phase with it. Look into it, bend your thoughts on it, don't move until you see the lights waken inside it. . . ."

He tried deliberately to relax; he realized that he was tensing every muscle against remembered pain. He finally looked into the pale jewel, feeling only a tiny shock of awareness, but something inside the jewel glimmered faintly. He bent his thoughts on it, reached out, reached out . . . deep, deep inside. Something stirred, trembled, flared into a living spark. Then it was as if he had blown his breath on a coal from the fireplace: the spark was brilliant blue fire, moving, pulsing with the very rhythm of his blood. Excitement crawled in him, an almost sexual thrill.

"Enough!" Javanne said. "Look away quickly or you'll be trapped!"

No, not yet. . . . Reluctantly, he wrenched his eyes from the stone. She said, "Start slowly. Look into it only a few minutes at a time until you can master it or it will master you. The most important lesson is that you must always control *it,* never let it control *you.*"

He gave it a last glance, wrapped it again with a sense of curious regret, feeling Javanne's protective touch/embrace withdraw. She said, "You can do with it what you will, but that is not much, untrained. Be careful. You are not yet immune to threshold sickness and it may return. Can a few days matter so much? Neskaya is only a little more than a day's ride away."

"I don't know how to explain, but I feel that every moment matters. I'm afraid, Javanne, afraid for Danilo, afraid for all of us. I must go now, tonight. Can you find me some old riding-clothes of Gabriel's, Javanne? These will attract too much attention in the mountains. And will you have your women make me some food for a few days? I want to avoid towns nearby where I might be recognized."

"I'll do it myself; no need for the women to see and gossip." She left him to his neglected supper while she went to find the clothing. He did not feel hungry, but dutifully stowed away a slice of roast fowl and some bread. When she came back, she had his saddlebags, and an old suit of Gabriel's. She left him by the fire to put them on, then he followed her down the hall to a deserted kitchen. The servants were long gone to bed. She moved around, making up a package of dried meat, hard bread and crackers, dried fruit. She put a small cooking-kit into the saddlebags, saying it was one which Gabriel carried on hunting trips. He watched her silently, feeling closer to this little-known sister than he had felt since he was six years old and she left their home to marry. He wished he were still young enough to cling to her skirts as he had then. An ice-cold fear gripped at him, and then the thought: before going into danger, a Comyn heir must himself leave an heir. He had refused even to think of it, as Dyan had refused, not wanting to be merely a link in a chain, the son of his father, the father of his sons. Something inside him rebelled, deeply and strongly, at what he must do. Why bother? If he did not return, it would all be the same, one of Javanne's sons named his heir. . . . He could do nothing, say nothing. . . .

He sighed. It was too late for that, he had gone too far. He said, "One thing more, sister. I go where I may never return. You know what that means. You must give me one of your sons, Javanne, for my heir."

Her face blanched and she gave a low, stricken cry. He felt the pain in it but he did not look away, and finally she said, her voice wavering, "Is there no other way?"

He tried to make it a feeble joke. "I have no time to get one in the usual way, sister, even if I could find some woman to help me at such short notice."

Her laughter was almost hysterical; it cut off in the middle, leaving stark silence. He saw slow acceptance dawning in her eyes. He had known she would agree. She was

Hastur, of a family older than royalty. She had of necessity married beneath her, since there was no equal, and she had come to love her husband deeply, but her duty to the Hasturs came first. She only said, her voice no more than a thread, "What shall I say to Gabriel?"

"He has known since the day he took you to wife that this day might come," Regis said. "I might well have died before coming to manhood."

"Come, then, and choose for yourself." She led the way to the room where her three sons slept in cots side by side. By the candlelight Regis studied their faces, one by one. Gabriel, sturdy and swarthy and taller than his brother; Rafael, slight and dark, close-cropped curls tousled around his face, Mikhail, who was four, was still pixie-small, fairer than the others, his rosy cheeks framed in light waving locks, almost silvery white. Grandfather must have looked like that as a child, Regis thought. He felt curiously cold and bereft. Javanne had given their clan three sons and two daughters. He might never father a son of his own. He shivered at the implications of what he was doing, bent his head, groping through an unaccustomed prayer. "Cassilda, blessed Mother of the Domains, help me choose wisely. . . ."

He moved quietly from cot to cot. Rafael was most like him, he thought. Then, on some irresistible impulse, he bent over Mikhail, lifted the small sleeping form in his arms.

"This is my son, Javanne."

She nodded, but her eyes were fierce. "And if you do not return he will be Hastur of Hastur; but if you *do* return, what then? A poor relation at the footstool of Hastur?"

Regis said quietly, "If I do not return, he will be *nedestro,* sister. I will not pledge you never to take a wife, even in return for this great gift. But this I swear to you: he shall come second only to my first legitimately born son. My second son shall be third to him, and I will take oath no other *nedestro* heir shall ever displace him. Will this content you. *breda*?"

Mikhail opened his eyes and stared about him sleepily, but he saw his mother and did not cry. Javanne touched the blond head gently. "It will content me, brother."

Holding the child awkwardly in unpracticed arms, Regis carried him out of the room where his brothers slept.

"Bring witnesses," he said, "I must be gone soon. You know this is irrevocable, Javanne, that once I take this oath, he is not yours but mine, and must be sealed my heir. You must send him to Grandfather at Thendara."

She nodded. Her throat moved as she swallowed hard, but she did not protest. "Go down to the chapel," she said. "I will bring witnesses."

It was an old room in the depths of the house, the four old god-forms painted crudely on the walls, lights burning before them. Regis held Mikhail on his lap, letting the child sleepily twist a button on his tunic, until the witnesses came, four old men and two old women of the household. One of the women had been Javanne's nurse in childhood, and his own.

He took his place solemnly at the altar, Mikhail in his arms.

"I swear before Aldones, Lord of Light and my divine forefather, that Hastur of Hasturs is this child by unbroken blood line, known to me in true descent. And in default of any heir of my body, therefore do I, Regis-Rafael Felix Alar Hastur y Elhalyn, choose and name him my *nedestro* heir and swear that none save my first-born son in true marriage shall ever displace him as my heir; and that so long as I live, none shall challenge his right to my hearth, my home or my heritage. Thus I take oath in the presence of witnesses known to us both. I declare that my son shall be no more called Mikhail Regis Lanart-Hastur, but—" He paused, hesitating among old Comyn names for suitable new names which would confirm the ritual. There was no time to search the rolls for names of honor. He would commemorate, then, the desperate need which had driven him to this. "I name him Danilo," he said at last. "He shall be called Danilo Lanart Hastur, and I will so maintain to all challenge, facing my father before me and my sons to follow me, my ancestry and my posterity. And this claim may never be renounced by me while I live, nor in my name by any of the heirs of my body." He bent and kissed his son on the soft baby lips. It was done. They had a strange beginning. He wondered what the end would be. He turned his eyes on his old nurse.

"Foster-mother, I place you in charge of my son. When the roads are safe, you must take him to the Lord Hastur at Thendara, and see to it that he is given the Sign of Comyn."

Javanne was dropping slow tears, but she said nothing except, "Let me kiss him once more," and allowed the old woman to carry the child away. Regis followed them with his eyes. His son. It was a strange feeling. He wondered if he had *laran* or the unknown Hastur gift; he wondered if he would ever know, would ever see the child again.

"I must go," he said to his sister. "Send for my horse and someone to open the gates without noise." As they waited together in the gateway, he said, "If I do not return—"

"Speak no ill-omen!" she said quickly.

"Javanne, do you have the Hastur gift?"

"I do not know," she said. "None knows till it is wakened by one who holds it. We had always thought that you had no *laran*. . . ."

He nodded grimly. He had grown up with that, and even now it was too sore a wound to touch.

She said, "A day will come when you must go to Grandfather, who holds it to waken in his heir, and ask for the gift. Then, and only then, you will know what it is. I do not know myself," she said. "Only if you had died before you were declared a man, or before you had fathered a son, it would have been wakened in me so that, before my own death, I might pass it to one of my sons."

And so it might pass, still. He heard the soft clop-clop-clop of hooves in the dark. He prepared to mount, turned back a moment and took Javanne briefly in his arms. She was crying. He blinked tears from his own eyes. He whispered, "Be good to my son, darling." What more could he say?

She kissed him quickly in the dark and said, "Say you'll come back, brother. Don't say anything else." Without waiting for another word, she wrenched herself free of him and ran back into the dark house.

The gates of Edelweiss swung shut behind him. Regis was alone. The night was dark, fog-shrouded. He fastened his cloak about his throat, touching the small pouch where the matrix lay. Even through the insulation he could feel it, though no other could have, a small live thing, throbbing. . . . He was alone with it, under the small horn of moon lowering behind the distant hills. Soon even that small light would be gone.

He braced himself, murmured to his horse, straightened his back and rode away northward, on the first step of his unknown journey.

CHAPTER SIXTEEN

(Lew Alton's narrative)

Until the day I die, I am sure I shall return in dreams to that first joyous time at Aldaran.

In my dreams, everything that came after has been wiped out, all the pain and terror, and I remember only that time when we were all together and I was happy, wholly happy for the first and last time in my life. In those dreams Thyra moves with all her strange wild beauty, but gentle and subdued, as she was during those days, tender and pliant and loving. Beltran is there, too, with his fire and the enthusiasm of the dream from which we had all taken the spark, my friend, almost my brother. Kadarin is always there, and in my dreams he is always smiling, kind, a rock of strength bearing us all up when we faltered. And Rafe, the son I shall never have, always beside me, his eyes lifted to mine.

And Marjorie.

Marjorie is always with me in those dreams. But there is nothing I can say about Marjorie. Only that we were together and in love, and as yet the fear was only a little, little shadow, like a breath of chill from a glacier not yet in sight. I wanted her, of course, and I resented the fact that I could not touch her even in the most casual way. But it wasn't as bad as I had feared. Psi work uses up so much energy and strength that there's nothing much left. I was with her every waking moment and it was enough. *Almost* enough. And we could wait for the rest.

I wanted a well-trained team, so I worked with them day by day, trying to shape us all together into a functioning circle which could work together, precisely tuned. As yet we were working with our small matrices; before we joined together to open and call forth the power of the big one, we must be absolutely attuned to one another, with no hidden weaknesses. I would have felt safer with a circle of six or eight, as at Arilinn. Five is a small circle, even with

Beltran working outside as a psi monitor. But Thyra and Kadarin were stronger than most of us at Arilinn—I knew they were both stronger than I, though I had more skill and training—and Marjorie was fantastically talented. Even at Arilinn, they would have chosen her the first day as a potential Keeper.

Deep warmth and affection, even love, had sprung up among all of us with the gradual blending of our minds. It was always like this, in the building of a circle. It was closer than family intimacy, closer than sexual love. It was a sort of *blending,* as if we all melted into one another, each of us contributing something special, individual and unique, and somehow all of us together becoming more than the sum of us.

But the others were growing impatient. It was Thyra who finally voiced what they were all wanting to know.

"When do we begin to work with the Sharra matrix? We're as ready as we'll ever be."

I demurred. "I'd hoped to find others to work with us; I'm not sure we can operate a ninth-level matrix alone."

Rafe asked, "What's a ninth-level matrix?"

"In general," I said dryly, "it's a matrix not safe to handle with less than nine workers. And that's with a good, fully trained Keeper."

Kadarin said, "I told you we should have chosen Thyra."

"I won't argue with you about it. Thyra is a very strong telepath; she is an excellent technician and mechanic. But no Keeper."

Thyra asked, "Exactly how does a Keeper differ from any other telepath?"

I struggled to put it into language she could understand. "A Keeper is the central control in the circle; you've all seen that. She holds together the forces. Do you know what *energons* are?"

Only Rafe ventured to ask, "Are they the little wavy things that I can't quite see when I look into the matrix?"

Actually that was a very good answer. I said, "They're a purely theoretical name for something nobody's sure really exists. It's been postulated that the part of the brain which controls psi forces gives off a certain type of vibration which we call energons. We can describe what they do, though we can't really describe them. These, when directed and focused through a matrix—I showed you—become immensely amplified, with the matrix acting as a transformer. It is the *amplified* energons which transform energy. Well, in a matrix circle, it is the Keeper who receives the flow of energons from all members of the circle and weaves them all into a single focused beam, and this, the focused beam, is what goes through the large matrix."

"Why are Keepers always women?"

"They aren't. There have been male Keepers, powerful ones, and other men who have taken a Keeper's place. I can do it myself. But women have more positive energon flows, and they begin to generate them younger and keep them longer."

"You explained why a Keeper has to be chaste," Marjorie said, "but I still don't understand it."

Kadarin said, "That's because it's superstitious drivel. There's nothing to understand; it's gibberish."

"In the old days," I said, "when the really enormous matrix screens were made, the big synthetic ones, the Keepers *were* virgins, trained from early childhood and conditioned in ways you wouldn't believe. You know how close a matrix circle is." I looked around at them, savoring the closeness. "In those days a Keeper had to learn to be part of the circle and yet completely, *completely* apart from it."

Marjorie said, "I should think they'd have gone mad."

"A good many of them did. Even now, most of the women who work as Keepers give it up after a year or two. It's too difficult and frustrating. The Keepers at the towers aren't required to be virgins any more. But while they are working as Keepers, they stay strictly chaste."

"It sounds like nonsense," Thyra said.

"Not a bit of it," I said. "The Keeper takes and channels all that energy from all of you. No one who has ever handled these very high energy-flows wants to take the slightest chance of short-circuiting them through her own body. It would be like getting in the way of a lightning-bolt." I held out the scar again. "A three-second backflow did that to me. Well, then. In the body there are clusters of nerve fibers which control the energy flows. The trouble is that the same nerve clusters carry two kinds of energy: they carry the psi flows, the energons which carry power to the brain; they also carry the sexual messages and energies.

This is why some telepaths get threshold sickness when they're in their teens: the two kinds of energy, sexual energies and *laran*, are both wakening at once. If they aren't properly handled, you can get an overload, sometimes a killer overload, because each stimulates the other and you get a circular feedback."

Beltran asked, "Is that why—"

I nodded, knowing what he was going to ask. "Whenever there's an energon drain, as in concentrated matrix work, there's some nerve overloading. Your energies are depleted—have you noticed how we've all been eating?—and your sexual energies are at a low ebb, too. The major side effect for men is temporary impotence." I repeated, smiling reassuringly at Beltran, "*Temporary* impotence. Nothing to worry about, but it does take some getting used to. By the way, if you ever find you can't eat, come to one of us right away for monitoring; that can be an early-warning signal that your energy flows are out of order."

"Monitoring. That's what you're teaching me to do, then?" Beltran asked, and I nodded. "That's right. Even if you can't link into the circle, we can use you as a psi monitor." I knew he was still resentful about this. He knew enough by now to know it was the work usually done by the youngest and least skilled in the circle. The worst of it was that unless he could stop projecting this resentment, we couldn't even use him near the circle. Not even as a psi monitor. There are few things that can disrupt a circle faster than uncontrolled resentments.

I said, "In a sense, the Keeper and the psi monitor are at the two ends of a circle—and almost equally important." This was true. "Often enough, the life of the Keeper is in the hands of the monitor, because she has no energy to waste in watching over her own body."

Beltran grinned ruefully, but he grinned. "So Marjorie is the head and I'm the old cow's tail!"

"By no means. Rather she's at the top of the ladder and you're on the ground holding it steady. You're the lifeline." I remembered suddenly that we had come far astray from the subject, and said, "With a Keeper, if the nerve channels are not *completely* clear they can overload, and the Keeper will burn up like a torch. So while the nerve channels are being used to carry these tremendous energy overloads, they cannot be used to carry any other form of energy. And only complete chastity can keep the channels clear enough."

Marjorie said, "I can feel the channels all the time now. Even when I'm not working in the matrices. Even when I'm *asleep*."

"Good." That meant she was functioning as a Keeper now. Beltran looked at her with half shut eyes and said, "I can *see* them, almost."

"That's good, too," I said. "A time will come when you'll be able to sense the energy flows from across the room—or a mile away—and pinpoint any backflows or energy disruptions in any of us."

I deliberately changed the subject. I asked, "Precisely what do we want to do with the Sharra matrix, Beltran?"

"You know my plans."

"Plans, yes, precisely what do you want to do *first*? I know that in the end you want to prove that a matrix this size can power a starship—"

"Can it?" Marjorie asked.

"A matrix this size, love, could bring one of the smaller moons right down out of its orbit, if we were insane enough to try. It would, of course, destroy Darkover along with it. Powering a starship with one might be possible, but we can't *start* there. Among other reasons, we haven't got a starship yet. We need a smaller project to experiment with, to learn to direct and focus the force. This force is fire-powered, so we also need a place to work where, if we lose control for a few seconds, we won't burn up a thousand leagues of forest."

I saw Beltran shudder. He was mountain-bred too, and shared with all Darkovans the fear of forest fire. "Father has four Terran aircraft, two lights planes and two helicopters. One helicopter is away in the lowlands, but would the other be suitable for experiment?"

I considered. "The explosive fuel should be removed first," I said, "so if anything *does* go wrong it won't burn. Otherwise a helicopter might be ideal, experimenting with the rotors to lift and power and control it. It's a question of developing control and precision. You wouldn't put Rafe, here, to riding your fastest racehorse."

Rafe said shyly, "Lew, you said we need other telepaths.

Lord Kermiac . . . didn't he train matrix mechanics before any of us were born? Why isn't he one of us?"

True. He had trained Desideria and trained her so well that she could use the Sharra matrix—

"And she used it alone," said Kadarin, picking up my thoughts. "So why does it worry you that we are so few?"

"She didn't use it alone," I said. "She had fifty to a hundred believers focusing their raw emotion on the stone. More, she did not try to control it or focus it. She used it as a weapon, rather, she let it use *her*." I felt a sudden cold shudder of fear, as if every hair on my body were prickling and standing erect. I cut off the thought. I was tower-trained. I had no will to wield it for power. I was sworn.

"As for Kermiac," I said, "he is old, past controlling a matrix. I wouldn't risk it, Rafe."

Beltran grew angry. "Damn it, you might have the courtesy to ask him!"

That seemed fair enough, when I weighed the experience he must have had against his age and weakness. "Ask him, if you will. But don't press him. Let him make his own choice freely."

"He will not," Marjorie said. She colored as we all turned on her. "I thought it was my place, as Keeper, to ask him. He called it to my mind that he would not even teach me. He said a circle was only as strong as the weakest person in it, and he would endanger all our lives."

I felt both disappointed and relieved. Disappointed because I would have welcomed a chance to join him in that special bond that comes only among the members of a circle, to feel myself truly one of his kin. Relieved, because what he had told Marjorie was true, and we all knew it.

Thyra said rebelliously, "Does he understand how much we need him? Isn't it worth some risk?"

I would have risked the hazards to us, not those to him. At Arilinn they recommended gradual relinquishing of the work after early middle age, as vitality lessened.

"Always Arilinn," Thyra said impatiently, as if I had spoken aloud. "Do they train them there to be cowards?"

I turned on her, tensing myself against that sudden inner anger which Thyra could rouse in me so easily. Then, sternly controlling myself before Marjorie or the others could be caught up in the whirlpool emotion which swirled and raced between Thyra and me, I said, "One thing they *do* teach us, Thyra, is to be honest with ourselves and each other." I held out my hands to her. If she had been taught at Arilinn she would have known already that anger was all too often a concealment for less permissible emotions. "Are you ready to be so honest with me?"

Reluctantly, she took my extended hand between her own. I fought to keep my barriers down, not to barricade myself against her. She was trembling, and I knew this was a new and distressing experience to her, that no man except Kadarin, who had been her lover for so long, had ever stirred her senses. I thought, for a moment, she would cry. It would have been better if she had, but she bit her lip and stared at me, defiant. She whispered, half-aloud, "Don't—"

I broke the trembling rapport, knowing I could not force Thyra, as I would have had to do at Arilinn, to go into this all the way and confront what she refused to see. I couldn't. Not before Marjorie.

It was not cowardice, I told myself fiercely. We were all kinsmen and kinswomen. There was simply no need.

I said, changing the subject quickly, "We can try keying the Sharra matrix tomorrow, if you want. Have you explained to your father, Beltran, that we will need an isolated place to work, and asked leave to use the helicopter?"

"I will ask him tonight, when we are at dinner," Beltran promised.

After dinner, when we were all seated in the little private study we had made our center, he came to us and told us permission had been given, that we could use the old airstrip. We talked little that night, each thinking his or her own thoughts. I was thinking that it had certainly cost Kadarin a lot to turn the matrix over to me. All along, he had expected that he and Beltran would be wholly in charge of this work, that I would be only a helper, lending skill but with no force to decisions. Beltran probably still resented my taking charge, and his inability to be part of the circle was most likely the bitterest dose he had ever had to swallow.

Marjorie was a little apart from us all, the heartbreaking isolation of a Keeper having already begun to slip down over her, forcing her away from the rest. I hated myself for having condemned her to this. With one part of myself I wanted to smash it all and take her into my arms. Maybe Kadarin was right, maybe the chastity of a Keeper was the stupidest of Comyn superstitions, and Marjorie and I were going through all this hell unnecessarily.

I let myself drift out of focus, trying to see ahead to a day when we would be free to love one another. And strangely, though my life was here and I felt I had wholly renounced my allegiance to Comyn, I still tried to see myself breaking the news to my father.

I came up to ordinary awareness and saw that Rafe was asleep on the hearth. Someone should wake him and send him to bed. Was this work too strenuous for a boy his age? He should be playing with button-sized matrices, not working seriously in a circle like this!

My eyes dwelt longest, with a cruel envy, on Kadarin and Thyra, side by side on the hearthrug, gazing into the fire. No prohibition lay between them; even separated, they had each other. I saw Marjorie's eyes come to rest on them, with the same remote sadness. That, at least, we could share . . . and for now it was all we could share.

I turned my hand over and looked with detached sorrow at the mark tattooed on my right wrist, the seal of Comyn. The sign that I was *laran* heir to a Domain. My father had sworn for me, before that mark was set there, for service to Comyn, loyalty to my people.

I looked at the scar from my first year at Arilinn. It ached whenever I was doing matrix work like this; it ached now. That, not the tattoo mark of my Domain, was the real sign of my loyalty to Darkover. And now I was working for a great rebirth of knowledge and wisdom to benefit all our world. I was breaking the law of Arilinn by working with untrained telepaths, unmonitored matrices. Breaking their letter, perhaps, to restore their spirit all over Darkover!

When, yawning wearily, Rafe and the women went their way to bed, I detained Kadarin for a moment. "One thing I have to know. Are you and Thyra married?"

He shook his head. "Freemates, perhaps, we never sought formal ceremonies. If she had wished I would have been willing, but I have seen too many marriage customs on too many worlds to care about any of them. Why?"

"In a tower circle this would not arise; here it must be

taken into account," I said. "Is there any possibility that she could be carrying a child?"

He raised his eyebrow. I knew the question was an inexcusable intrusion, but it was necessary to know. He said at last, "I doubt it. I have traveled on so many worlds and been exposed to so many things . . . I am older than I look, but I have fathered no children. Probably I cannot. So I fear if Thyra really wants a child she will have to have it fathered elsewhere. Are you volunteering?" he asked, laughing.

I found the question too outrageous even to think about. "I only felt I should warn you that matrix circle work could be dangerous if there was the slightest chance of pregnancy. Not so much for her, but for the unborn child. There have been gruesome tragedies. I felt I should warn you."

"I should think you'd have done better to warn *her,*" he said, "but I appreciate your delicacy." He gave me an odd, unreadable look and went away. Well, I had done no more than my duty in asking, and if the question distressed him, he would have to absorb and accept it, as I absorbed my frustration over Marjorie and accepted the way Thyra's physical presence disturbed me. My dreams that night were disturbing, Thyra and Marjorie tangling into a single woman, so that again and again I would see one in dreams and suddenly discover it was the other. I should have recognized this as a sign of danger, but I only knew that when it was too late.

The next day was gray and lowering. I wondered if we would have to wait till spring for any really effective work. It might be better, giving us time to settle into our work together, perhaps find others to fit into the circle. Beltran and Kadarin would be impatient. Well, they would just have to master their impatience.

Marjorie looked cold and apprehensive; I felt the same way. A few lonesome snowflakes were drifting down, but I could not make the snow an excuse for putting off the experiment. Even Thyra's high spirits were subdued.

I unwrapped the sword in which the matrix was hidden. The forge-folk must have done this; I wondered if they had known, even halfway, what they were doing. There were old traditions about matrices like this, installed in weapons.

They came out of the Ages of Chaos, when, it is said, everything it's possible to know about matrices was known, and our world nearly destroyed in consequence.

I said to Beltran, "It's very dangerous to key into a matrix this size without a very definite end in mind. It must always be controlled or it will take control of us."

Kadarin said, "You speak as if the matrix was a live thing."

"I'm not so sure it's not." I gestured at the helicopter, standing about eighty feet away at the near edge of the deserted airfield, the snow faintly beginning to edge its tail and rotors. "What I mean is this. We cannot simply key into the matrix, say 'fly' and stand here watching that thing take off. We must know precisely *how* the mechanism works, in order to know precisely what forces we must exert, and in what directions. I suggest we begin by concentrating on turning the rotor blade mechanism and getting enough speed to lift it. We don't really need a matrix this size for that, nor five workers. I could do it with this." I touched the insulated bag which held my own. "But we must have some precise way of learning to direct forces. We will discover, then, how to lift the helicopter and, since we don't want it to crash, we'll limit ourselves to turning the rotors until it lifts a few inches, then gradually diminish the speed again until we set it down. Later we can try for direction and control in flight." I turned to Beltran. "Will this demonstrate to the Terrans that psi power has material uses, so they'll give us help in developing a way to use this for a stardrive?"

It was Kadarin who answered, "Hell yes! If I know the Terrans!"

Marjorie checked Rafe's mittened hands. "Warm enough?" He pulled away indignantly, and she admonished, "Don't be silly! Shivering uses up too much energy; you have to be able to concentrate!" I was pleased at her grasp of this. My own chill was mental, not physical. I placed Beltran at a little distance from the circle. I knew it was a bitter pill to swallow, that the twelve-year-old Rafe could be part of this and he could not, and I was intensely sorry for him, but the first necessity of matrix work was to know and accept for all time your own limitations. If he couldn't, he had no business within a mile of the circle.

There was really no need for a physical circle, but I drew us close enough that the magnetic energy of our bodies would overlap and reinforce the growing bond.

I knew this was folly, a partly trained Keeper, a partly trained psi monitor . . . an illegal, unmonitored matrix . . . and yet I thought of the pioneers in the early days of our world, first taming the matrices. Terran colonists? Kadarin thought so. Before the towers rose, before their use was guarded by ritual and superstition. And it was given to us to retrace their steps!

I separated hilt and blade, taking out the matrix. It was not yet activated, but at its touch the old scar on my palm contracted with a stab of pain. Marjorie moved with quiet sureness into the center of the circle. She stood facing me, laying one hand on the blue stone . . . *a vortex seeking to draw me into its depths, a maelstrom.* . . . I shut my eyes, reaching out for contact with Marjorie, steadying myself as I made contact with her cool silken strength. I felt Thyra drop into place, then Kadarin; the sense of an almost-unendurable burden lessened with his strength, as if he shifted a great weight onto his shoulders. Rafe dropped in like some small furry thing nestling against us.

I had the curious sense that power was flowing *up* from the stone and into the circle. It felt like being hooked up to a powerful battery, vibrating in us all, body and brain. That was wrong, that was very wrong. It was curiously invigorating, but I knew we must not succumb to it even for a moment. With relief I felt Marjorie seize control and with a determined effort direct the stream of force, focusing it through her, outward.

For a moment she stood bathed in flickering, transparent flames, then for an instant she took on the semblance of a woman . . . *golden, chained, kneeling, as the forge-folk depicted their goddess.* . . . I knew this was an illusion, but it seemed that Marjorie, or the great flickering fire-form which seemed to loom around and over and through her, reached out, seized the helicopter's rotors and spun them as a child spins a pin-wheel. With my physical ears I heard the humming sound as they began to turn, slowly at first under the controlling force, then winding to a swift spinning snarl, a drone, a shriek that caught the air currents. Slowly, slowly, the great machine lifted, hovering lightly a foot or so above the ground.

Straining to be gone . . .

Hold it there! I was directing the power outward as Marjorie formed and shaped it; I could feel all the others pressed tightly against me, though physically none of us were touching. As I trembled, feeling the vast outflow of that linked conjoined power, I saw in a series of wild flashes the great form of fire I had seen before, Marjorie and not Marjorie, a raw stream of force, a naked woman, sky-tall with tossing hair, each separate lock a streamer of fire . . . I felt a curious rage surging up and through me. *Take the helicopter, hanging there useless a few inches high, hurl it into the sky, high, high, fling it down like a missile against the towers of Castle Aldaran, burning, smashing, exploding the walls like sand, hurling a rain of fire into the valley, showering fires on Caer Donn, laying the Terran base waste.* . . . I struggled with these images of fire and destruction, as a rider struggles with the bit of a hard-mouthed horse. *Too strong, too strong.* I smelled musk, a wild beast prowled the jungle of my impulses, rage, lust, a constellation of wild emotions . . . a small skittering animal bolting up a tree in terror . . . the shriek of the rotor blades, a scream, a deafening roar. . . .

Slowly the noise lessened to a whine, a drone, a faint whir, silence. The copter stood vibrating faintly, motionless. Marjorie, still flickering with faint glimmers of invisible fire, stood calm, smiling absently. I felt her reach out and break the rapport, the others slipping away one by one until we stood alone, locked together. She withdrew her hand from the matrix and I stood cold and alone, struggling against spasms of lust, raging violence spinning in my brain, out of control, my heart racing, the blood pounding in my head, vision blurred. . . .

Beltran touched me lightly on the shoulder; I felt the tumult subside and with a shudder of pain managed to withdraw my consciousness. I covered the matrix quickly and drew my aching hand over my forehead. It came away dripping.

"Zandru's hells!" I whispered. Never, not in three years at Arilinn, had I even guessed such power. Kadarin, looking at the helicopter thoughtfully, said, "We could have done anything with it."

"Except maybe controlled it."

"But the power is *there,* when we do learn to control it," Beltran said. "A spaceship. Anything."

Rafe touched Marjorie's wrist, very lightly. "For a minute I thought you were on fire. Was that real, Lew?"

I wasn't sure if this was simply an illusion, the way generations upon generations of the forge-folk had envisioned their goddess, the power which brought metal from the deeps of the earth to their fires and forges. Or was this some objective force from that strange otherworld to which the telepath goes when he steps out of his physical body? I said, "I don't know, Rafe. How did it seem, Marjorie?"

She said, "I saw the fire. I even felt it, a little, but it didn't burn me. But I *did* feel that if I lost control, even for an instant, it would burn up inside and . . . and take over, so that I *was* the fire and could leap down and . . . and destroy. I'm not saying this very well. . . ."

Then it was not only me. She too had felt the weapon-rage, the lust for destruction. I was still struggling with their physical aftereffects, the weak trembling of adrenalin expended. If these emotions had actually arisen from within *me,* I was not fit for this work. Yet, searching within myself, with the discipline of the tower-trained, I found no trace of such emotion within me now.

This disquieted me. If my own hidden emotions—anger I did not acknowledge, repressed desire for one of the women, hidden hostility toward one of the others—had been wrested out of my mind to consume me, then it was a sign I had lost, under stress, my tower-imposed discipline. But those emotions, being mine, I could control. If they were not mine, but had come from elsewhere to fasten upon us, we were all in danger.

I said, "I'm more disturbed than ever about this matrix. The power's there, yes. But it's been used as a weapon. . . ."

"And it wants to destroy," Rafe said unexpectedly, "like the sword in the fairy tale; when you drew it, it would never go back into the scabbard until it had had its drink of blood."

I said soberly, "A lot of those old fairy tales were based on garbled memories of the Ages of Chaos. Maybe Rafe's right and it *does* want blood and destruction."

Thyra, her eyes brooding, asked, "Don't all men, just a little? History tells us they do. Darkovans and Terrans too."

Kadarin laughed. "You were brought up in the Comyn, Lew, so I'll forgive you for being superstitious." He put his arm around my shoulders in a warm hug. "I have more faith in the human mind than in forge-folk superstitions." We were still linked; again I felt the strength that lifted a great weight from my shoulders. I let myself lean against him. He was probably right. My mind had been filled from childhood with these old gods and powers. The science of matrix mechanics had been formulated to get rid of that. I was a skilled technician; why was I letting imagination run away with me?

Kadarin said, "Try again. Now that we know we *can* control it, it's all a matter of learning how."

"It's always up to the Keeper to decide that," I said. It troubled me that Marjorie still deferred to me. It was natural enough, for I had trained her, but she must learn that the initiative was hers, to lead, not follow.

She stretched her hand to me, setting up the primary line of force. One by one she brought us into the circle, each of us dropping into his appointed place as if we were scouts on a battlefield. This time I felt her touch Beltran, too, and *place* him so that he could maintain rapport just outside the circle. This time the force was easier to carry . . . *chained fire, electricity firmly stored in a battery, a firmly bridled racehorse.* . . . I saw the fire leap up around Marjorie, but this time I could see through it. It wasn't real, just a way of visualizing a force with no physical reality.

We stood linked, holding the pulsing power suspended. *If the Terrans will not give us what we need and deserve, we can force them to it, we need not fear their bombs nor their blasters. Do they think we are barbarians armed with swords and pitchforks?*

Clearly now, as the form of fire built up, I saw a woman, a sky-tall goddess clothed in flame, restlessly reaching to strike.

. . . *fire raining on Caer Donn, smashing the city into rubble, starships falling like comets out of the sky* . . .

Firmly Marjorie reached for control, like at one of those riding-exhibitions where a single rider controls four horses with one rein, bringing us back to the physical airfield. It shimmered around us, but it was there. The helicopter blades began to hum again, to turn with a clattering roar.

We need more power, more strength. For a moment I clearly saw my father's face, felt the strong line of rapport. He had awakened my gift; we were never wholly out of touch. I felt the amazement, the *fear* with which he felt the matrix touch him, momentarily draw him in. . . . He was gone. Had never been there. Then I felt Thyra reach out with a sure touch and draw Kermiac within the circle as if he had been physically present. For an instant the circle expanded with his strength, burning brilliantly, and the helicopter rose easily from the ground, hung there, quivering, rotors spinning with emphasis and force. I saw, I *felt* Kermiac crumple, withdraw. The lines of force went ragged . . . Kadarin and I locked hard together, supporting Marjorie as she controlled the wavering forces, lowering, lowering. . . . The helicopter bumped, hard, and the sound shattered the link. Pain crashed through me. Marjorie collapsed, sobbing. Beltran had seized Thyra by the shoulders, was shaking her like a dog shaking a rodent. He swung back his hand and slapped her full in the face. I felt—we all felt—the stinging pain of that blow.

"Vicious bitch! Damned she-devil," Beltran shouted. "How dare you, damn you, how dare you—"

Kadarin grabbed him, pulled him from Thyra by main force. Beltran was still fighting, struggling. Cold terror clutching at me, I reached out for Kermiac. *Uncle, have they killed you?* After a moment, sick with relief, I felt his presence, a thread of life, weak, collapsed, but alive. Alive, thank God!

Kadarin was still holding Beltran off Thyra; he let him go, flinging him violently to the ground. He said, raging, "Lay a hand on her again, Beltran, and I'll kill you with my own hands!" He hardly looked human at all now.

Marjorie was crying, trembling so violently I feared she would fall senseless. I caught and supported her. Thyra put a hand to her bruised face. She said, trying to be defiant, "What a fuss about nothing! He's stronger than any of us!"

My fear for Kermiac had turned to anger almost as great as Beltran's own. How dared Thyra do this against his will and Marjorie's judgment? I knew I couldn't trust her, damned sneaking bitch! I turned on her, still holding Marjorie with one arm; she shrank away as if from a blow. That shocked me back to my senses. Strike a woman? Slowly, lowering my head, I thrust the wadding around the matrix. This rage was ours. It was as dangerous as what Thyra did.

Marjorie could stand alone now. I put the matrix in her hand and went toward Thyra. I said, "I'm not going to hurt you, child. But what possessed you to do such a thing?" One of the strongest laws of every telepath was never to force another's will or judgment. . . .

The defiance was gone from her face. She fingered the cheek Beltran had struck. "Truly, Lew," she said, almost in a whisper, "I don't know. I felt we *needed* someone, and in days past this matrix had known the Aldarans, wanted Kermiac—no, that doesn't make sense, does it? And I felt that I could and I must because Marjorie wouldn't . . . I couldn't stop myself, I watched myself do it and I was afraid. . . ." She began to cry helplessly.

I stepped forward and took her into my arms, holding her against me, her face wet on my shoulder. I felt a shaking tenderness. We had all been helpless before that force. My own emotion should have warned me, but I was too distressed to feel alarm. The feel of her warm body in my arms should have warned me, too, at that stage, but I let her cling to me, sobbing, for a minute or two before I patted her shoulders tenderly, wiped her tears away and turned to help Beltran rise. He stood up stiffly, rubbing his hip. I sighed and said, "I know how you feel, Beltran. It was a dangerous thing to do. But you were in the wrong, too, losing your temper. A matrix technician must have control, must at all times."

Defiance and contrition warred in his face. He fumbled for words, I should have waited for them—I was responsible for this whole circle—but I felt too sick and drained to try. I said curtly, "Better see if any harm was done to the helicopter when it crashed."

"From three inches off the ground?" He sounded contemptuous now. That also troubled me but I was too tired to care. I said, "Suit yourself. It's your craft. If this is what comes of having you in the circle, I'll make damned sure you're a good long way away from it." I turned my back on him.

Marjorie was leaning on Rafe. She had stopped crying but her eyes and nose were red. Absurdly I loved her more than ever like that. She said in a small shaking voice, "I'm all right now, Lew. Honestly."

I looked at the ground at our feet. It was covered with more than an inch of snow. You always lost track of time inside a matrix. It was snowing harder than ever, and the sky was darkening. The shaking of my own hands warned me. I said, "We all need food and rest. Run ahead, Rafe, and ask the servants to have a meal ready for us."

I heard a familiar clattering roar and looked up. The other helicopter was circling overhead, descending. Beltran was walking away toward it. I started to call after him, summon him—he too would be drained, needing the replenishment of food and sleep. At that moment, though, my only thought was to let him collapse. It would do him good to learn this wasn't a game! We left him behind.

I'd have an apology to make to Kermiac, too. It didn't matter that it had been done against my orders. I was operating the matrix. I had trained this circle. I was responsible for everything that happened to it.

Everything.

Everything. Aldones, Lord of Light . . . everything: Ruin and death, a city in flames and chaos, Marjorie . . .

I shook myself out of the maelstrom of misery and pain, staring at the quiet path, the dark sky, the gently falling snow. None of it was real. I was hallucinating. Merciful Avarra, if, after three years at Arilinn, any matrix ever built could make *me* hallucinate, I was in trouble!

Kermiac's servants had laid a splendid meal for us, though I was so hungry I could as readily have eaten bread and milk. As I ate the drained weakness receded, but the vague, formless guilt remained. Marjorie. Had she been burned by the flare of fire? I kept wanting to touch her and make sure she was there, alive, unhurt. Thyra ate with tears running down her face, the bruise gradually swelling and darkening until her eye was swollen shut. Beltran did not come. I supposed he was with Kermiac. I didn't give a damn where he was. Marjorie self-consciously thrust aside her third plateful, saying, "I'm ashamed to be so greedy!"

I began to reassure her. Kadarin did it instead. "Eat, child, eat, your nerves are exhausted, you need the energy. Rafe, what's the matter, child?" The boy was restlessly pushing his food around on his plate. "You haven't touched a bite."

"I can't, Bob. My head aches. I can't swallow. If I try to swallow anything I'm afraid I'll be sick."

Kadarin met my eyes. "I'll take care of him," he said. "I know what to do, I went through it when I was his age." He lifted Rafe in his arms and carried him, like a small child, out of the room. Thyra rose and went after them.

Left alone with Marjorie, I said, "You should rest, too, after all that."

She said in a very small voice, "I'm afraid to be alone. Don't leave me alone, Lew."

I didn't intend to, not until I was sure she was safe. A Keeper in training has stresses no other matrix mechanic suffers, and I was still responsible for her. Although emotional upheavals were common enough when first keying into one of the really big matrices, such frightful blowups as this between Beltran and Thyra were not common. Fortunately. No wonder we were all literally sick from it.

I had never seen Marjorie's room before. It was at the top of a small tower, isolated, reached by a winding stair, a wedge-shaped room with wide windows. In clear weather it would have looked out on tremendous mountain ranges. Now it was all a dismal gray, gloomy, with hard beating snow rattling and whining against the glass. Marjorie slipped off her outdoor boots and knelt by the window, looking into the storm. "It's lucky we came in when we did. I've known the snow to come up so quickly you can lose your way a hundred paces from your own doorway. Lew, will Rafe be all right?"

"Of course. Just stress, maybe a touch of threshold sickness. Beltran's tantrum didn't help any, but it won't last long." Once a telepath gained full control of his matrix, and to do this he must have mastered the nerve channels, recurrences of threshold sickness were not serious. Rafe was probably feeling rotten, but it wouldn't last.

Marjorie leaned against the window, pressing her temples to the cold glass. "My head aches."

"Damn Beltran anyway!" I said, with violence that surprised me.

"It was Thyra's fault, Lew. Not his."

"What Thyra did is Thyra's responsibility, but Beltran must bear the responsibility for losing control, too."

My mind slid back to that strange interval within the matrix—whether it had been a few seconds or an hour I had no way of knowing—when I had sensed my father's presence. It occurred to me to wonder if at any of the towers, Hali or Arilinn or Neskaya, they had sensed the wakening of this enormous matrix, stirring to life. My father was an extraordinary telepath; he had served in Arilinn under the last of the old-style Keepers. He must have felt Sharra's wakening.

Did he know what we were doing?

As if following my thoughts Marjorie said, "Lew, what is your father like? My guardian has always spoken well of him."

"I don't want to talk about my father, Marjorie." But my barriers had been breached and that furious parting came back to me, with all the old bitterness. *He had been willing to kill me, to have his own way. He cared no more for me than a . . .*

Marjorie said in a low voice, "You're wrong, Lew. Your father loved you. Loves you. No, I'm not reading your mind. You were . . . broadcasting. But you are a loving person, a gentle person. To be so loving, you must have been loved. Greatly loved."

I bent my head. Indeed, indeed, all those years I had been so secure in his love, he could never have lived a lie. Not to me. We had been open to one another. Yet somehow that made it worse *Loving me, to risk me so ruthlessly . . .*

She whispered, "I know you, Lew. You could not have lived—would you have wanted to be without *laran*? Without the full potential of your gift? He knew your life wouldn't have been worth living without it. Blind, deaf, crippled . . . so he let you risk it. To become what he knew you *were*."

I laid my head on her knees, blind with pain. She had given me back something I never knew I had lost; she had returned to me the security of my father's love. I couldn't look up, couldn't let her see my face was contorted, that I was crying like a child. She knew anyway. I supposed this was my form of throwing a tantrum. Thyra disobeyed orders. Rafe got threshold sickness, Kadarin and Beltran started slamming each other . . . I started crying like a child. . . .

After a time I lifted her hand and kissed the slender fingertips. She looked worn and exhausted. I said, "You must rest too, darling." I was deeply proud of the skill with which she had seized control. She lay back against her pillows. I bent and, as I would have done at Arilinn, ran my fingertips lightly along her body. Not touching her, of course, simply feeling out the energy flows, monitoring the nerve centers. She lay quietly, smiling at the touch that was not a touch. I felt that she was still depleted, drained of energy, but that would not last. The channels were clear. I was glad she had come through this strenuous beginning so well, so undamaged.

I was not, at the moment, actively suffering because she was forbidden to me, that even a kiss would have been unthinkable. I was remotely aware of her but there was no sexual element in it. I simply felt an intense and overwhelming love such as I had never known for anyone alive. I didn't have to speak of it. I knew she shared it.

If I couldn't have reached Marjorie's mind I'd have gone mad with wanting her, needing her with every nerve in me. But we had this, and it was enough. Almost enough, and we had the promise of the rest.

I knew the answer, but I wanted to say the words aloud. "When this is over, you will marry me, Marjorie?"

She said, with a simplicity that made my heart turn over, "I want to. But will the Comyn let you?"

"I won't ask them. By then the Comyn may have learned it's not for them to arrange everyone's life!"

"I wouldn't want to make trouble, Lew. Marriage doesn't mean that much to me."

"It does to *me,*" I said fiercely. "Do you think I want our children to be bastards? I want them at Armida after me, without the struggle my father had to get it for me. . . ."

Her laugh was adorable. Quickly, she sobered. "Lew, Lew, I'm not laughing at *you,* darling. Only it makes me so happy, to think that it means all this to you—not just wanting me, but thinking of all that will come afterward, our children, our children's children, a household to stand into the future. Yes, Lew. I want to have your children, I'm sorry we have to wait so long for them. Yes, I'll marry you if you want me to, in the Comyn if they'll have it, if not, then any way we can, any way you choose." For a moment, a feather-touch, she laid her lips against the back of my hand.

My heart was so full I could bear no more. I had desired women before, but never with this wholeness, going far beyond any moment of desire, stretching into the future, all our lives. For a moment time went out of focus again . . .

. . . I was kneeling beside the cot of a little girl, five or six perhaps, a tiny child with a heart-shaped face and wide eyes fenced in long lashes, golden eyes just the color of Marjorie's . . . I felt a strange wonder, pain in my right hand, *dismayed, torn with anguish* . . .

Marjorie whispered, "What is it, Lew?"

"A flash of precognition," I said, coming back to myself, strangely shaken. "I saw—I saw a little girl. With your eyes." But why had I felt so bewildered, so agonized? I tried to see it again, but as these flashes come unbidden, so they can never be recalled. I felt Marjorie's thoughts, and hers were wholly joyful: *It will be all right then. We will be together as we wish, we will see that child.* Her lashes were dropping shut with weariness and, kneeling beside her, I looked into her face again. She thought drowsily, *We should have a son first,* and I knew she had seen the child's face in my mind. She smiled with pure happiness and her lids slipped shut. Her hand tightened on my own.

"Don't leave me," she whispered, half asleep.

"Never. Sleep, beloved." I stretched out beside her, holding her fingers in mine, my love encircling her sleep. After a moment, I slept too, in the deepest happiness I had ever known.

Or was ever to know again.

It was dark when I woke, the snow still rattling the windows. Kadarin was standing above us, holding a light. Marjorie was still deeply asleep. His glance at her was filled with a deep tenderness that warmed me to him as nothing else could have done.

And then, for a moment, I felt his face wrenched, contorted with rage . . . It was gone. He said softly, "Beltran sent to ask if you would come down. Let Margie sleep if you like, she's very tired."

I slid from the bed. She stirred, made a faint protesting noise—I thought she had murmured my name. I covered her gently with a shawl, picked up my boots in my hand and noiselessly went out, feeling her sink back into deep sleep.

"Rafe?"

"He's fine. I gave him a few drops of *kirian,* got him to drink some hot milk and honey, left him asleep." Kadarin wore his sad, tender smile on his face. "I've been looking for you everywhere. After all your warnings, I never expected—it was Thyra who suggested you might be with Marjorie." He laughed. "But I hadn't expected to find you in her bed!"

I said stiffly, "I assure you—"

"Lew, in the name of all the damned obscene gods of the Dry-Towners, do you think it matters a damn to me?" He was laughing again. "Oh, I believe you, you're just scrupulous enough, and bound hand and foot with your own idiot superstitions! I think you're putting a considerable strain on human nature, myself—I wouldn't trust myself to lie down with a woman I loved and never touch her—but if you happen to enjoy self-torture, that's your own choice. As the Dry-Towner said to the *cralmac* . . ." And he launched into a long, good-humored and incredibly obscene tale which took my mind off my embarrassment as nothing else could have. Not a word of it was suitable for repeating in polite company, but it was exactly what the situation demanded.

When we reached the fireside room, he said, "You heard the helicopter land this afternoon?"

I was still chuckling at the adventures of the Dry-Towner, the spaceman and the three nonhumans; the sudden gravity of his voice shocked me back to normal.

"I saw it, yes. Has it to do with me?"

"A special guest," Kadarin said. "Beltran feels you should speak with him. You told us he is a catalyst telepath with no reason to love the Comyn, and Beltran sent to persuade him—"

Seated on one of the stone benches near the fire, his dark hair awry, looking cold and ruffled and angry, was Danilo Syrtis. Beltran said, "Perhaps you can explain that we mean no harm, that he is not a prisoner, but an honored guest."

Danilo tried to sound defiant, but despite his best efforts I could hear that his voice was shaking. "You carried me off with armed men and my father will be ill with fright! Is this how you mountain men welcome guests, taking them away in infernal Terran machines?" He looked no older than Rafe.

I called "Danilo—" and his mouth dropped open. He sprang up. "They told me you were here, but I thought it was just another of their lies." The childish face hardened. "Was it by your orders they had me kidnapped? How long will the Comyn persecute me?"

I shook my head. "Not my orders, nor Comyn. Until this moment I had no idea you were here."

He turned on Beltran in childish triumph. His voice, still unbroken, sounded shrill. "I knew you were lying, when you told me Lew Alton ordered me brought here—"

I swung toward Beltran and said in real anger, "I told you Danilo might be *persuaded* to join us! Did you take that as license to kidnap him?" I held out both hands to the boy and said, "Dani, forgive me. It is true I told them of you and your *laran;* I suggested that one day they might seek you out and persuade you to join us in what we are doing." His hands felt cold. He had been badly frightened. "Don't be afraid. I swear on my honor, no one will hurt you."

"I am not *afraid* of such rabble," he said scornfully, and I saw Beltran wince. Well, if he was going to behave like some Brynat Scarface or Cyrillon des Trailles, he must expect to be called uncomplimentary names! Danilo added, his voice shaking, "My father is old and feeble. He has already suffered my disgrace. Now to lose me again . . . he will surely grieve himself to death."

I said to Beltran, "You fool, you utter fool! Send a message at once, send it through the Terran relays if you must, that Danilo is alive and well, and that someone must inform his family that he is here, an honored guest! Do you want a friend and ally, or a mortal enemy?"

He had the grace to look ashamed. He said, "I gave no orders to hurt or frighten him or his father. Did anyone lay rough hands on either of you, lad?"

"I was certainly issued no polite invitation, Lord Aldaran. Do you disarm all your honored guests?"

I said, "Go and send that message, Beltran. Let me talk to him alone." Beltran went and I mended the fire, leaving Danilo to recover his composure. At last I asked, "Tell me the truth, Danilo, have you been ill-treated?"

"No, though they were not gentle. We were some days riding, then the sky-machine. I do not know its name. . . ."

The helicopter. I had seen it land. I knew I should have gone after Beltran. If I had been there when Danilo was brought from it—well, it was done. I said, "A helicopter is safer, in the peaks and crossdrafts of the Hellers, than any ordinary plane. Were you very frightened?"

"Only for a little, when we were forced down by weather. Mostly I feared for my father."

"Well, a message will be sent. Have you had anything to eat?"

"They offered me something when we first landed," he said. He did not say he had been too shaken and frightened to eat, but I surmised that. I called a servant and said, "Ask my uncle to excuse me from his table, and say that Lord Beltran will explain. Then send some food here for my guest and myself." I turned back to the boy. "Dani, am I your enemy?"

"Captain, I—"

"I've left the Guards," I said. "Not captain, now."

To my amazement he said, "Too bad. You were the only officer everybody liked. No, you're not my enemy, Lew, and I always thought your father was my friend. It was Lord Dyan—you *do* know what happened?"

"More or less," I said. "Whatever it may have been this time, I know damn well that by the time you drew your dagger he'd given you enough provocation for a dozen duels anywhere else. You don't have to tell me all the nasty little details. I know Dyan."

"Why did the Commander—"

"They were children together," I said. "In his eyes Dyan can do no wrong. I'm not defending him, but didn't you ever do anything you thought was wrong, for a friend's sake?"

"Did you?" he asked. I was still trying to think how to answer when our supper was brought. I served Dani, but found I was not hungry and sat nibbling at some fruit while the boy satisfied his appetite. I wondered if they had fed him at all since his capture. No, boys that age were always hungry, that was all.

While he ate I worried what Marjorie would think when she woke and found herself alone. Was Rafe really all right, or should I go and make certain? Had Kermiac suffered any lasting ill-effects from Thyra's rashness? I didn't approve of what Beltran had done, but I knew why he had been tempted to do it. We needed someone like Danilo so badly that it terrified me.

I poured Dani a glass of wine when he had finished. He merely tasted it for courtesy's sake, but at least now he was willing to go through the motions of courtesy again. I took a sip of mine and set it aside.

"Danilo, you know you have *laran*. You also have one of the rarest and most precious Comyn gifts, one we've thought extinct. If Comyn Council finds out, they'll be ready and willing to make all kinds of amends for the stupid and cruel thing Dyan did to you. They'll offer you anything you want, up to and including a seat in Comyn Council if you want that, marriage with someone like Linnell Aillard—you name it, you can probably have it. You attended that Council meeting among the Terrans. Are you interested in power of that sort? If so, they'll be lining up two and three deep to offer it to you. Is that what you want?"

"I don't know," he said, "I never thought about it. I expected, after I finished in the cadets, to stay quietly at home and look after my father while he lived."

"And then?"

"I hadn't thought about that either. I suppose I thought when that time came, I'd be grown up, and then I'd know what I wanted."

I smiled wryly. Yes, at fifteen I too had been sure that by the time I was twenty or so my life would have arranged itself in simple patterns.

"That's not the way it happens when you have *laran*," I said. "Among other things, you must be trained. An untrained telepath is a menace to himself and everyone around him."

He made a grimace of revulsion. "I've never wanted to be a matrix technician."

"Probably not," I said. "It takes a certain temperament." I couldn't see Danilo in a tower; I, on the other hand, had never wanted anything else. I still didn't. "Even so, you must learn to control what you are and what gifts you have. All too many untrained telepaths end up as madmen."

"Then whether I'm interested in Comyn Council or not, what choice do I have? Isn't this training only in the hands of the Comyn and the towers? And they can train me to do whatever they want me to do."

"That's true in the Domains," I said. "They do draw all telepaths to their service there. But you still have a choice." I began to tell him about Beltran's plan, and a little about the work we had begun.

He listened without comment until I had finished. "Then," he said, "it seems I have a choice between taking bribes for the use of my *laran* from the Comyn—or from Aldaran."

"I wouldn't put it that way. We're asking you to come into this of your own free will. If we do achieve what we want, then the Comyn will no longer have the power to demand that all telepaths serve them or be left prey to madness. And there would be an end to the kind of power-hunger that left you at the mercy of a man like Dyan."

He thought that over, sipping the wine again and making a childish wry face. Then he said, "It seems as if something like that's always going to be happening to people like me, like us. Someone's always going to be bribing us to use our gifts for their good, not our own." He sounded terribly young, terribly bitter.

"No, some of us may have a choice now. Once we are a legitimate part of the Terran Empire—"

"Then I suppose the Empire will find some way to use us," Danilo said. "The Comyn makes mistakes, but don't they know more about us and our world than the Terrans ever could?"

"I'm not sure," I said. "Are you willing to see them stay in power, controlling all our lives, putting corrupt men like Dyan in charge—"

"No, I'm not," he said, "nobody would want that. But if people like you and me—you said I could have a seat on the Council if I wanted it—if people like you and me were on the Council, the bad ones like Dyan wouldn't have everything their own way, would they? Your father's a good man but, like you said, Dyan can do no wrong in his eyes. But when *you* take a seat on the Council, you won't feel that way, will you?"

"What I want," I said with concealed violence, "is *not*

to be forced to take a seat on the Council, or do all the other damned things the Comyn wants me to do!"

"If good men like you can't be bothered," said Danilo, "then who's left, except the bad ones who *shouldn't*?"

There was some truth in that, too. But I said vehemently, "I have other skills and I feel I can serve my people better in other ways. That's what I'm trying to do now, to benefit everyone on Darkover. I'm not trying to smash the Comyn, Dani, only to give everyone more of a choice. Don't you think it's an ambition worth achieving?"

He looked helpless. "I can't judge," he said. "I'm not even used to thinking of myself as a telepath yet. I don't know what I ought to do."

He looked up at me with that odd, trustful look which made me think somehow, of my brother Marius. If it were Marius standing here before me, gifted with *laran,* would I try to persuade him to face Sharra? A cold chill iced my spine and I shivered, even though the room was warm. I said, "Can you trust me, then?"

"I'd like to," he said. "You never lied to me or hurt me. But I don't think I'd trust any of the Aldarans."

"Is your mind still full of schoolroom bogeymen?" I asked. "Do you believe they are all wicked renegades because they have an old political quarrel with Comyn? You have reason to distrust the Comyn too, Danilo."

"True," he said. "But can I trust a man who begins by kidnapping me and frightening my father to death? If he had come to me, explained what he wanted to do, and that you and he together thought my gift could be useful, then asked my father to give me leave to visit him . . ."

The hell of it was, Dani was entirely right. What had possessed Beltran to do such a thing? "If he had consulted me, that is exactly how I would have suggested he should do it."

"Yes, I know," Dani said. "You're *you.* But if Beltran isn't the kind of man to do it that way, how can you trust him?"

"He's my kinsman," I said helplessly. "What do you expect me to say? I expect his eagerness got the better of him. He didn't hurt you, did he?"

Dani raged. "You're talking just the way you said your father did about Lord Dyan!"

It wasn't the same, I knew that, but I couldn't expect Danilo to see it. Finally I said, "Can't you look beyond personalities in this, Dani? Beltran was wrong, but what we're trying to do is so enormous that maybe it blinds people to smaller aims and ends. Keep your eyes on what he's doing, and forgive him. Or are you waiting," and I spoke deliberately, with malice, to make him see how cynical it sounded, "for the Comyn to make a better offer?"

He flushed, stung to the depths. I hadn't overestimated either his intelligence or his sensitivity. He was a boy still, but the man would be well worth knowing, with strong integrity and honor. I hoped with all my heart he would be our ally.

"Danilo," I said, "we need you. The Comyn cast you out in disgrace, undeserved. What loyalty do you owe them?"

"The Comyn, nothing," he said quietly. "Yet I am pledged and my service given. Even if I wanted to do what you ask, Lew, and I'm not sure, I am not free."

"What do you mean?"

Danilo's face was impassive, but I could sense the emotion behind his words. "Regis Hastur sought me out at Syrtis," he said. "He did not know how or why, but he knew I had been wronged. He pledged himself to set it right."

"We're trying to set many wrongs right, Dani. Not just yours."

"Maybe," he said. "But we swore an oath together and I pledged him my sword and my service. I am his paxman, Lew, so if you want me to help you, you must ask *his* consent. If my lord gives me leave, then I am at your service. Otherwise I am his man: I have sworn."

I looked at the solemn young face and knew there was nothing I could say to that. I felt a quite irrational anger at Regis because he had forestalled me here. For a moment I wrestled with strong temptation. I could make him see it my way . . .

I recoiled in horror and shame at my own thoughts. The first pledge I had sworn at Arilinn was this: never, never force the will or conscience of another, even for his own good. I could persuade. I could plead. I could use reason, emotion, logic, rhetoric. I could even seek out Regis and beg him for his consent; he too had reason to be disaffected, to rebel against the corruption in the Comyn. But further than this I could not go. I could *not.* That I had even thought of it made me feel a little sick.

"I may indeed ask Regis for your aid, Dani," I said quietly. "He too is my friend. But I will never force you. I am not Dyan Ardais!"

That made him smile a little. "I never thought you were, Lew. And if my lord gives me leave, then I will trust him, and you. But until that time shall come, Dom Lewis"—he gave me my title very formally, though we had been using the familiar mode before this—"have I your permission to depart and return to my father?"

I gestured at the snow, a white torrent whipping the windows, sending little spits of sleet down the chimney. "In *this,* lad? Let me at least offer you the hospitality of my kinsman's roof until the weather suits! Then you shall be given proper escort and company out of these mountains. You cannot expect me to set you adrift in these mountains, at night and in winter, with a storm blowing up?" I summoned a servant again, and requested that he provide proper lodging for a guest, near my own quarters. Before Danilo went away to his bed, I gave him a kinsman's embrace, which he returned with a childlike friendliness that made me feel better.

But I was still deeply troubled. Damn it, I'd have a word with Beltran before I slept!

CHAPTER SEVENTEEN

Regis rode slowly, head down against the biting wind. He told himself that if he ever got out of these mountains, no place on Darkover would ever seem cold to him again.

A few days ago he had stopped in a mountain village and traded his horse for one of the sturdy little mountain ponies. He felt a sort of despairing grief at the necessity—the black mare was Kennard's gift and he loved her—but this one attracted less attention and was surer-footed along the terrible trails. Poor Melisande would surely have died of the cold or broken a leg on these steep paths.

The trip had been a long nightmare: steep unfamiliar trails, intense cold, sheltering at night in abandoned barns or shepherd's huts or wrapped in cloak and blanket against a rock wall, close curled against the horse's body. He tried in general to avoid being seen, but every few days he had gone into a village to bargain for food and fodder for his pony. He aroused little curiosity; he thought life must be so hard in these mountains that the people had no time for curiosity about travelers.

Now and again, when he feared losing his way, he had drawn out the matrix, trying by furious concentration to fix his attention on Danilo. The matrix acted like one of those Terran instruments Kennard had once told him about, guiding him, with an insistent subliminal pull, toward Aldaran and Danilo.

By now he was numbed to fear, and only determination kept him going, that, and the memory of his pledge to Dani's father. But there were times when he rode in a dark dream, losing awareness of Danilo and the roads where he was. Images would spin in his mind, which seemed to drink up pictures and thoughts from the villages he passed. The thought of looking again into the matrix filled him with such a crawling sickness that he could not force himself to draw it out. Threshold sickness again. Javanne had warned him. At the last few villages he had simply inquired the road to Aldaran.

All the morning he had been riding up a long slope where forest fires had raged a few seasons ago. He could see miles of scorched and blackened hillside, ragged stumps sticking up gaunt and leafless through the gullied wasteland. In his hypersuggestible state the stink of burned woods, ashes and soot swirling up every time his pony put a hoof down, brought him back to that last summer at Armida and his first turn on the fire-lines, the night the fire came so close to Armida that the outbuildings burned.

That evening he and Lew had eaten out of the same bowl because supplies were running short. When they had lain down the stink of ashes and burned wood was all around them. Regis had smelled it even in his sleep, the way he was smelling it now. Toward midnight something woke him, and he had seen Lew sitting bolt upright, staring at the red glow where the fire was.

And Regis had known Lew was afraid. He'd touched Lew's mind, and *felt* it: his fear, the pain of his burns, everything. He could feel it as if it had been in his own mind. And Lew's fear hurt so much that Regis couldn't stand it. He would have done anything to comfort Lew, to take his mind off the pain and the fear. It had been too much. Regis couldn't shut it out, couldn't stand it.

But he had forgotten. Had made himself forget, till now. He had blocked away the memory until, later that year, when he was tested for *laran* at Nevarsin, he had not even remembered anything but the fire.

And that, he realized, was why Lew was surprised when Regis told him he did not have *laran*. . . .

The mountain pony stumbled and went down. Regis scrambled to his feet, shaken but unhurt, taking the beast by the bridle and gently urging him to his feet. He ran his hand up and down the animal's legs. No bones were broken, but the pony flinched when Regis touched his rear right hock. He was limping, and Regis knew the pony could not bear his weight for a while. He led him along the trail as they crested the pass. The downward trail was even steeper, black and mucky underfoot where recent rains had soaked the remnants of the fire., The stench in his nostrils was worse than ever, restimulating again the memories of the earlier fire and the shared fear. He kept asking himself why he forgot, why he made himself forget.

The sun was hidden behind thick clouds. A few drifting snowflakes, not many but relentless, began to fall as he went down toward the valley. He guessed it was about midday. He felt a little hungry, but not enough to stop and dig into his pack and get out something to eat.

He hadn't been eating much lately. The villagers had been kind to him, often refusing to take payment for food, which was tasty, though unfamiliar. He was usually on the edge of nausea, though, unwilling to start up that reflex again by actually chewing and swallowing something. Hunger was less painful.

After a time he did dig some grain out of his pack for the horse. The trail was well-traveled now; there must be another village not far away. But the silence was disturbing. Not a dog barked, no wild bird or beast cried. There was no sound but his own footsteps and the halting rhythm of the lame pony's steps. And far above, the unending wind moaning in the gaunt snags of the dead forest.

It was too much solitude. Even the presence of a bodyguard would have been welcome now, or two, chatting about the small chances of the trail. He remembered riding in the hills around Armida with Lew, hunting or checking the herdsmen who cared for the horses out in the open uplands. Suddenly, as if the thought of Lew had brought him to mind again, Lew's face was before him, lighted with a glow—not forest fire now! It was aglow, blazing in a great blue glare, space-twisting, gut-wrenching, the glare of the matrix! The ground was reeling and dipping under his feet, but for a moment, even as Regis dropped the pony's reins and clapped his hands over his tormented eyes, he saw a great form sketch itself on the inside of his eyelids, inside his very brain.

. . . *a woman, a golden goddess, flame-clothes, flame-crowned, golden-chained, burning, glowing, blazing, consuming* . . .

Then he lost consciousness. Over his head the mountain pony edged carefully around, uneasily nuzzling at the unconscious lad.

It was the pony's nuzzling that woke him, some time later. The sky was darkening, and it was snowing so hard that when he got stiffly to his feet, a little cascade of snow showered off him. A faint sickening smell told him that he had vomited as he lay senseless. *What in Zandru's hells happened to me?*

He dug his water bottle from his saddlebag, rinsed his mouth and drank a little, but was still too queasy to swallow much.

It was snowing so hard that he knew he must find shelter at once. He had been trained at Nevarsin to find shelter in unlikely places, even a heap of underbrush would do, but on a road as well-traveled as this there were sure to be huts, barns, shelters. He was not mistaken. A few hundred feet further on, the outline of a great stone barn made a dark square against the swirling whiteness. The stones were blackened with the fire that had swept over it and a few of the roof slates had fallen in, but someone had replaced the door with rough-hewn planking. Drifted ice and snow from the last storm was banked against the door, but he knew that in mountain country doors were usually left unfastened against just such emergencies. After much struggling and heaving Regis managed to shove the rough door partway open and wedge himself and the pony through into a gloomy and musty darkness. It had once been a fodder-storage barn; there were still a few rodent-nibbled bales lying forgotten against the walls. It was bitterly cold, but at least it was out of the wind. Regis unsaddled his pony, fed him and hobbled him loosely at one end of the barn. Then he raked some more of the moldy fodder together, laid his blankets out on it, crawled into them and let sleep, or unconsciousness, take him again.

This long sleep was more like shock, or suspended animation, than any normal sleep. Regis could not know it was the mental and physical reaction of a telepath in crisis. Now it only seemed that he wandered for eternities—certainly for days—in restless nightmares. At times he seemed to leave his aching body behind and wander in gray formless space, shouting helplessly and knowing he had no voice. Once or twice, coming up to dim semiconsciousness, he found his face wet and knew he had been crying in his sleep. Time disappeared. He wandered in what he only dimly knew was the past or the future: now in the dormitories of Nevarsin where the memory of cold, loneliness and an aching frustration held him aloof, frightened, friendless;

now by the fireside at Armida, then bending with Lew and an unknown fair-haired girl over the bedside of an apparently dying child, again wandering through thick forests while strange aliens, red-eyed, peered at them through the trees.

Again he was fighting with knives along a narrow ledge, the ragged red-eyed aliens thrusting at him, trying to kick him off. He sat in the Council chamber and heard Terrans arguing; in the Guard hall of Comyn Castle he saw Danilo's sword breaking with that terrible sound of shattering glass. He was looking down with a sense of aching tragedy at two small children, pale and lifeless, lying side by side in their coffins, dead by treachery, so young, so young, and knew they were his own. Again he stood in the armory, numb and shamed into immobility while Dyan's hands ran along his bare bruised body, and then he and Danilo were standing by a fountain in the plaza at Thendara, only Danilo was taller and bearded, drinking from wooden tankards and laughing while girls threw festival garlands down from windows above them.

After a time he began to filter these random awarenesses more critically. He saw Lew and Danilo standing by a fireplace in a room with a mosaic pattern of white birds on the floor, talking earnestly, and he felt insanely jealous. Then it seemed as if Kennard was calling his name in the gray dim spaces, and he could see Kennard drifting far off in the dimness. Only Kennard was not lame now, but young and straight-backed and smiling as Regis could hardly remember him. He was calling, with a mounting sense of urgency, *Regis, Regis, where are you? Don't hide from me! We have to find you!* All Regis could make of this was that he had left the Guards without leave and the Commander wanted to have him brought back and punished. He knew he could make himself invisible here in these gray spaces, so he did, running from the voice full speed over a gray and featureless plain, though by this time he was perfectly well aware that he was lying half-conscious in the abandoned fodder-barn. And then he saw Dyan in the gray spaces, only Dyan as a boy his own age. Somehow he dimly realized that, in this gray world where bodies did not come but only minds, every man appeared as he saw himself in his own mind, so of course Kennard looked well and young.

Dyan was saying, *I can't find him, Kennard, he is nowhere in the overworld,* and Regis felt himself laughing inside and saying, *I'm here but I don't have to let you see me here.* Then Kennard and Dyan were standing close together, their hands joined, and he knew that together they were seeking him out. Their faces and figures disappeared, they were only eyes in the grayness, seeking, seeking. He knew he must leave the gray world or they would find him now. Where could he go? He didn't want to go back! He could see Danilo in the distance, then they were both back in the dark barracks room—that night!—and he was bending over his friend, touching him with aching solicitude. And then that terrible, strained whisper, the shock more mental than physical as he thrust him away: *Come near me again, you filthy* ombredin, *and I'll break your neck . . .*

But I was only trying to reach him, help him. Wasn't I? Wasn't I? And with a shuddering gasp Regis sat up, fully awake at last, staring into the dim light that filtered through a broken roof-slate above him. He was shaking from head to foot and his body ached as if he had been battered and beaten. He was completely conscious, though, and his mind was clear. At the far end of the barn the pony was stamping restlessly. Slowly, Regis got to his feet, wondering how long he had been there.

Far too long. The pony had eaten every scrap of the ample fodder and nosed the floor clear of chaff as far as he could reach.

Regis went to the door and swung it open. It had stopped snowing long since. The sun was out, and melted snow dripped in runnels from the roof. Regis was aware of a raging thirst, but like all lifelong horsemen he thought first of his pony. He led the horse to the door and released him; after a moment the pony made off, deliberately, around the corner to the rear of the building. Regis followed, finding an old well there, covered against the snow, with a workable though creaky and leaking bucket assembly. He watered the pony and drank deeply, then, shivering, stripped off his clothes. He was grateful for the austere discipline of Nevarsin, which made it possible for him to wash in the icy water of the well. His clothes smelled of sweat and sickness; he got fresh ones from his pack. Shivering, but feeling immensely better, he sat down on the well-side and chewed dried fruit. Cold as he was, the interior of the building seemed to reek of his nightmares and echo with the voices he had heard in his delirium, if it had all been delirium. What else could it have been?

Moving slowly until he knew he could rely on his body to do what he told it, he saddled the pony again and collected his belongings. He must be nearing the Aldaran lands now and there was no time to lose.

The snow had drenched the smell of forest fire and he was glad. He had not ridden more than an hour or two when he heard the sound of approaching horses and drew aside to let them pass. Instead they confronted him, blocking the road, demanding his name and business.

He said, "I am Regis-Rafael Hastur, and I am on my way to Castle Aldaran."

"And I," the leader, a big swarthy mountain man, said in a mincing voice that mocked Regis' careful *casta* accent, "am the Terran Legate from Port Chicago, Well, whoever you are, you'll go to Aldaran, and damn quick, too."

It had evidently been nearer than Regis believed; as they reached the top of the next hill he saw the castle, and beyond it the city of Caer Donn and the white Terran buildings.

Now that he was actually within sight of Aldaran his old fears returned. No man knew—or if they did it was the best kept secret on Darkover—why Aldaran had been exiled from the Seven Domains.

They couldn't be that bad, Regis thought. Kennard had married into their kin. And if they were once of the Seven Domains, they too must be of the sacred lineage of Hastur and Cassilda. And why should a Hastur fear his kindred? He asked himself this as he rode through the great gates. Yet he was afraid.

Mountain men dressed in curiously cut leather cloaks took their horses. One of the guards led Regis into a hall, where he talked at length with another guard, then finally said, "We'll take you to Lord Aldaran, but if you're not who you claim you are, you'd better plan on spending the rest of the day in the brig. The old lord is ill, and none of us takes kindly to the notion of bothering him with an impostor!"

They conducted him through long stone corridors and

along flights of stairs, pausing at last outside a great door. From inside they could hear voices, one low and indistinguishable, the other a harsh old man's voice, protesting angrily:

"Zandru's hells! *Kirian,* at my age! As if I were a schoolboy—oh, very well, very well! But what you are doing is dangerous if it can have side effects like this, and I want to know more—a great deal more—before I let it go on!"

The guards exchanged glances over Regis' head; one of them knocked lightly and someone told them to come in.

It was a large, high-arched stone chamber, gray with the outdoor light. At the far end, a thin old man lay in a raised bed, propped on many pillows. He glared at them in angry question. "What's this now? What's this?"

"An intruder on the borders, Lord Aldaran, maybe a spy from the Domains."

"Why, he's just a boy," the old man said. "Come here, child." The guards thrust Regis forward, and the old eyes focused, hawk-keen, on him. Then he smiled, an odd amused smile.

"Humph! No need to ask *your* name! If ever a man wore his lineage on his face! You might be Rafael's son. I thought his heir was still in the schoolroom, though. Which one are you, then, some *nedestro* or old Danvan's bastard, maybe?"

Regis lifted his chin. "I am Regis-Rafael Hastur of Hastur!"

"Then in hell's name," said the old man testily, "what were you doing sneaking around the borders alone? Where is your escort? The heir of Hastur should have ridden up to the front gates, properly escorted, and asked to see me. I've never refused a welcome to anyone who comes here in peace! Do you think this is still a bandit fortress?"

Regis felt stung, all the more because he knew the old man was right. "My Lord, I felt there might be warfare of which I had been told nothing. If there is peace between us, what have you done with my sworn man?"

"*I,* young Hastur? I know of no man of yours. Who?"

"My paxman and my friend, Danilo Syrtis. He was taken by armed men, in the hills near his home, men bearing your ensign, my lord."

Aldaran's face narrowed in a frown. He glanced at the

tall thin man in Terran clothing who stood near the head of the bed. He said, "Bob, do you know anything at all about this matter? You usually know what Beltran's up to. What's he been doing while I've been lying here sick?"

The man raised his head and looked at Regis. He said, "Danilo Syrtis is here and unharmed, young Hastur. Beltran's men only exceeded their orders; they were told to invite him here with all courtesy. And we were told he had no reason to love the Comyn; how should we know he was your sworn man?" Regis felt unspoken contempt, *And why should we give a damn?* But Kadarin's words were rigidly polite. "He is unharmed, an honored guest."

"I'll have a word with Beltran," Kermiac of Aldaran said. "This isn't the first time his enthusiasm has carried him away. I'm sorry, young Hastur, I didn't know we had anyone of yours here. Kadarin, take him to his friend."

So it was as simple as that? Regis felt vague disquiet. Kadarin said, "There's no need for such haste. Lew Alton talked to the Syrtis boy for hours last night, I'm sure he knows now that he's not a prisoner. Lord Regis, would you like to speak with your kinsman?"

"Is Lew still here? Yes, I would like to see him."

Kermiac looked at Regis' travel-stained garments. He said, "But this is a long journey alone for a boy. You are exhausted. Let us take you to a guest chamber, offer you some refreshment—a meal, a bath—"

Both of them sounded almost unendurably attractive, but Regis shook his head. "Truly, I need nothing now. I am deeply concerned about my friend."

"As you wish, then, lad." He held out a withered old hand, seeming to have trouble moving as he wished. "Damned if I'm going to call a boy your age lord anything! That's half what's wrong with our world!"

Regis bent over it as he would have done over his grandfather's. "If I have misjudged you, Lord Aldaran, I implore your pardon. Let anxiety for my paxman be my excuse."

"Humph," Aldaran said again, "it seems to me that we of Aldaran owe you some apology as well, my boy. Bob, send Beltran to me—at once!"

"Uncle, he is very much occupied with—"

"I don't give a damn what he's occupied with, bring him!

And fast!" He released Regis' hand, saying, "I'll see you again soon, lad. You are my guest, remain here in peace, be welcome."

Dismissed and ushered out of Aldaran's presence, Kadarin striding through the halls at his side, Regis felt more confused than ever. What was going on here? What had Lew Alton to do with this? It was warm in the hallway and he wished he had taken off his riding-cloak; he felt suddenly very tired and hungry. He had not had a hot meal, or slept in a bed, for more days than he could reckon, and during his sickness he had completely lost count.

Kadarin turned into a small room, saying, "I think Lew is here with Beltran." Regis blinked in astonishment, seeing, in the first moment, only the blazing fire, the floor inlaid with the mosaic of white birds! Fantasies spun in his mind. Danilo was not here, as in his dream, but Lew was standing near the fire, his back to Regis. He was looking down at a woman who had a small harp across her knees. She was playing and singing. Regis had heard the song at Nevarsin; it was immeasurably old, and had a dozen names and a dozen tunes:

How came this blood, on your right hand,
  Brother, tell me, tell me.
It is the blood of an old gray wolf
Who lurked behind a tree.

The song broke off in mid-chord; Lew turned, and looked at Regis in amazement.

"Regis!" he said, coming quickly toward the door. "What are you doing here?" He held out his arms to embrace him, then, seeing him clearly, took him by the shoulders, almost holding him upright. He said savagely, "If this is any more of Beltran's—"

Regis drew himself upright. He wanted to let himself collapse into Lew's arms, lean on him, break down with fatigue and long-drawn-out fear—but not before these strangers. "I came here in search of Danilo; Javanne saw in her crystal that he had been taken by men of Aldaran. Had you any hand in this?"

"God forbid," said Lew. "What do you think I am? It was a mistake, I assure you, only a mistake. Come and sit down, Regis. You look tired and ill. Bob, if he's been mishandled, I'll have someone's head for it!"

"No, no," said Kadarin. "Lord Kermiac welcomed him as his own guest, and sent him to you right away."

Regis let Lew lead him to the bench by the fire. The woman touched the harp again, in soft chords. Another woman, this one very young, with long straight red hair and a pretty, remote face, came and took his cloak, looking at him with bold eyes, straight at him. No girl in the Domains would look at him like that! He had an uncomfortable feeling that she knew what he was thinking and was greatly amused by it. Lew said the women's names but Regis was in no condition to pay attention. He was introduced to Beltran of Aldaran, too, who almost immediately left the room. Regis wished they would all go away. Lew sat beside him, saying, "How came you to ride this long road alone, Regis? Only for Danilo's sake?"

"I am sworn to him, we are *bredin,*" Regis said faintly. "He is truly unharmed, not a prisoner?"

"He is housed in luxury, an honored guest. You shall see him as soon as you like."

"But I do not understand all this, Lew. You came on a mission from Comyn, yet I find you here entangled in their affairs. What is this all about?" As soon as their hands touched they had fallen into rapport, and Regis found himself wondering, *Has Lew turned traitor to Comyn*? In answer Lew said quietly, "I am no traitor. But I have come to believe that perhaps service to Comyn and service to Darkover are not quite the same thing."

The woman had begun the song again, softly.

No wolf would prowl at this hour of the day,
  Brother, tell me, tell me!
It is the blood of my own brothers twain
Who sat at the drink with me.

How came ye fight with your own blood kin,
  Brother, tell me, tell me,
Your father's sons and your mother's sons
Who dwelled in peace with thee.

Lew was still talking, through the sound. "The Comyn has been too often unjust. They threw Danilo aside like a piece of rubbish, for no better reason than that he had offended a wicked and corrupt man who should never have been in power. Danilo is a catalyst telepath. I suggested they bring him here—I had no idea they would take him by force—and his services be enlisted to a larger loyalty. I had it in mind he could serve all our world, not a sick, power-mad clique of aristocrats bent on keeping themselves in power at whatever cost. . . ."

The mournful harp-chords were very soft, the woman's voice very sweet.

> We sat at feast, we fought in jest,
> Sister, I vow to thee;
> A berserker's rage came in my hand,
> And I slew them shamefully.

Lew said, "Enough of this, you are tired and anxious about Dani, and you must have some rest. When you are well recovered, I want you to know all about what we are doing. Then you will know why those who are really loyal to Darkover may serve us all best by putting some check on the Comyn powers."

Regis could feel Lew's sincerity through the touch on his hand, yet there was some hesitation too. He slid his hand up Lew's arm to touch the tattooed mark there. He said, "You're not completely sure of this either, Lew. You are sworn, sealed to Comyn."

Lew took his hand away, saying bitterly, "Sworn? No. Vows in which I had no part were sworn for me when I was five years old. But come, we'll talk of this another time. If you've been imagining Danilo a prisoner it will reassure you to find him in the best guest suite, the only one, I suppose, fit to entertain a Hastur. If he's your sworn man he should be lodged with you."

He turned, briefly making his excuses to the women. In his sensitized state Regis could feel their emotions, too: sharp resentment from the older, the singer. The younger one seemed aware of nothing but Lew. Regis didn't want to be part of these complexities! He was glad when they were alone in the corridor.

"Regis, what's really wrong with you? You're ill!"

Regis tried—he knew he didn't succeed too well—to cut off the rapport entirely. He knew that if he told Lew he had threshold sickness on the road, Lew would be immensely concerned. Even Javanne had treated it as a serious matter. For some reason he was anxious to avoid this. He said, "Nothing much; I'm very tired. I'm not used to mountain riding and I may have a chill." Actively he resisted Lew's solicitude. He could feel his kinsman's anxiety about him, and it made him irritable for some unknown reason. He wasn't a child now! And he could sense the bafflement with which Lew gently but definitely withdrew.

Lew paused at an ornate double door, scowling at the guard stationed there. "You guard a guest, sir?"

"Safeguard, Dom Lewis. Lord Beltran ordered me to see that no one disturbed him. Everybody's not friendly to the valley folk here. See?" the guard said, thrusting the door open. "He's not locked in."

Lew went in and called, "Danilo?" Regis, following him, took in at a glance the luxurious old-fashioned surroundings. Danilo came from an inner room, stopped short.

Regis felt overwhelming relief. He couldn't speak. Lew smiled. "You see," he said, "alive and well and unharmed."

Danilo flung back his head in an aggressive gesture. He said, "Did you send to have him captured, too?"

"How suspicious you are, Dani," Lew said. "Ask him yourself. I'll send servants to look after you."

He touched Regis lightly on the arm. "My own honor pledged on it, no harm shall come to either of you, and you shall depart unharmed when you are able to travel." He added, "Take good care of him, Dani," and withdrew, closing the door.

CHAPTER EIGHTEEN

When I came back to the fireside room, Thyra was still playing her harp, and I realized how short a time I had been away; she was still singing the ballad of the outlaw berserker.

And when will you come back again,
  Brother, tell me, tell me?
When the sun and the moon rise together in the West,
And that shall never be.

It must be immeasurably old, I thought, and alien, to speak of one moon instead of four! Beltran had returned and was gazing into the fire, looking angry and remote. He must have gotten the scolding he deserved from Kermiac. Before this, the old man's illness had kept any of us from telling Kermiac what Beltran had done. I was distressed because Beltran was distressed—I couldn't help it, I liked him, I understood what had prompted his rash orders. But what he had done to Danilo was unforgivable, and I was angry with him, too.

And he knew it. His voice, when he turned to me, was truculent.

"Now that you've put the child to bed—"

"Don't mock the lad, cousin," I said. "He's young, but he was man enough to cross the Hellers alone. I wouldn't."

Beltran said, "I've had that already from Father; he had nothing but praise for the boy's courage and good manner! I don't need it from you, too!" And he turned his back on me again. Well, I had little sympathy for him. He might well have lost us any chance of Danilo's friendship or help; and Danilo's help, as I saw it now, was all that could save this circle. If Beltran's *laran* could be fully opened, if with Danilo's aid we could discover and open up a few more latent telepaths, there was a chance, a bare chance but one I was willing to take, that we might somehow control the Sharra matrix. Without that it seemed hopeless.

Marjorie smiled and said, "Your friend wouldn't speak to me or look at me. But I would like to know him."

"He's a valley man, love, he'd think it rude and boorish to stare at a maiden. But he is my good friend."

Kadarin's lip curled in amusement. "Yet it wasn't for *your* sake he crossed the mountains, but for the Syrtis boy."

"I came here of my free will, and Regis knew it," I retorted, then laughed heartily. "By my probably nonexistent forefathers, Bob, do you think I am jealous? I am no lover of boys, but Regis was put in my charge when he was a little lad. He's dearer to me that my own brother born."

Marjorie smiled her heart-stopping smile and said, "Then I shall love him, too."

Thyra looked up and taunted, through the chords of her harp, "Come, Marjorie, you're a Keeper! If a man touches you you'll go up in smoke or something!"

Icy shudders suddenly racked me. *Marjorie, burning in Sharra's flame.* . . . I took one stride toward the fire, wrenched the harp from Thyra's hands, then caught myself, still rigid. What had I been about to do? Fling the harp across the room, bring it down crashing across that mocking face? Slowly, deliberately, forcing my shaking muscles to relax, I brought the harp down and laid it on the bench.

"*Breda,*" I said, using the word for sister, not the ordinary one but the intimate word which could also mean darling, "such mockery is unworthy of you. If I had thought it possible, or if I had had the training of you from the first, don't you think I would have chosen you rather than Marjorie? Don't you think I would rather have had Marjorie free?" I put my arm around her. For a moment she was defiant, gazing angrily up at me.

"Would you really have trusted me to keep your rule of chastity?" she flung at me. I was too shocked to answer. At last I said, "*Breda,* it isn't you I don't trust, it's your training."

She had been rigid in my arms; suddenly she went limp against me, her arms clinging around my neck. I thought she would cry. I said, still trembling with that mixture of fury and tenderness, "And don't make jests about the fires! Evanda have mercy, Thyra! You were never at Arilinn, you have never seen the memorial, but have you, who are a singer of ballads, never heard the tale of Marelie Hastur?

I have no voice for singing, but I shall tell it you, if you need reminding that there is no jesting about such matters!" I had to break off. My voice was trembling.

Kadarin said quietly, "We all saw Marjorie in the fire, but it was an illusion. You weren't hurt, were you, Margie?"

"No. No, I wasn't. No, Lew. Don't, please don't. Thyra didn't mean anything," Marjorie said, shaking. I ached to reach out for her, take her in my arms, keep her safe. Yet that would place her in more danger than anything else I could possibly do.

I had been a fool to touch Thyra.

She was still clinging to me, warm and close and vital. I wanted to thrust her violently away, but at the same time I wanted—and she knew it, damn it, she knew it!—I wanted what I would have had as a matter of course from any woman of my own circle who was not a Keeper. What would have dispelled this hostility and tension. Any woman tower-trained would have sensed the state I was in and felt responsible. . . .

I forced myself to be calm, to release myself from Thyra's arms. It wasn't Thyra's fault, any more than it was Marjorie's. It wasn't Thyra's fault that Marjorie, and not herself, had been forced by lack of any other to be Keeper. It wasn't Thyra who had roused me this way. It wasn't Thyra's fault, either, that she had not been trained to the customs of a tower circle, where the intimacy and awareness is closer than any blood tie, closer than love, where the need of one evokes a real responsibility in the others.

I could impose the laws of a tower circle on this group only so far as was needed for their own safety. I could not ask more than this. Their own bonds and ties went far back, beyond my coming. Thyra had nothing but contempt for Arilinn. And to come between Thyra and Kadarin was not possible.

Gently, so she would not feel wounded by an abrupt withdrawal, I moved away from her. Beltran, staring into the fire as if hypnotized by the darting flames, said in a low voice, "Marelie Hastur. I know the tale. She was a Keeper at Arilinn who was taken by mountain raiders in the Kilghard Hills, ravaged and thrown out to die by the city wall.

Yet from pride, or fear of pity, she concealed what had been done to her and went into the matrix screens in spite of the law of the Keepers. . . . And she died, a blackened corpse like one lightning-struck."

Marjorie shrank, and I damned Beltran. Why did he have to tell that story in Marjorie's hearing? It seemed a piece of gratuitous cruelty, very unlike Beltran.

Yes. And I had been about to tell it to Thyra, and I had come near to breaking her own harp across her head. That was very unlike me, too.

What in all the Gods had come to us!

Kadarin said harshly, "A lying tale. A pious fraud to scare Keepers into keeping their virginity, a bogeyman to frighten babies and girl-children!"

I thrust out my scarred hand. "Bob, *this* is no pious fraud!"

"Nor can I believe it had anything to do with your virginity," he retorted, laughing, and laid a kind hand on my shoulder. "You're giving yourself nightmares, Lew. For your Marelie Hastur I give you Cleindori Aillard, who was kinswoman to your own father, and who married and bore a son, losing no iota of her powers as Keeper. Have you forgotten they butchered her to keep *that* secret? That alone should give the lie to all this superstitious drivel about chastity."

I saw Marjorie's face lose a little of its tension and was grateful to him, even if not wholly convinced. We were working here without elementary safeguards, and I was not yet willing to disregard this oldest and simplest of precautions.

Kadarin said, "If you and Marjorie feel safer to lie apart until this work is well underway, it's your own choice. But don't give yourselves nightmares either. She's well in control. I feel safe with her." He bent down, kissing her lightly on the forehead, a kiss completely without passion but altogether loving. He put a free arm around me, drew me against him, smiling. I thought for a moment he would kiss me too, but he laughed. "We're both too old for that," he said, but without mockery. For a moment we were all close together again, with no hint of the terrible violence and disharmony that had thrust us apart. I began to feel hope again.

Thyra asked softly, "How is it with our father, Beltran?" I had forgotten that Thyra was his daughter too.

"He is very weak," Beltran said, "but don't fret, little sister, he'll outlive all of us."

I said, "Shall I go to him, Beltran? I've had long experience treating shock from matrix overload—"

"And so have I, Lew," Kadarin said kindly, releasing me. "*All* the knowledge of matrix technology is not locked up at Arilinn, *bredu*. I can do better without sleep than you young people."

I knew I should insist, but I did not have the heart to face down another of Thyra's taunts about Arilinn. And it was true that Kermiac had been training technicians in these hills before any of us were born. And my own weariness betrayed me. I swayed a little where I stood, and Kadarin caught and steadied me.

"Go and rest, Lew. Look, Rafe's asleep on the rug. Thyra, call someone to carry him to bed. Off with you now, all of you!"

"Yes," said Beltran, "tomorrow we have work to do, we've delayed long enough. Now that we have a catalyst telepath—"

I said somberly, "It may take a long time now to persuade him to trust you, Beltran. And you cannot use force on him. You know that, don't you?"

Beltran looked angry. "I won't hurt a hair of his precious little head, kinsman. But you'd better be damned good at persuading. Without his help, I don't know what we'll do."

I didn't either. We needed Danilo so terribly. We separated quietly, all of us sobered. I had a terrible feeling of weight on my heart. Thyra walked beside the burly servant who was carrying Rafe to bed. Kadarin and Beltran, I knew, were going to watch beside Kermiac. I should have shared that vigil. I loved the old man and I was responsible for the moment's lack of control which had struck him down.

I was about to leave Marjorie at the foot of her tower stairway, but she clung hard to my hand.

"Please, Lew. Stay with me. As you did the other day."

I started to agree, then realized something else.

I didn't trust myself.

Whether it was the brief disturbing physical contact with

Thyra, whether it was the upsetting force of the quarrel, or the old songs and ballads . . . I didn't trust myself!

Even now, it took all my painfully acquired discipline, all of it, to keep from taking her into my arms, kissing her senseless, carrying her up those stairs and into her room, to the bed we had shared so chastely . . .

I stopped myself right there. But we were deeply in contact; she had seen, felt, *shared* that awareness with me. She was blushing, but she did not turn her eyes from mine. She said at last, quietly, "You told me that when we were working like this, nothing could happen that would harm or . . . or endanger me."

I shook my head in bewilderment. "I don't understand it either, Marjorie. Normally, at this stage," and here I laughed, a short unmirthful sound, "you and I could lie down naked together and sleep like brothers or unweaned babies. I don't know what's happened, Marjorie, but I don't dare. Gods above!" I almost shouted at her. "Don't you think I *want* to?"

Now she did avert her eyes for a moment. She said in a whisper, "Kadarin says it's only a superstition. I'll . . . I'll risk it if you want to, Lew. If you need to."

Now I really felt ashamed. I was better disciplined than this. I made myself take a long breath, unclench my hands from the railings of the stair. "No, beloved. Perhaps I can find out what's gone wrong. But I have to be alone."

I heard her plea, not aloud but straight to my mind, straight to my heart: *Don't leave me! Don't go, Lew, don't* . . . I broke the contact harshly, cutting her off, shutting her out. It hurt horribly, but I knew that if this went on I would never be able to leave her, and I knew where it would end. And her discipline held. She closed her eyes, drawing a deep breath. I saw that curious look of distance, withdrawnness, isolation, slip down over her features. The look Callina had had, that Festival Night. The look I had seen so often on Janna's face, my last season at Arilinn. She had known I loved her, wanted her. It hurt, but I felt relieved, too. Marjorie said quietly, "I understand, Lew. Go and sleep, my darling." She turned and went away from me, up the long stairs, and I went away, blind with pain.

I passed the closed door of the suite where Regis and Danilo had been lodged. I knew I should speak to Regis.

He was ill, exhausted. But my own misery made me shrink from the task. He had made it clear he did not want my solicitude. He was reunited with his friend, why should I disturb them now? He would be asleep, I hoped, resting after that terrible journey alone through the Hellers.

I went to my own room and threw myself down without bothering to undress.

Something was wrong. Something was terribly wrong.

I had felt a disruption like this once before, like a vortex of fury, lust, rage, destruction, surging up through us all. It should not be like this. It *could* not be like this!

Normally, matrix work left the workers drained, spent, without anything left over for any violent emotion. Above all, I had grown accustomed to the fact that there was nothing left over for sexuality. It wasn't that way now.

I had been angry with Thyra at first, not aroused by her. I had been angry when it seemed she mocked Marjorie, and then suddenly I'd been so overcome by my own need that it would have been easy for me to tear off her clothes and take her there before the fire!

And Marjorie. A Keeper. I shouldn't have been capable even of *thinking* about her this way. Yet I *had* thought about it. Damn it, I still ached with wanting her. And she had wanted me to stay with her! Was she weeping now, alone in her room, the tears she had been too proud to shed before me? Should I have risked it? Sanity, prudence, long habit, told me no; no, I had done the only thing it was safe to do.

I glanced briefly at the wrapped bundle of the matrix and felt the faintest thrill of awareness along my nerves. Insulated like that, it should have been wholly dormant. Damn it, I trained at Arilinn and any first-year telepath learns to insulate a matrix! What I insulate stays insulated! I must be dreaming, imagining. I was living on my nerves and by now they were raw, hypersensitive.

That damned thing was responsible for all our troubles. I'd have liked to heave it out the window, or better, send it out on a Terran rocket and let it work its mischief on cosmic dust or something! I heartily wished that Beltran and the Sharra matrix and Kadarin and old Desideria, with all her forge-folk about her, were all frying together on one of their own forges.

I was still in accord with Beltran's dream, but standing between us and the accomplishment of the dream was this ravening nightmare of Sharra. I knew, I knew with the deepest roots of my self, that I could not control it, that Marjorie could not control it, that nothing human could ever control it. We had only stirred the surface of the matrix. If it was roused all the way it might never be controlled again, and tomorrow I would tell Beltran so.

Clutching this resolve, I fell into an uneasy sleep.

For a long time I wandered in confused nightmares through the corridors of Comyn Castle; whenever I met someone, his or her face was veiled or turned away in aversion or contempt. Javanne Hastur refusing to dance with me at a children's ball. Old Domenic di Asturien with his lifted eyebrows. My father, reaching out to me across a great chasm. Callina Aillard, turning away and leaving me alone on the rain-swept balcony. It seemed I wandered through those halls for hours, with no single human face turned to me in concern or compassion.

And then the dream changed. I was standing on the balcony of the Arilinn Tower, watching the sunrise, and Janna Lindir was standing beside me. I was dreamily surprised to see her. I was back again where I had been happy, where I had been accepted and loved, where there was no cloud on my mind and heart. But I had thought my circle had been broken and scattered, the others to their homes, I to the Guards where I was despised, Janna married . . . no, surely that had been only a bad dream! She turned and laid her hand in mine, and I felt a deep happiness.

Then I realized it was not Janna but Callina Aillard, saying softly, mockingly, "You do know what's really wrong with you," taunting me from the safe barrier of what she was, a Keeper, forbidden, untouchable. . . . Maddened by the surge of need and hunger in me, I reached for her, I tore the veils from her body while she screamed and struggled. I threw her down whimpering on the stones and flung myself atop her, naked, and through her wild cries of terror she *changed,* she began to flame and glow and burn, the fires of Sharra engulfing us, consuming us in a wild spasm of lust and ecstasy and terror and agony. . . .

I woke up shuddering, crying out with the mingled terror and enchantment of the dream. The Sharra matrix lay shrouded and dormant.

But I dared not close my eyes again that night.

CHAPTER NINETEEN

After Lew had gone away, closing the door behind him, it was Regis who moved first, stumbling across the floor as if wading through a snowdrift, to clasp Dani's shoulders in a kinsman's embrace. He heard his own voice, hoarse in his ears.

"You're safe. You really are here and safe." He had doubted Lew's word, though never in all his life had he reason to doubt. What kind of evil was here?

"Yes, yes, well and safe," Danilo said, then drew a harsh breath of dismay. "My lord Regis, you're soaked through!"

For the first time Regis became aware of the heat from the fireplace, the hangings sealing off drafts, the warmth after the icy blasts of the corridors. The very warmth touched off a spasm of shivering, but he forced himself to say, "The guards. You are really a prisoner, then?"

"They're here to protect me, so they say. They've been friendly enough. Come, sit here, let me get these boots off, you're chilled to the bone!"

Regis let himself be led to an armchair, so ancient in design that until he was in the seat he was not sure what it was. His feet came out of the boots numb and icy-cold. He was almost too weary to sit up and unlace his tunic; he sat with his hands hanging, his legs stretched out, finally with an effort put his stiff fingers to the tunic-laces. He knew his voice sounded more irritible than he meant.

"I can manage for myself, Dani. You're my paxman, not my body-servant!"

Danilo, kneeling before the fire to dry Regis' boots, jerked upright as if stung. He said into the fire, "Lord Regis, I am honored to serve you in any way I may." Through the stiff formality of the words, Regis, wide open again, *felt* something else, a wordless resonance of despair: *He didn't mean it, then, about accepting my service. It was . . . it was only a way of atoning for what his kinsman had done. . . .*

Without stopping to think, Regis was out of the chair, kneeling beside Dani on the hearth. His voice was shaking, partly with the cold which threatened to rip him apart with shudders, partly with that intense awareness of Dani's hurt.

"The Gods witness I meant it! It's only . . . only . . ." Suddenly he knew the right thing to say. "You remember what a fuss it caused, when I expected anyone to wait on me, in the barracks!"

Their eyes caught and held. Regis had no idea whether it was his own thought or Danilo's: *We were boys then. And now . . . how long ago that seems! Yet it was only last season!* It seemed to Regis that they were looking back, as men, across a great chasm of elapsed time, at a shared boyhood. Where had it gone?

With a sense of fighting off unutterable weariness—it seemed he had been fighting off this weariness as long as he could remember—he reached for Danilo's hands. They felt hard, calloused, real, the only firm anchor-point in a shifting, dissolving universe. Momentarily he felt his hands going *through* Danilo's as if neither of them were quite solid. He blinked hard to focus his eyes, and saw a blue-haloed form in front of him. He could see through Danilo now, to the wall beyond. Trying to focus against the swarming fireflies that spun before his eyes, he remembered Javanne's warning, fight it, move around, speak. He tried to get his voice back into his throat.

"Forgive me, Dani. Who should serve me if not my sworn man . . . ?"

And as he spoke the words he *felt,* amazed, the texture of Danilo's relief: *My people have served the Hasturs for generations. Now I too am where I belong.*

No! I do not want to be a master of men . . . !

But the swift denial was understood by both, not as a personal rejection, but the very embodiment of what they both were, so that the giving of Danilo's service was the pleasure and the relief it was, so that Regis knew he must not only accept that service, but accept it fully, graciously.

Danilo's face suddenly looked strange, frightened. His mouth was moving but Regis could no longer hear him, floating bodiless in the sparkling darkness. The base of his skull throbbed with ballooning pain. He heard himself whisper, "I am . . . in your hands . . ." Then the world slid sidewise and he felt himself collapse into Danilo's arms.

He never knew how he got there, but seconds later, it seemed, he felt searing pain all over his naked body, and found himself floating up to the chin in a great tub of boiling water. Danilo, kneeling at his side, was anxiously chafing his wrists. His head was splitting, but he could see solid objects again, and his own body was reassuringly firm. A servant was hovering around with clean garments, trying to attract Danilo's attention long enough to get his approval of them.

Regis lay watching, too languid to do anything but accept their ministrations. He noticed that Danilo unobtrusively kept his own body between Regis and the Aldaran servant. Danilo chased the man out quickly, muttering under his breath, "I'm not going to trust any of them alone with you!"

At first the water had seemed scalding to his chilled body; now he realized it was barely warm, in fact it must have been drawn for some time, was probably a bath prepared for Danilo before he came in. Danilo was still bending over him, his face tight with worry. Suddenly Regis was filled with such intolerable anxiety that he cut off the intense, sensuous pleasure of the hot water soothing his chilled and stiffened body—eleven nights on the trail and not warm once!—and drew himself upright, hauling himself out of the hot tub, reaching for a towel to wrap himself in. Danilo knelt to dry him, saying, "I sent the servant for a healer-woman. There must be someone of that sort here. Regis, I never saw anyone faint like that before; your eyes were open but you couldn't hear me or see me . . ."

"Threshold sickness." Briefly he sketched in an explanation. "I've had a few attacks before. I'm over the worst." I hope, he added to himself. "I doubt if the healer could do anything with this. Here, give me that. I can dress myself." Firmly he took the towel away from Danilo. "Go and tell her not to bother, and find out if there's anything hot to drink."

Skeptically Danilo retreated. Regis finished drying himself and clambered into the unfamiliar clothing. His hands were shaking almost too hard to tie the knots of his tunic. What's the matter with me, he asked himself why didn't I want Dani to help he dress? He looked at his hands in cold shock, as if they belonged to someone else. I didn't want him to touch me!

Even to him that sounded incongruous. They had lived together in the rough intimacy of the barracks room for months. They had been close-linked, even thinking one another's thoughts.

This was different.

Irresistibly his mind was drawn back to that night in the barracks, when he had reached out to Danilo, torn by an almost frenzied desire to share his misery, the spasm of loathing and horror with which Danilo had flung him away. . . .

And then, shaken and shamed and terrified, Regis knew what had prompted that touch, and why he was suddenly shy of Danilo now. The knowledge struck him motionless, his bare feet cold through the wolfskin rug on the tile floor.

To touch him. Not to comfort Dani, but to comfort his own need, his own loneliness, his own hunger. . . .

He moved deliberately, afraid if he remained motionless another instant the threshold sickness would surge up over him again. He knelt on the wolfskin, drawing fur-lined stockings up over his knees and deliberately tying the thongs into intricate knots. On the surface of his mind he thought that fur clothing was life-saving here in the mountains. It felt wonderful.

But, relentless, the memory he had barricaded since his twelfth year burst open like a bleeding wound; the memory he had let himself lose consciousness before recovering on the northward trail: Lew's face, alight with fire, his barriers down in the last extremity of exhaustion and pain and fear.

And Regis had shared it all with him, there were no barriers between them. None. Regis had known what Lew wanted and would not ask, was too proud and too shy to ask. Something Regis had never felt before, that Lew thought he was too young to feel or to understand. But Regis had known and had shared it.

And afterward, perhaps because Lew had never spoken of it, Regis was too ashamed to remember. And he had never dared open his mind again. Why? Why? Out of fear, out of shame? Out of . . . longing?

Until Danilo, without even trying, broke that barricade.

And now Regis knew why it was Dani who could break it . . .

He doesn't know, Regis thought, and then with a bleak and spartan pride, He must never know.

He stood up, felt the splitting pain at his forehead again. He knew a frightened moment of disquiet. How could he keep this from him? Dani was a telepath too!

Lew had said it was like living with your skin off. Well, his skin was off and he was doubly naked. Taking a grip on himself, he walked out into the other room, decided his boots weren't dry. Inside he felt cold and trembly, but physically he was quite warm and calm.

How could he face Lew again, knowing this? Coldly, Regis told himself not to be a fool. Lew had always known. He wasn't a coward, he didn't lie to himself! Lew remembered, so no wonder he was astonished when Regis had said he did not have *laran*!

Lew had asked him why he could not bear to remember. . . .

"You should have gone straight to bed and let me bring you supper there," Danilo said behind him, and Regis, firmly taking mastery of his face, looked around. Danilo was looking at him with friendly concern, and Regis remembered, with a shock, that Danilo knew nothing, nothing of the memory and awareness that had flooded him in the scant few minutes they had been parted. He said aloud, trying for a casual neutral tone, "I collapsed before I saw anything of the suite but this room. I have no idea where I'm going to be sleeping."

"And I've had days with nothing to do but explore. Come, I'll show you the way. I told the servant to bring your supper in here. How does it feel to be quartered in a royal suite, after the student dormitory at Nevarsin?"

There was room enough for a regent and all his entourage in this guest suite: enormous bedrooms, servants quarters in plenty, a great hall, even a small octagonal presence chamber with a throne and footstools for petitioners. It was more elaborate than his grandfather's suite in Thendara. Danilo had chosed the smallest and least elaborate bedroom, but it looked like a royal favorite's chamber. There was a huge bed on a dais which would, Regis thought irreverently, have held a Dry-Towner, three of his wives and six of his concubines. The servant he had seen before was warming the sheets with a long-handled warming pan, and there was a fire in the fireplace. He let Danilo help him into the big bed, put a tray of hot food beside him. Danilo sent the man away, saying gravely, "It is my privilege to wait on my lord with my own hands." Regis would have laughed at the solemn, formal words, but knew even a smile would hurt Danilo unspeakably. He kept his composure, until the man was out of earshot, then said, "I hope you're not going to take that formal my-lord tone all the time now, *bredu.*"

There was relief in Danilo's eyes too. "Only in front of strangers, Regis." He came and lifted covers off steaming bowls of food, clambered up on the bed and poured hot soup from a jug. He said, "The food's good. I had to ask for cider instead of wine the first day, that's all. I see they brought both tonight, and the cider's hot."

Regis drank the soup and the hot cider thirstily; but although it was his first hot meal in days, he found it almost too hard to chew and swallow.

"Now tell me how you found me here, Regis."

Regis' hand went to the matrix on the thong around his neck. Danilo shrank a little. "I thought such things were to be used only by technicians, with proper safeguards. Isn't it dangerous?"

"I knew no other way."

Danilo looked at him, visibly moved. "And you took that risk for me, *bredu*?"

Regis deliberately withdrew from the moment of emotion. "Take that last cutlet, won't you? I'm not hungry. . . . I'm here and alive, aren't I? I expect I'll have trouble with my kinfolk; I got away from Gabriel and my escort by a trick. I was supposed to be on my way to Neskaya Tower."

The diversion worked. Danilo asked with a faint revulsion, "Are you to be a matrix mechanic, now they know you have *laran*?"

"God forbid! But I have to learn to safeguard myself."

Danilo had made a long mental leap. "Is this—using a matrix, untrained—why you have been having threshold sickness?"

"I don't know. Perhaps. It couldn't help."

Danilo said, "I should have sent for Lew Alton, instead

of the healer-woman. He's tower-trained, he'd know what to do for it."

Regis flinched. He didn't want to face Lew just yet. Not till he had his own thoughts in order. "Don't disturb him. I'm all right now."

"Well, if you're sure," Danilo said uncertainly. "No doubt, by now, he's in bed with his girl and wouldn't thank anyone for disturbing him, but just the same—"

"His girl?"

"Aldaran's foster-daughter. The guards are lonely and have nothing to do but gossip, and I thought it just as well to learn as much as I could about what's going on here. They say Lew's madly in love with her, and old Kermiac's arranging a marriage."

Well, Regis thought, that made good sense. Lew had never been happy in the lowlands and he was lonely. If he took a wife from his mountain kinsmen, that was a good thing.

Danilo said, "There's wine, if you want it," but Regis firmly shook his head. He might sleep better for it, but he dared not risk anything that might break down his defenses. He took a handful of sugared nuts and began nibbling them.

"Now, Dani, tell me all about it. Old Kermiac did not know why they had brought you here, and I had no chance to ask Lew alone." He wondered suddenly which of the women in the fireside room was Lew's sweetheart. The hard-faced girl with the harp? Or the delicate remote, younger one in blue?

"But you must have known all about it," said Danilo, "or how could you have come after me? I tried . . . I tried to reach out for you with my mind, but I was afraid. I could *feel* them. I was afraid they'd use that somehow . . ." Regis sensed he was almost crying. "It's terrible! *Laran* is terrible! I don't want it, Regis! I don't want it!"

Impulsively Regis reached out to lay a steadying hand on his wrist, stopped himself. Oh no. Not that. Not so easy an excuse to . . . to touch him. He said, keeping his voice detached, "It seems we have no choice, Dani. It has come to us both."

"It's like—like lightning! It hits people who don't want it, hits them at random—" Danilo's voice shook.

Regis wondered how anyone lived with it. He said, "I don't much want it either, now that I've got it. No more than I want to be heir to Comyn." He sighed. "But we have no choice. Or the only choice we have is to misuse it—like Dyan—or to meet it like men, and honorably." He knew he was not talking only of *laran* now. "Laran cannot be all evil. It helped me find you."

"And if I've brought you into danger of death . . ."

"That's enough of that!" The words were a sharp rebuke; Danilo shrank as if Regis had slapped him, but Regis felt he dared not face another emotional outburst. "Lord Kermiac has called me *guest*. Among mountain people that is a sacred obligation. Neither of us is in danger."

"Not from old Kermiac perhaps. But Beltran wants to use my *laran* to awaken other telepaths, and what's he going to do with them when he's got them awakened? Whatever they're doing . . ." He stared right through Regis and whispered, "It's *wrong*. I can feel it, reaching for me even in my sleep!"

"Surely Lew wouldn't be a party to anything dishonorable?"

"Not knowingly, maybe. But he's very angry with the Comyn, and wholly committed to Beltran now," Danilo said. "This is what he told me."

He began to explain Beltran's plan for revival of the old matrix technology, bringing Darkover from a non-industrial, non-technological culture into a position of strength in a galactic empire. As he spoke of star-travel Regis' eyes brightened, recalling his own dreams. Suppose he need *not* desert his world and his heritage to go out among the stars, but could serve his people and still be part of a great star-spanning culture . . . it seemed too good to be true.

"Surely if it could have been done at all, it would have been done at the height of the strength of the towers. They must have tried this."

"I don't know," said Danilo humbly, "I'm not as well-educated as you, Regis."

And Regis knew so little!

"Let's not sit and make guesses about what they're doing," Regis said. "Let's wait till tomorrow and ask them." He yawned deliberately. "I haven't slept in a bed for a dozen nights. I think I'll try this one out." Danilo was taking away the mugs and bowls; Regis beckoned him back.

"I hope you have no foolish notion of standing guard while I sleep, or sleeping on the floor across my doorway?"

"Only if you want me to," said Dani, but he sounded hurt, and with that unwelcome sensitivity Regis knew he'd have liked to. The picture that had haunted him for days now returned, Dani's brother shielding his father with his body. Did Dani really want to die for him? The thought shocked him speechless.

He said curtly, "Sleep where you damn please, but get some sleep. And if you really like having me give you orders, Dani, that's an order." He didn't wait to see where Dani chose. He slid down into the great bed and dropped into a bottomless pit of sleep.

At first, exhaustion taking its toll of his aching body and overstrained emotions, he was too weary even to dream. Then he began to drift in and out of dreams: the sound of horses' hooves on a road, galloping . . . the armory in Comyn Castle, struggling weakly against Dyan, armed and fresh against an aching lassitude that would not let Regis lift his sword . . . a great form swooping down, touching Castle Aldaran with a finger of fire, flames rising skyward. By the firelight he saw Lew's face alight with terror, and reached out to him, feeling the strange and unfamiliar emotions and sensations, but this time he knew what he was doing. This time he was not a child, his child's body responding half-aware to the most innocent of caresses; this time he knew and accepted it all, and suddenly it was Danilo in his arms, and Danilo was struggling, trying to push him away in pain and terror. Regis, gripped by need and blind cruelty, gripped him more and more tightly, fighting to hold him, subdue him, and then, with a gasp, cried aloud, "No! Oh, *no*!" and flung him away, pulling himself upright in the great bed.

He was alone, the firelight burned down to coals. Across the foot of the enormous bed, like a dark shadow, Danilo slept, wrapped in a blanket, his back turned away. Regis stared at the sleeping boy, unable to shake off the horror of the dream, the shock of knowing what he had tried to do.

No. Not tried to do. Wanted to do. Dreamed of doing. There was a difference.

Or was there, for a telepath?

Once, one of the few times Kennard had spoken of his own years in the tower, Kennard had said, very seriously: "I am an Alton; my anger can kill. A murderous thought is, for me, almost a murder. A lustful thought is the psychological equivalent of a rape."

Regis wondered if he was responsible even for his dreams. Would he ever dare sleep again?

Danilo stirred with a moan. Abruptly he began to gasp and cry out and struggle in his sleep. He muttered aloud, "No—no, please!" and began to cry. Regis stared in horror. Did his own dream disturb Dani! Dyan had reached him, even in sleep. . . . He could not leave him crying. He leaned forward, saying gently, "Dani, it's all right, you were asleep."

Half asleep, Danilo made the safeguarding sign of *cristoforo* prayers. It must be comforting to have their faith, Regis thought. Danilo's smothered sobbing tore at Regis like claws. He had no way of knowing that far away in the castle Lew Alton had also started out of nightmare, shaking with the guilt of the most dreadful crime *he* could imagine, but Regis did find himself wondering what form Danilo's nightmare had taken. He dared not ask, dared not risk the intimacy of midnight confidences.

Danilo had his crying under control now. He asked, "It's not . . . not threshold sickness again?"

"No. No, only a nightmare. I'm sorry I woke you."

"This damned place is full of nightmares . . ." Danilo muttered. Regis felt him reach out for reassurance, for contact. He held himself aloof from the touch. After a long time he knew Danilo slept again. He lay awake, watching the dying remnants of the fire on the hearth. The fire that had been a raging forest fire from his troubled childhood, that had become the great form of fire. Sharra, of the legends. What, in the name of all the Gods, were they *doing* here at Aldaran? Something here was out of control, dangerous.

Fire was the key, he knew, not only because the memory of the forest fire had brought back the memory he'd buried, but it was worse than that. Lew looked as if he'd been doing something dangerous. And all this . . . this dislocation of memory, these nightmares of cruelty and lust . . . something terrible was going on here.

And Regis had Danilo to protect. He came here for that, and he vowed again to fulfill it.

Weighed down under the unendurable burden of *laran,* knowing guilt even for his dreams, shouldering the heavy knowledge of what he had forgotten, Regis dared not sleep again. He thought instead. The mistake was in sending him to Nevarsin, he knew. Anywhere else he could have come to terms with it. He knew, rationally, that what had happened to him, what was happening to him now, was nothing to bring such catastrophic guilt and self-hatred. He had not even minded when the cadets thought him Dyan's minon.

But that was before he knew what Dyan had done. . . .

Dyan's shadow lay heavy on Regis. And heavier on Danilo. Regis knew he could not bear it if Dani were to think of him as he thought of Dyan . . . even if Regis thought of him that way. . . .

His mind reeling under it, Regis knew suddenly that he *had* a choice. Faced by this unendurable self-knowledge, he could do again what he had done when he was twelve years old, and this time there would be no lifting of the barrier. He could forget again. He could cut off the unwelcome, unwanted self-knowledge, cut off, with it, the undesired, unendurable *laran.*

He could be free of it all, and this time no one would ever be able to break through it again. Be free of it all: heritage, and responsibility. If he had no *laran,* it would not matter if he left the Comyn, went out into the Empire never to return. He even left an heir to take his place. He had done it once. He could do it again. He could meet Danilo in the morning with no guilty knowledge and no fear, meet him innocently, as a friend. He need never again fear that Danilo could reach his mind and learn what Regis now felt he would rather die than reveal.

He had done it once. Even Lew could not break that barrier.

The temptation was almost unendurable. Dry-mouthed, Regis looked at the sleeping boy lying heavily across his feet. To be free again, he thought, free of it all.

He had accepted Dani's oath, though, as a Hastur. Had accepted his service, and his love.

He was no longer free. He'd said it to Danilo, and it was true for him, too. They had no choice, it had come to them, and they had only the choice to misuse it or meet it with honor.

Regis did not know if he could meet it with honor, but he knew he'd have to try. Chickens couldn't go back into eggs.

Either way, there was nothing but hell ahead.

CHAPTER TWENTY

(Lew Alton's narrative)

Shortly after sunrise I let myself fall into a fitful drowse. Some time later I was awakened by a strange outcry, women screaming—no, wailing, a sound I had heard only once before . . . on my trip into the backwoods, in a house where there was a death.

I threw on some clothes and ran out into the corridor. It was crowded, servants rushing to and fro, no one ready to stop and answer my questions. I met Marjorie at the foot of the little stair from her tower. She was as white as her chamber robe.

"Darling, what is it?"

"I'm not sure. It's the death-wail!" She put out a hand and forcibly stopped one of the women rushing by. "What is it, what's that wailing, what's happened?"

The woman gasped. "It's the old lord, *domna Marguerida,* your guardian, he died in the night—"

As soon as I heard the words I knew I had been expecting it. I felt stricken, grieved. Even in such a short time I had come to love my uncle, and beyond my personal grief I was dismayed at what this must mean. Not only for the Domain of Aldaran, but for all Darkover. His reign had been a long one, and a wise one.

"Thyra," Marjorie whispered, "Evanda pity us, what will she do, how will she live with this?" She clutched my arm. "He's her *father,* Lew! Did you know? My father owned to her, but she was none of his, and it was her doing, her mistake, that has killed him!"

"Not hers," I said gently. "Sharra." I had begun to believe, now, that we were all helpless before it. Tomorrow—no, today, the sooner the better—it should go back to the forge-folk. Desideria had been right: it had lain safe in their keeping, should never have left them. I quailed, thinking of what Beltran would say. Yet Kadarin had pledged Desideria to abide my judgment.

First I must visit the death chamber, pay a kinsman's respects. The high wailing of the death-cries went on from inside, fraying my already ragged nerves to shreds. Marjorie clutched desperately at my fingers. As we entered the great chamber I heard Thyra's voice, bursting out, almost screaming:

"Cease that pagan caterwauling! I'll have none of it here!"

One or two of the women stopped in mid-wail; others, half-hearted, stopped and started again. Beltran's voice was a harsh shout:

"You who killed him, Thyra, would you deny him proper respect?"

She was standing at the foot of the bed, her head thrown back, defiant. She sounded at the ragged end of endurance. "You superstitious idiot, do you really believe his spirit has stayed here to listen to the yowling over his corpse? Is this your idea of a seemly sound of mourning?"

Beltran said, more gently, "More seemly, perhaps, than this kind of brawling, foster-sister." He looked as you would expect after a long night of watching, and a death. He gestured to the women. "Go, go, finish your wailing elsewhere. The days are long gone when anyone must stand and wail to scare away demons from the dead."

Kermiac had been decently laid out, his hands laid crosswise on his breast, his eyes closed. Marjorie made the *cristoforo* sign across the old man's brow, then across her own. She bent and pressed her lips for a moment to the cold brow, whispering, "Rest in peace, my lord. Holy Bearer of Burdens, give us strength to bear our loss . . ." Then she turned quietly away and bent over the weeping Thyra.

"He is past all forgiveness or blame, darling. Don't torment yourself this way. It is for us to bear now, for the living. Come away, love, come away."

Thyra collapsed into terrible sobbing and let Marjorie lead her out of the room. I stood looking down at the calm, composed old face. For a moment it seemed my own father was lying here before me. I bent and kissed the cold brow, as Marjorie had done.

I said to Beltran, "I knew him such a little while. It is my great loss that I did not come here before." I embraced my kinsman, cheek to cheek, feeling the pain of his grief added to my own. Beltran turned away, pale and composed, as Regis came into the room, Danilo in his wake. Regis spoke a brief formal phrase of condolence, held out his hand. Beltran bowed over it but he did not speak. Had his grief dimmed his awareness of courtesy? He should have bidden Regis welcome as his guest; somehow it made me uneasy that he did not. Danilo made the *cristoforo* sign over the old man's brow, as Marjorie had done, whispering, I suppose, one of their prayers, then made a formal bow to Beltran.

I followed them outside. Regis looked as if he'd had the same nightmare-ridden sleep I had, and he was fully barriered against me—a new thing, and a disquieting one. He said, "He was your kinsman, Lew. I'm sorry for your grief. And I know my grandfather respected him. It's fitting there should be someone here from the Hasturs, to extend our condolences. Things will be different, now, in the mountains."

I had been thinking that myself. The sight of Regis almost automatically taking his place as the formal representative of Comyn was disquieting. I knew his grandfather would approve, but I was surprised.

"He told me, Regis, shortly before his death, that he hoped for a day when you and Beltran could sit down together and plan a better future for our world."

Regis smiled bleakly. "That will be for Prince Derik. The Hasturs are not kings now."

I gave him a skeptical smile. "Yet they stand nearest the throne. I have no doubt Derik will choose you for his nearest counselor, as his kinsmen chose your grandsire."

"If you love me, Lew, don't wish a crown on me," Regis said with a shudder of revulsion. "But enough of politics for now. I will remain for the funeral, of course; I owe Beltran no courtesies, but I'll not insult his father's death bed, either."

If Kermiac's untimely death had delayed Regis' immediate departure, it must also, in all decency, delay my ultimatum to Beltran. I anticipated less trouble now that he had had a bitter taste of the dangers inherent in Sharra. Kadarin might be less tractable. Yet I had faith in his good sense and his affection for all of us.

And so, all those days of mourning for the old lord of

Aldaran, none of us spoke of Sharra or Beltran's plans. During the days I could guard myself against the memory and the fear; only in terrifying dreams did it return, claw at me with talons of torment. . . .

The funeral services were over; the mountain lords who had come to pay their respects to the dead, and to give allegiance to Beltran, departed one by one. Beltran made an appearance of grave dignity, solemnly accepting their pledges of amity and support, yet I sensed in all of the mountain men an awareness that an era had irrevocably come to an end. Beltran was aware of it, too, and I knew it hardened his resolve not to run peaceably along the track his father had made—resting on his father's accomplishments and accepting their homage because of their goodwill to Kermiac—but to carve his own place.

We were so much alike, he and I, I have known twins less like. And yet we were so different. I had not known he was personally ambitious, too. I had lost the last traces of personal ambition at Arilinn, had resented Father's attempts to rouse it in me, in the Guards. Now I was deeply disturbed. Would he let his plans slip through his fingers without protest? It would take all my persuasion, all my tact, to convince him to a course less dangerous for all our world. Somehow I must make it clear to him that I still shared his dreams, that I would work for his aims and help him to the utmost, even though I had irrevocably renounced the means he and Kadarin had chosen.

When the mountain lords had departed, Beltran courteously asked Regis and Danilo to remain for a few more days. I had not expected either of them to agree and was ready to try to persuade them, but to my surprise, Regis had accepted the invitation. Maybe it was not so surprising. He looked dreadfully ill. I should have talked to him, tried to find out what ailed him. Yet whenever I tried to speak to him alone he rebuffed me, always turning the conversation to indifferent things. I wondered why. As a child he had loved me; did he think me a traitor, or was it something more personal?

Such was my state when we gathered that morning in the small fireside hall where we had met and worked together so often. Beltran bore the marks of stress and grief and he looked older, too, sobered by the new weight of responsibility. Thyra was pale and composed, but I knew how hard-won that composure had been. Kadarin, too, was haggard, grieved. Rafe, though subdued, had suffered the least; his grief was only that of a child who had lost a kindly guardian. He was too young to see the deeper implications of this.

Marjorie had that heartbreaking remoteness I had begun to see in her lately, the isolation of every Keeper. Through it I sensed a deeper disquiet. Beltran was her guardian now. If he and I were to quarrel, the future for us was not bright.

These were my kinsmen. Together we had built a beautiful dream. My heart ached that I must be the one to shatter it.

But when Danilo and Regis were ceremoniously escorted in, I felt again a glimmer of hope. Perhaps, perhaps, if I could persuade them to help us, there was still a way to salvage that dream!

Beltran began with the utmost courtesy, making formal apologies to Danilo for the way his men had exceeded their orders. If the words had more of diplomacy than real regret, I supposed only the strongest of telepaths could feel the difference. He ended by saying, "Let the end I am striving for outweigh personal considerations. A day is coming for Darkover when mountain men and the Domains must forget their ages-old differences and work together for the good of our world. Can we not agree on that at least, Regis Hastur, that you and I speak together for a world, and that our fathers and grandfathers should have wrought together and not separately for its well-being?"

Regis made a formal bow. I noticed he was wearing his own clothes again. "For your sake, Lord Beltran, I wish I were more skilled in the arts of diplomacy, so that I might more fittingly represent the Hasturs here. As it is, I can speak only for myself as a private individual. I hope the long peace between Comyn and Aldaran may endure for our lifetimes and beyond."

"And that it may not be a peace under the thumbs of the Terrans," Beltran added. Regis merely bowed again and said nothing.

Kadarin said with a grim smile, "I see that already you are skilled, Lord Regis, in the greatest of the Comyn arts, that of saying nothing in pleasant words. Enough of this fencing-match! Beltran, tell them what it is you hope to do."

Beltran began to outline, again, his plans to make Darkover independent, self-sufficient and capable of star-travel. I listened again, falling for the last time under the sway of that dream. I wished—all the gods there ever were *know* how I wished—that his plans might work. And they might. If Danilo could help us uncover enough telepaths, if Beltran's own latent powers could be wakened. *If, if, if!* And, above all, if we had some source of power other than the impossible Sharra. . . .

Beltran concluded, and I knew our thoughts ran for the moment at least along the same track: "We have reached a point where we are dependent on your help, Danilo. You are a catalyst telepath; that is the rarest of all psi powers, and if it is in our service, our chances of success are enormously raised. It goes without saying that you will be rewarded beyond your dreams. You will help us, will you not?"

Danilo met the ingratiating smile with a slight frown of puzzlement. "If what you are doing is so just and righteous, Lord Aldaran, why did you resort to violence? Why not seek me out, explain this to me, ask my aid?"

"Come, come," said Beltran good-naturedly, "can't you forgive me for that?"

"I forgive you readily, sir. Indeed, I am a little grateful. Otherwise I might have been charmed into doing what you wish without really thinking about it. Now I am not nearly so sure. I've had too much experience with people who speak fine words, but will do whatever they think justified to get what they want. If your cause is as good as you say, I should think any telepath would be glad to help you. If I am made sure of that by someone I can trust, and if my lord gives me leave"—he turned and made Regis a formal bow—"then I am at your service. But I must first be wholly assured that your motives and your methods are as good as you say"—he looked Beltran straight in the eyes, and I gasped aloud at his audacity—"and not just fine words to cover a will to power and personal ambition."

Beltran turned as red as a turkey-cock. He was not used to being crossed, and for this shabby nobody to read him a lesson in ethics was more than he could face. I thought for a moment that he would strike the boy. Probably he remembered that Danilo was the only catalyst telepath known to be adult and fully functioning, for he controlled himself, although I could see the signs of his inward wrath. He said, "Will you trust Lew Alton's judgment?"

"I have no reason not to trust it, but . . ." And he turned to Regis. I knew he had reached the end of his own defiance.

I knew Regis was as frightened as Danilo, but just as resolute. He said, "I will trust no man's judgment until I have heard what he has to say."

Kadarin said shortly, "Will you two boys, who know nothing of matrix mechanics, presume to sit in judgment upon a trained Arilinn telepath about matters of his own competence?"

Regis gave me a pleading look. After a long pause, during which I could almost feel him searching for the right words, he said, "To judge his competence—no. To judge whether I can conscientiously support his . . . his means and motives—for that I can trust no man's judgment but my own. I will listen to what he has to say."

Beltran said, "Tell them, then, Lew, that we must do this if Darkover is to survive as an independent world, not a slave colony of the Empire!"

All their eyes were suddenly on me. This was the moment of truth, and a moment of great temptation. I opened my mouth to speak. Darkover's future was a cause justifying all things, and we needed Dani.

But did I serve Darkover or my own private ends? Before the boy whose career was ruined by a misuse of power, I discovered I could not lie. I could not give Danilo the reassurance it would take to enlist his aid, then frantically try to find some way to make the lie true.

I said, "Beltran, your aims are good and I trust them. But we cannot do it with the matrix we have to work with. Not with Sharra, Beltran. It is impossible, completely impossible."

Kadarin swung around. I had seen his rage only once before, turned on Beltran. Now it was turned on me, and it struck me like a blow. "What folly is this, Lew? You told me Sharra has all the power we could possibly need!"

I tried to barrier that assault and hold my own wrath

firmly under control. The unleashed anger of an Alton can kill, and this man was my dear friend. I said, "Power, yes, all the power we could ever need, for this work or any. But it's essentially uncontrollable. It's been used as a weapon and now it's unfit for anything but a weapon. It is—" I hesitated, trying to formulate my vague impressions. "It's hungry for power and destruction."

"Comyn superstition again!" Thyra flung at me. "A matrix is a machine. No more and no less."

"Most matrices, perhaps," I said, "though I am beginning to think that even at Arilinn we know far too little of them to use them as recklessly as we do. But this one is more." I hesitated again, struggling for words for a knowledge, an *experience* which was basically beyond words. "It brings something into our world which is not of this world at all. It belongs to other dimensions, other places or spaces. It's a gateway, and once it's opened, it's impossible to shut completely." I looked from face to face. "Can't you see what it's *doing* to us?" I pleaded. "It's rousing recklessness, a failure of caution, a lust for power—" I had felt it myself, the temptation to lie ruthlessly to Regis and Danilo, just to enlist their aid. "Thyra, you know what you did under its impulse, and your foster-father lies dead. I'll never believe you would have done that, knowingly, on your own! It's so much stronger than we are, it's playing with us like toys!"

Kadarin said, "Desideria used it with none of this fuss."

"But she used it as a weapon," I said, "and in a righteous cause. She had no wish for personal power, so that it could not take her and corrupt her, as it has done with us; she gave it over to the forge-folk, to lie unused and harmless on their altars."

Beltran said harshly, "Are you saying it has corrupted *me*?"

I looked squarely at him and said, "Yes. Even your father's death has not made you see reason."

Kadarin said, "You talk like a fool, Lew. I hadn't expected this sort of whining cant from you. If we have the power to give Darkover its place in the Empire, how can we shrink from anything we must do?"

"My friend," I pleaded, "listen to me. We cannot use Sharra's matrix for the kind of controlled power you wish to show the Terrans. It cannot be used to power a spaceship; I would not trust it even to control the helicopter now. It is a weapon, only a weapon, and it is not weapons we need. It is technology."

Kadarin's smile was fierce. "But if a weapon is all we have, then we will use that weapon to get what we must from the Terrans! Once we show them what we can do with it—"

My spine iced over with a deadly cold. I saw again the vision: *flames rising from Caer Donn, the great form of fire bending down with a finger of destruction*. . . .

"No!" I almost shouted. "I'll have nothing to do with it!"

I rose and looked around the circle, saying desperately, "Can't you see how this has corrupted us? Was it for war, for murder, for violence, blackmail, ruin, that we forged our link in such love and harmony? Was this your dream, Beltran, when we spoke together of a better world?"

He said savagely, "If we must fight, it will be the fault of the Terrans for denying us our rights! I would rather do it peacefully, but if they force us to fight them—"

Kadarin, coming and laying his hands on my shoulders with real affection said, "Lew, you're foolishly squeamish. Once they know what we can do, there will certainly be no need to do it. But it places us in a position of equal power with the Terrans for once. Can't you see? Even if we never use it, we must have the power, simply in order to control the situation and not be forced to submit!"

I knew what he was trying to say, but I could see the fatal flaw. I said, "Bob, we cannot bluff with Sharra. It *wants* ruin and destruction . . . can't you feel that?"

"It *is* like the sword in the fairy tale," Rafe said. "Remember what it said on the scabbard? 'Draw me never unless I may drink blood.' "

We swung to look at the child and he smiled nervously under all our eyes.

"Rafe's right," I said harshly. "We can't loose Sharra unless we really mean to use it, and no sane human beings would do that."

Kadarin said, "Marjorie. You're the Keeper. Do you believe this superstitious drivel?"

Her voice was not steady, but she stretched her hand to me. "I believe Lew knows more about matrices than any of us, or all of us together. You pledged, Bob, you swore to Desideria to be guided by Lew's judgment. I won't work against it."

Beltran said, "You're both part-Terran! Are you two on their side then, against Darkover?"

I gasped at the old slur. I would never have believed it of Beltran. Marjorie flared. "It was you, yourself, who pointed out not a moment ago that we are *all* Terran! There is no 'side,' only a common good for all! Does the left hand chop off the right?"

I felt Marjorie struggle for control, felt Kadarin, too, fighting to overcome his flaming anger. I had confidence still in his integrity, when he took the time to control that vicious rage which was the one chink in the strong armor of his will.

Kadarin spoke gently at last: "Lew, I know there is some truth in what you say. I trust you, *bredu*." The word moved me more than I could express. "But what alternative have we, my friend? Are you trying to say that we should simply give up our plans, our hopes, our dream? It was your dream, too. Must we forget what we all believed in?"

"The Gods forbid," I said, shaken. "It is not the dream I would see put aside, only Sharra's part in it." Then I appealed directly to Beltran. He was the one I must convince.

"Let Sharra go back to the forge-folk's keeping. They have held it harmless all these years. No, kinsman, hear me out," I pleaded. "Do this, and I will go to Arilinn; I will speak with telepaths at Hali, at Neskaya and Corandolis and Dalereuth. I will explain to all of them what you are doing for Darkover, plead for you, if need be, before the Comyn Council itself. Do you honestly believe that you are the only man on Darkover who chafes under Terran rule and control? I am as certain as that I stand here, that they will come to your support and work with you freely and wholeheartedly, far better than I alone can do. And they have access to every known, monitored matrix on Darkover, and to the records of what was done with them in old times. We can find one safe for our purpose. Then I will work with you myself, and as long as you like, for your *real* aims. Not bluff with a terrible weapon, but a total, concerted effort by all of us, every one of us together, to recover the *real* strengths of Darkover, something positive to give the Terrans and the Empire, in return for what they can give us."

I met Regis' eyes, and suddenly time was out of focus again. I saw him in a great hall, crowded with men and women, hundreds and hundreds of them, *every telepath on Darkover*! It slid away and the eight of us were alone in the little fireside room again. I said to Regis and Danilo, "You would cooperate in such an endeavor, wouldn't you?"

Regis, his eyes gleaming with excitement, said, "With all my heart, Lord Beltran. I am certain that even Comyn Council would put all the telepaths and towers of Darkover at your service!"

This was a greater dream than the one which had drawn us together! It must be! I had seen it! Beltran must catch fire from it too!

Beltran stared at us all, and before he spoke my heart sank. There was icy contempt in his voice and words.

"You damnable forsworn *traitor*!" he flung at me. "Get me under the heel of Comyn, would you? That I should get on my knees before the *Hali'imyn* and take from them as a gift the power which is my right? Better even to do as my doddering old father did, and grovel to the Terrans! But I am lord of Aldaran now, and I will plunge all Darkover into red chaos first! Never! Never, damn you! Never!" His voice rose to a hoarse shriek of rage.

"Beltran, I beg of you—"

"Beg! Beg, you stinking half-caste! As you would make *me* beg, grovel—

I clenched my fists, aching with the need to fall on him, beat that sneer off his face . . . no. That was not his true self, either, but Sharra.

"I am sorry, kinsman. You leave me no choice." Whatever happened after, the closeness of this circle was broken; nothing could ever be the same. "Kadarin, you placed Sharra in my hands and pledged to abide my judgment. Before it is too late, the circle must be broken, the link destroyed, the matrix insulated before it controls us all."

"No!" Thyra cried. "If you dare not handle it, I do!"

"Breda—"

"No," Marjorie said, her voice shaking, "no, Thyra. It is the only way. Lew's right, it can destroy us all. Bob." She faced Kadarin, her golden eyes swimming in tears. "You made me Keeper. By that authority, I have to say it." Her voice broke in a sob. "The link must be broken."

"No!" Kadarin said harshly, repulsing her outstretched hands. "I did not want you to be Keeper; I feared just this—that you would be swayed by Lew! Sharra's circle must be preserved! You know you cannot break it without my consent!" He stared fiercely at her, and I thought of a hawk I had once seen, hovering over its prey.

Beltran stood in front of Danilo, facing him down. "I ask you for the last time. Will you do what I ask?"

Danilo was trembling. I recalled that he had been the youngest and most timid of the cadets. His voice shook as he said, "N-no, my lord Aldaran. I will not."

Beltran turned his eyes on Regis. His voice was level and grim. "Regis Hastur. You are not now in the Domains, but in Aldaran's stronghold. You came here of your own free will, and you will not depart from here until you command your minion to use his powers as I shall direct."

"My *paxman* is free to follow his own will and conscience. He has refused you; I support his decision. Now, Lord Aldaran, I respectfully request your leave to depart."

Beltran shouted in the mountain tongue. The doors suddenly burst open and a dozen of his guards burst into the fireside room. I realized, in sudden consternation, that he must have meant this all along. One of them approached Regis, who was unarmed; Danilo quickly drew his dagger and stepped between them, but was swiftly disarmed. Beltran's men dragged them back out of the way.

Marjorie faced Beltran is angry reproach.

"Beltran, you cannot! This is treachery! He was our father's guest!"

"But not *my* guest," Beltran said, and the words were a snarl, "and I have no patience with barbarian codes under a pretense of honor! Now for you, Lew Alton. Will you honor your pledge to us?"

"*You* speak of honor?" The words seemed to rise from some hidden spring within me, and I spat on the floor at his feet. "I honor my pledge to you as you honor your father's memory!" I turned my back on him. Within the hour I would be in touch with Arilinn by matrix, and the Comyn would know what Beltran planned . . .

I had forgotten the link still strong between us all. Kadarin said, "Oh, no, you won't," and gestured to the guards. "Take him!"

My hand fell to sword-hilt—and found, of course, nothing. *Wear no sword, at kinsman's board.* I had trusted in my safety in my cousin's own house! Two guards seized me, held me motionless between them. Kadarin came to where I was held and raised his hand to my throat, jerking the laces of my tunic undone. He raised his hand to the leather bag containing my personal matrix.

I began to struggle now in deadly fear. It had never been more than a few inches from my body since I had been keyed into it when I was twelve years old. I had been warned what it meant to have anyone else touch it. Kadarin hauled at the leather bag; I brought my knee up into his groin. He yelled with pain, and I felt the shock of the agony through my own body, doubling me up, but it only strengthened his fury. He beckoned to the rest of the guards. It took four of them to do it, but before long I was spread-eagled on the floor, arms and legs pinioned down, while Kadarin knelt atop me, straddling my helpless body, his fists flailing blows on my face. I felt blood breaking from my nose, my eyes; I gagged on my own blood, streaming down my throat from a broken tooth. I could no longer see Marjorie for the blood in my eyes, but I heard her shrieking, sobbing, begging. Were they hurting her too?

Kadarin drew his dagger. He stared straight down into my eyes, his face flickering with that unholy flame. He said between his teeth, "I should cut your throat now and save us all some trouble."

With a swift, downward slash, he cut the throng that held the leather bag; seized it between his hands and wrenched it away.

Until the day I die, I shall never forget that agony. I heard Marjorie scream, a long, death-like shriek of pain and terror, felt my whole body arch backward in a convulsive spasm, then fall limp. I heard my own voice screaming hoarsely, felt steel fingers clutch at my heart, felt my breathing falter. Every nerve in my body was in spasm. I had never known I could live through such anguish. Red haze blurring what was left of my sight, I felt myself dying and instinctively I heard my own tortured shriek:

"Father! *Father!*"

Then it all went dark and blind and I thought, This is death.

I don't know what happened in the next three days. For all I know, I was dead. I know it was three days because I was told so later; it might have been thirty seconds or thirty years later that I came up to foggy awareness that I was alive, and that I would much rather *not* be.

I was lying on the bed in my quarters in Castle Aldaran. I felt bruised, sick, every separate bone and muscle in my body with a separate ache. I staggered into the bathroom and stared at my reflection in the mirror. From the way my face looked, I can only imagine that my body kept on fighting long after I wasn't in it any more.

There were a couple of broken teeth ragged in my mouth, and they hurt like hell. My eyes were so bruised and swollen I could hardly get them open to see. My face had been cut by something hard, the big rings Kadarin wore, maybe. There were going to be scars.

Worse than the physical pain, which was bad enough, was the terrible sense of *emptiness*. Drearily, I wondered why I had not died. Some telepaths do die of shock, if they are forcibly severed from their own personal keyed matrices. I was just one of the unlucky ones.

Marjorie. My last memory was hearing her scream. Had they tortured her too?

If Kadarin had harmed her I would kill him . . .

The thought was wrenching pain. He had been my friend—he could not have pretended—not to a telepath. Sharra had corrupted him. . . .

I wished he *had* cut my throat instead.

Sharra. I went to look for the matrix, but it was gone. I was glad to be rid of the damnable thing, but I was afraid, too. Would it let us go?

I drank cold water, trying to lessen the dry sickness in me. My hand kept fumbling for the place around my neck where the matrix should have been. I couldn't think straight or see properly, and there was a constant dull ringing in my ears. I was really surprised I had survived this shock.

Slowly I realized something else. Sore and aching as I was, there was no blood anywhere on my face or garments.

Nor had I fouled my clothes. Someone had therefore been here, tended my wounds after a fashion, put clean clothes on me. Kadarin, when he came to take away the Sharra matrix?

I found I very much disliked the thought of Kadarin coming here, handling my unconscious body. I clenched my teeth, found out it hurt too much and made myself relax. Another score to settle with him.

Well, he'd done his worst, and I was still alive.

I tried the door cautiously. As I had suspected, it was bolted on the outside.

I ached so much that the thought of a long hot bath was tempting. The thought of being surprised naked and defenseless in the bathtub, however, removed all temptation from the idea. I soaked a cloth in the hot water and bathed my bruised face.

I ransacked the apartment, but of course my sword was gone, and the dagger, too. When I rummaged in my saddlebags for my heavy traveling boots, even the small *skean-dhu* in the boot was gone from its sheath.

A grim smile touched my face. Did they think me helpless? I had my Guardsman training still, and Kadarin might—he just might—despise me enough to come back alone.

I dragged up a chair—I still wasn't steady enough on my feet to stand for what might be hours waiting for him—and sat down facing the bolted door.

Sooner or later someone would come. And I would be ready.

It was a long time before I heard a tiny metallic rasp from the door. Someone was stealthily fumbling to draw the bolt back. Finally the door began, very slowly, to open inward.

I leaped, grabbed the hand that had just begun to steal inward and jerked hard—and felt the delicate wrist too late to arrest the force of the swing. Marjorie skidded inside, gasping, slammed against the door-frame. I dropped her wrist as if it was burned. She staggered and I held her quickly upright.

"Quick," she whispered, "shut the door!"

"Gods defend us," I whispered, staring in horror at her. "I could have killed you!"

"I'm glad you're able—" She drew a quick gasp. "Lew, your face! Oh God . . ."

"The loving attention of my kinsmen." I shut the door, shoved the heavy chair up against it.

"I begged them—I begged them—"

I laid my arms around her. "Poor love, I know, I heard you. Did they hurt you?"

"No, even Beltran didn't hurt me, though I scratched and bit him." She said, her voice coming in gasps, "I have your matrix for you. Here, quick." She held the small leather bag out to me. I thrust it inside my tunic, next to my skin. It seemed that my vision cleared at once, the dull ringing inside my head quieted. Even my heart beat more solidly. I was still battered and aching from the terrible beating I had taken, but I felt alive again. "How did you get it?"

"Bob made me take it," she said. "He said I was Keeper, only I could handle it without hurting you. He said you'd die otherwise. So I took it. Lew, only to save you. I swear it—"

"I know. If anyone but a Keeper had kept it long, I would certainly have died." Not that I credited Kadarin with that much kindness for my well-being. He probably knew what too much handling of someone else's keyed matrix would do to *him*.

"Where is the Sharra matrix?"

"Thyra has it, I think," she said doubtfully. "I'm not sure."

"How did you get in here, Marjorie? Are there guards watching me?"

She nodded slowly. "All the guards know me," she said at last. "Most of them were my father's friends and have known me since they held me on their knees. They trust me . . . and I brought them drugged wine. I'm ashamed of that, Lew, but what else could I do? But we must get away at once, as quickly as we can. When they wake up they will know, and tell Beltran . . ." Her voice failed.

"He should thank you for saving the small remnant of his honor," I said grimly. Then I realized she had said "we."

"You will come with me?"

"I must, I dare not stay after what I have done. Lew, don't you *want* me? Do you think I had any part in . . . *oh*!"

I held her tight. "Can you doubt it? But in these mountains, at this season—"

"I was born in these mountains; I've traveled in worse weather than this."

"We must be gone, then, before the guards wake. What did you give them?"

She told me and I shook my head. "No good. They'll wake within the hour. But maybe I can do better now." I touched the matrix. "Let's go." Hastily I gathered my things together. She had dressed warmly, I saw, heavy boots, a long riding-skirt. I looked out the windows. It was nightfall, but by some god's mercy it was not snowing.

In the dim hallway two figures sprawled in sodden, snoring sleep. I bent and listened to their breathing. Marjorie gasped, "Don't kill them, Lew. They've done you no harm!"

I wasn't so sure. My ribs still ached from the weight of somebody's boots. "I can do better than killing them," I said, cradling the matrix between my palms. Swiftly, incisively, I drew into the minds of the drugged men. *Sleep, I commanded, sleep long and well, sleep till the rising sun wakes you. Marjorie never came here, you drank no wine, drugged or wholesome.*

The poor devils would have to answer to Beltran for sleeping at their post. But I'd done what I could.

I tiptoed down the corridor, Marjorie hugging the wall behind me. Outside the great guest suite were two more drugged guards; Marjorie had been thorough. I stooped over them, sent them, too, more deeply into their dreams.

My hands are strong. I made shorter work of the bolts than Marjorie had done. Briefly I wondered at the kind of hospitality that puts a bolt on the outside of a guest room door for any contingency. As I stepped inside, Danilo quickly stepped between me and Regis. Then he recognized me and fell back.

Regis said, "I thought they'd killed you—" His eyes fell on my face. "It looks as if they'd tried! How did you get out?"

"Never mind," I said. "Get on your riding-things, unless you love Aldaran's hospitality too well to leave it!"

Regis said, "They came and took away my sword, and Danilo's dagger." For some reason the loss of the dagger seemed to grieve him most. I had no time to wonder why. I went and hauled at the senseless guardsmen's sword-belts, gave one to Regis, belted the other around my own waist. It was too long for me, but better than nothing. I gave the daggers to Marjorie and Danilo. "I have repaid my kinsman's theft," I said, "now let's get out of here."

"Where shall we go?"

I had made my decision swiftly. "I'll take Marjorie to Arilinn," I said. "You two just get away as fast and far as you can, before all hell breaks loose."

Regis nodded. "We'll take the straight road to Thendara, and get the word to Comyn."

Danilo said, "Shouldn't we all stay together?"

"No, Dani. One of us may get through if the others are recaptured, and the Comyn must be warned, whatever happens. There is an out-of-control, unmonitored matrix being used here. Tell them that, if I cannot!" Then I hesitated. "Regis, don't take the straight road! It's suicide! It's the first place they'll look!"

"Then maybe I can draw pursuit away from you," he said. "Anyway, it's you and Marjorie they'll be after. Danilo and I are nothing to them."

I wasn't so sure. Then I saw what I could not mistake. I said, "No. We cannot separate while I send you on the route of danger. You are ill." Threshold sickness, I finally realized. "I cannot send the heir to Hastur into such danger!"

"Lew, we *must* separate." He looked straight up into my eyes. "Someone *must* get through to warn the Comyn."

What he said was true and I knew it. "Can you endure the journey?" I asked.

Danilo said, "I'll look after him, and anyway he's better off on the road than in Beltran's hands, especially once you've escaped." This was true also and I knew it. Danilo was quickly separating the contents of Regis' saddlebags, discarding nearly everything. "We've got to travel light. There's food here from Regis' journey north . . ." He quickly divided it, rolling meat and fruit, hard bread, into two small parcels. He handed the larger one to me and said, "You'll be on the back roads, further away from villages."

I stuffed it into the inside pocket of my riding cloak and looked at Marjorie. "Can we get out unseen?"

"That's easy enough, word won't have reached the stables. We'll get horses, too."

Marjorie led us out a small side door near the stables. Most of the stablemen were sleeping; she roused one old man who knew her as Kermiac's ward. It was eccentric, perhaps, for her to set forth at nightfall with some of Beltran's honored guests, but it wasn't for an old horse-keeper to question. Most of them had seen me with her and had heard the castle gossip that a marriage was being arranged. If he had heard of the quarrel, this would have accounted for it in his mind, that Marjorie and I had run away to marry against Beltran's will. I'm sure this accounted for the looks of sympathy the old groom gave us. He found mounts for us all. I thought tardily of the escort from Comyn, who had come here with me.

I could order them to go with Regis and Danilo, protect them. But that would make a stir. Marjorie said softly, "If they don't know where you've gone, they cannot be made to tell," and that decided me.

If we rode hard till morning, and Beltran's guards slept as I had insured they would, we might be beyond pursuit. We led our horses toward the gates; the groom let us out. I lifted Marjorie to her saddle, readied myself to mount. She looked back with a faint sadness but, seeing me watching, she smiled bravely and turned her face to the road.

I turned to Regis, holding him for a moment in a kinsman's embrace. Would I ever see him again? I thought I had turned my back on Comyn, yet the tie was stronger than I knew. I had thought him a child, easily flattered, easily swayed. No. Less so than I was myself. I told myself firmly not to be morbid, and kissed him on the cheek, letting him go. "The Gods ride with you, *bredu*." I said, turning away. His hand clung to my arm for a moment, and in a split second I saw, for the last time, the frightened child I had taken into the fire-lines; he remembered, too, but the very memory of conquered fear strengthened us both. Still, I could not forget that he had been placed in my charge. I said hesitantly, "I am not sure . . . I do not like letting you take the road of most danger, Regis."

He gripped my forearms with both hands and looked straight into my eyes. He said fiercely, "Lew, you too are the heir to your Domain! And I have an heir, you don't!

If it comes to that, better me than you!" I was shocked speechless by the words. Yet they were true. My father was old and ill; Marius, so far as we knew, was without *laran*.

I was the last male Alton. And it had taken Regis to remind me!

This was a man, a Hastur. I bowed my head in acquiescence, knowing we stood at that moment before something older, more powerful than either of us. Regis drew a long breath, let go of my hands, and said, "We'll meet in Thendara, if the Gods will it, cousin."

"I knew my voice was shaking. I said, "Take care of him, Dani."

He answered, "With my life, Dom Lewis," as they swung into their saddles. Without a backward glance, Regis rode away down the path, Danilo a pace behind him.

I mounted, taking the opposite fork of the road, Marjorie at my side. I thanked all the gods I had ever heard of, and all the rest I hadn't, for the time I had spent with maps on my northward journey. It was a long way to Arilinn, through some of the worst country on Darkover, and I wondered if Marjorie could endure it.

Overhead two of the moons swung, violet-blue, green-blue, shedding soft light on the snow-clad hills. We rode for hours in that soft night light. I was wholly aware of Marjorie: her grief and regret at leaving her childhood home, the desperation which had driven her to this. She must never regret it! I pledged my own life that she should not regret.

The green face of Idriel sank behind the crest of the pass; above us was a bank of cold fog, stained blood color with the coming sunrise. We must begin to look somewhere for shelter; I was sure the hunt would be up soon after daylight. I was enough in contact with Marjorie to know when her weariness became almost unendurable. But when I spoke of it, she said, "Another mile or so. On the slope of the next hill, far back from the roadway, is a summer pasture. The herdwomen have probably taken their beasts down into the valley, so it will be empty."

The herdwomen's hut was concealed within a grove of nut trees. As we drew near my heart sank, for I could hear the soft lowing of herd animals, and as we dismounted I saw one of the women, barefoot in the melting snow, her hair long and tangled around her face, clad in a ragged leather skirt. Marjorie, however, seemed pleased.

"We're in luck, Lew. Her mother was one of *my* mother's people." She called softly, "Mhari!"

The woman turned, her face lighting up. *"Domna Marguerida!"* She spoke a dialect too ancient for me to follow; Marjorie answered her softly in the same patois. Mhari grinned widely and led us into the hut.

Most of the inside was taken up with a couple of dirty straw pallets on which an older woman lay, entangled with half a dozen small children and a few puppies. The only furniture was a wooden bench. Mhari gestured to us to sit on it, and ladled us out bowls of hot, coarse, nut-porridge. Marjorie almost collapsed on the bench; Mhari came to draw off her riding-boots.

"What did she say to you, Marjorie? What did you tell her?"

"The truth. That Kermiac was dead, that on his deathbed he had promised me to you, and that you and Beltran had quarreled, so we are going into the lowlands to marry. She has promised that neither she nor her friend, nor any of the children, will say a word of our being here." Marjorie took another spoonful of the porridge. She was almost too weary to lift her spoon to her mouth. I was glad to down my portion, to put aside my sword and haul off my boots and later, when the conglomeration of babies and puppies had vacated the mattress, to lie down there in my clothes beside Marjorie.

"They should have gone, days ago," Marjorie said, "but Caillean's husband has not come for them. She says they'll be out all day with the beasts and we can sleep safely here." And indeed, very shortly the clamoring crew of babies and puppies had been fed on the rest of the porridge and hustled outside. I drew Marjorie into the circle of my arm, then realized that in spite of the noise made by children and dogs she was already deeply asleep. The straw smelled of dogs and dirt, but I was too tired to be critical. Marjorie lying in the curve of my arm, I slept too.

The next thing I knew it was late evening, the room was full of puppies and children again, and we rose and ate big hot bowlfuls of vegetable soup that had been simmering over the fire all day. Then it was time to pull on our boots and go. The women, from their vantage point high on the slopes, had seen no riders, so we were not pursued yet. Marjorie kissed Mhari and the smallest of the babies, and warned me not to offer them money. Mhari and her friend insisted that we take bags of nuts and a loaf or two of the hard-baked bread, telling us they had too much to load on their pack animals on the way down into the valley for winter. I didn't believe a word of it, but we could not refuse.

The next two or three nights of travel were duplicates of that one. We were blessed with good weather and there was no sign of pursuit. We slept by day, concealed in herd-huts, but these were deserted. We had food enough, although we were almost always cold. Marjorie never complained, but I was desperately concerned about her. I could not imagine any woman I had ever known enduring such a journey. When I said so to Marjorie, she laughed.

"I am no pampered lowland lady, Lew, I am used to hard weather, and I can travel whenever I must, even in dead winter. Thyra would be a better companion, perhaps, she is hardened to long journeys with Bob, in and out of season . . ." She fell silent, and quickly turned her face away. I kept silent. I knew how close she had been to her sister and how she felt about this parting. It was the first time she spoke of her life at Castle Aldaran. It was also the last.

On the fourth or fifth morning we had to ride far into daylight to find any shelter at all. We were now in the wildest part of the mountains, and the roads had dwindled away to mere trails. Marjorie was dropping with weariness; I had half resolved that for once we must find a sheltered place in the woods and sleep in the open, when suddenly, riding into a small clearing, we came on a deserted farmstead.

I wondered how anyone had ever managed to farm these bleak hills, but there were outbuildings and a small stone house, a yard which had once been fenced, a well with wooden piping still splashing water into a broken stone trough in the yard—all wholly deserted. I feared it had become the haunt of birds or bats, but when I forced the door open it was weathertight and almost clean.

The sun was high and warm. While I unsaddled, Marjorie had taken off her cloak and boots and was splashing her hands in the stone trough. She said, "I am past my first sleepiness, and I have not had my clothes off since we set out. I am going to wash; I think it will refresh me better than sleep." She was suiting action to words, pulling off her riding-skirt and fur-lined tunic, standing before me in her long heavy shift and petticoat. I came and joined her. The water was icy cold, coming straight down from a mountain spring above us, but it was marvelously refreshing. I marveled how Marjorie could stand barefoot in the last melting runnels of the last night's snowfall, but she seemed not as cold as I was. We sat in the growing warmth of the sun afterward, eating the last of the herdwomen's coarse bread. I found a tree in the yard where the former owners had farmed mushrooms, an intricate system of small wooden pipes directing water down the trunk. Most of the mushrooms were hard and woody, but I found a few small new ones high up, and we ate them at the end of our meal, savoring their sweet freshness.

She stretched a little, sleepily. "I would like to sleep here in the sun," she said. "I am beginning to feel like some night-bird, never coming out into the light of day."

"But I am not hardened to your mountain weather," I said, "and we may have to sleep in the open, soon enough."

She made a mock-serious face. "Poor Lew, are you cold? Yes, I suppose we must go inside to sleep." She gathered up our heavy outer clothes and carried them. She spread them out on an old, abandoned pallet in the farmhouse, wrinkling a fastidious nose at the musty smell. I said, "It is better than dog," and she giggled and sat down on the heap of clothing.

She had on a thick woolen shift, knee-length and with long sleeves; I had seen her far more lightly clothed at Aldaran, but there was something about being here like this that roused an awareness that fear and weariness had almost smothered. All during this trip she had slept within the circle of my arm, but innocently. Perhaps because I was still recovering from the effects of Kadarin's brutal beating. Now, all at once, I was aware again of her physical presence. She felt it—we were lightly in rapport all the time now—and turned her face a little away, color rising along her cheekbones. There was a hint of defiance as she said, "Just the same, I am going to take down my hair and comb and braid it properly, before it gets tangled like Mhari's and I have to cut it off!" She raised her arms, pulled out the butterfly-shaped clasp that held her braids pinned at the nape of her neck, and began to unravel the long plaits.

I felt the hot flush of embarrassment. In the lowlands a sister who was already a woman would not have done this even before a grown brother. I had not seen Linnell's hair loose like this since we were little children, although when we were small I had sometimes helped her comb it. Did customs really differ so much? I sat and watched her move the ivory comb slowly through her long copper hair; it was perfectly straight, only waved a little from the braiding, and very fine, and the sun, coming in cracks through the heavy wooden shutters, set it all ablaze with the glint of the precious metal. I said at last, hoarsely, "Don't tease me, Marjorie. I'm not sure I can bear it."

She did not look up. She only said softly, "Why should you? I am here."

I reached out and took the comb away from her, turning her face up to meet my eyes. "I cannot take you lightly, beloved. I would give you all honor and all ceremony."

"You cannot," she said, with the shadow of a small smile, "because I no longer . . ." the words were coming slowly now, as if it were painful to speak them. "—no longer acknowledge Beltran's right to give me in marriage. My foster-father meant to give me to you. That is ceremony enough." Suddenly she spoke in a rush. "And I am not a Keeper now! I have renounced that, I will not keep myself separate from you, I will not, *I will not*!"

She was sobbing now. I flung the comb away and drew her into my arms, holding her to me with sudden violence. "Keeper? No, no, never again," I whispered against her mouth. "Never, never again—"

What can I say? We were together. And we were in love.

Afterward I braided her hair for her. It seemed almost as intimate as lying down together, my hands trembling as they touched the silken strands, as they had when I first touched her. We did not sleep for a long time.

When we woke it was late and already snowing heavily. When I went to saddle the horses, the wind was whipping the snow in wild stinging needles across the yard. We could not ride in this. When I came inside again, Marjorie looked at me in guilty dismay.

"I delayed us. I'm sorry—"

"I think we are beyond pursuit now, *preciosa*. But we would only have had to turn back; we cannot ride in this. I'll put the horses into the outbuilding and give them some foder."

"Let me come and help—"

"Don't go out in the snow, beloved. I'll attend to the horses."

When I came in, Marjorie had kindled a fire on the long-dead hearth and, finding an old battered stone kettle discarded in a corner, had washed it, filled it at the well and put some of our dried meat to stew with the mushrooms. When I scolded her for going into the yard—in these snow-squalls men have been lost and frozen between their own barnyard and doorway—she said shyly, "I wanted us to have a fireside. And a . . . a wedding-feast."

I hugged her close and said, "The minute he sees you my father will be delighted to arrange all that."

"I know," she said, "but I'd rather have it here."

The thought warmed me more than the fire.

We ate the hot soup before the fire. We had to share one spoon and eat it straight from the old kettle. We had little fuel and the fire burned down quickly, but as it sank into darkness Marjorie whispered, "Our first fireside."

I knew what she meant. It was not the formal ceremony, *di catenas,* the elaborate wedding-feast for my kin, her proclamation before Comyn Council, that would make her my wife. Everywhere in the hills, where ceremonies are few and witnesses sparse, the purposeful sharing of "a bed, a meal, a fireside" acknowledges the legal status of a marriage, and I knew why Marjorie had risked losing her way in the snow to kindle a fire and cook us up some soup. By the simple laws of the hills, we were wedded, not in our own eyes alone, but in a ceremony that would stand in the eyes of all men.

I was glad she had been sure enough of me to do this without asking. I was glad the weather kept us here for another night. But something was troubling me. I said, "Regis and Danilo are nearer to Thendara now than we are to Arilinn, unless they have been recaptured. But neither of them is a skilled telepath, and I doubt if a message has gone through. I should send a message, either to Arilinn or to my father. I should have done it before."

She caught my hand as I pulled the matrix from its resting place. "Lew, is it really safe?"

"I must, love, safe or not. I should have done it the moment I had my matrix back. We must face the possibility that they will try again. Beltran won't abandon his aims so quickly, and I fear Kadarin is unscrupulous." I backed off from speaking the name of Sharra aloud, but it was there between us and we both knew it.

And if they did try again, without my knowledge or control, without Marjorie for Keeper, what then? Playing with forest fire would be child's play, next to the risk of waking that thing without a trained Keeper! I had to warn the towers.

She said hesitantly, "We were all in rapport. If you . . . use your matrix . . . can they *feel* it, trail us that way?"

That was a possibility, but whatever happened to us, Sharra must be controlled and contained, or none of us would ever be safe again. And in all these days I had sensed no touch, no seeking mind.

I drew out the matrix and uncovered it. To my dismay, I felt a faint, twisting tinge of sickness as I gazed into the blue depths. That was a danger signal. Perhaps during the days I had been separated from it, I had become somewhat unkeyed. I focused on it, steadying my mind to the delicate task of establishing rapport again with the starstone; again and again I was forced to turn my eyes away by the pain, the blurring of vision.

"Leave it, Lew, leave it, you're too tired—"

"I cannot." If I delayed, I would lose mastery of the matrix, be forced to begin again with another stone. I fought the matrix for nearly an hour, struggling with my inability to focus it. I looked at Marjorie with regret, knowing that I was draining my strength with this telepathic struggle. I cursed the fate that had made me a telepath and a matrix mechanic, but it never occurred to me that I should abandon the struggle unfinished.

If this had—unimaginably—happened in Arilinn, I would have been given *kirian* or one of the other psi-activator drugs and helped by a psi monitor and my own Keeper. Now I had to master it alone. I myself had made it impossible and dangerous for Marjorie to help me.

At last, my head splitting, I managed to focus the lights in the stone. Quickly, while I still had the strength, I reached out through the gray and formless spaces that we call the underworld, looking for the light-landmark that was the relay-circle at Arilinn.

For a moment I had it. Then, within the stone, there was a wild flaring flame, a rush of savage awareness, a too-familiar surge of fiery violence . . . flames rising, the great form of fire blotting out consciousness . . . a woman, dark and vital, bearing a living flame, a great circle of faces pouring out raw emotion. . . .

I heard Marjorie gasp, fought to break the raport. *Sharra! Sharra! We had been sealed to it, we were caught and drawn to the fires of destruction. . . .*

"No! *No!*" Marjorie cried aloud, and I saw the fires thin out and vanish. They had never been there. They were reflected in the dying coals of our ritual marriage-fire; the eerie edge of light around Marjorie's face was only the last firelight there. She whispered, trembling, "Lew, what was it?"

"You know," I hesitated to say the name aloud, "Kadarin. And Thyra. Working directly with the sword. Zandru's hells, Marjorie, they are trying to use it the old way, not with a Keeper-controlled circle of telepaths in an orderly energon ring—and it's uncontrollable even that way, as we found out—but with a single telepath, focusing raw emotion from a group of untrained followers."

"Isn't that terribly dangerous?"

"Dangerous! The word's inadequate! Would you kindle a forest fire to cook your supper? Would you chain a dragonfire to roast your chops or dry your boots? I wish I thought they would only kill *themselves*!"

I strode up and down by the dead fire, restlessly listening to the battering of the storm outside. "And I can't even warn them at Arilinn!"

"Why not, Lew?"

"So close to—to Sharra—my own matrix won't work," I said, and tried to explain how Sharra evidently blanked out smaller matrices.

"How far will that effect reach, Lew?"

"Who knows? Planet-wide, maybe. I've never worked with anything that strong. There aren't any precedents."

"Then, if it reached all the way to Arilinn, won't the telepaths there know that *something* is wrong?"

I brightened. That might be our only hope. I staggered suddenly and she caught at my arm.

"Lew! You're worn out. Rest here by me, darling." I flung myself down at her side, dizzy and despairing. I had not even spoken of my other fears, that if I used my personal matrix, I, who had been sealed to Sharra, might be drawn back into that vortex, that savage fire, that corner of hell. . . .

She knew, without my saying it. She whispered, "I can feel it reaching for us. . . . Can it draw us back, back into itself?" She clung to me in terror; I rolled over and took her to me, holding her with savage strength, fighting an almost uncontrollable desire. And that frightened hell out of me. I should be drained, spent, exhausted, incapable of the slightest sexual impulse. That was frustrating, but it was normal, and I had long since come to terms with it.

But this wild lust—and it was pure lust, a hateful dark animal thing with no hint of love or warmth—set my pulses racing, made me gasp and fight against it. It was too strong; I let it surge up and overwhelm me, feeling the fire burn up in my veins as if some scalding ichor had replaced the blood in my body. I smothered her mouth under mine, felt her weakly struggling to fight me away. Then the fire took us both.

It is the one memory I have of Marjorie which is not all joy. I took her savagely, without tenderness, trying to slake the burning need in me. She met me with equal violence, hating it equally, both of us gripped with that uncontrollable savage desperation. It was fierce and animal—no! Not animal! Animals meet cleanly, driven only by the life-force in them, knowing nothing of this kind of dark lust. There was no innocence in this, no love, only raw violence, insatiable, a bottomless pit of hell. It *was* hell, all the hell either of us would ever need to know. I heard her sobbing helplessly and knew I was weeping, too, with shame and self-hatred. Afterward we did not sleep.

CHAPTER TWENTY-ONE

Even at Nevarsin, Regis thought, it had never snowed so hard, or so persistently. His pony picked its way deliberately along, following in the steps of Danilo's mount, as mountain horses were trained to do. It was snowing again.

He wouldn't mind any of it, he thought, the riding, the cold or the lack of sleep, if he could see properly, or keep the world straight under him.

The threshold sickness had continued off and on, more on than off in the last day or so. He tried to ignore Danilo's anxious looks, his concern for him. There wasn't anything Danilo could do for him, so the less said about it, the better.

But it was intensely unpleasant. The world kept thinning away at irregular intervals and dissolving. He had had no attacks as bad as the one he'd had at Thendara or on the way north, but he seemed to live in mild chronic disorientation all the time. He didn't know which was worse, but suspected it was whichever form he happened to have at the time.

Danilo waited for him to draw even on the path. "Snowing already, and it's hardly midafternoon. At this rate it will take us a full twelve days to reach Thendara, and we'll lose the long start we had."

The more quickly they reached Thendara, the better. He knew a message *must* get through, even if Lew and Marjorie were recaptured. So far there was no sign of pursuit. But Regis knew, cursing his own weakness, that he could not take much more of the constant exertion, the long hours in the saddle and the constant sickness.

Earlier that day they had passed through a small village, where they had bought food and grain for the horses. Perhaps they could risk a fire tonight—if they could find a place to build it!

"Anything but a hay-barn," Danilo agreed. The last night they had slept in a barn, sharing warmth with several cows and horses and plenty of dry hay. The animals had made it a warm place to sleep, but they could not risk a fire or even a light, with the tinder-dry hay, so they had eaten nothing but hard strips of cured meat and a handful of nuts.

"We're in luck," Danilo said, pointing. Away to the side of the road was one of the travel-shelters built generations ago, when Aldaran had been the seventh Domain and this road had been regularly traveled in all seasons. The inns had all been abandoned, but the travel-shelters, built to stand for centuries, were still habitable, small stone cabins with attached sheds for horses and proper amenities for travelers.

They dismounted and stabled their horses, hardly speaking, Regis from weariness, Danilo from reluctance to intrude on him. Dani thought he was angry, Regis sensed; he knew he should tell his friend he was not angry, just tired. But he was reluctant to show weakness. He was Hastur: it was for him to lead, to take responsibility. So he drove himself relentlessly, the effort making his words few and sharp, his voice harsh. It only made it worse to know that if he had given Danilo the slightest encouragement, Dani would have waited on him hand and foot and done it with pleasure. He wasn't going to take advantage of Danilo's hero-worship.

The Comyn had done too much of that. . . .

The horses settled for the night, Danilo carried the saddle-bags inside. Pausing on the threshold, he said, "This is the interesting time, every night. When we see what the years have left of whatever place we've found to stay."

"It's interesting, all right," Regis said dryly. "We never know what we'll find, or who'll share our beds with us." One night they had had to sleep in the stables, because a nest of deadly scorpion-ants had invaded the shelter itself.

"Um, yes, a scorpion-ant is a lower form of life than I care to go to bed with," Danilo said lightly, "but tonight we seem to be in luck." The interior was bare and smelled dusty and unaired, but there was an intact fireplace, a pair of benches to sit on and a heavy shelf built into the wall so they need not sleep on the floor at the mercy of spiders or rodents. Danilo dumped the saddlebags on a bench. "I saw some dead branches in the lee of the stable. The snow won't have soaked them through yet. There may not be enough to keep a fire all night, but we can certainly cook some hot food."

Regis sighed. "I'll come and help you get them in." He opened the door again on the snow-swept twilight; the world toppled dizzily around him and he clung to the door.

"Regis, let me go, you're ill again."

"I can manage."

"Damn it!" Suddenly Danilo was angry. "Will you stop pretending and playing hero with me? How the hell will I manage if you fall down and can't get up again? It's a lot easier to drag a couple of armfuls of dry branches in, than try to carry *you* through the snow! Just stay in here, will you?"

Pretending. Playing hero. Was that how Danilo saw his attempt to carry his own weight? Regis said stiffly, "I wouldn't want to make things harder for you. Go ahead."

Danilo started to speak but didn't. He set his chin and strode, stiff-necked, into the snowy darkness. Regis started to unload the saddlebags but became so violently dizzy that he had to sit down on one of the stone benches, holding on with both hands.

He was a dead weight on Danilo, he thought. Good for nothing but to hold him back. He wondered how Lew was faring in the mountains. He'd hoped to draw pursuit away from him, that hadn't worked either. He felt like huddling on the bench, giving way to the surges of sickness, but remembered Javanne's advice: move around, fight it. He hauled himself to his feet, got his flint-and-steel and the wisps of dry hay they had kept for tinder, and knelt before the fireplace, clearing away the remnants of the last travelers' fire. How many years ago was that one built? he wondered.

Wind, and cold slashes of snow blew through the open doorway; Danilo, laden with branches, staggered inside, shoved them near the fireplace, went quickly out again. Regis tried to separate the driest branches to lay a fire, but could not steady his hands enough to manipulate the small mechanical flint-and-steel, fed with resinous oil, which kept the spark alive. He laid the device on the bench and sat with his head in his hands, feeling completely useless, until Danilo, bent under another load of branches, came in and kicked the door shut behind him.

"My father calls that a lazy man's load," he said cheerfully, "carrying too much because you're too lazy to go back for another. It ought to keep the cold out awhile. Anyway, I'd rather be cold here than warm in Aldaran's royal suite, damn him." He strode to where Regis had laid the fire, kneeling to spark it alight with Regis's lighter. "Bless the man who invented this gadget. Lucky you have one."

It had been part of Gabriel's camping-kit that Javanne had given him, along with the small cooking pots they carried. Dani looked at Regis, huddled motionless and shivering on the bench. He said, "Are you very angry with me?"

Silently, Regis shook his head.

Danilo said haltingly, "I don't want to . . . to offend you. But I'm your paxman and I have to do what's best for you. Even if it's not always what you want."

"It's all right, Dani. I was wrong and you were right," Regis said. "I couldn't even light the fire."

"Well, I don't mind lighting it. Certainly not with that gadget of yours. There's water piped in the corner, there, if the pipes aren't frozen. If they are, we'll have to melt snow. Now, what shall we cook?"

The last thing Regis cared about at that moment was food, but he forced himself to join in a discussion about whether soup made from dried meat and beans, or crushed-grain porridge, would be better. When it was bubbling over the fire, Danilo came and sat beside him. He said, "Regis, I don't want to make you angry again. But we've got to have this out. You're no better. Do you think I can't see that you can hardly ride?"

"What do you want me to say to you, Dani? I'm doing the best I can."

"You're doing *more* than you can," said Danilo. The light of the blazing fire made him look very young and very troubled. "Do you think I'm blaming you? But you must let me help you more." Suddenly he flared out, "What am I to say to them in Thendara, if the heir to Hastur dies in my hands?"

"You're making too much of this," Regis said. "I never heard that anyone died of threshold sickness."

Yet Javanne had looked genuinely frightened . . .

"Maybe not," Danilo said skeptically, "but if you cannot

sit your horse, and fall and break your skull, that's fatal, too. Or if you exhaust yourself and take a chill, and die of it. And you are the last Hastur."

"No I'm not," Regis said, at the end of endurance. "Didn't you hear me tell Lew? I have an heir. Before I ever came on this trip I faced the fact that I might die, so I named one of my sister's sons as my heir. Legally." Danilo sat back on his heels, stunned, wide open, and his thought was as clear as if he had spoken aloud, *For my sake?* Regis forcibly stopped himself from saying anything more. He could not face the naked emotion in Danilo's eyes. This was the time of danger, the forced intimacy of these evenings, when he must barricade himself continually against revealing what he felt. It would be all too easy to cling to Danilo for strength, to take advantage of Danilo's emotional response to him.

Danilo was saying angrily, "Even so, I won't have your death on my head! The Hasturs need you for *yourself,* Regis, not just for your blood or your heir!"

"What do you suggest I do about it?" Regis did not know, himself, whether it was an honest question or a sarcastic challenge.

"We are not pursued. We must rest here till you are well again."

"I don't think I shall ever be well again until I have a chance to go to one of the towers and learn to control this." *Laran?* Gift? Curse, he thought. In his blood, in his brain. But that was not the only thing making him ill, he knew. It was the constant need to barrier himself against his feelings, against his own unwelcome thoughts and desires. And for that there was no help, he decided. Even in the towers they could not make him other than he was. They might teach him to conceal it, though, live with it.

Danilo laid his hand on Regis' shoulder. "You must let me look after you. It is my duty." He added after a moment, "And my pleasure."

By an effort that literally made his head spin, Regis remained motionless under the touch. Rigidly, refusing the proffered rapport, he said, "Your porridge is burning. If you're so eager to do something, attend to what you're supposed to be doing. The damned stuff is inedible even when properly cooked."

Danilo stiffened as if the words had been a blow. He went to the fire and took off the boiling concoction. Regis did not look at him or care that he had hurt him. He was beyond thinking about anything, except his own attempt *not* to think.

He felt a violent anger with Danilo for forcing this intimate confrontation on him. Suddenly he recalled the fight Danilo had picked in the barracks; a fight which, had it not been for Hjalmar's intervention, might have gone far beyond a single blow. He wanted to lash out at Danilo now, flay him with cruel words. He felt a need to put distance between them, break up this unendurable closeness, keep Dani from looking at him with so much love. If they fought, perhaps Regis would no longer have to be constantly on guard, afraid of doing and saying what he could not even endure to think. . . .

Danilo came with porridge in a small pannikin. He said tentatively, "I don't think this is burned . . ."

"Oh, stop being so damned *attentive*!" Regis flung at him. "Eat your supper and let me alone, damn you, just stop hovering over me! What must I do to make you realize I don't want you, I don't need you? *Just let me alone!*"

Danilo's face went white. He went and sat on the other bench, his head bent over his own porridge. His back to Regis, he said coldly, "Yours is there when you want it, my lord."

Regis could see clearly, as if time had slid out of focus, that searing moment in the barracks, when Danilo had flung him off with an insult. It was clear in Danilo's mind, too: *He has done to me, knowing, what I did to him, unknowing.*

By main force Regis held himself back from immediate apology. The smell of the porridge made him feel violently sick. He went to the stone shelf and laid himself down, wrapping himself in his riding-cloak and trying to suppress the racking shudders that shook his whole body. It seemed to him that he could hear Danilo crying, as he had done so often in the barracks, but Danilo was sitting on the bench, quietly eating his supper. Regis lay looking at the fire, until it began to flare up, flame—hallucination. Not forest fire, not Sharra. Just hallucination again. Psi out of control.

Still, it seemed that he could see Lew's face, vividly, by firelight. Suppose, Regis thought, when I reached up toward him, drew him down beside me, he had flung me off, slapped me? Suppose he had thought the comfort I offered him a thing too shameful to endure or acknowledge?

I was only a child. I didn't know what I was doing.

He wasn't a child. And he knew.

Unable to endure this train of thought, he let the swaying sickness take him again. It was almost a relief to let the world slide away, go dim and thin out to nothing. Time vanished. He heard Danilo's voice after a time, but the words no longer made sense; they were just vibration, sound without sense or relevance. He knew with the last breath of sanity that his only hope of saving himself now was to cry out, get up and move around, call out to Danilo, hang on to him as an anchor in this deadly nowhere—

He could *not.* He could not surrender to this; he would rather die . . . and he heard some curious remote little voice in his mind say *Die, then, if it is so important to you.* And he felt something like a giant swing to take him, toss him high, further out into nowhere with every swooping breath, seeing stars, atoms, strange vibrations, the very rhythm of the universe—or was it his own brain cells vibrating, madly out of control?

He'd done this to himself, he knew. He'd let it happen, too much of a coward to face himself.

Call out to Dani, that inner voice said. *He'll help you, even now, if you ask him. But you'll have to ask, you've made it impossible for him to come to you again unless you call him. Call quickly, quickly, while you still can.*

I can't—

He felt his breathing begin to come in gasps, as if he hung somewhere in the far spaces which were all he could see now, with every breath coming for an instant back to that struggling, dimming body lying inert on the shelf. *Quickly! Cry out now for help or you will die, here and now with everything left undone because of your pride . . .*

With the last of his strength Regis fought for enough voice to shout, call aloud. It came out as the faintest of stifled whispers.

"Dani . . . help me . . ."

Too late, he thought, and felt himself slide off into nothingness. He wondered, with desperate regret, if he was dying . . . because he could not bear to be honest with himself, with his friend. . . .

He swung in darkness, immobile, numb, paralyzed. He felt Danilo, only a dim blue haze through his closed eyes, bending over him, fumbling at his tunic-laces. He could not even feel Danilo's hands except that they were at his throat. He thought insanely, Is he going to kill me?

Without warning his body convulsed in a spasm of the most hideous pain he had ever known. He was *there* again, Danilo's face visible through a reddish blood-colored mist, standing over him, his hand just touching the matrix around Regis' neck. Regis said hoarsely, "No. Not again—" and felt the bone-cracking spasm return. Danilo dropped the matrix as if it burned him and the hellish pain subsided. Regis lay gasping. It felt as if he had fallen into the fire.

Danilo gasped, "Forgive me—I thought you were dying! I knew no other way to reach your mind. . . ." Carefully, without touching it, Danilo covered the matrix again. He dropped down on the stone bed beside Regis, as if his knees were too weak to hold him upright.

"Regis, Regis, I thought you were dying—"

Regis whispered, "I thought so too."

"I told myself, if I let you die because I could not forgive a harsh word, then I was a disgrace to my father and all those who had served Hastur. I am a catalyst telepath, there had to be *something* I could do to reach you—I shouted and you didn't hear, I slapped and pinched you, I thought you were dead already, but I could *feel* you calling me. . . ." He was entirely unstrung. Regis whispered, "What was it that you did? I felt you—"

"I touched the matrix—nothing else seemed to reach you, I was so sure you were dying—" He broke down and sobbed. "I could have killed you! I could have killed you!"

Regis drew Danilo down beside him, holding him tight in his arms. "*Bredu,* don't cry," he whispered. "See, I'm not dead." He felt suddenly shy again. Danilo's face, wet with tears, was pressed against his cheek. Regis patted it clumsily. "Don't cry any more."

"But I hurt you so—I can't bear to hurt you," Danilo said wildly.

"I don't think anything less would have brought me

back," Regis said. "It's my life I owe you this time, *bredu*." He was still dizzy and aching with the aftermath of what he now knew must have been a convulsion. Later he was to learn that this last-resort heroic treatment, gripping a matrix, was used only at the point of death; when stronger telepaths determined that without it, the sufferer might wander endlessly in the corridors of his own brain, cutting off all outside stimuli, until he died. Danilo had done it by pure instinct. Now Regis remembered what Javanne had said. "I've got to get up and move around or it may come back. But you'll have to help me, Dani, I'm too weak to walk alone."

Danilo helped him upright. By the last light of the dying fire Regis could see the tears on his face. He kept his arm around Regis, steadying him. "I should never have quarreled with you when you were sick."

"It was I who picked the quarrel, Dani. Can you forgive me?"

He was cruel to Dani out of fear, Regis knew, fear of what he was himself. Perhaps Dyan, too, turned to cruelty out of fear and came at last to prefer cruelty to fear—or to shame—at knowing himself too well.

Laran was terrible. But they had no choice, only to meet it with honor.

Danilo said shyly, "I kept your porridge hot for you. Can you try to eat it now?"

Regis took the hot pottery pannikin, burning his fingers a little on the edges. The thought of food made him feel sick, but obediently he chewed a few mouthfuls and discovered that he was actually very hungry. He ate the hot unsweetened stuff, saying after a time, "Well, it's no worse than what we got in barracks. If you ever find yourself a masterless man, Dani, we'll get you a job as an army cook."

"God forbid I should be a masterless man while you live, Regis."

Regis reached for Danilo's hand, holding it tight. He felt exhausted and aching, but at peace. He finished the porridge and Danilo took the bowl away to rinse it out. Regis lay down on the shelf again. The fire was dying down and it was cold. Danilo came and spread out his own cloak and blanket beside Regis, sat beside him, pulling off his boots.

"I wish I knew more about threshold sickness."

"Be damn glad you don't," Regis said harshly, "it's hell. I hope you never have it."

"Oh, I *had* it," Dani said. "I know now that's what it must have been when I began . . . reading minds. There was no one to tell me what it was, and I never had it so seriously. The trouble is, I don't know what to do about it. Or I could help you." He looked at Regis hesitantly in the dim light and said, "We're still in rapport a little. Let me try."

"Do what you want to," Regis said, "I won't drive you away again. Only be careful. Your last experiment was painful."

"I did find out one thing," Danilo said. "I could see and feel things. There's a kind of . . . of *energy*. Look." He bent over Regis, running his fingertips lightly above his body, not touching him. "I can feel it this way, without touching you, and certain places it's strong, and others I feel it ought to be and isn't. . . . I don't know how to explain it. Do you feel it?"

Regis remembered the very little the *leronis* had told him when she tested him, unsuccessfully, for *laran*. "There are certain . . . energy centers in the body, which waken with the wakening of *laran*. Everybody has them, but in a telepath they're stronger and more . . . perceptible. If that's true, you should have them, too." He reached out toward Danilo, running his hands over his face, feeling the definite, tangible flow of power. "Yes, it's like an . . . an extra pulsebeat here, just above your brow." He had once been shown a drawing of these currents, but at that time he had no reason to believe it applied to him. Now he struggled to remember, sensing it must be important. "There's one at the base of the throat."

"Yes, I can see it," Danilo said, touching it lightly with a fingertip. The touch was not painful, but Regis felt it like a faint, definite electric shock. Yet once he was fully aware of the pulse, his perceptions cleared and the dizziness which had been with him for weeks now seemed to clear and shift somehow. He felt that he had discovered something very important, but he didn't know what. Danilo went on, trying to trace out the flows of power with his fingertips. "I don't really have to touch you to feel them. I seem to know—"

"Probably because you've got them yourself," Regis said.

"Matrix work needs training, but it must be possible to learn to control *laran,* or the techniques couldn't have evolved. Unless you want to believe all those old stories about gods and demigods coming down to teach the Comyn how to use them, and I don't." It was very dark, but he could see Danilo clearly, as if his body were outlined with the pale, pulsing energy flows. Danilo said, "Then maybe we can find out how to keep you from going into that kind of . . . of crisis again."

Regis said, "I seem to be in your hands, Dani. Quite literally. I don't know if I could live through another attack like that one." He knew that the physical shock Danilo had given him by touching his matrix had revived him, but that he was drained, dangerously weak. "You had threshold sickness? And got over it?"

"Yes. Though, as I say, I had no idea what it was. But finding out about these energy currents helped. I could make them flow smoothly, most of the time, and it seemed that I could *use* that energy. I'm not saying this very well, am I? I don't know the right words."

Regis smiled ruefully and said, "Maybe there aren't any." He lay watching the energy flows in Danilo's body and had the strange sensation that, although they were both heavily clothed against the cold, they were both, somehow, naked, a different kind of naked. Maybe this is what Lew meant: living with your skin off. He could feel the energy flows in Danilo, too, pulsing, moving smoothly and steadily with the forces of life. Danilo went on, gently searching out the flows, not touching him; even so, the touch that was not a touch stirred physical awareness again. Regis had not heard Lew explain how the same currents carried telepathic force and sexual energy, but he sensed just enough to be self-conscious about it. He gently reached out and held Danilo's hand away from him.

"No," he said, not angry now, but honestly, facing it—they could not lie to each other now. "You don't want to stir *that* up, do you, Dani?"

There was a frozen instant while Danilo almost stopped breathing. Then he said, in a smothered whisper, "I didn't think you knew."

"So when you called me names—you were nearer right than you knew yourself, Dani. I didn't know it then, either.

But I would rather not . . . approach you as Dyan did. So take care, Dani."

He was not touching Danilo now, but just the same he felt the steady currents of energy in Danilo begin to halt, the pulse go ragged and uneven, like an eddy and whirlpool in a smooth-running river. He didn't know what it meant, but he sensed without knowing why that it was important, that he had discovered something else that he really needed to know, something on which his very life might depend.

Danilo said hoarsely, "You? Like Dyan? *Never!*"

Regis fought to steady his own voice, but he was aware of the energy currents now. The steady pulsing which had eased and cleared his perceptions was beginning to back up, eddy and move unevenly. He said, fighting for control, "Not in any way that . . . that you have to fear. I swear it. But it's true. Do you hate me, then, or despise me for it?"

Danilo's voice was rough. "Don't you think I can tell the difference? I will not speak your name in the same breath—"

"I am very sorry to disillusion you, Dani," Regis said very quietly, "but it would be worse to lie to you now. That's what went wrong before. I think it was trying so hard to . . . to keep it from you, to keep it from *myself,* even, that has been making me so sick. I knew about your fears; you have good reason for them. I tried very hard to keep you from knowing: I almost died rather than let you think of me like Dyan. I know you are a *cristoforo,* and I know your customs are different."

He should know, after three years in one of their monasteries. And now Regis knew what cut off his *laran*: the two things coming together, the emotional response, wakening that time with Lew, and the telepathic awareness, *laran.* And for three years, the years when they should have been wakening and strengthening, every time he had felt any kind of emotional or physical impulse, he had cut it off again; and every time there was the slightest, faintest telepathic response, he had smothered it. To keep from rousing, again, all the longing and pain and memory. . . .

Saint-Valentine-of-the-Snows, saint or no, had nearly destroyed Regis . Perhaps, if he had been less obedient, less scrupulous . . .

He said, "Just the same, I must speak the truth to you,

Dani. I am sorry if it hurts you, but I cannot hurt myself again by lying, to you or myself. I *am* like Dyan. Now, at least. I will not do what he has done, but I feel as he felt, and I think I must have known it for a long time. If you cannot accept this, you need not call me lord or even friend, but please believe I did not know it myself."

"But I know you've been honest with me," Danilo gasped. "*I* tried to keep it from *you*—I was so ashamed—I wanted to die for you, it would have been easier. Don't you think I can tell the difference?" he demanded. Tears were streaming down his face. "Like Dyan? *You?* Dyan, who cared nothing for me, who found his pleasure in tormenting me and drank in my fear and loathing as his own joy—" He drew a deep, gasping breath, as if there were not enough air anywhere to breathe. "And you. You've gone on like this, day after day, torturing yourself, letting yourself come almost to the edge of death, just to keep from *frightening* me—do you think I am *afraid* of you? Of anything you could say or . . . or do?" The lines of light around him were blazing now, and Regis wondered if Danilo, in the surge of emotion blurring them both, really knew what he was saying.

He stretched both hands to Danilo and said, very gently, "Part of the sickness, I think, was trying to hide from each other. We've come close to destroying each other because of it. It's simpler than that. We don't have to talk about it and try to find words. Dani— *bredu*—will you speak to me, now, in the way we cannot misunderstand?"

Danilo hesitated for a moment and Regis, frightened with the old agonizing fear of a rebuff, felt as if he could not breathe. Then, although Regis could feel the last aching instant of fear, reluctance, shame as if it were in himself, Danilo reached out his hands and laid them, palm to palm, guided by a sure instinct, against Regis' own hands. He said, "I will, *bredu*."

The touch was that small but definite electric shock. Regis felt the energy pulses blazing up in him like live lightning for an instant. He felt the current, then, running through them both, from Danilo into him, into his whole body—the centers in the head, the base of the throat, beneath the heart, down deep inside his whole body—and back again through Danilo. The muddied, swirling eddies in the currents began to clear, to run like a smooth pulse, a swift current. For the first time in months, it seemed, he could see clearly, without the crawling sickness and dizziness, as the energy channels began to flow in a straightforward circuit. For a moment this shared life energy was all either of them could feel and, under the relief of it, Regis drew what seemed his first clear breath in a long time.

Then, very slowly, his thoughts began to merge with Danilo's. Clear, together, as if they were a single mind, a single being, joined in an ineffable warmth and closeness.

This was the real need. To reach out to someone, this way, to feel this togetherness, this blending. Living with your skin off. This is what laran *is.*

In the peace and comfort of that magical blending, Regis was still aware of the tension and clawing need in his body, but that was less important. *But why should either of us be afraid of that now?*

This, Regis knew, was what had twisted his vital forces into knots, blockading the vital energy flows until he was near death. Sexuality was only part of it; the real trouble was the unwillingness to face and acknowledge what was within him. He knew without words that the clearing of these channels had freed him to be what he was, and what he would be.

Some day he would know the trick of directing those currents without making them flow through his body. But now this is what he needed, and only someone who could accept him entirely, all of him, mind and body and emotions, could have given it to him. And it was a closer brotherhood than blood. Living with your skin off.

And suddenly he knew that he need not go to a tower. What he had learned now was a simpler way of what he would have been taught there. He knew he could use *laran* now, any way he needed to. He could use his matrix without getting sick again, he could reach anyone he needed to reach, send the message that had to be sent.

CHAPTER TWENTY-TWO

(Lew Alton's narrative)

For the ninth or tenth time in an hour I tiptoed to the door, unfastened the leather latch and peered out. The outside world was nothing but swirling, murky grayness. I backed away from it, wiping snow from my eyes, then saw in the dim light that Marjorie was awake. She sat up and wiped the rest of the snow from my face with her silk kerchief.

"It's early in the season for so heavy a storm."

"We have a saying in the hills, darling. Put no faith in a drunkard's prophecy, another man's dog, or the weather at any season."

"Just the same," she said, struggling to put my own thoughts into words, "I *know* these mountains. There's something in this storm that frightens me. The wind doesn't rage as it should. The snow is too wet for this season. It's *wrong* somehow. Storms, yes. But not like this."

"Wrong or right, I only wish it would stop." But for the moment we were helpless against it. We might as well enjoy what small good there was in being snowbound together. I buried my face in her breast; she said, laughing, "You are not at all sorry to be here with me."

"I would rather be with you at Arilinn," I said. "We would have a finer bridal chamber."

She put her arms around me. It was so dark we could not see one another's faces, but we needed no light. She whispered, "I am happy with you wherever we are."

We were exaggeratedly gentle with one another now. I hoped a time might come, some day, when we could come into one another's arms without fear. I knew I would never forget, not while I lived, that terrifying madness that had gripped us both, nor those dreadful hours, after Marjorie had cried herself into a stunned, exhausted sleep, while I lay restless, aching with the fear she might never trust or love me again.

That fear had vanished a few hours later, when she opened her eyes, still dark and bruised in her tear-stained face, and impulsively reached for me, with a caress that healed my fears. But one fear remained: could it seize us again? Could anyone, ever, be sane, after the touch of Sharra?

But for now we were without fear. Later Marjorie slept; I hoped this prolonged rest would help her recover her strength after long traveling. I moved restlessly away, peering into the storm again. Later, I knew, I must brave the outdoors to give the last of our grain and fodder to the horses.

There was something very wrong with the storm. It made me think of Thyra's trick with the waterfall. No, that was foolish. No sane person would meddle with the weather for some private end.

But I said it myself: Could anyone be sane, after the touch of Sharra?

I dared not even look into my matrix, check what, if anything, was behind the undiminished strangeness of the storm. While Sharra was out and raging, seeking to draw us back, my matrix was useless—worse than useless, dangerous, deadly.

I fed the horses, came back inside to find Marjorie still sleeping and knelt to kindle a fire with a little of our remaining wood supply. Food was running low, but a few days of fasting would not hurt us. Worse was the shortage of fodder for the horses. As I put some grain to cook for porridge, I wondered if I had yet made Marjorie pregnant. I hoped so, of course, then caught myself with a breath of consternation. Evanda and Avarra, not yet, not yet! This journey was hard enough on her already. I felt torn, ambivalent. With a deep instinct I hoped she was already bearing my child, yet I was afraid of what I most desired.

I knew what to do, of course. Celibacy is impossible in the tower circles, except for the Keepers, and it takes an unimaginable toll of them. Yet pregnancy is dangerous for the women working in the relays, and we cannot risk interruption of their term. I suspected Marjorie would be shocked and indignant if I tried to protect her this way. I would not have had her feel otherwise. But what were we to do? At least we should talk about it, honestly and openly. It would have to be her own choice, either way.

Behind me Marjorie stirred restlessly in her sleep, cried

out "No! No! Thyra, no—" and sat bolt upright, holding her hands to her head as if in wild terror. I ran to her. She was sobbing with fright, but when I got her fully awake she could not tell me what she had seen or dreamed.

Was Thyra doing this to her? I didn't doubt she was capable of it, and now I had no faith in her scruples. Nor in Kadarin's. I braced myself against the hurt of that. We had been friends. What had changed them?

Sharra? If the fires of Sharra could break through the discipline of years at Arilinn, what would it do to a wild telepath without it?

Marjorie said, a little wistfully, "You were a little in love with Thyra, weren't you?"

"I desired her," I said quietly, facing it. "That kind of thing is unavoidable in a close circle of that sort. It might have happened with any woman who could reach my mind. But she did not want it; she tried to fight against it. I, at least, knew it could happen. Thyra was trying very hard not to be aware of it."

How much had that battle with herself damaged and disrupted her? Had I failed Thyra, too? I should have tried harder to help her confront it, face it in full awareness. I should have made us all—*all*—be honest with one another, as my training demanded, especially when I saw where our undisciplined emotions were leading us—to rage and violence and hate.

We could never have controlled Sharra. But if I had known sooner what was happening among us all, I might have seen the way we were being warped, distorted.

I had failed them all, my kinsmen, my friends, by loving them too much, not wanting to hurt them with what they were.

The experiment, noble as Beltran's dream had been, lay in ruins. Now, whatever the cost, the Sharra matrix must be monitored, then destroyed. But again, what of those who had been sealed to Sharra?

The snow continued to fall all that day and night, and was still falling when we woke the next morning, drifting high around the stone buildings. I felt we should try to pass on, nevertheless, but knew it was insanity. The horses could never force their way through those drifts. Yet if we were trapped here much longer, without food for them, they would not be able to travel.

It must have been the next afternoon—events of that time are blurred in my mind—when I roused from sleep to hear Marjorie cry out in fear. The door burst inward and Kadarin stood in the doorway, half a dozen of Beltran's guards crowding behind him.

I snatched up my sword but within seconds I was hopelessly outmatched, and with a horrible sense of infinite repetition, stood struggling, helplessly pinioned between the guards. Marjorie had drawn back into a corner. As Kadarin went toward her I told myself that if he handled her roughly I would kill him, but he only lifted her gently to her feet and draped his own cloak over her shoulders. He said, "Foolish child, didn't you know we couldn't let you go like that?" He thrust her into the arms of two of the guards and said, "Take her outside. Don't hurt her, treat her gently, but don't let her go or I'll have your heads!"

"Do you make war on women? Can't you settle it with me, man to man?"

He was still holding my sword; he shrugged, flung it into a corner. "So much for your lowland toys. I learned long ago to fight my battles with sounder weapons. If you think I'd hurt Marjorie, you're more of a fool than I ever believed you. I'll die first."

"Do you think I'll ever work with you again? No, damn you, I'll die first."

"Yes, you will," he said in an almost amiable tone. "There isn't the slightest use in your heroics, dear boy."

"What did you do, find you couldn't handle Sharra alone? How much did you destroy before you found it out?"

"I don't have to account to *you,*" he said with sudden brutality. I fought momentarily against the men holding me and at the same time lashed out with a murderous mental assault. I had always been told that the unleashed rage of an Alton can kill, had been disciplined never, *never* to let my anger wholly free. Yet now . . .

I let my rage go, visualizing hands at Kadarin's throat, my mind raining hatred and fury on him . . . I felt him wince under the onslaught, saw him go white, sag to his knees . . .

"Quick," he gasped in a strangled voice, "knock him—out—"

A fist connected with my jawbone, darkness crashed through my mind. I felt myself go limp, hang helpless between my captors. Kadarin came and took over the beating himself, his ring-laden hands slashing hard at my face, blow after blow until I went down into a blurred, red-shot darkness. Then I realized they were hauling me out into the snowstorm; the cold sleet on my face revived me a little. Kadarin's face hung in a red mist before my eyes.

"I don't want to kill you, Lew. Come quietly now."

I said thickly, through my torn and bleeding mouth, "Better kill me . . . brave man, who beats a man held helpless by . . . a couple of others. . . . Give me two men to hold you and I'll beat you half dead too . . . dishonored . . ."

"Oh, save your Domain cant," he said. "I went beyond all that jabber of honor and dishonor long ago. I've no use for you dead. You are coming with me, so choose if you will come quietly, like the sensible lad you always were and will be again, or whether you will be carried, after these fellows beat you senseless? They don't like beating helpless men, either. Or shall I make it easy and immobilize you?" His hand went out toward the matrix on my neck.

No! No! Not again! I screamed, a frenzied cry which actually made him step back a pace. Then quietly—there had never been anything in the world as terrible as his low, even voice—he said, "You can't endure that again, can you? I'll do it if I must. But why not spare us both the pain?"

"Better . . . kill me . . . instead." I spat out the blood filling my mouth. It struck him in the face. Unhurriedly, he wiped it away. His eyes glinted like some bird of prey, mad and inhuman. He said, "I hoped you'd save me the worst threat. Nascar, go and get the girl. Get her marix stone off of her. She carries it in—"

I cursed him, straining. "You devil, you fiend from hell! Do what you damn please with me, but let her alone!"

"Will you come, then, with no more of this?"

Slowly, defeated, I nodded. He smiled, a silky, triumphant smile, and jerked his head at the men to bring me along. I went between them, not protesting. If I, a strong man, could not endure that torment, how could I let them inflict it on Marjorie?

The men shoved us along through the blinding snow. A couple of hundred feet from the house, past the wall of trees, the snow stopped as if a water faucet had been turned off; the woodland road lay green before us. I stared, unbelieving. Kadarin nodded. "Thyra has always wanted to experiment with storms," he said, "and it kept you in one place until we were ready for you."

My instinct had been right. We should have pressed through it. I should have known. Despair took me. A helicopter was waiting for us; they lifted me into one seat, set Marjorie in another. They had tied her wrists with her silk scarf, but had not otherwise harmed her. I reached out to touch her hand. Kadarin, swiftly coming between us, gripped my wrist with fingers of steel.

I jerked away from him as if he had been a cold corpse. I tried to meet Marjorie's eyes. Together we might master him . . .

"It's no use, Lew. I cannot fight you and keep threatening you all the way to Aldaran," Kadarin said tonelessly. He reached into a pocket, brought out a small red vial, uncapped it. "Drink this. And don't waste time."

"No—"

"I said drink it. Quickly. If you contrive to spill it, I shall have no recourse except to tear off your matrices; first Marjorie's, then yours. I shall not threaten again."

Glancing at those inhuman eyes—Gods! This man had been my friend! Did he even know what he had become?—I knew we were both defenseless in his hands. Defeated, I raised the flask to my lips and swallowed the red liquid.

The helicopter, the world slid away.

And did not return.

I did not know then, what drug he had given me. I am still not entirely sure. Nor have I ever known how much of what I remember from the next few days is dream and how much is underlaid by some curious core of reality.

For a long time I saw nothing but fire. Forest fire raging in the hills beyond Armida; fire raining down on Caer Donn; the great form of fire, stretching out irresistible arms and breaking the walls of Storn Castle as if they had been made of dough. Fire burning in my own veins, raging in my very blood.

I stood, once, on the highest point of Castle Aldaran and looked down on a hundred assembled men and felt the fire blazing behind me, sweeping through me with its wild lust and terror. I felt the men's raw emotions surging up to where I stood, the Sharra sword between my hands, feeding my nerves with crude fear, lust, greed. . . .

Again, a terrified child, I stood between my father's hands, docilely awaiting the touch that could give me my heritage or my death. I felt the fury rising in me, raving in me, and I let the fire take him. He went up in flames, burning, burning. . . .

I saw Regis Hastur, lying in a small dark hut somewhere on the road between Aldaran and Thendara, and knew he had failed. He lay there dying, his body torn with the last dying convulsions, unable to cross that dark threshold, failed, dying, burning. . . .

I felt Dyan Ardais seize me from behind, felt my arm snap in his hands, felt through his touch the combined cruelty and lust. I turned on him and rained hatred and violence on him, too, and saw him go up under the flame of my hatred, burning, burning. . . .

Once I heard Marjorie crying helplessly and fought up to consciousness again, and then I was in my room in Castle Aldaran, but I was tied down with enormous weights. Someone wedged my jaws open and poured down another dose of the pungent red drug, and I began to lose myself again in the dreams that were not dreams.

I stood atop a great flight of stairs, leading down and down and down forever into a great burning pit of hell, and Marjorie stood before me with the Sharra matrix between her hands and her face white and empty, and the matrix gripped in my hands burned me like fire, burned through my hand. Down below, the faces of the men, upturned to me, poured wave upon wave of raw emotion through me again, so that I burned endlessly in a hell-fire of fury and lust, burning, burning. . . .

Once I heard Thyra crying out "No, no, I can't, I won't," and a terrible sound of weeping. Even at the deathbed of her father she had not wept like this. . . .

And then without transition Marjorie was there in my arms and I threw myself on her as I had done before. I covered her with frenzied and despairing kisses; I plunged gratefully into her warmth, my body and the very blood in my veins, burning, burning, trying in a single act to slake the frenzy of rage and lust which had tormented me, helpless, for days, months, years, eternities. . . . I tried to stop myself, feeling that there was some dimension of *reality* to this which had not been in most of the other dreams or illusions. I tried to cry out, it was happening again, the thing I feared and I hated, the thing I desired . . . the thing I dared not see—I was responsible for all this cruelty and violence! It was my own hate, never acknowledged, never admitted, which they were using, channeling through me! I was powerless to stop myself now; a world of frenzy was shaking me, endlessly tearing at me with great claws. Marjorie was crying helplessly, hopelessly, and I could feel her fear and pain burning in me, burning, burning. . . . Lightning ripped through my body, thunder crashing inside and out, a world of lust and fury was pouring through my loins . . . burning, burning. . . .

I was alone. I lay spent, drained, still confused with the dreams. I was alone. Where was Marjorie? Not here, thanks to all the Gods, not here, not here! None of it had been real.

My mind and body at peace, I slept, but far away in the blackness, someone was crying. . . .

CHAPTER TWENTY-THREE

"It's not threshold sickness this time, *bredu,*" Regis said, raising his head from the matrix. "This time I'm doing it right, but I can't see anything but the . . . the image that struck me down on the northward road. The fire and the golden image. *Sharra.*"

Danilo said, shuddering, "I know. I saw it too."

"At least it didn't strike me senseless this time." Regis covered the matrix. It roused no sickness in him now, just an overwhelming sense of heightened perception. He should have been able to reach Kennard, or someone at Arilinn, but there was nothing—nothing but the great, burning, chained image he knew to be Sharra.

Yes, something terrible was happening in the hills.

Danilo said, "I'd think every telepath on Darkover must know it by now, Regis. Don't they keep a lookout for such things in the towers? No need for you to feel guilty because you can't do it alone, without training."

"I don't feel exactly guilty, but I am dreadfully worried. I tried to reach Lew, too. And couldn't."

"Maybe he's safe at Arilinn, behind their force-field."

Regis wished he could think so. His head was clear and he knew the sickness would not return, but the reappearance of the image of Sharra troubled him deeply. He had heard stories of out-of-control matrices, most of them from the Ages of Chaos, but some more recent. A cloud covered the sun and he shivered with cold.

Danilo said, "I think we should ride on, if you've finished."

"Finished? I didn't even start," he said ruefully, tucking the matrix into his pocket again. "We'll go on, but let me eat something first." He accepted the chunk of dried meat Danilo handed him and sat chewing it. They were sitting side by side on a fallen tree, their horses cropping grass nearby through the melting snow. "How long have we been on the road, Dani? I lost count while I was sick."

"Six days, I think. We aren't more than a few days from Thendara. Perhaps tonight we'll be within the outskirts of the Armida lands and I can send word somehow to my father. Lew told Beltran's men to send word, but I don't trust him to have done it."

"Grandfather always regarded Lord Kermiac as an honorable man. Beltran is a strange cub to come from such a den."

"He may have been decent enough until he fell into the hands of Sharra," Danilo said. "Or perhaps Kermiac ruled too long. I've heard that the land which lives too long under the rule of old men grows desperate for change at any cost."

Regis wondered what would happen in the Domains when his grandfather's regency ended, when Prince Derik Elhalyn took his crown. Would his people have grown desperate for change at any cost? He was remembering the Comyn Council where he and Danilo had stood watching the struggle for power. They would not be watching, then, they would be part of it. Was power always evil, always corrupt?

Dani said, as though he knew Regis' thoughts, "But Beltran didn't just want power to change things, he wanted a whole world to play with."

Regis was startled at the clarity of that and pleased again to think that if the fate of their world ever depended on the Hasturs he would have someone like Dani to help him with decisions! He reached out, gave Danilo's hand a brief, strong squeeze. All he said was, "Let's get the horses saddled, then. Maybe we can help make sure he doesn't get it to play with."

They were about to mount when they heard a faint droning, which grew to a sky-filling roar. Danilo glanced up; without a word, he and Regis drew the horses under the cover of the trees. But the helicopter, moving steadily overhead, paid no attention to them.

"Nothing to do with us," said Danilo when it was out of sight, "probably some business of the Terrans." He let out his breath and laughed, almost in apology. "I shall never hear one again without fear!"

"Just the same, a day will come when we'll have to use them too," Regis said slowly. "Maybe the Aldaran lands and the Domains would understand each other better if it were not ten days' ride from Thendara to Caer Donn."

"Maybe." But Regis felt Danilo withdraw, and he said no more. As they rode on, he thought that, like it or not, the Terrans were here and nothing could ever be as it was before they came. What Beltran wanted was not wrong, Regis felt. Only the way he chose to get it. He himself would find a safer way.

He realized, with astonishment and self-disgust, the direction his thoughts were taking. What had he to do with all that?

He had ridden this road from Nevarsin less than a year ago, believing then that he was without *laran* and free to shrug his heritage aside and go out into space, follow the Terran starships to the far ends of the Empire. He looked up at the face of Liriel, pale-violet in the noonday sky, and thought how no Darkovan had ever set foot even on any of their own moons. His grandfather had pledged to help him go, if Regis still wanted to. He would not break his word.

Two years more, given to the cadets and the Comyn. Then he would be free. Yet an invisible weight seemed to press him down, even as he made plans for freedom.

Danilo drew his horse suddenly to a stop.

"Riders, Lord Regis. On the road ahead."

Regis drew even with him, letting his reins lie loose on his pony's neck. "Should we get off the road?"

"I think not. We are well within the Domains by now; here you are safe, Lord Regis."

Regis lifted his eyebrows at the formal tone, suddenly realizing its import. In the isolation of the last days, in stress and extremity, all man-made barriers had fallen; they were two boys the same age, friends, *bredin*. Now, in the Domains and before outsiders once again, he was the heir to Hastur, Danilo his paxman. He smiled a little ruefully, accepting the necessity of this, and let Danilo ride a few paces ahead. Looking at his friend's back, he thought with a strange shiver that it was literally true, not just a word: Dani would die for him.

It was a terrifying thought, though it should not have been so strange. He knew perfectly well that any one of the Guardsmen who had escorted him here and there when he was only a sickly little boy, or ridden with him to and from Nevarsin, were sworn by many oaths to protect him with their lives. But it had never been entirely real to him until Danilo, of his free will and from love, had given him that pledge. He rode steadily, with the trained control he had been taught, but his back was alive with prickles and he felt the very hairs rise on his forearms. Was this what it meant, to be Hastur?

He could see the riders now. The first few wore the green-and-black uniform he had worn himself in the past summer. Comyn Guardsmen! And a whole group of others, not in uniform. But there were no banners, no displays. This was a party of war. Or, at least, one prepared to fight!

Ordinary travelers would have drawn off the road, letting the Guardsmen pass. Instead Regis and Danilo rode straight toward them at a steady pace. The head Guardsman—Regis recognized him now, the young officer Hjalmar—lowered his pike and gave formal challenge.

"Who rides in the Domains—" He broke off, forgetting the proper words. "Lord Regis!"

Gabriel Lanart-Hastur rode quickly past him, bringing his horse up beside Regis. He reached both hands to him. "Praise to the Lord of Light, you are safe! Javanne has been mad with fear for you!"

Regis realized that Gabriel would have been blamed for letting him ride off alone. He owed him an apology. There was no time for it now. The riders surrounded them and he noted many members of the Comyn Council among Guardsmen and others he did not recognize. At the head of them, on a great gray horse, rode Dyan Ardais. His stern, proud face relaxed a little as he saw Regis, and he said in his harsh but musical voice, "You have given us all a fright, kinsman. We feared you dead or prisoner somewhere in the hills." His eyes fell on Danilo and his face stiffened, but he said steadily, "Dom Syrtis, word came from Thendara, sent by the Terrans and brought to us; a message was sent to your father, sir, that you were alive and well."

Danilo inclined his head, saying with frigid formality, "I am grateful, Lord Ardais." Regis could tell how hard the civil words came. He looked at Dyan with faint curiosity, surprised at the prompt delivery of the reassuring message, wondering why, at least, Dyan had not left it to a subordinate to give. Then he knew the answer. Dyan was in charge of this mission, and would consider it his duty.

Whatever his personal faults and struggles, Regis knew, Dyan's allegiance to Comyn came first. Whatever he did, everything was subordinate to that. It had probably never occurred to Dyan that his private life could affect the honor of the Comyn. It was an unwelcome thought and Regis tried to reject it, but it was there nevertheless. And, even more disquieting, the thought that if Danilo had been a private citizen and not a cadet, it genuinely would *not* have mattered how Dyan treated or mistreated him.

Dyan was evidently waiting for some explanation; Regis said, "Danilo and I were held prisoner at Aldaran. We were freed by Dom Lewis Alton." Lew's formal title had a strange sound in his ears. He did not remember using it before.

Dyan turned his head, and Regis saw the horse-litter at the center of the column. His grandfather? Traveling at this season? Then, with the curiously extended senses he was just beginning to learn how to use, he knew it was Kennard, even before Dyan spoke.

"Your son is safe, Kennard. A traitor, perhaps, but safe."

"He is no traitor," Regis protested. "He too was held a prisoner. He freed us in his own escape." He held back the knowledge that Lew had been tortured, but Kennard knew it anyway: Regis could not yet barricade himself properly.

Kennard put aside the leather curtains. He said, "Word came from Arilinn—you know what is going on at Aldaran? The raising of Sharra?"

Regis saw that Kennard's hands were still swollen, his body bent and bowed. He said, "I am sorry to see you too ill to ride, Uncle." In his mind, the sharpest of pains, was the memory of Kennard as he had been during those early years at Armida, as Regis had seen him in the gray world. Tall and straight and strong, breaking his own horses for the pleasure of it, directing the men on the fire-lines with the wisdom of the best of commanders and working as hard as any of them. Unshed tears stung Regis' eyes for the man who was closest to a father to him. His emotions were swimming near the surface these days, and he wanted to weep for Kennard's suffering. But he controlled himself, bowing from his horse over his kinsman's crippled hand.

Kennard said, "Lew and I parted with harsh words, but I could not believe him traitor. I do not want war with Lord Kermiac—"

"Lord Kermiac is dead, Uncle. Lew was an honored guest to him. After his death, though, Beltran and Lew quarreled. Lew refused . . ." Quietly, riding beside Kennard's litter, Regis told him everything he knew of Sharra, up to the moment when Lew had pleaded with Beltran to renounce his intention, and promising to enlist the help of Comyn Council . . . and how Beltran had treated them all afterward. Kennard's eyes closed in pain when Regis told of how Kadarin had brutally beaten his son, but it would not have occurred to Regis to spare him. Kennard was a telepath, too.

When he ended, telling Kennard how Lew had freed them with Marjorie's aid, Kennard nodded grimly. "We had hoped Sharra was laid forever in the keeping of the forgefolk. While it was safely at rest, we would not deprive them of their goddess."

"A piece of sentiment likely to cost us dear," Dyan said. "The boy seems to have behaved with more courage than I had believed he had. Now the question is, what's to be done?"

"You said that word came from Arilinn, Uncle. Lew is safe there, then?"

"He is not at Arilinn, and the Keeper there, seeking, could not find him. I fear he has been recaptured. Word came, saying only that Sharra had been raised and was raging in the Hellers. We gathered every telepath we could find outside the towers, in the hope that somehow we could control it. Nothing less could have brought me out now," he added, with a detached glance at his crippled hands and feet, "but I am tower-trained and probably know more of matrix work than anyone not actually inside a tower."

Regis, riding at his side, wondered if Kennard was strong enough. Could he actually face Sharra?

Kennard answered his unspoken words. "I don't know, son," he said aloud, "but I'm going to have to try. I only hope I need not face Lew, if he has been forced into Sharra again. He is my son, and I do not want to face him as an enemy." His face hardened with determination and grief. "But I will if I must." And Regis heard the unspoken part of that, too: *Even if I must kill him this time.*

CHAPTER TWENTY-FOUR

(Lew Alton's narrative concluded)

To this day I have never known or been able to guess how long I was kept under the drug Kadarin had forced on me. There was no period of transition, no time of incomplete focus. One day my head suddenly cleared and I found myself sitting in a chair in the guest suite at Aldaran, calmly putting on my boots. One boot was on and one was off, but I had no memory of having put on the first, or what I had been doing before that.

I raised my hands slowly to my face. The last clear memory I had was of swallowing the drug Kadarin had given me. Everything after that had been dreamlike, hallucinatory quasi-memories of hatred and lust, fire and frenzy. I knew time had elapsed but I had no idea how much. When I swallowed the drug, my face had been bleeding after Kadarin had ripped it to ribbons with his heavy fists. Now my face was tender, with raised welts still sore and painful, but all the wounds were closed and healing. A sharp pain in my right hand, where I bore the long-healed matrix burn from my first year at Arilinn, made me flinch and turn the hand over. I looked, without understanding, at the palm. For three years and more, it had been a coin-sized white scar, a small ugly puckered patch with a couple of scarred seams at either side. That was what it *had* been.

Now—I stared, absolutely without comprehension. The white patch was gone, or rather, it had been replaced by a raw, red, festering burn half the breadth of my palm. It hurt like hell.

What had I been doing with it? At the back of my mind I was absolutely certain that I had been lying here, hallucinating, during all that time. Instead I was up and half dressed. What in the hell was going on?

I went into the bath and stared into a large cracked mirror.

The face which looked out at me was not mine.

My mind reeled for a moment, teetering at the edge of madness. Then I slowly realized that the eyes, the hair, the familiar brows and chin were there. But the face itself was a ghastly network of intersection scars, flaming red weals, blackened bluish welts and ridges. One lip had been twisted up and healed, puckered and drawn, giving me a hideous permanent sneer. There were stray threads of gray in my hair; I looked years older. I wondered, suddenly, in insane panic, if they had kept me here drugged while I grew old. . . .

I calmed the sudden surge of panic. I was wearing the same clothes I had worn when I was captured. They were crushed and dirty, but not frayed or threadbare. Only long enough for my wounds from the beating to heal, then, and for me to acquire some new ones somehow, and that atrocious burn on my hand. I turned away from the mirror with a last rueful glance at the ruin of my face. Whatever pretensions to good looks I might ever have had, they were gone forever. A lot of those scars had healed, which meant they'd never look any better than they did now.

My matrix was back in its bag around my neck, though the thong Kadarin had cut had been replaced with a narrow red silk cord. I fumbled to take it out. Before I had the stone bared, the image flared, golden, burning . . . *Sharra!* With a shudder of horror, I thrust it away again.

What had happened? Where was Marjorie?

Either the thought had called her to me or had been summoned by her approaching presence. I heard the creaking of the door-bolts again and she came into the room and stopped, staring at me with a strange fear. My heart sank down into my boot soles. Had that dream, of all the dreams, been true? For an aching moment I wished we had both died together in the forests. Worse than torture, worse than death, to see Marjorie look at me with fear. . . .

Then she said, "Thank God! You're awake this time and you know me!" and ran straight into my arms. I strained her to me. I wanted never to let her go again. She was sobbing. "It's really you again! All this time, you've never looked at me, not once, only at the matrix. . . ."

Cold horror flooded me. Then some of it had been true.

I said, "I don't remember anything, Marjorie, nothing at all since Kadarin drugged me. For all I know, I have been in this room all that time. What do you mean?"

I felt her trembling. "You don't remember *any* of it? Not the forge-folk, not even the fire at Caer Donn?"

My knees began to collapse under me; I sank on the bed and heard my voice cracking as I said, "I remember nothing, nothing, only terrible ghastly dreams. . . ." The implications of Marjorie's words turned me sick. With a fierce effort I controlled the interior heaving and managed to whisper, "I swear, I remember nothing, nothing. Whatever I may have done . . . Tell me, in Zandru's name, did I hurt you, mishandle you?"

She put her arms around me again and said, "You haven't even *looked* at me. Far less touched me. That was why I said I couldn't go on." Her voice died. She put her hand on mine. I cried out with the pain and she quickly caught it up, saying tenderly, "Your poor hand!" She looked at it carefully. "It's better, though, it's much better."

I didn't like to think what it must have been, if this was *better*. No wonder fire had flamed, burned, raged through all my nightmares! But how, in the name of all the devils in all the hells, had I done this?

There was only one answer. Sharra. Kadarin had somehow forced me back into the service of Sharra. But how, *how*? How could he use the skills of my brain while my conscious mind was elsewhere? I'd have sworn it was impossible. Matrix work takes deliberate, conscious concentration. . . . My fists clenched. At the searing pain in my palm I unclenched them again, slowly.

He dared! He dared to steal my mind, my consciousness . . . But how? *How?*

There was only one answer, only one thing he could have done; use all the free-floating rage, hatred, compulsion in my mind, when my conscious control was gone—and take all that and channel it through *Sharra*! All my burning hatred, all the frenzies of my unconscious, freed of the discipline I kept on them, fed through that vicious thing.

He had done that to me, while my own conscious mind was in abeyance. Next to that, Dyan's crime was a boy's prank. The ruin of my face, the burn of my hand, these were nothing, nothing. He had stolen my conscious mind, he had *used* my unconscious, uncontrolled, repressed passions. . . . *Horrible!*

I asked Marjorie, "Did they force you, too, into Sharra?"

She shivered. "I don't want to talk about it, Lew," she said, whimpering like a hurt puppy. "Please, no, no. Just . . . just let's be together for now."

I drew her down on the bed beside me, held her gently in the circle of my arms. My thoughts were grim. She stroked her light fingers across my battered face and I could feel her horror at the touch of the scars. I said, my voice thick in my throat. "Is my face so . . . so repulsive to you?"

She bent down and laid her lips against the scars. She said with that simplicity which, more than anything else, meant *Marjorie* to me, "You could never be horrible to me, Lew. I was only thinking of the pain you have suffered, my darling."

"Fortunately I don't remember much of it," I said. How long would we be here uninterrupted? I knew without asking that we were both prisoners now, that there was no hope of any such trick as we had managed before. It was hopeless. Kadarin, it seemed, could force us to do anything. *Anything!*

I held her tight, with a helpless anguish. I think it was then that I knew, for the first time, what impotence meant, the chilling, total helplessness of true impotence.

I had never wanted personal power. Even when it was thrust on me, I had tried to renounce it. And now I could not even protect this girl, my wife, from whatever tortures, mental or physical, Kadarin wanted to inflict on her.

All my life I had been submissive, willing to be ruled, willing to discipline my anger, to accept continence at the peak of early manhood, bending my head to whatever lawful yoke was placed on it.

And now I was helpless, bound hand and foot. What they had done they could do again. . . . And now, when I needed strength, I was truly impotent. . . .

I said, "Beloved, I'd rather die than hurt you, but I *must* know what has been going on." I did not ask about Sharra. Her trembling was answer enough. "How did he happen to let you come to me now, after so long?"

She controlled her sobs and said, "I told him—and he

knew I meant it—that unless he freed your mind, and let us be together, I would kill myself. I can still do that and he cannot prevent me."

I felt myself shudder. It went all the way to the bone. She went on, keeping her voice quiet and matter-of-fact, and only I, who knew what discipline had made her a Keeper, could have guessed what it cost her. "He can't control the . . . the matrix, the *thing*, without me. And under drugs I can't do it at all. He tried, but it didn't work. So I have that last hold over him. He will do almost anything to keep me from killing myself. I know I should have done it. But I had to"—her voice finally cracked, just a little—"to see you again when you knew me, ask you . . ."

I was more desperately frightened than ever. I asked, "Does Kadarin know that we have lain together?"

She shook her head. "I tried to tell him. I think he hears only what he wants to hear now. He is quite mad, you know. It would not matter to him anyway, he thinks it is only Comyn superstition." She bit her lip and said, "And it cannot be as dangerous as you think. I am still alive, and well."

Not well, I thought, looking at her pallor, the faint bluish lines around her mouth. Alive, yes. But how long could she endure this? Would Kadarin spare her, or would he use her all the more ruthlessly to achieve his aims—whatever, in his madness, they were now—before her frail body gave way?

Did he even know he was killing her? Had he even bothered to have her monitored?

"You spoke of a fire at Caer Donn . . . ?"

"But you were there, Lew. You really don't remember?"

"I don't. Only fragments of dreams. Terrible nightmares."

She lightly touched the horrible burn on my hand. "You got this there. Beltran made an ultimatum. It was not his own will—he has tried to get away—but I think he is helpless in Kadarin's hands now too. He made threats and the Terrans refused, and Kadarin took us up to the highest part of the city, where you can look straight down into the city, and—oh, God. Lew, it was terrible, terrible, the fire striking into the heart of the city, the flames rising everywhere, screams . . ." She rolled over, hiding her head in the pillow. She said, muffled, "I can't. I can't tell you. Sharra is horrible enough, but this, the fire . . . I never dreamed, never imagined. . . . And he said next time it would be the spaceport and the ships!"

Caer Donn. Our magical dream city. The city I had seen transformed by a synthesis of Terran science and Darkovan psi powers. Shattered, burned. Lying in ruins.

Like our lives, like our lives. . . . And Marjorie and I had done it.

Marjorie was sobbing uncontrollably. "I should have died first. I will die before I use that—that destruction again!"

I lay holding her close. I could see the seal of Comyn, deeply marked in my wrist a few inches above the dreadful flaming burn. There was no hope for me now. I was traitor, doubly condemned and traitor.

For a moment, time reeling in my mind, I knelt before the Keeper at Arilinn and heard my own words: ". . . swear upon my life that what powers I may attain shall be used only for the good of my caste and my people, never for personal gain or personal ends . . ."

I was forsworn, doubly forsworn. I had used my inborn talents, my tower-trained skills, to bring ruin, destruction on those I was doubly sworn, as Comyn, as tower telepath, to safeguard and protect.

Marjorie and I were deeply in rapport. She looked at me, her eyes wide in horror and protest. "You did not do it willingly," she whispered. "You were forced, drugged, tortured—"

"That makes no difference." It was my own rage, my own hate, they had used. "Even to save my life, even to save *yours,* I should never have let them bring us back. I should have made him kill us both."

There was no hope for either of us now, no escape. Kadarin could drug me again, force me again, and there was no way to resist him. My own unknown hatred had set me at his mercy and there was no escape.

No escape except death.

Marjorie—I looked at her, wrung with anguish. There was no escape for her either. I should have made Kadarin kill her quickly, there in the stone hut. Then she would have died clean, not like this, slowly, forced to kill.

She fumbled at the waist of her dress, and brought out a small, sharp dagger. She said quietly, "I think they forgot I still have this. Is it sharp enough, Lew? Will it do for both of us, do you think?"

That was when I broke down and sobbed, helplessly, against her. There was no hope for either of us. I knew that. But that it should come like this, with Marjorie speaking as calmly of a knife to kill us both as she would have asked if her embroidery-threads were the right color—that I could not bear, that was beyond all endurance.

When at last I had quieted a little, I rose from her side, going to the door. I said aloud, "We will lock it from the inside this time. Death, at least, is a private affair." I drew the bolt. I had no hope that it would hold for long when they came for us, but by that time we would no longer care.

I came back to the bed, hauled off the boots I had found myself putting on for some unknown purpose. I knelt before Marjorie, drawing off her light sandals. I drew the clasps from her hair, laid her in my bed.

I thought I had left the Comyn. And now I was dying in order to leave Darkover in the hands of the Comyn, the only hands that could safeguard our world. I drew Marjorie for a moment into my arms.

I was ready to die. But could I force myself to kill her?

"You must," she whispered, "or you know what they will make me do. And what the Terrans will do to all our people after that."

She had never looked so beautiful to me. Her bright flame-colored hair was streaming over her shoulders, faintly edged with light. She broke down then, sobbing. I held her against me, straining her so tightly in my arms I must have been hurting her terribly. She held me with all her strength and whispered, "It's the only way, Lew. The only way. But I didn't want to die, Lew, I wanted to live with you, to go with you to the lowlands, I wanted . . . I wanted to have your children."

I knew no pain in my life, nothing would ever equal the agony of that moment, with Marjorie sobbing in my arms, saying she wanted to have my children. I was glad I would not live long to remember this; I hoped the dead did not remember. . . .

Our deaths were all that stood between our world and

terrible destruction. I took up the knife. Touching my finger to the edge left a stain of blood, and I was insanely glad to feel its razor sharpness.

I bent down to give her a long, last kiss on the lips. I said in a whisper, "I'll try not to . . . to hurt you, my darling. . . ." She closed her eyes and smiled and whispered, "I'm not afraid."

I paused a moment to steady my hand so that I could do it in a single, swift, painless stroke. I could see the small vein throbbing at the base of her throat. In a few moments we would both be at peace. Then let Kadarin do his worst. . . .

A spasm of horror convulsed me. When we were dead, the last vestige of control was gone from the matrix. Kadarin would die, of course, in the fires of Sharra. But the fires would never die. Shara, roused and ravening, would rage on, consume our people, our world, all of Darkover. . . .

What would we care for that? The dead are at peace!

And for a painless death for ourselves, would we let our world be destroyed in the fires of Sharra?

The dagger dropped from my hand. It lay on the sheets beside us, but for me it was as far away as if it were on one of the moons. I regretted bitterly that I could not give Marjorie, at least, that swift and painless death. She had suffered enough. It was right that I should live long enough to expiate my treason in suffering. It was cruel, unfair, to make Marjorie share that suffering. Yet, without her Keeper's training, I would not live long enough to do what I must.

She opened her eyes and said tremulously, "Don't wait, Lew. Do it now."

Slowly, I shook my head.

"We cannot take such an easy way, beloved. Oh, we will die. But we must *use* our deaths. We must close the gateway into Sharra before we die and destroy the matrix if we can. We have to go into it. There's no chance—you know there's no chance at all—that we will live through it. But there *is* a chance that we will live long enough to close the gateway and save our world from being ravaged by Sharra's fire."

She lay looking at me, her eyes wide with shock and dread. She said in a whisper, "I would rather die."

"So would I," I said, "but such an easy way is not for us, my precious."

We had sacrificed that right. I looked with longing at the little dagger and its razor sharpness. Slowly, Marjorie nodded in agreement. She picked up the little dagger, looked at it regretfully, then rose from the bed, went to the window and flung it through the narrow window-slit. She came back, slipped down beside me. She said, trying to steady her voice, "Now I cannot lose my courage again." Then, though her eyes were still wet, her voice held just a hint of the old laughter. "At least we will spend one night together in a proper bed."

Can a night last a lifetime?

Perhaps. If you know your lifetime is measured in a single night.

I said hoarsely, drawing her into my arms again, "Let's not waste any of it."

Neither of us was strong enough for much physical lovemaking. Most of that night we spent resting in each other's arms, sometimes talking a little, more often caressing one another in silence. From long training at disciplining unwelcome or dangerous thoughts, I was able to put away almost completely all thought of what awaited us tomorrow. Strangely enough, my worst regret was not for death, but for the long, quiet years of living together which we would never know, for the poignant knowledge that Marjorie would never know the hills near Armida, that she would never come there as a bride. Toward morning Marjorie cried a little for the child she would not live long enough to bear. Finally, cradled in my arms, she fell into a restless sleep. I lay awake, thinking of my father and of my unborn son, that too-fragile spark of life, barely kindled and already extinguished. I wished Marjorie had been spared that knowledge, at least. No, it was right that someone should weep for it, and I was beyond tears.

Another death to my account . . .

At last, when the rising sun was already staining the distant peaks with crimson, I slept too. It was like a final grace of some unknown goddess that there were no evil dreams, no nightmares of fire, only a merciful darkness, the dark robe of Avarra covering our sleep.

I woke still clasped in Marjorie's arms. The room was

full of sunlight; her golden eyes were wide, staring at me with fear.

"They will come for us soon," she said.

I kissed her, slowly, deliberately, before I rose. "So much the less time of waiting," I said, and went to draw back the bolt. I dressed myself in my best, defiantly digging from my packs my finest silk under-tunic, a jerkin and breeches of gold-colored dyed leather. A Comyn heir did not go to his death like a common criminal being hanged! Some such emotion must have been in Marjorie yesterday, for she had evidently put on her finest gown, pale blue, woven of spider-silk and cut low across the breasts. Instead of her usual plaits, she coiled her hair high atop her head with a ribbon. She looked beautiful and proud. Keeper, *comynara*.

Servants brought us some breakfast. I was grateful that she could smile proudly, thanking them in her usual gracious manner. There were no traces in her face of the tears and terror of yesterday; we held our heads high and smiled into each other's eyes. Neither of us dared speak.

As I had known he would, Kadarin came in as we were silently sharing the last of the fruits on the tray. I did not know how my body could contain such hate. I was physically sick with the lust to kill him, to feel my fingers meeting in the flesh of his throat.

And yet—how can I say this?—there was nothing left there to hate. I looked up just once and quickly looked away. He was not even a man any more, but something else. A demon? Sharra walking like a man? The real man Kadarin was not there any more. Killing him would not stop the thing that used him.

Another score against Sharra: this man had been my friend. The destruction of Sharra would not only kill him, it would avenge him, too.

He said, "Have you managed to make him see sense, Marjorie? Or must I drug him again?"

Her fingertips touched mine out of his sight. I knew he did not see, though he would always have noticed before. I said, "I will do what you ask me." I could not bring myself to call him Bob or even Kadarin. He was too far from what I had known.

As we walked through the corridors, I looked sidewise

at Marjorie. She was very pale; I felt the life in her flaring fitfully. Sharra had drained her, sapped her life-forces nearly to the death. One more reason not to go on living. Strange, I was thinking as if I had a choice.

We stepped out onto the high balcony overlooking Caer Donn and the Terran airfield. On a lower level I saw them all assembled, the faces I had seen in my . . . what? Dream, drugged nightmare? Or had that part been real? It seemed I knew the faces. Some ragged, some in rich garments, some knowing and sophisticated, some dulled and ignorant, some not even entirely human. But one and all, their eyes gleamed with the same glassy intensity.

Sharra! Their eagerness burned at me, tearing, ravaging.

I looked down at Caer Don. My breath stuck in my throat. Marjorie had told me, but no words could have prepared me for this kind of destruction, ruin, desolation.

Only after the great forest fire that had ravaged the Kilghard Hills near Armida had I seen anything like this. The city lay blackened; for wide areas not one stone remained upon another. All the old city lay blasted, wasted, the damage spreading far into the Terran Zone.

And I had played a part in this!

I had thought I knew how dangerous the great matrices could be. Looking down on this wasteland which had been a beautiful city, I knew I had never known anything at all. And all these deaths were on my single account. I could never expiate or atone. But perhaps, perhaps, I might live long enough to end the damage.

Beltran stood on the heights. He looked like death. Rafe was nowhere to be seen. I did not think Kadarin would have hesitated to destroy him now, but I hoped, with a deep-lying pain, that the boy was alive and safe somewhere well away from this. But I had no hope. If the Sharra matrix was actually smashed, no one who had been sealed into it was likely to live.

Kadarin was unwrapping the long, bundled length of the sword which contained the Sharra matrix. Beyond him I saw Thyra, her eyes burning into mine with an ineradicable hatred. I had hurt her beyond bearing, too. And, unlike Marjorie, she had not even consented to her death. I had loved her, and she would never know.

Kadarin placed the sword in my hand. The matrix,

throbbing with power at the junction of hilt and blade, made my burned hand stab blindly with a pain that reached all the way up my arm, made me feel sick. But I must be in physical contact with it, not mental touch alone. I took it from the sword, held it in my hand. I knew my hand would never be usable again after this, but what matter? What did a dead man care for a hand burned from his corpse? I had been trained to endure even such terrible pain, and it could not last long. If I could endure just long enough for what I had to do . . .

We know what you are trying to do, Lew. Stand firm and we will help.

I felt my whole body twitch. It was my father's voice!

It was cruel, a stabbing hope. He must be very near or he could never have reached us through the enormous blanking out field of the Sharra matrix.

Father! Father! It was a great surge of gratitude. Even if we all died, perhaps his strength added to mine could help us live long enough to destroy this thing. I locked firmly with Marjorie, made contact through the Sharra matrix, felt the old rapport flame into life: Kadarin's enormous sustaining strength, Thyra like a savage beast, giving the linkage claws, savagery, a wild prowling frenzy. And it all flooded through me. . . .

It was not the way we had used it before, the closed circle of power. As I raised the matrix this time I felt a mighty river of energy flooding through Kadarin, the vast floods of raw emotion from the men standing below: worship, rage, anger, lust, hatred, destruction, the savage power of fire, burning, burning . . .

This was what I had felt before, the dream, the nightmare.

Marjorie was already etched in the aureole of light. Slowly, as the power grew, pouring into my mind through the linked focus, then channeling through me into Marjorie, I saw her begin to change, take on power and height and majesty. The fragile girl in the blue dress merged, moment by moment, into the great looming goddess, arms tossed to the sky, flames shaking exultantly like tossed tresses, a great fountain of flame . . .

Lew, hold steady for me. I cannot do this without your full cooperation. It will hurt, you know it may kill you, but you know what hangs on this, my son. . . .

My father's touch, more familiar than his voice. And almost the same words he had spoken before.

I knew perfectly well where I was, standing in the matrix circle of Sharra on the heights of Castle Aldaran, the great form of fire towering over me. Marjorie, her identity lost, dissolved in the fire and yet controlling it like a torch-dancer with her torches in her hands, swooped down to touch the old spaceport with a fingertip of fire. Far below us there was a vast booming explosion; one of the starships shattered like a child's toy, vanishing skyward in flames. And yet, though all of me was here, now, still I stood again in my father's room at Armida, waiting, sick with that terrible fear—and elation! I reached for him with a wild and reckless confidence. *Go on! Do it! Finish what you started! Better at your hands than Sharra's!*

I felt it then, the deep Alton focused rapport, blazing alive in me, spreading into every corner of my brain and being, filling my veins. It was such agony as I had never known, the fierce, violent traumatic *tearing* rapport, a ripping open of every last fiber of my brain. Yet this time I was in control. I was the focus of all this power and I reached out, twisting it like a steel rope in my hand, a blazing rope of fire. The hand was searing with flame but I barely felt it. Kadarin was motionless, arched backward, accepting the stream of emotions from the men below, transforming them into energons, focusing them through me and into Sharra. Marjorie . . . Marjorie was there somewhere in the midst of the great fire, but I could see her face, confident, unafraid, laughing. I looked at her for a brief instant, wishing in anguish that I could bring her, even for a fraction of a second, out and free from Sharra, see her again—no time. No time for that. I saw the goddess pause to strike. I must act now, quickly, before I too was caught up in that mindless fire, that rage for violence and destruction. I looked for a last instant of anguish and atonement into my father's loving eyes.

I braced myself against the terrible throbbing agony in the hand that held the matrix. *Just a little more. Just a moment more,* I spoke to the screaming agony as if it were a separate living entity, *you can bear it just an instant more.* I focused on the black and wavering darkness behind the form of fire where, instead of the parapets and towers of

Castle Aldaran, a blurring darkness grew, out of focus, a monstrous doorway, a gate of fire, a gate of power, where *something* hovered, swayed, bulged as if trying to break through that gateway. I gathered all the power of the focused minds, all of them, my father's strength, my own, Kadarin's and all the hundred or so mindless, focused believers behind him pouring out all their raw lust and emotion and strength. . . .

I held all that power, fused like a rope of fire, a twisted cable of force. I focused it all on the matrix in my hand. I smelled burning flesh and knew it was my own hand burning and blackening, as the matrix glowed, flared, flamed, ravened, a fire that filled all the worlds, the gateway between the worlds, the reeling and crashing universes. . . .

I smashed the gateway, pouring all that fire back into it. The form of fire shrank, died, scattered and dimmed. I saw Marjorie, reeling, collapse forward; I leaped to snatch her within the circle of my arm, clinging to the matrix still. I heard her screaming as the fires turned back, flaring, blazing up in her very flesh. I caught her fainting body in my arms and with a final, great thrust of power, hurled myself between space, into the gray world, *elsewhere.*

Space reeled under me; the world disappeared. In the formless gray spaces we were bodiless, painless. Was this death? Marjorie's body was still warm in my arms, but she was unconscious. I knew we could remain between worlds only an instant. All the forces of balance tore at me, pulling me back, back to that holocaust and the rain of fire and the ruin at Castle Aldaran, where the men who had spent their powers collapsed and died, blackened and burned, as the fires burned out. Back there, back there to ruin and death? No! *No!* Some last struggle, some last vitality in me cried out *No!* and in a great final thrust of focused power, draining myself ruthlessly, I pushed Marjorie and myself through the closing gates and *escaped.* . . .

My feet struck the floor. It was cool daylight in a curtained, sunlit room; there was hellish pain in my hand, and Marjorie, hanging between my arms, was moaning senselessly. The matrix was still clutched in the blackened, crisped ruin that had been a hand. I knew where I was: in the highest room of the Arilinn Tower, within the safety-field. A girl in the white draperies of a psi-monitor was staring at me, her eyes wide. I knew her; she had been in her first year at Arilinn, my last year there. I gasped "Lori! Quick, the Keeper—"

She vanished from the room and I gratefully let myself fall to the floor, half senseless, next to Marjorie's moaning body.

We were here at Arilinn. Safe. And alive!

I had never been able to teleport before, but for Marjorie's sake I had done it.

Consciousness came and went, wavering like a gray curtain. I saw Callina Aillard looking down at me, her gray eyes reflecting pain and pity. She said softly, "I am Keeper here now, Lew. I will do what I can." Her hand insulated in the gray silk veil, she reached out to take the matrix, thrusting it quickly within the field of a damper. The cessation of the vibration behind the matrix was a moment of almost heavenly comfort, but it also turned off the near-anesthesia of deep focused effort. I had felt hellish pain in my hand before, but now it felt flayed and dipped anew in molten lead. I don't know how I kept from screaming.

I dragged myself to Marjorie's side. Her face was contorted, but even as I looked, it went slack and peaceful. She had fainted and I was glad. The fires that had burned my hand to a sickening, charred ruin had struck inward, through her, as the fire of Sharra withdrew back through that opened gateway. I dared not let myself think what she must have suffered, what she must still suffer if she lived. I looked up at Callina with terrible appeal and read there what Callina had been too gentle to tell me in words.

Callina knelt beside us, saying with a gentleness I had never heard in any woman's voice, "We will try to save her for you, Lew." But I could see the faint, blue-lighted currents of energy pulsing dimmer and dimmer. Callina lifted Marjorie in her arms, kneeling, held her head against her breast. Marjorie's features flickered for a moment in renewed consciousness and renewed pain; then her eyes blazed into mine, golden, triumphant, proud. She smiled, whispered my name, rested her head peacefully on Callina's breast and closed her eyes. Callina bent her head, weeping, and her long dark hair fell like a mourning veil across Marjorie's stilled face.

I let consciousness slip away, let the fire in my hand take my whole body. Maybe I could die too.

But there was not even that much mercy anywhere in the universe.

EPILOGUE

The Crystal Chamber, high in Comyn Castle, was the most formal of all the meeting places for Comyn Council. An even blue light spilled through the walls; flashes of green, crimson, violet struck through, reflected from the prisms everywhere in the glass. It was like meeting at the heart of a rainbow, Regis thought, wondering if this was in honor of the Terran Legate. Certainly the Legate looked suitably impressed. Not many Terrans had ever been allowed to see the Crystal Chamber.

". . . in conclusion, my lords, I am prepared to explain to you what provisions have been made for enforcing the Compact on a planet-wide basis," the Legate said, and Regis waited while the interpreter repeated his words in *casta* for the benefit of the Comyn and assembled nobles. Regis, who understood Terran Standard and had heard it the first time around, sat thinking about the young interpreter, Dan Lawton, the redheaded half-Darkovan whom he had met at the spaceport.

Lawton could have been on the other side of the railing, listening to this speech, not interpreting it for the Terrans. Regis wondered if he regretted his choice. It was easy enough to guess: no choice ever went wholly unregretted. Regis was mostly thinking of his own.

There was still time. His grandfather had made him promise three years. But he knew that for him, time had run out on his choices.

Dan Lawton was finishing up the Legate's speech.

". . . every individual landing at any Trade City, whether at Thendara, Port Chicago or Caer Donn, when Caer Donn can be returned to operation as a Trade City, will be required to sign a formal declaration that there is no contraband in his possession, or to leave all such weapons under bond in the Terran Zone. Furthermore, all weapons imported to this planet for legal use by Terrans shall be treated with a small and ineradicable mark of a radioactive substance, so that the whereabouts of such weapons can be traced and they can be recalled."

Regis gave a faint, wry smile. How quickly the Terrans had come around, when they discovered the Compact was not designed to eliminate Terran weapons but the great and dangerous Darkovan ones. They had had enough of Darkovan ones on the night when Caer Donn burned. Now they were all too eager to honor the Compact, in return for a Darkovan pledge to continue to do so.

So Kadarin accomplished something. And for the Comyn. What irony!

A brief recess was called after the Legate's speech and Regis, going to stretch his legs in the corridor, met Dan Lawton briefly face to face.

"I didn't recognize you," the young Terran said. "I didn't know you'd taken a seat in Council, Lord Regis."

Regis said, "I'm anticipating the fact by about half an hour, actually."

"This doesn't mean your grandfather is going to retire?"

"Not for a great many years, I hope."

"I heard a rumor—" Lawton hesitated. "I'm not sure it's proper to be talking like this outside of diplomatic channels . . ."

Regis laughed and said, "Let's say I'm not tied down to diplomatic channels for half an hour yet. One of the things I hope to see altered between Terran and Darkovan is this business of doing everything through diplomatic channels. It's your custom, not ours."

"I'm enough of a Darkovan to resent it sometimes. I heard a rumor that there would be war with Aldaran. Any truth to it?"

"None whatever, I'm glad to say. Beltran has enough trouble. The fire at Caer Donn destroyed nearly eighty years of loyalty to Aldaran among the mountain people—and eighty years of good relations between Aldaran and the Terrans. The last thing he wants is to fight the Domains."

"Rumor for rumor," Lawton said. "The man Kadarin seems to have vanished into thin air. He'd been seen in the Dry Towns, but he's gone again. We've had a price on his head since he quit Terran intelligence thirty years ago—"

Regis blinked. He had seen Kadarin only once, but he would have sworn the man was no more than thirty.

"We're watching the ports, and if he tries to leave Darkover we'll take him. Personally I'd say good riddance. More likely he'll hide out in the Hellers for the rest of his natural life. If there's anything natural about it, that is."

The recess was over and they began to return to the Crystal Chamber. Regis found himself face to face with Dyan Ardais. Dyan was dressed, not in his Domain colors, but in the drab black of ritual mourning.

"Lord Dyan—no, Lord Ardais, may I express my condolences."

"They are wasted," Dyan said briefly. "My father has not been in his right senses for years before you were born, Regis. What mourning I made for him was so long ago I have even forgotten what grief I felt. He has been dead more than half of my life; the burial was unduly delayed, that was all." Briefly, grimly, he smiled.

"But formality for formality, Lord Regis. My congratulations." His eyes held a hint of bleak amusement. "I suspect those are wasted too. I know you well enough to know you have no particular delight in taking a seat in Council. But of course we are both too well trained in Comyn formalities to say so." He bowed to Regis and went into the Crystal Chamber.

Perhaps these formalities were a good thing, Regis thought. How could Dyan and he ever exchange a civil word without them? He felt a great sadness, as if he had lost a friend without ever knowing him at all.

The honor guard, commanded today by Gabriel Lanart-Hastur, was directing the reseating of the Comyn; as the doors were closed, the Regent called them all to order.

"The next business of this assembly," he said, "is to settle certain heirships within the Comyn. Lord Dyan Ardais, please come forward."

Dyan, in his somber mourning, came and stood at the center of the rainbow lights.

"On the death of your father, Kyril-Valentine Ardais of Ardais, I call upon you, Dyan-Gabriel Ardais, to relinquish the state of Regent-heir to the Ardais Domain and assume that of Lord Ardais, with wardship and sovereignty over the Domain of Ardais and all those who owe them loyalty and allegiance. Are you prepared to assume wardship over your people?"

"I am prepared."

"Do you solemnly declare that to your knowledge you are fit to assume this responsibility? Is there any man who will challenge your right to this solemn wardship of the people of your Domain, the people of all the Domains, the people of all Darkover?"

How many of them could truly declare themselves fit for that? Regis wondered. Dyan gave the proper answer.

"I will abide the challenge."

Gabriel, as commander of the Honor Guard, strode to his side and drew Dyan's sword. He called in a loud voice, "Is there any to challenge the worth and rightful wardship of Dyan-Gabriel, Lord of Ardais?"

There was a long silence. Hypocrisy, Regis thought. Meaningless formality. That challenge was not answered twice in a score of years, and even then it had nothing to do with fitness but with disputed inheritance! How long had it been since anyone seriously answered that challenge?

"I challenge the wardship of Ardais," said a harsh and strident old voice from the ranks of the lesser peers. Dom Felix Syrtis rose and slowly made his way toward the center of the room. He took the sword from Gabriel's hand.

Dyan's calm pallor did not alter, but Regis saw that his breathing had quickened. Gabriel said steadily, "Upon what grounds, Dom Felix?"

Regis looked around quickly. As his sworn paxman and bodyguard, Danilo was seated just beside him. Danilo did not meet Regis' eyes, but Regis could see that his fists were clenched. This was what Danilo had feared, if it came to his father's knowledge.

"I challenge him as unfit," Dom Felix said, "on the grounds that he contrived unjustly the disgrace and dishonor of my son, while my son was a cadet in the Castle Guard. I declare blood-feud and call formal challenge upon him."

Everyone sat silent and stunned. Regis picked up Gabriel Lanart-Hastur's scornful thought, unguarded, that if Dyan had to fight a duel over every episode of that sort he'd be here fighting until the sun came up tomorrow, lucky for him he was the best swordsman in the Domains. But aloud Gabriel only said, "You have heard the challenge, Dyan Ardais, and you must accept it or refuse. Do you wish to consult with anyone before making your decision?"

"I refuse the challenge," Dyan said steadily.

Unprecedented as the challenge itself had been, the refusal was even more unprecedented. Hastur leaned forward and said, "You must state your grounds for refusing a formal challenge, Lord Dyan."

"I do so," Dyan said, "on the grounds that the charge is justified."

An audible gasp went around the room. A Comyn lord did not admit that sort of thing! Everyone in that room, Regis believed, must know the charge was justified. But everyone also knew that Dyan's next act was to accept the challenge, quickly kill the old man and go on from there.

Dyan had paused only briefly. "The charge is just," he repeated, "and there is no honor to be gained from the legal murder of an old man. And murder it would be. Whether his cause is just or unjust, a man of Dom Felix' years would have no equitable chance to prove it against my swordsmanship. And finally I state that it is not for him to challenge me. The son on whose behalf he makes this challenge is a man, not a minor child, and it is he, not his father, who should rightly challenge me in this cause. Does he stand ready to do it?" And he swung around to face Danilo where he sat beside Regis.

Regis heard himself gasp aloud.

Gabriel, too, looked shaken. But, as protocol demanded, he had to ask:

"Dom Danilo Syrtis. Do you stand ready to challenge Lord Dyan Ardais in this cause?"

Dom Felix said harshly, "He does or I will disown him!"

Gabriel rebuked gently, "Your son is a man, Dom Felix, not a child in your keeping. He must answer for himself."

Danilo stepped into the center of the room. He said, "I am sworn paxman to Lord Regis Hastur. My Lord, have I your leave to make the challenge?" He was as white as a sheet. Regis thought desperately that the damned fool was no match for Dyan. He couldn't just sit there and watch Dyan murder him to settle this grudge once and for all.

All his love for Danilo rebelled against this, but before his friend's leveled eyes he knew he had no choice. He could not protect Dani. He said, "You have my leave to do whatever honor demands of you, kinsman. But there is no compulsion to do so. You are sworn to my service and by law that service takes precedence, so you have also my leave to refuse the challenge with no stain upon your honor."

Regis was giving Dani an honorable escape if he wanted it. He could not, by Comyn immunity, fight Dyan in his place. But he could do this much.

Danilo made Regis a formal bow. He avoided his eyes. He went directly to Dyan, faced him and said, "I call challenge upon you, Lord Dyan."

Dyan drew a deep breath. He was as pale as Danilo himself. He said, "I accept the challenge. But by law, a challenge of this nature may be resolved, at the option of the one challenged, by the offer of honorable amends. Is that not so, my lord Hastur?"

Regis could feel his grandfather's confusion like his own, as the old Regent said slowly, "The law does indeed give you this option, Lord Dyan."

Regis, watching him closely, could see the almost-involuntary motion of Dyan's hand toward the hilt of his sword. This was the way Dyan had always settled all challenges before. But he steadied his hands, clasping them quietly before him. Regis could feel, like a bitter pain, Dyan's grief and humiliation, but the older man said, in a harsh, steady voice, "Then, Danilo-Felix Syrtis, I offer you here before my peers and my kinsmen a public apology for the wrong done you, in that I did unjustly and wrongfully contrive your disgrace, by provoking you willfully into a breach of cadet rules and by a misuse of *laran;* and I offer you any honorable amends in my power. Will this settle the challenge and the blood-feud, sir?"

Danilo stood as if turned to stone. His face looked completely stunned.

Why did Dyan do it? Regis wondered. Dyan could have killed him now with impunity, legally, and the matter could never be raised against him again!

And suddenly, whether or not he received the answer directly from Dyan, or his own intuition, he knew: they had all had a lesson in what could happen when Comyn misused their powers. There was disaffection among the subjects and even among themselves, in their own ranks, their own sons turned against them. It was not only to their subjects that they must restore public trust in the integrity of the

Comyn. If their own kinsmen lost faith in them they had lost all. And then, as for an instant Dyan looked directly at him, Regis knew the rest, right from Dyan's mind:

I have no son. I thought it did not matter, then, whether I passed on an unsullied name. My father did not care what his son thought of him and I had no son to care.

Danilo was still standing motionless and Regis could feel his thoughts, too, troubled, uncertain: I have wanted for so long to kill him. It would be worth dying. But I am sworn to Regis Hastur, and sworn through him to the good of the Comyn. Dani drew a long breath and wet his lips before he could speak. Then he said, "I accept your honorable amends, Lord Dyan. And for myself and my house, I declare no feud remains and the challenge withdrawn—" Quickly he corrected himself: "The challenge settled."

Dyan's pallor was gradually replaced by a deep, crimson flush. He spoke almost breathlessly. "What amends will you ask, sir? Is it necessary to explain here, before all men, the nature of the injustice and the apology? It is your right . . ."

Regis thought that Dani could make him crawl. He could have his revenge, after all.

Danilo said quietly, "It is not necessary, Lord Ardais. I have accepted your apology; I leave the amends to your honor."

He turned quietly and returned to his place beside Regis. His hands were shaking. More advantages to the custom of formality, Regis thought wryly. Everyone knew, or guessed, and most of them probably guessed wrong. But now it need never be spoken.

Hastur spoke the formal words which confirmed Dyan's legal status as Lord Ardais and warder of the Ardais Domain. He added: "It is required, Lord Ardais, that you designate an heir. Have you a son?"

Regis could feel, through the very air, his grandfather's regret at the inflexibility of this ritual, which must only inflict more pain on Dyan. Dyan's grief and pain, too, was a knife-edge to everyone there with *laran*. He said harshly, "The only son of my body, my legitimate heir, was killed four years ago in a rockslide at Nevarsin."

"By the laws of the Comyn," Hastur instructed him needlessly, "You must then name your choice of near kinsmen as heir-designate. If you later father a son, that choice may be amended."

Regis was remembering their long talk in the tavern and Dyan's flippancy about his lack of an heir. He was not flippant now. His face had paled to its former impassivity. He said, "My nearest kinsman sits among the Terrans. I must first ask if he is prepared to renounce that allegiance. Daniel Lawton, you are the only son of the eldest of my father's *nedestro* daughters, Rayna di Asturien, who married the Terran David Daniel Lawton. Are you prepared to renounce your Empire citizenship and swear allegiance to Comyn?"

Dan Lawton blinked in amazement. He did not answer immediately, but Regis sensed— and knew, when he spoke a minute later—that the hesitation had been only a form of courtesy. "No, Lord Ardais," he said in *casta,* "I have given my loyalty and will not now renounce it. Nor would you wish it so; the man who is false to his first allegiance will be false to his second."

Dyan bowed and said, with a note of respect, "I honor your choice, kinsman. I ask the Council to bear witness that my nearest kinsman has renounced all claim upon me and mine."

There was a brief murmur of assent.

"Then I turn to my privileged choice," Dyan said. His voice was hard and unyielding. "Second among my near kinsmen was another *nedestro* daughter of my father; her son has been confirmed by the Keeper at Neskaya to be one who holds the Ardais gift. His mother was Melora Castamir and his father Felix-Rafael Syrtis, who is of Alton blood. Danilo-Felix Syrtis," Dyan said, "upon the grounds of Comyn blood and Ardais gift, I call upon you to swear allegiance to Comyn as heir to the Ardais Domain; and I am prepared to defend my choice against any man who cares to challenge me." His eyes moved defiantly against them all.

It was like a thunderclap. So these were Dyan's honorable amends! Regis could not tell whether the thought was his own or Danilo's, as Danilo, dazed, moved toward Dyan.

Regis remembered how he'd thought Dani should have a seat on Comyn Council! But like this? Did Kennard engineer this?

Dyan said formally, "Do you accept the claim, Danilo?"

Danilo was shaking, though he tried to control his voice. "It is . . . my duty to accept it, Lord Ardais."

"Then kneel, Danilo, and answer me. Will you swear allegiance to Comyn and this Council, and pledge your life to serve it? Will you swear to defend the honor of Comyn in all just causes, and to amend all evil ones?" Dyan's speaking voice was rich, strong and musical, but now he hesitated, his voice breaking. "Will you grant to me . . . a son's duty . . . until such time as a son of my body may replace you?"

Regis thought, suddenly wrung by Dyan's torment, who has taken revenge on whom? He could see that Danilo was crying silently as Dyan's wavering voice went out: "Will you swear to be a . . . a loyal son to me, until such time as I yield my Domain through age, unfitness or infirmity, and then serve as my regent under this Council?"

Dani was silent for a moment and Regis, close in rapport with him, knew he was trying to steady his voice. At last, shaking, his voice almost inaudible, he whispered, "I will swear it."

Dyan bent and raised him to his feet. He said steadily, "Bear witness that this is my *nedestro* heir; that none shall take precedence from him; and that this claim"—his voice broke again—"may never be renounced by me nor in my name by any of my descendants."

Briefly, and with extreme formality, he embraced him. He said quietly, but Regis heard, "You may return for the time to your sworn service, my son. Only in my absence or illness need you take a place among the Ardais. You must attend this Council and all its affairs must be known to you, however, since you may need to assume my place unexpectedly."

As if he were walking in his sleep, Danilo returned to his place beside Regis. Bearing himself with steady pride, he slid into the seat beside him. Then he broke and laid his head on the table before them, his head in his arms, crying. Regis reached his hand to Danilo, clasped his arm above the elbow, but he did not speak or reach out with his thoughts. Some things were too painful even for a sworn brother's touch. He did think, with a curious pain, that Dyan had made them equals. Dani was heir to a Domain; he need be no man's paxman nor vassal, nor seek Regis' protection now. And no one could ever again speak of disgrace or dishonor.

He knew he should rejoice for Danilo, he did rejoice for him. But his friend was no longer dependent on him and he felt unsure and strange.

"Regis-Rafael Hastur, Regent-heir of Hastur," Danvan Hastur said. In the shock of Dyan's act, Regis had wholly forgotten that he, too, was to speak before the Council. Danilo lifted his head, nudged him gently and whispered, in a voice that could be heard two feet away, "That's *you,* blockhead!"

For a moment Regis thought he would break into hysterical giggles at this reminder. Lord of Light, he could not! Not at a formal ceremony! He bit his lip hard and would not meet Danilo's eyes, but as he rose and went forward he was no longer worried about what their relationship might become after this. He had been a fool to worry at all.

"Regis-Rafael," his grandfather said, "vows were made in your name when you were six months old, as heir-designate of Hastur. Now that you have reached the age of manhood, it is for you to affirm them or reject them, in full knowledge of what they entail. You have been affirmed by the Keeper of Neskaya Tower as possessing full *laran,* and you are therefore capable of receiving the Hastur gift at the proper time. Have you an heir?" He hesitated, then said kindly, "The law provides that until your twenty-fourth year you need not repeat formal vows of allegiance nor name an heir-designate. And you cannot be legally compelled to marry until that time."

He said quietly, "I have a designated heir." He beckoned to Gabriel Lanart-Hastur, who stepped into the hallway, taking from a nurse's arms the small plump body of Mikhail. Gabriel carried him to Regis, and Regis set the child down in the center of the rainbow lights. He said, "Bear witness that this is my *nedestro* heir, a child of Hastur blood, known to me. He is the son of my sister Javanne Hastur, who is the daughter of my mother and of my father, and of her lawful consort *di catenas,* Gabriel Lanart-Hastur. I have given him the name of Danilo Lanart Hastur. Because of his tender years, it is not yet lawful to ask him for any formal oath. I will ask him only, as it is my duty to do: Danilo Lanart Hastur, will you be a good son to me?"

The child had been carefully coached for the ceremony but for a moment he did not answer and Regis wondered if he had forgotten. Then he smiled and said, "Yes, I promise."

Regis lifted him and kissed his chubby cheek; the little boy flung his arms around Regis' neck and kissed him heartily. Regis could not help smiling as he handed him back to his father, saying quietly, "Gabriel, will you pledge to foster and rear him as my son and not your own?"

Gabriel's face was solemn. He said, "I swear it on my life and my honor, kinsman."

"Then take him, and rear him as befits the heir to Hastur, and the Gods deal with you as you with my son."

He watched Gabriel carry the child away, thinking soberly that his own life would have been happier if his grandfather had given him entirely up to Kennard to foster, or to some other kinsman with sons and daughters. Regis vowed not to make that mistake with Mikhail.

And yet he knew his grandfather's distant affection, and the harsh discipline at Nevarsin, too, had contributed to what he had become. Kennard was fond of saying, "The world will go as it will, not as you or I would have it." And for all Regis' struggles to escape from the road laid out before birth for the Hastur heir, it had brought him here, at the appointed time. He turned to the Regent, thinking with pain that he did not have to do this. He was still free. He had promised three years. But after this he would never again be wholly free.

He met Danilo's eyes, felt that somehow their steady, affectionate gaze gave him strength.

He said, "I am ready to repeat my oath, Lord Hastur."

Hastur's old face was drawn, tense with emotion. Regis felt his thoughts, unbarriered, but Hastur said, with the control of fifty years in public life, "You have arrived at years of manhood; if it is your free choice, none can deny you that right."

"It is my free choice," Regis said.

Not his wish. But his will, his choice. His fate.

The old Regent left his place, then, came to the center of the prismed lights. "Kneel, then Regis-Rafael."

Regis knelt. He knew he was shaking.

"Regis-Rafael Hastur, will you swear allegiance to Comyn and this council, pledge your life to serve it? Will you . . ." He went on. Regis heard the words through a wavering mist of pain: never to be free. Never to look at the great ships bound outward to the stars and know that one day he would follow them to those distant worlds.

Never to dream again. . . .

". . . pledge yourself to be a loyal son to me until I yield my place through age, unfitness or infirmity, and then to serve as Regent-heir subject to the will of this Council?"

Regis thought, for a moment, that he would break into weeping as Danilo had done. He waited, summoning all his control, until he could lift his head and say, in a clear, ringing voice, "I swear it on my life and honor."

The old man bent, raised Regis, clasped him in his arms and kissed him on either cheek. His hands were trembling with emotion, his eyes filled with tears that ran, unheeded, down his face. And Regis knew that for the first time in his life, his grandfather saw him, him alone. No ghost, no shadow of his dead son, stood between them. Not Rafael. Regis, himself.

He felt suddenly, immensely lonely. He wished this council were over. He walked back to his seat. Danilo respected his silence and did not speak or look at him. But he knew Danilo was there and it warmed, a little, the cold shaking loneliness inside him.

Hastur had mastered his emotion. He said, "Kennard, Lord Alton."

Kennard still limped heavily, and he looked weary and worn, but Regis was glad to see him on his feet again. He said, "My lords, I bring you news from Arilinn. It has been determined there that the Sharra matrix can neither be monitored nor destroyed at present. Until such time as a means of completely inactivating it can be devised, it has been decided to send it offworld, where it cannot fall into the wrong hands and cannot raise again its own specific dangers."

Dyan said, "Isn't that dangerous, too, Kennard? If the power of Sharra is raised elsewhere—"

"After long discussion, we have determined that this is the safest course. It is our opinion that there are no telepaths anywhere in the Empire who are capable of using it. And at interstellar distances, it cannot draw upon the activated spots near Aldaran, which is always a risk while it remains on Darkover. Even the forge-folk could not hold it inactive now. Offworld, it will probably be dormant until a means of destroying it can be devised."

"It's a risk," Dyan said.

"*Everything* is a risk, while anything of such power remains active in the universe anywhere," Kennard said. "We can only do the best we can with the tools and techniques we have."

Hastur said, "You are going to take it offworld yourself, then? What of your son? He was at least partly responsible for its use—"

"No," said Danilo suddenly, and Regis realized that Danilo now had as much right as anyone there to speak in Council, "he refused to have any part in its misuse, and endured torture to try to prevent it!"

"And," Kennard said, "he risked his life and came near to losing it, to bring it to Arilinn and break the circle of destruction. If he and his wife had not risked their lives—and if the girl had not sacrificed her own—Sharra would still be raging in the hills and none of us would sit here peacefully deciding who is to sit in Council after us!" Suddenly the Alton rage flared out, lashing them all. "Do you know the price he paid for you Comyn, who had despised him and treated him with contempt, and not one of you, not a damned one of you, have so much as asked whether he will live or die?"

Regis felt flayed raw by Kennard's pain. He was sent to Neskaya, but he knew he should somehow have contrived to send a message.

Kennard said harshly, "I came to ask leave to take him to Terra, where he may regain his health, and perhaps save his reason."

"Kennard, by the laws of the Comyn, you and your heir may not both go offworld at once."

Kennard looked at Hastur in open contempt and said, "The laws of the Comyn be damned! What have I gained for keeping them, what have my ten years in Council gained me? Try to stop me, damn you. I have another son, but I'm not going through all that rigamarole again. You accepted Lew, and look what it's done for him!" Without the slightest vestige of formal leave-taking, he turned his back on them all and strode out of the Crystal Chamber.

Regis got hurriedly to his feet and went after him; he

knew Danilo followed noiselessly at his heels. He caught up with Kennard in the corridor. Kennard whirled, still hostile, and said, "What the hell—"

"Uncle, what of Lew? How is he? I have been in Neskaya, I could not—don't damn me with them, Uncle."

"How would you expect him to be?" Kennard demanded, still truculent, then his face softened. "Not very well, Regis. You haven't seen him since we brought him from Arilinn?"

"I didn't know he was well enough to travel."

"He isn't. We brought him in a Terran plane from Arilinn. Maybe they can save his hand. It's still not certain."

"You're going to Terra?"

"Yes, we leave within the hour. I haven't time to argue with your damned Council and I won't have Lew badgered."

Angry as he sounded, Regis knew it was despair, not hostility, behind Kennard's harsh voice. He tried to barricade himself against the despairing grief. At Neskaya he had been taught the basic techniques of closing out the worst of it; he no longer felt wholly naked, wholly stripped. He could face Dyan now, and even with Danilo they need not lower their barriers unless they both wished it.

"Uncle, Lew and I have been friends since I was only a little boy. I—I would like to see him to say farewell."

Kennard regarded him with hostility for some seconds, at last saying, "Come along, then. But don't blame me if he won't speak to you." His voice was not steady either.

Regis could not help recalling the last time he had stood here in the great hall of the Alton rooms, before Kennard and his grandfather. And the time before that. Lew was sitting on a bench before the fireplace. Exactly where he was sitting that night when Regis appealed to him to waken his *laran*.

Kennard asked gently, "Lew, will you speak to Regis? He came to bid you farewell."

Lew's barriers were down and Regis felt the naked surge of pain, rejection: *I don't want anyone, I don't want anyone to see me now.* It was like a blow, sending Regis reeling. But he braced himself against it, saying very softly, *"Bredu—"*

Lew turned and Regis shrank, almost with horror, from the first sight of that hideously altered face. Lew had aged twenty years in the few short weeks since they had parted. His face was a terrible network of healed and half-healed scars. Pain had furrowed deep lines there, and the expression in his eyes was of someone who has looked on horrors past endurance. One hand was bundled in clumsy bandages and braced in a sling. He tried to smile but it was only a grimace.

"Sorry. I keep forgetting, I'm a sight to frighten children into fits."

Regis said, "But I'm not a child, Lew." He managed to block out the other man's pain and misery and said as calmly as he could manage, "I suppose the worst of the scars will heal."

Lew shrugged, as if that was a matter of deadly indifference. Regis still looked uneasily at him; now that they were together he was uncertain why he had come. Lew had gone dead to all human contact and wanted it that way. Any closer contact between them, any attempt to reach him with *laran,* to revive their old closeness, would simply breach that merciful numbness and revive Lew's active suffering. The quicker he said goodbye and went away again, the better it would be.

He made a formal bow, resolving to keep it that way, and said, "A good journey, then, cousin, and a safe return." He started to move backward. He bumped into Danilo in his retreat, and Danilo's hand closed over his wrist, the touch opening a blaze of rapport between them. As clearly as if Danilo had spoken aloud, Regis felt the intense surge of his distress:

No, Regis! Don't shut it all out, don't withdraw from him! Can't you see he's dying inside there, locked away from everyone he loves? He's got to know that you know what he's suffering, that you don't shrink from him! I can't reach him, but you can because you've loved him, and you must, before he slams down the last barrier and locks everyone out forever. It's his reason at stake, maybe his life!

Regis recoiled. Then, torn, agonized, he realized that this, too, was the burden of his heritage: to accept that nothing, nothing in the human mind, was too fearful to face, that what one person could suffer, another could share. He had known that when he was only a child, before his *laran* was fully awake. He hadn't been afraid then, or ashamed, because he wasn't thinking of himself then at all, but only of Lew, because he was afraid and in pain.

Hew let go of Danilo's hand and took a step toward Lew. One day—it flashed through his mind at random and, it seemed, irrelevantly—as the telepathic men of his caste had always done, he would go down, with the woman bearing his child, into the depths of agony and the edge of his death, and he would be able, for love, to face it. And for love he could face this, too. He went to Lew. Lew had lowered his head again. Regis said, "Bredu," and stood on tiptoe, embracing his kinsman, and deliberately laying himself open to all of Lew's torment, taking the full shock of rapport between them.

Grief. Bereavement. Guilt. The shock of loss, of mutilation. The memory of torture and terror. And above all, guilt, terrible guilt even at being alive, alive when those he had loved were dead. . . .

For a moment Lew fought to shut away Regis' awareness, to block him out, too. Then he drew a long, shaking breath, raised his uninjured arm and pressed Regis close.

. . . you remember now. I know, I know, you love me, and you have never betrayed that love . . .

"Goodbye, *bredu,*" he said, in a sharp aching voice which somehow hurt Regis far less than the calm controlled formality, and kissed Regis on the cheek. "If the Gods will, we shall meet again. And if not, may they be with you always." He let Regis go, and Regis knew he could not heal him, nor help him much, not now. No one could. But perhaps, Regis thought, perhaps, he had kept a crack open, just enough to let Lew remember that beside grief and guilt and loss and pain, there was love in the world, too.

And then, out of his own forfeited dreams and hope, out of the renunciation he had made, still raw in his mind, he offered the only comfort he could, laying it like a gift before his friend:

"But you have another world, Lew. And you are free to see the stars."

A Note From The Author

Like all previous Darkover novels, this story is complete in itself and does not depend on knowledge of any other. More than any other Darkover book, however, this one was written by popular demand.

One result of writing novels as they occured to me, instead of following strict chronological order, was that I began with an attempt to solve the final problems of the society; each novel thus suggested one laid in an earlier time, in an attempt to explain how the society had reached that point. Unfortunately, that meant that relatively mature novels, early in the chronology of Darkover, were followed by books written when I was much younger and relatively less skilled at storytelling; and of all these, the least satisfactory was *The Sword of Aldones,* perhaps because this book was, in essence, dreamed up at the age of fifteen.

In 1975 I made a landmark decision; that in writing *The Heritage of Hastur,* I would not be locked into the basically immature concepts set forth in *Sword,* even at the sacrifice of consistency in the series. After *Heritage* appeared in print, *Sword of Aldones* seemed even less satisfactory—for years, it seemed that everyone I met asked me when I was going to rewrite it. For years I replied "Never," or "I don't want to go back to it." But I finally decided that I had, in *Sword of Aldones,* developed a basically good idea, without the skill or maturity to handle it as well as it deserved; and that the characters deserved serious treatment by a matured writer. I decided not to rewrite, but to write an entirely new book based on events in the same time frame as *Sword.* The present book is the result.

—MARION ZIMMER BRADLEY

SHARRA'S EXILE

Prologue

The second year of exile

This was the home of my ancestors.

But I knew, now, that it would never be *my* home.

My eyes ached as I stared at the horizon where the sun sank out of sight—a strange yellow sun, not red as a sun should be, a glaring sun that hurt my eyes. But now, for a moment just before twilight, it was suddenly red and huge and sinking behind the lake in a sudden crimson glory that made me ache with homesickness; and across the water a streak of crimson. . . . I stood staring until the last gleams of crimson faded; and over the lake, pale and silver, the solitary moon of Terra showed the thinnest of elegant crescents.

Earlier in the day there had been rain, and the air was heavy with alien smells. Not alien, really; they were known, somehow, in the very depth of my genes. My ancestors had climbed down from the trees of this world, had lived out the long evolution which had patterned them into human, and had later sent out the seedling ships, one of which—I had heard the tale—had crash-landed on Darkover and settled there, rooting into the new world so deeply that I, exiled from my race's homeworld and returning, found homeworld alien and longed for the world of my people's exile.

I did not know how long ago, or for how long my people had dwelt on Darkover. Travel among the stars has strange anomalies; the enormous interstellar distances play strange tricks with time. There would never be any way for the folk of the Terran Empire to say, three thousand years ago, or fifteen thousand years ago, which particular colony ship founded Darkover. . . . The elapsed time on Terra was something like three thousand years. Yet elapsed time on Darkover was somehow more like ten thousand, so that Darkover had a history nearly as long as Earth's own history of civilization and chaos. I knew how many years ago Terra, in the days long before the Terran Empire had spread from star to star, had sent out the ship. I knew how many years had elapsed on Darkover. And there was no way for even the most accurate historian to reconcile them: I had long ago stopped trying.

Nor was I the only one with hopelessly torn loyalties, as deep as the very DNA in my cells. My mother had been earth born under this impossibly blue sky and this colorless moon; yet she had loved Darkover, had married my Darkovan father and borne him sons and, at last, been laid to rest in an unmarked grave in the Kilghard Hills on Darkover.

And I wish I were lying there beside her. . . .

For a moment I was not sure that the thoughts were not my own. Then I shut them out, savagely. My father and I were too close . . . not the ordinary closeness of a Comyn telepath family (though that in itself would have been freakish enough to the Terrans around us) but entangled by common fears, common loss . . . shared experience and pain. Bastard, rejected by my father's caste because my mother had been half Terran, my father had gone to endless pains to have me accepted as a Comyn Heir. To this day I did not know whether it was for my sake or his own. My futile attempts at rebellion had entrapped us all in the abortive rebellion under the Aldarans, and Sharra. . . .

Sharra. Flame burning in my mind . . . the image of a woman of flame, chained, restless, tresses of fire rising on a firestorm wind, hovering . . . rising, ravening . . . Marjorie caught in the fires, screaming, dying . . .

No! Merciful Avarra, no. . . .

Black dark. Shut out everything. Close my eyes, bend my head, go away, not there at all, nowhere at all. . . .

Pain. Agony flaming in my hand. . . .

"Pretty bad, Lew?" Behind me I felt the calming presence of my father's mind. I nodded, clenching my teeth, slamming the painful stump of my left hand against the railing, letting the cold strangeness of the white moon-rim flood me.

"Damn it, I'm all right. Stop—" I fought for the right word and came up with "stop hovering."

"What am I supposed to do? I can't shut it out," he said quietly. "You were—what shall I say? Broadcasting. When you can keep your thoughts to yourself, I'll leave you alone with them. In the name of all the Gods, Lew, I was a technician in the Arilinn Tower for ten years!"

He didn't elaborate. He didn't have to. For three years, the happiest years of my life, perhaps, I too had been matrix mechanic in the Arilinn Tower, working with the complex matrix crystals which linked telepaths and minds in linkages to provide communication, technology to our metal-poor, machinery-poor world. I had learned, in Arilinn, what it was to be a telepath, Comyn of our caste, gifted or cursed with the linking of minds and the hypersensitivity to the other minds around me. You learned not to pry; you learned not to let your own thoughts entangle with others, not to be hurt too much by the pain, or the needs, of others, to remain exquisitely sensitive and at the same time to live without intruding or demanding.

I had learned this, too. But my own control had been burned out by the ninth-level matrix which I had tried, insanely, to handle with a circle of half-trained telepaths. We had hoped, vainly, to restore the old, high-level Darkovan technology, handed down as legend from the Ages of Chaos. And we had nearly done it, too, experimenting with the old Darkovan crafts, called sorcery and magic by the commoners. We knew that in truth they were a complex technology, which could have done anything—powered spaceships for Darkover to stand equal to the Empire, rather than remain poor relations, dependents of the Terran Empire, a cold, metal-poor planet.

We had nearly done it . . . but Sharra was too powerful for us, and the matrix which for years had been chained, peacefully bringing fire to the forges of the mountain smiths, had been freed, ravening and raging in the hills. A city had been destroyed. *And I, I had been destroyed too, burnt in those monstrous fires, and Marjorie, Marjorie was dead. . .*

And now within my matrix, now I could see nothing but flame and destruction and Sharra. . . .

A telepath keys himself into the matrix stone he uses. At eleven I had been given such a matrix: if it had been taken from me, I would swiftly have died. I do not know what the matrix stones are. Some people say they are crystals which amplify the psychoelectrical emanations of the brain's activity in the "silent" areas where the Comyn powers reside. Others call them an alien life-form, symbiotic with the special powers of the Comyn. Whatever the truth, a Comyn telepath works through his own matrix; the larger matrixes, multi-level, are never keyed to the body and brain of the individual matrix worker, but relayed and transformed through his stone.

But Sharra had reached out for us, and taken us into the fire . . .

"Enough!" My father spoke with the particular force of an Alton, forcing his mine on mine, wresting the image away. Grateful darkness descended behind my eyes; then I could see the moon again, see something other than flames.

He said quietly, as I rested my eyes, covering them with my good hand, "You don't believe it now, but it *is* better, Lew. It comes when you let your guard down, yes. But there are long periods when you can break the domination of the Sharra matrix. . . ."

"When I don't talk about it, you mean," I interrupted angrily.

"No," he said, "when it isn't there. I've been monitoring you. It's not nearly as bad as it was that first year. In the hospital, for instance . . . I couldn't get you out of it for more than a few hours at a time. Now there are days, even weeks. . . ."

Yet I would never be free. When we went offworld, from Darkover, hoping to save the hand burned in Sharra's fires, I had taken the Sharra matrix, hidden in its elaborate sword; not because I wished to take it, but because after what had happened, I could no more be separated from it than parted from my own matrix. My own matrix hung around my neck; it had hung there since my twelfth year, and I could not remove it without pain and probably brain damage. Once it had been taken from me—a kind of deliberate torture—and I had come nearer to death than I like to think. Probably if it had been kept from me another day, I would have died, of heart failure or cerebral accident.

But the Sharra matrix . . . somehow it had overpowered my own. I need not wear it hanging round my neck, or be in physical contact with it, but I could not go beyond a certain critical distance, or the pain would begin, and the fire images surge in my brain, like static blurring out all else. My father was a competent technician, but he could do nothing; the technicians in the Arilinn Tower, where they had tried to save my hand, could do nothing. Finally they had taken me offworld, in a vain hope that Terran science could do more. It was illegal for the Warden of the Alton Domain, my father, Kennard Alton, to leave Darkover at the same time as his Heir. He had done it anyway, and for that I knew that I should have been grateful to him. But all I felt was weariness, rage, resentment.

You should have let me die.

My father stepped out into the light of the dim moon and stars. I could only barely see his outline; tall, once heavy and imposing; now stooped with the bone disease which had crippled him for many years; but still powerful, dominating. I was never sure whether I saw my father's physical presence or the mental, commanding force which had overpowered my life since, at eleven, he had forced my mind open to the telepathic Alton Gift—the gift of forced rapport even with non-telepaths, which characterizes the Alton Domain. He had done it because there was no other way to prove to the Comyn Council that I was worthy to be the Alton Heir. But I had had to live with it—and with his domination—ever since.

My hand throbbed where I had slammed down what was left of the arm. Peculiar, that ache; I could feel it in my fourth and sixth fingers . . . as if I had burned off a nail. And yet there was nothing there, nothing but the empty scar . . . they had explained it to me; phantom pain, nerves remaining in the rest of the arm. Damned real for a phantom. At least the Terran medics, and even my father, now realized there was nothing more to be done for the hand, and they had done what they should have done at first, and taken it off. Nothing to be done, even with their (rightly) fabled medical science. My mind still flinched away from the memory of the twisted, terrifying thing which had crowned their latest, experimental technique at regeneration. Whatever it is in the cells of the body which bids a hand be a hand, with palm and fingers and nails, and not a claw or a feather or an eye, had been burned away by Sharra, and once, through the drugs, I had seen what my hand had become. . . .

Force my mind away from that too . . . was there anything

safe to think about? I stared into the quiet sky from which the last lingering trace of crimson had faded.

He said quietly "It's worse at twilight, I think. I wasn't even full-grown yet when I came first to Terra; I used to come here at sunset so that my cousins and foster-brothers wouldn't see. You get so tired—" His back was to me, and in any case it was too dark to see anything but the dark loom of his presence, but still, somewhere in my mind, I could see the wry deprecating half-smile, "of the same old moon. And my Terran cousins thought it shameful for anyone my age to cry. So I made sure, after the first time, that they wouldn't see it."

There is a saying on Darkover; *only men laugh, only men dance, only men weep.*

But it had been different for my father, I thought in fierce envy. He had come here of his free will, and for a purpose; to build a bridge between our peoples, Terran and Darkovan. Larry Montray, his Terran friend, remaining on Darkover to be fostered in the Alton Domain: Kennard Alton coming here for a Terran education in the sciences of this world.

But I?

I had come here an exile, broken, maimed, my beloved Marjorie dead because I, like my father before me, had tried to build a bridge between Terran Empire and Darkover. And I had better reason: I was a son of both worlds, because Kennard, all Comyn, had married Montray's half-sister, Elaine. So I tried; but I had chosen the wrong instrument—the Sharra matrix—and failed, and lived on, with everything that made life real for me dead or abandoned on a world half a Galaxy away. Even the hope which had persuaded my father to bring me here—that my hand, burned in the fires of Sharra, might somehow be salvaged or regenerated—had proved worse than a mirage; even after all I had endured, that was gone too. And I was here on a hated world, alien and familiar at once.

My eyes were growing used to the darkness; I could see my father now, a man in late middle age, stooped and lame, his once-blazing hair all gray; his face was deeply lined with pain and conflict.

"Lew, do you want to go back? Would it be easier? I was here for a reason; I was an exchange student, on a formal mission. It was a matter of honor. But nothing binds you here. You can take ship and return to Darkover whenever you will. Shall we go home, Lew?" He did not glance at my hand; he didn't need to. *That* had failed, there was no reason to stay here hoping for a miracle.

(But I could still feel that dull pain like a torn-off nail around the thumb. And the sixth finger ached as if I had pinched it in a vise, or burnt it. Strange. Haunted by the ghost of a hand that wasn't there.)

"Lew, shall we go home?" I knew he wanted it; this alien land was killing him, too. But then he said the wrong thing.

"The Council wants me back. They know, now, I will father no other sons. And you are acknowledged Heir to Alton; when I went away, they said it was unlawful for the lord of Alton Domain and his Heir to leave the Domains at the same time. If you returned, the Council would be forced to acknowledge—"

"Damn the Council!" I said, so loudly that my father flinched. The same damned old political maneuvering. He had never stopped trying to get the Council to acknowledge me—it had made a nightmare of my childhood, forced him into the painful and dangerous step he had taken, forcing premature awakening of my *laran* gift. Later it had driven me to my Aldaran kinsfolk, and the ill-fated attempt to raise power through Sharra, and Marjorie. . . . I slammed the door shut in my mind, a closed place, black, blank. I would not think about that, *I would not*. . . . I wanted no part of their damned Council, nor of the Comyn, nor Darkover. . . . I turned my back and walked away toward the lake cabin, feeling him behind me, close, too close. . . .

Get out of my mind! Get—out Leave me alone! I slammed my mind shut like the cabin door, heard the door open and close, felt him there though I stood with closed eyes. I did not turn or look.

"Lew. No, damn it, don't shut me out again, listen to me! Do you think you are the only one in the world who has known what it is to lose a loved one?" His voice was rough but it was a roughness I knew; it meant that if his voice had been less rough he might have wept. It had taken me twenty-two years to know that my father could weep.

"You were two years old; and your sister died at birth. We both knew there should be no more. Elaine—" he had never before spoken her name in my hearing, though I knew it from his friends; always it had been the distant, formal *your mother.* *"Yllana,"* he said again, saying the Darkovan version of the name this time. "She knew as well as I, how fragile is the rule of a man with only one son. And you were not a hardy child. Believe me, I did not demand it of her. It was her free choice. And for fifteen years I have borne *that* burden, and tried never to let Marius feel it . . . that I grudged him life at the cost of Yllana's. . . ."

He had never said so much before. I could feel in his harsh voice what it had cost him to say it.

But it had been my mother's free choice, to risk her life in bearing my brother Marius. Marjorie had had no choice. . . .

Fire. Ravening flames shooting into the sky, the great hovering wings of flame. Marjorie, burning, burning in the flames of Sharra. . . . Caer Donn, the world, Darkover, all in flames. . . .

I slammed the barrier and the blackness down into my mind, heard myself shouting "No!" at the top of my voice, and once again brought up my maimed arm and slammed it down on anything, anything that would send pure physical pain crashing through my mind to the point where I could think of nothing else. *He should not make me look at this, that I had killed the only thing I had ever loved or would ever love. . . .*

From very far away I heard him calling my name, felt the concerned touch of his thoughts . . . I slammed the barrier tighter, felt the dark close down. I stood there, not hearing, not seeing, until he went away.

BOOK ONE

The Exile

Darkover: the third year of exile

CHAPTER ONE

Regis Hastur stood on a balcony of Comyn Castle, high over Thendara and the valley which lay ahead, looking over the city and the Terran Trade city beyond.

Behind him lay the castle, shadowed beneath the mountains. Before him lay the Terran Trade City, the spaceport beyond it—and the rising skyscrapers of the Terran Headquarters building. As he had thought many times before, he thought: *This has its own alien beauty.*

For many years he had had a dream. When he had come of age, he would leave Darkover behind him, take passage on one of those Terran starships, and go outward, among the stars, strange suns and worlds multiple beyond all telling. He would leave behind him all that he hated about his life; his own uneasy position, heir to an ancient household and a Regency which was more of an anchoronism with every passing year; the continuing pressure to marry, young as he was, and provide heirs to the legacy of the Hasturs: the unknown potential of *laran,* the inbred psychic ability bred into bones and brain and genes. He would leave behind him the rulership of the contending Domains, each striving for something different in the ever-changing world that was modern Darkover. Regis was eighteen; legally of age three years ago, sworn to Hastur. Now he knew he would never have his dream.

He would not have been the first of the Comyn to leave Darkover and go into the Empire. Adventure, the lure of an alien society and a vast complex universe, had drawn more than one Darkovan, even of the highest nobility, into the Empire.

The Ridenow Domain, he thought. *They make no secret*

of their belief that Darkover should align with the Empire, become a part of this modern world. Lerrys Ridenow has traveled widely in the empire, and no doubt at Council this season he will be singing their praises again. Kennard Alton was educated on Terra, and he is there now, with his son Lew. And then Regis wondered how Lew fared, somewhere in that alien universe.

If I were free of the burden of the Hastur heritage, I too would go forth and never return. And again the temptation struck him, as he had planned it when he was a rebellious child in his first year in the Cadets of the Guard—the necessary apprenticeship served by all Comyn sons. He and his friend Danilo had plotted it together; they would ship outward on one of the Terran ships, find a place for themselves there . . . lose themselves in the immensities of a thousand alien worlds. Regis smiled, reminiscently, knowing it had been the dream of children. For better or worse, he was Heir to Hastur, and the fate of Darkover was a part of his life, as intimately as body or brain. Danilo was Heir to Ardais, adopted by the childless Lord Dyan Ardais, being prepared for that high office as Regis was prepared for his own. Last year had been their third year in the cadets together; junior officers, learning command and self-command. It had been a peaceful time; but it was over. Regis had spent the winter past in the city of Thendara, attending sessions of the *cortes,* dealing with city magistrates, diplomatic envoys from the other Domains and the Dry Towns beyond the Domains, the representatives of the Terrans and the Empire; learning, in short, to take his grandfather's place as representative of the Domains.

Danilo had paid only one or two fleeting visits to the city since that Festival Night when Council Season had ended; he had had to return to Castle Ardais with Dyan and learn the ordering of the Domain which, if Dyan died still childless, would be his own. Then, Regis had heard, Danilo had been called back to Syrtis by the grave illness of his own father.

Why is Danilo on my mind now, so suddenly? And then he knew; he was not a powerful telepath, but the bond sworn between himself and Danilo was a strong one, and he turned abruptly away from the view of city and spaceport which lay before him, thrusting the curtains closed behind him as he went inside.

It is a boy's idle dream, to stand there and dream of the stars. My world lies here. He went into the outer room of the Hastur apartments just as one of the servants came in search of him.

"*Dom* Danilo Syrtis, Heir and Warden of Ardais," he announced, and Danilo came into the room, a slender, handsome young man, dark-haired and dark-eyed. Regis moved to take him into a formal kinsman's embrace, but over his shoulder he saw the servant leave the room and the formal greeting somehow transformed itself into an enthusiastic mutual hug.

"Dani! I'm so glad to see you! You can't imagine how dull the city is in winter!"

Danilo chuckled, looking down at Regis affectionately. He was a little taller, now, than his friend. "I'd have chosen it. I swear to you that the climate of Ardais has much in common with that of Zandru's coldest hell. I don't think Lord Dyan was any colder than that in Nevarsin monastery!"

"Is Dyan still at Nevarsin?"

"No, he left it early last winter. We were at Ardais together all the winter; he taught me many things he said I should know as Regent of the Domain. Then we traveled south to Thendara together . . . Strange, I never thought I would take pleasure in his company, yet he has taken great pains to have me properly educated for the place I will have—"

"He would do that for the honor of his own house," said Regis dryly.

"Yet when my poor father died he was kindness itself."

"I am not surprised at that either," Regis said. "You have grown handsome, Dani, and Lord Dyan has always had an eye for beauty in a boy—"

Danilo laughed. They could laugh together about it, now, though three years ago it had been no laughing matter. "Oh, I am too old for Dyan now—he prefers lads who have not yet grown their beards, and you can see—" with a nervous finger he twisted the small, dark moustache on his upper lip.

"Why, I wonder, then, that you have not grown a full beard!"

"No," said Danilo, with a strange, quiet persistence. "I know Dyan better now. And I give you my word, never once has he offered me a word or a gesture unseemly between father and son. When my own father died, he showed him all honor; he said it was a pleasure to do honor to one who had deserved it; it made amends, perhaps, for the honor he had had to show to those of his kinsmen who deserved it not." The old Lord of Ardais had died three years ago, mad and senile after a long and disgraceful life of debauchery.

"Dyan said something like that to me once," Regis agreed. "But enough of that—I am glad you are here, *bredu.* I suppose you are to sit in Council this year among the Ardais?"

"So Dyan said," Danilo agreed. "But Council will not begin till tomorrow, and tonight—well, I have not been in Thendara for years."

"I seldom go into the streets," said Regis, so quietly that it did not even sound bitter. "I cannot walk half a mile without a crowd following me . . ."

Danilo started to make a flippant answer; then withheld it, and the old sympathy began to weave between them again, a touch closer than words; the telepathic touch of *laran,* of sworn brotherhood and more.

Well, you are Heir to Hastur, Regis; it is part of the burden of being what you are. I would lighten it if I could, but no one alive can do that. And you would not have it otherwise.

You lighten it by understanding; and now that you are here I am not altogether alone . . .

No spoken words were necessary. After a time Danilo said lightly, "There is the tavern where the Guard officers go; they at least have grown used to Comyn and do not think we are all freaks or monsters, or that we walk without touching the ground like some heroes from old legends. We could have a drink there without anyone staring."

The Castle Guard of Thendara at least know that we are human, with all the human faults and failings, and sometimes more. . . . Regis was not entirely sure whether the thought was his own, or whether he picked it up from Danilo. They went down through the great labyrinth of the Comyn Castle, and out into the crowded streets of the first night of Festival.

"Sometimes, at Festival, I come here masked," Regis said.

Danilo grinned. "What—and deprive every girl in the city of the joys of hopeless love?"

Regis made a nervous gesture—the gesture of a fencer who concedes a hit. Danilo knew he had struck too close to the nerve, but did not make it worse with an apology. Regis picked up the thought anyway; *The Regent is pressuring him to marry again, damned old tyrant! At least my foster-father understands why I do not.* Then Danilo managed to shield his thoughts; they went into the tavern near the gates of the Guard Hall.

The front room was crowded with young cadets. A few of the boys saluted Regis and he had to speak a word or two to them, but they finally got through to the quieter back room, where the older officers were drinking. The room was semi-dark even at this hour, and some of the men nodded in a friendly fashion to Regis and his companion, but immediately turned back to their own affairs; not unfriendliness but a way of giving the Hastur Heir the only privacy and anonymity he ever could have these days. Unlike the boys in the outer room, who enjoyed the knowledge that even the powerful Hastur-lord was required by law and custom to return their salutes and acknowledge their existence, these officers knew a little of Regis's burden and were willing to let him alone if he wished.

The tavernkeeper, who knew him too, brought his usual wine without asking. "What would you like, Dani?"

Danilo shrugged. "Whatever he's brought."

Regis began to protest, then laughed and poured the wine; the drinking was only an excuse, anyway. He raised his rough mug, sipped and said, "Now tell me everything that's been happening while you were away. I'm sorry about your father, Dani; I liked him and hoped to bring him to court someday. Did you spend all that time in the Hellers?"

Hours slipped away while they talked, the wine half forgotten between them. At last they heard the drum-roll of "Early Quarters" beat out from the Guard Hall, and Regis started, half rising, then laughed, remembering that he was no longer obliged to answer to it. He sat down again.

"What a soldier you've become!" Danilo teased.

"I liked it," Regis said, after a moment. "I always knew exactly what was expected of me, and who expected it, and what to do about it. If there were war, it would have been a different thing. But the worst trouble I ever had was in breaking up street riots, or escorting drunks to the lockup if they were making a nuisance of themselves, or investigating when a house was robbed, or making somebody tie up a troublesome dog. Last year there was a riot in the marketplace—no, this one is funny, Dani; a cattle-drover's wife had left him because, she said, she had caught him in her *own* bed with her *own* cousin! So she slipped into his stall, and stampeded the animals he'd brought to sell! There were upset stalls and broken crockery all over the place . . . I happened to be officer of the day, so I caught it! One of the cadets complained that he'd left home so he *wouldn't* have to chase dairy animals all day long! Well, we finally got them all rounded up again, and I had to go and testify before the city magistrate. So the *cortes* fined the woman twelve *reis* for all the damage the beasts had caused, and it was the husband who had to pay the fine! He protested that he had been the victim, and it was his wife who let the animals loose, and the magistrate—she was a Renunciate—said that it would teach him to conduct his love affairs in decent privacy, in a way that didn't insult or humiliate his wife!"

Danilo laughed, more at the reminiscent amusement in Regis's face, than at the story. Out in the other room, he heard the cadets jostling each other and bickering as they paid their accounts and went back to barracks. "Did I see one of your sister's sons among the cadets out there? They must be great boys now."

"Not yet this year," said Regis. "Rafael is only twelve, and young Gabriel only eleven . . . I suppose Rafael might have been just old enough, but with his father the Commander of the Guard, I suppose he felt it was early for that. Or my sister did, which is the same thing."

Danilo looked startled. "Gabriel Lanart-Hastur is Commander of the Guards? How did that happen? Has Kennard Alton not returned?"

"There's been no word from him; not even whether he is dead or alive, my grandfather said."

"But the Command of Castle Guard is an Alton post," Danilo protested. "How comes it into Hastur hands?"

"Gabriel is one of the nearest kin to the Altons of Armida. With Kennard and his Heir both offworld, what else could they do?"

"But surely there are Altons nearer of kin than your brother-in-law," protested Danilo. "Kennard's other son, Marius—he must be fifteen or sixteen now."

"Even if he were acknowledged Heir to Alton," Regis said, "he would hardly be old enough to command the Guard. And Kennard's elder brother had a son, the one they found on Terra . . . but he's chief technician at Arilinn Tower, and knows no more of commanding soldiers than I know of embroidery stitches! Anyway, his Terran education's a handicap—it doesn't hurt him out there at Arilinn, but they don't want him in Thendara to remind them that there are Terrans in the very heart of Comyn Council!" His voice sounded bitter. "After all, they managed to get rid of Lew Alton, and the Council refused again last year to give Marius any of the rights—or duties—of a Comyn son. My grandfather told me—" his smile only stretched his mouth a little— "that they had made that mistake with Lew, and they're not going to make it again, they said. Terran blood, bad blood, treachery."

"Lew deserves better of them than that," said Danilo quietly. "And if he does not, Kennard at least is guiltless of any treachery and should be consulted."

"Do you think I did not say that? I am old enough to sit in Council and listen to my elders, Dani, but do you think they listen to me when I speak? My grandfather said that he knew Lew and I had been *bredin* when I was a child—implying that would warp my judgment. If Kennard were *here* to be consulted, they might listen to him. Most people do. But they are not neglecting Marius, even though they have not allowed him status as Alton of Armida; they appointed Gabriel as his Guardian, and he has been sent to the Terran Headquarters for a proper Terran education. He's better educated than either you or I, Dani, and what he has learned there probably makes more sense in this day of Empire and star-travel than *this*—" He gestured around the tavern, at the Guardsmen wearing swords. Regis fully agreed with the Darkovan Compact, which forbade use of any weapon beyond arm's reach of the man using it, insisting that he who would kill must take his own chance with death. Still, swords were not weapons alone, but tokens of a way of life which seemed to make little sense in the presence of an interstellar Empire. Danilo followed his thoughts, but shook his head stubbornly.

"I don't agree with you, Regis. Marius deserves better of the Council than a Terran education. I don't think Kennard should have gone offworld, and certainly he should not have stayed this long. Hastur should recall him at once—unless your grandfather is greedy for another Domain to pass under the rule of the Hasturs. Already, it seems, he has taken over the Elhalyn Domain—or why is Derik not yet crowned, at eighteen?"

Regis made a wry face. "You do not know our Prince. He may be eighteen, but he is a child of ten—or might as well be. My grandsire wants nothing more than to be free of the burden of the Regency of Thendara—"

Danilo raised a skeptical eyebrow but said nothing. Regis repeated, "Derik is not yet ready to rule. The Council has deferred his crowning till he is twenty-five. There is precedent for that, and if Derik is simply slow to reach manhood and wisdom, well, that will give him time. If not—well, we will fly that falcon when his pinions are grown."

"And what if Derik, in Hastur's opinion, is never fit to rule?" Danilo asked. "There was a time when the Hasturs ruled all these Domains, and the rebellion against their tyranny split the Domains into a hundred little kingdoms!"

"And it was the Hasturs who united them all again, in the days of King Carolin," said Regis. "I have read history, too. In Aldones's name, Dani, do you think my grandsire is anxious to be King over all this country? Or do I look to you like a tyrant?"

Danilo said, "Certainly not. But in principle, each of the Domains should be strong—and independent. If Lord Hastur cannot crown Derik—and from what little I have seen of him, he looks not much like a King—he should look elsewhere for an Heir to Elhalyn. Forgive me, Regis, but I like it not, to see so much power in Hastur hands; first the Regency which controls the Heir to the Crown, and now the Altons under Hastur rule too. And the Alton Domain carries with it the command of Castle Guard.

Where will Hastur turn next? Lady Callina of Valeron is unmarried; will he marry her, perhaps, to you, and bring the Aillard Domain as well under the Hasturs?"

"I am old enough to be consulted about my marriage," said Regis dryly. "And I assure you that if he has any such plan, he has not spoken of it to me. Do you think my grandfather is a spider at the center of such a web as that?"

"Regis, I am not trying to pick a quarrel with you." Danilo raised the wine pitcher; Regis shook his head, but Danilo poured it anyway, raised the rough mug to his lips and set it down untasted. "I know your grandsire is a good man, and as for you—well, you know well what I think, *bredhyu.*" He used the intimate inflection, and Regis smiled, but Danilo went on earnestly, "All this sets a dangerous precedent. After you, Hasturs may reign who are really not fit for such power. A day could come when all the Domains would be Hastur vassals."

"Zandru's hells, Dani!" said Regis impatiently. "Do you really think Darkover will remain independent of the Empire that long, or that the Comyn will rule over the Domains when that day comes? I think Marius Alton is the only one of us who will be properly prepared for the direction in which Darkover will go."

"That day will come," Danilo told him quietly, "over the dead bodies of the Ardais Domain."

"No doubt, on that day, there will be Hastur bodies lying dead too, but it will come for all that. Listen, Dani," he said urgently, "do you *really* understand the situation? A few generations ago, when the Terrans came here, it was because we happened to be in the wrong place at the right time—a planet located between the upper and lower spiral arms of the Galaxy, exactly where they needed to set up a spaceport as a crossroads and transit point for Empire traffic. They'd have preferred an uninhabited planet, and I'm sure they debated making us into one. Then they discovered that we were a lost Terran colony—"

"And Saint-Valentine-of-the-Snows lies buried in Nevarsin," Danilo said, exasperated. "I heard all that when we were prisoners in Aldaran three years ago, Regis!"

"No, listen—the Terrans found us, speaking languages long dead on Terra itself; but we were a primitive world, which had lost its technology, or so they thought. They gave us Closed World status, so that we would not be disturbed by too-rapid social upheavals—they do that with all primitive societies, so that they can evolve at their own rate. Then they found out that we were not so primitive a planet after all, and they found out about our *laran,* our matrix technology. They found that the linked minds in the Tower circles could mine metals, power aircraft, all those other things—well, they wanted matrix technology, and they tried all sorts of things to get some of it."

"Regis, I know all that, but—"

"Will you *listen?* You know as well as I; some Darkovans wanted, and still want, the advantages of Terran technology, a place in the Empire, status for Darkover as a colony with political strength, representation in the Empire Senate—all those things. Others, especially in the Comyn, felt that Empire citizenship would destroy our world and our people. That we'd become just another colony like a dozen others, dependent on Terran trade, offworld metals and luxuries, tourists. . . . They've had their way so far. I can see that there will have to be changes on Darkover. But I want them to come at a rate we can assimilate."

"And I don't want them to come at all," Danilo said.

"Who would? But the Terrans are *here,* like it or not. And I will not be accused of trying to keep our people primitives, barbarians, so that my family and I can maintain our superstitious powers over them!"

He had spoken more forcefully than he realized, forgetting where they were. A languid voice said, "Bravo! The Heir to Hastur has come of age and learned that Terrans are a reality, not a crew of bogeymen to frighten little children!"

Regis started. He had forgotten they were not alone. He turned to see a tall thin man, fair-haired, with the stamp of the Comyn on his angular features, elegantly dressed in foppish Darkovan clothing, but with rich alien furs adorning his cloak. Regis bowed, his face set in rigid politeness.

"Cousin," he acknowledged. "I did not see you, Lerrys."

"Nor I you, *Dom* Regis," said Lerrys Ridenow, "but when you shout so loudly that the Terrans in their Headquarters could hear you across the city, why should I pretend I did not hear? I am glad to know that you understand the situation. I hope this means there will be another advocate for sanity in the Council this year, and that the Ridenow need not stand alone against that doddering conclave of maiden ladies of either sex!"

Regis said stiffly, "Please don't believe that I am altogether in agreement with you, *Dom* Lerrys. I do not like to think of the kind of social upheavals there would be, if we became just another Terran colony—"

"But we *are* another Terran colony," Lerrys said. "And the sooner we recognize it, the better. Social upheavals? Bah! Our people want the good things Terran citizenship will bring them, and they would accept the rest, once they were confronted with an accomplished fact. They simply haven't enough education to know what they want, and the Hasturs, and the worthy lords of the Comyn, have made sure they won't have it!" He half-rose. "Must we shout this from table to table? Will you not join us, cousin—and your friend as well?" He used the intimate inflection of the world, with its implications, and Regis, flicked raw, glanced at Danilo, half-wishing the other would refuse; but there was no reasonable cause for denial. Lerrys was Comyn and his kinsman. There was no reason for his distaste.

Only, perhaps, that we have more in common than I could wish. He flaunts abroad what I must, for the sake of my grandfather, keep discreetly within bounds. I envy him, perhaps, that he is a younger son of a minor Comyn house, that he is not always in the public eye. Everything he does, does not immediately become public property for gossip or censure.

They took a seat at Lerry's table and accepted a fresh round of drinks, which neither of them wanted. After another round or two, he thought, he would make some excuse, then he and Danilo would go somewhere and dine; Early Quarters had been some time ago. Soon there would be the sound of Night Quarters from the Guard Hall and he could invent an engagement somewhere. The places he chose to dine would be too tame for Lerrys and his elegant hangers-on; most of them, he could see, were Darkovan, but they wore elaborate Terran clothing; not the functional uniform of the spaceports, but brilliant and colorful things from the far corners of the Empire.

Lerrys, pouring the wine he had ordered, went on, taking up the conversation he had interrupted, "After all, we *are*

Terrans; we deserve all the privileges of our heritage. Everyone in the Domains could benefit from Terran medicine and science—not to mention education! I happen to know you can read and write, Regis, but you must admit you are a happy exception. How many, even of the cadets, can do more than scribble their names and spell their way through the arms manual?"

"I think they have enough education for what they must do in the world," said Regis. "Why should they burden themselves with idle nonsense, which is what most written matter turns out to be? There are enough idle scholars in the world—and in the Empire, for that matter."

"And if they are uneducated," Lerrys said with a sardonic smile, "it is easier to keep them in superstitious bondage to the Comyn, fabulous tales about the God-given rulership of the Hasturs, kinfolk to the Gods. . . ."

"Certainly I would agree with you that there is no excuse for that kind of mental slavery," said Regis. "If you heard what I was saying before, you would hear that I was protesting against that sort of tyranny. But you cannot say that we are Terrans and no more." He reached across the table; took Lerrys's hand and laid his own palm-to-palm with it, counting the six fingers; then touched the small leather bag at his throat, where the matrix stone rested; a small warmth, a pulse. . . .

"The powers of the Comyn are real."

"Oh—*laran,*" said Lerrys with a shrug. "Even some of the Terrans who come among us have developed it; it, too, is part of our Terran heritage, and we can teach them something of this, too . . . Why should it be limited to the Comyn? In return we will have their sciences; knowledge of weather control, which would be like a blessing from the Gods in some of the country across the Hellers; the Drytown desert, perhaps, reclaimed for agriculture, and some of the impassable mountains across the Wall Around the World, brought into contact with the Domains; astronomy, star-travel—and in return, *laran* and knowledge all through the Galaxy. . . ."

"That could be dangerous, too dangerous to spread indiscriminately through the Empire," said one of Lerry's young companions diffidently. "Were you there when Caer Donn burned, Lerrys?"

"I was," Regis said, and looked sharply at the young stranger. "I know you. Rakhal—Rafe—"

"Rakhal Darriell-Scott, *z'par servu,*" said the young man. "They call me Rafe Scott, in the Terran Zone. I saw then what *laran* uncontrolled can do—and hope never to see it again!"

"No fear of that," Lerrys said. "The Sharra matrix was destroyed. As far as we know, that was the only one of those old matrixes from the Ages of Chaos left on our world. Besides, if there are such things, we should learn how to control and use them, not hide like banshee-birds in the sunlight, and pretend they do not exist. Believe me, the Terrans are no more anxious than you to see *laran* out of control that way."

"And, no matter what happens, there will always be those who can use *laran* and those who cannot," said another youngster. There was something familiar about him, too; Regis thought he was probably one of Rafe Scott's kinsmen. He was not eager to remember that time at Castle Aldaran, and the frightful time when Sharra had raged and ravened in the hills across the river. He and Danilo, escaping from Aldaran, had come near to dying in those hills. . . .

"Still, we are all Terrans," said Lerrys, "and the Empire is our heritage, as of right, not a privilege; we should not have to ask for Empire citizenship or the benefits of Empire. They gave us Closed World status, but it's high time to rectify that mistake. Before we can do that, we must acknowledge that the Terran Empire is our lawful government, not the local bigwigs and aristocracy! I can understand that you, Regis, would like to keep your place of power, but listen to me! In the face of an Empire which spans a thousand worlds, what does it matter what the peasants think of our nobles? As long as this is a Closed World, the local aristocrats can maintain their personal power and privilege. But once we acknowledge that we are a part of the Terran Empire—not that we wish to become part of the Empire, but that we are already so, and thus subject to their laws—then every citizen of Darkover can claim that privilege; and—"

"Perhaps there are many who do not consider it such a privilege—" Danilo began hotly, and Lerrys drawled, "Does it matter what such people think? Or, in denying them that privilege, are you simply demanding your own, Lord Danilo, as warden of Ardais—"

But before Danilo could answer that, there was a commotion in the front room; then Dyan Ardais strode into the back room, where the few remaining senior officers, and the Comyn, were sitting. He came directly to their table.

"Greetings, kinsmen." He bowed slightly. Danilo, as befitting a foster-son in the presence of the Head of his Domain, rose and stood awaiting recognition or orders.

Dyan was tall and spare, mountain Darkovan from the Hellers; his features aquiline, his eyes steel-gray, almost colorless, almost metallic. Ever since Regis had known him, Dyan had affected a dress of unrelieved black whenever he was not in uniform or clad in the ceremonial colors of his Domain: it gave him a look of chilly austerity. Like many hillmen, his hair was not the true Comyn red, but coarse, curly and dark.

"Danilo," he said, "I have been looking for you. I might have known I would find you here; and Regis with you, of course."

Regis felt the little ironic flicker of telepathic touch, recognition, awareness, annoyingly intimate, as if the older man had taken some mildly unsuitable liberty in public, tousled his hair as if he were a boy of eight or nine; nothing serious enough so that he could object without loss of dignity. He knew Dyan liked to see hm ill at ease and off balance; what he did not know was *why*. But the Ardais Lord's face was blank and indifferent.

He said, "Will you both dine with me? I have something to say to you, Danilo, which will affect your plans for Council season, and since I know your first move afterward would be to tell it to Regis, I might as well say it to both of you at once and save the time."

"I am at your orders, sir," said Danilo with a slight bow.

"Will you join us, cousin?" Lerrys asked, and Dyan shrugged. "One drink, perhaps."

Lerrys slid along the bench to make room for Dyan and for his young companion; Regis did not recognize the younger man, and Lerrys, too, looked questioningly at Dyan.

"Don't you know one another? Merryl Lindir-Aillard."

Dom Merryl was, Regis thought, about twenty; slender, red-haired, freckled, good-looking in a boyish way. With a mental shrug—Dyan's friends and favorites were no business of his, Aldones be praised—he bowed courteously to young Merryl. "Are you kin to *Domna* Callina, *vai dom?* I do not think we have met."

"Her step-brother, sir," Merryl said, and Regis could hear in the other young man's mind, like an echo, the question he was too diffident to ask: *Lord Dyan called him Regis, is this the Regent's grandson, the Hastur Heir, what is he doing here just like anyone else, like an ordinary person. . . .* It was the usual mental jangle, wearying to live with.

"Are you to sit in Council this year, then?"

"I have that honor; I am to represent her in Council while she is held at Arilinn by her duties as Keeper there," he said, and the annoying telepathic jangle went on: *in any other Domain it would be* my *Council seat, but in this one, damn all the Council, rank passes in the female line and it is my damned bitch of a half-sister, like all women, coming the mistress over us all. . . .*

Regis made a strong effort to barricade himself and the trickle of telepathic leakage quieted. He said politely, "Then I welcome you to Thendara, kinsman."

The dark, slender youngster sitting between Lerrys and Rafe Scott said shyly, "You are Callina's brother, *dom* Merryl? Why, then, I shall welcome you as kinsman too; Callina's half-sister Linnell was fostered with me at Armida, and I call her *breda.* She has spoken of you, kinsman."

"I'm afraid I don't know all of *Domna* Callina's relatives," Merryl returned, in the most indifferent formal mode. Regis winced at the direct snub he had given the boy, and suddenly knew who the other must be; Kennard's younger son, Marius, never acknowledged by the Council, and educated among the Terrans. Regis hadn't recognized Marius, but that wasn't surprising; they moved in different orbits and he had not seen the boy since he was the merest child. Now he must be all of fifteen. He seemed indifferent to Merryl's snub; was he merely so accustomed to insults that he had truly learned to ignore them, or had he only learned not to seem to care? With a little extra courtesy, Regis said, "Dom Marius; I did not recognize you, cousin."

Marius smiled. His eyes were dark, like a Terran's. "Don't apologize, Lord Regis; there aren't many in Council who do." And again Regis heard the unspoken part of that, *or would admit it if they did.* Lerrys covered the small, awkward silence by pouring wine, passing it to Dyan with some offhand comment about the quality of wine here not being the best.

"But as a Guardsman, cousin, no doubt you've learned to ignore that."

"One would never think, now, that you had worn a Guardsman's uniform, Lerrys," Dyan returned, affably enough.

"Well, I did my share of it for a Comyn son," Lerrys said, with a grin, "as did we all. Though I do not remember seeing you among the cadets, Merryl."

Merryl Lindir-Aillard said with a grimace, "Oh, I caught one of the fevers about the time I should have done service in the cadets, and my mother was a timid woman, she thought I'd melt in the summer rains . . . and later, when my father died, she said I was needed at home." His voice was bitter. Danilo said, smiling, "My father felt so too; and he was old and feeble. He let me go, willingly enough, knowing I should better myself there; but he was glad to have me home again. It's not easy to judge where one is needed most, kinsman."

"I think we have all had experience of that," said Dyan.

"You didn't miss anything," said Lerrys. "Zandru's hells, kinsman, who needs sword practice and training at knife play in this day and age? The Cadets—saving your presence, Lord Regis—are an anachronism in this time, and the sooner we admit it, and call them an honor guard in fancy dress, the better off we'll be. The Guardsmen police the city, but we ought to take advantage of the Terran offer to send Spaceforce to teach them modern police techniques. I know you must feel as if you missed what every Comyn kinsman should have, Merryl, but I spent three years in the Cadets and two more as an officer, and I could have done as well without it. As long as you look handsome in a Guardsman's cloak—and I can see by looking at you that you'll have no trouble with that—you already know all you'll need for *that.* As I'm sure Dyan's told you."

"There's no need to be offensive, Lerrys," Dyan said

stiffly. "But I might have expected it of you—you spend more time on Vainwal exploring alien pleasures than here in Thendara doing your duty as a Comyn lord! It seems to be the climate of the day. I can't blame you; when the Altons neglect their duty, what can one expect of a Ridenow?"

"Are you jealous?" Lerrys asked. "On Vainwal, at least I need not conceal my preferences, and if the Altons can spend their time idling throughout the Empire, by what right do you criticize me?"

"I criticize them no less—" Dyan began hotly.

"Lord Dyan," said Marius Alton angrily. "I thought you at least were my father's friend—or friend enough not to judge his motives!"

Dyan looked him straight in the eye and drawled, "Who the hell are you?"

"You know who I am," Marius retorted, "even if it amuses you to pretend you do not! I am Marius Montray-Lanart of Alton—"

"Oh, the Montray woman's son," Dyan said, in the derogatory mode implying *brat* or *foundling.*

Marius drew a deep breath and clenched his fists. "If Kennard, Lord Alton, acknowledges me his son, it matters nothing to me who else does not!"

"Wait a minute—" Lerrys began, but Merryl Lindir said, "Must we listen to this even here in Thendara? I did not come here to drink with Terran bastards—and with Terran spies!"

Marius sprang angrily to his feet. "Terran spies? Captain Scott is *my* guest!"

"As I said, Terran spies and toadies—I did not come here for that!"

"No," retorted Marius, "it seems you came here for a lesson in manners—and I am ready to give you one!" He kicked the chair back, came around the table, his hand on his knife. "Lesson one: you do not criticize the invited guest of anyone—and I am here as the guest of the Lord Lerrys, and Captain Scott as mine. Lesson two: you do not come into Thendara and cast aspersions on any man's lineage. You will apologize to Captain Scott, and retract what you said about my father—and my mother! And you too, Lord Dyan, or I shall call you to account as well!"

Good for him, Regis thought, looking at the angry youngster, knife in hand, crouched into a stance of readiness for a fight. Meryl blinked; then whipped out his knife and backed away, giving himself room to move. He said, "It will be a pleasure, Alton bastard—"

Lerrys tried to move toward them, laid a hand on Marius's wrist. "Wait a minute—"

"Keep out of this, sir," Marius said, between gritted teeth.

Good, the boy has courage! Good-looking, too, in his own way! Zandru's hells, why didn't Kennard— For a moment Regis could not identify the source of the thought, then Dyan said aloud, "Put your knife up, Merryl! Damn it, that's an order! You too, Marius, lad. Council never acknowledged your father's marriage, but it's not hard to see you're your father's son."

Marius hesitated, then lowered the knife in his hand. Merryl Lindir-Aillard snarled, "Damn you, are you afraid to fight me, then, like all you coward Terrans—ready to kill with your coward's weapons and guns from a distance, but frightened of bare steel?"

Lerrys stepped between them, saying, "This is no place for a brawl! In Zandru's name—"

Regis saw that the others in the tavern had drawn back, making something like a ring of spectators. *When kinsmen quarrel, enemies step in to widen the gap! Does it give them pleasure to see Comyn at odds?* "Stop it, both of you! This is not a house of bandits!"

"Get back, both of you," said a new, authoritarian voice, and Gabriel Lanart-Hastur, Commander of the Guard, stepped forward. "If you want to fight, make it a formal challenge, and let's not have any stupid brawls here! Are you both drunk? Lerrys, you are an officer, you know no challenge is valid unless both challengers are sober! Marius—"

Marius said, fists clenched, "He insulted my father and mother, kinsman! For the honor of the Alton Domain—"

Gabriel said quietly, "Leave the honor of the Domain in my hands until you are older, Marius."

"I am sober enough to challenge him!" Marius said, angrily, "and here I call challenge—"

"Merryl, you damned fool—" Dyan said urgently, laying a hand on his shoulder, "this is serious—"

"I'm damned if I'll fight a Terran bastard with honor," shouted Merryl, enraged, and rounded on Gabriel Lanart-Hastur. He said, "I'll fight *you,* or your whole damned Domain—if I can get any of them back here on Darkover where they belong! But your Lord Alton is no better than any of his bastards, off gallivanting all over the Empire when they're needed in Council—"

Gabriel took a step forward, but there was a glare of blue fire and Merryl went reeling back staggering. The telepathic slap was like a thunder in the minds of everyone there.

BRIDLE YOUR STUPID TONGUE, LACK-WIT! I HAVE LONG SUSPECTED THAT DOMNA CALLINA IS TRULY THE MAN OF YOUR HOUSEHOLD, BUT MUST YOU PROVE IT HERE IN PUBLIC LIKE THIS? ARE YOUR BRAINS ALL WHERE YOU CAN SIT UPON THEM? It was followed by an obscene image; Regis saw Merryl cringe. He felt it in Danilo's mind too; Danilo had known what it was to be abused by Dyan, mercilessly, with sadistic strength, until Danilo had cracked and drawn a knife on him. . . . Regis, feeling Danilo cower, felt his friend's agony and stepped back, blindly, to stand close to him. Merryl was dead white; for a moment Regis thought he would weep, there before them all.

Then Dyan said aloud, coldly, "Lord Regis, Danilo, I believe we have an engagement to dine. *Dom* Lerrys, I thank you for the drink." He nodded to Regis, then turned away from them all. There was nothing Regis or Danilo could do but follow him. Merryl was still numbly holding the knife; he slid it into his sheath and went after them. With a swift look backward, Regis saw the tension had evaporated; Gabriel was talking in an urgent undertone to Marius, but that was all right; there was no malice, Regis knew, in his brother-in-law; and after all, in Kennard's absence, Gabriel was Marius's guardian.

Outside, Dyan frowned repressively at Merryl. "I had intended to ask you to join us; I want you and Regis to know one another. But you'd better stay away until you learn how to behave in the city, boy! The first time I take you into the company of the Comyn, you get yourself into a stupid brawl!"

Neither tone nor words need have been changed a fraction if he had been speaking to a boy of eight or nine who had bloodied his nose in a dispute over a game of marbles. Inexcusable as Merryl's behavior had been, Regis felt sorry for the youngster, who stood, crimson, accepting Dyan's tongue-lashing without a word. Well, he deserved it. Merryl said, swallowing, "Was I to stand there and be insulted by Terrans and half-Terrans, kinsman?" He used the word in the intimate mode which could mean Uncle, and Dyan did not reprove him; he reached out and slapped him very lightly on the cheek.

"I think you did the insulting. And there's a right way and a wrong way to do these things, *kiyu.* Go think about the right way. I'll see you later."

Merryl went, but he no longer looked quite so much like a puppy that had been kicked. Regis, acutely uncomfortable, followed Dyan through the street. The Comyn lord turned into the doorway of what looked like a small, discreet tavern. Inside, he recognized the place for what it was, but Dyan shrugged and said, "We'll meet no other Comyn here, and I can endure to be spared the company of any more like the last!" The flicker of unspoken thought again, *if you value your privacy, lad, you might as well get used to places like this one,* was so indifferent that Regis could ignore it if he chose.

"As you wish, kinsman."

"The food's quite good," Dyan said, "and I have ordered dinner. You needn't see anything else of the place, if you prefer not to." He followed a bowing servant into a room hung with crimson and gilt, and talked commonplaces—about the decorations, about the soft stringed music playing—while young waiters came and brought all kinds of food.

"The music is from the hills; they are a famous group of four brothers," said Dyan. "I heard them while they were still in Nevarsin, and it was I who urged them to come to Thendara."

"A beautiful voice," said Regis, listening to the clear treble of the youngest musician.

"Mine was better, once," said Dyan, and Regis, hearing the indifference of the voice, knew it covered grief. "There are many things you do not know about me; that is one. I have done no singing since my voice broke, though when I was in the monastery for a time last winter, I sang a little with the choir. It was peaceful in the monastery, though I am not a *cristoforo* and will never be so; their religion is too narrow for me. I hope a day will come when you will find it so, Danilo."

"I am not a good *cristoforo,*" Danilo said, "but it was my father's faith and will be mine, I suppose, till I find a better."

Dyan smiled. He said, "Religion is an entertainment for idle minds, and yours is not idle enough for that. But it does a man in public life no harm to conform a little to the religion of the people, if the conformity is on the surface and does not contaminate his serious thinking. I hold with those who say, even in Nevarsin, *There is no religion higher than the truth.* And that is not blasphemy either, foster-son; I heard it from the lips of the Father Master. But enough of this—I had something to say to you, Danilo, and I thought to save you the trouble of running at once to pour it into Regis's ears. In a word; I am a man of impulse, as you have known for a long time. Last year I dwelt for a time at Aillard, and Merryl's twin sister bore me a son ten days since. Among other business of the Comyn, I am here to have him legitimated."

Danilo said correctly, "My congratulations, foster-father."

Regis said a polite phrase also, but he was puzzled.

"You are surprised, Regis? I am a bit surprised myself. In general, even for diversion, I am no lover of women—but as I say, I am . . . a creature of impulse. Marilla Lindir is not a fool; the Aillard women are cleverer than the men, as I have reason to know. I think it pleased her to give Ardais a son, since sons to Aillard have no chance of inheriting that Domain. I suppose you know how these things can happen—or are you both too young for that?" he asked with a lift of the eyebrows, and a touch of malice. "Well, so it went—when I found she was pregnant, I said nothing. It might have been a daughter for Aillard, rather than an Ardais son—but I took the trouble to have her monitored and to be sure the child was mine. I did not speak of it when we met at Midwinter, Danilo, because anything might have befallen; even though I knew she bore a son, she might have miscarried, the child might have been stillborn or defective—the Lindirs have Elhalyn blood. But he is healthy and well."

"Congratulations again, then," said Danilo.

"Do not think this will change anything for you," said Dyan. "The lives of children are—uncertain. If he should come to misfortune before he is grown, nothing will change; and should I die before he is come to manhood, I should hope you will be married by then and be named Regent for him. Even so, when he leaves his mother's care, I am no man to raise a child, nor would I care, at my age, to undertake it; I should prefer it if you would foster him. I will soon apply myself to finding you a suitable marriage—Linnell Lindir-Aillard is pledged to Prince Derik, but there are other Lindirs, and there is Diotima Ridenow, who is fifteen or sixteen now, and—well, there is time enough to decide; I do not suppose you are in any too great a hurry to be wedded," he added ironically.

"You know I am not, foster-father."

Dyan shrugged. "Then any girl will do, since I have saved you the trouble of providing an Heir to Ardais; we can choose one who is amiable, and content to keep your house and run your estate," he said. "A legal fiction, if you wish." He turned his eyes to Regis, and added, "And while I am about it, my congratulations are due to you, too; your grandfather told me about the Di Asturien girl, and your son—will he be born this tenday, do you suppose? Is there a marriage in the offing?"

Shock and anger flooded through Regis. He had intended to tell Danilo this in his own time. He said stiffly, "I have no intention of marrying at this time, kinsman. No more than you."

Dyan's eyes glinted with amused malice. He said, "Why, have I said the wrong thing? I'll leave you to make your peace with my foster-son, then, Regis." He rose and bowed to them with great courtesy. "Pray command anything here you wish, wine or food or—entertainment; you are my guests this evening." He bowed again and left them, taking up his great fur-lined cloak, which flowed behind him over his arm like a living thing.

After a minute Danilo said, and his voice sounded numb, "Don't mind, Regis. He envies our friendship, no more than that, and he is striking out. And, I suppose, he feels foolish; to father a bastard son at his age."

"I swear I meant to tell you," Regis said miserably, "I

was waiting for the right time. I wanted to tell you before you heard it somewhere as gossip."

"Why, Regis, what is it to do with me, if you have love affairs with women?"

"You know the answer to that," said Regis, low and savage, "I have no *love affairs* with women. You know that things like this must happen, while I am Heir to Hastur. Comyn Heirs at stud in the Domains—that's what it amounts to! Dyan doesn't like it any better than you do, but even so, he spoke of getting you married off. And I am damned if I'll marry someone they choose for me, as if I were a stud horse! That's what it was, and that is *all* it was. Crystal di Asturien is a very nice young woman; I danced with her at half a dozen of the public dances, I found her friendly and pleasant to talk to, and—" He shrugged. "What can I say to you? She wanted to bear a Hastur son. She's not the only one. Do I have to apologize for what I must do, or would you rather I did not enjoy it?"

"You certainly owe me no apologies." Danilo's voice was cold and dead.

"Dani—" Regis pleaded, "are we going to let Dyan's malice drive a wedge between us, after all this time?"

Danilo's face softened. "Never, *bredhyu.* But I don't understand. You already have an Heir—you have adopted your sister's son."

"And Mikhail is still my Heir," Regis retorted, "but the Hastur heritage was hung too long on the life of a single child. My grandfather will not force me to marry—as long as I have children for the Hastur lineage. And I don't want to marry," he added. The unspoken awareness hung in the air between them.

A waiter came, bowing, and asked if the *vai domyn* had any other pleasure: wine, sweets, young entertainers. . . . He weighted this last heavily, and Danilo could not conceal a grimace of distaste.

"No, no, nothing more." He hesitated, glancing at Regis. "Unless you—"

Regis said wryly, "I am a libertine only with women, Dani, but no doubt I have given you cause to think otherwise."

"If we have to quarrel," Dani said, with a gulp, "Let us at least do it in clean air and not in a place like this!"

Regis felt a great surge of enormous bitterness. Dyan had done this, damn it! He said, "Oh, no doubt, this is the place for lovers' quarrels of this kind—and I suppose if the Heir to Hastur and his favorite must quarrel, better here than in Comyn Castle, where all the Domains, sooner or later, will hear!"

And again he felt, it is more of a burden than I can bear!

Vainwal: Terran Empire
Fifth year of exile

CHAPTER TWO

Dio Ridenow saw them first in the lobby of the luxury hotel serving humans, and humanoids, on the pleasure-world of Vainwal. They were tall, sturdy men, but it was the blaze of red hair on the elder of them that drew her eyes; Comyn red. He was past fifty and walked with a limp: his back was bent, but it was easy to see that once he had been a large and formidable man. Behind him walked a younger man in nondescript clothing, dark-haired and black-browed, sullen, with steel-gray eyes. Somehow he had the look of deformity, of suffering, which Dio had learned to associate with lifetime cripples; yet he had no visible defect except for a few ragged scars along one cheek. The scars drew up one half of his mouth into a permanent sneer, and Dio turned her eyes away with a sense of revulsion; why would a Comyn lord have such a person in his entourage?

For it was obvious that the man was a Comyn lord. There were redheads in other worlds of the Empire, and plenty on Terra itself; but there was a strong facial stamp, an ethnic likeness; Darkovan, Comyn, unmistakable. And the older man's hair, flame-red, now dusted with gray. But what was he doing here? For that matter, who was he? It was rare to find Darkovans anywhere but on their home world. The girl smiled; someone might have asked her that question, as well, for she was Darkovan and far from home. Her brothers came here because, basically, neither of them was interested in political intrigue; but they had had to defend and justify their absence often enough.

The Comyn lord moved across the great lobby slowly limping, but with a kind of arrogance that drew all eyes;

Dio framed it to herself, in an unfocused way; he moved as if he should have been preceded by his own drone-pipers, and worn high boots and a swirling cloak—not the drab, featureless Terran clothing he actually wore.

And having identified his Terran clothing, suddenly Dio knew who he was. Only one Comyn lord, as far as anyone knew, had actually married, *di catenas* and with full ceremony, a Terran woman. He had managed to live down the scandal, which in any case had been before Dio was born. Dio herself had not seen him more than twice in her life; but she knew that he was Kennard Lanart-Alton, Lord Armida, self-exiled Head of the Alton Domain. And now she knew who the younger man must be, the one with the sullen eyes; this would be his half-caste son Lewis, who had been horribly injured in a rebellion somewhere in the Hellers a few years ago. Dio took no special interest in such things, and in any case she had still been playing with dolls when it happened. But Lew's foster-sister Linnell Aillard had an older sister, Callina, who was Keeper in Arilinn; and from Linnell Dio had heard about Lew's injuries, and that Kennard had taken him to Terra in the hope that Terran medical science could help him.

The two Comyn were standing near the central computer of the main hotel desk; Kennard was giving some quietly definite order about their luggage to the human servants who were one of the luxury touches of the hotel. Dio herself had been brought up on Darkover, where human servants were commonplace and robots were not; she could accept this kind of service without embarrassment. Many people could not overcome their shyness or dismay at being waited on by people rather than servomechs or robots. Dio's poise about such things had given her status among the other young people on Vainwal, many of them among the new-rich in an expanding Empire, who flocked to the pleasure worlds like Vainwal, knowing little of the refinements of good living, unable to accept luxury as if they had been brought up to it. Blood, Dio thought, watching Kennard and the exactly right way he spoke to the servants, would always tell.

The younger man turned; Dio could see now that one hand was kept concealed in a fold of his coat, and that he moved awkwardly, struggling one-handed to handle some piece of their equipment which he seemed not to want touched by anyone else. Kennard spoke to him in a low voice, but Dio could hear the impatient tone of the words, and the young man scowled, a black and angry scowl which made Dio shudder. Suddenly she realized that she did not want to see any more of that young man. But from where she stood she could not leave the lobby without crossing their path.

She felt like lowering her head and pretending they were not there at all. After all, one of the delights of pleasure worlds like Vainwal was to be anonymous, freed of the restraints of class or caste on one's own home world; she would not speak to them, she would give them the privacy she wanted for herself.

But as she crossed their path, the young man, not seeing Dio, made a clumsy movement and banged full into her. Whatever he was carrying slid out of his awkward one-handed grip and fell to the floor with a metallic clatter; he muttered some angry words and stooped to retrieve it.

It was long, narrow, closely wrapped; more than anything else it looked like a pair of dueling swords, and that alone could explain his caution; such swords were often precious heirlooms, never entrusted to anyone else to handle. Dio stepped away, but the young man fumbled with his good hand and succeeded only in sending it skidding farther away across the floor. Without thinking, she bent to retrieve it and hand it to him—it was right at her feet—but he actually reached out and shoved her away from it.

"Don't touch that!" he said. His voice was harsh; raw, with a grating quality that set her teeth on edge. She saw that the arm he had kept concealed inside his coat ended in a neatly folded empty sleeve. She stared, open-mouthed with indignation, as he repeated, with angry roughness, "Don't touch that!"

She had only been trying to help!

"Lewis!" Kennard's voice was sharp with reproof; the young man scowled and muttered something like an apology, turning away and scrambled the dueling swords, or whatever the untouchable package was, into his arms, turning ungraciously to conceal the empty sleeve. Suddenly Dio felt herself shudder, a deep thing that went all the way to the bone. But why should it affect her so? She had seen wounded men before this, even deformed men; surely a lost hand was hardly reason to go about as this one did, with an outraged, defensive scowl, a black refusal to meet the eyes of another human being.

With a small shrug she turned away; there was no reason to waste thought or courtesy on this graceless fellow whose manners were as ugly as his face! But, turning, she came face to face with Kennard.

"But surely you are a countrywoman, *via domna?* I did not know there were other Darkovans on Vainwal."

She dropped him a curtsy. "I am Diotima Ridenow of Serrais, my lord, and I am here with my brothers Lerrys and Geremy."

"And Lord Edric?"

"The Lord of Serrais is at home on Darkover, sir, but we are here by his leave."

"I had believed you destined for the Tower, mistress Dio."

She shook her head and knew the swift color was rising in her face. "It was so ordained when I was a child; I—I was invited to take service at Neskaya or Arilinn. But I chose otherwise."

"Well, well, it is not a vocation for everyone," said Kennard genially, and she contrasted the charm of the father with the sneering silence of the son, who stood scowling without speaking even the most elementary formal phrases of courtesy! Was it his Terran blood which robbed him of any vestige of his father's charm? No, for good manners could be learned, even by a Terran. In the name of the blessed Cassilda, couldn't he even *look* at her? She knew that it was only the scar tissue pulling at the corner of his mouth which had drawn his face into a permanent sneer, but he seemed to have taken it into his very soul.

"So Lerrys and Geremy are here? I remember Lerrys well from the Guards," Kennard said. "Are they in the hotel?"

"We have a suite on the ninetieth floor," Dio said, "but they are in the amphitheater, watching a contest in gravity-dancing. Lerrys is an amateur of the sport, and reached the semi-finals; but he tore a muscle in his knee and the medics would not permit him to continue."

Kennard bowed. "Convey them both my compliments,"

he said, "and my invitation, lady, for all three of you to be my guests tomorrow night, when the finalists perform here."

"I am sure they will be charmed," Dio said, and took her leave.

She heard the rest of the story that evening from her brothers.

"Lew? That was the traitor," said Geremy, "Went to Aldaran as his father's envoy and sold Kennard out, to join in some kind of rebellion among those pirates and bandits there. His mother's people, after all."

"I had thought Kennard's wife was Terran," Dio said.

"Half Terran; her mother's people were Aldarans," Geremy said. "And believe me, Aldaran blood isn't to be trusted."

Dio knew that; the Domain of Aldaran had been separated from the original Seven Domains so many generations ago that Dio did not even know how long it had been, and Aldaran treachery was proverbial. She said, "What were they doing?"

"God knows," Geremy said. "They tried to hush it up afterward. It seems they had some kind of super-matrix back there, perhaps stolen from the forge-folk; I never heard it all, but it seems Aldaran was experimenting with it, and dragged Lew into it—he'd been trained at Arilinn, after all, old Kennard gave hm every advantage. We knew no good would come of it; burned down half of Caer Donn when the thing got out of hand. After that, I heard Lew switched sides again and sold out Aldaran the way he sold us out; joined up with one of those hill-woman bitches, one of Aldaran's bastard daughters, half-Terran or something, and got his hand burned off. Served him right, too. But I guess Kennard couldn't admit what a mistake he'd made, after all he'd gone through to get Lew declared his Heir. I wonder if they managed to regenerate his hand?" He wiggled three fingers, lost in a duel years ago and regenerated good as new by Terran medicine. "No? Maybe old Kennard thought he ought to have something to remember his treachery by."

"No," Lerrys said. "You have it wrong way round, Geremy. Lew's not a bad chap; I served with him in the

Guards. He did his damnedest, I heard, to control the fire-image when it got out of hand but the girl died. I heard he'd married her, or something. I heard from one of the monitors of Arilinn, how hard they'd worked to save her. But the girl was just too far gone, and Lew's hand—" He shrugged. "They said he was lucky to have gotten off that easy. Zandru's hells, what a thing to have to face! He was one of the most powerful telepaths they ever had at Arilinn, I heard; but I knew him best in the guards. Quiet fellow, standoffish if anything, nice enough when you got to know him; but he wasn't easy to know. He had to put up with a lot of trouble from people who thought he had no right to be there, and I think it warped him. I liked him, or would have if he'd let me; he was touchy as the devil, and if you were halfway civil to him, he'd think he was being patronized, and get his back up." Lerrys laughed soundlessly.

"He was so standoffish with women that I made the mistake of thinking he was—shall we say—one who shared my own inclinations, and I made him a certain proposition. Oh, he didn't *say* much, but I never asked him *that* again!" Lerrys chuckled. "Just the same, I'll bet he didn't have a good word for you, either? That's a new thing for you, isn't it, little sister, to meet a man who's not at your feet within a few minutes?" Teasing, he chucked her under the chin.

Dio said, pettishly, "I don't like him; he's rude. I hope he stays far away from me!"

"I suppose you could do worse," Geremy mused. "He *is* Heir to Alton, after all; and Kennard isn't young, he married late. He may not be long for this world. Edric would like it well if you were to be Lady of Alton, sister."

"No." Lerrys put a protecting arm around Dio. "We can do better than that for our sister. Council will never accept Lew again, not after that business with Sharra. They never accepted Kennard's other son, in spite of the best Ken could do; and Marius's worth two of Lew. Once Kennard's gone, they'll look elsewhere for a Head of the Alton Domain—there are claimants enough! No, Dio—" gently he turned her around to look at him—"I know there aren't many young men of your own kind here, and Lew's Darkovan, and, I suppose, handsome, as women think of these things. But stay away from him. Be polite, but keep your distance. I like him, in a way, but he's trouble."

"You needn't worry about that," Dio said. "I can't stand the sight of the man."

Yet inside, where it hurt, she felt a pained wonder. She thought of the unknown girl Lew had married, who had died to save them all from the menace of the fire-Goddess. So it had been Lew who raised those fires, then risked death and mutilation to quench them again? She felt herself shivering again in dread. What must his memories be like, what nightmares must he live, night and day? Perhaps it was no wonder that he walked apart, scowling, and had no kind word or smile for man or woman.

Around the ring of the null-gravity field, small crystalline tables were suspended in midair, their seats apparently hanging from jeweled chains of stars. Actually they were all surrounded by energy-nets, so that even if a diner fell out of his chair (and where the wine and spirits flowed so freely, some of them did), he would not fall; but the illusion was breathtaking, bringing a momentary look of wonder and interest even to Lew Alton's closed face.

Kennard was a generous and gracious host; he had commanded seats at the very edge of the gravity ring, and sent for the finest of wines and delicacies; they sat suspended over the starry gulf, watching the gravity-free dancers whirling and spinning across the void below them, soaring like birds in free flight. Dio sat at Kennard's right hand, across from Lew, who, after that first flash of reaction to the illusion of far space, sat motionless, his scarred and frowning face oblivious. Past them, galaxies flamed and flowed, and the dangers, half-naked in spangles and loose veils, flew on the star-streams, soaring like exotic birds. His right hand, evidently artificial and almost motionless, lay on the table unstirring, encased in a black glove. That unmoving hand made Dio uncomfortable; the empty sleeve had seemed, somehow, more honest.

Only Lerrys was really at ease, greeting Lew with a touch of real cordiality; but Lew replied only in monosyllables, and Lerrys finally tired of trying to force conversation and bent over the gulf of dancers, studying the finalists with unfeigned envy, speaking only to comment on the skills, or lack of them, in each performer. Dio knew he longed to be among them.

When the winners had been chosen and the prizes awarded, the gravity was turned on, and the tables drifted, in gentle spiral orbits, down to the floor. Music began to play, and dancers moved onto the ballroom surface, glittering and transparent as if they danced on the same gulf of space where the gravity-dancers had whirled in free-soaring flight. Lew murmured something about leaving, and actually half-rose, but Kennard called for more drinks, and under the service Dio heard him sharply reprimanding Lew in an undertone; all she heard was "Damn it, can't hide forever—"

Lerrys rose and slipped away; a little later they saw him moving onto the dance floor with an exquisite woman whom they recognized as one of the performers, in starry blue covered now with drifts of silver gauze.

"How well he dances," Kennard said genially. "A pity he had to withdraw from the competition. Although it hardly seems fitting for the dignity of a Comyn lord—"

"Comyn means nothing here," laughed Geremy, "and that is why we come here, to do things unbefitting the dignity of Comyn on our own world! Come, kinsman, wasn't that why *you* came here, to be free for adventures which might be unseemly or worse, in the Domains?"

Dio was watching the dancers, envious. Perhaps Lerrys would come back and dance with her. But she saw that the woman performer, perhaps recognizing him as the contestant who had had to withdraw, had carried him off to talk to the other finalists. Now Lerrys was talking intimately with a young, handsome lad, his red head bent close to the boy. The dancer was clad only in nets of gilt thread, and the barest possible gilt patches for decency; his hair was dyed a striking blue. It was doubtful, now, that Lerrys remembered that there were such creatures as women in existence, far less sisters.

Kennard watched the direction of her glance. "I can see you are longing to be among the dancers, Lady Dio, and it is small pleasure to a young maiden to dance with her brothers, as I have heard my foster-sister and now my foster-daughters complain. I have not been able to dance for many years, *damisela,* or I would give myself the pleasure of dancing with you. But you are too young to dance in such a public place as this, except with kinsmen—"

Dio tossed her head, her fair curls flying. She said, "I do as I please, Lord Alton, here on Vainwal, and dance with anyone I wish!" Then, seized by some imp of boredom or mischief, she turned to the scowling Lew. "Yet here sits a kinsman—will you dance with me, cousin?"

He raised his head and glared at her, and Dio quailed; she wished she had not started this. This was no one to flirt with, to exchange light pleasantries with! He gave her a murderous glance, but even so, he was shoving back his chair.

"I can see that my father wishes it, *damisela.* Will you honor me?" The harsh voice was amiable enough—if you did not see the look deep in his eyes. He held out his good arm to her. "You will have to forgive me if I step on your feet. I have not danced in many years. It is not a skill much valued on Terra, and my years there were not spent where dancing was common."

Damn him, Dio thought, this was arrogance; he was not the only crippled man in the universe, or on the planet, or even in this room—his own father was so lame he could hardly put one foot before the other, and made no bones about saying so!

He did not step on her feet, however; he moved as lightly as a drift of wind, and after a very little time, Dio gave herself up to the music, and the pure enjoyment of the dance. They were well matched, and after a few minutes of moving together in the perfect rhythm—she knew she was dancing with a Darkovan, nowhere else in the civilized Empire did any people place so much emphasis on dancing as on Darkover—Dio raised her eyes and smiled at him, lowering mental barriers in a way which any Comyn would have recognized as an invitation for the telepathic touch of their caste.

For the barest instant, his eyes met hers and she felt him reach out to her, as if by instinct, attuned to the sympathy between their bodies. Then, without warning, he slammed the barrier down between them, hard, leaving her breathless with the shock of it. It took all her self-control not to cry out with the pain of that rebuff, but she would not give him the satisfaction of knowing that he hurt her; she simply smiled and went on enjoying the dance at an ordinary level, the movement, the sense of being perfectly in tune with his steps.

But inside she felt dazed and bewildered. What had she done to merit such a brutal rejection? Nothing, certainly; her gesture had indeed been bold, but not indecently so. He was, after all, a man of her own caste, a telepath and a kinsman, and if he felt unwilling to accept the offered intimacy, there were gentler ways of refusing or withdrawing.

Well, since she had done nothing to deserve it, the rebuff must have been in response to his own inner turmoil, and had nothing to do with her at all. So she went on smiling, and when the dance slowed to a more romantic movement, and the dancers around them were moving closer, cheek against cheek, almost embracing, she moved instinctively toward him. For an instant he was rigid, unmoving, and she wondered if he would reject the physical touch, too; but after an instant his arm tightened round her. Through the very touch, though his mental defenses were locked tight, she sensed the starved hunger in him. . . . How long had it been, she wondered, since he had touched a woman in any way? Far too long, she was sure of that. The telepath Comyn, particularly the Alton and Ridenow, were well-known for their fastidiousness in such matters; they were hypersensitive, much too aware of the random or casual touch. Not many of the Comyn were capable of tolerating casual love affairs.

There were exceptions, of course, Dio thought; the young Heir to Hastur had the name of a follower of women; though he was likely to seek out musicians or matrix mechanics, women who were sensitive and capable of sharing emotional intensity, not common women of the town. Her brother Lerrys, too, was promiscuous in his own way, though he too tended to seek out those who shared his own consuming interests. . . . A quick glance told her that he was dancing with the youngster in the gilded nets, a quick-flaring, overflowing intimacy of shared delight in the dance.

The dance slowed, the lights dimming, and she sensed that all around them couples were moving into each other's arms. A miasma of sensuality, almost visible, seemed to lie like mist over the whole room. Lew held her tight against him, bending his head; she raised her face, again gently inviting the touch he had rebuffed. He did not lower his mental barriers, but their lips touched; Dio felt a slow, drowsy excitement climbing in her as they kissed. When they drew apart his lips smiled, but there was still a great sadness in his eyes.

He looked around the great room filled with dancing couples, many now entwined in close embraces. "This—this is decadent," he said.

She smiled, snuggling closer to him. "Surely no more than Midsummer festival in the streets of Thendara. I am not too young to know what goes on after the moons have set."

His harsh voice sounded gentler than usual. "Your brothers would seek me out and call challenge on me."

She lifted her chin and said angrily, "We are not now in the Kilghard Hills, *Dom* Lewis, and I do not allow any other person, not even a brother, to tell me what I may or may not do! If my brothers disapprove of my conduct, they know they may come to me for an accounting of it, not to you!"

He laughed and with his good hand touched the feathery edges of her hair. It was, she thought, a beautiful hand, sensitive and strong, without being over-delicate. "So you have cut your hair and declared the independence of a Free Amazon, kinswoman? Have you taken their oath too?"

"No," she said, snuggling close to him again. "I am too fond of men ever to do that."

When he smiled, she thought, he was very handsome; even the scar that pulled his lip into distortion only gave his smile a little more irony and warmth.

They danced together much of the evening, and before they parted, agreed together to meet the next day for a hunt in the great hunting preserves of the pleasure planet. When they said good night, Kennard was smiling benevolently, but Geremy was sullen and brooding, and when the three of them were in their luxurious suite, he demanded wrathfully, "Why did you do that? I told you, stay away from Lew! We don't really want an entanglement with that branch of the Altons!"

"How dare you try to tell me whom I can dance with? I don't censure your choice of entertainers and singing women and whores, do I, Geremy?"

"You are a lady of the Comyn! And when you behave so blatantly as that—"

"Hold your tongue!" Dio flared at him. "You are insulting! I dance one evening with a man of my own caste, because my brothers have left me no other dancing partner, and already you have me bedded down with him! And even if it were so, Geremy, I tell you once again, I will do as I wish, and neither you nor any other man can stop me!"

"Lerrys," Geremy appealed, "Can't you reason with her?"

But Lerrys stood regarding his sister with admiration. "that's the spirit, Dio! What is the good of being on an alien planet in a civilized Empire, if you keep the provincial spirit and customs of your backwater? Do what you like, Dio. Geremy, let her alone!"

Geremy shook his head, angry, but he was laughing too. "You too! Always one in mind, as if you had been born twins!"

"Certainly," said Lerrys. "Why, do you think, am I a lover of men? Because, to my ill-fortune, the only woman I have ever known with a man's spirit and a man's strength is my own sister!" He kissed her, laughing. "Enjoy yourself, *breda,* but don't get hurt. He may have been on his good behavior last night, or even in a romantic mood, but I suspect he could be savage."

"No." Suddenly Geremy was sober. "This is no joke. I don't want you to see him again, Diotima. One evening, perhaps, to do courtesy to our kinsmen; I grant you that, and I am sorry if I implied it was more than courtesy. But no more, Dio, not again. Lerrys said as much last night, when he wasn't devilling me! If you don't think I have your good at heart, certainly you know Lerrys does. Listen to me, sister; there are enough men on this planet to dance with, flirt with, hunt with—yes, damn it, and to lie with too, if that's your pleasure! But let Kennard Alton's half-caste bastard alone—do you hear me? I tell you, Dio, if you disobey me, I shall make you regret it!"

"Now," said Lerrys, still laughing, as Dio tossed her head in defiance, "you have made it certain, Geremy; you have all but spread the bridal bed for them! Don't you know that no man alive can forbid Dio to do anything?"

In the hunting preserve next day, they chose horses, and the great hawks not unlike the *verrin* hawks of the Kilghard

Hills. Lew was smiling, good-natured, but she felt he was a little shocked, too, at her riding breeches and boots. "So you are the Free Amazon you said you were not, after all," he teased.

She smiled back at him and said, "No. I told you why I could never be that." *And the more I see him,* she thought, *the more sure I am of it.* "But when I ride in the riding-skirts I would wear on Darkover, I feel like a housecat in leather mittens! I like to feel free when I ride, if not, why not stay on the ground and embroider cushions?"

"Why not, indeed?" he asked, smiling, and in his mind, painless for once, she saw, reflected, a quick memory of a laughing woman, red-headed, riding bareback and free over the hills. . . . The picture slammed shut; was gone. Dio wondered who the woman had been and felt a faint, quick envy of her.

Lew was a good rider, though the lifeless artificial hand seemed to be very much in his way; he could use it, after a fashion, but so clumsily that she wondered if, after all, he could not have managed better one-handed. She would have thought that even a functional metal hook would have been more use to him. But perhaps he was too proud for that, or feared she would think it ugly. He carried the hawk on a special saddleblock, as women on Darkover did, instead of holding it on his wrist as most hillmen did; when she looked at it, he colored and turned angrily away, swearing under his breath. Again Dio thought, with that sudden anger which Lew seemed able to rouse in her so quickly, *why is he so sensitive, so defensive, so self-indulgent about it? Does he think most people know or care whether he has two hands, or one, or three?*

The hunting preserve had been carefully landscaped and terraformed to beautiful and varied scenery, low hills which did not strain the horses, smooth plains, a variety of wild life, colorful vegetation from a dozen worlds. But as they rode she heard him sigh a little. He said, just loud enough for her to hear, "It is beautiful here. But the sun here—is wrong, somehow. I wish—" and he closed off the words, the way he could close off his mind, sharp and swift, brutally shutting her out.

"Are you homesick, Lew?" she asked.

He tightened his mouth. "Yes. Sometimes," he said, but

he had warned her off again, and Dio turned her attention to the hawk on her saddle.

"These birds are very well trained."

He made some noncommittal remark, but she managed to catch his thought that birds which were well enough trained to be used by all comers were like whores, not at all interesting. All he said aloud was, "I would rather train my own."

"I like to hunt," she said, "but I am not sure I could train a bird from the beginning. It must be very difficult."

"Not difficult for anyone with the Ridenow gift, I should think," Lew said. "Most of your clan have sensitivity to all animals and birds, as well as the gift you were bred for, to sense and make contact with alien intelligences—"

She smiled and shrugged. "In these days there is little of that. The Ridenow gift, in its original form—well, I think it must be extinct. Though Lerrys says it would be very useful in the Terran Empire, to make communication possible with non-humans. It is very difficult to train hawks?"

"It is certainly not easy," said Lew. "It takes time and patience. And somehow you must put your mind into touch with the bird's mind, and that is frightening; they are wild, and savage. But I have done it, at Arilinn; so did some of the women. Janna Lindir is a fine hawk trainer, and I have heard it is easier for women . . . though my foster-sister Linnell would never learn it, she was frightened of the birds. I suppose it is like breaking horses, which my father used to do . . . before he was so lame. He tried to teach me that, a little, a long time ago." Talking easily of these things, Dio thought, Lew was transformed.

The preserve was stocked with a variety of game, large and small. After a time they let their hawks loose, and Dio watched in delight as hers soared high, wheeled in midair and set off on long, strong wings after a flight of small white birds, directly overhead. Lew's hawk came after, swiftly stooping, seizing one of the small birds in midair. The white bird struggled pitiably, with a long, eerie scream. Dio had hunted with hawks all her life; she watched with interest, but as drops of blood fell from the dying bird, spattering them, she realized that Lew was staring upward, his face white and drawn with horror. He looked paralyzed.

"Lew, what is the matter?"

He said, his voice strained and hoarse, "That sound—I cannot bear it—" and flung up his two arms over his eyes. The black-gloved artificial hand struck his face awkwardly; swearing, he wrenched it off his wrist and flung it to the ground under the horse's hoofs.

"No, it's not pretty," he mocked, in a rage, "like blood, and death, and the screams of dying things. If you take pleasure in them, so much the worse for you, my lady! Take pleasure, then, in this!" He held up the hideously scarred bare stump, shaking it at her in fury; then wheeled his horse, jerking at the reins with his good hand, and riding off as if all the devils in all the hells were chasing him.

Dio stared in dismay; then, forgetting the hawks, set after him at a breakneck gallop. After a time they came abreast; he was fighting the reins one-handed, struggling to rein in the mount; but, as she watched in horror, he lost control and was tossed out of the saddle, falling heavily to the ground, where he lay without moving.

Dio slid from her horse and knelt at his side. He had been knocked unconscious, but even as she was trying to decide whether she should go to bring help, he opened his eyes and looked at her without recognition.

"It's all right," she said. "The horse threw you. Can you sit up?"

He did so, awkwardly, as if the stump pained him; he saw her looking, flinched and tried to thrust it into a fold of his riding cloak, out of sight. He turned his face away from her, and the tight scar tissue drew up his mouth into an ugly grimace, as if he were about to cry.

"Gods! I'm sorry, *domna,* I didn't mean—" he muttered, almost inaudibly.

"What was it, Lew? Why did you lose your temper and rush off like that? What did I do to make you angry?"

"Nothing, nothing—" Dazed, he shook his head. "I—I cannot bear the sight of blood, now, or the thought of some small helpless thing dying for my pleasure—" he said, and his voice sounded exhausted. "I have hunted all my life, without ever thinking of it, but when I saw that little white bird crying out and saw the blood, suddenly it all came over me again and I remembered—oh, Avarra have mercy on me, I remembered. . . . Dio, just go away, don't, in the name of the merciful Avarra, Dio—"

His face twisted again and then he was crying, great hoarse painful sobs, his face ugly and crumpled, trying to turn away so that she would not see. "I have seen . . . too much pain . . . Dio, don't—go away, go away, don't touch me—"

She put out her arms, folded him in them, drawing him against her breast. For a moment he resisted frantically, then let her draw him close. She was crying too.

"I never thought," she whispered. "Death in hunting—I am so used to it, it never seemed quite real to me. Lew, what was it, who died, what did it make you remember?"

"Marjorie," he said hoarsely. "My wife. She died, she died, died horribly in Sharra's fire—Dio, don't touch me, somehow I hurt everyone I touch, go away before I hurt you too, I don't want you to be hurt—"

"It's too late for that," she said, holding him, feeling his pain all through her. He raised his one hand to her face, touching her wet eyes, and she felt him slam down his defenses again; but this time she knew it was not rejection, only the defenses of a man unbearably hurt, who could bear no more.

"Were you hurt, Dio?" he asked, his hand lingering on her cheek. "There's blood on your face."

"It's the bird's blood. It's on you too," she said, and wiped it away. He took her hand in his and pressed the fingertips to his lips. Somehow the gesture made her want to cry again. She asked, "Were you hurt when you fell?"

"Not much," he said, testing his muscles cautiously. "They taught me, in the Empire hospital on Terra, how to fall without hurting myself, when I was—before this healed." Uneasily he moved the stump. "I can't get used to the damned hand. I do better one-handed."

She had thought he might. "Why do you wear it, then? If it's only for looks, why do you think I would care?"

His face was bleak. "Father would care. He thinks, when I wear the empty sleeve, I am—flaunting my mutilation. Making a show of it. He hates his own lameness so much, I would rather not—not flaunt mine in his face."

Dio thought swiftly, then decided what she could say. "You are a grown man, and so is he. He has one way of coping with his own lameness, and you have another; it is easy to see that you are very different. Would it really make him angry if you chose another way to deal with what has happened to you?"

"I don't know," Lew said, "but he has been so good to me, never reproached me for these years of exile, nor for the way in which I have brought all his plans to nothing. I do not want to distress him further." He rose, went to collect the grotesque lifeless thing in its black glove, looked at it for a moment, then put it away in his saddlebag. He fumbled one-handed to pin his empty sleeve over the stump; she started to offer, matter-of-factly, to help him, and decided it was too soon. He looked into the sky. "I suppose the hawks are gone beyond recall, and we will be charged for losing them."

"No." She blew the silver whistle around her neck. "They are birds with brains modified so they cannot choose but come to the whistle—see?" She pointed as two distant flecks appeared in the sky, growing larger and larger; spiraling down, then landing on the saddle blocks where they sat patiently, awaiting their hoods. "Their instinct for freedom has been burnt out."

"They are like some men I know," said Lew, slipping the hood on his bird. Dio followed suit, but neither of them moved to mount. Dio hesitated, then decided he had probably had far too much of politely averted eyes and pretenses of courteous unawareness.

"Do you need help to mount? Can I help you, or shall I fetch someone who can?"

"Thank you, but I can manage, though it looks awkward." Again, suddenly, he smiled and his ugly scarred face seemed handsome again to her. "How did you know it would do me good to hear that?"

"I have never been really hurt," she said, "but one year I had a fever, and lost all my hair, and it did not grow in for half a year; and I felt so ugly you couldn't imagine. And the one thing that bothered me worst was when everyone would say how nice I looked, tell me how pretty my dress or sash or kerchief looked, and pretended nothing at all was wrong with me. So I felt so bad about how miserable I was, as if I was making a dreadful fuss about nothing at all. So if I was—was really lamed or crippled, I think I would hate it if people made me go on acting as if nothing at all was wrong and there was nothing the matter with me. Please don't ever think you have to pretend with me."

He drew a deep breath. "Father flies into a rage if anyone seems to notice him limping, and once or twice when I have tried to offer him my arm, he has nearly knocked me down."

Yet, Dio thought, *Kennard used his lameness, last night, to manipulate me into dancing with Lew. Why?* She said, "That is the way he manages *his* life and *his* lameness. You are not your father."

Suddenly he started shaking. He said, "Sometimes—sometimes it is hard to be sure of that," and she remembered that the Alton gift was forced rapport. Kennard's intense closeness to his son, his deep ambition for him, was well-known on Darkover; that closeness must become torture sometimes, make it hard for Lew to distinguish his own feelings and emotions. "It must be difficult for you; he is such a powerful telepath—"

"In all fairness," said Lew, "it must be difficult for him too; to share everything I have lived through in these years, and there was a time when my barriers were not as strong as they are now. It must have been hell for him. But that does not make it less difficult for me."

And if Kennard will not accept any weakness in Lew . . . but Dio did not pursue that. "I'm not trying to pry. If you don't want to answer, just say so, but . . . Geremy lost three fingers in a duel. The Terran medics regrew them for him, as good as new. Why did they not try to do that with your hand?"

"They did," he said. "Twice." His voice was flat, emotionless. "Then I could bear no more. Somehow, the pattern of the cells—you are not a matrix technician, are you? It would be easier to explain this if you knew something about cell division. I wonder if you can understand—the pattern of the cells, the *knowledge* in the cells, that makes a hand a hand, and not an eye, or a toenail, or a wing, or a hoof, had been damaged beyond renewing. What grew at the end of my wrist was—" he drew a deep breath and she saw the horror in his eyes. "It was not a hand," he said flatly, "I am not sure just *what* it was, and I do not want to know. They made a mistake with the drugs, once, and I woke and saw it. They tell me I screamed my throat raw.

I do not remember. My voice has never been right since. For half a year I could not speak above a whisper." His harsh voice was completely emotionless. "I was not myself for years. I can live with it now, because—because I must. I can face the knowledge that I am—am maimed. What I cannot face," he said, with sudden violence, "is my father's need to pretend that I am—am whole!"

Dio felt the surge of violent anger and was not even sure whether it was her own, or that of the man before her. She had never been so wholly aware of her own *laran;* the Ridenow gift, which was a sharing of emotions, full empathy, even with nonhumans, aliens . . . She had never had much experience with it before. Now it seemed to shake her to the core. Her voice was unsteady. "Never pretend with me, Lew. I can face you as you are—exactly as you are, always, all of you."

He seized her in a rough grip, dragged her close. It was hardly an embrace. "Girl, do you know what you're saying? You can't know."

She felt as if her own boundaries were dissolving, as if somehow she was melting into the man who stood before her. "If you can endure what you have endured, I can endure to know what it is that you have had to endure. Lew, let me prove it to you."

In the back of her mind she wondered, *why am I doing this?* But she knew that when they had come into each other's arms on the dancing floor last night, even behind the barriers of Lew's locked defenses, their bodies had somehow made a pact. Barricade themselves from the other as they would, something in each of them had reached out to the other and accepted what the other was, wholly and forever.

She raised her face to him. His arms went round her in grateful surprise, and he murmured, still holding back, "But you are so young, *chiya,* you can't know. . . . I should be horsewhipped for this . . . but it has been so long, so long. . . ." and she knew he was not speaking of the most obvious thing. She felt herself dissolve in that total awareness of him, the receding barricades . . . *the memory of pain and horror, the starved sexuality, the ordeals which had gone on past human endurance . . . the black encompassing horror of guilt, of a loved one dead, self-knowledge, self-*

blame, mutilation almost gladly accepted as atonement for living on when she was dead. . . .

In a desperate, hungering embrace she clasped him close, knowing it was this for which he had longed most; someone who knew all this, and could still accept him without pretense, love him nevertheless. *Love; was this love, the knowledge that she would gladly take on herself all this suffering, to spare him another moment of suffering or guilt . . . ?*

For an instant she saw herself as she was, reflected in his mind, hardly recognizing herself, warm, glowing, woman, and for a moment loved herself for what she had become to him; then the rapport broke and receded like a tide, leaving her awed and shaken, leaving tears and tenderness that could never grow less. Only then did he lower his lips to hers and kiss her; and as she laughed and accepted the kiss, she said in a whisper, "Geremy was right."

"What, Dio?"

"Nothing, my love," she said, lighthearted with relief. "Come, Lew, the hawks are restless, we must get them back to the mews. We will have our fee refunded because we have claimed no kill, but I, for one, have had full value for my hunt. I have what I most wanted—"

"And what is that?" he asked, teasing, but she knew he did not need an answer. He was not touching her now, as they mounted, but she knew that somehow they were still touching, still embraced.

He flung up one arm and called, "We may as well have a ride, at least! Which of us will be first at the stables?"

And he was off; Dio dug her heels into her horse's sides and was off after him, laughing. She knew as well as he did, how and where this day would end.

And it was only the beginning of a long season on Vainwal. It would be a long, beautiful summer.

Even though she knew there was darkness ahead, and that she moved into it, unafraid and willing, she was willing to face it. Beyond the darkness she could see what Lew had been and what he could be again . . . if she could have the strength and courage to bring him through. She raced after him, crying out "Wait for me—Lew, we'll ride together!" and he slowed his horse a little, smiling, and waited for her.

Lew Alton's narrative:
Vainwal: sixth year of exile

CHAPTER THREE

I thought I had forgotten how to be happy.

And yet, that year on Vainwal, I was happy. The planet is more than the decadent city of the pleasure world. Perhaps we would have left it altogether—though not, perhaps, to return to Darkover—but my father found the climate beneficial to his lameness, and preferred to stay in the city where he could find hot springs and mineral baths, and sometimes, I suspect, companionship he could tolerate. I've wondered, sometimes, about that; but, close as we were, there are some things we could not—quite—share, and that was one area of itchy privacy I tried, hard, to stay away from. I suppose it's hard enough with ordinary sons and their fathers.

When both father and son are telepaths, it becomes even more difficult. During my years in Arilinn, working in the telepathic relays as a matrix mechanic, I had learned a lot about privacy, and what it has to be when all around you are closer than your own skin. There used to be an old taboo preventing a mother and her grown son from working in the relays at the same time; or a father and his nubile daughter. My father could mask his thoughts better than most. Even so, I described that sort of thing, once, to somebody, as living with your skin off. During these years of exile, we'd been so close that there were times when neither of us was sure which thought belonged to whom. Any two solitary men are going to get on each other's nerves from time to time. Add to that the fact that one of them is seriously ill and at least (let me not pass too lightly over this) intermittently insane, and it adds another turn of the screw. And we were both extremely powerful telepaths, and there had been long periods of time when I had no control over what I was sending. By the time I was halfway sane again there were long periods of time where there was at least as much hate as there was love. We had been too close, too long.

Not the least of what I had to be grateful to Dio for was this; that she had broken that deadlock, broken into that unhealthy, over-preoccupation with one another's every thought. If we had been mother and son, father and daughter, brother and sister, at least there would have been a taboo we could break. For a father and son there was no such dramatic exit from the trap; or so it seemed to us that there was not, though I cannot swear it never entered either of our minds. We were both old enough to make such a decision, we were away from the world which had ingrained such taboos, and we were alone together in an alien universe, among the headblind who would neither know nor care what levels of decadence we might choose to explore. Nevertheless, we let it alone; it was, perhaps, the only thing we never tried to share, and I think it may have been the only way we kept our sanity.

My father was quickly enchanted with Dio, too, and I think he was genuinely grateful to her; not least because she had come between our unhealthy preoccupation with one another. Yet, glad as he was to have some degree of freedom from my constant presence and to be free of fears for my continued sanity (and, though he had shielded them carefully from me, I was always aware of it, and a man watched constantly for signs of insanity will doubt his own sanity the more), the coming of Dio had left him alone. He could not admit his helplessness; Kennard Alton never would. Yet daily I saw him growing worse, and knew that a time would come, even if it had not come yet, when he needed me. He had always been there when I needed him, and I would not leave him alone, a prey to age and infirmity. So Dio and I found a home at the edge of the city, where he could call upon us when he needed us, and in the overflow of our own happiness, it was easy enough to spare him some time for companionship.

Well, we were happy. When I lost Marjorie, in the horror of that last night when Caer Donn had gone up in flames and we had tried, with our two lives thrust into the gap, to close the breach Sharra had made in the fabric of the world, we had both been ready to die. But it hadn't happened that way; Marjorie died, and I—lived on, but something had been destroyed in me that night. Not cut clean away, but, like my hand, rotting and festering and growing into terrifying inhuman shapes. Dio had gone unflinching into all that horror, and somehow, after that, I had healed clean.

Neither of us thought of marriage. Marriage *di catenas,* the ritual formalized marriage of the Domains, was a solemn joining of property, a mutual matter concerning two families, two houses, for the raising of children to inheritance and *laran.* What Dio and I had was so deeply personal that we had no wish or need to bring either family into it. With Marjorie, half my love for her had been a desire to see her as my wife, living with me at Armida, bringing up children we would share in common, the desire for the long quiet years of peace in our beloved home. With Dio it was something different. When Dio found herself pregnant, in the second year we were together, we were not really happy about it. But perhaps our bodies had spoken to what our minds refused to know. It lay deep in both of us, of course, a desire for continuity, something to come after us when we were gone, the deep-rooted desire for the only immortality anyone can ever know.

"I needn't have the child, if you don't want it," she said, curled up at my side in our living room, which was high above the lights of Vainwal, below us; colored lights, strung gaily in ribbons along the streets; there was always some kind of festival here, noise and gaiety and confusion and the seeking of pleasure.

She was close enough to me to feel my instinctual flinching. She said, "You *do* want it—don't you, Lew?"

"I don't know, and that's the truth, Dio."

Truth; I resented the intrusion of our idyll by any third party, however beloved; someone who would inevitably destroy the deepest closeness between us; Dio would no longer be altogether preoccupied with my needs and wishes, and in that way, selfishly, I resented the knowledge that she was pregnant.

Truth, equally; I remembered with anguish that night—the very night before her death—when I knew that Marjorie was carrying the child she would not live long enough to bear. I had sensed the tentative life as I now sensed the new and growing seed of life in Dio and my very soul shrank from seeing it extinguished. Maybe it was only squeamishness. But, selfishly, I wished *this* child to live.

I said, "I want it and I do not. It is you who will have to bear it; you must make the choice. Whatever you decide, I will try to be happy with your decision."

For a long time she watched the changing play of lights in the city below us. At last she said, "It will change my life in ways I can't even imagine. I'm a little afraid to change that much. It's you I want, Lew, not your child," and she laid her head on my shoulder. Yet I sensed she was as ambivalent as I. "At the same time, it's something that—that came out of our love. I can't help wanting—" She stopped and swallowed, and laid her hand, almost protectively, over her belly. "I love you, Lew, and I love your child because it's yours. And this is something that could be—well, different and stronger than either of us, but *part* of what we have together. Does that make any sense to you?"

I stroked her hair. At that moment she seemed so infinitely precious to me, more so than she had ever been before; perhaps more than she would ever be again.

"I'm frightened, Lew. It's too big. I don't think I have the right to decide something as big as that. Maybe the decision was made by something beyond either of us. I never thought much about God, or the Gods, or whatever there is. I keep feeling that there's something terrible waiting for us, and I don't want to lose even a minute of what happiness we could have together." Again the little gesture, holding her hand over her womb, as if to shield the child there. She said, in a scared whisper, "I'm a Ridenow. It's not just a *thing,* Lew, it's alive, I can feel it alive—oh, not moving, I won't feel it moving for months yet, but I can sense it there. It's alive and I think it wants to live. Whether it does or not, I *want* it to live—I want to feel it living. I'm scared of the changes it will make, but I want to have it, Lew. I want this baby."

I put my hand over hers, trying to sense it, feeling—maybe it was my imagination—the sense of something living. I remembered the depthless, measureless grief I had felt, knowing Marjorie would not live to bear me her child. Was it only the memory of *that* grief, or did I really sense deeper sorrow awaiting us? Perhaps it was at that moment that I fully accepted that Marjorie was gone, that death was forever, that there would be no reunion in this world or the next. But under my hand and Dio's was life, a return of hope, something in the future. We were not only living from day to day, grasping for pleasure wholly our own, but life went on, and there was always more life to live. I kissed her on the forehead and on the lips, then bent to kiss her belly too.

"Whatever comes of it," I said, "I do too, *preciosa.* Thank you."

My father, of course, was delighted; but troubled, too, and he would not tell me why. And now that we were not so close he could shield his thoughts from me. At first Dio was well and blooming, quite free of the minor troubles which some women feel in pregnancy; she said she had never been happier or healthier. I watched the changes in her body with amusement and delight. It was a joyful time; we both waited for the child's birth, and even began to talk about the possibility—which I had never been willing, before, to acknowledge—that someday we would return to Darkover together, and share the world of our birth with our son or daughter.

Son or daughter. It troubled me, not to know which, Dio had not a great deal of *laran* and had not been trained to use what little she had. She sensed the presence and the life of the child, but that was all; she could not tell which, and when I could not understand this, she told me with spirit that an unborn child probably had no awareness of its own gender, and therefore, not being aware of its own sex, she could not read its mind. The Terran medics could have taken a blood sample and a chromosome analysis and told us which, but that seemed a sick and heartless way to find out. Perhaps, I thought, Dio would develop the sensitivity to find it out, or if all else failed, I would know when the child was born. Whichever it might be, I would love it. My father wanted a son but I refused to think in those terms.

"This child, even if it is a son, will not be Heir to Armida. Forget it," I told him, and Kennard said with a sigh, "No, it will not. You have Aldaran blood; and the Aldaran gift is precognition. I do not know why it will not, but it will not." And then he asked me if I had had Dio monitored to make certain all was well with the child.

"The Terran medics say that all is well," I told him, defensively. "If you want her monitored, do it yourself!"

"I *cannot,* Lew." it was the first time he had ever confessed weakness to me. I looked at my father carefully for the first time, it seemed, in months, his eyes sunken deep in his face, his hands twisted and almost useless now. It seemed as if the flesh was wasting off his bones. I reached out to him and as I had often enough done to him, he rebuffed the touch, slamming down barriers. Then he drew a long breath and looked me straight in the eye. "*Laran* sometimes fails with age. Probably it is no more than that. You are free from Sharra now, are you not? You have Ridenow blood; you and Dio are cousins. My father's wife was a Ridenow, and so was his mother. A woman who bears a child with *laran* should be monitored."

I sighed. This was the simplest of the techniques I had learned in Arilinn; a child of thirteen can learn to monitor the body's functions, nerves, psychic channels. Monitoring a pregnant woman and her child is a little more complex, but even so, there was no difficulty in it. "I'll—try."

But I knew he could feel my inner shrinking. The Sharra matrix was packed away into the farthest corner of the farthest closet of the apartments I shared with Dio, and not twice in ten days, now, did I think of that peculiar bondage. But then, I did not use my own personal matrix, either, or seek to use any *laran* except the simplest, that reading of unspoken thoughts which no telepath can ever completely blockade from his mind.

"When?" he insisted.

"Soon," I said, cutting him off.

Get out! Get out of my mind! Between you and Sharra, I have no mind of my own! He winced with the violence of the thought, and I felt pain and regret. In spite of all that had been between us, I loved my father, and could not endure that look of anguish on his face. I put my hand out to him.

"You are not well, sir. What do the Terran medics say to you?"

"I know what they would say, and so I have not asked them," he said, with a flicker of humor, then returned to the former urgency. "Lew, promise me; if you find you cannot monitor Dio, then promise me—Lerrys is still on Vainwal, though I think he will soon leave for Council season. If you cannot monitor her, send for Lerrys and make him do it. He is a Ridenow—"

"And Dio is a Ridenow, and has *laran* rights in the estate, and the legal right to sit in Council," I said. "Lerrys quarreled with her because she had not married me; he said her children should have a legal claim to the Alton Domain!" I swore, with such violence that my father flinched again, as if I had struck him or gripped his thin crippled hands in a vise-grip.

"Like it or not, Lew," my father said, "Dio's child is the son to the Heir to Alton. What you say or think cannot change it. You can forswear or forgo your own birthright, but you cannot renounce it on your son's behalf."

I swore again, turned on my heel and left him. He came after me, his step uneven, his voice filled with angry urgency.

"Are you going to marry Dio?"

"That's *my* business," I said, slamming down a barrier again. I could do it, now, without going into the black nothingness. He said, tightening his mouth, "I swore I would never force or pressure you to marry. But remember; refusing to decide is also a decision. If you refuse to decide to marry her, you have decided that your son shall be born *nedestro,* and a time may come when you will regret it bitterly."

"Then," I said, my voice hard, "I will regret it."

"Have you asked Dio how she feels?"

Surely he must know that we had discussed it endlessly, both of us reluctant to marry in the Terran fashion, but even less willing to bring my father, and Dio's brothers, into the kind of property-based discussions and settlements there would have to be before I could marry her *di catenas.* It had no relevance here on Vainwal, in any case. We had considered ourselves married in what Darkovans called freemate marriage—the sharing of a bed, a meal, a fireside—and desired no more; it would become as legal as any *catenas* marriage when our child was born. But now I faced that, too; if our son was born *nedestro,* he could not inherit from me; if I should die Dio would have to turn to her Ridenow kin. Whatever happened, I must provide for her.

When I explained it that way, as a matter of simple and practical logic, Dio was willing enough, and the next day we went to the Empire HQ on Vainwal and registered our marriage there. I settled the legal questions, so that if I died before her, or before our child had grown to maturity, she could legally claim property belonging to me, on Terra or on Darkover, and our son would have similar rights in my estate. I realized, somewhere about halfway through these procedures, that both of us, without any prearrangement, had mutually begun referring to the child as "he." Father had reminded me that I was part Aldaran, and precognition was one of those gifts. I accepted it as that. And knowing that, I knew all that I needed to know, so why trouble myself with monitoring?

A day or two later, Dio said, out of a clear blue sky, as we sat at breakfast in our high room above the city, "Lew, I lied to you."

"Lied, *preciosa?"* I looked at her candid fair face. In general one telepath cannot lie to another but there are levels of truth and deceit. Dio had let her hair grow; now it was long enough to tie at the back of her neck, and her eyes were that color so common in fair-haired women, which can be blue or green or gray, depending on the health, and mood, and what she is wearing. She had on a loose dress of leaf-green—her body was heavy, now—and her eyes glowed like emeralds.

"Lied," she repeated. "You thought it was an accident—that I had become pregnant by accident or oversight. It was deliberate. I am sorry."

"But why, Dio?" I was not angry, only perplexed. I had not wanted this to happen, at first, but now I was altogether happy about it.

"Lerrys—had threatened to take me back to Darkover for this Council season," she said. "A pregnant woman cannot travel in space. It was the only way I could think of to make sure he would not force me to go."

I said, "I am glad you did." I could not, now, envision life without Dio.

"And now, I suppose, he will use the knowledge that I am married, and have a son," I said. It was the first time I had been willing to ask myself what would become of the Alton Domain, with both my father and myself self-exiled. My brother Marius was never accepted by the Council; but if there really was no other Alton Heir, they might make the best of a bad bargain and accept him. Otherwise it would probably go to my cousin Gabriel Lanart; he had married a Hastur, after all, and he had three sons and two daughters by his Hastur wife. They had wanted to give it, and the command of the Guards, to Gabriel in the first place, and my father would have saved a lot of trouble if he had permitted it.

It would all be the same in the end anyhow, for I would never return to Darkover.

Time slid out of focus. I was kneeling in a room in a high tower, and outside the last crimson light of the red sun set across the high peaks of the Venza mountains behind Thendara. I knelt at the bedside of a little girl, five or six years old, with fair hair, and golden eyes . . . Marjorie's eyes . . . I had knelt at Marjorie's side like this . . . and we had seen her together, our child, that *child . . . but it had never been, it would never be, Marjorie was dead . . . dead . . . a great fire blazed, surged through my brain . . . and Dio was beside me, her hand on the hilt of a great sword. . . .*

Shaken, I surfaced, to see Dio looking at me in shock and dismay.

"Our child, Lew—? And on Darkover—"

I gripped at the back of a chair to steady myself. After a time I said shakily, "I have heard of a *laran*—I thought it was only in the Ages of Chaos—which could see, not only the future, but many futures, some of which may never come to pass; all of the things which *might* someday happen. Perhaps—perhaps, somewhere in my Alton or Aldaran heritage there is a trace of that *laran,* so that I see things which may never be. For I have seen that child once before—with Marjorie—and I thought it was *her* child." Dimly I realized that I had spoken Marjorie's name aloud for the first time since her death. I would always remember her love; but she had receded very far, and I was healed of that, too. "Marjorie," I said again. "I thought it was our child, our daughter; she had Marjorie's eyes. But Marjorie died before she could bear me any child, and so what I thought was a true vision of the future never came to be. Yet now I see it again. What does it mean, Dio?"

She said, with a wavering smile, "Now I wish my *laran* were better trained. I don't know, Lew. I don't know what it means."

Nor did I; but it made me desperately uneasy. We did not talk about it any more, but I think it worked inward, coloring my mood. Later that day she said she had an appointment with one of the medics at the Terran Empire hospital; she could have found any kind of midwife or birth-woman in Vainwal, which spanned a dozen dozen cultures, but since she could not be tended as she would be on Darkover, the cool impersonality of the Terran hospital suited her best.

I went with her. Now, thinking back, it seems to me that she was very quiet, shadowed, perhaps, by some weight of foreknowledge. She came out looking troubled, and the doctor, a slight, preoccupied young man, gestured to me to come and talk with him.

"Don't be alarmed," he said at once. "Your wife is perfectly well, and the baby's heartbeat is strong and sound. But there are things I don't understand. Mr. Montray-Lanart—" my father and I both used that name on Terra, for Alton is a Domain, a title, rather than a personal name, and *Lord Armida* meant nothing here—"I notice your hand; is it a congenital deformity? Forgive me for asking—"

"No," I said curtly. "It was the result of a serious accident."

"And you did not have it regenerated or regrown?"

"No." The word was hard and final and this time he understood that I would not talk about it. I understand there are cultures where there are religious taboos against that kind of thing, and it was all right with me if he thought I was that sort of idiot. It was better than trying to talk about it. He looked troubled, but he said, "Are there twins in your family, or other multiple births?"

"Why do you ask?"

"We checked the fetus with radiosound," he said, "and there seems to be—some anomaly. You must prepare yourself for the fact that there might be some—minor deformity, unless it is twins and our equipment did not pick up exactly what we intended; twins or multiple births lying across one another can create rather odd images."

I shook my head, not wanting to think about that. But my hand was *not* a congenital deformity, so why was I worried? If Dio was carrying twins, or something like that, it was not surprising that we could not clearly identify male or female.

Dio asked, when I came out, what the doctor had said.

"He said he thought you might be carrying twins."

She looked troubled, too. She said, "He told me the placenta was in a difficult position—could not see the baby's body as clearly as he could wish," she said. "But it would be nice to have twins. A boy *and* a girl, perhaps." She leaned on my arm and said, "I'm glad it won't be long now. Not forty days, perhaps. I'm tired of carrying him, or them, around—it will be nice to let you hold him for a while!"

I took her home, but when we arrived we found a message on the communicator which was an integral part of all Empire apartments; my father was ill and asking for me. Dio offered to go with me; but she was tired after the morning's excursion, so she sent him loving messages, and begged his pardon for not attending him, and I set off for the city alone.

I had expected to find him abed, but he was up and around, his step dragging. He motioned me to a chair, and offered me coffee or a drink, both of which I refused.

"I thought I'd find you laid up. You look as if you ought to be in bed," I said, risking his wrath, but he only sighed. He said, "I wanted to say good-bye to you; I may have to go back to Darkover. A message has come from Dyan Ardais—"

I grimaced. Dyan had been my father's friend since they were children together; but he has never liked me, nor I him. My father saw my expression and said sharply, "He has befriended your brother when I was not there to guard his interests, Lew. He has sent me the only news I had—"

"Don't you throw that up at me," I said sharply. "I never asked you to bring me here! Or to Terra, either."

He waved that aside. "I won't quarrel with you about that. Dyan has been a good friend to your brother—"

"If I had a son," I said deliberately, "I would want a better friend for him than that damned sandal-wearer!"

"We've never agreed on that, and I doubt we ever will," said my father, "but Dyan is an honorable man, and he has the good of the Comyn at heart. Now he tells me that they are about to pass over Marius, and formally give over the Alton Domain to Gabriel Lanart-Hastur."

"Is that such a tragedy? Let him have it! I don't want it."

"When you have a son of your own, you will understand, Lew. That time is not very far away, either. I think you should come back with me to Darkover, and settle things at this Council season."

He heard my refusal, like a shout of rage, before what I actually said, which was a quiet "No. I cannot and I will not. Dio is too pregnant to travel."

"You can be back before the child is born," he said reasonably. "And you will have settled his future properly."

"Would you have left my mother?"

"No. But your son should be born at Armida—"

"It's no good thinking about that," I said. "Dio is here, and here she must stay until the baby is born. And I will stay with her."

His sigh was heavy, like the rustling of winter leaves. "I am not eager for the journey, alone, but if you will not go, then I must. Would you trust me to stay with Dio, Lew? I do not know if I can bear the climate of the Kilghard Hills. Yet I will not let Armida go by default, nor let them pass over Marius's rights without being sure how Marius feels about it." And as he spoke I was overwhelmed with the flood of memories—Armida lying in the fold of the Kilghard Hills, flooded with sunlight, the great herds of horses grazing in the upland pastures, the streams rushing, or frozen into knotted and unruly floods, torrents arrested in motion and midair; snow lying deep on the hills, a line of dark trees against the sky; the fire that had ravaged us in my seventeenth year, and the long line of men, stooped over their fire-shovels in back-breaking work; camping on the fire-lines, sharing blankets and bowls, the satisfaction of seeing the fires die and knowing that our home was safe for another season . . . the smell of resins, and bloom of *kireseth,* gold and blue with the blowing pollen in a high summer . . . sunset over the roofs . . . the skyline of Thendara . . . the four moons hanging behind one another in the darkening sky of Festival . . . my home. My home, too, loved and renounced. . . .

Get . . . out! Were even my memories not my own?

"There's still time, Lew. I won't leave for more than a tenday. Let me know what you decide."

"I've already decided," I said, and slammed out, not waiting for the concerned questions I knew would follow, his scrupulous inquiries about Dio, his kind wishes for her well-being.

The decision had been made for me. I would not return with my father. Dio could not go and so I would not go, it was as simple as that, I need not listen to the thousand memories that pulled me back. . . .

It was that night that she asked me to monitor the child. Perhaps she sensed my agitation; perhaps, in that curious way that lovers share one another's preoccupations and fears (and Dio and I, even after the year and more we had spent together, were still very much lovers), she felt the flood of my memories and it made her eager for reassurance.

I started to refuse. But it meant so much to her. And I was free now, free of it for months at a time; surely a time would come when I was wholly free. And this was such a simple thing.

And what the Terran medic had said made me uneasy, too. Twins; that was the simplest answer, but when he had asked about congenital deformities, I knew I was uneasy, had been uneasy since the child was conceived.

"I'll try, love. I'd have to try sometime. . . ."

One more thing, perhaps, to rediscover with Dio; one more healing, one more freedom, like the manhood I had rediscovered in her arms. I fumbled one-handed with the little leather bag around my neck, where the blue crystal hung in its shielded wrapping of pale insulating silks.

The crystal dropped into my hand. It felt warm and alive, a good sign, without the instant flare, blaze, fire. I cupped the blue stone in my palm, trying not to remember the last time I had done this.

It had been the other hand, the stone had burned *through* my hand . . Not my own matrix, but the Sharra matrix . . . *enough!* I forced the memories away, closing my eyes for a moment, trying to settle myself down to the smooth resting rhythm of the stone. It had been so long since I had touched the matrix. Finally I sensed that I had keyed into the stone, opening my eyes, glancing dispassionately into the blue depths where small lights flickered and curled like live things. Maybe they were.

I had not done monitoring for many years. It is the first task given to young apprentices in the Towers; to sit outside a matrix circle, and through the powers of the starstone, amplifying your own gifts, to keep watch on the bodies of the workers while their minds are elsewhere, doing the work of the linked matrix circles. Sometimes matrix workers, deep in rapport with one another through the starstones, forget to breathe, or lose track of things which should be under the control of their autonomic nervous systems, and it is the monitor's work to make sure all is well. Later, the monitor learns more difficult techniques of medical diagnosis, going *into* the complex cells of the human body . . . it had been a long time. Slowly, carefully, I made the beginning scan; heart and lungs were doing their work of bringing oxygen to the cells, the eyelids blinked automatically to keep the eye surfaces lubricated, there was stress on the back muscles because of the weight of pregnancy . . . I was running through surface things, superficial things. She sensed the touch; though her eyes were closed, I felt her smile at me.

I hardly believed this; that, once again, slowly, stumbling like a novice, I was making contact with the matrix stone after six years, though I had, as yet, barely touched the surface. I dared a deeper touch. . . .

Fire. Blazing through my hand. Pain . . . outrageous, burning agony—in a hand that was not there to burn. I heard myself cry out . . . or was it the sound of Marjorie screaming . . . before my locked eyes the fire-form rose high, locks tossing in the firestorm wind, like a woman, tall and chained, her body and limbs and hair all on fire. . . .

Sharra!

I let the matrix stone drop as if it had burned through my good hand; felt the pain of having it away from my body, tried to scrabble for it with a hand that was no longer part of my arm . . . *I felt it there, felt the burning pain through every finger, pain in the lines of the palm, in the nails burning* . . . Sobbing with pain, I fumbled the matrix into its sheath around my neck and wrenched my mind away from the fire-image, feeling it slowly burn down and subside. Dio was staring at me in horror.

I said, my mouth stiff and fumbling on the words, "I'm—I'm sorry, *bredhiya,* I—I didn't mean to frighten you—"

She caught me close to her, and I buried my head in her breast. She whispered, "Lew, it is I should beg forgiveness—I did not know that would happen—I would never have asked—Avarra's mercy, what was that?"

I drew a deep breath, feeling the pain tearing at the hand that was not there. I could not speak the words aloud. The fire-form was still behind my eyes, blazing. I blinked, trying to make it go away, and said, "You know."

She whispered, "But how . . ."

"Somehow, the damned thing is keyed into my own matrix. Whenever I try to use it, I see . . . only *that.*" I swallowed and said thickly, "I thought I was free. I thought I was—was healed, and free of *that* . . ."

"Why don't you destroy it?"

My smile was only a painful grimace. "That would probably be the best answer. Because I am sure I would die with it . . . very quickly and not at all pleasantly. But I was too cowardly for that."

"Oh, no, no, no—" She held me close, hugging me desperately. I swallowed, drew several deep breaths, knowing this was hurting her more than me; Ridenow, empath, Dio could not bear any suffering . . . there were times when I wondered whether what she felt for me had been love, or whether she had given me her body, her heart, her comfort, as one soothes a screaming baby because one cannot bear his crying and will do anything, anything to shut him up. . . .

But it had helped me, to know my pain hurt Dio and I must somehow try and control it. "Get me a drink, will you?" When she brought it, calming herself a little by the need to collect her thoughts and look for something, I sipped, trying to quiet my mind. "I am sorry, I thought I was free of that."

"I can't bear it," she said fiercely. "I can't bear it, that *you* think you should apologize to *me.* . . ." She was crying, too. She laid her hand over the baby and said, trying to make a joke of it, "Already he is troubled when he hears his mother and father yelling at each other!"

I picked up on it at once and made a joke of it too, saying with exaggerated humor, "Well, we must be very quiet and not wake up the baby!"

She came and curled up next to me on the couch, leaning against my breast. She said seriously, "Lew, on Darkover—there are matrix technicians who could free you—aren't there?"

"Do you think my father hasn't done his best? And he was First at Arilinn for almost ten years. If he can't do it, it probably can't be done."

"No," she said, "but you *are* better; it doesn't happen now as often as it did in the first years—does it? Maybe, now, they could find a way. . . ."

The communicator jangled and I went to answer it. I might have known it would be my father's voice.

"Lew, are you all right? I felt uneasy. . . ."

I wasn't surprised. Every telepath on this planet, if there were any others, must have felt that shock. Even the distant voice of my father tried to reassure me. "It hasn't happened for a long time, has it? Don't get discouraged, Lew, give yourself time to heal. . . ."

Time? The rest of my life, I thought, holding the voice-piece of the communicator under my chin with the stump of my left hand, the fingers of my remaining hand nervously smoothing the insulating silks over my matrix. Never again. I would never touch the matrix again, not when—this—was waiting for me. What I said to my father was surface noise, mouthed platitudes of reassurance, and he must have known it, but he did not press me; he probably knew I would have slammed down the communicator and refused to answer it again. All he said was, "In ten days there is a ship which will touch at Darkover. I have booked a double passage; and a reservation on the ship which leaves ten days after *that,* so that if something should prevent my taking ship on the first, I will be on the second, and your place is reserved too. I think you should come; has this, tonight, not proved it to you, that you must face it soon or late?"

I managed not to shout at him the furious refusal storming in my mind. The distance, and the mechanical communicator, blocked out thoughts; this was the best way to talk to my father, after all. I even managed to thank him for his attempt at kindness. But after I had refused him again and replaced the communicator set, Dio said, "He's right, you know. You can't live the rest of your life with this. It started on Darkover and it should end there. You can't go through your life dragging that—that horrible link behind you. And I understand—you said something, once—that you cannot leave it. . . ."

I shook my head. "No. It—it *nags* me. Believe me, I've tried."

I had tried to abandon it, when we left the lake cabin on Terra where we had been living while my hand healed after the final failure and the amputation. I had gone half-way round the world and then . . . the fire-form behind my eyes, blurring out all sight and sense. . . . I had had to return, to pack it among our luggage . . . to carry it with me, a monstrous incubus, a demon haunting me; like my father's presence within my mind, something of which I would never be free.

"The question's academic," I said, "You can't go, and I won't leave you. That's what my father wanted."

"The baby might not be born for forty days, at least . . . you could go and return. . . ."

"I don't know about babies," I said, "but I do know they come when they will and not when we expect them." But why did the thought bring such anguish and fear? Surely it was only the aftermath of Sharra's impact on my shattered nerves.

"What about the others? You were a whole matrix circle, linked to the Sharra matrix—weren't you? Why didn't they die?"

"Maybe they did," I said. "Marjorie did. She was our—you'd have to say, our Keeper. And I took it from her when she—when she burned out." I could talk about it, now, almost dispassionately, as if I were talking of something that had happened a long time ago to someone else. "The others were not linked quite so tight to Sharra. Rafe was only a child. Beltran of Aldaran—my cousin—he was outside the circle. I don't think they would die when they lost contact with the matrix, or even when it went offworld. The link was made *through* me." In a matrix circle, where there is a high-level matrix, it is the Keeper who links with the matrix, and then with the individual matrix stones of the telepaths in her circle. I was a high-level matrix mechanic; I had taught Marjorie to make that link, so that in a very real sense, I had been Keeper to the Keeper. . . .

"And the others?" Dio persisted. I resented her dragging

it out of me this way, but I supposed I would have to think of this sooner or later, or she would never believe I had really explored all avenues to be free. And I owed her this; Sharra had touched her too, now, although at a safe remove, and even touched our child.

I said, "The others? Kadarin and Thyra? I don't know; I don't know what happened to them, or where they were when—when everything went up."

She persisted. "If you couldn't leave the matrix behind, wouldn't they have died when the matrix went offworld?"

Again I grimaced when I tried to smile. I said, "I hope so," and even as I spoke, knew it was not true. Kadarin. We had been friends, brothers, kinsmen, united in a shared dream which would bring Darkover and Terra close together, heal our shattered heritage . . . at last, that had been what we shared at first. Without knowing I was doing it, I fingered the scars on my face. He had given me those scars. And Thyra. Marjorie's half-sister; Kadarin's woman. I had loved her, hated her, desired her . . . I could not think that she was dead. Somewhere, somehow, I knew she lived, and that Kadarin lived. I could not explain it; but I knew.

Reason beyond all reasons, the thousandth reason I could never return to Darkover . . .

After Dio was asleep I sat long in the outer room of the apartment, looking down at the lights of the city below me, the lights which were never extinguished, far into the night. On Vainwal the pursuit of pleasure goes on, deepening and growing more frantic as the day's rhythms subside, when other people are sleeping. Down there, perhaps, I could find some kind of forgetfulness. Wasn't that, after all, why I had come to Vainwal, to forget duty and responsibility? But now I had a wife and a child, and I owed them something. Dio's little finger meant more to me than all the unexplored pleasures of Vainwal.

And my son. . . . I had been angry when my father said it. But it was true. He should be born at Armida; when he was five years old I would take him out, as my father had taken me riding on his shoulder, to see the great river of wild horses flowing down through the valley. . . .

No; that was gone, renounced. There would be other worlds for my son. Dozens, hundreds of them, an Empire of them, and beyond. I went and laid myself down beside my sleeping wife and slept. But even through my sleep, uneasy dreams moved, I saw my hand again, the horror that had grown there . . . and it reached out, reached *into* Dio's body, clawing at the child, pulling it forth bloody, dripping, dying . . . I woke with my own shriek in my ears, and Dio staring at me in shock. I covered her carefully, kissed her and went to sleep in the other room where my nightmares would not disturb her dreams.

This time I slept peacefully without nightmares; it was Dio who woke me in the graying dawn, saying hesitantly "Lew, I feel so strange—I think the baby's coming. It's early—but I think I should go and be certain."

It was far too early; but the Terrans have made something of a specialty of this, artificial wombs for babes cast from their mothers too young, and most of them, in that artificial life-support, do quite well, though they are beyond the thoughts and tenderness of their mothers; I have wondered, sometimes, if this is why so many Terrans are headblind, without any traceable *laran,* the distance from that most intimate of contacts, where the mother teaches the little heart to beat, and all things in the unborn body to function as they should . . . the body can grow, artificially supported and nourished, but what of the mind and *laran?*

Well, if this should damage the unborn child's *laran,* so be it, if it saved his life . . . my own *laran* had done me little good. And surely it would not hurt this child to be away from our troubled thoughts and fears, and such torment as it had certainly overheard during my ill-fated attempt to monitor. That attempt had certainly brought on this premature labor, and Dio must have known it, but she did not reproach me, and once, when I spoke of it, she hushed me, saying, "I wanted it, too."

So I was cheerful as we made our way through the streets, from which all but a hardy few pleasure-seekers had vanished in these last gray hours before sunrise. The Terran hospital was pale and austere in the growing light, and Dio flinched as fast elevators swooped us upward to the highest floors, where they kept maternity cases; high above the sound and clamor of the noisy pleasure-world. I told them who I was and what was happening, and some functionary assured Dio that a technician would be there in a few moments to take her to a room.

We sat on characterless, comfortless furniture, waiting. After a time, a young woman entered the room. She was wearing Medic clothing, bearing the curious staff-and-serpents of Terran medical services; I had been told that it was an antique religious symbol, but the medics seemed to know no more than I about what it meant. But there was something in the voice that made me look up and cry out with pleasure.

"Linnell!"

For the girl in uniform was my own foster-sister. Avarra alone knew what she was doing on Darkover, or in that curious uniform, but I hurried to her, took her hands, repeating her name. I could have kissed her, and I nearly did, but the young nurse drew back in outrage.

"What—I don't understand!" she exclaimed, indignant, and I blinked, realizing I had made an insane blunder. But even now, staring, I could only shake my head and say, "It's amazing—it's more than just a resemblance! You *are* Linnell!"

"But I'm not, of course," she said, with a puzzled, chilly smile. Dio laughed. She said, "It's true, of course, you are very like my husband's foster-sister. Very, *very* like. And how strange to meet a double of a close relative, here on Vainwal, of all places! But of course Linnell would never have come here, Lew; she's too conventional. Can you imagine Linnell wearing that kind of outfit?"

And of course I couldn't; I thought of Linnell, in her heavy tartan skirt and embroidered over-tunic, her hair hanging in shining brown braids down her neck. This woman was wearing a white tunic and close-fitting trousers . . . a Darkovan in such costume would have feared incipient lung-fever, and Linnell would have died of outraged modesty. There was a little patch with a name written on it. I could read the Terran letters now, after a fashion, not well, but better than Dio. I spelled them out, slowly.

"K-a-t-h—"

"Kathie Marshall," she said, with a friendly smile. She even had the little dimple near the right corner of her mouth, and the small scar on her chin which she'd gotten when we'd gone riding in a forbidden canyon on Armida land and our horses had stumbled and fallen under us. I asked her, "If you don't mind, could you tell me where you got that scar?"

"Why, I've had it since I was ten," she said. "I think it was an accident with an air-sled; I had four stitches."

I shook my head, baffled. "My foster-sister has one just like it, in the same place." But Dio made a sharp movement, as of pain, and instantly the woman, familiar-strange, Linnell—Kathie, was all professional solicitude.

"Have you timed the contradictions? Good. Here, I'll take you and get you into bed—" and as Dio turned to me, grabbing at my hand in sudden panic, she reassured, "Don't worry about it; your husband can come and stay with you, as soon as the doctor's had a look at you and seen what's going on. Don't worry," she said to me, and the expression on her face was exactly like Linnell's, sober and sweet and gentle. "She's very healthy, and we can do a lot, even if the baby is born too soon. Don't worry about your wife, or the baby either."

And within the hour they called me into her room. Dio was lying in bed in a sterile hospital gown, but the surroundings were pleasant enough in the Vainwal fashion, green plants everywhere, patterns of shimmering rainbows beyond the windows; laser holograms, I supposed, but pleasant to watch, distracting the mind of the prospective mother from what was going on.

"Our *coridom* behaves like this when a prize mare is about to foal," Dio said wryly. "Petting her and fussing over her and whispering reassuring words into her ears, instead of leaving her alone to get on with it. They're all over me with machines supposed to tell them everything about the baby including the color of his eyes, but they won't tell me anything."

They let me stay with her in the early stages, rubbing her back, giving her sips of water, reminding her of the proper breathing; but we all knew it was too soon, and I was afraid. And I sensed Dio's fear too, the tensing of fright, even through her careful attempts to relax, to cooperate with the inexorable process that was thrusting our child, unready, too soon into the world. We watched the rainbows, played a game or two with cards, but even I noticed one omission; neither of us discussed the future, or spoke of a name for the coming child. I told myself we were waiting until we knew whether we were really naming a son or daughter, that was all. Every hour or so they would send me out into the hall, while they came and examined her; and as the day moved on toward nightfall, after one of these intervals, the young nurse, Kathie, said, "You'll have to stay down here, Mr. Montray; they're taking her up to surgery. Things aren't going quite as they should, and this baby will be *very* premature, so we need all kinds of support for him, or her, right at hand the minute he's born."

"But I want Lew with me—" Dio cried, almost in tears, and clung, hard, to my good hand.

Kathie said gently, "I know. I'm sure it would comfort both of you. But, you see, we have to think first of the baby. As soon as the baby's born we'll let your husband come up and stay with you again. But not now, I'm afraid. I'm sorry."

I held Dio close, trying to reassure her with my touch. I knew how she felt, let myself sink into her body, into her pain—on Darkover, no telepath, no Comyn, would have considered being apart from the woman who bore his child, sharing her ordeal, so that he too should know the price of a child . . . but we were not on our home world, and there was nothing to be done.

"He is frightened," Dio whispered, her voice shaken, and it frightened me too, to see her cry; I had grown so accustomed to her courage, her unflinching strength which had so often supported my own fears. Well, it was my turn to be strong.

"They'll do the best for you that they can, *preciosa.*" I tried to send forth all kinds of soothing, calming thoughts, to enfold Dio and the child in a wash of calm and comfort; under it I saw the pain go out of her face, and she sighed and smiled up at me.

"Don't worry about me, Lew; we'll be all right," she said, and I kissed her again, and Kathie motioned to the other nurse to stand aside so that I could lift Dio onto the rolling bed they would use to take her away into their inner sanctuaries. Her arms tightened around me, but I knew I had to let her go.

I paced the halls, smelling the sharp hospital smells that reminded me of my own ordeal, sharply aware of the phantom pain in my missing hand. I would rather live in Zandru's ninth and coldest hell than within the reach of those damnable smells. Blurred by distance, and my own growing weariness, I could feel Dio's fear, and hear her crying out for me. . . . I would have tried to fight my way to her side, but it would have done no good, not here on this alien world. At home, beneath our own red sun, I would have been sharing her ordeal, in close mental rapport with her . . . no man could allow his wife to go through childbirth alone. How, now, could we share our child, when I, his father, had been isolated from the birth? Even in the distance, I could feel her fright, bravely concealed, her pain, and then it all went into the blurring of drugs. Why had they done that? She was healthy and strong, well prepared for childbirth, she should not have needed nor wanted this unconsciousness, and I knew she had not asked for it. Had they drugged her against her will? I berated myself, that my own distaste for the hospital surrounding, my own revived horror at the memory of the Terran hospital where they had tried, and failed, to save my hand, had prevented me from what I should have done. I should have stayed in rapport with her mind, been present with her in every moment, telepathically, even if I was prevented from being physically present. I had failed her, and I was full of dread.

I tried to quiet my growing dismay. In a few hours, we would have our son. I should have called my father, at some time during this endless day. He would have come to the hospital, kept me company here. Well, I would send him word as soon as our son was born.

Could I be to my son such a father as Kennard had been to me, fighting endlessly to have me accepted, trying to protect me from any insult or slight, fighting to have me given every privilege and duty of a Comyn son? I hoped I would not have to be as hard on my son as my father had been on me; would have less reason. Yet I could understand now, a little, why he had been so harsh.

What would we call the boy? Would Dio object if I wanted to name him Kennard? My own name was Lewis-Kennard; my father's older brother had been named Lewis. Kennard-Marius, perhaps, for my brother and my father. Or would Dio want, perhaps, to name him for one of her own brothers, her favorite, Lerrys, perhaps? Lerrys had quarreled with me, perhaps he would not want his name given to my son . . . I played with these thoughts to hide my own desperate unease, my growing concern at the delay—why was I told nothing?

Perhaps I should go now—there was a communicator screen in the lower lobby of the hospital—and call Kennard, telling him where I was, and what was happening. He would want to know, and I realized that at this moment I would welcome his company. What would he think, I wondered, when he saw the young nurse Kathie, who was so much like Linnell? Maybe he would not even see the resemblance, perhaps I was simply in a hypernormal state which had exaggerated a slight likeness into a near-identity. After all, most young girls have a dimple somewhere and a small scar somewhere else. Nor is it unusual for a young woman of Terran ancestry—and whether we liked it or not, Darkover had been colonized from a single homogeneous stock, which accounted for our strong ethnic similarity—to be brown-haired, blue-eyed, with a heart-shaped face and a sweet husky voice. My own agitation had done the rest, and exaggerated. She was probably not at all like Linnell, and I would certainly see it, in the unlikely event that I could see them standing side by side . . .

Perhaps it was my own growing exhaustion, the effort I was making to hold sleep at bay; it seemed for a minute that I could see them standing side by side, Linnell in her Festival gown, and somehow Linnell looked older, worn, and Kathie, by her side, somehow was wearing Darkovan clothing too . . . and behind them, it seemed, there was a wavering darkness. . . .

There was a soft sound and I turned to see the young nurse who looked so much like Linnell . . . yes, she *did* look like her, the resemblance was not an illusion; calling up Linnell's picture in my mind had made me surer than ever.

Ah, to be at home, in the hills near Armida, riding with Marius and Linnell over those hills, with the old Terran coridom Andres threatening to beat us for racing and riding at so breakneck a pace that Marius and I tore our breeches and Linnell's hair tangled in the wind too much for her governess to brush it properly . . . by now Linnell was prob-

ably married to Prince Derik, and Derik crowned, so that my foster-sister was a Queen. . . .

"Mr. Montray?"

I whirled. "What is it? Dio? The baby? Is everything all right?" I thought she looked subdued, deeply troubled; and she would not meet my eyes.

"Your wife is perfectly all right," she said gently, "but Doctor DiVario wants to see you, about the baby."

The young doctor was a woman; I was grateful for that, glad Dio had been spared the indignity of male attendance, Sometimes a strong telepath or empath can transcend the difference of gender, but here among the head-blind, I knew Dio would prefer a doctor of her own sex. The woman looked tired and strained, and I knew that, if she had not empathy, not in the strong sense of the Ridenow gift, she at least had that rudimentary awareness that differentiates the indifferent doctor from the good one.

"Mr. Montray-Lanart? Your wife is well; you can see her in a few minutes," she said, and I whispered a prayer of thanks to the Mother Avarra, a prayer I had not known I remembered. Then I said, "Our child?"

She bent her head and already I knew—I thought, the worst. "Dead?"

"It was simply too soon," she said, "and we could do nothing."

"But," I protested, like a fool, "the life-support, the artificial wombs—babies born even more prematurely than this have lived. . . ."

She waved that aside. She looked strained. She said, "We did not let your wife see. The minute we knew, we—drugged her. I am sorry, but I felt it the safest way; she was very agitated. She should be coming out of the anesthetic any moment, now, and you should be with her. But first—" she said, and looked at me with what I recognized, uncomfortably, as pity, "you must see. It is the law, so that you cannot accuse us of making away with a healthy child—" and I remembered there was a thriving market in adoptive children, for women who did not want to be bothered bearing their own. I sensed the young doctor's distress, and somehow it made me remember a dream—I could not remember the details, something about the doctor who had said to me here, a few days ago, that I should be prepared for some degree of deformity . . . something dreadful, blood, horror . . .

She took me into a small bare room, with cabinets and closed doors and sinks, and a tray lying covered with a white cloth. She said, "I am sorry," and uncovered it.

Once I came up through the veils of the drug and saw the horror which had grown at the end of my arm. The messages, deep within the cells, which bid a hand be a hand and not a foot or a hoof or a bird's wing . . .

I had screamed my throat raw. . . .

But no sound escaped me this time. I shut my eyes, and felt the young doctor's compassionate hand on my shoulder. I think she knew I was glad our child lay there, lifeless, for I would surely—I could not have let it live. Not like that. But I was glad it was not my hand which had. . . .

. . . thrust through Dio's body and wrenched the child forth bloody, clawed, feathered, a horror past horror . . .

I drew a long breath and opened my eyes, looking stony-eyed at the dreadfully deformed thing lying lifeless before me. *My son. Had Kennard felt like this when he saw what Sharra had left of me?* For a moment I wished I could still take refuge in the darkness of insanity. But it was too late for that. I said meaninglessly, "Yes, yes, I see," and turned away from the thing. So the damage, cell-deep, had gone deeper than I knew, into the very germ plasm of my seed.

No son of mine would ever sit on my shoulder and watch the horses at Armida. . . . turned away, I still seemed to see the horror behind my eyes. Not even human. And yet, monstrously, it had been alive as recently as last night. . . .

The Goddess has shown us mercy . . .

"Does Dio know?"

"I think she knows it was—too deformed to live," said the doctor gently, "but she does not know quite how, and if you are wise you will never tell her. Tell her some quite simple lie—she will believe you; women do not want to know, I think, beyond what they must. Tell her a simple truth, that the child's heart stopped." She led me out of that room, away from the thing I would see again and again in nightmares. She touched me again compassionately on the shoulder and said, "We could have—re-started the heart. Would you have wanted that? Sometimes a doctor must make such decisions."

I said, heartfelt, "I am very grateful to you."

"Let me take you to your wife."

Dio was lying in the bed where they had brought her, looking stunned and very small, like a child who had cried herself to sleep, with traces of tears still on her face. They had covered her hair with a white cap, and tucked her up warmly under blankets; one of her hands gripped the softness of the blanket like a child clutching a toy. I could smell the sharpness of the drug all around her; her skin smelled of it when I bent to kiss her.

"Presciosa . . ."

She opened her eyes and started to cry again.

"Our baby's dead," she whispered. "Oh, Lew, our baby, it couldn't live. . . ."

"You're safe, darling. That's all that matters to me," I whispered, gathering her into my arms.

But behind my eyes it was still there, that thing, the horror, not human. . . . She reached in her weakness for the comfort of rapport, she who had always been the stronger of us two, reached for my mind. . . .

I could feel her recoil from what she saw there, see it lying cold and impersonal in that cold bare room on a surgical tray, not human, terrible, nightmare. . . .

She screamed, struggling away from me; she screamed and screamed, as I had screamed when I saw what had taken the place of my hand, screamed and screamed and fought to be free of me when I would have comforted her, struggled away from the horror. . . .

They came and drugged her, afraid she would hurt herself again, and they sent me away from her. And when, having shaved and washed and eaten and made grotesque legal arrangements for the cremation of what should have been our son, I went back, resolved that if she wished to blame me I could bear it . . . she had lived with me through all of my horrors and nightmares. . . . I could be strong for her now. . . . She was not there.

"You wife checked out of the hospital hours ago," the doctor told me, when I made a scene and demanded to know what they had done with my wife. "Her brother came, and took her away."

* * *

"She could be anywhere," I said, "anywhere in the Empire."

My father sighed, leaning his head on his thin distorted hand. "She should not have done that to you."

"I don't blame her. No man should do that to any woman. . . ." and I clenched my teeth against the flood of self-blame. If I had been able to barricade my thoughts. If I had had myself monitored to be sure there was no such damage to the germ plasm . . . I could have known; I *should* have known, seeing that my hand had not grown back as a hand, but as a nightmare—the pain in the arm was nightmarish now, distant, dreadful, welcome, blurring the pain of losing Dio. But I did not blame her. She had borne so much for me already, and then this . . . no. If I had been Dio I would not have stayed for a tenday, and I had had her presence, her comfort, for a year and a half. . . .

"We could have her found," my father said. "There are detectives, people who specialize in tracing the lost; and citizens of Darkover do not find it exactly easy to blend into the general citizenry of the Empire. . . ."

But he had spoken diffidently, and I shook my head.

"No. She is free to come and go. She is not my prisoner or my slave." If the love between us had crashed in the wake of tragedy, was she to blame? Even so I was grateful to her. Two years ago, something like this would have broken me, sent me into a tailspin of agony and despair and suicidal self-pity. Now I felt grief immeasurable, but what Dio had given me could not be destroyed by her absence. I was not healed—I might never heal—but I was alive again, and I could live with whatever happened. What she had given me was a part of me forever.

"She is free to go. Someday, perhaps, she may learn to live with it, and come back to me. If she does, I will be ready. But she is not my prisoner, and if she returns it must be because she wishes to return."

My father looked a long time at me, perhaps expecting me to break again. But after a time, perhaps, he believed that I meant what I said, and began to talk of something else.

"There is no reason, now, why you should not come with me to Darkover, to settle what remains of the Alton heritage—"

I thought of Armida, lying in a fold of the Kilghard Hills. I had thought of going there with my son on my shoulder, showing him the horses, teaching him what I had been taught, watching him grow up there, do his first fire-watch duty at my side . . . no. That had been a mad hope. Marius was undamaged; it would be *his* sons that would carry on the Alton lineage, if there was one. I no longer cared; it no longer had anything to do with me. I was transplanted, cut off from my roots, exiled . . . and the pain of that was less than the pain of trying to return. I said, "No," and my father did not try to persuade me. I think he knew I was at the end of endurance, that I had borne enough, had no further strength to struggle.

"You don't want to go back to the place you shared with Dio, not yet," he said, and I wondered how he knew. It was too full of memories. Dio, curled in my arms, looking down with me at the lights of the city. Dio, her hair down her back, in her night-dress, gigglingly playing at a domesticity which was new and amusing to us both. Dio. . . .

"Stay here a few days," he said.

If she comes back, wants me . . .

"She will know where to find you," he said. And as he spoke I knew she would not come back.

'Stay here with me a few days. Then I will be taking ship for Darkover . . . and you can return to your own place, or come and stay here alone. I won't—" he looked at me with a pity he was too wise to speak aloud, and said, "I won't—intrude." For the first time in my life, I felt my father spoke to me as to an equal, to another man, not to his child. I sighed and said, "Thank you, Father. I'd be glad to come."

I did not think again of the Sharra matrix, wrapped and insulated and packed away in the farthest corner of the farthest closet of the apartment I had shared with Dio at the very outskirts of the city. Nor did either of us speak of it again, in those days, the final ten days we spent in that apartment. He was not on the first of the outbound ships. I think he wanted to spend that remaining time with me, that he would not leave me wholly alone on a planet which had become as strange to me as if I had not lived there for the best part of two years.

There were still five days to go before the second of the ships on which he had tentatively booked passage would depart from the Vainwal spaceport. Not many ships had a final destination at Cottman IV, as the Terrans called Darkover. But many ships touched down there; it was located between the upper and lower spiral arms of the Galaxy, a logical transfer point. Around midday, my father asked me, rather tentatively it is true, if I cared to accompany him to one of the great pleasure palaces of the city, one whose main attraction was a giant bath, modeled after that of some famous old Terran city which had raised bathing to a fine art.

My father had been crippled for years; one of my earliest memories was of the hot springs at Armida, and soaking, after an icy day in the saddle, neck-deep in the boiling water. It was not only the lame or infirm who enjoyed that. But all over the Empire, and more especially on pleasure-worlds where nothing is taboo, bathhouses serve as a gathering place for those whose interest is in something other than hot water and soothing mineral baths. Maybe the atmosphere of relaxed nudity contributes to the breakdown of inhibitions. Many sorts of entertainment are offered there which have little to do with bathing.

My father's infirmity and his noticeable lameness gave him the most obvious and respectable reasons for being there; also, he found masseurs who could give his aching muscles considerable ease. I seldom visited such places—there had been a time when it was agony to me to be in the midst of such things, and the women who gathered there seeking men whose inhibitions had been loosened by the atmosphere of the baths were not, to put it mildly, the kind of women who attracted me much. But my father seemed more lame than usual, his steps more uneasy. He could have called to summon a masseur who could have accompanied him there, or even someone to carry him in a sedan chair—on Vainwal you can have literally any kind of attention or care, for a price—but in his present condition I would not leave him to hired attendants. I accompanied him to the bathhouse, took him to the door of the hot pools, and went off to the restaurant for a drink. There I sat watching a group of dancers doing the most astonishing things with their anatomy, later waved away the women—and men—who went round afterward trying to find clients sufficiently roused by the display to pay for a more private exhibition. Later I watched another entertainment, this time in hologram, a musical drama telling an ancient legend of the love and revenge of the fire-God; one of his fellow-Gods had had his wife stolen, ravished away by a third, and the fire-God had declared her chaste, though the one who had lost his wife was jealous and would not accept assurances. But the illusion of flames surrounding the actor who mimed the fire-God made me nervous, and I rose and uneasily left the restaurant. I went into one of the bars for another drink, and there my father's masseur found me.

"You are Lewis-Kennard Lanart—"

Quickly, I was troubled, knowing something was wrong, braced for more tragedy. "My father—what is wrong with my father?"

"He is not in danger now," the masseur said, fidgeting with the towel in his hands, "but the heat of the steam room was too much for him, and he collapsed. I sent for a medic," he added defensively. "They wanted to take him to the Terran hospital, but he would not go. He said all he wanted was a few minutes of rest, and for you to come and take him home."

They had sent for a valet to help him dress, and he was sipping a glass of strong brandy. He looked very pale, thinner than I had noticed. Pain and compunction struck me. I said, "Let me take you home, Father," and sent for one of the little skycabs which lifted us directly to the roof-platform of our own building.

I had not felt his distress, nor his collapse; I had been watching the stupid dancers!

"It's all right, Lew," he said gently. "You're not my keeper." And somehow that made me feel raw-edged too, troubled. For once, instead of staying on his feet, he was willing to lie down on a piece of furniture, a soft flotation couch in the apartment, though he would not go to bed.

"Father, you're not planning, surely, to travel to Darkover in five days? You'll never be able to endure the trip! And the climate of Thendara—"

"I was born there," he said tightly. "I can endure it. And

I have no choice, unless you choose to go and save me the trouble."

I said, anger and pity fighting in me, "That's not fair! You can't ask it—!"

"I do ask it," he said. "You're strong enough, now, to do it. I didn't ask it of you before you were ready. But now there is no reason you should not—"

I considered it. Or tried to. But everything in me flinched away. Return; walk back on my own two feet into that corner of hell where I had found death and mutilation, rebellion, love and treachery. . . .

No. No. Avarra's mercy, no. . . .

He sighed, heavily. "You'll have to face it some day, Lew. And I don't want to face the Council alone. I can count on only one ally there—"

"Dyan," I said, "and he'll do more for you if I'm not there. He hates my guts, Father."

My father shook his head. "I think you're mistaken. He promised—" and then he sighed. "Still, be that as it may, you'll have to go back some day. . . ."

You cannot live like this, Lew. On Darkover there are some experts in matrix technology who might be able to find a way to free you from Sharra. . . .

"They tried," I said. "You told me they tried before you brought me offworld, and they couldn't; which is why we had to bring the matrix offworld, you couldn't separate me from it without killing me—"

"You were weaker then. That was years ago. You could survive it, now."

A thousand regrets, terrors, agonies flooded me; if it had not been for my ill-fated attempt to monitor her, perhaps Dio would not have gone into premature labor . . .

And that monstrous horror might have lived, breathed . . .

But Dio might have understood. Might not have—loathed me. Might not have shrunk in horror from the monster I had fathered, the monster I had become. . . .

Free of Sharra, might the damage somehow have been reversed? The link with that giant matrix which had somehow damaged my very cells . . . if I had had the courage to endure it, being freed of Sharra, perhaps the horror would not have reached out and touched our child . . . at least I could have been monitored, to know enough, beforehand, avoid fathering a child . . . could have warned Dio, so she need not have suffered that loss. . . .

"I don't think it would have made any difference. The damage was done before ever I met Dio." I knew he shared the image in my mind, of that monstrous failure with my hand . . . but we would never be sure.

"Some day. Some day. Maybe."

He started to speak; then shut his mouth, and although I could hear the words he did not speak, clearly in his mind . . . *I need you, Lew, I cannot go alone* . . . I was grateful that he did not use that last weapon, his weakness, to persuade me. I felt guilty that I did not offer it, unasked. But I could not, *I could not. . . .*

He shut his eyes. "I would like to rest." I went out and left him alone.

I paced the apartment, debating whether or not I should go down into the multiformed world of the pleasure planet below me, get myself blind drunk; too drunk to know or care what horrors pulled at my mind, what guilt and self-blame. My father needed me; he had done, unsparing, whatever I needed when I was sick and helpless, and now I would not, could not force myself to give to him as generously as he had given to me. But I would not leave him alone. I could not do what he wished of me; but I would do what I could.

I do not know how long it was before I heard his voice, that cry of terrible pain, ringing and echoing in my mind and crashing through the rooms. I know, now, that there was no cry, it had been so swift that he could never have uttered a sound, but it was a scream of agony. Even as I ran toward his room, stumbling in haste, his voice crashed through my mind as it had done in that first rapport where he had shocked my *laran* awake when I was eleven years old; pain like death and the harsh command, inflexible, that I could not shut out.

LEW! YOU MUST GO, I CANNOT—YOU MUST GO BACK TO DARKOVER, FIGHT FOR YOUR BROTHER'S RIGHTS AND FOR THE HONOR OF ALTON AND THE DOMAIN—YOU MUST GO BACK AND FREE YOURSELF FROM SHARRA—LEW, I COMMAND YOU. IT IS MY DYING WISH, THE LAST WISH—

And then a flood of love and tenderness and a moment of pure joy.

"Elaine," he cried out in my mind. *Yllana. Beloved.*

Then I broke into his room, and he lay there, quite dead. But on his face was a tender smile of happiness.

BOOK TWO:

The Form of Fire

Darkover: The end of exile

CHAPTER ONE

There was someone at the door. Regis Hastur struggled up through confused dreams and found himself in his own rooms in Comyn Castle, his body-servant arguing in dogged whispers with someone who stood at the door, insisting. Regis threw a furred bedgown about his shoulders and went to see what it was.

"*Via dom,* this—this *person* is insisting on seeing you, even at this godforgotten hour. . . ."

"Well, I'm awake now anyhow," he said, blinking. For a moment he did not recognize the sturdy, dark-eyed youngster who stood there, and the youngster's wry smile told Regis that he knew it.

"We haven't met many times and I don't think we've ever been formally introduced," he said. "Not since I was eight or nine years old, anyhow. My name is Marius, and I won't argue about the rest of it when I'm here to ask a favor of you."

Now Regis recognized Kennard's younger son. He had seen him, briefly, somewhere in Thendara, about three years ago; perhaps in the company of Lerrys Ridenow? He said, "Of course I remember you, kinsman." And when he had spoken that word, *kinsman,* a formal recognition as to an equal, he thought, tardily, how vexed his grandfather would have been. The Council, after all, had gone to considerable lengths to avoid extending that formal recognition to Kennard's younger son.

Yet they had placed Regis himself in Kennard's hands for fostering between the ages of nine and twelve. Regis and Lew had been *bredin,* sworn brothers. How could he now refuse that recognition to Kennard's son and Lew's brother, who, by all standards of honor and decency, was

Regis's foster-brother too. But he had neglected that obligation. Even now, his body-servant was staring at Marius as if the youngster were something with a hundred legs which the man had found in his porridge-bowl.

Regis said, "Come in, Marius; what can I do for you?"

"It's not me," Marius said, "but for my friend. I have been living, this season, in my father's town house in Thendara. I haven't been made to feel exactly welcome in Comyn Castle."

"I know, and I'm sorry, Marius. What can I say? I don't make Council decisions, but that doesn't mean I agree with them, either. Come in, won't you? Don't stand here in the hallway. A drink? Erril, take his cloak."

Marius shook his head. "There's no time for that, I'm afraid. My friend—you know him; he told me, once, you were prisoners together at Aldaran, and you know something of—" Marius fidgeted, lowered his voice as if he spoke a gutter obscenity—*"of Sharra."*

Now Regis remembered his dream, the monstrous fire-form flaring and ravaging in his nightmare, ships bursting in flame. . . . "I remember," he said, "all too well. Your friend—Rafe Scott, isn't it?" He remembered, too, that he had seen them together in Thendara. Yes; in the company of Lerrys Ridenow, who liked the society of Terrans. "What's happened, Marius?"

And yet his mind was running quick counterpoint, *this can't happen, all these years I have not even dreamed of Sharra, and now . . . this is more than coincidence.*

"He was my guest," Marius said, "and the servants heard him crying out and came and wakened me; but when I went to him he didn't know me, just kept crying out, raving about Sharra. . . . I couldn't make him hear me. Could you—could you come?"

"What you want is a healer," Regis said. "I don't have any skill at that kind of thing . . ." and he found himself wondering if Danilo, who had been prisoner with him during those weeks at Aldaran, who also had been touched by the fire-form, had wakened in terrifying nightmares of Sharra. And what did it mean?

"Lord Regis," said the body-servant in outrage, "you're not thinking of going out with this—at this hour of night, at the beck and call of just anybody?"

Regis had been thinking of refusal. What Marius needed was a healer or a licensed matrix technician. Regis had spent a season in a Tower, learning to manage to own *laran* so that it would not make him ill or drive him mad, but he had none of the advanced skills for matrix healing of mind or body, and what he knew of Sharra was very little. Only that for all that time his own matrix had been overshadowed, so that he could not touch it without seeing that ravaging form of fire. . . . but the servant's words made him angry again.

"I don't know if I can help you very much, Marius, and I don't know the Scott youngster at all. I haven't seen him since then, not to speak to. But I'll come as a friend," he said, disregarding his servant's look of outrage. "Get me my clothes, Erril, and my boots. If you'll excuse me while I get dressed—"

Hurrying into his clothes, he thought that he was perhaps the only telepath still in the Domains who had had even that much indirect experience with Sharra. What little he knew of it did not tempt him to learn more.

But what can this mean? The matrix is not even on Darkover! It went with Lew and Kennard into exile . . .

He splashed his face with icy water, hoping to clear his confusion. And then he realized what could have happened . . .

I am responsible for this. I sent the message, and my grandfather will be very angry when he finds out that it was I. And already I am suffering the consequences of my actions.

It flashed through his mind, relived in an instant as it had happened. It had been a score of tendays ago; and he had, as Heir to Hastur, been privy to a decision made by the *cortes,* the ruling body of Thendara. He was in honor bound not to discuss their decisions with any outsider; *but what to do when honor conflicts with honor?* And in the end he had gone to the one man on Darkover who might have a stake in reversing this decision.

Dyan Ardais had heard him out, a faint smile playing ironically over his lips, as if he could sense how Regis hated this . . . the necessity that he, Regis, should come as a suppliant, begging favors of Dyan. Regis had concluded, angrily, "Do you want to see them do this to Kennard?"

Dyan had frowned, then, and made him go all over it again. "What exactly are they intending to do?"

"At the first session of Council, this year, they are going to declare Kennard's estates forfeit because he has abandoned Darkover; and they are going to give Armida into the hands of Gabriel Lanart-Hastur! Just because he commands the Guards and because he's married to my sister!"

"I don't see what choice they have."

"Kennard *must* come home," Regis said angrily. "They shouldn't do this behind his back! He should have a chance to protest this! And Kennard has another son!"

After a long silence, Dyan had said, "I'll make certain that Kennard knows, at least. Then, if he chooses not to return and press his claim—well, I suppose the law must take its course. Leave it to me, Regis. You've done all you can."

And now, weeks later, hurrying to join Marius, Regis wondered about that. Even if Kennard had returned, he would not be fool enough to bring the Sharra matrix back to Darkover, would he?

Perhaps, he thought, perhaps it is only nightmare . . . perhaps it is not the frightening coincidence I think. Perhaps Rafe's nightmare reached out to the one person in Thendara who had been touched by Sharra and so I, too, dreamed. . . .

He slung his cloak about his shoulders and said to Marius, "Let's go. Erril, call my bodyguard." He didn't want the man; but he also knew, even at this hour, he could not walk the streets of Thendara wholly unattended; and even if he could, he had been forced to promise his grandfather that he would not.

I am past twenty and a grown man. Yet as my grandfather's Heir, the Heir to Hastur, I am forced to do his will. . . . He waited for the man in Guardsman's uniform to come, and went down through the hallways of Comyn Castle and down into the empty streets of Thendara, Marius moving quietly at his side.

It had been many years since Regis had entered Kennard Alton's Thendara town house. It stood at the edge of a wide cobbled square, and tonight it was all dark except for a single light at the back. Marius led him to a side door; Regis said to the Guardsman, "Wait here." The man argued a little in an undertone—the *Vai Dom* should be careful, it might be a trap—but Regis said wrathfully that such a statement was an offense to his kinsman, and the Guardsman, who had, after all, known Kennard as his Commander, and probably Lew too as cadet and officer, growled and subsided.

But after he had left them Regis thought he would have been glad of the man's company after all. He tended to trust Marius, but Rafe Scott was a Terran, and they were noted for their indifference to codes of honor. And Rafe was also blood kin somehow, to that arch-traitor Kadarin, who had been Lew's sworn friend, but had betrayed him, beaten and tortured him, drugged him and forced him, unwilling, to serve Sharra. . . .

From inside the darkened house rose a cry, a scream, a howl of terror, as if no human throat could quite compass that cry. For a moment, behind Regis's eyes he felt the blaze of fire—the primal terror of the fire-form, raging, ravening. . . . then he shut it out, knowing it was the terror in the other's mind that he picked up and read. He managed to barrier his mind, and turned to Marius, white with dread, at his side. He wondered if the younger man had enough *laran* to pick up the image, or whether it was Rafe's distress that troubled him.

Kennard had proved to the Council that Lew had the Alton gift and they had accepted him. They had not accepted Marius; did that mean that Kennard's younger son was wholly without laran?

"Remember, Marius, I don't know if I can do anything at all for him. But I ought to see him."

Marius nodded, and led the way into an inner room. A frightened servant stood shaking by the door, afraid to go in. "There hasn't been any change, *dom* Marius. Andres is with him."

Regis just flicked the barest glance of recognition at the burly, graying man in Darkovan clothing—though Regis knew he was a Terran—who had been chief *coridom*, or steward, at Armida when Regis was there as a child. Rafe Scott was sitting bolt upright, staring at nothing Regis could see, and as Regis came into the room, again there was that infernal, animal howl of terror and dread. Even through his strong barriers, Regis could sense the blaze of heat, fire, torment . . . a woman, locks of fiery hair blazing, tossing. . . .

Regis felt the hair on his forearms, every separate hair on his body bristling and standing upright; like some animal in the presence of a primordial enemy. Marius had asked Andres something in a low, concerned tone, and the man shook his head. "All I could do was hold him so he wouldn't hurt himself."

"I wish Lerrys was in the city," Marius said. "The Ridenow are trained to deal with alien intelligences—presences that aren't on this dimension at all."

Regis looked at the terrified face of the young man before him. He had seen Rafe only once, and that briefly; he remembered him best as a child, a boy of thirteen, at Aldaran. He had thought, then, that the boy was young to be admitted into one of the matrix circles. He must be nineteen or twenty now—

Not a boy, then. A young man. But, living among Terrans, he has not had the training which would teach him to cope with such things.

. . . but Lew was trained at Arilinn, and the best they could do could not keep him unburned by the fires of Sharra. . . .

It would do no good to send for an ordinary matrix technician. They could do many things—unfasten locks without a key, trace lost objects through clairvoyance matrix-amplified, set truthspell for business dealings where ordinary trust would not serve, diagnose obscure complaints, even perform simple surgery without knife or blood. But Sharra would be beyond their knowledge or their competence. For better or for worse, Regis, who knew little, knew as much of Sharra as anyone.

He felt the most terrible revulsion against touching that horror; but he reached out, steadying his mind by gripping the matrix around his neck, and tried to make a light contact with Rafe's mind. At the strange touch, Rafe convulsed all over, as if in the grip of horror again, and cried out, "No! No, Thyra! Sister, don't—"

For just a fraction of a second Regis saw and recognized the picture in Rafe's mind, a woman, not the flame-haired horror that was Sharra, but a woman, red-haired, red-lipped, with eyes of a curious golden color. . . .

And then Rafe blinked and in the twinkling of an eye it was gone and he looked at Regis with intelligence in his eyes. Regis noted, with mild surprise, that his eyes too were golden, like the woman he had seen. Rafe said, "What's the matter, why are you staring at me? What are you doing here—" He blinked again and looked round him wildly. "Marius, what happened?"

"You tell *me* that," said Marius angrily. "All I know is that you wakened the whole house screaming and raving of—of—" Again the hesitation and Rafe finally, matter-of-factly, supplied the word. He said "Sharra," and Regis was relieved, obscurely, as if a deadlock had been broken.

Marius said, "I couldn't make you hear me; you didn't know me."

Rafe frowned and said, "I'm sorry for having disturbed you—in hell's name, did you go and fetch the Hastur out of bed at this hour of the night?" He looked at Regis in apology and dismay. "I'm sorry. It must have been a bad dream, no more."

Outside the dawn was graying into pale light. Marius said, embarrassed, "Will you honor my house, Lord Regis, and take some breakfast here? It is a poor apology for disturbing your rest—"

"It will be my pleasure, cousin," Regis said, using the word just a trace more intimate than the formal *kinsman,* not quite as intimate as *foster-brother.* His grandfather would be very angry when he heard; but all the smiths in Zandru's forges can't mend a broken egg, and done was done. Marius gave orders to Andres, and Regis added, "Ask the servants to feed my Guardsman in the kitchens, will you?"

When the servants were gone, Marius said, "What happened, Rafe? Or don't you really know?"

Rafe shook his head. "I don't think it was a dream," he said. "I saw my sister Thyra, and she—she turned into Sharra again. I was afraid—"

Regis demanded, "But why should it happen now, of all times, when nothing like it has happened for six years?"

Rafe said, "I'm almost afraid to find out. I thought Sharra was gone—dormant, at least here on Darkover—"

"But it isn't here on Darkover," Regis said, "The Altons took it offworld; perhaps to Terra. I've never known why—"

"Perhaps," Rafe said, "because, here on Darkover, it could never be controlled and might do more harm—" and he was silent, but Regis, seeing the picture in his mind, remembered that the old Terran spaceport at Caer Donn, in the mountains, had gone up in flames. "If it had been here, Kadarin might have gotten it back."

"I didn't know he was still alive," said Regis.

Rafe sighed. "Yes. Though I haven't seen either of them for years. They were—in hiding for a long time." He seemed about to say something more, then shrugged and said, "Under ordinary circumstances, I would have been glad to know that Thyra was still alive, but now—"

With shaking fingers he fumbled at the matrix around his neck. "I was only a child when the Sharra circle was broken, and then I—I was in shock. I was ill for a long time. When I recovered, they told me Marjorie was dead, that Lew had taken the matrix offworld and would never return, and I—I found I could not use my starstone; I had been part of it, and when the link with the Sharra matrix was broken, my own starstone was—was burned out, I thought. But now I am not sure. . . ."

He unwrapped the stone. It was, Regis thought dispassionately, a very small one, a blue jewel, faceted, flawed. He bent his eyes on it; it flamed crimson within, so clearly that even Regis and Marius could see the form of fire. He put the stone way, with fingers that wobbled as he tried to draw the strings of the little leather pouch.

"What does it mean?" he asked in a whisper.

"There's only one thing it can mean," Regis said. "It means that Kennard has come home. Or Lew. Or both. And that, for some reason or other, they have brought the Sharra matrix home with them."

On the first day of Council season, Regis Hastur came early to the Crystal Chamber. He debated, for a moment, going in through the Hastur entrance—in the hallway around the Chamber, there was a private entrance for each Domain, and a small antechamber to each railed-off segment, so that the members of the Domain might meet privately for a moment before making formal appearance in Council—but then shrugged, and, pausing for a friendly word with the Guardsman at the door, went into the main entrance.

Outside it was a day of brilliant sun, and the light

streamed through the prisms in the ceiling which gave the chamber its name; it was like standing at the multicolored heart of a rainbow. The Crystal Chamber was eight-sided, and spacious—at least, Regis thought, it seemed spacious now; at the height of Comyn powers it must have seemed small for all those who had Domain-right in the Comyn. Where Regis stood was a central dais, the wide double doors at the back protected by trusty Guardsmen; the other seven sides were allotted, each to one of the Domains, and each was a section divided off by wooden railings and lined with benches, boxes, and a few curtained-off enclosures so that the lords and ladies of each Domain might watch unseen or maintain their privacy until the time came for the full Council session. One segment was empty, and had been empty since Regis, or any of his living relatives, could remember; and he remembered that his grandfather had told him once, when he was a boy, that the Domain of Aldaran had been untenanted since *he,* or any of *his* relatives, could remember. The old Seventh Domain, Aldaran, had been exiled from the Comyn for so long that no one could remember why; the reasons, if indeed there were reasons, had been lost in the Ages of Chaos. He had seen it every year since he was old enough to attend Council; empty, dusty benches and seats, a bare space on the wall where once the double-eagle banner of Aldaran had hung.

The curtains were drawn around the Alton Domain's enclosure too. It had been empty for the last five seasons; now, at the beginning of the sixth, Regis supposed that either Lew or Kennard or both would be there, to head off the threatened action—to declare the Alton Domain vacant and place it formally in the hands of Gabriel Lanart-Hastur as Warden of the Domain. But had either of them returned? He could not believe that Kennard would return without paying at least a courtesy call on Lord Hastur, and there had been no such call. On the other hand, if Lew had returned, Regis found it unlikely that he would not have sent some word to Regis himself.

We were friends. I think Lew would have let me know.

But there had been no word, and Regis was beginning to be troubled. Perhaps Lew and Kennard had decided to let the Domain go by default. In the days that were inevitable, a feudal lordship over an enormous Domain might have no meaning. Marius was well-to-do; Kennard owned a good deal of property aside from the Great House at Armida. Perhaps, Regis thought, he was better spared that kind of feudal Wardenship of the ancient Domain, as Regis himself would as soon have been spared the changes that were certainly coming in Darkovan society; let Gabriel have the thankless task of dealing with them.

He looked around the Chamber. He could see someone stirring behind the partially closed curtains of the Ridenow enclosure; perhaps Lord Edric's wife or any of her grown daughters. Well, there were enough Ridenow sons and daughters; they were not, apparently, cursed by the barrenness which plagued some of the older Domains. The direct line of the Aillard was extinct; a collateral line, the Lindir-Aillard family, ruled that house, with Lady Callina as formal head of the Domain; she had a younger sister Linnell, who had been another of Kennard's fosterlings, and a brother who was one of Dyan Ardais's circle, though Regis was not sure (and did not care) whether the boy was Dyan's lover and favorite, or simply a hanger-on. Latterly, Merryl Lindir-Aillard had been seen more often in the company of young Prince Derik Elhalyn. On one occasion Regis's grandfather, Danvan, Lord Hastur, had expressed some distress at the company the prince kept.

"I don't think you need to worry, sir," Regis had said, a little wryly. "No matter what Merryl is, Derik's a lover of women. Merryl flatters him, that's all."

And because of what he was, telepath—and, although there were telepathic dampers all around the crystal Chamber, they had not yet been set or adjusted—Regis was not surprised to hear the Guardsman at the door, his voice changed from the friendly, though respectful tone he had used with Regis to a flat deference.

"No, *vai dom*, you have come early; there is no one here but the Lord Regis Hastur."

"Oh, good," said the high voice of the young prince. "I haven't seen Regis since last season," and Regis turned and bowed to Derik Elhalyn. But Derik disregarded that and came to give Regis a kinsman's embrace.

"Why have you come so early, cousin?"

Regis smiled and said, "I might ask the same of you, my lord. I wasn't aware I was all that early—I hadn't expected to be the first one here." There were one or two, even in the Comyn, to whom he might have said, forthrightly, *Grandfather was badgering me again about letting my marriage be arranged this season, and I walked out because I didn't want to quarrel with him again.* But, although Derik was three years older than Regis himself, tall and good-looking, such adult affairs seemed out of place when talking to Derik.

The Domain of Elhalyn had once been a Hastur sept—although, in fact, all the Domains had once been descended from the legendary Hastur and Cassilda, the Elhalyn had retained their kinship to Hastur longer than the rest. A few hundred years ago, the Hastur kings had ceded their ceremonial functions, and the throne itself, to the Hasturs of Elhalyn. Regis's mother had been a sister of King Stephen, and so the "cousin" was not courtesy alone. Regis had known Derik since they were little children; but by the time Regis was nine years old, it was already apparent that Regis was quicker and more intelligent, and he had begun to treat Derik almost as a younger brother. The adult Regis wondered sometimes if that was why they had separated them and sent Regis to be fostered at Armida, so that the young prince might not feel his inferiority too much. As they all grew older, it had become painfully obvious that Derik was dull-witted and slow. He might have been crowned at fifteen, the age at which a boy was legally a man; at that age, Regis had been declared Heir to Hastur, and given all the responsibilities that went with that position; but Derik's crowning had been delayed, first until he was nineteen, then till he should reach twenty-five.

And what then, Regis wondered. *What will my grandfather do when it becomes painfully obvious that Derik is no readier to rule at five-and-twenty than he was at fifteen?* Most likely he would crown the youngster, retaining the unofficial Regency in the eyes of all Darkover, as many Hasturs had done over the centuries.

"We should have a new banner when I am crowned," said Derik, standing outside the rails of the Elhalyn enclosure. "The old one is threadbare."

Merryl Lindir-Aillard, standing behind him, said softly, "But the old one has seen the crowning of a hundred Elhalyn kings, sir. It holds all the tradition of the past."

"Well, it's time we had some new traditions around here," said Derik. "Why aren't you in uniform, Regis? Aren't you in the Guards anymore?"

Regis shook his head. "My grandfather needs me in the *cortes.*"

"I don't think it was fair that they never let me serve in the cadets as all the Comyn sons do," said Derik. "There are so many things they don't let me do! Do they think I haven't the wit for them?"

That, of course, was exactly what they thought; but Regis had not the heart to say so. He said, "My grandfather told me once that he was cadet-master for a few seasons, but they had to replace him because all the young cadets were too much in awe of him as a Hastur."

"I'd have liked to wear a cadet uniform, though," said Derik, still sulky, and Merryl said smoothly. "You *wouldn't* have liked it, my prince. The cadets resent having Comyn among them—they made your life miserable, didn't they, Dom Regis?"

Regis started to say, *only during the first year, only until they knew I wasn't trying to use the privileges of rank to get special favors I hadn't worked for.* But he supposed that was beyond Derik's understanding. He said, "They certainly gave me a lot of trouble," and left it at that.

"Even if they've delayed my crowning, they won't delay my marriage again," said Derik. "Lord Hastur said that he would speak to Lady Callina about announcing the betrothal with Linnell at this Council. I think I should ask *you* instead, Merryl. *You* are her guardian—aren't you?"

Merryl said, "As the Comyn is now arranged, sir, the Aillard line is ruled by the female line. But Lady Callina is very busy with her work in the Towers; perhaps it can be arranged so that the lady need not be troubled with such minor matters as this."

Regis asked, "Is Callina still Keeper at Neskaya—no—Arilinn, *Dom* Merryl?" He used the formal address, annoyed by the way in which the youngster was planting the thought in Derik's mind that perhaps he, Merryl, should be consulted before the rightful Warden of the Domain. Merryl scowled and said, "No, I believe she has been brought here to serve as Keeper to work with the Mother Ashara."

"Merciful Avarra, is old Ashara still alive?" Derik asked.

"She was a bogey for my nurse to frighten me with when I was six years old! Anyway, Callina won't be there long, will she, Merryl?" He smiled at his friend, and Regis thought there was some secret understanding there. "But I've never seen Ashara, and I don't think anyone else has—my great-aunt Margwenn was under-Keeper for her a long time ago, before I was born; she said *she* had hardly seen her. Ashara must be as old as Zandru's grandmother!"

Regis was trying to remember what he had heard of the ancient Keeper of the Comyn Tower. "I think we would have heard if she was dead," he said. "But surely she is too old to take any real part in Comyn affairs. Is she Hastur, or Elhalyn? I don't think I ever knew."

Derik shook his head. "For all I know," he said, "she could have been foster-sister to the Cassilda of the legends! I suppose she has *chieri* blood—I have heard they are incredibly long-lived."

"I have never seen a *chieri,*" Regis said. "Nor has anyone, I think, in our lifetimes; though Kennard told me once that once, on a journey into the mountains with his foster-brother, he had been guested in a *chieri* dwelling; he was not out of his teens then. For that matter, our grandfather seems likely to live as long as a *chieri,*" and he smiled. "That is fine as far as I am concerned—may his reign be long! I am not at all eager to take over the Domain of Hastur!"

"But I am ready for the Domain of Elhalyn," said Derik sullenly. "My first act will be to find you a noble wife, Regis."

But before they could pursue it further, there was a stir in the Ardais sector, and Dyan Ardais came in through the entrance at the back of the Ardais section, and went into one of the private boxes. Danilo was with him, and Regis went to speak to him, briefly, while he saw Derik and Merryl separate and go to their individual Domains.

"Dom Regis." As always before strangers, Danilo was excessively formal. "Is your Heir to sit in Council today?"

"No; Mikhail's only eleven. Time enough for that when he's declared a man," said Regis. Six years ago, under the spur of danger, he had adopted the youngest son of his sister Javanne for his Heir.

Mikhail is eleven. In two more years he will be old enough for the Cadet Corps, and then for all the responsibilities of a Comyn son. Javanne's elder sons, Gabriel and Rafael, are in the cadets now—fifteen and fourteen. If their father, the older Gabriel, is made Warden of the Alton Domain, will they be Alton or Hastur? Rank follows the higher parent; they are Hastur, then . . .

He glanced at Dyan Ardais. Today the Ardais lord wore, not his usual unrelieved black, but the glimmering black and silver of his Domain, somber and elegant. He said to Dyan, not quite a question:

"There is no one in the Domain of Alton—"

Dyan, if anyone, would know if Kennard had returned—

Perhaps I should tell him about—about what happened two nights ago, about Marius, and Rafe Scott—and Sharra.

But Dyan said, "Regis, the Domain will not fall unchallenged into the hands of the Hasturs. I promise you that." And Regis, looking at the flat, metallic eyes of the Ardais lord, unreadable as if shuttered, knew he could not ask Dyan exactly what he had arranged. He bowed and went to his own place in the railed-off section, beneath the blue and silver fir-tree banner of the Hasturs.

Other men and women were coming in now, arranging themselves under the banners of the different Domains. A faint distant hum told him that someone was setting the telepathic dampers; when the Comyn Castle and the Crystal Chamber were built, it had been assumed that everyone here, everyone with blood-right in the Domains, was *laran*-gifted, and by tradition there were telepathic dampers set all about the Chamber at strategic intervals, to prevent involuntary (or voluntary) telepathic eavesdropping.

Everyone here, Regis thought, is my kinsman, or should be. Everyone in the Comyn held descent from the legendary seven sons of Hastur and Cassilda. Legend, all of that; legend called Hastur a god, son of Aldones who was Lord of Light. Hastur the god, so they said, had put off his godhead for love of a mortal woman. Whatever truth might lie behind the legend was veiled in time and prehistory, before ever the Ages of Chaos came down to split the country of the Domains into a hundred little kingdoms, and at the end of those ages, though the Hastur-kin had reclaimed their powers, all but a few Towers lay shattered and the *laran* of the Comyn had never recovered.

And yet, he thought, *the Terrans claim, and say they can prove it that we here on Darkover, Seven Domains, Comyn and all, are descended from a colony ship which crashed here, Terran colonists. What is the truth?* Even more, what does the truth mean? Whence came the legends? If we are all Terrans, where had the *laran* come from, the Comyn powers? In the Ages of Chaos, Regis knew from the history he had read at Nevarsin, there had been a time of great tyranny, when the Comyn Council had ruled over a breeding program which would fix the gifts of each Domain into their sons and daughters; matrix technology had reached its height, even meddling with the genes of the Comyn children.

And we are suffering still from that great inbreeding and genetic meddling. Look at Derik. And many of the Ardais are unstable; Dyan's father was mad for decades before his death, and there are those in Council who think Dyan himself is none too sane.

Javanne Lanart-Hastur, with her husband, Gabriel, came in through the rear doors of the Hastur enclosure. She embraced Regis, in a flurry of scent, curls, ruffles, and took her seat. Gabriel—tall burly, wearing the uniform of the Castle Guard as Commander—nodded good-naturedly to Regis as he took his place. Their second son, Rafael, a scrawny, dark-haired youngster of thirteen, who reminded Regis of his own mirrored face at that age, bowed to Regis and sat down on one of the back benches. He wore cadet uniform and side-arms.

Two more years and I will be expected to enroll Mikhail in the cadet corps. And in the name of Aldones, Lord of Light, and Zandru, lord of all the hells, what sense does it make for me to send the Heir to Hastur into the cadets, as I was sent, as Javanne is dutifully sending her sons? Yes, of course, if Mikhail is one day to inherit the power and might of the Hasturs—and I have never seen the woman I wish to marry, so it's likely Mikhail will inherit—he must learn to command himself, and others. But with the Empire on Darkover, with the inevitability of an interstellar empire at our very doorstep, surely there is a better way to educate the Heir to Hastur than sending him to be schooled in swordplay and the code duello, and taught unarmed combat and the best way to keep drunks off the streets! Regis sighed, thinking of the inevitable outcry it would cause if he, Heir to Hastur, should choose to have his son given the Terran education which Marius, Kennard's son, had had.

And where was Marius? Surely he should have come into the Alton Domain's enclosure! He was old enough, now, and if he wished to lay claim to the Domain, before it was declared vacant, surely it should be now!

Perhaps he too has bowed to the inevitable, or decided he would rather leave the Wardenship of the Domain to Gabriel. Again, Regis sighed, remembering a time when he had told his grandfather that he would as soon leave the Domain to Javanne's sons.

One, at least, of my sons, should have a Terran education. If not Mikhail, he thought, then his son by Crystal di Asturien. It was early to think about that—the boy was a hearty toddler not yet two years old, and Regis had seen him fewer than a dozen times. He had two other children, too, daughters, through similar liaisons. *Terrans educate their daughters. I will see that the girls, at least, are educated, though I suppose there will be trouble about it; their mothers are conventional enough to think it an honor to bear a child to a Hastur Heir.* He knew perfectly well the women had not had much interest in him aside from that, and his undoubted good looks—women pursued him for that and it grew a little wearying.

At this point his train of thought was interrupted by a loud cry from the Guardsmen at the door.

"Danvan Hastur of Hastur, Warden of Hastur, Regent of Elhalyn and of the Comyn!"

Regis rose with the rest as his grandfather—Hastur of Hastur, an aging man, his light hair still retaining some gold among the gray, clad in the ceremonial blue and silver of the Hasturs—came into the Crystal Chamber and went slowly to his seat. He seated himself in the front row and looked round the Crystal Chamber.

"Kinsmen, nobles, *Comynari,*" he said, in his rich voice. "I welcome you to Council. Highness—" he bowed to Derik—"will it please you to call the roll of the Domains?"

So Lord Hastur had decided that he must give Derik some privileges and responsibilities, however empty and ceremonial! Derik rose and came forward; like the Hasturs, he was wearing blue and silver with the golden crown of the Elhalyns across the fir-tree emblem.

"I speak for Hastur of Elhalyn," he said. "Hastur of Hastur?"

Danvan Hastur rose and bowed. He said, "I am here at your service, my lord Derik."

"Ardais?"

Dyan Ardais stood up and bowed. "Dyan-Gabriel, Warden of Ardais."

"Aillard?"

There was a small stir behind the curtains of one of the boxes in the enclosure of the Aillards, and Callina Aillard, thin and pale, in the formal gray and crimson draperies of the Aillards, said quietly, *"Para servirte, vai dom."* Regis saw Merryl, looking sullen, in a seat somewhat below his half-sister; then a handful of loosely related families, Lindir, Di Asturien, Eldrin. Regis did not know most of them by sight at all.

"Ridenow of Serrais."

This was out of order, Regis thought; the Alton Domain was higher in rank than the Ridenow. But perhaps he was giving them ample time to answer.

"I speak for Ridenow, and I am here at your command, *vai dom,"* said Edric Ridenow. An enormously fat man, well into middle age, he sat with his half-grown sons and a small herd of his brothers; Regis recognized Lerrys, and Auster who had been in the Guards as officers. There were others he didn't know. There were a few women behind the curtains in the private boxes; the Ridenow lived at the very borders of the Dry Towns and were of Dry-town blood, and while they did not follow Dryland customs and chain their women, they did keep them in somewhat greater seclusion than most of the mountain Domains.

"Alton?" Derik called, and for some reason he looked pleased.

Silence.

"Alton of Armida, Alton of Mariposa—"

Gabriel Lanart-Hastur rose within the Hastur enclosure and said, "For the sixth time I answer for the Domain of Alton, as Regent during the absence of the rightful claimants."

Derik bowed and then he turned toward Lord Hastur. He asked, "Do I ask him now?"

Regis saw his grandfather flinch slightly. But he nodded and Derik said, "This answer has been acceptable for five years. On the sixth year it is time to declare the Domain of Alton of Armida vacant, and accept the claim of the next Heir. Gabriel Lanart-Hastur of Edelweiss, come forward."

Regis tightened his lips. Gabriel, or Old Hastur himself, had put Derik up to this; the young prince had not the wit to think it out for himself. Gabriel stood up and went forward into the center of the room, the rainbow lights playing over him. He was, Regis thought, a reasonable claimant. He was an honorable man; he was the grandson of one of the sisters of Kennard's father, giving him Ridenow and Alton blood; he had commanded the Guards for six years in Kennard's absence; he was married and had fathered several sons.

Dyan promised it should not go unchallenged. What is he waiting for? Regis looked over at the Ardais enclosure, but Dyan sat without moving, unsmiling, his face blank and grim.

Danvan Hastur made his way slowly down into the central area and stood before Gabriel. Regis could see that Javanne was hugging herself with excitement.

"Gabriel Lanart-Hastur, Alton of Mariposa," said Hastur quietly, "for six years you have ruled the Domain of Alton in the absence of Kennard-Gwynn Lanart-Alton of Armida, and of his lawful heir Lewis-Kennard. In the continuing absence of these two, I call upon you to relinquish the state of Regent-Heir to the Domain, and assume that of Warden of Alton and Lord Alton of Armida, over the entire Domain of Alton and those who owe them loyalty and allegiance. Are you prepared to assume wardship over your people?"

"I am prepared," said Gabriel quietly.

"Do you solemnly declare that to your knowledge you are fit to assume this responsibility? Is there any man who will challenge your right to this solemn wardship of the people of your Domain?"

Gabriel made the correct ritual answer: "I will abide the challenge."

Ruyven di Asturien, second-in-command of the Guardsmen, commander of the Honor Guard, strode to Gabriel's side and drew his sword. He cried out in a loud voice, "Is there any here to challenge the worth and rightful wardship of Gabriel-Alar, Lord Alton?"

There was a minute of silence. Regis looked at Dyan, but he was as impassive as ever. Young Gabriel, on the back benches of the Hastur enclosure, was watching his father with excitement. Regis wondered, will Gabriel declare young Gabriel his Heir? Or will he do the decent thing and declare himself willing to adopt Marius as his Heir, giving him Council recognition? I swear by the Lord of Light, if he does not, I shall do so myself. . . .

Then, from two corners of the room, there were two answers.

"I challenge."

"And I."

Slowly, Marius came forward from the curtained box in the empty Alton enclosure. He said, "None could challenge my cousin Gabriel's worth, my lords; but I challenge his rightful wardship. I am Marius-Gwynn Lanart Alton y Aldaran, son of Kennard Alton, and his rightful Heir in the absence of my elder brother, Lewis-Kennard, and I claim the Domain of Alton and the household of Armida."

And from the rear of the Ardais enclosure came a man Regis did not recognize: a tall, broad-shouldered man with flaming red hair just touched with gray. He came slowly down the steps and said, "I challenge Gabriel-Alar Lanart-Hastur, worth and wardship; he is Regent, not Heir. I can rightfully claim the Domain of Alton, though many years ago I renounced it in favor of Kennard Alton: now I claim it as Regent for Kennard, since Dom Gabriel has violated his Regency by making claim to the Domain on his own part."

Danvan Hastur said formally, "I do not recognize you; state the nature of your claim." Yet Regis knew from the look on his grandfather's face that he knew the man, or at least knew who he was. A quick look at Dyan, and in spite of the telepathic dampers he picked up the thought, *you see, Regis, I promised you the Domain should not go unchallenged, and now I have confused them with not one claimant but two.*

The strange red-haired man said, "My mother was Cleindori Aillard; my father was Lewis Lanart-Alton, elder son of Valdir, Lord Alton. And my name, though I have never used it, in all my years at Arilinn, is Damon Lanart-Aillard; and for twenty years I have been Second in the Arilinn Tower as Technician and *tenerézu.*" He used the archaic word which could mean Keeper or Guardian. "I can claim Council-right, both through my mother and my father; and I was married to Elorie Ardais, daughter of Lord Kyril, and a half-sister to Lord Dyan."

"We do not recognize this man as Aillard!" shouted Merryl, half leaping down the steps almost into the central space. "He is a Terran imposter!"

"Silence, sir!" said Lord Hastur sharply. "You do not speak for your Domain! Lady Callina?"

She said quietly, "I have known Jeff—*Dom* Damon—for many years at Arilinn. His Heritage is Alton and Aillard; if he had had a daughter, she would stand where I stand now. It is true that he was fostered on Terra; yet he has come within the Veil at Arilinn and I am here to witness that he has the Alton gift in full measure."

"Are we going to let a woman testify about this kind of thing?" demanded Merryl. And Derik said, "*Dom* Merryl has the right to speak for Aillard—"

"Not in the presence of Lady Callina, but only in her absence," said Hastur sharply. "So here we have two claimants to Alton, and the day when such claims could be settled by the sword is over forever." Regis, unwilling, remembered the last time such a challenge had been made in this room; Dyan had been challenged, and he, a superb swordsman, could have settled it at once that way; but he had wisely refused to do so. It seemed that Dyan had set a precedent. "For Gabriel's claim we have his Regency of the affairs of the Domain for the last six years, and his command of the Castle Guard, and certainly there is none can say he has commanded unworthily. Marius Lanart-Montray—" he said, turning to Marius and speaking directly to him, and Regis reflected that this was the first time Lord Hastur had admitted that Marius existed. He had not given him his title claimed as Kennard's heir, Lanart-Alton, but he had acknowledged his existence, and that was more than he had ever done before. "Marius Lanart-Montray, since you have appealed to justice here before Comyn, we are required by law to hear the nature of your claim."

Marius had dressed himself in the green and black of his Domain; he wore a ceremonial cloak bearing the device of the Altons and their standard. He had, Regis noticed, Kennard's own sword. No doubt Andres had kept it for him till this day.

He said, and his voice was not entirely steady, "I declare that I am the true and lawful son of Kennard, Lord Alton, and Elaine Aldaran-Montray."

Hastur said, "We do not recognize the Domain of Aldaran as having any claims among the Comyn."

"But that is due to change," said Prince Derik, stepping forward, "for on this day I have betrothed the sister of my dear friend and cousin and loyal paxman, Merryl Lindir-Aillard, to Lord Beltran of Aldaran; and through his marriage to the Lady Callina, who will be my sister-in-law after my marriage to Linnell Lindir-Aillard, the Domain of Aldaran will be restored to the Comyn."

Callina made a short, sharp exclamation: Regis realized that she had been told nothing of this! Merryl was grinning like a housecat which had just devoured a cagebird and is pretending to lick nothing more than cream from his whiskers. Dyan leaned forward, with a dismayed stare.

Danvan Hastur said, and he could not keep the reproach from his voice. "My prince, you should have informed me privately about this!"

"Why?" Derik demanded, not even trying to conceal his insolent stare. "You have delayed my crowning well past the age when every other King in Thendara has taken his throne, my Lord Hastur, but you cannot refuse me the right to make a good marriage for my loyal paxman."

Hastur muttered something under his breath. It sounded like an oath—or was it a prayer? He could not openly refuse the Heir to the throne, and, Regis thought, it serves him right for never facing the fact that Derik simply is not fit to be crowned—and that he should have tried to have him legally set aside.

He said, sharply reproving, "We will speak of this later, my prince; may I venture to remind you that it is the Alton Domain now at stake?"

"But Marius is part Aldaran, and the Aldaran claim is legitimate now—" said Derik, insisting. Hastur was at a point where he was, Regis could see, ready to tell Derik that if he did not sit down and be quiet, he would have him removed, and that, Regis realized, would blow the pretense of Derik's competence sky-high. But Linnell Aillard, leaning over the railing, said something softly to Derik, and he fell silent.

Marius was obviously trying to collect his thoughts. He said, "I challenge Gabriel's wardship; he has not the Alton gift and he has not arranged to have me tested to prove whether or not I have it."

Gabriel asked, staring directly at Marius, "*Do* you claim to have the Alton gift?"

"I don't know," said Marius. "I have not been tested. Do *you* claim to have it?"

Gabriel said, "In these days—" but was interrupted by a cry of surprise from the Guardsman at the door.

"Gods above! Is it you, sir?"

And then a tall, gaunt man strode into the Crystal Chamber. He was wearing Terran clothing; one arm ended in a folded sleeve at his wrist. His dark hair, thick and curling, was streaked with gray, and his face was scarred and emaciated.

"I am Lewis-Kennard, Lord Alton, Warden of Armida," he said in a harsh voice that sounded raw and strained, "and I claim your indulgence, my lords, for coming late to this assembly; as you can see, I have but just landed here, and have come at once without even delaying to clothe myself in the ceremonial colors of my Domain."

General uproar, exploding in all directions from the walls of the Crystal Chamber. In the middle of it, Old Hastur's voice crying out uselessly for order; and finally he spoke urgently to Gabriel, who bellowed in his best drill-sergeant voice, "Council is recessed for half an hour! We will reconvene then and make some sense out of all this!"

CHAPTER TWO

(Lew Alton's narrative)

I'm no good at handling crowds; no telepath is, and I'm worse than most. Within seconds after Hastur called a recess, they were all around me, and despite the telepathic dampers, the blend of curiosity, horror, shock—malice from somewhere—was more than I could take. I elbowed a way into the corridor outside, and moments later, Marius was beside me.

"Lew," he said, and we hugged each other. I stood back a little to look at him.

"I wouldn't have recognized you. You were just a skinny little tadpole—" I said. Now he was tall, almost as tall as I, sturdy, broad-shouldered—a man. I could see the shock in his eyes as he took in the scars on my face, the arm that ended in the folded sleeve. I don't know what, if anything, my father had told him—and he had only been a child when it happened—but God only knows what gossip he had heard in the Comyn. Well, I was used to that shock in people's faces when they saw me first; I only had to remember the first time I'd looked in a mirror after it all happened. They got used to it, and if they didn't, they weren't likely to stay around in my life long enough for it to matter. So I didn't say anything except, "It's good to see you, brother. Where's Andres?"

"Home," Marius said. "Waiting. I wouldn't let him come with me this morning. Whatever happened, I didn't want him mixed up in it. He's not as young as he used to be." I caught the unspoken part of that, too. He didn't want it thought that the claimant for the Alton Domain wanted, or needed, a Terran bodyguard. I never thought of Andres as Terran anymore; he'd been a second father to me, and all the father Marius had had during these crucial years between boy and man.

That had been my fault, too. Then, angrily, I put that

thought aside. No law had required our father to spend all his attention on his elder son. It was not my doing, but Marius had been neglected for me, and I wondered, even as we embraced, just how much he resented it. Even now, he might feel that I had turned up just in time to snatch the Domain from his hands.

But there were those in the Comyn who would see nothing in Andres but his Terran background and name. Andres was one of the half dozen or less people here on Darkover that I cared to see.

One of the others was waiting quietly behind Marius until our embrace loosened and we stood back from each other. I said, "Well, Gabriel?"

"Well, Lew?" he replied, in almost the same inflection. "You certainly picked one hell of a moment to walk in!"

"I'm sure you'd have preferred him to wait a day or two, until you had the Domain neatly tied up in your own wallet," Marius retorted sharply.

"Don't be a fool, youngster," Gabriel said without heat, and I remembered that Gabriel's oldest son must be close to Marius's own age; a bit younger, perhaps, but not much. "What was I to think, with no word from Kennard? And by the way, Lew, where is the old man? Not well enough to travel?"

I hadn't wanted Marius to find it out that way, but Gabriel picked it up from my mind before I spoke and so did Marius. Gabriel said something shocked and sympathetic, and Marius began to cry. Gabriel put an arm around him as Marius struggled for self-control. He was still young enough to be ashamed of weeping in public. But behind him my other kinsman made no attempt to conceal the tears streaming down his face.

I hadn't seen him since I'd left Arilinn, and there, though everyone knew that he was the son of my father's elder brother and could have been the rightful claimant, before my father or me, to Armida, he had made a great thing, a point of honor, of bearing the name of his Terran foster-father; he was *Lord Damon* only on ceremonial occasions. The rest of the time we knew him—and thought of him—only as Jeff Kerwin. As he looked at me, tears falling down his face, I remembered the close ties among the Arilinn circle. It was the only time, perhaps, I had been truly happy, truly at peace, in my entire life. He asked now, "Did you—did you at least bring him home to rest here on Darkover, cousin?"

I shook my head. "You know the Terran law," I reminded him. "I came as soon as I had—had buried him."

Jeff sighed and said, "He was like a father to me, too, or an elder brother." He turned to Marius, embracing him, and said, "I have not seen you since you were a child—a baby, really."

"So here we have all four claimants for the Alton Domain," said a harsh, musical voice behind us. "But instead of disputing manfully for the Domain as one would expect of hillmen, they are indulging in a love-feast! What a touching spectacle, this reunion!"

Marius whirled on him and said, "Listen, you—" His fists clenched, but I touched his arm with my good hand. "Let it go, brother. He doesn't know. Lord Dyan, you were my father's friend, you'll want to know this. He is buried on Vainwal. And on the last day of his life, a few minutes before his death—which was very sudden and unexpected—he spoke kindly of you and said you had been a good friend to my brother."

But as I spoke of that last day, remembering—my head was ringing.

—My last command! Go back, Lew, go back and fight for your brother's rights—

With that final command still ringing in my mind, drowning out everything else, I was even prepared to be civil to Lord Dyan.

Dyan stared straight ahead, his jaw tight, but I saw the muscles in his throat move. At that moment I came closer to liking Dyan Ardais than ever before, or ever again. Somehow his struggle not to weep, as if he were a boy still young enough to be ashamed of tears, touched me as no display could have done. Jeff actually dared to lay a compassionate hand on Dyan's shoulder. I remembered that Jeff had been married to Dyan's half-sister—I had never seen her; she had died before I came to Arilinn—and watching them, I knew how Jeff had been persuaded to leave Arilinn and come here, when Jeff had about as much interest in the Regency of Alton—or the politics of the Comyn—as he had in the love life of the banshee. Less, really; he might have had some intellectual curiosity about the banshee.

The silence stretched.

. . . *back and fight for your rights, your brother's rights . . . last command* . . .

Endless, a never-ending loop battering my mind . . . It seemed, for a moment, impossible that they did not hear. Gabriel said finally, "All my life he's been there; bigger than life. I simply can't believe he's gone."

"Nor I," said Jeff. Abruptly he looked at me, and I saw my face mirrored in his mind and was shocked. "Zandru's hells, Lew! Did you come here directly from the spaceport?" I nodded and he asked, "When did you eat last?"

I thought about that and said at last, "I can't remember. They shot me so full of drugs aboard ship . . . I'm still fuzzy."

. . . *My last command* . . . *go back* . . . it was to drown that unending clamor in my mind, that I put my hand to my head, but Jeff put his hand under my arm. He said, "You can't think straight in this condition, and thinking straight is the first thing you have to be able to do. Besides, you ought not to appear before Council wearing Terran clothes. It made a dramatic point, perhaps, for a few minutes, but it would start people thinking the wrong things. Dyan—?"

The Ardais lord nodded, and Jeff said, "I am guested here in the Ardais quarters—I don't know who, if anyone, is living in the Alton ones—"

"Caretakers," said Gabriel, with a wry twist of his mouth. "I may be presumptuous, but not *that* presumptuous!"

"Come along," Jeff said. "We can find you something to eat, and some decent clothes—"

Dyan said, "Yours would go round him twice, Jeff." He looked me up and down. "You're thinner than you used to be. Tell them to find something of mine for him."

Jeff led me quickly along the corridor; I was glad to get away, for some others of the Comyn and the others in the Crystal Chamber had come out into the hallway. I saw someone wearing Ridenow colors, and the flash of golden and green made me think of Dio.

Was she here, would she confront me at any moment, shrieking Monster! *Would she think I had come to force her back as if the Terran ceremony had made her my prisoner? . . .*

Her touch, her understanding . . . it might even have quieted the shrieking in my mind . . . yet the love between us had not been strong enough to hold through tragedy. How could I ask it . . . that horrible thing . . . *no man had any right to do that to a woman . . .*

"Steady," said Jeff. "There in a minute. Sit down." He shoved me onto a piece of furniture. It was dreamlike, *déjà vu,* for I could not remember ever being in the Ardais apartments before. Yet my father had known them well, I supposed, Dyan had been his closest friend when they were young. . . . *Zandru's hells, would I never again be sure which thoughts, feelings, emotions were mine, which my father's? The forced rapport which had wakened my Alton gift when I was eleven years old had been bad enough, but that last dying death-grip on my mind* . . . I shuddered, and when Dyan thrust a drink into my hand I leaned for a moment against his shoulder, letting him support me. Memories of a younger Dyan flooded me with an affection warm, almost sensual, which shocked me to the bone, and I slammed the barrier shut, straightening up and easing free of his support. I drained the glass without noticing the taste. It was the strong *firi* cordial of the Kilghard Hills.

"Thanks. I needed that, but some soup would be better, I suppose, or something solid—"

"If I remember rightly," Dyan said, "your father was allergic to the Terran drugs too." He used the Terran word "allergic"; there wasn't one in *casta.* "I wouldn't try to eat anything solid for a few hours, if I were you. They'll bring you something to eat in a few minutes, but you don't really have that much time. We could call for a day or two delay, if you want." He looked around, saw Marius hovering, and asked, "Where's Gabriel?"

Marius said, "He's honor guard there; he had to go back, he said."

"Damn." Jeff scowled. "We need a family conference of some kind."

Dyan's lip curled. "Keep Gabriel out of it," he said. "He's a Hastur lackey. I've always suspected that's why old Hastur married him to the girl . . . his granddaughter. I don't suppose you had sense enough to get yourself married and father a son, did you, Lew?"

With an effort that made me tremble, I slammed down a barrier. It was enough that I would never be free of the memory of that inhuman *thing* which should have been my son. If it were ever to be shared, it would not be with Dyan. He might have been my father's chosen friend and confidant; he was not mine. I shrugged off his supporting arm as I rose.

"Let's see about those clothes. No, I don't mind wearing Ardais colors . . ."

But it turned out Marius had sent a servant at a run to the townhouse, with orders to fetch a cloak and Domain colors for me. I glanced in the mirror, saw myself transformed. And I could hide the missing hand in a fold of the cloak, if I wished. Marius gave me my father's sword and I fastened it at my side, trying not to think of the Sharra matrix.

It wasn't too far; I could tolerate that much distance . . . I had tried, again, to leave it on Vainwal. Had thought, this time, I could be free . . . and then the burning, the blurring clamor . . . I had nearly missed the ship because I had realized I could not abandon it, to abandon it would be death . . . not that I would have minded death . . . better dead than enslaved this way . . .

"At least now you look proper Comyn," said Jeff. "You have to fight them on their own ground, Lew."

I hurried with the tunic-laces, making a little extra display of my one-handed skill because I was still damnably sensitive about Marius watching. Dyan's eyes flicked over the empty sleeve.

"I told Kennard that hand would have to come off," he said. "They should have had it off at Arilinn. He kept on hoping the Terrans could do something. Terran science was one of the few things he kept on believing in, even after he lost faith in damned near everything else."

The silence stretched, came to a full stop. Jeff, who had seen the hand at Arilinn, and had tried to save it, would have spoken, but I mentally commanded him to be silent. I might manage to discuss it, some day, with Jeff; but not with Dyan; and not with anyone here, not yet.

Dio had accepted it . . . I cut off that train of thought, afraid of what it would lead to.

Sooner or later, I supposed, I would see her again, and I would have to make it clear . . . she was free, not my prisoner or slave, not bound to me . . .

There was a tentative knock at the door, and one of Hastur's servants, liveried in blue and silver, came in to convey the Regent's compliments and request that the Ardais and Alton lords would return to Council.

Dyan said, with a faint curl of his lip, "At least there is now no reason to declare the Domain vacant."

That was true. At first there had been no rightful claimant; now there were four. I asked Marius, as we went down the hallway toward the Crystal Chamber, "Do you have the Alton Gift?"

Marius had the dark eyes of our Terran mother. I have always thought dark eyes were expressionless, unreadable. "I haven't the faintest idea," he said. "What with one thing and another, I've been given to understand that it would be . . . insufferable insolence . . . to try and find out. I'm fairly sure Gabriel doesn't, though."

"The reason I asked," I said, exasperated, "is that they'll be badgering me to declare an Heir." And I knew he could pick up the part of that I did not speak aloud; that I would prefer to assume he had it, without the shock tactics my father had had to use on my own Gift.

"It's probably irrelevant," Dyan said. "Everyone knew I didn't have the Ardais Gift; it didn't stop them from declaring me as Heir and Regent to my father." The Ardais gift—catalyst telepathy, the gift of awakening latent *laran*—had been thought extinct, until it had been discovered in Danilo. That made me think about Regis, and wonder why he had not come to greet me. Well, if there was a plot to take the Alton Domain under Hastur wardship, I wasn't surprised he didn't care to face me just yet.

. . . fight for your brother's rights . . . last command . . .

I shook my head to clear it of the insistent jangling, and, between my kinsmen, walked back into the Crystal Chamber.

Some kind of hurried conference was going on behind the curtained enclosure of the Hastur Domain. For once in my life I was glad of the telepathic dampers, which lessened the jangle in my head to a manageable ache. When they called us to order again, Danvan Hastur rose and said, "From having no rightful claimant to the Alton Domain, we now have four, and the situation must be investigated further. I ask that we delay the formal investiture of Lord Alton for another seven days, until the period of Council mourning for Kennard Alton is finished."

I could hardly protest it, that they should give my father his due.

Marius had taken a seat beside me in the Alton enclosure; I noticed that Gabriel's wife, Javanne Hastur, had seated herself among the Hasturs, with a dark, slender boy who looked like Gabriel and was, I supposed, Gabriel's elder son. Gabriel himself, down with the honor Guard, was thus spared any confusion about whether he should seat himself among Hasturs or Altons, and I supposed he had planned it that way. I had always liked Gabriel; I preferred to think that he meant precisely what he said. My own whereabouts and my father's being unknown, he had claimed the Domain on Hastur's orders. I didn't think I needed to worry about Gabriel. My eyes sought old Hastur, a small squarish unbending figure, graying, upright, like the rock of the castle itself, and just as unchanging. Was this the real enemy I must face?

And why? I know he had never cared much for me, but I had done him the courtesy, before this, to believe it was not personal; I was simply an uncomfortable reminder of my father's stubbornness in marrying the wrong woman, and he had acted as if my Terran and Aldaran blood were simply a mistake for which I was not to blame. But now all was in confusion; Hastur was behaving like my enemy, and Dyan, who had always disliked me, as a kinsman and friend. I couldn't figure it out. Near the back of the Hastur enclosure I saw Regis. He did not seem to have changed much; he was taller, and his shoulders somewhat broader, and the fresh boyish face was now shadowed by faint reddish beard, but he still had the Hastur good looks. The change must have been inside; I would have expected him to come and greet me, and the boy I had known would have done it, even more quickly than Marius. I had, after all, been closer to Regis than to the little brother from whom six years had separated me.

Hastur was calling us all to order again, and I saw Prince

Derik, in the Elhalyn enclosure with some people whom I did not know. I supposed they were his elder sisters and their families, or some of the Elhalyn connections: Lindirs, perhaps, Di Asturiens, Dellerays. Mentally I counted on my fingers; why had Derik not been crowned? I remembered that he had been somewhat too immature at sixteen, but now he must be well into his twenties. There was so much I did not know; I was being thrown into Council without any time to find out what had happened! Why, in the name of all the probably nonexistent Gods of the Comyn, had I agreed to come?

. . . . *last command. . . .fight for your brother's rights* . . . . despite the dampers, the mental command kept reverberating in my mind till I began seriously to wonder, as I had done several times on the ship which brought me from Vainwal, if there had been damage to the brain! The unbridled anger of an Alton can kill—I had always known that; and my father's mental Gift was unusually powerful. Now, when he was dead and I should have been free of that dominating voice in my mind, I seemed more bound than ever, more hag-ridden. Would I ever be free of it?

Marius saw the nervous gesture, hand to head, and leaned close to whisper, "What's wrong, Lew?" But I shook my head restlessly and muttered, "Nothing." I had that eerie sense of being *watched* from somewhere. Well, I had always had that, in Council. I tried to pull myself together and focus on what was going on.

Hastur said gravely, "My lord Derik, before the Council was interrupted—" I could *hear* him saying what he had started to say, *disrupted,* "—by the arrival of an unexpected Heir to Alton—" *at least he admitted I was that*— "you had spoken of an alliance which you had made. Will it please you to explain it to us, *vai dom?*"

"I think I should let Merryl do that," Prince Derik said, "since it concerns the Aillards."

Merryl came down slowly from the enclosure; but was stopped by a clear feminine voice.

"I object to this," said the voice, which I recognized. "*Dom* Merryl does not speak for the Aillards." And I looked up and saw my cousin Callina coming slowly down the center of the enclosure. She paused at the rails and waited. That clear voice troubled me; I had heard it last when Marjorie . . . died. She had died in Callina's arms. And I . . . once again it seemed that I could feel the old agony in my wounded hand, tearing through every nerve and finger and nail which had been long gone . . . This was madness; I caught at vanishing self-control and listened to what Callina was saying.

"In courtesy, Lord Hastur, if something concerns the Domain of the Aillards, I should be asked to give my consent before *Dom* Merryl speaks."

She was slight and slender; she wore the ceremonial regalia and the crimson veils of a Keeper in Council, and I, who had spent years on Vainwal seeing women who looked as if they were free and alive, thought that she looked like a prisoner, with the heavy robes, the ceremonial ornaments weighing down her slight body so that she appeared fettered, like a child trying to wear the garments of an adult. Her hair was long and dark as spun black glass, what little I could see of it shining through the veil.

Merryl turned on her, with a look of pure hatred. He said, "I have been left to manage the affairs of the Domain while you were isolated at Neskaya and then at Arilinn, my lady; am I now to turn all these things over to you again at your whim? I think my management of the Domain speaks for my competence; what of yours?"

"I do not question your competence," she said, and her voice was like molten silver. "But where your arrangements for the Domain alliances concern me, I have a legitimate right to question, and if need be, to veto. Answer what Hastur has asked you, my brother." She used the most formal and distant mode of that word. "I cannot comment until I know what is being proposed."

Merryl looked disconcerted. I didn't know him; I didn't know most of the younger Aillards, even though Callina's younger sister Linnell was my foster-sister. Now he stood shifting nervously from foot to foot, glanced at Derik, who was grinning and gave him no help, and finally said, "I have made arrangements that the Lady Callina should consolidate a new alliance by marriage with *Dom* Beltran of Aldaran."

I saw shock come over Callina's face, but I could not keep silent. I burst out, "You people must all have gone mad! Did you say—alliance with Aldaran? Beltran of Aldaran?"

Hastur glanced repressively at me, and Derik Elhalyn said, "I see no reason against it." He sounded defensive, very young. "The Aldarans are already allied to one major Domain by marriage, as you of all people should know, *Dom* Lewis. And in this day and age, with the Terrans at our very doorstep, it seems well to me that we should take this opportunity to line up their allegiance with the Comyn."

He repeated this as a child repeats his lesson. I wondered who had schooled him in that theory. Glancing at Merryl, I decided that the answer was not far to seek.

But—*ally with Aldaran? With that damned renegade clan—?*

Callina said, "When before this has a Keeper been subjected to the whims of the Council? I am the head of the Aillard Domain in my own right; and not subject to *Dom* Merryl. I think there need be no further discussion of this—" I could almost hear her sorting through her mind for an inoffensive adjective, and she finally compromised—"this ill-advised plan. I am sorry, my prince; I refuse."

"You—refuse?" Derik turned to stare at her. "On what grounds, lady?"

She made an impatient gesture; her veil fell back, revealing dark hair braided with gems. She said, "I have no will to marry at this time. And if I should, and when I do, I shall, no doubt, be capable of finding myself a husband who will be suitable. And I do not think I will look for him among the Aldaran Domain. I know more of that Domain than I wish to know, and I tell you, we might as well hand ourselves over here and now to the accursed Terrans than ally with that—" again the mental sorting, the visible search for a word—"with that renegade, exiled Domain."

Dyan said, "*Domna,* you have been misinformed." His voice held that exquisite, indifferent courtesy which he always had when speaking to women. "The Aldaran are no longer in the laps of the Terrans. Beltran has broken that alliance to Terra, and for that reason, if for no other, I do not think we can afford to hold aloof from Aldaran." He turned to the Council and explained: "Alliance with Aldaran would give us more strength, and that is what we need now, to stand united against the pull of the Terran Empire. Granted, there are those among us who would turn us over to the Terrans—" His eyes moved toward the Ridenow enclosure—"but there are also those who remain loyal to our world and to the old ways. And of these, I am convinced, Beltran of Aldaran is one. Our forefathers—for reasons which seemed good to them, no doubt—cast out the Domain of Aldaran from the Comyn. But there were seven Domains; there should be seven Domains again, and this move, I am sure, would catch the imagination of the common people."

She said, "I am a Keeper—"

He shrugged and said, "There are others. If Beltran has asked for alliance to the Aillard Domain—"

"Then I say for the Aillards that we will have none of it," said Callina. And, unexpectedly she turned to me. "And here sits one who can prove the truth of what I say!"

"You damned, incredible fools!" I heard my own voice, and as Hastur turned to me, there was first a stir of voices, then a mutter, then a clamor, and I realized that once again I had disrupted Council, that I had jumped head-first into an argument I really knew nothing about. But I had started and I must go on.

"The Terrans are bad enough. But what the Aldarans got us into—" I fought for control. I would not, I *would not* speak the name of that ravening terror, which had flared and raged in the hills, which had sent Caer Donn up in flames, which had burned away my hand and my sanity. . . .

"You ought to be in favor of this alliance," said Derik. "After all, if we recognize the Aldarans, there won't be so much question about whether you are legitimate or not, will there?"

I stared at him, wondering if Derik were really this much of a fool, or whether the statement had a profundity that somehow escaped me; no one else seemed inclined to question it. It was like some nightmare, where perfectly ordinary people said the most outrageous things and they were taken for granted.

Dyan Ardais said bluntly, "There's no question of legitimacy. Council accepted Kennard's eldest son, and that's that. Sit down and listen, Lew. You've been away a long time, and when you know what's been happening while you were away, you may change your mind. It might not change your status, but it could change your brother's."

I glanced at Marius. It was certain that the recognition of Aldaran would do a great deal to alter his legitimacy or otherwise. But did Dyan honestly think that would make the rest of the Council overlook his Terran blood? Dyan went on, his rich musical voice persuasive and kind, "I think it's your hate speaking, not your good sense. Comyn—" he said, looking around, "I think we can all agree that *Dom* Lewis has reason for prejudice. But it was a long time ago. Listen to what we have to say, won't you?"

There was a general murmur of approval. I could have dealt with hostility from Dyan, but this—! Damn him! He had hinted—no, he had said right out—that I was to be pitied, a cripple with an old grudge, coming back and trying to take up the old feud where I left off! By skillfully focusing all the unspoken feelings, their pity, the old admiration and friendship for my father, he had given them a good reason to disregard what I said.

The worst of it was, I wasn't sure he was wrong. The rebellion at Aldaran, in which I had played so disastrously wrong-headed a part, had been, like all civil wars, a symptom of something seriously wrong in the culture; not an end in itself. The Aldarans were not the only ones on Darkover who had been lured by the Terran Empire. The Ridenow brothers had almost given up pretending loyalty to the Comyn . . . and they were not the only ones. The Comyn, officially at least, had stood out almost alone against the lure of the Terran Empire, promising a world made easier, simpler, with Terran technology and a star-spanning alliance. I had been an easy scapegoat for both sides, with my Terran blood on the one hand and, on the other, the fact that Kennard, educated on Terra, had nevertheless turned his back on the Empire and become one of the staunchest supporters of the Comyn conservatives. Maybe all sons rebel against their fathers as a matter of course, but few can have had their personal rebellion escalated into such tragedy, or brought down such disaster on their own heads or their families'. I had been drawn into the rebellion, and my tremendous *laran,* trained at Arilinn, had been put to the service of Beltran's rebellion and to . . . even now I flinched and could not say the name to myself. My good hand clutched at the matrix and let it go as if it burned me.

Sharra. Ravening, raging, a city in flames . . .

What the hell was I doing here, twice haunted, hag-ridden by my father's voice . . .

Lerrys Ridenow stood up, turning to Lord Edric for formal permission to speak; Edric gave him the slightest gesture of recognition. He said, "By your leaves, my lords, I would like to say that perhaps this whole argument is futile. The day is past when alliances can be cemented by marriages with unwilling women. Lady Callina is a Keeper, and the independent head of a Domain. If Aldaran wishes to marry into Comyn—"

"You'd like that, wouldn't you?" said Merryl. "Make this fine alliance for one of your own, and line Aldaran up with the rest of the toadies licking Terran arses—"

"Enough!" Callina spoke sharply, but I could see the faint stain of color etching her cheek. She was too old, and too well-bred, to reprove him for the obscenity directly, but she said, "I did not give you leave to speak!"

"Zandru's hells," shouted Merryl. "Will you silence that woman, Lord Hastur? She knows nothing about this—she has spent her life shut up in one Tower after another—now she is here as a puppet of old Ashara, but are we to keep up this nonsensical farce that a cloistered professional virgin knows anything at all about the conduct of her Domain? Our world is on the edge of destruction. Are we going to sit and listen to a girl squalling that she doesn't want to marry this one or that?"

Callina was white to the lips; she stepped forward, her hand clasped at her throat where I knew her matrix was concealed. She said, very low, but her voice carried to the heights of the Crystal Chamber, "Merryl, the rulership of the Domain is not at issue here. A time may come when you wish to dispute it. I cannot keep it by force of arms, perhaps—but I shall keep it by any means I must." She laid her hand on the matrix, and it seemed to me that somewhere there was a dim rumble as of distant thunder. Without taking the slightest notice, she turned her face to Gabriel and said, "My lord commander, you are charged with keeping peace in this chamber. Do your duty."

Gabriel laid his hand on Merryl's arm and spoke to him, in a low, urgent voice. Despite the telepathic dampers, I had no trouble in following the general import of what Gabriel said: that if Merryl didn't sit down and shut up, he would have him carried out by force. Teeth clenched, Merryl glanced at Dyan Ardais, as if for support, then at Prince Derik.

Derik said uneasily, "Come, come, Merryl, that's no way to talk before ladies. We'll discuss it later, my dear fellow. Let's have peace and quiet here, by all means."

Merryl sank into a seat, glowering.

Callina said quietly, "As for this marriage, I think everyone here knows that it is not marriage which is being discussed. It is *power,* my lords, power in the Comyn. Why should we not call things by their right names? The question before us, and I think my brother knows it as well as I do, is this: do we want to put that kind of power within Comyn in the hands of the Aldarans? I think not. And there sits one who can attest to the truth of what I say. Would you like to tell them, *Dom* Lewis, why it would be—unwise—to put that much power in the hands of Aldaran, or to trust him with it."

I felt my forehead breaking out in cold sweat. I knew I should explain myself, calmly and quietly, how at one time I had trusted Beltran, and how I had been—betrayed. Now I must speak calmly, without undue emotion.

Yet, to drag it all out here, in Council, before all those kinsmen who had tried to deny me my very place in this room . . . I could not. My voice failed me, I felt it strangle in my throat, and knew if I spoke aloud I would crack completely. My father's voice, the ravening flames of Sharra, the continuous unrhythmic waves of the telepathic jangle—my head was pandemonium. Yet Callina was standing there, waiting for me to speak, and I opened my mouth, trying to force myself to find words. I heard only a raw meaningless croak. I finally managed to say, "You—know. You were there at Arilinn—"

And I cringed before the pity in her eyes. She said, "I was there when Lew came to Arilinn with his wife, after they both risked their lives to break the link with Sharra."

"Sharra is not relevant here," said Dyan harshly. "The link was broken and the matrix controlled again. We are talking now of Beltran of Aldaran. And he, too, has a strong interest in seeing that nothing like that ever happens again. As for Lew—" his eyes turned on me. "I am sorry to say this, kinsman, but those who meddle with forces as strong as Sharra should not complain if they are—hurt. I cannot but think that Lew brought his trouble upon himself, and he has had his lesson—as Beltran has had his."

I bent my head. Perhaps he was right, but that made it no easier. I had learned to live with what had happened, after a fashion. That did not mean I was willing to hear Dyan lecture me about it.

Regis Hastur rose to his feet within the Hastur enclosure. He said, not looking at me, "I cannot see that Lew was so much to blame. But whether or nor, I do not think we can trust Beltran. It was Beltran's doing, and Kadarin's. And Lew was Beltran's kinsman, his guest and under the safeguard of hospitality. He imprisoned him; he imprisoned me; he kidnapped Danilo and attempted to force him to use his *laran* for the Sharra circle. And if Beltran did *this* to a kinsman—" he turned and gestured, with what seemed mute apology for turning all eyes to me—"how could anyone trust him?"

I could read the horror in the eyes turned on me; even through the telepathic damper their horror surged into my mind, the shock and horror . . . *the scars on my face, the arm ending abruptly at the wrist, the horror that had surged into my mind from Dio when she saw in my mind the horror that had been our child . . . Merciful Avarra, was there no end to this agony?* I dropped my forehead on my arms, hiding my face, hiding my mutilated arm. Marius laid his hand on my shoulder; I hardly felt it there.

Danilo's voice, shaken with emotion, took up the tale where Regis had left off.

"It was Beltran's doing; he had Lew tied and beaten. He stripped him of his matrix. All of you Comyn who have been in a Tower know what that means! And why? Because Lew begged him to use caution with Sharra, to turn it over to one of our own Towers and see if a safe way could be found for its harnessing! And look at Lew's face! This—this torturer is the man you want to invite courteously into Comyn, to marry the head of a Domain and Ashara's Keeper?"

Dyan's voice lashed. "I did not give you leave to speak!"

Danilo turned to him. He was very pale. "My Lord, with all respect, I am testifying only to the truth of what I witnessed with my own eyes. And it is relevant to what is being discussed in the Comyn. I have Council-right; am I to sit silent?"

Hastur said, his displeasure evident in his voice, "It seems this is the day for all the unruly younger members of the Domains to speak in Council without leave of their elders!" His eyes rested on Merryl, on Danilo, then on Regis, and the younger man drew a deep breath.

"By your leave, sir, I can only repeat what my paxman said: I am testifying to what I myself saw and witnessed. When we see our elders and—and our betters, about to take a step which they could not honorably take if all the facts were known to them, then, for the—" again he hesitated, almost stammering—"for the honor of the Comyn, we must bring it to the light. Or are we to believe, sir, that the Comyn consider it of no importance that Beltran was capable of betraying, and torturing, a kinsman?" The words were impeccably courteous, and the tone; but his eyes were blazing.

"All this," said Dyan, "took place a long time ago."

"Still," said Regis, "before we bring Beltran of Aldaran into Comyn itself—whether by marriage-right or any other way—should we not first assure ourselves that he has come to think otherwise about what has happened?" And then he said what I knew I should have said myself. "In the names of all the Gods, do we want the kind of thing that happened in Caer Donn to happen in Thendara? Do we want—Sharra?"

Lerrys Ridenow came down to the center of the dais. I had not seen him since shortly after my marriage to Dio; but he had not changed: slender, elegant, dressed now in Darkovan clothing, the green and gold of the Ridenow Domain, but exhibiting the same foppish grace as he had had in the clothing he had worn on the pleasure world.

He said, "Are you going to raise the bogey of Sharra again? We all know the link was broken and the matrix controlled again. The Sharra matrix is no trouble to anyone now—or rather," he said, raising his head and cocking it a little to one side with a calculating glance at me, "it may be very grave trouble to Lew Alton, but he asked, after all, for his trouble."

How could he have known that? Dio must have told him! How could she . . . how could she have betrayed to him what was so personal to me? And what else had she told him, what else had she betrayed? I had trusted her implicitly. . . . My hand clenched and I bit back a rising surge of nausea. I did not want to believe that Dio could have betrayed me this way.

But next to me, Marius rose to his feet. I was startled, almost turned to him to remind him sharply that he had no voice here—then I remembered. He was one of the official claimants for the Alton Domain; they could no longer refuse to acknowledge his existence.

He said, and his voice was only a shred of sound. "That's not true, *Dom* Lerrys. The matrix is—is active again. Lord Regis, tell them what you saw . . . in my father's house, not three days ago."

"It's true," Regis said, and he was very pale. "The Sharra matrix is alive again. But I did not know, at that time, that Lew Alton had returned to Darkover. I think he must have brought it back with him."

I had had no choice, but there was no way I could tell them that. While Regis spoke, I listened, transfixed with horror. I clutched at Marius's sleeve and said, "Rafe. He is in Thendara. . . ."

But I hardly heard Marius's reply.

Rafe was in Thendara.

That meant Kadarin and Thyra were—somewhere.

And so was the Sharra matrix.

And so—all the Gods of Darkover be merciful—so was I.

CHAPTER THREE

Even as he told the story of what he had seen in Kennard's house the night Marius had come in panic to summon him, Regis watched Lew, thinking that he would hardly have known the older man, who had been like a brother in his childhood. Lew looked, he formed the thought without volition, like something hung up in a field to scare the birds! Not so much the gauntness, though he was thin enough, and looked worn, nor even the dreadful scars. No, it was something in the eyes, something haunted and terrible.

In six years, has he found no peace?

Surely it was only that Lew was travel-worn, still suffering with the shock of his father's sudden death. Regis knew that when he could stop to think, he too would mourn the kindly and genial man who had been foster-father and friend, who had trained him in swordplay and given him the only family and home he had ever known. But this was no time for mourning. Tersely, he completed the tale.

". . . and when I tried to look within my own matrix, it was as it had been in the Hellers, during that time when Sharra was freed and Lew was—enslaved. I saw nothing but the Form of Fire."

From his place among the Altons, the big red-headed man who had come from Arilinn, and who was one of Lew's kinsmen—Regis had only heard his name briefly and did not remember it—said, "I find this disturbing, Lord Regis. For look, my own matrix is free of any taint." With the big fingers which looked better suited to the hilt of a sword—or to a blacksmith's hammer—he deftly untwisted the silk about the cord at his neck; briefly, Regis saw a glow of pallid blue before the man covered it again.

"And mine," said Callina quietly but without moving. Regis assumed that, as a Keeper, she would know the condition of her matrix without touching it. Sometimes he wished he had chosen to remain in a Tower, to be trained in the skills of using all of his latent *laran,* whatever it was.

Usually, when this wish came upon Regis, it was when he saw a trained technician working with a matrix. It had not been strong enough to hold him in a Tower against the other claims of clan and caste, and he supposed that for a true mechanic or technician, that call must supersede other claims and needs.

Callina said quietly to Lew, "What of yours?"

He shrugged, and to Regis it seemed like the last hopeless movement of a man so defeated that there was no longer strength in him to fight this ultimate shame and despair. He wanted to cry out to Callina, *Can't you see what you are doing to him?* At last Lew said tonelessly, "I have never been—free of it."

But the others in the Crystal Chamber were growing restless. Already the quality of the light had altered, as the Bloody Sun beyond the windows sank toward the horizon and was lost in the evening mists; now the light was cold, chill and austere. At last someone, some minor noble somewhere within the Ardais Domain, called out, "What has this to do with the Council?"

Callina said in her sombre voice, "Pray to all the Gods you never find out how much this can have to do with us, *comynari.* There is nothing that can be done here, but we must investigate this. . . ." She looked at Lew's kinsman from Arilinn and said, "Jeff, are there any other technicians here?"

He shook his head. "Not unless the mother Ashara can supply some." He turned back to the Hasturs and addressed himself to Regis's grandfather.

"Vai Dom, will you dismiss the Council for a few days, until we can look into this and find out why there has been this—this outbreak of a force we thought safely controlled."

Hastur frowned, and Derik said shrilly, "It is too late to stop this alliance, Lord Hastur, and anyway I don't think Beltran has anything to do with the Sharra people—not now. I think he's had his lesson about that! Don't you think so, Marius?"

Regis saw Lew start and stare in dismay at Marius, and wondered if Lew had not known about the ties between his brother and Rafe Scott—ties that probably meant with the Aldarans too. Well, they were Marius's kinsmen, his mother's people. *We made a great mistake,* he thought drearily, *we should have kept Marius allied to us in bonds of friendship, kin-ties. We cast him out; where could he turn, save to the Terrans, or Aldarans, or both? And now it seems we must deal with him as Heir to Alton.* It seemed fairly obvious that Lew was in no shape to take upon himself the rulership of the Alton Domain, even if the Council could be brought to accept him there.

There was once a laran *which could foretell the future,* Regis thought, *and it was among the Hasturs. Would that I had some of that gift!*

He had missed what Marius had said, but his grandfather looked distressed. Then he said, "There can be no question of alliance with Aldaran until we know something of this—" he hesitated and Regis saw the old man's lip curl in fastidious distaste—"this—reappearance of Sharra."

"But that's what I am trying to tell you," said Derik in exasperation. "We have sent the message to Beltran, and he will be here on Festival Night!" And, as he read the anger and dismay in old Hastur's face, Derik added, defensive, petulant, like a small boy who has been caught at some mischief, "Well, I am Lord of Elhalyn! It was my right—wasn't it?"

Danvan Hastur took the cup of warmed spiced wine that his body-servant had set in his hand, and propped his feet up on a carven footstool. Around him the servants were moving quietly, lighting lamps. Night had fallen; the same night after which he had had no choice but to dismiss the Council.

"I should send a message to see how Lew does," Regis said, "or go and greet him. Kennard was my friend and foster-father; Lew and I were *bredin.*"

Hastur said with asperity, "You could surely find yourself a less dangerous friend in these days. That alliance won't do you any good."

Regis said angrily, "I don't choose my friends for their political expediency, sir!"

Hastur shrugged that away. "You're still young enough for the luxury of friendships. I remained convinced that Kennard was a good friend—perhaps for too long." As Regis stirred, he said, "No, wait. I need you here. I have sent for Gabriel and Javanne. The question before us is this: what are we going to do about Derik?" As Regis looked blank he said impatiently, "Surely you don't still think we can have him crowned! The boy's not much better than a halfwit!"

Regis shrugged. "I don't see what choice you have, Grandfather. It's worse than if he were a halfwit; then everyone would agree that he can't be crowned. The trouble is that Derik has nine-tenths of his wits, and he's missing only the most important tenth." He smiled, but knew there was no mirth in the joke.

But Danvan Hastur did not smile, he said, "In some lesser walk of life—even as the ordinary Head of a Domain—it wouldn't be so important; he's going to marry Linnell Lindir-Aillard, and she's no fool. Derik loves her, he's grown up with the knowledge that the Aillard women are the Heads of Council in their own right, and he would let himself be guided by her. I remember when my father married off one of the less stable Ardais to an Aillard woman; Lady Rohana was the real head of that clan well into Dyan's time. But—to wear the crown of the Hasturs of Elhalyn—" he shook his head slowly, "and in the days that are coming now? No, I can't risk it."

"I don't know that you have the power to risk it or not risk it, sir," Regis pointed out. "If you had faced the fact, years ago, that Derik would never be fit for his crown, perhaps when he was twelve or fifteen, and instead had him put under Guardianship and had him set aside—who is the next Heir to Elhalyn?"

Danvan Hastur scowled, lines running down sharply from his jaw to his chin. "I can't believe you are *that* naïve, Regis."

"I don't know what you mean, Grandfather."

Danvan Hastur sighed and said heavily, as if he were explaining a thing to a child with the use of colored pictures, "Your mother, Regis, was King Stephen's sister. His only sister." Just in case Regis might have missed the implications of *that,* he added baldly, "You are the nearest to the crown—even before the sons of Derik's sisters. The oldest of those sons is three years old. There is also an infant at the breast."

"Aldones! Lord of Light!" Regis muttered, and the imprecation was nevertheless a prayer. Words he had said, joking, to Danilo years before, came back to him now. *"If you love me, Dani, don't wish a crown upon me!"*

"If I had had him set aside," his grandfather said, "who would have believed that I was not simply trying to consolidate power in my own hands? Not that it would have been such a bad thing, in these days—but it would have lost me the popular support that I needed to keep order in a crownless realm. I delayed, hoping it would become clear to everyone that Derik was really unfit."

"And now," said Regis, "everyone will think that you are trying to depose Derik the first time he makes a decision contrary to yours."

"The trouble is," his grandfather said, and he sounded despondent, "this proposed alliance with Aldaran might not be such a bad idea, if we could be absolutely certain that the Aldarans are once and for all out of the Terran camp. What happened during that Sharra business seemed to have broken off the closeness between Terrans and Aldaran. If we could get the Aldarans firmly on our side—" he considered for a moment.

"Grandfather, do you honestly think that the Terrans are going to pack up their spaceport and go away?"

The old man shook his head. "I want us to turn our backs on them completely. I think my father made a very great mistake when he allowed Kennard to be educated on Terra, and I think I compounded that mistake when I recognized Lew for Council. No, of course the Terran Empire won't go away. But the Terrans might have respected us, if we hadn't kept looking over the wall. We should never have let the Ridenow go offworld. We should have said to the Terrans, 'Build your spaceport if you must, but in return for that, let us alone. Leave us with our own way of life, and go about your business without involving us.' "

Regis shook his head. "It wouldn't have worked. You can't ignore a fact, and the Terran Empire is a fact. It's *there.* Sooner or later it's going to affect us one way or the other, no matter how strictly we try to pretend it doesn't exist. And you can't ignore the fact that we are Terran colonists, or that we were once—"

"What we were once doesn't matter," Danvan Hastur said. "Chickens can't go back into eggs."

"The very point I'm trying to make, sir. We were cut off from our roots, and we found a way of life which meant we accepted ourselves as belonging to this world, compelled to live within its restrictions. That worked while we were still isolated, but once we had come back into contact with a—" he stopped, and considered—"with an empire which spans the stars, and takes world-hopping for granted, we can't pretend to continue as we were."

"I don't see why not," Hastur said. "The Terrans have nothing that we want."

"Nothing *you* want, perhaps, sir." Regis made a point of not staring markedly at the silver coffee service on his grandfather's table, but the old man saw his look anyhow and said, "I am willing to do without any Terran luxuries, if it will encourage the rest of our people to do likewise."

"Once again, sir, won't work. We had to turn to the Terrans during the last epidemic of Trailmen's fever. There's some evidence the climate's changing, too, and we need some technological help there. People will die if they don't see an alternative, but if we let them die when Terran medicine can help them, are we anything but tyrants? Sir, one thing no one can control is *knowledge.* We can use it or misuse it—like *laran,*" he added grimly, remembering that his own laran had brought him such unendurable self-knowledge that, at one time, he would willingly have had it burned forever from his brain. "But we can't pretend it's never happened, or that it's our destiny to stay on this one world as if it was all there would ever be in the universe."

"Are you trying to say that we must inevitably become part of the Terran Empire?" his grandfather asked, scowling so furiously that Regis wished he had never started this.

"I am saying, sir, that whether we join into it or not, the Terran Empire is now a fact of our existence, and whatever decisions we make, must be made in the full knowledge that the Terrans are *there.* If we had refused them permission to build their spaceport, at first, they might—I say they *might,* not that they *would*—have turned their backs, gone away and built it somewhere else. I doubt it. Most likely they would have used just enough force to stop our open rebellion against it, and built it anyhow. We could have tried to resist—and perhaps, if we still had the weapons of the Ages of Chaos, we might have been able to drive them away. But not without destroying ourselves in the process. You remember what happened in a single night when Beltran turned *Sharra* against them—" He stopped, shivering. "That is not the worst of the Ages of Chaos weapons, but I pray I will never see a worse one. And we do not, now, have the technology of the Ages of Chaos, so that those weapons are uncontrollable. And even you, sir, don't think we can drive away the Terrans with the swords of the Guardsmen—not even with every swordsman on Darkover under arms."

His grandfather sat silent, head on hands, for so long that Regis wondered if he had said the unforgivable, if the next thing Danvan Hastur did would be to disown and disinherit him as a traitor.

But everything I said was true, and he is honest enough to know it.

"That's right," said Danvan Hastur, and Regis was, guiltily, startled; he had grown used to the knowledge that his grandfather was only the most minimal of telepaths, and never used mindspeech if he could possibly help it; so little, in fact, that sometimes he forgot there was any *laran* they shared.

"I should be as witless as Derik if I tried to pretend that Darkover alone could stand out against anything the size of the Terran Empire. But I absolutely refuse to let Darkover become a Terran colony, and nothing more. If we can't retain our integrity in the face of Terran culture and technology, perhaps we don't deserve to survive at all."

"It's not that bad," Regis pointed out. "That's one reason Kennard was educated on Terra in the first place—to point out that our way of life is viable, even for us, and that we don't need the worst of their technology—that we needn't adopt it, for instance, to the level where our own ecology suffers. We can't support the kind of technology they have on some of the city worlds, for instance; we're metal-poor, and even too-intensive agriculture would strip our topsoil and forests within two generations. I was brought up with that fact and so were you. The Terrans know it, too. They have laws against world-wrecking, and they're not going to give us anything we don't demand. But with all respect, Grandfather, I think we've gone too far in the other direction and we're insisting that we keep our people in a state—" he groped for words—"a state of barbarism, a feudal state where we maintain hold over people's very minds."

"They don't know what's good for them," Hastur said despairingly. "Look at the Ridenow! Spending half their time on places like Vainwal—deserting our people when they most need responsible leadership! As for the common people, they look at the luxuries Terran citizenship would give them—they think—and forget the price that would have to be paid."

"Maybe I trust people more than you do, sir. I think that if we gave them more education, more knowledge—maybe they'd know what they were fighting and know why you were refusing it."

"I've lived longer than you have," pointed out the old man dryly, "long enough to know that most people want what's going to give them the most profit and the least effort, and they *won't* think about the long-range consequences."

"That's not always true," said Regis. "Look at the Compact."

Hastur said, "That was forced on the people by one singleminded fanatic, when they were already frightened and exhausted by a series of suicidal wars. And it was kept only because the keepers of those old weapons destroyed them before they could be used again, and took the knowledge to their graves. Look how it's been kept!" His lip curled. "Every now and then someone digs up an old weapon and uses it—or so they say—in self-defense. You're not old enough to remember the time when the catmen darkened all the lands of the Kilghard Hills, or when some of the forge-folk—I suppose—raised Sharra against some bandits a couple of generations ago. If the weapons are *there,* people are going to use them, and to hell with the long-range consequences! Your own father was blown to pieces by smuggled contraband weapons from the Terran Zone. So much for the strength of our way of life against the Terrans!"

"I still think that could have been avoided if people had been dully warned against the consequences," Regis said, "but I'm not saying we must become a Terran colony. Even the Terrans aren't demanding that."

"How do you know what they want?"

"I've talked with some of them, sir. I know you don't really approve, but I feel it's better to know what they're doing—"

"And as a result," said his grandfather coldly, "you stand here and defend them to me."

Regis fought back a surge of exasperation. He said at last, "We were speaking of Derik, Grandfather. If he can't be crowned, what's the alternative? Why can't we just marry him to Linnell and rely on her to keep him within bounds?"

"Linnell's too good for him," Danvan Hastur said, "and I hate to see him come any further under the influence of Merryl. I don't trust that man."

"Merryl's a fool and a hothead," said Regis, "and dangerously undisciplined. But I imagine Lady Callina can help there—if you don't tie her hands by letting Merryl marry her off. I don't, and won't, trust the Aldarans. Not with Sharra loose again."

"I cannot go directly against the heir to the Throne, Regis. If I cause him to lose *kihar*—" deliberately, Danvan Hastur used the untranslatable Dry-Town word meaning personal integrity, honor, dignity—less and more than any of these, "before the Council, how can he ever rule over them after that?"

"He can't anyway, Grandfather. Will you let him marry off Callina to save his face before Council? If you have to crown him—and I think perhaps you do—you must let him know *before* he's crowned that the Council can always veto his decisions, or you'll have him playing the tyrant over us in all kinds of foolish ways. Callina Lindir is Head of a Domain in her own right, and has been Keeper of Neskaya and Arilinn, and now here under Ashara. What about *Callina's* loss of *kihar?*"

His grandfather scowled; Regis knew, though it was not—quite—telepathy, that Hastur was reluctant to allow Callina also that much Council power.

Not unless he's sure she'll support him and his isolationist notions. Otherwise he'll marry her off just to get her out of the Council!

"I don't suppose you'd be willing to marry her yourself?"

"Callina?" he asked in horror. "She must be twenty-seven!"

"Hardly senile," said the old man dryly, "but I was speaking of Linnell. She's too good for that fool Derik."

Evanda's mercy, is the old man harping on that string again? "Sir, Derik and Linnell have been sweethearts since Linnie's hair was too short to braid! And you've encouraged it. She's the only woman Derik would, perhaps, consent to be ruled by. You'd break both their hearts! Why separate them now?"

"I'd like to be firmly allied to the Aillards—"

"We're that already, sir, with Linnell handfasted to Derik. But we won't be if you alienate them by losing face for Callina by marrying her off against her will—and to Aldaran," Regis said. "And you're forgetting the most important thing, Grandfather."

"What's that?" The old man snorted, getting up and pacing the room restlessly. "All this business about Sharra?"

"Don't you see what's happening, Grandfather? Derik did this behind our backs, and Beltran will be here on Festival Night. Which means he's already on the road, unless he's patched things up enough with the Terrans to get an aircraft or two, and it's not very easy to fly through the Hellers." He remembered someone telling him that they had been, profanely, dubbed worse things than that by the only Terrans to try to fly over them in anything slower and lower than a rocketplane; they were a nightmare of updrafts, down-drafts and wild thermal patterns. "So when he gets here, what do you say? *Please, Lord Aldaran, turn around and go home again, we've changed our minds!*"

Old Hastur grimaced. "Wars have been fought for a lot less than that on Darkover."

"And the Aldarans haven't always observed the Compact that well," Regis pointed out. "Either we have to let him marry Callina—or we have to insult Beltran by saying, maybe in public, 'Sorry, Lord Aldaran, the woman won't have you,' or by telling him that our Prince and Ruler is a ninny who can't be entrusted even with the making of a marriage for his paxman! Either way, Beltran will have a grievance! Grandfather, I find it hard to believe you couldn't have foreseen this day!"

Hastur came and dropped in his carved and gilded presence-chair. He said, "I knew Derik couldn't be trusted to make any important decision. I said again and again that

I didn't like him going about with Merryl! But could I have foreseen that Merryl would have the insolence to speak for the head of his Domain—or that Aldaran would listen?"

"If you had faced the fact that Derik was witless—well, not witless, not a ninny who should be in leading-strings with a he-governess to look after him, but certainly without the practical judgment of a boy of ten, let alone the presumptive Heir to the Throne—" Regis began, then sighed. He said, "Sir, done is done. There's no point in arguing what we should have done. The question now is, how do we get out of this without a war?"

"I don't suppose Callina would consent to marry him, just to go through the ceremony as a formality—" Hastur began, but broke off as his servant entered and stood near the door.

"Yes?"

"*Domna* Javanne Lanart-Hastur and her consort, Dom Gabriel."

Regis went to kiss his sister's hand and draw her into the room. Javanne Hastur was a tall, handsome woman, well into her thirties now, with the strong Hastur features. She glanced at both of them and said, "Have you been quarreling with Grandfather again, Regis?" She spoke as if reproving him for climbing trees and tearing his best holiday breeches.

"Not quarreling," he said lightly. "Simply exchanging views on the political situation."

Gabriel Lanart grimaced and said, "That's bad enough."

"And I was reminding my grandson and Heir," said Danvan Hastur sharply, "that he is old to be unmarried, and suggesting that we might even marry him to Linnell Aillard-Lindir, if that will convince him to settle down. In Evanda's name, Regis, what are you waiting for?"

Regis tried to control the anger surging up in him and said, "I am waiting, sir, to meet a woman with whom I can contemplate spending the rest of my life. I'm not refusing to marry—"

"I should hope not," his grandfather snorted. "It's—undignified for a man your age, to be still unmarried. I don't say a word against the Syrtis youngster; he's a good man, a suitable companion for you. But in the times that are coming, one of the things we don't need is for anyone to name the Heir to Hastur in contempt as a lover of men!"

Regis said evenly, "And if I *am,* sir?"

His grandfather was denying too many unpalatable facts this evening. Now let him chew on this one. Javanne looked shocked and dismayed. Granted, it was not the right thing to say before one's sister, but after all, Regis defended himself angrily, his grandfather knew perfectly well what the situation was.

Danvan Hastur said, "Nonsense! You're young, that's all. But if you're old enough to have such pronounced views, and if I'm supposed to take them seriously, then you ought to be willing to convince me you're mature enough to be worth hearing. I want you married, Regis, before this year is out."

Then you will be in want for a long time, Grandfather, Regis thought, but he did not say it aloud. Javanne frowned, and he knew that she, who had somewhat more telepathic sensitivity than his grandfather, had followed the thought. She said, "Even Dyan Ardais has provided his Domain with an Heir, Regis."

"Why, so have I," said Regis. "Your own son, Javanne. Would it not please you if he were Hastur-lord after me? And I have other sons by other women, even though they are *nedestro.* I am perfectly capable of—and willing—to father sons for the Domain. But I do not want a marriage which will simply be a hoax, a sham, to please the Council. When I meet a woman I wish to marry, I wish to be free to marry her." And as he spoke, it seemed to him that he walked side by side with someone, and the overpowering emotion that surged up in him was like nothing he had ever felt, except in the first sudden outpouring of love and gratitude when Danilo had awakened his *laran* and he had allowed himself to accept it, and himself. But although he knew there was a woman by his side, he could not see her face.

"You are a romantic fool," said Javanne. "Marriage is not like that." But she smiled and he saw the kindly look she gave Gabriel. Javanne was fortunate; she was well content in her marriage.

"When I find a woman who suits me as well as Gabriel suits you, sister, then I will marry her," he said, and tried to keep his voice light. "And that I pledge to you. But I have not found such a woman yet, and I am not willing to marry just because it would please the Council, or you, or grandfather."

"I don't like hearing it said," Javanne said, frowning, "that the Heir to Hastur is a lover of men. And if you do not marry soon, Regis, it will be said, and there will be scandal."

"If it is said, it will be said and there's an end to it," Regis said, in exasperation. "I will not live my life in fear of Council tongues! There are many things that would trouble me more than Council's speculation on my love life—which, after all, is none of their affair! I thought we came here to discuss Derik, and the other troubles we had in Council! And to have dinner—and I've seen no sign of food or drink! Are we to stand about wrangling over my personal affairs while the servants try to keep dinner hot, afraid to interrupt us while we are quarreling about when to hold my wedding?"

He was ready to storm out of the apartments, and his grandfather knew it. Danvan Hastur said, "Will you ask the servants to set dinner, Javanne?" As she went to do it, he beckoned a man to take Gabriel's cloak. "You could have brought your son, Gabriel."

Gabriel smiled and said, "He has guard duty this night, sir."

Hastur nodded. "How does he do in the cadets, then? And Rafael, he's in the first year, isn't he?"

Gabriel grinned and said, "I'm trying hard not to notice Rafael, kinsman. He's probably having the same trouble any lad of rank does in the cadets—young Gabe last year, or Regis, or Lew Alton—I still remember having to give Lew some extra skills in wrestling. They really had it in for him, they made his life miserable! I suppose Kennard himself had the same trouble when he was a first-year cadet. I didn't, but I was out of the direct line of Comyn succession." He sighed and said, "Too bad about Kennard. We'll miss him. I'll go on commanding the Guardsmen until Lew is able to make decisions—he's really ill, and this business of Sharra hasn't helped. But when he recovers—"

"You certainly don't think Lew's fit to rule the Alton Domain, do you?" Hastur asked, shocked. "You saw it as well as I did! The boy's a wreck!"

"Hardly a boy," Regis said. "Lew is six years older than

I, which means he is halfway through his twenties. It's only fair to wait until he's recovered from the loss of his father, and from the journey from Vainwal. Kennard told me, once, that most long passages have to be made under heavy sedation. But when he recovers from that—"

Hastur opened his mouth to speak, but before he could say anything, Javanne said, "Dinner is on the table. Shall we go in?" and took her husband's arm. Regis followed, with his grandfather. Dinner had been laid on a small table in the next room, with elegant cloths and the finest dishes and goblets; Javanne, at her grandfather's nod, signaled for service and poured wine. But Gabriel said, as he spread his napkin on his knees, "Lew's sound enough, I think."

"He has only one hand; can he command the Guards as a cripple?"

"Precedent enough for that too," said Gabriel. "Two or three generations ago, Dom Esteban—who was my great-grandfather and Lew's too, I think—commanded the Guards for ten years from a wheelchair after he lost the use of his legs in the Catmen's War. For that matter, there was Lady Bruna, who took up her sword and made a notable commander, once, when the Heir was but a babe—" he shrugged. "Lew can dress himself and look after himself one-handed—I saw him. As for the rest—well, he was a damned good officer once. And if he wants me to go on commanding the Guards—well, he's the head of my Domain, and I'll do what he says. And the boys coming up—and there's Marius. He hasn't had military training, but he's perfectly well-educated."

"Terran education," Hastur said dryly.

Regis said, "Knowledge is knowledge, Grandfather." He remembered what he had been thinking in Council, that it made more sense to have Mikhail, perhaps, instructed under the Terrans than to shove him into the cadets for military discipline and training in swordplay. "Marius is intelligent—"

"And has some unfortunate Terran friends," said Javanne scornfully. "If he hadn't involved himself with the Terrans, he wouldn't have brought out all that business about Sharra today at Council!"

"And then we wouldn't know what was going on," said Regis. "When a wolf is loose in the pastures, do we care if the herdsman loses a night's sleep? And whose fault is it that Marius was not given cadet training? I'm sure he would have done as well there as I did. We chose to turn him over to the Terrans, and now, I'm afraid, we have to live with what we have made of him. We made certain that one Domain, at least, would remain allied to the Terrans!"

"The Altons have always been too ready to deal with the Terrans," said Hastur. "Ever since the days when Andrew Carr married into that Domain—"

"Done is done," Gabriel said, "there's no need to hash it over now, sir. I didn't see any signs that Lew was so happy among the Terrans that he can't rule the Altons well—"

"You're acting as if he were going to be Head of the Domain," said Hastur.

Gabriel laid down his spoon, letting the soup roll out on the tablecloth. "Now look here, Grandfather. It's one thing for me to claim the Domain when we had no notion whether Lew was alive or dead. But Council accepted him as Kennard's Heir, and that's all there is to it. It's up to him, as head of the Domain, to say what's to be done about Marius, but I suppose he'll name him Heir. If it were Jeff Kerwin I might challenge—he doesn't want the Domain, he wasn't brought up to it—"

"A Terran?" asked Javanne in amazement.

"Jeff isn't a Terran. I ought to say, *Dom* Damon—he has no Terran blood at all. His father was Kennard's older brother. He was fostered on Terra and brought up to think he was Terran, and he bears his Terran foster-father's name, that's all," Gabriel explained, patiently, not for the first time. "He has less Terran blood than I do. My father was Domenic Ridenow-Lanart, but it was common knowledge that he was fathered by Andrew Carr. Twin sisters married Andrew Carr and Damon Ridenow—"

Danvan Hastur frowned. "That was a long time ago."

"Funny, how a generation or two wipes out the scandal," said Gabriel with a grin. "I thought that had all been hashed over, back when they tested Lew for the Alton Gift. He had it, I didn't, and that was that."

Danvan Hastur said quietly "I want you at the head of the Alton Domain, Gabriel. It is your duty to the Hastur clan."

Gabriel picked up his spoon, frowned, rubbed it briefly on the napkin and thrust it back into his soup. He took a mouthful or two before he said, "I did my duty to the Hastur clan when I gave them two—no, three—sons, sir, and one of them to be Regis's Heir. But I swore loyalty to Kennard, too. Do you honestly think I'm going to fight my cousin for his rightful place as Alton Heir?"

But that, Regis thought, watching the old man's face, *is exactly what Danvan Hastur does think. Or did.*

"The Altons are allied to Terra," he said. "They've made no secret of it. Kennard, now Lew, and even Marius, have Terran education. The only way we can keep the Alton Domain on the Darkovan side is to have a strong Hastur man in command, Gabriel. Challenge him again before the Council; I don't even think he wants to fight for it."

"Lord of Light, sir! Do you honestly think—" Gabriel broke off. He said, "I can't do it, Lord Hastur, and I won't."

"Do you want a half-Terran pawn of Sharra at the head of the Alton Domain?" Javanne demanded, staring at her husband.

"That's for him to say," said Gabriel steadily. "I took oath to obey any lawful command you gave me, Lord Hastur, but it isn't a lawful command when you bid me challenge the rightful Head of my Domain. If you'll pardon my saying so, sir, that's a long way from being a lawful command."

Old Hastur said impatiently "The important thing at this time is that the Domains should stand fast. Lew's unfit—"

"If he's unfit, sir—" and Gabriel looked troubled—"it'll be apparent soon enough."

Javanne said shrilly, "I thought they had deposed him as Kennard's successor after the Sharra rebellion. And now both he and his brother are still tied up with Sharra—"

Regis said, "And so am I, sister; or weren't you listening?"

She raised her eyes to him and said, disbelieving, "You?"

Regis reached, with hesitant fingers, for his matrix; fumbled at taking it from its silk wrapping. He remembered that Javanne had, years ago, taught him to use it, and she remembered too, for she raised her angry eyes and suddenly softened, and smiled at him. There was the old image in her mind, *as if the girl she had been—herself motherless, trying to mother her motherless baby brother—had bent over him as she had so often done when he was small, swung him up into her arms—* For a moment the hard-faced woman, the mother of grown sons, was gone, and she was the gentle and loving sister he had once known.

Regis said softly, "I am sorry, *breda,* but things don't go away because you are afraid of them. I didn't want you to have to see this." He sighed and let the blue crystal fall into his cupped hand.

Raging, flaming in his mind, the form of fire . . . a great tossing shape, a woman, tall, bathed in flame, her hair rising like restless fires, her arms shackled in golden chains . . . Sharra!

When he had seen it six years ago at the height of the Sharra rebellion, his *laran* had been newly waked; he had been, moreover, half dead with threshold sickness, and Sharra had been only another of the horrors of that time. When he had seen it briefly in Marius's house, he had been too shocked to notice. Now something cold took him by the throat; his flesh crawled on his bones, every hair on his body rose slowly upright, beginning with his forearms, slowly moving over all his body. Regis knew, without knowing how he knew, that he looked upon a very ancient enemy of his race and his caste, and something in his body, cell-deep, bone-deep, knew and recognized it. Nausea crawled through his body and he felt the sour taste of terror in his mouth.

Confused, he thought, *but Sharra was used and chained by the forge-folk, surely I am simply remembering the destruction of Sharra loosed, a city rising in flame . . . it is no worse than a forest fire*—but he knew this was something worse, something he could not understand, something that fought to draw him into itself. . . . *recognition, fear, a fascination almost sexual in its import . . .*

"Aaahh—" It was a half-drawn breath of horror; he heard, saw, *felt* Javanne's mind, her terror reaching out, entangled. She clutched at the matrix under her own dress as if it had burned her, and Regis, with a mighty effort, wrenched his mind and his eyes from the Form of Fire blazing from his matrix. But Javanne clung, in terror and fascination. . . .

And something in Regis, long dormant, unguessed, seemed to uncoil within him; as a skilled swordsman takes the hilt in his hand, without knowing what moves he will make, or which strokes he will answer, knowing only that he can match his opponent, he felt that strangeness rise, take over what he did next. He *reached out* into the depths of the fire, and delicately picked Javanne's mind loose, focusing so tightly that he did not even touch the Form of Fire . . . as if she were a puppet, and the strings had been cut, she slumped back fainting in her chair, and Gabriel caught her scowling.

"What did you do?" he demanded, "What have you done to her?"

Javanne, half-conscious, was blinking. Regis, with careful deliberation, wrapped up his matrix. He said, "It is dangerous to you too, Javanne. Don't come near it again."

Danvan Hastur had been staring, bewildered, as his grandson and granddaughter stared in terror, paralyzed, then, as they withdrew. Regis remembered, wearily, that his grandfather had little *laran*. Regis himself did not understand what he had done, only knew he was shaking down deep in the bones, exhausted, as weary as if he had been on the fire-lines for three days and three nights. Without knowing he was doing it, he reached for a plateful of hot rolls, smeared honey thickly on one and gobbled it down, feeling the sugar restoring him.

"It was Sharra," Javanne said in a whisper. "But what did you do?"

And Regis could only mumble, shocked, "I haven't the faintest idea."

CHAPTER FOUR

(Lew Alton's narrative)

I've never been sure how I got out of the Crystal Chamber. I have the impression that Jeff half-carried me, when the Council broke up in discord, but the next thing I remember clearly, I was in the open air, and Marius was with me, and Jeff. I pulled myself upright.

"Where are we going?"

"Home," said Marius, "The Alton town-house; I didn't think you'd care for the Alton apartments, and I've never been there—not since Father left. I've been living here with Andres and a housekeeper or two."

I couldn't remember that I'd been to the town house since I was a very young child. It was growing dark; thin cold rain stung my face, clearing my mind, but fragments of isolated thought jangled and clamored from the passersby, and the old insistent beat:

. . . *last command. . . . return, fight for your brother's rights* . . . Would I never be free of that? Impatiently I struggled to get control as we came across the open square; but I seemed to see it, not as it was, dark and quiet, with a single light somewhere at the back, a servant's night-light; but I saw it through someone else's eyes, alive with light and warmth spilling down from open doors and brilliant windows, companionship and love and past happiness . . . I realized from Jeff's arm around my shoulders that he was seeing it as it had been, and moved away. I remembered that he had been married, and that his wife had died long since. He, too, had lost a loved one. . . .

But Marius was up the steps, calling out in excitement as if he were younger than I remembered him.

"Andres! Andres!" and a moment later the old *coridom* from Armida, friend, tutor, foster-father, was staring at me in astonishment and welcome.

"Young Lew! I—" he stopped, in shock and sorrow, as

he saw my scarred face, the missing hand. He swallowed, then said gruffly, "I'm glad you're here." He came and took my cloak, managing to give my shoulder an awkward pat of affection and grief. I suppose Marius had sent word about father; mercifully, he asked no questions, just said "I've told the housekeeper to get a room ready for you. You too, sir?" he asked Jeff, who shook his head.

"Thank you, but I am expected elsewhere—I am here as Lord Ardais's guest, and I don't think Lew is in any shape for any long family conferences tonight." He turned to me and said, "Do you mind?" and held his hand lightly over my forehead in the monitor's touch, the fingers at least three inches away, running his hand down over my head, all along my body. The touch was so familiar, so reminiscent of the years at Arilinn—the only place I could remember where I had been wholly happy, wholly at peace—that I felt my eyes fill with tears.

That was all I wanted—to go back to Arilinn. And it was forever too late for that. With the hells in my brain that would not bear looking into, with the matrix tainted by Sharra . . . no, they would not have me in a Tower now.

Jeff's hand was solid under my arm; he shoved me down in a seat. Through the remnant of the drugs which had destroyed my control, I felt his solicitude, Andres's shock at my condition, and turned to face them, clenching my hand, aware of phantom pain as by reflex I tried to clench the missing hand too; wanting to scream out at them in rage, and realizing that they were all troubled for me, worrying about me, sharing my pain and distress.

"Keep still, let me finish monitoring you." When he finished Jeff said, "Nothing wrong, physically, except fatigue and drug hangover from that damned stuff the Terrans gave him. I don't suppose you have any of the standard antidotes, Andres?" At the old man's headshake he said dryly, "No, I don't suppose they're the sort of thing that one can buy in an apothecary shop or an herb-seller's stall. But you need sleep, Lew. I don't suppose there's any *raivannin* in the house—"

Raivannin is one of the drugs developed for work among Tower circles, linked in the mind of a telepathic circle. . . . There are others: *Kirian,* which lowers the resistance to telepathic contact, is perhaps the most common. *Raivannin* has an action almost the opposite of that of *kirian*. It tends to shut down the telepathic functions. They'd given it to me, in Arilinn, to quiet, a little, the torture and horror which I was broadcasting after Marjorie's death . . . quiet it enough so that the rest of the Tower circle need not share every moment of agony. Usually it was given to someone at the point of death or dissolution, or to the insane, so that they would not draw everyone else into their inner torment. . . .

"No," Jeff said compassionately. "That's not what I mean. I think it would help you get a night's sleep, that's all. I wonder—There are licensed matrix mechanics in the City, and they know who I am; First in Arilinn. I will have no trouble buying it."

"Tell me where to go," said a young man, coming swiftly into the room, "and I will get it; I am known to many of them. They know I have *laran*. Lew—" he came around and stood directly before me. "Do you remember me?"

I focused my eyes with difficulty, saw golden-amber eyes, strange eyes . . . Marjorie's eyes! Rafe Scott flinched at the agony of that memory, but he came up and embraced me. He said, "I'll find some *raivannin* for you. I think you need it."

"What are you doing in the city, Rafe?" He had been a child when I had drawn him, with Marjorie, into the circle of Sharra. Like myself, he bore the ineradicable taint, fire and damnation. . . . *no!* I slammed my mind shut, with an effort that turned me white as death.

"Don't you remember? My father was a Terran, Captain Zeb Scott. One of Aldaran's tame Terrans." He said it wryly, with a cynical lift of his lip, too cynical for anyone so young. He was Marius's own age. I was beyond curiosity now; though I had heard Regis describing what he had seen, and knew that he was Marius's friend. He didn't stay, but went out into the rainy night, shrugging a Darkovan cloak over his head.

Jeff sat on one side of me; Marius on the other. We didn't talk much; I was in no shape for it. It took all my energy for me to keep from curling up under the impact of all this.

"You never did tell me, Jeff, how you came to be in the city."

"Dyan came to bring me," he said. "I don't want the Domain and I told him so; but he said that having an extra claimant would confuse the issue, and stall them until Kennard could return. I don't think he was expecting you."

"I'm sure he wasn't," Marius said.

"That's all right, brother, I can live without Dyan's affection," I said. "He's never liked me . . . " but still I was confused by that moment of rapport, when for a moment I had seen him through my father's eyes . . .

. . . *dear, cherished, beloved, sworn brother . . . even, once or twice, in the manner of lads, lovers* . . . I slammed the thought away. In a sense the rejection was a kind of envy. Solitary in the Comyn, I had had few *bredin,* fewer to offer such affection even in crisis. Could it be that I envied my father that? His voice, his presence, were a clamor in my mind. . . .

I should tell Jeff what had happened. Since Kennard had awakened the latent Alton gift, the gift of forced rapport, by violence when I was hardly out of childhood, he had been there, his thoughts overpowering my own, choking me, leaving me all too little in the way of free will, till I had broken free, and in the disaster of the Sharra rebellion, I had learned to fear that freedom. And then, dying, his incredible strength closing over my mind in a blast I could not resist or barricade . . .

Ghost-ridden; half of my brain burnt into a dead man's memories . . .

Was I never to be anything but a cripple, mutilated mind and body? For very shame I could not beg Jeff for more help than he had given me already . . .

He said neutrally, "If you need help, Lew, I'm here," but I shook my head.

"I'm all right; need sleep, that's all. Who is Keeper at Arilinn now?"

"Miranie from Dalereuth; I don't know who her family was—she never talks about them. Janna Lindir, who was Keeper when you were at Arilinn, married Bard Storn-Leynier, and they have two sons; but Janna put them out to foster, and came back as Chief Monitor at Neskaya. We need strong telepaths, Lew; I wish you could come back, but I suppose they'll need you on the Council—"

Again I saw him flinch, slightly, at my reaction to that. I

knew the state I was in, as well as he did; every transient emotion was broadcasting at full strength. Andres, Terran and without any visible *laran,* still noticed Marius's distress; he had, after all, lived with a telepath family since before I was born. He said stolidly, "I can find a damper and put it on, if you wish."

"That won't be—" I started to say, but Jeff said firmly, "Good. Do that." And before long the familiar unrhythmic pulses began to move through my mind, disrupting it. It blanked it out for the others—at least the specific content—but for me it substituted nausea for the sharper pain. I listened with half an ear to Marius telling Andres what had happened at the Council. Andres, as I had foreseen, understood at once what the important thing was.

"At least they recognized you; your right to inherit was challenged, but for once the old tyrant had to admit you existed," snorted Andres. "It's a beginning, lad."

"Do you think I give a damn—" Marius demanded. "All my life I haven't been good enough for them to spit on, and suddenly—"

"It's what your father fought for all his life," Andres said, and Jeff said quietly, "Ken would have been proud of you, Marius."

"I'll bet," said the boy scornfully. "So proud he couldn't come back even once—"

I bent my head. It was my fault, too, that Marius had had no father, no kinsman, no friend, but was left alone and neglected by the proud Comyn. I was relieved when Rafe came back, saying he had found a licensed technician in the street of the Four Shadows, and he had sold him a few ounces of *raivannin.* Jeff mixed it, and said, "How much—"

"As little as possible," I said. I had had some experience with the chemical damping-drugs, and I didn't want to be helpless, or unable to wake if I got into one of those terrible spiraling nightmares where I was trapped again in horrors beyond horrors, where demons of fire flamed and raged between worlds. . . .

"Just enough so you won't have to sleep under the dampers," he said. To my cramping shame, I had to let him hold it to my lips, but when I had swallowed it, wincing at its biting astringency, I felt the disruptions of the telepathic damper gradually subsiding, mellowing, and slowly, gradually, it was all gone.

It felt strange to be wholly without telepathic sensitivity; strange and disquieting, like trying to hear under water or with clogged ears; painful as the awareness had been, now I felt dulled, blinded. But the pain was gone, and the clamor of my father's voice; for the first time in days, it seemed, I was free of it. It was there under the thick blankets of the drug, but I need not listen. I drew a long, luxurious breath of calm.

"You should sleep. Your room's ready," Andres said. "I'll get you upstairs, lad—and don't bother fussing about it; I carried you up these stairs before you were breeched, and I can do it again if I have to."

I actually felt as if I could sleep, now. With another long sigh, I stood up, catching for balance.

Andres said, "They couldn't do anything about the hand, then?"

"Nothing. Too far gone." I could say it calmly now; I had, after all, before that ghastly debacle when Dio's child was born and died, learned to live with the fact. "I have a mechanical hand but I don't wear it much, unless I'm doing really heavy work, or sometimes for riding. It won't take much strain, and gets in my way. I can manage better, really, without it."

"You'll have your father's room," Andres said, not taking too much notice. "Let me give you a hand with the stairs."

"Thanks. I really don't need it." I was deathly tired, but my head was clear. We went into the hallway, but as we began to mount the stairs, the entry bell pealed and I heard one of the servants briefly disputing; then someone pushed past him, and I saw the tall, red-haired form of Lerrys Ridenow.

"Sorry to disturb you here; I looked for you in the Alton suite in Comyn Castle," he said. "I have to talk to you, Lew. I know it's late, but it's important."

Tiredly, I turned to face him. Jeff said, "Dom Lerrys, Lord Armida is ill." It took me a moment to realize he was talking about me.

"This won't take long." Lerrys was wearing Darkovan clothing now, elegant and fashionable, the colors of his Domain. In the automatic gesture of a trained telepath in the presence of someone he distrusts, I reached for contact; remembered: I was drugged with *raivannin*, at the mercy of whatever he chose to tell me. It must be like this for the head-blind. Lerrys said, "I didn't know you were coming back here. You must know you're not popular."

"I can live without that," I said.

"We haven't been friends, Lew," he said. "I suppose this won't sound too genuine; but I'm sorry about your father. He was a good man, and one of the few in the Comyn with enough common sense to be able to see the Terrans without giving them horns and tails. He had lived among the Terrans long enough to know where we would eventually be going." He sighed, and I said, "You didn't come out on a rainy night to give me condolences about my father's death."

He shook his head. "No," he said, "I didn't. I wish you'd had the sense to stay away. Then I wouldn't have to say this. But here you are, and here I am, and I do have to say it. Stay away from Dio or I'll break your neck."

"Did she send you to say that to me?"

"I'm saying it," Lerrys said. "This isn't Vainwal. We're in the Domains now, and—" He broke off. I wished with all my heart that I could read what was behind those transparent green eyes. He looked like Dio, damn him, and the pain was fresh in me again, that the love between us had not been strong enough to carry us through tragedy. "Our marriage ceremony was a Terran one. It has no force in the Domains. No one there would recognize it." I stopped and swallowed. I had to, before I could say, "If she wanted to come back to me, I'd—I'd welcome it. But I'm not going to force it on her, Lerrys, don't worry about that. Am I a Dry-towner, to chain her to me?"

"But a time's coming when we'll all be Terrans," Lerrys said, "and I don't want her tied to you then."

It was like struggling under water; I could not reach his mind, his thoughts were blank to me. Zandru's hells, was this what it was like to be without *laran,* blind, deaf, mutilated, with nothing left but ordinary sight and hearing? "Is this what Dio wants? Why doesn't she tell me so herself, then?"

Now there was blind rage exploding in Lerrys's face; it

needed no *laran* to see that. His face tightened, his fists clenched; for a moment I braced myself, thinking he would strike me, wondering how I could manage, with one hand, to defend myself if he did.

"Damn you, can't you see that's what I want to spare her?" he demanded, his voice rising to hysteria. "Haven't you put her through enough? How much do you think she can stand, you—you—you damned—" His voice failed him. After a time he got control of it again.

"I don't want her to have to see you again, damn you. I don't want her left with any memory of what she had to go through!" he said, raging. "Go to the Terran HQ and dissolve your marriage there—and if you don't, I swear to you, Lew, I'll call challenge on you and feed your other hand to the *kyorebni*!"

Through the drugs I was too dulled to feel sorrow. I said heavily, "All right, Lerrys. If that's what Dio wants, I won't bother her again."

He turned and slammed out of the house; Marius stood staring after him. He said, "What, in the name of all the Gods, was that all about?"

I couldn't talk about it. I said, "I'll tell you tomorrow," and, blindly, struggled up the stairs to my father's room. Andres came, but I paid no attention to him; I flung myself down on my father's bed and slept like the dead.

But I dreamed of Dio, crying and calling my name as they took her away from me in the hospital.

When I woke my head was clear; and I seemed, again, to be in possession of it alone. It had assumed the character of any family reunion; Marius came and sat on my bed and talked to me as if he were the young boy I'd known, and I gave him the gifts I'd remembered to bring from Vainwal, Terran lensed goods: binoculars, a camera.

He thanked me, but I suspected he thought them gifts for a child; he referred to them once as "toys." I wondered what would have been a proper gift for a man? Contraband blasters, perhaps, in defiance of the Compact? After all, Marius had had a Terran education. Was he one of those who considered the Compact a foolish anachronism, the childish ethic of a world stuck in barbarism? I suspected, too, that he felt little grief for our father. I didn't blame him; father had abandoned Marius a long time ago.

I told them I had business at the Terran HQ, without telling them much about it.

"You've got seven days, after all," Jeff pointed out to me after breakfast. "They deferred the formal transfer of the Domain until ritual mourning for Kennard was completed. And now it's only a formality—they accepted you as his Heir when you were fifteen.

There was the question as to whether they would accept Marius.

"Stupid bigots," Andres grumbled, "to decide a man's worth on the color of his eyes!"

Or the color of his hair; I could feel Jeff thinking that, remembering a time when, in Arilinn, most Comyn had had hair of the true Comyn red. I said, only half facetiously, "Maybe I should dye mine—and Marius's—so we'll look more like Comyn."

"I couldn't change my eyes," Marius said dryly, and I thought, with a pang, of the changeable sea-colors in Dio's eyes. But Dio hated me now, and that was all past; and who could blame her?

"They'll challenge me," I said. "And if they do—hell, I can't fight them with one hand."

"Stupid anachronism in this day and age," Marius said predictably, "to settle anything as important as the Heirship of a Domain with a sword."

Andres—we had demanded he sit with us at table; *coridom* or no, he had been guardian and foster-father much of our lives—asked, with equal dryness, "Would it make more sense to fight it out with blasters or invade each other's Domains and fight a war over it?"

Jeff was leaning back in his chair, a half-empty cup in front of him. "I remember hearing, in the Tower, why it was that the formal challenge with swords was instituted. There was a time when a formal challenge for the rulership of a Domain was made with the Gift of that Domain—and the one whose *laran* was the stronger won it. There was a day when the Domains bred men and women like cattle for these Gifts—and the Alton Gift, full strength, can kill. I doubt Gabriel wants to try *that* kind of duel against you."

"I'm not so sure, after last night, that I could win it if he did," I said. "I had forgotten where Comyn immunity came from." At Arilinn, matrix mechanics and technicians in training sometimes fought mock battles with *laran,* but I had been taught control since I was into my teens; real battles with *laran* were forbidden.

The Compact was not invented to ban blasters and firearms, but the older laran *weapons which were as dreadful as anything the Terran empire could produce . . .*

"I don't think Gabriel will challenge you," Andres said. "But they'll ask why, at your age, you're not married, and whether you have a legitimate child for an Heir."

I felt the scars at my mouth pull as I grimaced. "Married, yes, but not for long; that was what Lerrys came here about," I said. "And no children, nor likely to have."

Marius started to ask questions; Jeff stared him down. He knew what I was talking about. "We were afraid, at Arilinn, that would happen, but the technique of cell-monitoring at that level was lost sometime in the Ages of Chaos. Some of us are working to master it again—it's quicker and safer than some of the DNA work they do in the Empire. I don't suppose you fathered any bastards before you went offworld?"

There had been adventures in my youth, but if I had fathered a child—I put it bluntly to myself—the girl involved would have been proud to tell me so. And Marjorie had died, her child unborn.

"They'd accept Marius if I tested him for the Alton Gift, perhaps," I said. "They might have no choice. Comyn law says there *must* be an Heir named, a succession insured. By letting Kennard take me offworld, they gave tacit consent for Marius as presumptive Heir, I'd think. The law is clear enough." I didn't want to test Marius for the Alton Gift—not by the shock tactics my father had used on me, and I knew no others. Not now. And with my matrix in the shape it was in . . . about all I could do would be to give a demonstration of the powers of Sharra!

It wanted me, the fires sought to call me back. . . .

But there were other things to think about now.

"Marius should be tested before the formal challenge," I said. "You're First at Arilinn; you can do that, can't you?"

"Certainly," Jeff said. "Why not? I suspect he has some *laran,* perhaps Ridenow gift—there's Ridenow in the Alton lineage, and Ardais, too; Kennard's mother was Ardais and I always suspected he had a touch of catalyst telepathy."

Marius had been tearing a buttered roll to pieces. He said now, without looking up, "What I have, I think, is—is the Aldaran Gift. I can see—ahead. Not far, not very clearly; but the Aldaran gift is precognition, and I—I have that."

That he would have had from our half-Terran mother. In these days the gifts were entangled anyhow, bred out by intermarriage between the Domains. But I stared at him and demanded, "How would you know about the Aldaran Gift?"

He said impatiently, "The Aldarans are all the kin I have! And hell, Lew, the Comyn weren't very eager to claim me as kin! I spent one summer with Beltran—why not?"

This was a new factor to be reckoned with.

"I know he didn't treat you well," Marius went on, defensively, "but your quarrel was a private one, after all. What do you expect, that I should declare blood-feud for three generations because of that? Are we the barbarians the Terrans call us, then?"

There was no answer to that, but I didn't know what to say.

"We could all use some information about the future," I said. "If you've got *that* Gift, for the love of Aldones tell me what's going to happen if I claim the Domain? Will they accept you as my Heir?"

"I don't know," he confessed, and once again he seemed young, vulnerable, a boy half his age. "I—I tried to find out. They told me that sometimes that happened, you couldn't see too clear for yourself or anyone close to you . . ."

That was true enough, and since it was true, I wondered, not for the first time, what good that Gift was to anyone. Perhaps, in the days when Aldarans could see the fate of rulers, kingdoms, even of the planet . . . and that was another disquieting thought. Maybe the Aldarans, with their foresight, saw that Darkover would go the way of the Terran Empire and that was why they had joined forces, for so long, with Terra. I wondered if Beltran had entirely broken with them after the Sharra rebellion.

Well, there was one way to find out, but there was no time for it now. I strode restlessly to the window, looked out across the bustle of the cobbled square. Men were leading animals to the market, workmen going about carrying tools; a quiet familiar bustle. Because of the season, there was only a light thin powdering of snow on the stones; Festival, and High Summer, were upon us. Still it seemed cold to me after Vainwal and I dressed in my warmest cloak. Let the Terrans call me *barbarian* if they liked, I was home again, I would wear the warm clothes my own world demanded. The fur lining felt good even at this season as I drew it round me. Both Marius and Jeff offered to accompany me; but this was private business and I must attend to it by myself, so I refused.

It was a bright day; the sun, huge and red—the Terrans called it Cottman's Star, but to me it was just the sun, and just the way a sun should be—hung on the horizon, coming free of layers of morning cloud, and there were two small shadows in the sky where Liriel and Kyrddis were waning. Once I could have told you what month we were in, and what tenday of which month, by the position of the moons; as well as what to plant, in season, or what animals would be rutting or dropping their young; there is a month called Horse Month because more than three-quarters of the mares will foal before it fades, and there are all kinds of jokes about Wind Month because that is when the stallions and chervines and other animals run in rut; I suppose, where people live very close to the land, they work too hard to have much time for rutting, like the stallions, except at the proper season, and it becomes an uneasy joke.

But all that land . . . knowledge was only a dim memory, though I supposed, as I lived here longer, it would come back to me. As I strode through the morning streets, I felt comfortable under morning light and shadowed moons, something in my brain soothed and fed by the familiar lights. I've been on several planets, with anywhere from one to six moons—with more than that, the tides make the place uninhabitable—and suns yellow, red and blazing blue-white; at least I knew this one would not burn my skin red or brown!

So Marius, in addition to a Terran education, had the Aldaran Gift. That could be a dangerous combination, and I wondered how the Council would feel when they knew. Would they accept him, or would they demand that I adopt one of Gabriel's sons?

It was a fairly stiff walk from the quarter of the city where my father and his forefathers had kept their town house, to the gates of the Terran Zone. A high wind was blowing, and I felt stiff. I wasn't used to this kind of walk, and for six years I had lived on a world, Terra or Vainwal, where urgent business could be settled by mechanical communicators—anywhere in the Empire I could have settled the formalities for the dissolution of a marriage by communicator and video-screens—and where, if personal appearance had really been necessary, I could have all kinds of mechanical transport at a moment's notice. Darkover has never had much interest in roads—it takes either machine labor, man-hours or matrix work to build good roads, and our world has never wanted to pay the price of any of those three. I'd spent my share of time in a Tower, providing the kind of communication you can get through the relays, telepathically operated; and I'd done my share of mining, too, and chemically purifying minerals. I'd monitored, and trained monitors. But I knew how hard it was to find enough talent for the matrix work, and it was no longer required of my caste, who had *laran,* that they spend their lives behind Tower walls working for the people they served.

Were we Comyn the rulers of our people, because of our laran . . . *or were we their slaves? And which was which? A slave is a slave, even if, for his* laran *work, the people he serves surround him in every luxury and bow to his every word. A protected class quickly becomes an exploited and exploiting class. Look at women.*

The gates of the Terran HQ, stark and sombre, loomed before me, a black-leathered spaceman at their gates. I gave my name and the guard used his communicator; they admitted I was on legitimate business, and let me in. My father had gone to some trouble to arrange double citizenship for me, and the Terrans claimed that Darkover was a lost Terran colony anyhow, which meant it was part of their policy to grant citizens rights to anyone who went to the trouble of applying for them. I had never troubled to vote for a representative in the Imperial Senate or Parliament, but I had a shrewd suspicion that Lerrys always did. I don't have much faith in parliamentary governments—they tend to pick, not the best man, but the one who appeals to the widest mass temperament, and, in general, majorities tend to be always wrong—as the long history of culture and the constant return of certain types of slavery and religious bigotry show us. I didn't trust the Empire to make decisions for Darkover, and why in all of Zandru's nine hells—or the four hundred known and inhabited worlds of the Empire—should the Darkovans have any voice in making decisions for such worlds as Vainwal? Even in small groups—such as Comyn Council—politicians are men who want to tell their fellows what to do; and thus criminal at heart. I seldom thought about it much, and preferred it that way. My father had tried, many times, to point out the flaws in that reasoning, but I had better things to do with my life than worry about politics.

Better things? Had I anything to do with my life at all? At the back of my brain it seemed there was a familiar mutter. I kept my thoughts resolutely away from it, knowing that if I focused on it, it would be the clamor of my father's voice, the nag of the Sharra matrix at my brain. . . . no, I wouldn't think of it.

The marriage was a line in a computer, hardly more than that. My occupation? When I went offworld, drugged and only half alive after being seared in Sharra's fires, my father had had to name his occupation and he had put both his and mine down as *Matrix mechanic.* What a joke that was! He could have called himself *rancher*—Armida produces about a twentieth of the horses traded in the Kilghard Hills—or, because of his post as commander of the Guards, *soldier;* or, for that matter, because of his Council seat, claimed equal rank with a Senator or Parliamentarian. But, knowing the mystique the Terrans attach to our matrix technology, he had called himself, *Matrix Technician,* and me, *mechanic.* What a joke that was! I couldn't monitor a pebble from the forge-folk's cave! Not with my matrix still overshadowed by Sharra. . . .

There were technicians and Keepers on Darkover still. Perhaps I could be freed . . . but later, later. The business at hand was trouble enough. Lewis-Kennard Montray-Lanart, Lord Alton, resident of Cottman Four—which is what the Empire calls Darkover—occupation, matrix mechanic, residence, Armida in the Kilghard Hills, temporary residence—I gave them the name of the street and the square of the town house. Damned if I wanted Comyn Castle brought into this! Wife's name: Diotima Ridenow-Montray. Wife's middle name. I didn't think she had any, I said. I was sure she did, and probably didn't use it; half the Ridenow of Serrais named their daughters *Cassilda,* perhaps because there was some doubt about their status as genuine descendants of Hastur and Cassilda, who probably never existed anyhow. Wife's residence. Well, she was certainly in the custody of her brother, so I gave the estate of Serrais, where the Ridenow ought to live, and I heartily wished they were all out there. Reason for dissolution of marriage?

Here I stopped, not sure what to say, and the clerk, who acted as if loves like this were disrupted a hundred times a day, and in the anthill population of the Empire they probably were, told me irritably that I must state a reason for dissolving the marriage. Well, I could hardly say that her brother threatened to murder me otherwise!

The clerk prompted: "Barrenness if you both wish for children; impotence; irreconcilable differences in life-styles; desertion . . ."

That would do; she had certainly deserted me.

But the clerk was yammering on.

"Allergy to the other's planet or residence; failure to support the children of the marriage; inability to father viable offspring if both wish for children . . ."

"That will do," I said, though I knew in principle that this, or barrenness, were seldom actually cited for divorces; usually they cited less offensive reasons by mutual consent, such as desertion or irreconcilable difference of life-styles. But Dio had asked for it, and I would state the real reason.

Slowly he put it into the computer in code; now it was on record that I was incapable of fathering viable offspring. Well, they must have it somewhere in the records of that Terran hospital on Vainwal. . . . what had been born to Dio on that night of disaster. I smothered an agonized picture of

Dio, smiling up at me as she talked about our son . . . no. It was over. She wanted to be free of me, I would not cling to a woman who had every reason to despise me.

While the clerk was finishing up the details, a communicator beeped somewhere, and he answered it, looked up.

"Mr. Montray, if you will stop at the Legate's office on your way out—"

"The Legate?" I asked, raising my eyebrows. I had seen the Terran Legate once, a stuffy functionary named Ramsay, when he attended a conference where I had been Honor Guard; I was still one of my father's officers, then. Perhaps he too wished to pay courtesy condolences after my father's death, the sort of meaningless social formality not limited to Darkover *or* to Terra. The clerk said, "That's finished, then," and I saw our marriage, and our love, reduced to meaningless lines of print, stored somewhere in a computer. The thought filled me with revulsion.

"Is that all there is to it?"

"Unless your wife contests the divorce within a tenday," said the clerk, and I smiled bitterly. She wouldn't. I had caused enough havoc in her life; I could not blame her if she wanted no more.

The clerk pointed me in the direction of the Legate's office, but when I got there, (wishing, because of the stares, that I had worn my hand) I found the Legate was not the man I remembered, but that his name was Dan Lawton.

I had known him briefly. He was actually a distant relative of mine, though closer kin to Dyan—who was, after all, my father's cousin. Lawton's story was something like mine; only reversed, Terran father, a mother who was a kinswoman of Comyn. He could have claimed a seat in Comyn Council if he had chosen; he had chosen otherwise. He was tall and lean, his hair nearer to Comyn red than my own. His greeting was friendly, not over-hearty, and he did not, to my great relief, offer to shake hands; it's a custom I despise, all the more since I had no longer a proper handshake to offer. But he didn't evade my eyes; there are not many men who can, or will, look a telepath full in the eyes.

"I heard about your father," he said. "I suppose you're sick of formal condolences; but I knew him and liked him. So you've been on Terra. Like it there?"

I said edgily, "Are you implying I should have stayed there?"

He shook his head. "Your business. You're Lord Armida now, aren't you?"

"I suppose so. It's up to Council to confirm me."

"We can use friends in Council," he said. "I don't mean spies; I mean people who understand our ways and don't automatically think all Terrans are monsters. Danvan Hastur arranged for your younger brother to be educated here at the Terran HQ; he got the same education a Senator's son would have had: politics, history, mathematics, languages—you might encourage him to go in that direction when he's old enough. I always hoped your father would apply for a place in the Imperial Senate, but I had no chance to persuade him. Maybe your brother."

"That would be one direction for Marius, if the Council won't accept him as my formal Heir," I said, temporizing. It did make more sense than putting him at the head of the Guards. Gabriel wanted *that* and would be good at it. "I'll talk to him about it."

"Before he would be eligible for Imperial Senate," he said, "he must live on at least three different planets for a year apiece, and demonstrate understanding of different cultures. It's not too soon to start arranging it. If he's interested, I'll put him in the way of a minor diplomatic post somewhere—Samarra, perhaps. Or Megaera."

I did not know if Marius was interested in politics. I said so, adding that I would ask him. It might be a viable alternative for my brother.

And I need not test him for the Alton Gift, need not risk his death at my hands . . . as my father had risked mine . . .

"Is he, too, a matrix mechanic?"

I shook my head. "I don't think so. I don't even know how much of a telepath he is."

"There are telepaths on some worlds," he said. "Not many, and this is the only culture where they're really taken for granted. But if he'd be more comfortable on a world where the population accepted telepathic and psi powers as a matter of course—"

"I'll ask him." I hoped that when I broached the subject Marius wouldn't think I was trying to get rid of him. In history, brothers were allies; in fact they had all too often been rivals. Marius ought to know how little I cared to dispute with him for the Domain! I made a move to rise. "Was there anything else?"

"As a matter of fact," Lawton said, "there was. What do you know about a man named Robert Raymon Kadarin?"

I flinched. I knew too much about the accursed traitor Kadarin, who had—once—been friend, almost brother; who had brought the Sharra matrix from its forges, given it over to me, given me these scars, forced Marjorie to the pole of Sharra's power. . . . *no!* I made myself stop thinking about that; my teeth clenched. "He's dead."

"We thought so too," said Lawton. "And even in the course of nature and time, he *ought* to be dead. He was in Terran Intelligence considerably before I was born—hell, before my grandfather was born, which means he's probably about a hundred, or older."

I remembered the gray eyes, colorless. . . . there was *chieri* blood in the Hellers, as there had been in Thyra, in Majorie herself and her unknown mother. And the mountain men with the half-human *chieri* blood were abnormally long-lived, as some of the old Hastur kings had been.

"He's dead anyway if he crosses my path," I said. "His life is mine, where, as and how I can; if I see him, I warn you, I will kill him like a dog."

"Blood-feud—?" Lawton asked, and I said, "Yes." He was one of the few Terrans who would understand. Unsettled blood-feud outweighs any other obligation, in the hills. . . . I could, if need be, stall the formal proceedings for claiming the Alton Domain by speaking of blood-feud in the old way.

I should have killed him before. . . . I thought he was dead. I had been offworld, forgetting my duty, my honor. . . . I thought him dead already. . . . and a voice whispered in my mind, but ready to roar again, *my last command . . . return to Darkover, fight for your brother's rights. . . .* the Alton Domain could not survive with the stain of unsettled blood-feud. . . .

"What makes you think he's alive?" I asked. "And why do you ask me about him anyway? I've been offworld, in any case, even if I hadn't, he'd hardly be likely to hide himself under my cloak!"

"Nobody accused you of sheltering him," Lawton

pointed out. "I understood, though, that you and he were allies during the rebellion and the Sharra troubles, when Caer Donn burned. . . ."

I said quickly, to ward off questions, "No doubt you've heard some of the story from Beltran—"

"I haven't. I've never met the present Lord Aldaran," Lawton said, "though I saw him once. Did you know there's a very strong resemblance? You're cousins, aren't you?"

I nodded. I have seen twins who were less like than Beltran and I; and there had been a time when I had been glad of that resemblance. I said, touching the scars on my face, "We're not so much alike now."

"Still, at a quick look, anyone who knew you both might take either of you for the other," Lawton said. "Half a gram of cosmetic would cover those scars. But that's neither here nor there . . . what did Kadarin have to do with Beltran, and with you?"

I gave him a brief, bald, emotionless outline of the story. Spurred on by Beltran of Aldaran, when old Lord Aldaran—who was my great-uncle—lay dying, the old man who called himself Kadarin had brought the Sharra matrix from the forge-folk.

"The name Kadarin is just defiance," I said. "In the Hellers, any—bastard—is known as a 'son of the Kadarin' and he adopted it."

"He was one of our best intelligence men, before he left the Service," Lawton said, "or so the records say. I wasn't out of school then. Anyhow, there was a price on his head—he'd served on Wolf; nobody knew he'd come back to Darkover until the Sharra trouble broke out."

I fought against a memory: Kadarin, lean, wolfish, smiling, telling me of his travels in the Empire; I had listened with a boy's fascination. So had Marjorie. Marjorie. . . . *time slid, for a moment, I walked the streets of a city which now lay in burned ruins, hand in hand with a smiling girl with amber eyes . . . and we shared a dream which would bring Terran and Darkovan together as equals.*

I told the story flatly, as best I could.

"Beltran, with Kadarin, had a plan, to form a circle around one of the old, high-level matrixes; show the Terrans that we had a technology, a science, of our own. It was one of the matrixes that could power aircraft, mine metals—we thought, when we learned to handle it, we could offer it to the Empire in return for some of the Empire sciences. We formed a circle—a Tower circle, but without a Tower; a mechanic's circle—"

"I'm no expert at matrix technology," said Lawton, "but I know something about it. Go on. Just you and Kadarin and Beltran, or were there others?"

I shook my head. "Beltran's half-sister Thyra; her mother was said to be part *chieri,* a foundling of the forest-folk. She—the *chieri* woman, I don't remember her name—also had two children by one of Lord Aldaran's Terran officers, a Captain Scott."

"I know his son," said Lawton. "Rafael Scott—do you mean to tell me he was one of you? He wouldn't have been more than nine or ten years old, would he? You'd take a *child* into a thing like that?"

"Rafe was twelve," I said, "and his *laran* was awake, or he couldn't have been one of us. You know enough about Darkover to know that if a child's old enough to function as a man—or a woman—then he's old enough, and that's all there is to it. I know you Terrans tend to keep young men and women in the playroom long after they're grown; we don't. Do we have to debate social customs now? Rafe was one of us. And so was Thyra, and so was Rafe's sister Marjorie." And then I stopped. There was no way I could talk about Marjorie; not now, with old wounds torn fresh.

"The matrix got out of control. Half of Caer Donn went up in flames. I suppose you know the story. Majorie died. I—" I shrugged, moving the stump of my arm slightly. "Rafe didn't seem much the worse when I saw him last. But I thought Kadarin, and Thyra, were both dead."

"I don't know about the woman," Lawton said. "I haven't heard. Wouldn't know her if she walked into this office. But Kadarin's alive. He was seen in Thendara, less than a tenday ago."

"If he's alive, she's alive," I said. "Kadarin would have died before letting her be hurt." Guilt clawed me again; *as I should have died before Marjorie, Marjorie . . .* and then I had a disquieting thought. Thyra was Aldaran as well as *chieri.* Had she foreseen the return of Sharra to Darkover . . . and come to Thendara, drawn by that irresistible pull, even before I knew, myself, that I would bring it back?

Were we nothing more than pawns of that damned thing?

Lawton said, "What *is* Sharra? Just a matrix—"

"It's that, certainly," I said. "A very high-level one; ninth or tenth," and I forestalled his question. "In general, a ninth-level matrix is a matrix which can only be operated or controlled by at least nine qualified telepaths of mechanic level."

"But I gather it's more—"

"Yes," I said. "It's probably—I'm not sure what it is. The forge-folk thought it was the talisman controlling a Goddess who brought fire to their forges . . . "

Lawton said, "I was not asking for an account of Darkovan superstitions about Sharra. I've heard the stories of the flame-hair—"

"They're not stories," I said. "You weren't there when Caer Donn burned, were you? Sharra *appeared*—and struck fire down on the ships—"

He said restlessly, "Hypnotism. Hallucination."

"But the fire was real," I said, "and believe me, the Form of Fire is real." I shut my eyes as if I could see it there, as if my matrix was keyed to the burning in that older, larger matrix—

Lawton may have had a touch of *laran;* I have never been sure. Many Terrans do, not knowing what it is or how to use it. He asked, "Do you suppose he came to Thendara because you were here—to try and recover the Sharra matrix?"

That was what I feared. Above all, that was what I feared; the matrix in the hands of Kadarin again . . .

and I unwilling slave to the matrix, burning, burning, sealed to the form of fire . . . "I would kill him before that," I said.

Lawton's eyes dwelt a moment past courtesy on my one hand. Then he said, "There is a price on his head in the Empire. And you are an Empire citizen. If you like, I will issue you a weapon, to protect yourself against a known criminal under sentence of death, and give you the legal right to execute him."

To my eternal shame, I considered it; I was afraid of Kadarin. And the ethics of the Compact—my father said it cynically once—crumble in the face of fear or personal advantage. Regis Hastur's father had died, twenty years ago, leaving the Domains to be ruled by an unborn son, because some band of rebels had accepted contraband weapons with what, I am sure, they thought were reasons important enough to overthrow their allegiance to Compact.

Then I said, with a shudder, "Forget it. I may not be much good with a sword just now, but I doubt if I can shoot well enough to make it worth the trouble. I'll fight him if I must. He'll have the Sharra matrix only over my dead body."

"Your dead body wouldn't do any of us a damned bit of good if Kadarin had the Sharra matrix," said Lawton impatiently, "and I'm not concerned at this moment with your honor or the Compact. Would you consider moving the matrix—and yourself—into the Terran Zone so that we could protect you with effective weapons?"

This was a Darkovan affair. Should I hide behind the hem of a Terran's robe, guarded by their guns and blasters, coward's weapons?

"Stubborn damned fool," Lawton said without heat. "I can't force you, but be careful, damn it, be careful, Lew." It was the first time he had called me by my name, and even through my anger, I was warmed; I needed friends, even Terran friends. And I respected this man. He said, "If you change your mind, or want a gun, or a bodyguard with a gun, tell me. We need friends in Council, remember."

I said reluctantly, "I can't promise to be your friend, Lawton."

He nodded and said, "I understand. But—" he hesitated and looked me straight in the eye, "I can promise to be yours. Remember that if you need it. And my offer stands."

I thought about that, as I went out, and down the long elevators and lifts to the ground level. Outside the wind was chilly, and the sky was covered with cloud; later it would snow. I was amazed how quickly my weather skills returned to me. Snow, at high summer! Not unprecedented. Once a summer snow had saved Armida, in a terrifying forest fire when half our buildings had gone up in the backfire. But not common, either, and perhaps an omen of ill-luck. Well, that would be no surprise.

* * *

I didn't tarry to look at the starships. I had seen enough of them. Quickly, drawing my cloak close about my shoulders against the chill, I walked through the streets. I should move as quickly as possible, back into the Alton apartments in Comyn Castle, establish possession; show that I regarded myself as legitimate head of the Alton Domain, Lord Armida. The Sharra matrix too, left alone in the town house, safeguarded only by the fact that no one knew where it was—it too would be safer in Comyn Castle. Better yet, take it to the Comyn Tower and ask my cousin Callina, who was Keeper now for the incredibly ancient keeper there, old Ashara, to put it in the Tower matrix laboratory under a matrix lock. Kadarin could break into the town house, he might even manage to break into the Castle, but I did not believe he could break into a matrix-locked laboratory in Comyn Tower, in the hands and under the wardship of a Keeper. But if he could do that, then we were all dead anyhow and it did not matter.

Having made this resolve, I felt better. It was good to breathe, not the mechanical smells of the Terran Zone, but the clean natural smells of my own part of the city; spices from a cookshop, heat from a forge where someone was shoeing a string of pack animals; a group of Renunciates, their hair cut so short it was hard to tell whether they were men or women, dressed in bulky trail clothing, readying an expedition into the hills; a shrouded and heavily veiled lady in a sedan chair in the midst of them. The clean smell of animals, fresh smells of garden plants. Thendara was a beautiful city, though I would rather have been out in the Kilghard Hills. . . .

I could go. I owned estates that needed me. Armida was mine now . . . my home. But it was Council season and I was needed here. . . .

Across a square I heard a soft call and challenge; a patrol of young Guardsmen. I looked up, and Dyan Ardais left the patrol and came striding toward me, his military cloak flying briskly behind him.

This encounter was the last thing I wanted. As a boy I had detested Dyan with a consuming hatred; older, I had wondered whether a part of my dislike might not be that he had been my father's friend, and I, bastard, lonely, friendless, had envied every attention that my father had paid to anyone else. The unhealthy closeness between my father and myself had not all been his doing, and I knew that now. In any case, Kennard was dead and, one way or another, I must free myself of his influence, the real or imagined voice in my mind.

Dyan was my kinsman, he was Comyn, and he had befriended my brother and my father. So I greeted him civilly enough, and he returned the formal greeting, Comyn to Comyn, the first time in my life that he had greeted me as an equal.

Then he dropped formality and said, "I need to talk to you, cousin." The word, a degree more intimate than "kinsman," seemed to come as hard to him as to me. I shrugged, though I wasn't pleased. The talk with Lawton had made me, even more than before, desperately uneasy about the Sharra matrix; I wanted it put into a safe place before anyone—for anyone read *Kadarin,* who was the only one I knew who could get it—could know its presence on Darkover through the reawakening of his matrix—and if that had happened to my matrix, it would certainly have happened to his. And once he knew the matrix was back on Darkover, what would he do? I didn't have to ask; I knew.

"There's a tavern; will you drink with me? I need to talk with you, cousin,"

I hesitated; I'm not that much of a drinker at any time. "It's early for me, thank you. And I am rather in a hurry. Can it wait?"

"I'd rather not," said Dyan. "But I'll walk with you, if you like." Too late I realized: it had been meant as a friendly gesture. I shrugged. "As you like. I don't know this end of the city so well."

The tavern was clean enough, and not too dark, though my spine prickled a little as I went into the unlighted room, Dyan behind me. He evidently knew the place, because the potboy brought him a drink without asking. He poured some for me; I put out my hand to stop him.

"Only a little, thanks." It was more a ritual than anything else; we drank together, and at the back of my mind I thought, if my father knew, he would have been pleased to see me drinking in all amiability with his oldest friend. Well, I could do that much homage to his memory. He caught my eye and I knew he shared the thought; we drank silently to my father's peace.

"We'll miss him in Council," Dyan said. "He knew all the Terran ways and wasn't seduced by them. I wonder—" and his eyes dwelt on me a moment past courtesy, looking at the scar, the folded sleeve. But I was enough used to that. I said, "I'm not exactly enthralled by the Terran—more strictly, by the Empire ways. Terra itself—" I shrugged. "I suppose it's a beautiful world, if you can stand living under a yellow sun and having the colors all wrong. There's a certain—status—in being of old Terran stock, or living there, but I didn't like it. As for the Empire—"

"You lived on Vainwal a long time," he said, "and you're not a decadent like Lerrys, bound on pleasure and—exotic entertainment."

It was half a question. I said, "I can live without Empire luxuries. Father found the climate good for his health. I—" I broke off, wondering just why I had stayed. Inertia, deadly lassitude, one place no worse than another to me, until I met Dio, and then any place as good as another, as long as she was with me. If Dio had asked me, would I have come back to Darkover? Probably, if the subject had been broached before it became impossible for her to travel. Why had we not come before she became pregnant? At least, here, she could have been monitored, we would have had some forewarning of the tragedy—I stopped myself. Done was done; we had done the best we could, unknowing, and I would not carry that burden of guilt along with all the rest.

"I stayed with Father. After he died, he wanted me to come back; it was his dying wish." I said it gingerly, afraid the clamor in my mind would begin again, once invoked, but it was only a whisper.

"You could hold Kennard's place in Council," he said, "and have the same kind of power he held."

My face must have flinched, because he said half angrily, "Are you a fool? You are needed in Council, provided you don't take the part of the Ridenow and try to pull us all into the Empire!"

I shook my head. "I'm no politician, Lord Dyan. And—without offense—I'd like a little time to size it up on my own, before being told what to think by each of the interested parties!"

I had expected him to fly into a rage at the rebuke, but he only grinned, that fierce and wolfish grin which was, in its own way, handsome. "Good enough; at least you're capable of thinking. While you're sizing up the situation, try and take the measure of our prince. There's precedent enough—Council knew my own father was mad as a *kyorebni* in the Ghost wind, and they took care to draw his fangs."

They had appointed Dyan his father's regent, and in one of the old man's lucid intervals, old Dom Kyril had agreed to it. But I said, "Derik has no near kinsman; isn't he the only adult Elhalyn?"

"His sisters are married," Dyan said, "though not, perhaps, as near to nobility as they would have been if we had known one of their husbands might have to be regent of the Elhalyns. Old Hastur wants to set Regis up in Derik's place, but the boy's kicking about that, and who can blame him? It's enough to rule over Hastur, without a crown as well. A crown is nonsense in these days, of course; what we need is a strong Council of equals. And there's the Guard—not that a few dozen men carrying swords can do much against the Terrans, but they can keep our own people on the right side of the wall."

"Who's commanding the Guard now?" I asked, and he shrugged.

"Anybody. Nobody. Gabriel, mostly. I took it myself for the first two years—Gabriel seemed a bit young." I remembered Dyan had been one of the best officers. "After that it went to him."

"He's welcome to it," I said. "I never had much taste for soldiering."

"It goes with the Domain," Dyan said fiercely. "I suppose you would be willing to do your duty and command it?"

"I'll have to get my bearings first," I said, and then I was angry. "Which is more important? To get someone who's competent at commanding the Guards, and likes it, or to get someone who has the right blood in his veins?"

"They're both important," he said, and he was deadly serious. "Especially in these times. With the Hasturs gobbling up one Domain after another, Gabriel's *exactly* the wrong man to command the Guards; you should force the issue and take them away from him as soon as possible."

I almost laughed. "Force the issue? Gabriel could tie me up into a bow for his wife's hair, and do it with one hand tied—" I broke off; that particular figure of speech was, to say the least, unfortunate. "I could hardly fight a duel with him; are you suggesting assassination?"

"I think the Guard would be loyal to you for your father's sake."

"Maybe."

"And if you don't take over the Guard? What are you intending to do? Go back to Armida and raise horses?" He put all his scorn into the words. Pain flooded through me, remembering how I had wanted to take my son there. "I could probably do worse."

"Just sit at home and attend to your own affairs while Darkover falls into Empire hands?" he asked scornfully. "You might as well hide behind Tower walls! Why not go back with Jeff to Arilinn—or did they burn *that* out of you too?"

Rage flooded through me. How dared Dyan, under the pretense of kinship and his friendship for my father, probe old, unhealed wounds this way? "I was taught at Arilinn," I said deliberately, "to speak of such matters only to those who were concerned in them. Are you monitor, mechanic, or technician, Lord Dyan?"

I had always thought that the phrase *black with rage* was only a manner of speaking; now I saw it, the blood rising dark and congested in Dyan's face until I thought he would fall down, stricken by a stroke. Too late, I remembered; Dyan had been briefly in a Tower, and no one, not even my father, knew why he had left it. What I had meant as a freezing rebuke, a way of telling him to keep his distance, had been interpreted as deadly personal insult—an attack on his weakest spot.

"Neither monitor, mechanic nor technician, damn you," he said at last, his chair going over backward as he rose, "nor power-pole for the forces of Sharra, you damned insolent bastard! Go back to Armida and raise horses, or to a Tower if they'll have you, or back to the Empire, or to hell if Zandru will take you in, but stay out of Council politics—hear me?"

He turned and strode away, and I stared after him, in shock and dismay, knowing I had made, from a man who had been ready to befriend me, the most dangerous of enemies.

CHAPTER FIVE

The Comyn Tower rose high above the Castle, part of the great sprawling mass that looked down on Thendara, and yet apart from it, older than any part of it; immeasurably old, built of an ancient reddish sandstone which, otherwise, appeared only in the oldest, ruined houses of the Old Town. Regis had never come here before.

He said to the nonhuman servant, "Will you ask the *Domna* Callina Lindir-Aillard if she will receive Regis Hastur?"

It surveyed him for a long moment, the dark eyes alert and responsive; a humanlike form, a humanlike intelligence, but Regis could not dismiss the feeling that he had been speaking to a large and not altogether friendly dog. He had seen the silver-furred *kyrri* during his brief training session in Neskaya Tower; but he had never grown used to them. The thing stared at him longer, he thought, than a human would have done. Then it gave a brief graceful nod of its sleek silver head and glided noiselessly away.

Regis wondered, remotely and at the edge of awareness, how the *kyrri* would deliver its message to Callina. The origin of the *kyrri* was lost in the Ages of Chaos—had they, after all, been part of that monstrous breeding program which the Hastur-kin had carried on for centuries to fix the Comyn gifts in the families of the Seven Domains? Stranger games than the *kyrri* had been played with genetics modified by *laran* power and matrix technology.

Or did they go back further yet, part of the prehistory of Cottman's star before a lost Terran colony came to call it Darkover? He suspected that even in the Towers they were not sure what the *kyrri* were or how they had come to be traditional servants of the Tower. He took them for granted, had learned to stay out of range of the painful electric shocks they could give when they were excited or threatened, had been tended by their odd thumbless hands when it would have been unendurable to have near him human telepaths who could read his mind or reach it.

But all this was with the surface of his mind and had nothing to do with the underlying unease which had brought him here; and for a moment he wondered if he should have sought out Callina in the Aillard suite, presuming somewhat on his acquaintance with Linnell—who, like himself, had been fostered at Armida and was foster-sister to Lew and Marius. He had never spoken more than a dozen words to Callina, and those formal and ceremonious. He could have talked to Linnell as to a kinswoman, but Callina was something else again . . . Keeper at Neskaya and then at Arilinn, then sent here to be under-Keeper in the oldest of the Towers, long inactive, but still sheltering the ancient Ashara, who had not been seen outside the Tower in living memory—nor, Danvan Hastur had told him once, in the living memory of anyone *he* had ever known; and his grandfather was nearing his hundredth year. He supposed Ashara's own circle, if she had one, and her attendants, must see her sometime. . . .

She must have been an ordinary woman once; at least as ordinary as any of the Comyn could be said to be ordinary; and not immortal, only long-lived as some of the Hasturs were long-lived. There was *chieri* blood mixed with the blood of the Domains. Regis knew little of the *chieri*, but they were said to be immortal and beautiful, still dwelling somewhere in a remote valley where humankind never came. But his own grandfather showed signs of being one of those Hasturs whose reign could span generations . . . *it was a lucky thing for the Comyn, that Danvan Hastur had been there to reign as Regent during these troubled years* . . . Regis found his thoughts sliding into unexpected channels, as if some other mind had briefly touched his own; he started, blinked as if he had fallen asleep on his feet for a moment; his skin crawled, and something *touched* him . . . . Regis felt a faint nausea deep in his body. A shadow had fallen across the doorway and Callina Aillard was standing there.

He had not seen her come. *Lord of Light!* Regis swore to himself, sweating; had he stood there, sound asleep on his feet, an idiot's grin on his face, his clothing disarranged or worse? He felt exposed, desperately uncomfortable; Callina was a Keeper, and uncanny. He managed to get out a formal, *Su serva, Domna* . . ."

She was not now wearing the formal crimson robes she had worn in the Crystal Chamber, the traditional garb which marked out a Keeper as apart, untouchable, sacrosanct. Instead she had on a long, fleecy gown of blue wool, close-cut, high-necked. It was girdled with a copper belt, squared plaques of the precious metal, a large blue semiprecious stone at the center of each plaque; and her hair, coiled low on her neck, was caught into a priceless clasp of copper filigree.

"Come through here, and then we can talk if you wish. Hush; do not disturb the relays." Her voice was so low it barely stirred the air between them, and Regis followed on tiptoe, as if a normal step would be like a shout. They passed through a large silent chamber, bare, with relay screens staring blank and glassy blue, and other things which Regis did not recognize; before one of the screens a young girl was curled up on a soft seat. Her face had the strange, not-quite-present look of a telepath whose mind was fixed in the relays communicating with other Towers, other telepaths. Regis did not know the girl and Callina of course did not notice her in any way; in fact, only her body was there in the room with them at all.

Callina opened a noiseless door at the far end of the room, and they went through into a small, comfortable private room, with low divans and chairs, and a high window with colored glass, throwing prism lights across the room; but it was dark outside, and if it had not been high summer Regis would have thought it might be snowing. Callina shut the door soundlessly behind them, gestured him to a seat and curled up in one of them herself, tucking her feet under her, and drawing the hem of the blue gown over them. She said in her stilled voice, "Well, Regis, did Old Hastur send you to me to ask if I'd go through the marriage ceremony with Beltran, just to save the Council some embarrassment?"

Regis felt his face burning; had she read his mind while he stood there, asleep on his feet like a gaby? He said truthfully, "No, he didn't, though he did mention it to me at dinner last night. I don't think he would have the arrogance actually to ask it, Lady Callina."

Callina said, sighing, "Derik is an accursed fool. And I had no idea what that foolish brother of mine was doing behind my back, or that Derik was stupid enough to listen to him. Linnell loves Derik; it would break her heart to separate them now. How she can care for such a fool—!" Callina shook her head in exasperation. "Merryl's never reconciled himself to being born an Aillard, and subject to the female Head of the Domain. And I doubt he ever will."

"Grandfather did suggest that you might go through the ceremony—no more than that—as a matter of form," Regis said.

"It might be easier than telling Beltran what he otherwise must say to him," Callina said, "that this marriage was contrived by a young man greedy for power and a prince too dull to see how he's being manipulated."

"Don't forget," Regis said dryly, "a Regent too lazy or forgetful to keep a strong hand over his not-too-intelligent princeling."

"Do you really think it was only laziness or forgetfulness?" Callina asked, and Regis said, "I don't like to think my grandfather would have plotted against the Head of a Domain. . . ."

Then he remembered a conversation he had had with Danilo three years ago, as fresh as today: *so Domain after Domain falls into Hastur hands; the Elhalyn is already under Hastur Regency, then the Aillard with Derik married to Linnell,* Regis thought, all the easier if Callina was married off and exiled in distant Aldaran. And he had watched his grandfather's machinations against the Altons.

"No, he couldn't plot it," Callina said, and a faint smile stirred her lips, "but he could sit back while Merryl and that fool of a Derik create such a situation that I must fall into place or seriously embarrass the Comyn."

"Callina, even Hastur cannot marry off the Head of a Domain without her own consent. And you are Keeper for Ashara; what will she say to that?"

"Ashara . . ." Callina was silent for a moment, as if the very sound of the name stirred unease in her calm face. She looked troubled. "I seldom see Ashara. She spends much of her time in meditation. I could hold all her power in the Council, but I am afraid—" she stopped herself in mid-sentence. "You are not Tower-trained, Regis?"

He shook his head. "I had enough training so that I could manage my Gift without becoming ill, but I'm not that powerful a telepath, and Grandfather needed me in Thendara, he said."

"I think you are more of a telepath than you believe, kinsman," Callina said, with a skeptical look.

The quiet, assured statement somehow made him uneasy; he frowned, ready to protest. "I'm useless in the relays, and they couldn't teach me much about monitoring—"

"That may be," she said. "In the Towers we test only for those gifts which are useful to their functions; monitoring, the skill to stay in rapport with a matrix screen for mining and manipulating power. . . . in this day and age, that seems the only kind of *laran* the Towers find useful. But you are finding out that there is more to your *laran* than you believed—is it not so, cousin?"

Regis flinched as if she had put her fingers directly on a bruise he did not know he had.

"You had better tell me about it," she said, "I saw how you had picked up the presence of Sharra, in Council. Let me see your matrix, Regis."

Apprehensively, Regis touched the small velvet bag, undid the strings, tilted the small blue crystal into his palm. It lay there blue and placid, small distant lights glimmering inside the stone; no sign of fire, no sign of the ravening Form of Fire . . .

"It's gone!" he said in surprise.

"And you expected it to be there," Callina said. "Really, I think you had better tell me everything about it."

Regis was still staring at his matrix in disbelief. After a moment he managed to blurt out something about it; how Javanne had been trapped by the image, how he had, without thinking about it, freed her mind from the matrix.

"It was like—I watched her, once, unpicking a design that had gone wrong in her tapestry—I think it must have felt like that, though I don't know how to do tapestry. . . ."

"I do," Callina said, "and that's just what it would have felt like."

"What did I do?" Regis had not known how frightened he was until he heard his own voice trembling. "How could I do that? I thought—it would take a powerful telepath, perhaps a Keeper—to match resonances like that—"

"There have been male Keepers in history," Callina said abstractedly. "Good ones, powerful ones. Only for the last few hundred years have Keepers been women. And until a few generations ago, they were locked up, treated like sorceresses, sacred virgins, ritual objects of great power and veneration." Her face was cool, ironic. "Now, of course, in these enlightened days, we know better . . . a Keeper today need be no more than centerpolar—the center of their matrix circles, the one who holds the energon rings. Regis, have you had enough Tower training to have the faintest idea what I'm talking about?"

"I think so. I know the language, though I don't think I really understand it all. They never thought I had had enough strength as a telepath to let me work in a circle, and besides, I was needed here. But if I wasn't even able to work as a monitor, I couldn't have done a Keeper's work, not completely untrained, not like that, could I?" His voice cracked, but he was not quite so afraid; Callina had talked about it as a technical problem, not some strange and terrifying flaw in himself.

"But a Keeper's work, in these days, is no more than any well-trained technician can do, as I said," she told him. "Kennard was a technician, and he could do almost everything Elorie of Arilinn could do, except actually hold the center of a circle. I think Jeff could do that if he had to, if tradition would let him. And you're a Hastur, and your mother was Hastur of Elhalyn—what do you know about the Hastur Gift, Regis?"

"Not much," he said frankly. "When I was a boy, a *leronis* told me I had not even the ordinary *laran.*" The memory of that, as always, was multiple layers of pain, the sense that he was unworthy to follow in the steps of the forefather Hasturs who had come before him; and at the same time freedom, freedom from the path laid out for the Hastur sons, a path he must walk whether he would or no . . .

"But your laran wakened . . ." she said, half a question, and he nodded. Danilo Syrtis, friend, paxman, sworn brother, and the last known to hold the almost-extinct gift of catalyst telepathy—Danilo had wakened Regis's *laran,* given him the heritage of the Comyn; but it was not altogether a blessing, for it had meant the loss of his freedom. Now he must shoulder the burden, take up the heritage of all the Hasturs, and abandon his dream of freedom from those unendurable bonds. . . .

I have been a good Heir to the Hasturs; I have done my

duty, commanded in the Guard, sat in the Council, adopted the son of my sister for an Heir in turn. I have even given sons and daughters to the Hastur clan, even though I would not marry the women who bore them to me. . . .

"I know something of those bonds," she said, and it seemed to him that her passionless voice was sympathetic. "I am a Keeper, Regis, not a Keeper in the new way, only a highly specialized technician, but Keeper in the old way; I was trained under Elorie of Arilinn. She was Dyan's half-sister, you know . . . Cleindori, Dorilys of Arilinn, freed the Keepers by reducing the old superstition to what they now call the science of matrix mechanics, and now the Keepers need not give up their lives, and live cloistered, virgin . . . but I had been trained in the old fashion, Regis, and after I had served at Arilinn and Neskaya, then I came here, just *because* I was the only woman in the Domains who had been trained in the ancient way. Ashara demanded it, and I, who had had the ancient training and was still virgin, because I had never felt any wish to marry, or leave my post even for a few years to marry or take a lover. . . ." her smile was faint, almost absent. "I was content with my work, nor had I ever met any man who would tempt me to leave my calling. So I was sent, willy-nilly, to serve under Ashara, I who was ruler of a Domain in my own right . . . simply because I was what I was." For a moment it seemed that there was terror in her eyes, and he wondered: *is she so afraid of Ashara?* Fear seemed an unlikely emotion for a Keeper.

What had women to be afraid of? They didn't have to fight in the coming wars, they would be safe and protected. . . .

She said, "What do you know of the Hastur Gift?" again, insistently.

"Not much, as I told you. I grew up thinking I didn't even have ordinary *laran*. . . ."

"But whatever it may be, it's latent in you," she mused.

He asked her point-blank, "Do *you* know what the Hastur Gift is?"

She said, biting her lip, "Ashara must know . . ." and he wondered what that had to do with it. As if speaking to herself, she said, "The Ardais Gift; catalyst telepathy, the ability to awaken *laran* in others. The Ridenow make the best monitors because they are empaths . . . the Gifts are all so muddled, now, by inbreeding, by marriage with non-telepaths, it's rare to find the full strength of any of the old Gifts. And there is so much superstition and tradition cluttering any clear knowledge of the Gifts . . . there is a tradition that the original Gift of the Hasturs may have been what was trained into the Keepers: the ability to work with other matrixes, without the elaborate safeguards a Keeper must have. Originally the word Keeper—" she used the casta, *tenerésteis*—"meant *one who holds, one who guards* . . . a Keeper, in the simplest terms, putting aside a Keeper's function of working at the center of the energon rings, is one who keeps the other matrixes in the group resonating together; it's a special skill of working with other matrixes, not just her own. As I say, some high-level technicians can do it. I wonder . . ." she hesitated a little, then said, "Hasturs, in general, are long-lived and mature late. Ordinary *laran* waked in you late—you were fifteen, weren't you? And perhaps that was only a first stirring of the *laran* you will eventually have. How old are you now? Twenty-one? That would mean your matrix was wakened at about the time as the Sharra troubles—"

"I was in the mountains then; and my matrix was overshadowed, like all the matrixes in the vicinity of the Sharra matrix," Regis said.

And he had, furthermore, been going through an intolerable personal crisis with the wakening of his heritage; his decision to accept himself as he was, and not as his grandfather and the Comyn wanted him to be; to accept self-knowledge and the unwanted burden of the Hasturs, or to bury it all, live a life without either, an uncomprehending, unburdened life without *laran,* without responsibility. But now there was this new dimension to his *laran,* and he could not even guess what further burdens it would demand of him.

"Let me be sure about this," Callina said. "While you were in the mountains during the Sharra rebellion, your matrix was overshadowed; you could not use it because of—of what I saw in Lew's at that time: the Form of Fire. But later, when Sharra was offworld—"

"It was clear," he said, "and I learned to use it, my matrix I mean, without any sign of Sharra. Only when Lew brought the Sharra matrix back to Darkover—"

She nodded. "And yet, you cleared your matrix," she said. "It will be easy enough to see if you have natural talent for a Keeper's skills." She unrolled her own from the tiny leather bag at her throat. She held it naked on her palm and said, "Can you match resonances and touch it without hurting me?"

Regis looked away, gulping; his mind was full of that day in Castle Aldaran, when he had seen Kadarin strip away Lew's matrix and send Lew to the floor in violent convulsions, a shrieking mindless wreck . . . He muttered, "I wouldn't know where to start. And I'd be afraid to try. I could—I could kill you."

She shook her head. "No, you couldn't, not here, not safeguarded as I am," she said. "Try it."

Her voice was low and indifferent, but it was a command, and Regis, sweating, tried to think himself into the blue crystal that lay in Callina's palm. He tried to remember how he had gone into Javanne's mind, reaching out to unpick her mind from the matrix as if it were interwoven threads of tapestry. . . . He felt a strange, unpleasant force against his mind and moved squeamishly against it. *Was that Callina?* He glanced up, hesitant, unable to reconcile that cold stony force with the smiling, gentle woman before him.

"I—can't," he said.

"Forget about me! Match resonances with the matrix, I said!"

This is foolish. I have known Callina most of my life. It is absurd to be afraid of her! He reached out again, tentative, feeling the pulsing life-force, her guarded thoughts—she had the strongest barrier he had ever touched; he supposed it had something to do with being a Keeper. He caught only fragments, the light hurting her eyes from a window, subliminal awareness of him, Regis, *he's a good-looking boy,* how tired he was of that reaction from women. . . . Again he felt the pulsing of the matrix, tried to match his breathing against it. . . . A face sketched itself lightly on his mind, cold, distant, making him shiver as if he stood naked in frost . . . beautiful, terrible, alien. . . . He banished that, too, and the fear, and forced himself into the matrix, feeling the resonance, the cold life of stone, the glowing lights in tune with his breathing, the blood in his veins . . . He felt himself reach out, not conscious of movement, and closed his fingers over it, lifting it lightly from her hand. . . . distant cold eyes, gray and colorless as metal. . . . Cold seas washing over his mind. . . .

Pain splintered through Callina's head and Regis quickly let the matrix go, tilting it back into her hand. She blinked and he felt her controlling the stab of pain. She said, "Well, you have the talent for that . . . but I don't know how much further it goes. I saw something, like a vision . . ." She was fumbling for words; she felt him share the fumbling and stopped it cold.

It was not at all like his contact with Javanne; it was not at all like the contact he had had with any of the women who had briefly been his lovers. . . . was it because she was a Keeper, that cold stony alien thing in her mind, a *leronis* of the old kind, vowed to virginity, to touch no man with even a hint of sexuality? *Or had it been Callina at all?* His own head was aching.

She said, "If you can do that, and if you could clear a matrix which had touched Sharra. . . ." She bit her lip and he saw the pain move across her face again. "You have a gift we don't know about. Maybe it can be helpful . . ." and he picked up the words she was hesitant to speak, *perhaps it could help to control the Sharra matrix, free Kennard's son from the domination of that—that terrible thing. . . .*

A second of terror; something greedy, ravenous, reaching out . . .

Then it was gone, or had it ever been there? "Go and tell Lew Alton that he should bring the Sharra matrix here, where it will be safe. . . . there is no time to lose. Perhaps you can help to free him . . ."

"I'd be afraid to try," he said, shaking.

"But you must not be afraid," she said, demanding. "If you have such a Gift as that . . ." and Regis felt she was not seeing him as a human being, not as Regis at all, just as a Gift, a strange and puzzling problem for a matrix technician, something to be solved and unraveled. It troubled him; for a moment he wanted to force her to see him as a human, a man standing before a woman; she was all cool aloofness, the woman in her subdued, her features cold and static, and for an instant Regis remembered the curious stony face that had briefly crossed his mind like a vision in the matrix. . . . *Was that Callina too? Which was real?* Then, so swiftly he could not be sure of it, it was gone, and Callina was only a frail-looking woman, slender, troubled, in a fuzzy blue robe, looking up at him and pressing her temples with her two hands as if they hurt her.

She said, "You must go now, but make sure the Sharra matrix is brought here . . ." and opened the door into the relay chamber. But as they went through, the young girl curled up before the relay screen raised her head and beckoned, and Callina, motioning Regis to go out into the outer chamber, stole on silent feet to her side. After a few minutes she joined him in the outer chamber. Her face was white, and she looked dazed.

"It is worse than I thought," she said. "Lilla has had word from the relays. . . . Beltran has set forth. And he is traveling with an escort so great that it could be called an army. He will be here by Festival Night, here at our gates in Thendara. Merciful Avarra," she whispered, "this will mean war in the Domains! How could Hastur allow this to happen? How could even Merryl do this to me? Does he really hate me that much?"

And Regis had no answer for her.

Because there was nothing else to do, he went back to his own rooms, half intending to face his grandfather, to tell him that Derik's plan had borne unexpected fruit; that it could indeed mean war in the Domains if Callina refused to do their will. But his grandfather's steward told him that the Regent had gone to confer with the *cortes,* and Regis set out for the Alton town house. At least he could convey the message that the Sharra matrix would be safer in the Comyn Tower.

But as he neared the house, he saw a familiar figure in the green and black of the Alton Domain. Lew had changed in the intervening years; Regis had barely recognized him in Council; but his walk was unchanged, and Regis recognized him now, though his back was turned. Regis walked faster to catch up with him, hesitant about reaching out for the old touch of minds.

But Lew must have sensed a presence behind him, for he turned and waited for Regis to come up with him.

"Well, Regis, it's been a long time."

"It has, cousin," said Regis, and took him into a kinsman's embrace, pressing his cheek to the scarred face. He stood back and smiled. "I was coming to find you, and here you are in my pathway . . . where are you going so early?"

"Not as early as all that," Lew said, looking into the sky with a practiced eye. "Not too early for Dyan to offer me a drink, or for a quarrel—damn him!"

"Dyan's not a good man to quarrel with," said Regis soberly, "How did you get into that?"

Lew sighed. "I hardly know. Something he said to me—I suppose what he really meant was, *go to hell*, some version of, *you've offended me,* but it sounded like a declaration of war. I—" he broke off, troubled. "Will you walk with me to my house? I'm uneasy, for no reason at all. But I wanted to talk to you."

"And I had a message for you from the *leronis,*" Regis said. He started to speak, then stopped, overcome by an overpowering conviction that he should not speak that ill-omened name, *Sharra,* here in the street. That was for privacy, and a well-shielded room. Instead he said, "You should move back into the Comyn Castle, into the Alton suite. It's expected at Council season, and if you're actually inhabiting the proper quarters, they'll have a harder time challenging your rights . . ."

"I've thought of that," Lew said, "The Terrans have a saying; possession is nine points of the law. Though I don't think I have to worry about Jeff, and the main problem may be to get them to accept Marius as my Heir. I don't know if he's even had the regular testing when he was thirteen or so—we haven't had any time to talk about such things."

"It may not mean anything," Regis said, "even if he has; remember, they told me I had no *laran* at all." Briefly, there was an old memory of bitterness. "At least if Marius turns out *not* to have laran, you won't send him to Nevarsin, will you, to be brought up there?"

"Not unless he wants to go," Lew said amiably. "A lad who's of a scholarly turn and wants a good education might enjoy the chance to study there, but Marius, I've heard, has already had the best education the Terrans could give. I owe your grandfather thanks for arranging that."

"He didn't do it to please you. On the contrary." It had been, and they both knew it, a way of emphasizing that Marius must seek his destiny among Terrans, not his father's people. "While you were away, I suppose you learned much of what the Terrans had to offer. . . ."

"Not as much as I'd have liked to; I was in hospitals a good deal of the time," Lew said, and behind his scarred face Regis sensed much of what Lew would never tell him, pain and final acceptance of mutilation. "But while I was convalescing, yes, I'd have gone mad without something to do. I tried some surveying, map-making; there are parts of the Kilghard Hills, and most of the Hellers, that have never been properly mapped. Better to do it ourselves than to let the Terrans do it because we can't be bothered to teach our own people measurements. It seems preposterous, that *they* have a Mapping and Survey unit on Darkover, and we don't!"

Regis said, "I've thought of having my sons educated by the Terrans. Though, I suppose, I'd have to fight grandfather every step of the way. It might be better to have someone who's had a Terran education—like Marius, or you—educate them, instead of sending them offworld, or into the Trade City—"

Lew said, with that sudden irradiating smile which made Regis, finally and forever, forget the gargoyle scarring of the face, "I've lived in the empire too long; you seem young to me to have a family. But you're twenty-one now, I should have known Hastur would have married you off long since. I'd be proud to foster your sons. Who is your wife? How many children—"

Regis shook his head. "That's been a constant argument with Grandfather, too. But I adopted my sister's son, just before you went offworld—" He paused, hesitant, remembering; Lew had been in no state to remember that. But Lew nodded and said, "I remember. You told me at Aldaran."

"I have a *nedestro* son and two daughters," Regis said. "The oldest is past three; in a couple more years, I shall bring him before the Council. And Mikhail is already eleven. When he is twelve, I shall bring him to Thendara and take his education into my own hands." He grinned and said, "I've had a lot of experience fighting Grandfather on that subject; I suppose I can supervise my son's education. I won't let him grow up ignorant."

"You're right, we've kept to the old ways too long," Lew said. "I remember my father saying that when he was fifteen, he was an officer in the Guards, but he could neither read nor write, and was proud of it; when he went among the Terrans, they thought him an idiot because no one with a sound mind is allowed to let it lie fallow—"

"The monks at Nevarsin deplore it just as much as a Terran would," Regis said. "I ought to be grateful to Grandfather that he made certain I had that much education at least." In Nevarsin monastery, he had at least learned to read and write, done some elementary ciphering, and read such Darkovan history as was available, which wasn't much.

"Kennard had me taught to read and write, though I must admit I wasn't tremendously apt at either," Lew said. "Lying in the hospital, I made up for lost time; but boys are still being brought up as if it was unmanly—I imagine it's because a scholar hasn't enough time to master weapons, and of course when the Domains were one constant battleground year after year, that was the most important thing in a boy's education, to be good with a sword and weapons. Even when I was a boy, there were bandits enough in the Kilghard Hills. For centuries Armida had to be kept like an armed camp. Kennard would never have been criticized, if he'd kept me there to defend his lands instead of sending me into a Tower. . . ."

Regis picked up the unspoken part of that too: that Lew's work in the Arilinn Tower, his skill at matrix technology, had led to the Sharra rebellion, and to the sword that was not a sword, the sword which concealed *Sharra*. . . .

And he saw it growing, blossoming behind Lew's eyes, the look of horror that slid over Lew's face, felt his own hair rising as the flames flared in his mind. . . . *Sharra!* He looked at Lew. The smiling man, the kinsman with whom he had been calmly discussing the merits of Darkovan versus Terran education, was gone; Lew's face was dead white, so that the scars stood out like crimson brands, and his eyes were—blank horror, staring at nothing Regis could see. But they could both see it, the raging, ravening form of the fire-Goddess, straining against the chains, fire-locks tossing high against the sky . . . She was not in the quiet street around them, she was not in this world at all, but she was there, *there* in their minds, horribly present for both of them. . . .

Regis breathed hard, forcing himself to control the trembling of his hands, reached out for Lew's mind, tried to do what he had done with Javanne's, to pick the fire-form out of the texture of Lew's thoughts . . . and found something he had never touched. Javanne had seen Sharra only in his mind; Rafe had only seen the matrix . . . this was something else, something more dangerous; he saw a face, lean, wolfish, colorless hair, colorless gray eyes, and a woman's face like a restless flame. . . .

"Kadarin—" he gasped, and never knew whether he had spoken aloud or not. The frozen, static horror left Lew's eyes. He said grimly, "Come on. I've been afraid of this—"

He began to run, and Regis, following, could feel the jolting pain, like fire in Lew's hand—a hand that was not there, a phantom fire . . . but real enough to make sweat stand out on Lew's forehead as he ran, jolting, uneven, his good hand gripping a dagger in his belt. . . .

They turned into an open square, heard shrieks, cries. Regis had never been inside the Alton town house, though he had seen it from the outside. Half a dozen of the uniformed City Guard were fighting in the center of the square; Regis could not see who they were fighting. Lew cried out, "Marius!" and ran up the steps. The door suddenly burst open, and at the same time Regis saw flames shooting from an upper window. One of the Guardsmen officers was trying to organize people into a fire-fighting line, water being passed from hand to hand from the nearest well and from a smaller well in the garden behind the house, but it was utter confusion.

Lew was fighting, on the steps, with a tall man whose face Regis could not see, fighting one-handed with his knife. *Gods! He has only one hand!* Regis ran, whipping his sword from its sheath; saw Andres struggling with a bandit who wore the garb of the mountains . . . *but what are mountain men doing here in Thendara?* The Guards flowed up the steps, an officer shouting to rally them. It was hard, in the press, to tell friend from foe; Regis managed to get himself back to back with Lew, covering him, and for a moment, as his sword went up, he saw a face he recognized. . . .

Gaunt, gray-eyed, lips drawn back in a feral scowl. . . . The man Kadarin looked older, more dangerous. His face was bleeding; Lew had somehow slashed him with his dagger. Behind Regis there was a great cracking roar, like an explosion; then Guardsmen were hurrying everyone down the steps, shouting urgently, and the house buckled slowly and erupted skyward. Regis was driven to his knees by the force of the blast. And then there was a high, clear call, in a woman's voice, and suddenly the bandits were gone, melting away across the square, evaporating like mountain mist into the labyrinth of streets. Dazed, Regis picked himself up, watching the Guardsmen struggling with the remains of the burning house. A cluster of scared servant women were crying in a corner of the garden. Andres, his jacket unlaced, his face streaked and grimed with smoke, one boot unlaced, limped down the stairs and bent over Lew. Jeff came and helped Lew to sit up.

Lew said in a sick, dazed voice, "Did you see him?"

Regis bent and pressed him back. "Don't try to sit up." Blood was flowing down Lew's face from a cut on his forehead; he tried to wipe it out of his eyes with his good hand. Lew said, "I'm all right," and tried to struggle to his feet. "What happened?"

Jeff Kerwin stared at the knife in his hand. It was not even bloody. "It all happened so fast. One minute all was quiet, the next, there were bandits all over the place and one of the serving-women shouted that the house was on fire . . . and I was fighting for my life. I haven't held a knife since my first year in Arilinn!"

Lew said urgently, "Marius! Gods of hell, Marius! Where is my brother?" Again he started up, disregarding Andres's restraining hands. The horror was in his eyes again, and Regis could see in his mind the great flaming image, Sharra, rising higher and higher over Thendara . . . but there was nothing there. The street was quiet, the Guardsmen had the fire out; though there had been something like an explosion in the upstairs floors and there was a great gaping hole in the roof. Regis thought, with wild irrelevancy, that now Lew had no choice but to move into the suite in Comyn Castle which had, from time out of mind, been reserved for the Alton Domain. Jeff was touching, with careful hands, the cut on Lew's head.

"Bad," he said, "it will need stitches—"

But Lew struggled away from them. Regis grabbed him; laid his hand urgently over his eyes, and reached out with his mind, struggling to banish the ravening form of fire from his mind. . . . slowly, slowly, the flames died in Lew's mind and his eyes came back to reality; he staggered, letting himself lean on Jeff's arm.

"Did you see him?" he asked again urgently. "Kadarin! It was Kadarin! *Do they have the Sharra matrix?"*

Regis, staggering with that thought, compelled by Lew's horror, suddenly knew this was what Callina had feared. Lew demanded, "Marius! Marius—" and stopped, his voice strangling and catching in a sob.

Merciful Gods! Not this too! My brother, my brother . . . He collapsed on the steps like a puppet whose strings are cut, his shoulders shaking with grief and shock. Jeff came and held him as if he were a child; with Andres, somehow they got him up the steps. But Regis stood still, looking at horror beyond horror.

Kadarin had the Sharra matrix.

And Marius Alton lay dead somewhere inside the burning house, with a Terran bullet through his heart.

CHAPTER SIX

(Lew Alton's narrative)

"Here." Jeff shoved a mirror into my hand. "Not as good as a Terran medic might have done—I'm out of practice—but it's stopped the bleeding, anyhow, and that's what counts."

I shoved the mirror away. I could—sometimes—make myself look at what Kadarin had left of my face; but not now. But none of it was Jeff's fault; and he had done his best. I said, trying to be flippant, "Just what I needed—another scar, to balance the top and the bottom of my face."

He had gone all over me very carefully, to make sure that the blow to the head had left no aftereffects; but the cut was only a surface wound and fortunately had missed my eye. I had a headache roughly the size of Comyn Castle, but otherwise there seemed to be no damage.

Through it all was the haunting cry that would not be silenced, like a roaring in my mind; . . . *to Darkover, fight for your brother's rights.* . . . and now would never be stilled. Marius was gone, and my grief was boundless; not only for the little brother I had lost, for the man he was beginning to be, that I would never, now, know. Grief, and guilt too, for while I had stayed away, Marius was neglected, perhaps, but alive. He might have lost the Domain; but as a Terran he might have made a good life somewhere, somehow. Now life and choice were gone. (And beneath grief and guilt a deeper layer of ambivalence I would not let myself see; a trickle of relief, that I need never, now, risk that frightful testing for the Alton gift, never risk death for him as my father had risked it for me . . .)

"You have no choice, now, but to move into the Alton apartments in Comyn Castle," Jeff said, and I nodded, with a sigh. The house, at least for the moment, was uninhabitable. Gabriel had come, with the final crew of Guards who had gotten the fire out. He offered to arrange for men to guard the ruins and prevent looting until we could get workmen to repair the roof and make the place weather-proof again. Every room was filled with smoke, furniture lying blackened and ruined. I tried without success to close my eyes and nostrils to the sight and smell. I have . . . a horror of fire, and now, I knew, somewhere at the back of my mind, if I gave it mental lease, the form of fire was there, raging, ravening, ready to destroy. . . . and destroy me with it.

Not that I cared a damn, now. . . .

Andres looked twenty years older. He came to me now and said, hesitantly, "Where—where shall we take Marius?"

It was a good question, I thought; a damned good question, but I didn't know the answer. There had never been any room for him in the Comyn Castle, not since he was old enough to notice his existence; they had never noticed it, in life, and now, in death, they would not care.

Gabriel said quietly, "Have him carried to the chapel in Comyn Castle." I looked up, startled and ready to protest, but he went on: "Let him have that much in death, kinsman, even though he didn't have it in life."

I looked on his dead face only once. The bullet that had smashed out his life had somehow left his face unmarked; and he looked, dead, like the little brother I remembered.

Now indeed I was alone. I had laid my father to rest on Vainwal, near my son, who had never lived except in the dreams I had shared with Dio before his birth. Now my brother would lie in an unmarked grave, as the custom was, on the shores of the Lake of Hali, where all the Hastur-kin were laid to rest. A thousand legalities separated me from Dio.

I should never have come back here! I stared at the lightly falling snow in the street outside, and realized that it did not matter where I was, here or elsewhere. Andres, crushed and old; Jeff, who had left his adopted world behind for Darkover; and Gabriel, who had his own family, but who, now, in default of any other, was Alton. Let him have the Domain; I should have sent for Marius, taken him away before it came to this. . . .

No. That way lay only endless regret, a time when I would listen and hunger for my father's voice in my mind because it was all I had left of the past, live complacently with ghosts and grief and guilt . . . no. Life went on, and someday, perhaps, I would give a damn. . . . for now there were two things that must be done.

"Kadarin is somewhere in the City," I said to Gabriel. "He must be found. I can't possibly emphasize it enough—how dangerous he is. Dangerous as a banshee, or a wolf maddened by hunger. . . ."

And he had the Sharra matrix! And somehow he might manage to raise it again, the raging form of fire which would break the Comyn Castle and the walls of Thendara like kindling-sticks in a forest fire . . .

And there was worse . . . I too had been sealed to Sharra . . .

I could not speak of that to Gabriel. Not even to Jeff. I tried to tell myself; Kadarin could do nothing, nothing alone. Even if he managed to raise the Sharra forces, alone or with Thyra . . . who must, somehow, be alive too. . . . the fires would turn on them and consume them, as they had burned and ravaged me. I could feel my hand burning again, burning in the fires of Sharra. . . . could feel it now, the burning that the Terran medics had called *phantom pain*. . . . haunted, I told myself at the edge of hysteria, haunted by the ghost of my father and the ghost of my hand. . . . and stopped myself, hard. That way I could go mad, too. I said grimly to Andres, "Get me something to eat, find us all some dinner. Then we will take Marius to the chapel at Comyn Castle, and go there for the rest of the Council. The caretakers there will be Alton men; they'll know me as my father's Heir. And there's one more person who has to be told. Linnell."

Andres's eyes softened. "Poor Linnie," he muttered. "She was the only person in Comyn who cared about him. Even when no one else remembered he was alive, he was always her foster-brother. She sent him Festival gifts, and went riding with him on holidays. . . . She had promised him, when they were children, that if he married first she would be his wife's bride-woman and if she married first he should give her away. She came here last not a tenday ago, to tell him that her wedding with Derik had been set, and they were laughing together and talking about the wedding—" and the old man stopped, quite overcome.

I had not seen Linnell to speak to since I came back. I had thought, when I went to speak with Callina about making the Sharra matrix safe, I would pay Linnell my respects. . . . she was nearer to Marius's age, but we had been friends, brother and sister. But there had been no time. Now time was running out for us; and I must speak with Callina too, not only as kinswoman but as Keeper.

I too had been sealed to Sharra . . . they could draw me into that unholy thing, at any moment. . . .

I bent over Marius's body; took the little dagger from his waist. I had given it to him when he was ten years old; I had not realized that he had borne it all these years. In the years on Vainwal, I had not remembered to wear side-arms. I slipped it into the empty sheath in my boot, startled at how easily the gesture came after all these years.

Before Sharra can draw me again into itself, this dagger will find my heart. . . .

"Take him to the Castle," I said, and followed slowly behind the small, weary procession through the lightly falling summer snow. I was almost glad for the roaring pain in my head, which kept me from thinking, too much, about Linnell's face when I must tell her of this death.

Marius rested that night in the Comyn Castle, in the chapel, beneath the old stone arches, the paintings on the wall; from her silent niche the blessed Cassilda, clad in blue and with a starflower in her hand, watched forever over her children. My father had cared little for the Gods, and brought me up the same way. Marius in death was closer to the Comyn than ever he had been in life. But I looked up at the Four Gods portrayed at the four corners of the Chapel—Avarra, dark mother of birth and death, Aldones, Lord of Light, Evanda, bright mother of life and growth, Zandru, the dark lord of the Nine Hells. . . . and, like pressing a sore tooth, felt the burning touch of Sharra somewhere in my mind. . . .

Sharra was bound in chains, by Hastur, who was the son of Aldones, who was the Son of Light. . . .

Fables, fairy tales to frighten children or console them in the dark. What had the Gods to do with me, who bore Sharra's fires like a raging torrent that might some day burn out my brain . . . *as she had burned my hand away. . . .*

But as I went out of the Chapel, I thought: the fire is

real, real enough to burn away the city of Caer Donn, real enough to destroy Marjorie, to sear my hand to scars that would never heal; and in the end to destroy me, cell-deep, so that even the child I fathered came forth a monstrous, nonhuman *thing*. . . . that much is no fable. *Something* must lie behind the legends. If there is any answer anywhere under the four moons, it must be known to the Keepers, or it will not be known anywhere. As I came out, I looked up at the night sky, which had cleared somewhat, and at the darkness of the Tower behind the Castle. Ashara, oldest of the Keepers on Darkover, might know the answer. But first I would see my brother buried. And I must go and tell his foster-sister, so that she could weep for him the tears I could no longer shed.

Marius was buried two days later. It was a small procession that rode to Hali; Gabriel and I, Linnell, Jeff and Andres; and, to my surprise, Lerrys Ridenow. At my questioning look he said roughly, "I was fond of the boy. Not as you might think, damn you, but he was a good lad, and he didn't have many kinsmen who'd give him such a kind word as they'd throw to a dog. We needed him as Heir to Alton; he would have had some sense on the Council, and all the Gods know, in these days we can use some plain good sense!"

He said something like that at the graveside, where it was traditional to speak good memories of the dead; words that would transcend grief and give everyone something else to remember of the one who was buried. I remembered my father's bitterness when my mother had not been buried here; it was almost my first memory. *Elaine gave two sons to the Comyn, and yet they would not let her body rest among the children of Hastur.* Now, standing by the grave of my mother's son, who had been accepted in death though never in life, I found myself remembering my father's dying cry, ripping through my mind; but afterward . . . afterward, too, I had heard his last thought, the surprised cry of joy; *Elaine! Yllana . . . beloved!* Had his dying mind seen a vision, was there that kind of mercy in death, or was there, somehow, something beyond death? I had never thought so; death was the end. Yet, though my father had never believed, either, but in his last moments he had cried out to greet *someone, something,* and his last emotion had been astonishment and joy. What was the truth? Marius, too, even though his death had been terribly sudden, had looked peaceful.

Perhaps, then, somewhere, in spite of the galaxy of stars that lay between, somewhere beyond time and space, Marius knew that my father's last thought had been of him . . . *fight for your brother's rights* . . . or even that now, somewhere, he was with the mother whose life he had taken in birth. . . .

No, this was morbid nonsense, fables to comfort the bereaved.

Yet, that cry of joy, delight. . . .

I thought, cynically, *Well, I will know when I am dead, or I will never know the difference.*

Lerrys finished his short speech and stepped back. I could not bring myself to speak, save for a brief sentence or two. "My father's last words or thoughts were of his younger son. He was greatly loved, and it is my sorrow that he never knew it."

Linnell wore a dark cloak, thick gray, almost too heavy for her slight body. She said, in a voice thick with tears, "I never knew my own brothers; they were fostered away from me. When Marius and I were very little, before we knew we were boy and girl, or what that means, he said to me once, "Linnie, I'll tell you what, you can be my brother and I'll be your sister." Even weeping, she laughed through it.

No doubt, I thought, Marius was more a brother to her than that arrogant young scamp Merryl!

It was near noon; the red sun stood high in the sky, casting sharp shadows across the clouds which covered the surface of the Lake of Hali. Here on this shore, so legend among the Comyn said, the forefather of all the Comyn, Hastur, son of the Lord of Light, had fallen to earth, and here he had met with Cassilda the Blessed, and here she had borne the son who had fathered all of the Comyn . . . what was the truth of the legend? The hills rose beyond Hali, distant, shadowed, and above them a small shadow of moon, pale blue in the colored sky. And on the far shore the chapel of Hali, where rested the sacred things of the Comyn, from the days when the fullest powers of their minds were known . . . we were a shadow; a remnant, an echo of the powers that had been known in the Seven Domains in the old days. Once many Towers had risen over the Domains, telepaths in the relays had sped messages back and forth more quickly than the mechanical signals of the Terran Empire; the powers of mind allied to matrix had flown air-cars, brought metal to the ground from deep within the core of the planet, looked deep within the body and cured disease, healed wounds, controled the minds of animals and birds, looked deep within the cell plasm and knew whether the unborn child would be gifted with *laran* of a specific kind . . . yes, and in those days there had been wars fought with strange and terrible weapons, ranging into other dimensions, and of these weapons Sharra was one of the least . . . somewhere within the white gleaming walls of that chapel were there other weapons, one which could be effective against *Sharra* . . . ?

I would never know. In the days of the Compact, knowledge of those weapons had been destroyed, too, and perhaps it was as well that it should be so. Who could have foreseen, in those days, that descendants of the Comyn should somehow discover the ancient talisman of Sharra, and raise that raging fire?

I looked around the shores of the Lake with a sudden shiver.

Kadarin! Kadarin had the Sharra matrix, and he would try, perhaps, to force me back within it. . . .

In the old days at Aldaran, Kadarin and Beltran had raised dozens of fanatical believers, ready to let their own raw emotion rage forth, be drawn into the raging fires of Sharra, feeding all that raw hungry mind power into the destroying flames to be loosed on the city . . . could he bring such a force to Thendara, could he recapture me to loose that destroying power in my mind? . . . I trembled, looking at the hills, feeling that somehow I was being *watched,* that Kadarin lurked somewhere, waiting to seize me, force me back to the power-pole of Sharra, *feeding* that unholy flame!

And Sharra will rise and destroy and burn me wholly away in fire . . . all my hate, all my rage and torment . . .

Rafe Scott was not at the graveside. Yet he had been one of my brother's few friends. *Had Kadarin seized him too, drawn him back into Sharra?* Dizziness seized me, I saw men riding, an army on the road, marching on Thendara. . . .

Andres's hand on my shoulder steadied me. "Easy, Lew," he muttered. "There's not much more. We'll be away from here soon, and then you can rest."

Rest be damned! With all this closing in on us, Sharra's matrix free and in Kadarin's hands once more, there would be no rest for me for some time.

Hoofbeats! I tensed, my hand gripping the hilt of the light ceremonial sword I had been persuaded to wear for this occasion. Kadarin with his rabble, ready to capture me and drag me into slavery to Sharra once more? But the riders came slowly to the graveside, and I saw they wore the uniform of the Castle Guard. Regis Hastur slid from his horse and came slowly to the graveside. I had wondered what had happened to him; he had been there when Marius died and the house was burned. . . .

He stood for a moment over the grave and said quietly, "I did not know Marius well, and it is my sorrow. But once I heard him speak, in a tavern, the kind of words which we need in Council. His death is upon all our heads here; and here I promise that I will have the courage to speak the words he never had a chance to say in Council."

He looked up expectantly, and behind Regis I saw the tall, lean figure of Dyan Ardais, in the ceremonial gray and black of his Domain. He came to the graveside, and looked at the open grave; but he did not speak, merely picked up a handful of soil and cast it quietly into the grave. Then, after a long silence, he said, "Rest well, kinsman; and may all the folly and wrong which brought you to birth rest here with you." He turned away from the grave and said, "Lord Regis persuaded me that it was well to guard you; in these days there are enemies and Comyn should not ride unguarded. We will escort you in safety back to the Castle."

In silence, then, I turned from my brother's grave, and we went to our horses. As Lerrys mounted, I said quietly, "It was good of you to come, kinsman. Thank you."

His fair face darkened and he said fiercely, "It wasn't for you, damn you, it was for Marius!" He turned his back on me, pulling himself up, with a dancer's agile movement, into the saddle. He wore Darkovan dress and was heavily cloaked against the fierce cold of the hills, in wool and leather, not the elegant silks and synthetics of the pleasure worlds.

I hauled myself, awkwardly, one-handed, into the saddle. Regis said from his horse, "I would have come sooner. But I felt it necessary to get leave to bring guards. I never had a chance to tell you; Beltran is on the road, and he brings what could almost be called an army. Beltran has no love for you. And if Kadarin's at large—"

I said, grimacing, "Don't tell me Hastur wouldn't be relieved if Beltran caught up with me—or I broke my neck!"

He looked down at his saddlehorn. Then he said very quietly, "I am Hastur too, Lew. My grandfather and I have had differences before this, and we will have them afterward. But you must believe me: he would not wish you to fall into Kadarin's hands. That would be true no matter what he felt about you personally. And he bears you no ill will. He was stupid and wrong-headed about Marius, perhaps. But whatever he may have felt, you are Lord Armida, and head of the Alton Domain, and there is nothing he can do about that; and he will accept it with such grace as he must. Your father was his friend."

I looked away across the hills. Danvan Hastur had never been unkind to me. I took up the reins, and we rode, side by side, for a little while. Mist from the Lake of Hali floated in wisps on our trail, covered Marius's silent grave, where he lay among the Comyn before him. Their troubles were over; mine lay ahead of me, on the trail. My hand was busy about the reins; I could not let it go to grip at the hilt of my sword, and I felt uneasy, as if somewhere at the back of my mind I could *see* Kadarin, surrounded by his fanatics, could see Thyra's strange golden eyes so much like Marjorie's. Where was Rafe? Had Kadarin seized on him too? Rafe feared Sharra, almost as much as I, but could he stand against Kadarin?

Could I? Would I let them force me back again into those fearful fires? I had not had the courage to die, before. . . . Would I live, craven, in Sharra, without courage to die . . . ?

Gabriel was riding at the head of the Guards, and in the small detachment I noticed he had brought both his sons; the slender, dark, gray-eyed Rafael, like a younger, darker Regis, and sturdy young Gabriel, whose reddish hair made me think of my father. I supposed that sooner or later I would have to adopt one of them as my Heir, since I would father no more sons. . . .

I heard Regis speaking and realized I had drifted very far away.

"Do you know if Marius had a son, Lew?"

"Why, no," I said. "If he did, he never told me. . . ." But there had been so many things he had never had any time to tell me. He had not been a boy, though Lerrys had called him so; when he died he was twenty, and at that age I had been three years at Arilinn, three years as cadet and officer in the Guard, had sold myself into slavery and fire in Sharra. "I suppose it's possible. Why?"

"I'm not sure," Regis said. "But my foster-son, Mikhail—Javanne's son—told me that his brother Gabriel said something about a rumor going round among the Guards, just before Council. Everybody knew, of course, that the Alton Domain was to be declared forfeit, and—forgive me, Lew—that they wouldn't hear of Kennard's younger son taking it, because of his Terran education. But that the Council, or somebody, had found an Alton child, and they were going to declare it Head of the Domain, under Hastur Regency. Something of that sort. You know what sort of rumors get around in the cadet corps; but this seemed more persistent than most."

I shook my head. "I suppose it's not impossible Marius could have fathered a son. Or, for that matter, that my father might have left a bastard or two; he didn't tell me everything about his life. Though, I should think, I would have known—"

"It's possible that someone might have had his child, from a casual love affair, and not told anyone till he was gone," Regis said, and I caught the unspoken part of that, that there were women enough who would enjoy the status of bearing a *laran* child to Comyn, he should know. . . .

"And," I finished, "no woman would dare lie about it, not to a telepath, not to Comyn. But I'd think if it were true, your grandfather would have acted before this."

"I'd think so too," Regis said, and raised a hand to motion to Gabriel Lanart-Hastur to ride beside us. I think I myself would have questioned the boys, who had passed the rumor around, but perhaps Regis thought it beneath his dignity to interrogate boys in their teens. When Gabriel came riding close to us he said, "Brother-in-law, what's this tale going about in the cadets about an Alton child?"

"I don't know anything about it, Regis. Rafael said something, and the way I heard it, it was some bastard son of my own," said Gabriel good-humoredly, while I found myself thinking: if I had a sharp-tongued wife like the lady Javanne, I would make damned sure she never found out anything about any bastard child I had fathered! Gabriel's smile was rueful. "I could assure my son that it was none of mine, but there are other Alton kinsmen in the Domains. No doubt, if there's anything to it, whoever's backing him will bring the child forward when Council meets again." His eyes apologized to me as he said, "You're not all that popular anymore, Lew. The Guardsmen would follow you to hell—they still talk about how good an officer you were—but that's a long way from being Warden of Alton."

And for a moment I was heartily sick of the whole business. It occurred to me that the best thing to do, when I reached Thendara, was to come to some understanding with Gabriel about the Domain, then find a ship and take passage out, away from Darkover and Sharra and all of it . . . but I thought of Armida, far in the Kilghard Hills, and my homeland there. And I remembered, like a pain gripping me in the vitals.

Kadarin had the Sharra matrix. Twice I had tried to leave it behind, on another planet. Twice I had been drawn back to it. . . . I was slave and exile for Sharra and it would never let me go, and somehow I must fight it and destroy it . . . fight Kadarin, too, if need be, and all his wild-eyed madman and followers. . . .

Fight them? Alone? As soon face, with my single ceremonial sword, and my one hand, all of Beltran's armies . . . and I was no legendary Comyn hero, armed with a magical spell-sword out of legend!

I twisted my head, looking back toward the Lake of Hali and the low, gleaming chapel on the shore. I could feel Regis and Gabriel thinking that I was saying farewell to the last resting place of my brother. But instead I was wondering if, in all the history of the Comyn, there was a weapon against Sharra.

Ashara must know. And if she knew, perhaps, my kinswoman Callina would know.

I said, "Gabriel, Regis, excuse me, I must go and speak to Linnell. She loved Marius and she is crying again." I rode forward, feeling the prickling again in my back as if I were being watched, and I *knew,* that from somewhere, whether with some small band of ruffians or through the matrix, Kadarin was watching me . . . but because Regis and Dyan had brought a detachment of the Guard, with swordsmen, he would not, quite, dare attack us now.

He had access to Terran weapons. Marius had died with a bullet through his head. But even so, he could not face a whole detachment of Guardsmen . . . so for the moment I was safe.

Maybe.

Disregarding the pricking of warning, I rode forward to speak to Linnell, to try to comfort my foster-sister.

Linnell's eyes were red and her face blotched, but she had begun to look peaceful again. She tried to smile at me. "How your head must ache, Lew—it's a bad cut, isn't it? Jeff told me he put ten stitches in it. You should be in bed."

"I'll manage, little sister," I said, using the word *bredilla* as if she were the child she had been. But Linnell must be two or three and twenty now, a tall poised young woman, with soft brown hair and blue eyes. I supposed she was pretty; but in every man's life there are two or three women—his mother, his sisters—who simply don't register on his mind as women. Linnell was, always, no more to me than my little sister. Before her big, sympathetic eyes, I wished suddenly that I could tell her about Dio. But I would not burden her with that dreadful story; she was still sick with grief about Marius.

She said, "At least he was buried as a full member of the Comyn, with all honors; even Lord Ardais came to do him honor, and Regis Hastur." I started to say something bitter—what good is the honor of the dead?—and then held my peace; if Linnell could find comfort in that, I was glad. Life went on.

"Lew, would you be very upset if Derik and I were married soon after Festival?"

"Upset? Why, *breda*? I would be glad for you." That marriage had been in the air since Linnie put away her dolls. Derik was slow-witted and not good enough for her, but she loved him, and I knew it.

"But—I should still do mourning for—for Kennard, and for my brother—"

I reached over, clumsily, letting go of the reins for a moment, to pat her on the shoulder. "Linnie, if Father or Marius is anywhere where they can know about it—" which I did not believe, at least not most of the time, but I would not say that to Linnell—"do you think their ghosts could be jealous of your happiness? They loved you and would be glad to see you happy."

She nodded and smiled at me.

"That's what Callina told me; but she is so unworldly. I wouldn't want people to think I wasn't paying proper respect to their memory—"

"Don't you worry about that," I said. "You need kinsmen and family, and now more than ever; without foster-father or brother, you should have a husband to look after you and love you. And if anyone says anything suggesting you are not properly respecting them, you send that person to me and I will tell them so myself."

She blinked back tears and smiled, like a rainbow through cloud. "And you are the Lord of the Domain now," she said, "and it is for you to say what mourning shall be held. And Callina is Head of my Domain. So if both of you have given permission, then I will tell Derik. We can be married the day after Festival. And at Festival, Callina's to be handfasted to Beltran—"

I stared at her, open-mouthed. In spite of all, was the Council still bent on this suicidal madness?

I must certainly see Callina, and there was no time for delay.

Andres asked me, as we rode through the gates of the city, if I would come and speak to the workmen who had been hired to repair the town house. I started to protest—I had always obeyed him without question—and suddenly I recalled that I need not, now, even explain myself.

"You see to it, foster-father," I said. "I have other things I must do."

Something in my voice startled him; he looked up, then said in a queerly subdued voice, "Certainly, Lord Armida," and inclined his head in what was certainly a bow. As he rode away, I identified what had been in his tone; he had spoken to me as he had always spoken to my father.

Linnell's eyes were still red, but she looked peaceful. I said, "I must see Callina, sister. Will she receive me?"

"She's usually in the Tower at this time, Lew. But you could come and dine with us—"

"I would rather not wait that long, *breda.* It's very urgent." Even now I could still feel the prickling, as if Kadarin were watching me behind some clump of trees or from some dark and narrow alleyway. "I will seek her out there."

"But you can't—" she began, then stopped, remembering: I had spent three years in a Tower.

I had never been in the Comyn Tower before, though I had come to the Castle every summer of my life except for the Arilinn years. I had spoken to the technicians in the relays, but I did not think there were many living telepaths who had actually stepped through the insulating veils. And even among those who kept the relays going, I did not think there were many who had ever seen the ancient Keeper, Ashara. Certainly my father said she had not been seen in the memory of anyone he had ever known. Maybe, I thought, there was no such person!

Perhaps Callina knew I was coming; she met me and beckoned me softly through the relay chamber—I noted that there was a young girl at the screen, but I did not recognize her—and through an inner chamber into what must have been the ancient matrix laboratory—at least that is what we would have called it at Arilinn. I could believe it had been built long before that, in the Ages of Chaos or before; there were matrix monitor screens, and other equipment the use of which I had not the foggiest notion. I found I did not like to think of the level of matrix it would have taken to use some of these things. I could feel the soothing vibrations of a specially modulated telepathic damper which filtered out telepathic overtones without inhibiting ordinary thought. There was an immense panel about whose molten-glass shimmer I could not even make guesses; it might have been one of the almost-legendary psychokinetic screens. Among all these things were the ordinary prosaic tools of the matrix mechanic's art; cradles, lattices, blank crystals, a glass-blower's pipe, screwdrivers and soldering irons, odd scraps of insulating cloth. Beyond them she motioned me to a seat.

"I've been expecting you," she said, "ever since I heard that they got away with the Sharra matrix. I suppose it was Kadarin?"

"I didn't see him," I said, "but no one else could have touched it without killing me. I'm still here—worse luck!"

"You're still keyed into it, then? It's an illegal matrix, isn't it?"

"It's not on the screens at Arilinn," I said. They had found that out when Marjorie died. But this was an older Tower; some memory of it might linger here. She said, "If you can give me the pattern, I'll try to find it." She led me to the monitor screen, flashing with small glimmers, one for every known and licensed matrix on Darkover. She made a gesture I remembered; I fumbled one-handed with the strings of the matrix crystal around my neck, averted my eyes as it dropped into my hand, seeing the crimson fires within. . . . It still resonated to the Sharra matrix; it was no good to me.

And while I bore it, anyone with the Sharra matrix could find me . . . and it seemed, though it could have been my imagination, that I could feel Kadarin, watching me through it. . . .

She took it from me, matching resonances so carefully that there was no shock or pain, and laid it in a cradle before the screen. The lights on the screen began to wink slowly; Callina leaned forward, silent, intent, her face shut-in and plain. At last she sighed. "It's not a monitored matrix. If we could monitor and locate it, we might even destroy it—though destroying a ninth-level matrix is not a task I am eager to attempt, certainly not alone. Perhaps Regis—" she looked thoughtfully at my matrix, but she did not explain and I wondered what Regis had to do with it. "Can you give me the pattern? If the others—Kadarin, Thyra—were using matrixes which resonated to Sharra—"

"Thyra, at least, was a wild telepath. I don't know where she got her matrix, but I'm sure it's not a monitored one," I said. I supposed she had it from old Kermiac of Aldaran; he had been training telepaths back in those hills since before my father was born. If he had lived, the whole story of the Sharra circle would have been different. I tried to show her the pattern against the blank screen, but only blurs swirled against the blue surface, and she gestured me to take up my own matrix and put it away.

"I shouldn't have let you try that, so soon after a head injury. Come through here."

In a smaller, sky-walled room, I relaxed, in a soft chair, while Callina watched me, aloof and reflective. She said at last, "Why did you come here, Lew? What did you want from me?"

I wasn't sure. I did not know what, if anything, she could do about the ghost-voice in my mind, my father's voice. Whether a true ghost or a reverberation from brain-cells injured in his dying grip on my mind, it would fade away at last; of that I was certain. Nor could she do anything much about the fact that the Sharra matrix was in the hands of Kadarin and Thyra, and that they were here in Thendara. I said harshly, "I should never have brought it back to Darkover!"

"I don't know what choice you had," she pointed out reasonably. "If you are keyed into it. . . ."

"Then I shouldn't have come back!"

And this time she did not argue with me, only shrugged a little. I was here on Darkover and so was the matrix. I said, "Do you suppose Ashara knows anything about it? She goes back a long way . . ." and paused, hesitant. Callina's voice rebuked: "No one asks to see Ashara!"

"Then maybe it's time they did."

Her voice was still, stony and remote. "Perhaps she would consent to see you. I will inquire." For a moment she was nothing like the girl I had known, my cousin and kinswoman. I was almost afraid of her.

"There must have been a time when telepaths knew how to handle things like the Sharra matrix. I know it was used by the forge-folk to bring metal to their forges; and it was used as a weapon. If the weapon wasn't destroyed, why would they have destroyed the defenses against it?"

Callina started a little, as if she had been very far away and the sound of my voice had brought her back from whatever distance she had inhabited. I remembered that look on Marjorie's face, the heart-breaking isolation of a Keeper, alone even at the center of a great circle. Somehow it made me lonely for my days at Arilinn. Callina and I had not been there at the same time, but she was part of it, she remembered, we were comfortable together.

"What can Kadarin *do* with the matrix?" she asked.

"Nothing, himself," I said, "but he has Thyra to control it." Even at the beginning, he had wanted Thyra to control the matrix; she was more pliant to his will than Marjorie, who had, at the last, rebelled and tried to close the gate into that other world or dimension from which Sharra came into this world in raging fire . . . I said, "If he wanted to, he could burn Thendara around the heads of the Comyn, or go to the Trade City and bring one of their damned spaceships down out of the sky! The matrix is that powerful; and the thing is, he doesn't have enough telepaths to control it as if it were a proper ninth-level matrix. Which it isn't: it's something unholy, a weapon, a force—" I stopped myself. Like Callina I had been Tower-trained, I should know better. Old tales made matrixes magical, called them gates to sorcery and alien magic. I knew the science of which they were a part. A matrix is a tool, no more good or evil than the one who uses it; a device to amplify and direct the *laran*, the special hyper-developed psychic powers of the Comyn and those of their blood. The superstitious might speak of Gods and magical powers. I knew better. And yet the form of fire blazed in my mind, a woman, tall and imposing, overshadowing . . . and now she bore Marjorie's face. Marjorie, competent and unafraid in the midst of the rising illusion-flames of Sharra, and then—then crumpling, screaming in agony as the flames struck inward—my hand burning like a torch beneath the matrix. . . .

Callina reached out one hand, lightly touched my forehead, where Jeff had stitched the sword cut. Under her touch the fire went out. I found that I was kneeling at her feet, my head bent under the weight of it.

She said "But would he dare? Surely no sane man—"

I said, hearing the bitterness in my own voice, "I'm not sure he's a man—and I'm even less sure he is sane."

"But what could he hope to accomplish, unless he is simply mad for destruction?" she asked. "Surely he would not risk the woman—Thyra, you called her?—She was his—" she hesitated, and I shook my head. I had never understood the relationship between Kadarin and Thyra. It was not the ordinary relationship of lovers, but something at once less and more. I bent my head; I too had been glamored by the dark, glowing beauty of Thyra, so like and so unlike Marjorie. I had chosen. And Marjorie had been destroyed. . . . I turned on her in rage. She said softly, "I know, Lew. I know."

"You know! Thank the Gods you *don't* know—" I flung at her, in a blind fury. What could she know of that, that raging fire, that fury, ravening between the worlds. . . .

But under her steady eyes my rage dissolved. Yes, she did know. On that dreadful day when I had turned on Kadarin with the desperation of a man who knows himself already condemned to death, smashed the gate between the worlds and closed away Sharra from this world, I had thrust forth with my last strength and brought Marjorie and myself *between* the world-gates. The Terrans called it teleportation. I had brought us both to the matrix chamber in Arilinn, both of us terribly wounded, Marjorie dying. Callina had fought to save her; Marjorie had died in her arms. I bent my head, haunted again by that memory burned into my brain; Callina, holding Marjorie in her arms, the moment of peace that had descended in that last minute over her face. Yes, she knew.

I said, trying to think about it calmly without going into the horror again, "I don't think, if he was sane, he would risk Thyra; but I'm not sure he understands the danger, and if the matrix has them both in its grip. . . . I don't know if he would have any choice." I knew how the matrix could control a worker, how it had seized control even from our carefully balanced circle, going forth to do its ravening work of destruction.

"It—wants to destroy," I said unsteadily. "I think it was made in the Ages of Chaos, to burst forth from control, to kill as much as it could, burn, destroy. . . . I don't think anyone alive now knows how to control it." For years, I knew, the Sharra matrix had lain harmlessly on the altars of the forge-folk, a talisman invoking their fire Goddess, to light their altars. To bring fire to their forges and fires, and the Goddess within, content with her worshippers and their fires, had not been roused into this world. . . .

And I had loosed it on Darkover; I, a complacent puppet in Kadarin's hands. And he had used my own rage, my own lust, my own inner fires . . .

This was superstitious nonsense. I drew a deep breath and said, "In the Ages of Chaos there were many such weapons, and somewhere there must be defenses, or the memory of defenses against them. Maybe, then, Ashara would know." But would she care, if she had withdrawn so far from the world?

Callina picked up the unspoken question and said, "I do not know. I—I am afraid of Ashara—" I could see her shaking. She said, "You think I am here, safe, isolated—out of the troubles in the Council and the Comyn—Merryl hates me, Lew, he will do anything to keep me from having power in Comyn Council. And now there is this alliance with Aldaran—you do know Beltran is bringing an army to the very gates of Thendara, and if, at the last, they refuse him this alliance—do you suppose *he* knows about Sharra, or will use it as a weapon?"

I didn't know. Beltran was my kinsman; there had been a time when I had trusted him, even as I had trusted and liked Kadarin. But Sharra had seized on him, too, and I still felt that was why he had this lust for power . . . and he, too, would have been alerted to its presence.

I said, "They *can't* marry you off to Beltran, just like that! You are Head of a Domain and Keeper. . . ."

"So I thought," she said dispassionately. "But if I were not Head of a Domain, he would not want me—I do not think it is me he wants. If he simply wanted to marry into the Comyn, there are other women as close to the center of power; Derik's sister Alanna was widowed last year. As for my being Keeper—I do not think the Council wants a Keeper in power there, either. And if I marry—" she shrugged. "There's the end of that."

I remembered the old stories that a Keeper maintains her power only through her chastity. It's drivel, of course, superstitious rubbish, but like all superstitions, it has a core of truth. *Laran,* in a Comyn telepath, is carried in the same channels as the sexual forces of the body. The main side effect, for men, is that prolonged or heavy work in the matrixes temporarily closes off the channels to sex, and the man undergoes a prolonged period of impotence. It's the first thing a man, working in the Towers, has to get used to, and some people never learn to handle it. I suppose for many people it would seem a high price to pay.

A woman has no such physical safeguard. While a woman is working at the center of a circle, holding the tremendous forces of the amplified linked matrixes, she must keep the physical channels clear for that work, or she can burn up like a torch. A three-second backflow, when I was seventeen years old, had burned a scar in my hand that had never really healed, the size of a silver coin. And the Keeper is at the very center of those flows. While she is working at the center of the screens, a Keeper remains chaste for excellent and practical reasons which have nothing to do with morality. It's a heavy burden; few women want to live with it, more than a year or two. In the old days, Keepers were vowed to hold their office lifelong, were revered and treated almost as Goddesses, living apart from anything human. In this day and age, a Keeper is simply required to retain her chastity while she is actively working as a Keeper, after which she may lay down her post, conduct her life as she pleases, marry and have children if she wishes. I had always assumed that Callina would elect to do this; she was, after all, the female Head of the Domain, and her oldest daughter would hold the Domain of Aillard.

She followed my thoughts and shook her head. She said wryly, "I have never had any wish to marry, nor met any man who would tempt me to leave the Tower. Why should I bear a double burden? Janna of Arilinn—she was your Keeper, was she not?—left her post and bore two sons, then fostered them away, and came back to her work. But I have served my Domain well; I have sisters, Linnell will soon be married, even Merryl, I suppose, will some day find a woman who will have him. There is no need . . ." but she sighed, almost in despair. "I might marry if there was another who could take my place. . . . but not Beltran. Merciful Avarra, not Beltran!"

"He's not a monster, Callina," I said. "He's very like me, as a matter of fact."

She turned on me with wild anger, and her voice caught in her throat. "So you'd have me marry him too? A man who would bring an army against Thendara, and blackmail my kinsmen into giving him the most powerful woman in the Council for his own purposes? Damn you! Do you think I am a *thing,* a horse to be sold in the market, a shawl to be bartered for?" She stopped, bit her lip against a sob, and I stared at her; she had seemed so cold, remote, dispassionate, more like a mechanical doll than a woman; and now she was all afire with passion, like a struck harp still vibrating. For the first time I knew it; Callina was a woman, and she was beautiful. She had never seemed real to me, before this; she had only been a Keeper, distant, untouchable. Now I saw the woman, trapped and frantic behind that barricade, reaching out—reaching out to me.

She dropped her face into her hands and wept. She said, through her tears, "They have put it to me that if I do not marry Beltran it will plunge the Domains into war!"

I could not stop myself; I reached out, drew her into my arms.

"You shall *not* marry Beltran," I said, raging. "I will kill him first, kinswoman!" And then, as I held her against me I knew what had happened to us both. It was not as kinswoman that I had vowed to shelter and protect her. It went deeper than that; it went back to the time when she had been the only woman in the Comyn who understood my rebellion against my father, to the time when she had fought to save Marjorie's life and had shared my agony and despair. She was Tower-trained, she was a memory of the one good time in my entire life, she was home and Arilinn and a time when I had been happy and real and felt my life worthy; a time when I had not been damned.

I held her, trembling with fright, against me; clumsily, I touched her wet eyes. There was something else, some deeper, more terrible fear behind her.

I murmured, "Can't Ashara protect you? She is Keeper of the Comyn. Surely she would not let you be taken from her like this."

We were deeply in rapport now; I felt her rage, her dread, her outraged pride. Now there was terror. She whispered, her voice only a thread, as if she feared that she would be heard, "Oh, Lew, you don't know—I am afraid of Ashara, so afraid . . . I would rather marry Beltran, I would even marry him to be free of her . . . " and her voice broke and strangled. She clung to me in terror and despair, and I held her close.

"Don't be afraid," I whispered, and felt the shaking tenderness I had thought I would never know again. Burned and ravaged as I was, scarred, mutilated, too deeply haunted by despair to lift my one remaining hand to save myself—still, I felt I would fight to the death, fight like a trapped animal, to save Callina from that fate.

. . . still there was something between us. I dared not kiss her; was it only that she was still Keeper and the old taboo held me? But I held her head against my breast, stroking her dark hair, and I knew I was no longer rootless, alone, without kin or friends. Now there was some reason behind my desperate holding on. Now there was Callina, and I promised myself, with every scrap of will remaining to me, that for her sake I would fight to the end.

CHAPTER SEVEN

"There's only one good thing about Council season," said Regis sleepily, "I get to see you now and then."

Danilo, barefoot and half-dressed at the window, grinned back at him. "Come now, is that the spirit in which to face the final day of Council?"

Regis groaned and sat up. "I suppose you had to remind me. Shall I send for breakfast?"

Danilo shook his head, rubbing his chin thoughtfully. "I can't stay; Lord Dyan asked me to dine with him last night, he even said I could bring you if I wished; but I told him I'd be engaged elsewhere." He smiled at his friend. "So he said breakfast would do. I suppose, too, that I'll have to wear Council robes." He made a wry face. "Without disrespect to our worthy forefathers, did you ever see any robes as ugly as full Council ceremonial dress? I am sure the cut and fashion have not changed since the days of Stephen the Fourth!"

Regis chuckled, swinging his feet out of bed. "Longer than that, surely—I am certain they were designed by Zandru's great-grandmother."

"And she made him wear them as punishment when he was more wicked than usual," laughed Danilo. "Or do you suppose they were designed by *cristoforos,* so that while we sit at Council we will be doing suitable penance for our sins?"

"Sitting in Council is penance enough," said Regis glumly.

"And the Ardais colors—gray and black, how dismal! Do you suppose that is why Dyan is so morose—the result of wearing black and silver in Council for so many years? If I were no more than your paxman, at least I could wear blue and silver!"

"We shall have to design you a special robe for your divided loyalties," said Regis, mock-serious. "Patchwork of black and blue. Suitable enough, I suppose, for anyone who comes under Dyan's influence—like my ribs when he was my arms-master!" After all these years, Regis could make a joke of it. But Danilo frowned.

"He spoke again of my marriage, a day or two ago. It seems his *nedestro* son is three years old, and looks healthy, and likely to live to grow up; he wants me to foster the boy, he said. He has neither time nor inclination to bring him up himself—and to do this I must have a household and wife. He said that he understood why I was reluctant—"

"He should, after all," said Regis dryly.

"Nevertheless, he said it was my duty, and he would take care to find me a wife who would not trouble me too much."

"Grandfather speaks in the same vein—"

"I think," Danilo said, "that I shall take one who will find herself a devoted Lady-companion; and after I have given her a child or two to raise, she will not weep if I absent myself from her bed and fireside. Then we should both be content."

Regis pulled on tunic and breeches, slid his feet into indoor boots. "I must breakfast with Grandfather; time enough to haul myself into ceremonials later. There seems little sense in attending Council—most of the speeches I will hear today I could say over from memory!"

Danilo sighed. "There are times when I think Lord Dyan—and some others I could mention—would rather see the Ages of Chaos come again than wake up to realities! Regis! Does your grandsire really think the Terrans will go away if we pretend they are not there?"

"I don't know what my grandfather thinks, but I know what he will say if I do not breakfast with him," Regis said, fastening his tunic-laces. "And now that I think of it, Council may not be so predictable as all that—it seems we are to have seven Domains again, after all. Did you know Beltran has brought and quartered an army above Thendara?"

"I heard he was calling it an honor-guard," said Danilo. "I would not have thought, when were were his *guests*—" he gave the word an ironic inflection—"at Aldaran, that he had so much honor as all that to guard."

"I would say, rather, he needs an army to keep what little honor he has from escaping him," said Regis, remembering the time when he and Danilo had been imprisoned in Castle Aldaran. "Are they really going to accept him in Council, I wonder?"

"I don't think they have much choice," said Danilo. "Whatever his reasons, I don't like it."

"Then, if you are given a chance to speak in Council you had better say so," Regis said. "Dyan is expecting you, and Grandfather, no doubt, awaiting me. You had better go."

"Is this the hospitality of the Hasturs?" Danilo teased. But he gave Regis a quick, hard hug, and went. Regis stood in the door of his room, watching Danilo cross the outer hallway of the suite, and briefly come face to face with Lord Hastur.

Danilo bowed and said cheerfully, "A good morning to you, my lord."

Danvan Hastur scowled in displeasure, grunting the barest of uncivil greetings; it sounded like "H'rrumph!" He went on without raising his head. Danilo blinked in surprise, but went out the door without speaking. Regis, his mouth tightening with exasperation, went to comb his hair and ask his valet to lay out his ceremonial garb for Council.

Through the window the fog was lifting; high across the valley he could see the Terran HQ, a white skyscraper reddened with the glint of the red sun. His body-servant was fussing with the robes. Regis looked at them in distaste.

I am weary of doing things for no better reason than that the Hasturs have always done them that way, he thought, and the man flinched nervously as if Regis's uneasy thoughts could reach him. Maybe they could.

He stared morosely at the skyscraper, thinking: if his grandfather had been wise, he should have had the same kind of Terran education as poor Marius. If his grandfather indeed perceived the Terrans as the enemy, all the more so, then—a wise man will take the measure of his enemy, and know his powers.

Regis stopped, the comb halfway to his hair. Suddenly he knew why Danvan Hastur had not done just that.

Grandfather is sure that anyone who had a Terran education would, of necessity, choose the ways of Terra. He does not trust me, or the strength of what I have been taught. Are the Terrans and their ways so attractive, then?

His grandfather, in the little breakfast room, was still scowling as Regis drew up his chair. Regis said a polite good morning and waited until the servant had gone.

"Grandsire, if you cannot be courteous to my sworn man, I will find quarters elsewhere."

"Do you expect me to approve?" asked the old man in frigid displeasure.

"I expect you to admit I am a grown man with the right to choose my own companions," Regis said hotly. "If I brought a woman here for the night, and she was any sort of respectable woman, you would show her civility, at least. Danilo is as well born as I—or you yourself, sir! If I spoke like that to one of *your* friends, you would say I deserved a beating!"

Old Hastur clamped his lips tight, and even a non-telepath could have read his thoughts: *that was different.*

Regis said angrily, "Grandfather, it is not as if I were carousing in common taverns, disgracing the Hastur name by letting myself be seen in brothels and such places as the Golden Cage, or keeping a perfumed minion as the Dry-towners do—"

"Silence! How dare you speak of such things to me?" Hastur clamped his lips in anger. He gestured to the breakfast table. "Sit down and eat; you will be late for Council." As Regis hesitated he commanded dryly, "Do as you are told, boy. This is no time for tantrums!"

Regis clenched his fists. The quick wave of anger almost dizzied him. He said icily, "Sir, you have spoken to me as if I were a child for the last time!" He turned and went out of the room, disregarding his grandfather's shocked "Regis!"

As he walked through the labyrinthine corridors of Comyn Castle, his fists were clenched, and he felt as if a weight were pressing inward on his chest. It had been only a matter of time; this quarrel had been building for years, and it was just as well it should be in the open.

In all save this I have been an obedient grandson, I have done everything he asked of me; I am sworn to obey him as the Head of the Domain. But I will not be spoken to as if I were ten years old—never again. When he entered the Ardais apartments he was still fighting back a wholly uncharacteristic fury. The servant who let him in said an automatic, *"Su serva, dom . . ."* and broke off to ask, "Are you ill, sir?"

Regis shook his head. "No—but ask Lord Danilo if he will see me at once."

The message was carried, but answered by Danilo himself coming to the outer room. "Regis! What are you doing here?"

"I came to ask if I may join you at breakfast," said Regis, more calmly than he felt, and Dyan, appearing in the doorway, already in the ceremonial black and silver of Council, said quickly, "Yes, come and join us, my dear fellow! I wanted a chance to speak with you, in any case."

He went back toward the breakfast room, and Danilo murmured in an undertone, "What's wrong?"

"I'll tell you later, if I may. Grandfather and I had words," Regis muttered, "Leave it for now, will you?"

"Set another place for Dom Regis," Dyan ordered. Regis took a seat. Danilo looked at him, a swift questioning look, as he unfolded a napkin, but asked nothing aloud, and Regis was grateful.

He must know that I quarreled with Grandfather, and why. But he said nothing more, except for a complimentary remark about the food. Dyan himself ate sparingly, a little bread and fruit, but he had provided an assortment of hot breads, broiled meat and fried cakes; when Danilo commented on this, Dyan said, with a comical emphasis, "I am quite experienced at judging the—appetites—of young men." He caught Regis's eye for a moment, and Regis looked at his plate.

When they had finished and were idling over some fruits, Dyan said, "Well, Dani, I'm glad Regis joined us; I really wanted to talk to both of you. Most of the business of the Council has finished; this will be the final session, and because of the mourning for Kennard, everything's been put off to this last session. And there's much to be done. The heritage of Alton has to be settled—"

"I thought it was settled when Lew came back," Regis said, his heart sinking as he realized what Dyan was driving at.

Dyan sighed. "I know he is your friend, Regis, but look at realities, will you, without sentiment? It's a pity Kennard died without formally disinheriting him—"

"Why would he do that?" Regis asked, resentfully.

"Don't be a fool, lad! If he hadn't been mortally wounded and ill, you know as well as I that he'd have stood trial before the Comyn for treason, for that Sharra business, and been formally exiled. I don't have any ill will toward him—" but Dyan's glance slid uneasily away as Regis faced him, "and I've no desire to see Kennard's son cast out or stripped of wealth and power. Lew has no son, nor is likely to have, from something I heard—no, don't ask me where. A compromise might be worked out whereby he could have Armida, or its revenues, or both, for his lifetime, but—"

"I suppose you want to set up Gabriel in his place," Regis said. "I heard that song from Grandfather; I didn't think you would sing it too!"

"With Marius dead, it seems reasonable, doesn't it? I have no wish to see Alton heritage in Hastur hands. But there *is* an Alton child. Fostered in a good, loyal Domain—perhaps even in the care of Prince Derik and Linnell—that child could be trusted to bring back the honor of the Alton Domain."

"A child of Marius? Or of Kennard?"

"I'd rather not say anything about it until arrangements have been made," Dyan evaded, "but I give you my word of honor, the child's an Alton, and with potential *laran.* Regis, you are Lew's friend; can't you persuade him to step down and hand over the Domain in return for an assurance that during his lifetime he'll have Armida unquestioned? What do you think of that plan?"

It stinks to high heaven, Regis thought, but he cast about for some more diplomatic way of saying it. "Why not put it up to Lew? He's never been ambitious, and if this child is an Alton, he might perfectly well agree to adopt him and name the youngster his Heir."

"Lew's too damned much of a Terran," Dyan said. "He's lived in the Empire for years. I wouldn't trust him, now, to bring up a Comyn Heir."

"Kinsman," said Danilo, in the most formal mode; then he paused and walked restlessly to the window. Regis and Danilo were lightly in rapport, and Regis could see, through his friend's eyes, the view of the high mountain pass above Thendara and the scattered watch-fires of Beltran's army. Abruptly Danilo swung around and said to Dyan angrily,

"You pretend to be afraid of Lew because of his Terran education and because of Sharra! Have you forgotten that Beltran, out there, was part of the Sharra rebellion too? And *that's* the man you're trying to bring into the Comyn as full partner?"

"Beltran's devoted himself to undoing what his father did. Kermiac was a Terran lackey; but when Beltran became Lord Aldaran, he renounced that—"

"And renounced honor, decency and the laws of hospitality," said Danilo angrily. "You weren't there, sir, when he last decided to take action! I saw Caer Donn burning!"

Dyan shrugged slightly. "A Terran city. What a pity he didn't burn one or two more while he was at it! Don't you see, Beltran can use Sharra against the Terrans, to give us the upper hand if they continue to—encroach—on our good will and our world."

Regis and Danilo stared at him in horror. Finally Regis said, "Kinsman, I think you speak this way because you do not know much about Sharra. It cannot be tamed that way, and used as a weapon—"

"We would not have to use it," Dyan said. "The Terrans, too, remember Caer Donn and the burning of the spaceport there. The threat would be enough."

Why should we need such a threat against the Terrans? We live in the same world! We cannot destroy them without destroying ourselves!

Dyan asked angrily, "Have you too, Regis, been seduced by the Empire? I never thought to see the day when a Hastur would speak treason!"

"I think what you say is worse than treason, Dyan," Regis said, struggling for calm. "I cannot believe that you would do what you censured Lew for doing—make compromise with Beltran to bring back all those old terrors out of the Ages of Chaos! I know Beltran. You do not."

"Don't I?" asked Dyan, his eyes glinting strangely.

"If you do, and you still wish this alliance—"

"Look here," said Dyan harshly, interrupting him, "what we face now is the very survival of the Comyn—you know that. We need a strong Comyn, firmly allied against those who would hand us over to the Terrans. The Ridenow have already gone over—or haven't you heard Lerrys's favorite speech? Write off the Ridenow. Write off Lew—a cripple, half Terran, with nothing to lose! Write off the Elhalyn—" and as Danilo began a formal protest he gestured him imperatively to silence. "If you don't know that Derik's a halfwit, you're the only one in Council who doesn't. Forget about the Aillard—*Domna* Callina is a sheltered woman, a Keeper, a Tower-dweller; she can't do much, but I do have some influence, praise to Aldones, on *Dom* Merryl." His grin was wolfish. "What does that leave? The three of us in this room, Merryl, and your grandfather—who's over a hundred, and although he's still sharp-witted enough, he can't go on forever! In the name of all of Zandru's frozen hells, Regis, need I say anything more?"

And this is the burden of being a Hastur, Regis thought wearily. *This is only the beginning. More and more they will come to me for such decisions.*

"You think that means we must make an alliance with Aldaran, even at the cost of betraying the legitimate Heads of two Domains?" he asked.

"Two Domains? Lew would have been exiled six years ago, and it seems to me we are being generous with him," Dyan said.

"And *Domna* Callina? Is a Keeper nothing more than a woman to be married off for a political alliance?"

"If she wished to remain a Keeper," said Dyan savagely, "she should have remained within her Tower and refrained from trying to meddle in Council affairs! Tell me, Regis, will you stand with me in Council, or are you going to side with the Ridenow and hand us over to the Terrans without making a fight for Darkover?"

Regis bent his head. Put starkly like that, it seemed to give him no choice. Dyan had neatly mousetrapped him into seeming to agree, and either way, he betrayed someone. Lew was his sworn friend from childhood. Painfully he remembered the years he had spent at Armida, running about like a puppy at Lew's heels, wearing his outgrown clothes, riding, hawking, fighting at his side in the fire-lines when the Kilghard Hills went up in flame; remembered a tie even stronger, even older than that with Danilo; the first fierce loyalty of his life. Lew, his sworn friend and foster-brother.

Maybe this was best after all. Lew had said, again and again, that he wants no power in Comyn. Certainly Regis could not allow Dyan to believe that he would side against the Hasturs, and for the Terrans. Regis swallowed hard, trying to weigh loyalties. For all of Dyan's harshness, he knew that the older man was a shrewd judge of political reality. The thought of Darkover and the Domains in the hands of the Terrans, one more colony in a star-spanning Empire, came hard. But there seemed no middle way.

"I will never compromise with Sharra," he said wearily, "I draw the line there."

"If you stand firmly with me," said Dyan, "we will never need to use it. If we take a firm line, the threat is enough—"

"I don't believe that," said Danilo. "Sharra—" he stopped and Regis knew Danilo was seeing what he saw, the monstrous form of fire, blanking every matrix in the vicinity, drawing power even from those who hated it . . . death, destruction, burning!

Dyan shook his head. "You were children then, both of you, and you had a scare. The Sharra matrix is no more than a weapon—a mighty weapon. But nothing worse. Surely—" he grinned his wolfish grin—"you do not believe that it is a God from some other dimension, or the old legends that Hastur bound Sharra in chains and that she should be loosed only at the end of the world—or maybe you do?" Dyan grinned again, "and maybe, Regis, you will have to be the Hastur to bind her this time!"

He is making fun of me, Regis knew it, and yet a terrifying chill made every hair on his body stand again on end.

Hastur the God, father and forefather of all the Hastur-kin, bound Sharra in chains. . . . and I am Hastur. Is this my task?

Shaking his head to clear it, he reached out to pour himself another cup of *jaco,* and sipped it slowly, hardly tasting the bitter-chocolate fragrance. He told himself angrily not to be superstitious. The Sharra matrix was a matrix, a mechanical means of amplifying psychic powers; it had been made by human minds and hands, and by other human minds and hands it could be contained and made harmless. In Beltran's hands—and Kadarin's—it would be a fearful weapon, but then, there was no reason Beltran should be allowed to use it. Kadarin was human; and both Comyn and Terran had put a price on his head. Surely it was not as bad as he feared.

He said steadily to Dyan, "On the word of a Hastur, kinsman, I will never sit by and see our world handed over to the Terrans. We may not agree on the methods taken to avoid this; but we are in agreement otherwise."

And as he said it, he realized that he was trying to placate Dyan, as if he were still a boy and Dyan his cadet-master.

Dyan and his grandfather were on the same side, aiming at the same goal. Yet he had quarreled with his grandfather; and he was trying hard to agree with Dyan. Why? he wondered. Is it only because Dyan understands and accepts me as I am?

He said abruptly, "Thank you for a fine breakfast, cousin, I must go and get myself into those damnable Council ceremonials, and try to persuade my grandfather that Mikhail is still too young to sit through an entire Council session, Heir to Hastur or no—he is nevertheless only a boy of eleven! Dani, I will see you in the Crystal Chamber," and he went out of the room.

But it was Lerrys who caught up with him on the threshold of the Crystal Chamber. He was wearing the colors of his Domain, but not the full ceremonial robes, and he looked mockingly at Regis.

"Full fancy dress, I see. I hope Lew Alton has sense enough to turn up this morning wearing something like Terran clothes."

"I wouldn't call that very sensible," Regis said. "They wouldn't fit the climate, and it would just offend people without any reason. Why should it matter what we wear to Council?"

"It doesn't. That's the point. That's why it makes me so damnably angry to see a dozen or so grown men and women behaving as if it made a difference whether we wore one kind of dress or another!"

Regis had been thinking something rather like this himself, as he got into the cumbersome and archaic robes, but for some reason it exasperated him to hear Lerrys say it. He said, "In that case, what are you doing wearing your clan colors?"

"I'm a younger son, if you remember," said Lerrys, "and neither Head nor Heir to Serrais; if I did it, all they'd do would be to send me away for not following custom, like a horrid small boy who's dressed up for the fun of it. But if you, Heir to Hastur, or Lew, who's head of Armida by default—there's literally no one else now—should refuse to follow that custom, you might be able to change things . . . things which will never be changed unless you, or somebody like you, has the brains and the guts to change them! I heard that Lord Damon, what-do-they-call-him, Jeff, went back to Arilinn. I wish he'd stayed. He'd been brought up on Terra itself; and yet he was telepath enough to become a technician at Arilinn—that would have let some fresh air into Arilinn, and I think it's time to break a few windows in the Crystal Chamber, too!"

Regis said soberly, ignoring the rest of Lerrys's long speech, "I wish I were as sure as you that they'd accept Lew by default. Have you heard anything about a rumor that they've found a child of one of the Altons and they're going to set it up, like a figurehead, in Lew's place?"

"I know there's supposed to be such a child," said Lerrys. "I don't know all the details. Marius knew, but I don't think he ever got the chance to tell Lew. You got him first, didn't you?"

Regis stared at him in dismay and anger. "Zandru's hells! Are you daring to say that *I* had anything to do with Marius's death?"

"Not you personally," said Lerrys, "but I don't think we'd have to look too far for the murderer, do you? It's just too convenient for that group of power-mad old freaks in Council."

Regis shuddered but tried not to let Lerrys see his consternation. "You must be mad," he said at last. "If my grandsire—and I suppose it's Lord Hastur you're accusing—had intended to send assassins to deal with Marius, why would he have waited this long? He arranged it with the Terrans to have Marius given the best education they could provide, he always knew where Marius was—why in all the hells should he send anyone round to murder him now?"

"You're not going to tell me a boy Marius's age had any personal enemies, are you?" Lerrys demanded.

Not in the Comyn—no more than he had any personal friends there, Regis thought, and said stiffly, "That touches the honor of Hastur, Lerrys. I warn you not to repeat that monstrous slander beyond this room, or I will—"

"You'll what? Whip out your little sword and cut me to pieces with it? Regis, you're acting like a boy of twelve! Do you honestly believe all this stable-sweepings about the honor of Hastur?" Even through his rage, something in Lerrys's voice got through to Regis. His hand had gone to his dagger, without being fully aware of it; now he let go the hilt, and said, "Don't mock that honor, Lerrys, just because you don't know anything about it."

"Regis," said Lerrys, and now his voice was deadly serious, "believe me, I'm not implying that you are personally anything but a model of integrity. But it wouldn't be the first time that a Hastur had stood by and watched someone murdered, or worse, because that person didn't fit into the Comyn plan. Ask Jeff sometime who murdered his mother, because she dared to hint that a Comyn Keeper was not a sacrosanct virgin locked up in Arilinn to be worshipped. He himself had two or three narrow escapes from being murdered out of hand because the Council didn't find him too convenient to their long-range plans. We can't even blame the Terrans—assassination has been a favorite weapon here on Darkover since the Ages of Chaos. Do you know what the Terrans think of us?"

"Does it matter what the Terrans think of us?" Regis evaded.

"Damn right it matters! Whether you like it or not—" he broke off. "Ah, why should I waste this on you? You're no better than your grandfather, and why should I give you the full speech I'm going to try to make in Council, if they don't shut me up first?" He started to push on by Regis, who caught his arm and held him.

"My grandfather may not have mourned very much for Marius," he said, "but I'd swear with my hand in the fires of Hali that he had nothing to do with his murder! I was there when the Alton's town house was burned. Marius was killed by men trying to get the Sharra matrix—and they did get it, you know. You don't think my grandfather had anything to do with *that,* certainly?"

Lerrys stared at him for a moment; then said contemptuously, "You're worse than Lew—or you've been talking to him. He sees *Sharra* as the bogeyman under every bed! Damned convenient, isn't it?" He pushed past Regis and went into the Council Chamber.

Thoughtfully, Regis followed. Most of the Council members were inside their railed enclosures, and his grandfather had already risen for the roll call of the Domains. He scowled at Regis, seeing him enter almost with Lerrys Ridenow, but they parted and went to their separate enclosures.

Was Marius's death not the accidental death he had thought, killed in defending his father's house and home against invaders searching for something he did not even know about? Certainly Marius knew nothing about the Sharra matrix except its danger—he thought of the night Marius had come to seek his help for Rafe Scott.

I wonder where he is? Maybe Lew would know. If I were young Scott, I think I would be hiding inside the Terran Zone and never put my nose outside it while Kadarin is loose with the Sharra matrix; and I think if Lew had any sense he would do the same. But Lew is not that kind of person. *Terrans are cowards,* he thought, his mind sliding over what he had taken for granted all his life; his own father had been killed in a war because some coward had trusted to Terran weapons which kill at a distance; and then he stopped and began to think about that.

They can't all be cowards, any more than all Comyn lords are honorable and proud. . . . he thought. And, as Derik began to call the roll of the Domains, he thought: *I will have to go to the Terran Zone and find out what Rafe Scott knows about the Sharra matrix. Unless he's joined forces with Kadarin—and that was not the idea I got of Rafe Scott!*

One by one, from their enclosures, the Comyn of the Seven Domains answered for their Houses. When "Alton" was called, Regis saw Lew, dressed in the ceremonial robes of his house, step forward, and answer, "I am here for Alton of Armida." Regis had been braced for a challenge, but it did not come, not even from where Dyan sat beside Danilo beneath the Ardais banner. Was the challenge to be more insidious than this, simply pressure on Lew to remain quietly at Armida and adopt the Alton son they had found somewhere? Were they allowing him to keep the nominal leadership of Alton in return for some other concession? Regis discovered that he could not even guess. And why was Dyan so certain that Lew would have no children?

Even Dyan himself, who is a lover of men, has a son; and

he lost another in childhood. I have fathered several children. Why should Lew not marry and have as many children as he wants? He turned to look at Lew, and saw, as Callina Aillard rose to answer for her Domain, that Lew was watching her intently, so intently that it seemed, even through the thick disturbance of the telepathic dampers in the Crystal Chamber, that for an instant he could read Lew's thoughts.

But Callina is a Keeper. Nevertheless, she would not be the first Keeper to lay down her high office and marry. . . . not the first nor the last. She would have to train her successor first, but Lew is not an impulsive boy; he could wait long enough for that. I think they might even be happy. It would be good to see Lew happy again.

They had finished the roll-call of the Domains, without reference to Aldaran. It seemed to Regis that there was someone in that enclosure, behind the curtains, and he wondered at that, but Derik, his task finished, had stepped back, and Hastur was taking his place to preside over the session. Supposedly, this final session of Council was to complete any unfinished matters, anything left unsettled during the Council season. In actuality, Regis knew, any small time-consuming triviality would be brought up, anything to fill time until weariness, or even hunger, brought Council to an end; after which, the matter would be closed till next year. He supposed that was why Hastur had not challenged Lew when he spoke for Armida; the real problem of the Alton heritage would be settled quietly by personal pressures, behind the scenes, not argued out in Council.

He had seen those tactics used before. And now, ignoring Dyan's signal, Hastur gestured to Lerrys Ridenow, who had risen for recognition.

Lerrys came down into the central space where the rainbows from the prisms in the roof cast colored lights over the pale floor and walls. He bowed, and Regis thought, dispassionately, that the young man was beautiful as a cat; red-haired, slender, lithe, with the delicate chiseled features of the Ridenow; more beautiful, he thought, than any of the women in the Crystal Chamber. He wondered why he was noticing this in this solemn setting.

"My lords," Lerrys said, "I've heard a lot in this Chamber since Council began. All of you—" with one of those quick catlike movements, he swiveled his head to look around the room, "have been talking about such serious matters as marriages, and heritages, and repairs to the Castle roof—oh, not literally, perhaps, but that's what it amounts to, discussing things seriously which could be settled in three minutes by a little common sense. I want to know when we are going to talk about serious things. For instance—" and this time the sweep of his eyes around the Chamber was hard and challenging, "when are we going to send our proper representative to the Empire Senate? When are we going to appoint a Senator with proper credentials? I want to know when, or if, we are going to launch a *real* investigation of who murdered Marius Alton and burned the Alton house over his head? And I want to know when we are going to take our part as an equal in the Empire Senate, instead of being under a Terran protectorate as a primitive, barbarian world with a feudal culture which mustn't be touched, as if we were savages just evolving to the point where we rub two sticks together and worship the god of fire who makes the spark!"

The contempt in his voice was scathing.

"They let us alone, when they ought to be honoring us as the first and most prestigious of their colonies!"

"That kind of honor—" it was a whiplash from Dyan—"we can well do without!"

Lerrys turned on him. He said, "What in hell do *you* know about the Terrans? Have you ever gone far enough to take a walk inside the Terran Zone and go through one of their buildings? Have you ever done *anything* in the Terran Zone except visit one of their exotic whorehouses? With all due respect—which isn't much, Lord Dyan—you ought to shut your mouth until you know what you're talking about!"

"I know you are trying to make us all Terrans—" said Dyan, and Lerrys said, "*Make* us Terrans? Hell! We *are* Terrans, or has that significant fact been kept from you by your crazy father, and all our forefathers? If there's anyone here who doesn't know that we were a Terran colony once, it's time that sheltered idiot learned the truth!"

Danvan of Hastur said repressively, "This matter has been discussed before, by your elders, Dom Lerrys. We are all in agreement that we want no part of Terra—"

"You are all in agreement," mocked Lerrys. "How many of you are in agreement—all fifteen or sixteen of you? What's the population of Thendara, at the last census, or have we been too backward to number our people? What do you think *they* would say, if you asked them whether they wanted to go on worshipping you aristocrats as *the Hastur-kin, the children of Gods,* and all that balderdash? Or whether they preferred to be free citizens of the Empire, with a voice in their own government, and no need to bow down to you lofty Comyn? Just ask them sometime!"

Edric Ridenow, Lord Serrais, rose ponderously from his seat. He said, "We have ruled these lands from time out of mind and we know what our people want. Get back to your place, Lerrys; I did not give you leave to speak!"

"No, you didn't," retorted Lerrys at white heat, "and I spoke anyway. It needs saying! I am a citizen of the Empire, I want some real voice in what's happening!"

"Do you really believe that will give you such a voice?" inquired Lord Hastur. Regis thought he sounded genuinely curious. "You have accused Lord Dyan of speaking without real knowledge of the Terrans. Can you accuse me of the same? I have dealt with the Terrans during most of my long life, Lerrys, and I can assure you, they have nothing worth wanting. But I cannot sit here and let you speak out of turn in Council. I beg you, sit until your brother and lord gives you leave to speak."

"Who in all of Zandru's hells gave him godship over my voice?" demanded Lerrys in a rage. "I am Comyn, though you may not want to admit it, and I have a right to be heard—"

"Gabriel," said Hastur quietly, "your duty."

Regis said, "Let him speak, Grandfather. I want to hear what he has to say." But he was shouted down, and Gabriel, drawn sword of the honor-guard in hand, strode to Lerrys and said quietly, "Sit, *dom* Lerrys. Silence."

Lerrys said, "Like hell—"

"You leave me no choice, sir. Forgive me," Gabriel gestured to the Guardsmen, who collared Lerrys roughly; he elbowed and shoved, but he was lightly built and the Guards were two huge hefty men, and they had no trouble at all in restraining him. They frog-marched him toward his seat. Abruptly, with a swift kick or two well-placed, he managed to free himself, and stood defiant.

"Never mind. I'm not going to upset your precious fool's Council any more," he said. "You're not worth it. Now have me assassinated as you did with Marius Alton, because I'm on the wrong side of the political fence! Damned fools, all of you, and murderers, because you're afraid to listen to the facts! You're a damned bloody anachronism, all of you, sitting there playing at lords and ladies with a star-spanning Empire at your feet! All right, damn it, go to hell in your own way, and I'll stand there and watch while you do it!" He laughed, loud and mocking, swirled with a great flying toss of his cape and his long light hair, and turned his back, striding out of the Council Chamber.

Regis sat there, aghast. Lerrys had voiced the thoughts he had never dared, before, to voice—and he had sat there, like a lump, not daring to speak aloud, not challenging Gabriel. *Damn it, I should have stepped down there beside him and demanded some of those answers! I am Heir to Hastur, they could not have silenced me so easily!*

He told himself that he had had no choice; that Lerrys had been excluded because of his disregard of Council custom and courtesies, not because of what he was saying.

He all but accused them of murder, and no one spoke to deny it, Regis thought, with a sudden shiver. Was it only because they felt it too ridiculous to answer? He did not like to think about the alternative.

One of the lesser nobles, a Di Asturien from the shores of Lake Mirien—Regis knew him slightly; he had had a brief affair with one of the man's daughters—rose and gestured to Lord Hastur for recognition. Hastur nodded, and the man came down to the speaker's place.

"My lords," he said, "I do not question your wisdom, but I feel it needs explaining. In these days, when we in Council are so few, why should Prince Derik be married inside of Comyn? Their children will be divided between the two Domains involved; would it not be better for Prince Derik to marry outside the Council, and thus bring in a strong alliance? Linnell Lindir-Aillard, too, should be married to some man who will bring new blood into Council. I also wish to point out that the two of them are very closely akin. With all respect sir, I point out that the inner circle of Comyn has already been thinned overmuch by inbreeding. I'm not asking that we go back to the old days of keeping stud-books on *laran,* my lord, but any horse-breeder can tell you that too much inbreeding brings out bad things in the blood lines."

Yes, it does, Regis thought, looking at Callina, who looked so frail it seemed a puff of air would waft her off her feet; at Derik's shallow foolish face. Javanne had been lucky, being married outside direct Comyn lines. Her sons were all healthy and strong. Derik—looking at the young prince, Regis wondered if Derik would father anything but a string of halfwits like himself. And suddenly his blood iced; he looked at Derik and saw nothing, nothing but a grinning skull . . . *a skull, laughing* . . . he rubbed his hands over his eyes and Derik was simply sitting there with his good-natured dimwitted grin.

Hastur said quietly, "You have a good point, sir. But Prince Derik and *comynara* Linnell were childhood sweethearts, and it would be cruel to part them now. There are others who can bring fresh blood into Council."

Regis thought, cynically, *maybe that's a good name for what I am doing, fathering nedestro sons wherever I wish . . . the women don't seem to object, and neither do their fathers, since I am Hastur of Hastur* . . . and his thoughts slid aside, as he saw Lady Callina rise, looking tall and stately in her crimson ceremonial robes.

"This matter is not for Council meddling," she said, pale as death, "Linnell is *my* ward! I have given consent to her marriage and that is enough!"

"Meddling, lady?" asked Di Asturien, "That's a strange way to put it. Marriages in Comyn are supposed to be settled by the Council, aren't they?"

"I am Head of Aillard. Linnell's marriage is not for the Council to agree or disagree."

"But the prince's is," the old man insisted. "I protest it, and I'm sure there are others!"

Derik said amiably, "Can't you trust me to choose my own wife, sir? Or am I to imitate a Dry-Towner and have half a dozen wives and *barraganas*? Even a prince should have a few areas of private choice."

"What does the lady say about it?" asked old Di Asturien, and Linnell, sitting in Callina's shadow, colored and shrank away.

"This marriage was approved by the Council a long time

ago," she said, almost in a whisper. "If somebody was going to protest against it, they should have done so years ago. Derik and I were handfasted when I was fourteen and he was twelve. There's been time enough to protest it before this, and before we—before we had our hearts set on each other."

"That was a long time ago, and the Council was stronger then," said the old man, grumpily. "There are plenty of women in the Domains with good blood in 'em. He didn't have to choose a sister of another Domain Head."

"With respect, sir," said Lord Hastur, "we have heard what you have to say. Is there anyone within Comyn who wants to speak on this?"

"I will not hear," said Callina, in pale rage. "I have given consent to this marriage, and there is no other with the power by law to change it."

"And if anyone tries," said Derik, "I will challenge him anywhere." He laid his hand to sword-hilt.

And for a moment it seemed to Regis that he saw the Council as Lerrys had seen it; children, squabbling over toys, that contemptuous *You'll whip out your little sword and cut me to pieces with it.* Derik had spoken as honor and Comyn law demanded, yet he sounded like a blustering fool. Derik was a fool, of course. But had he ever had a chance to be anything else? Were they all, in Comyn, just such fools?

But Hastur was going, calmly, along with custom. He said to Di Asturien, "Sir, are you ready to accept Prince Derik's challenge?"

The old man shrank.

"All Gods forbid, sir! I, challenge Hastur of Elhalyn and my lawful prince? I was just putting the question, Lord Hastur, no more than that." He bowed to Derik. *"Su serva, Dom."* And Regis, watching the dignified old man retreat, almost servile, heard again Lerrys's question . . . *playing at lords and ladies* . . . why, because of his ancestry, should a fool like Derik make an old and honorable man, of excellent lineage and long service to his country, cringe like that?

I get it too. From the time I was ten years old, Guards following me around like so many governesses, for fear I would break a toenail—why, in heaven's name?

Preoccupied again, he missed the next words of Hastur, and roused suddenly to shock when Hastur called out, "The Seventh Domain! Aldaran!"

Then Regis heard a voice he had never thought to hear again, speaking from behind the curtain; then the curtain rings clashed with a small metallic clamor, and a tall man came and stood at the edge of the railing.

He looked like Lew; older, and unscarred, but the resemblance was still there; he might have been Lew's elder brother. He said, "I am here for Aldaran; Beltran-Kermiac, Lord of Aldaran and Scathfell."

And the shocked silence in the Crystal Chamber was shattered by Lew's loud cry.

"I protest!"

CHAPTER EIGHT

(Lew Alton's narrative)

I didn't know I was going to protest until I heard myself doing it.

I heard them call Aldaran's name, and realized that this was actually happening; it was not a nightmare. I had heard the voice in nightmares, often enough. He was still so much like me that I have seen twins less alike; although now, no one could mistake us . . . bitterness overwhelmed me. It was he who had worked to summon Sharra; and there he stood, unscathed; while I, who had suffered to stem the fire-storm he had raised, and contain Sharra again, so that it should not ravage our world from the Bay of Storms to the Wall Around the World—I stood here, scarred and mutilated, more of an outcast than he.

"I protest!" I shouted again, leaping down until I stood at the center of the open space, facing him.

Hastur said mildly, "We have not yet called for a formal challenge. You must state the reasons for your protest."

I fought to steady my voice. Whatever my own hate—and I felt that it would rise and swallow me—I must speak now calmly. Hysteria would only harm my cause; no matter what protests, incoherent accusations, were tumbling over one another in my mind, I must plead my cause with quiet rationality. I grasped at the presence in my mind, the alien memories I carried; how would my father have spoken? He had usually been able to make them do his will.

"I declare—" I began, trying to steady my voice against the flood, "I declare—the existence—of an unsettled blood feud." Blood feud was held, everywhere in the Domains, to be an obligation surmounting every other consideration. "His life is—is mine; I have claimed it."

To this moment our eyes had not met; now he raised his head, and looked at me, skeptical, concerned. I turned my own away. I did not want to remember that once I had called this man cousin and friend. Gods above, how could the man stand there and look me calmly in the eye and say, as he was saying now, "I did not know you felt that way, Lew. Do you blame me for everything then? How can I make amends? Certainly I was not aware of any such quarrel as that."

Amends! I clenched the stump of my arm with my good hand, wanting to shout, *can you make amends for this? Can you give me back six years of my life, can you bring back—Marjorie?* For once in my life I was grateful for the presence of the telepathic dampers without which all this would have blasted through the room with the full force of the hyper-developed Alton rapport—but I said doggedly, "Your life is mine; when, where and as I can."

Beltran spead his hands slightly, as if to say, "What is this all about?" Before the puzzled look in his eyes, I swear that for a moment I doubted my own sanity. Had I dreamed it all? My fingernails clenched in my wrist, and I reminded myself; *this* was no nightmare.

Hastur said sternly, "Your words are nothing here, Lord Armida." I remembered, after a shocked second; this was *my* name, not my father's; I was Lord Armida now.

"You have forgotten," Hastur went on, "blood feud is forbidden here in Comyn as among equals." The word was a counterplay on words; the word *comyn* meant, simply, *equals in rank or status.*

"And I state," said Beltran calmly, "that I have no grudge against my cousin of Alton; if he believes there is a bloodfeud between us, it must arise from a time in his life when he was—" and I could see everyone in Council saying what he seemed, so kindly, to forbear saying: *from a time when he was mad.* . . .

The very existence of Comyn, the Seven Domains of the Hastur's kin, was predicated on an alliance prohibiting bloodfeud, Comyn immunity. Which Beltran, damn him, now enjoyed. Zandru send him scorpion whips! Was there no way to stop this farce?

Where I was standing I could not see her; but Callina rose and came forward, her crimson Keeper's veils fluttering as if in an invisible breeze. I turned as she spoke; she stood there, strange, distant, remote, not at all like the woman I had held in my arms and pledged to support. Her voice, too, sounded faraway and overly distinct, as if it came, not *from* her, but somehow *through* her.

"My lord Aldaran, as Keeper of Comyn I have the right to ask this of you. Have you sworn allegiance to Compact?"

"When I am pledged Comyn," Beltran said, "I am ready to swear."

She gestured and said, "Your army stands out there, bearing Terran weapons, in defiance of Compact. Are we to allow you in Comyn when you have not yet sworn to observe the first law of Comyn, in return for welcoming you among us?"

"When I swear to Comyn," said Beltran with silken suaveness, "my Honor Guard shall give up those weapons into the hands of my promised wife."

I saw Callina flinch at the words. There were telepathic dampers all over the room, but still it seemed that I could read her thoughts.

If I do not agree to this marriage, it means war. The last war in the Domains decimated the Comyn. Beltran could wipe us out altogether.

She raised her eyes and looked at him. She said, her words dropping into deathly silence, "Why, then, my lord of Aldaran, if you are content with an unwilling bride—" she hesitated; I knew she did not turn or look at me, but I sensed the trapped despair behind her words—"then I agree. Let the handfasting be held on Festival Night."

"Be it so," said Beltran, with that smile that was like a mask over his true feelings, and bowed. I stood, without moving, as if my feet were rooted to the floor of the Crystal Chamber. Were they really going to do this? Were they going to sell Callina to Beltran, to prevent war? Was there no one who could lift a hand against this monstrous injustice?

In a final appeal I cried out, "Will you have him in Council, then? He is sealed to Sharra!"

He turned directly to me, then, and said, "So are you, cousin."

To that, there was nothing I could say. I felt at that moment like doing what Lerrys had done, and storming out of the Council, cursing them all.

I have never been quite sure what happened next. I know that I made a move to resume my seat, had taken a few steps toward the Alton enclosure, when I heard a cry, in a woman's voice. For a moment it sounded so like Dio's that I stood frozen; then Derik cried out, too, and I turned to see Beltran take a step back and thrust out his hands, as if to guard himself.

Then there were cries everywhere, shouts of dread and terror; backing a little away into the enclosure, I saw it, hanging in the air above us, growing, menacing. . . .

The form of a chained woman, hair of flame, tossing, ravening, growing higher, higher, with the crackling sound of forest-fire . . . Sharra! The fire-form, Sharra. . . . Now I know it was a nightmare from hell, I backed away, too, from the rising flames licking at us, the smell of burning, the flood of terror, of hate, the corner of hell which had opened up for me six years ago. . . .

I clutched at vanishing self-control before I could cry out again and disgrace myself by screaming like a woman. The Form of Fire was there, yes; it hovered and flickered and trembled above us, the shape of a woman, her head thrown back, three times the height of a tall man, the flames licking at her hair. *Marjorie! Marjorie, burning, overshadowed by Sharra* . . . then I caught at vanishing rationality.

No, this was not Sharra as I had known it. My heart was beating fast from fright, but there was no true smell of burning in the room, the curtains of the enclosures did not smolder or catch into flame where the fire touched them . . . this was illusion, no more, and I stood, clenching the fist of my good hand, feeling the nails cut into the flesh, feeling the old burning pain in the hand that was not there . . . *phantom pain, as this was no more than a phantom, an image of Sharra. . . . I would have known the real thing, I would feel my whole body and soul tied into that monstrous overshadowing. . . .*

The Form of Fire thrust out an arm . . . a woman's arm lapped in fire . . . and Beltran broke, backed away . . . bolted from the Crystal Chamber. Now that I knew what it was, I stood my ground, watching him go, wondering who had done it. Kadarin, wherever he was, drawing the Sword, evoking the Form of Fire? No. I was sealed to Sharra, body and soul; if Kadarin, who had also been sealed to that unholy thing, had summoned, I too would have been consumed in the flame. . . . I gripped my hand hard on the railing, wondering. The Comyn were milling around, crying out in confusion. Two or three others bolted, too, through their private entrances at the back of the enclosures.

Callina? No Keeper would profane her office that way, using it to terrify. I could have done it—even now I could feel the heat of flame in my useless matrix—but I knew I had not. Beltran, who also was Sharra-sealed? He had been the most frightened of all, for he had seen Caer Donn burning.

The Form of Fire flamed and died and was gone, like a candle blown out by the wind.

Danvan of Hastur, Regent of the Comyn, had stood his ground, but he was white as death, and he was holding the rail before him as he spoke, ritual words almost without significance.

"I declare . . . Council Session . . . closed for this year and all matters before it, adjourned until another year shall bring us together . . ."

One by one, those members who had not already run away went silently out of the Chamber, already shocked and ashamed of their terror. I, who had faced the reality of Sharra, found myself wondering how they would react to the real thing. Yet my own heart was still pounding a little; a fear bred in the bone, a gateway just dimly ajar between worlds to let in that monstrous shadow. . . . I had seen those gates open halfway, and knew that they opened into fire and hell, like the living heart of a volcano.

Then, behind Danvan Hastur, I saw Regis standing very still, his hand just touching his matrix. He did not look at me, he was not looking at anything, but I knew, as clearly as if I had spoken:

Regis! Regis had summoned that image! But why? Why and how!

He lowered his hand. I could see fine beads of sweat around his hairline, but his voice sounded normal. "Will you have my arm, Grandfather?"

The old man snarled, "When I need help I will be dressed in my shroud!" and, throwing his head erect, marched out of the Chamber. Now only Regis and I remained.

I found my voice, bitterly.

"You did that. I don't know how or why, but *you* did that! Cousin—can you play with such things as a joke?"

His hand fell away from his matrix, hanging limp at his side as if it hurt him. Maybe it did; I was too agitated to care. At last he said in a strained voice, only a whisper, "It gave us—time. Another year. They cannot—cannot challenge your right to the Alton Domain, or pledge Beltran to Council, for another year. Council has been—closed." Then he swayed, and caught weakly at the railing where he stood. I pushed him down in a chair.

"Put your head between your knees," I said roughly, and watched him as he sat there, his head bent, while a little color began to come back into his cheeks. At last he sat upright again.

"I am sorry if the—the image—frightened you," he said. "It was the only thing I could think of to stop this Council. This farce. I wanted them to see what it was that they had to fear. So many of them don't know."

I remembered Lerrys saying, *You see Sharra as the bogeyman under every bed* . . . no. He had not said that to me, but to Regis. I looked at him, dazed. I said, "There are supposed to be telepathic dampers in here. I should not be able to read your mind, nor you mine. Zandru's hells, Regis, what is going on?"

"Maybe the dampers aren't working," he said, in a stronger voice, and now he sounded completely rational; only afraid, as he had every right to be. I was afraid myself.

"The image didn't frighten me," I said, "except for a moment at first. I have seen the reality of Sharra. What frightens me, now, is the fact that you could do that, with dampers all over the room. I didn't know you had that much *laran,* though I knew, of course, that you had some. What sort of *laran* can do that?" I went to the nearest of the telepathic dampers and twisted dials until it was gone, the unrhythmic waves vanished. Now I could feel Regis's agitation and fear, full scale, and wished I could not. He said, in a strained voice, "I don't know how I did it. Truly I don't. I was standing here behind Grandfather, listening to Beltran talk so calmly, and wishing there was some way to show them what it had been. . . . and then—" he wet his lips with his tongue, and said shakily, "then it was there. The—the Form of Fire."

"And it scared Beltran right out of the room," I said. "Do you think he knows that Kadarin has the Sharra matrix?"

"I couldn't read him. I wasn't trying, of course. I—" his voice broke again. "I wasn't *trying* to do anything. It just—just happened!"

"Something in your *laran* you don't know about? We know so little of the Hastur Gift, whatever it was," I said, trying to calm him. "Hang on to the good part; it scared Beltran out of here. I wish it had scared him all the way back into the Hellers! I'm afraid there's no such luck!"

I was willing to leave it at that. But as I turned to the doorway, Regis caught at my shoulder.

"But how could I do that? I don't understand! You—you accused me of playing with it, like a joke! But I didn't, Lew, I didn't!"

I had no answer for him. I moved aimlessly around the room, turning out the rest of the dampers. I could feel his fear, mounting almost to panic, rising as the dampers were no longer there to interfere with telepathic contact. I even wondered, angrily, why *he* should be so afraid. It was I who was bound to Sharra, I who must live night and day with the terror that one day Kadarin would draw the Sword of Sharra and with that gesture summon me back into that terrible gateway between worlds, that corner of hell that I once had opened, which had swept away my hand, my love—my life . . .

Firmly I clamped down on the growing panic. If I did not stop this now, my own fear and Regis's could reinforce each other and we would both go into screaming hysterics. I caught at what I could remember of the Arilinn training, managed to steady my breathing, felt the panic subside.

Not so Regis; he was still sitting there, in the chair where I had shoved him, white with dread. I turned around and was surprised to hear my own voice, the steady, detached voice of a matrix mechanic, dispassionate, professionally soothing, as I had not heard it in more years than I liked to think about.

"I'm not a Keeper, Regis, and my own matrix, at the moment, is useless, as you know. I could try to deep-probe you and find out—"

He flinched. I didn't blame him. The Alton gift is nothing to play games with, and I have known experienced technicians, Tower-trained for many years, refuse to face that fully focused gift of rapport. I can manage it, if I must, but

I was not eager. It is not, I suppose, unlike rape, the deliberate overpowering of a mind, the forced submission of another personality, the ultimate invasion. Only the probably non-existent Gods of Darkover know why such a Gift had been bred into the Alton line, to force rapport on an unwilling other, paralyze resistance. I knew Regis feared it too, and I didn't blame him. My father had opened my own Gift in that way, when I was a boy—it had been the only way to force the Council to accept me, to show them that I, alien and half Terran, had the Alton Gift—and I had been ill for weeks afterward. I didn't relish the thought of doing the same thing to Regis.

I said, "It might be that they could tell you in a Tower; some Keeper, perhaps—" and then I remembered that here in Comyn Castle was a Keeper. I tended to forget; Ashara of the Comyn Tower must be incredibly old now, I had never seen her, nor my father before me . . . but now Callina was there as her surrogate, and Callina was my kinswoman, and Regis's too.

"Callina could tell you," I said, "if she would."

He nodded, and I felt the panic recede. Talking about it, calmly and detached, as if it were a simple problem in the mechanics of *laran,* had defused some of the fear.

Yet I too was uneasy. By the time I left the Crystal Chamber, even the halls and corridors were empty; the Comyn Council had scattered and gone their separate ways. Council was over. Nothing remained except the Festival Night ball, tomorrow. On the threshold of the Chamber, we encountered the Syrtis youngster; he almost ignored me, hurrying to Regis.

"I came back to see what had happened to you!" he demanded, and, as Regis smiled at him, I quietly took my leave, feeling I made an unwelcome third. As I went off alone, I identified one of my emotions; was I jealous of what Regis shared with Danilo? No, certainly not.

But I am alone, brotherless, friendless, alone against the Comyn who hate me, and there is none to stand by my side. All my life I had dwelt in my father's shadow; and now I could not bear the solitude when that was withdrawn. And Marius, who should have stood at my side—Marius too was dead by an assassin's bullet, and no one in the Comyn except Lerrys had even questioned the assassination.

And—I felt myself tensing as I identified another element of my deep grief for Marius. It was relief; relief that I would not have to test him as my father had tested me, that I need not invade him ruthlessly and feel him die beneath that terrible assault on identity. He had died, but not at my hands, nor beneath my *laran.*

I had known my laran could kill, but I had never killed with it.

I went back to the Alton rooms, thoughtfully. They were home, they had been home much of my life, yet they seemed empty, echoing, desolate. It seemed to me that I could see my father in every empty corner, as his voice still echoed in my mind. Andres, puttering around, supervising the other servants in placing the belongings which had been brought here from the town house, broke off what he was doing as I came in, and hurried to me, demanding to know what had happened to me. I did not know that it showed on my face, whatever it was, but I let him bring me a drink, and sat sipping it, wondering again about what Regis had done in the Crystal Chamber. He had scared Beltran. But, probably, not enough.

I did not think Beltran was eager to plunge the Domains into war. Yet I knew his recklessness, and I did not think we could gamble on that; not when his outraged pride was at stake, the pride of the Aldarans.

I said to Andres, "You hear servants' gossip; tell me, has Beltran moved into the Aldaran apartments here in Comyn Castle?"

Andres nodded glumly, and I hoped that he would find them filled with vermin and lice; they had stood empty since the Ages of Chaos. It said something about the Comyn that they had never been converted to other uses.

Andres stood over me, grumbling, "You're not intending to go and pay a call on him there, I hope!"

I wasn't. There was only one way in the world I would ever come again within striking range of my cousin, and that was if he had me bound and gagged. He had betrayed me before; he would have no further chance. Sunk in the misery of that moment, I confess, to my shame, that for a moment I played with the escape that Dan Lawton, in the Terran Zone, had offered me, to hide there out of reach of Sharra. . . . but that was no answer, and it left Regis and Callina at the mercy of whatever unknown thing was working in the Comyn.

I was not altogether alone. The thought of Callina warmed me; I had pledged to stand beside her. And I had not yet spoken alone with my kinswoman Linnell, except over the grave of my brother. It was the eve of Festival Night, when traditionally, gifts of fruit and flowers are sent to the women of every family, throughout the Domains. Not the meanest household in Thendara would let tomorrow morning pass without at least a few garden flowers or a handful of dried fruits for the women of the household; and I had done nothing about a gift for Linnell. Truly, I had been too long away from Darkover.

There would be flower sellers and fruit vendors doing business in the markets of the Old Town, but as I stepped toward the door, I hesitated, unwilling again to show myself. Damn it, during the time I had lived with Dio, I had almost forgotten my scarred face, my missing hand, and now I was behaving as if I were freshly maimed—Dio! Where was Dio, had I truly heard her voice in the Crystal Chamber? I told myself sternly that it did not matter; whether Dio was here or elsewhere, if she chose not to come to me, she was lost to me. But still I could not make myself go down to ground level of the enormous castle, go out into the Old Town through Beltran's damnably misnamed *Honor Guard.*

Some of them would have known me, remembered me. . . .

At last, hating myself for the failure, I told Andres to see about some flowers for Linnell tomorrow. Should I send some to Dio too? I truly did not know the courtesies of the situation. Out there in the Empire, I knew, a separated husband and wife can meet with common courtesy; here on Darkover, it was unthinkable. Well, I was on Darkover now, and if Dio wanted nothing from me, she would probably not want a Festival gift either. With surging bitterness I thought, *she has Lerrys to send her fruits and flowers.* If Lerrys had been before me, at that moment, I think I would have hit him. But what would that settle? Nothing. After a moment I picked up a cloak, flung it about my shoulders; but when Andres asked where I was going, I had no answer for him.

My feet took me down, and down into courtyards and

enclosed gardens, through unfamiliar parts of the castle. At one point I found myself in a court beneath the deserted Aldaran apartments—deserted all my life, till now. Half of me wanted to go in there and face Beltran, demand—demand what? I did not know. Another part of me wanted, cravenly, to walk through the city, take refuge in the Terran Zone, and then—then what? I could not leave Darkover, not while the Sharra matrix was here; I had tried. And tried again. It would mean death, a death neither quick nor easy.

Maybe I would be better dead, even that death, so that I was free in death of Sharra . . . and again it seemed to me that the Form of Fire raged before my eyes, a thrilling in my blood, cold terror and raging, ravening flame like ichor in my veins. . . .

No; this was real. I tensed, looking up at the hills behind the city.

Somewhere there, strange flames burned, an incredible ninth-level matrix twisted space around itself, a gateway opened, and the fire ran in my veins. . . . There was fire before my eyes, fire all through my brain. . . .

No! I am not sure that I did not scream that furious denial aloud; if I did no one heard me, but I heard the echoes in the courtyard around me, and slowly, slowly, came back to reality. Somewhere out there, Kadarin ran loose, and with him the Sharra matrix, and Thyra whom I had hated, loved, desired and feared . . . but I would die before they dragged me back into *that* again. Deliberately, fighting the call in my mind, I raised the stump of my arm and slammed it down, hard, on stone. The pain was incredible; it made me gasp, and tears came to my eyes, but that pain was *real;* outraged nerves and muscles and bones, not a phantom fire raging in my brain. I set my teeth and turned my back on the hills, and that call, that siren call which throbbed seductively in my mind, and went into the Castle.

Callina. Callina could drive these devils from my mind.

I had not been inside the Aillard wing of Comyn Castle for many years, not since I was a child. A silent servant met me, managed not to blink more than once at the ruin of my face. He showed me into a reception room where, he said, I would find *Domna* Callina and Linnell with her.

The room was spacious and brilliant, filled with sunshine

and silken curtains, green plants and flowers growing in every niche, like an indoor garden. Soft notes of a harp echoed through the room; Linnell was playing the *rryl.* But as I came in she pushed it aside and ran to me, taking an embrace and kiss with the privilege of a foster-sister, drawing back, hesitant, as she touched the stump of an arm.

"It's all right," I said. "You can't hurt me. Don't worry about it, little sister." I looked down at her, smiling. She was the only person on this world who had truly welcomed me, I thought; the only one who had had no thought of what my coming would mean. Even Marius had had to think of what it would mean in terms of Domain-right. Even Jeff; he might have had to leave Arilinn and take his place in Council.

"Your poor hand," she said. "Couldn't the Terrans do anything for it?"

Even to Linnell I didn't want to talk about it. "Not much," I said, "but I have a mechanical hand I wear when I don't want to be noticed. I'll wear it when I dance with you on Festival Night, shall I?"

"Only if you want to," she said seriously. "I don't care what you look like, Lew. You're always the same to me."

I hugged her close, warmed as much by her accepting smile as by the words. I suppose Linnell was a beautiful woman; I have never been able to see her as anything but the little foster-sister with whom I'd raced breakneck over the hills; I'd spanked her for breaking my toys or borrowing them without leave, comforted her when she was crying with toothache. I said, "You were playing the rryl . . . play for me, won't you?"

She took up the instrument again and began to play the ballad of Hastur and Cassilda:

> The stars were mirrored on the shore,
> Dark was the lone immortal moor,
> Silent were rocks and trees and stone—
> Robardin's daughter walked alone,
> A web of gold between her hands
> On shining spindle burning bright . . .

I had heard Dio singing it, though Dio had no singing voice to speak of—I wondered, where was Callina? I should speak with her—

Linnell gestured, and I saw, in a niche beyond the fireplace, Callina and Regis Hastur, seated on a soft divan and so absorbed in what they were saying that neither had heard me come into the room. I felt a momentary flare of jealousy—they looked so comfortable, so much at peace with each other—then Callina looked up at me and smiled, and I knew I had nothing to fear.

She came forward; I wanted to take her in my arms, into that embrace which was so much more than the embrace I would have given a kinswoman; instead she reached out and touched my wrist, the feather touch with which a working Keeper would have greeted me, and with that automatic gesture, frustration slipped between us like an unsheathed sword.

A Keeper. Never to be touched, never to be desired, even by a defiling thought . . . angry frustration, and at the same time, reassurance; this is how she would have greeted me if we were both back in Arilinn, where I had been happy . . . even had we been acknowledged lovers for years, she would no more have touched me than this.

But our eyes met, and she said gravely, "Ashara will see you, Lew. It is the first time, I think, in more than a generation, that she has agreed to speak with anyone from outside. When I spoke to her of the Sharra matrix, she said I might bring you."

Regis said, "I would like to speak with her, too. It may be that she would know something of the Hastur Gift . . ." but he broke off at Callina's cold frown.

"She has not asked for you. Even I cannot bring anyone into her presence unless she wishes it."

Regis subsided as if she had struck him. I blinked, staring aghast at this new Callina, the impassive mask of her face, the eyes and voice of a cold, stony stranger. Only a moment, and she was again the Callina I knew, but I had seen, and I was puzzled and dismayed. I would have said something more, even to reassure Regis that we would ask the ancient *leronis* to grant him an audience, but Linnell claimed me again.

"Are you going to take him away at once? When we have not seen each other for so many years? Lew, you must tell me about Terra, about the worlds in the Empire!"

"There will be time enough for that, certainly," I said, smiling, looking at the fading light. "It is not yet nightfall . . . but there's nothing good to tell of Terra, *chiya;* I have no good memories. Mostly I was in hospitals . . ." and as I said the word I remembered another hospital in which not I, but Dio had been the patient, and a certain dark-haired, sweet-faced young nurse. "Did you know, Linnie—no, of course, you couldn't know; you have a perfect double on Vainwal; so like you that at first I called her by your name, thought it was you yourself!"

"Really? What was she like?"

"Oh, efficient, competent—even her voice was like yours," I said. And then I stopped, remembering the horror of that night, the shockingly deformed, monstrous form that should have been my son . . . I was strongly barriered, but Linnell saw the twitching of my face and put up her hand to stroke my scarred cheek.

"Foster-brother," she said, giving the word the intimate inflection that made it a term of endearment, "don't talk about hospitals and sickness and pain. It's all over now, you're here at home with us. Don't think about it."

"And there are enough troubles here on Darkover to make you forget whatever troubles you may have had in the Empire," said Regis, with a troubled smile, joining us at the window, where the sun had faded, blurred by the evening clouds. "Council was not properly adjourned; I doubt we've heard the last of that. Certainly not the last of Beltran . . ." and Callina, hearing the name, shuddered. She said, looking impatiently at the clouds, "Come, we must not keep Ashara waiting."

A servant folded her into a wrap that was like a gray shadow. We went out and down the stairs, but at the first turning, something prompted me to turn back; Linnell stood there, framed in the light of the doorway, copper highlights caught in her brown hair, her face serious and smiling; and for a moment, that out-of-phase time sense that haunts the Alton gift, a touch perhaps of the precognition I had inherited from the Aldaran part of my blood, made me stare, unfocused, as past, present, future all collapsed upon themselves, and I saw a shadow falling on Linnell, and a dreadful conviction. . . .

Linnell was doomed. . . . the same shadow that had darkened my life would fall on Linnell and cover her and swallow her. . . .

"Lew, what's the matter?"

I blinked, turning to Callina at my side. Already the certainty, that sick moment when my mind had slid off the time track, was fading like a dream in daylight. The confusion, the sense of tragedy, remained; I wanted to rush up the stairs, snatch Linnell into my arms as if I could guard her from tragedy . . . but when I looked up again the door was closed and Linnell was gone.

We went out through the archway and into a courtyard. The light rain of early summer was falling, and though at this season it would not turn to snow, there were little slashes of sleet it in. Already the lights were fading in the Old City, or could not come through the fog; but beyond that, across the valley, the brilliant neon of the Trade City cast garish red and orange shadows on the low clouds. I went to the railed balcony that looked down on the valley, and stood there, disregarding the rain in my face. Two worlds lying before me; yet I belonged to neither. Was there any world in all the star-spanning Empire where I would feel at home?

"I would like to be down there tonight," I said wearily, "or anywhere away from this Hell's castle—"

"Even in the Terran Zone?"

"Even in the Terran Zone."

"Why aren't you, then? There is nothing keeping you here," Callina said, and at the words I turned to her. Her cobweb cloak spun out on the wind like a fine mist as I pulled her into my arms. For a moment, frightened, she was taut and resisting in my arms; then she softened and clung to me. But her lips were closed and unresponsive as a child's under my demanding kiss, and it brought me to my senses, with the shock of *déjà vu . . . somewhere, sometime, in a dream or reality, this had happened before, even the slashes of rain across our faces. . . .* She sensed it too, and put up her hands between us, gently withdrawing. But then she let her head drop on my shoulder.

"What now, Lew? Merciful Avarra—what now?"

I didn't know. Finally I gestured toward the crimson smear of garish neon that was the Trade City.

"Forget Beltran. Marry me—now—tonight, in the Terran Zone. Confront the Council with an accomplished fact and let them chew on it and swallow it—let them solve their own problems, not hide behind a woman's skirts and think they can solve them with marriages!"

"If I dared—" she whispered, and through the impassive voice of a trained Keeper, I felt the tears she had learned not to shed. But she sighed, putting me reluctantly away again. She said, "You may forget Beltran, but he will not go away because we are not there. He has an army at the gates of Thendara, armed with Terran weapons. And beyond that—" she hesitated, reluctant, and said, "Can we so easily forget—*Sharra*?"

The word jolted me out of my daydream of peace. For the first time in years, Sharra had not even been a whisper of evil in my mind; in her arms I had actually forgotten. Callina might be bound to the Tower by her vows as Keeper, but I was not free either. Silent, I turned away from the balconied view of the twin cities below me, and let her lead me down another flight of stairs and across another series of isolated courtyards, until I was all but lost in the labyrinth that was Comyn Castle.

Both of us, lost in the maze our forefathers had woven for us. . . .

But Callina moved unerringly through the puzzling maze, and at last led me into a door where stairways led up and up, then through a hidden door, where we stood close together as, slowly, the shaft began to rise.

This Tower—so the story goes—was built for the first of the Comyn Keepers when Thendara was no more than a village of wicker-woven huts crouching in the lee of the first of the Towers. It went far, far into our past, to the days when the fathers of the Comyn mated with *chieri* and bred strange nonhuman powers into our line, and Gods moved on the face of the world among humankind, Hastur who was the son of Aldones who was the son of light . . . I told myself not to be superstitious. This Tower was ancient indeed, and some of the old machinery from the Ages of Chaos survived here, no more than that. Lifts that moved of themselves, by no power I could identify, were commonplace enough in the Terran Zone, why should it terrify me here? The smell of centuries hung between the walls, in the shadows that slipped past, as if with every successive rising we moved further back into the very Ages of Chaos and before. . . . at last the shaft stopped, and we were before a small panel of glass that was a door, with blue lights behind it.

I saw no handle or doorknob, but Callina reached forward and it opened. And we stepped into . . . blueness.

Blue, like the living heart of a jewel, like the depths of a translucent lake, like the farther deeps of the sky of Terra at midday. Blue, around us, behind us, beneath us. Uncanny lights so mirrored and prismed the room that it seemed to have no dimensions, to be at once immeasurably large and terribly confined, to be everywhere at once. I shrank, feeling immense spaces beneath me and above me, the primitive fear of falling; but Callina moved unerringly through the blueness.

"Is it you, daughter and my son?" said a low clear voice, like winter water running under ice. "Come here. I am waiting for you."

Then and only then, in the frosty dayshine, could I focus my eyes enough in the blueness to make out the great carven throne of glass, and the pallid figure of a woman seated upon it.

Somehow I would have thought that in this formal audience Ashara would wear the crimson robes of ceremonial for a Keeper. Instead she wore robes that so absorbed and mirrored the light that she was almost invisible; a straight tiny figure, no larger than a child of twelve. Her features were almost fleshlessly pure, as unwrinkled as Callina's own, as if the very hand of time itself had smoothed its own marks away. The eyes, long and large, were colorless too, though in a more normal light they might have been blue. There was a faint, indefinable resemblance between the young Keeper and the old one, as if Ashara were a Callina incredibly more ancient, or Callina an embryo Ashara, not yet ancient but bearing the seeds of her own translucent invisibility. I began to believe that the stories were true; that she was all but immortal, had dwelt here unchanged while the worlds and the centuries passed over her and beyond her. . . .

She said, "So you have been beyond the stars, Lew Alton?"

It would not be fair to say the voice was unkind. It was not human enough for that. Detached, unbelievably remote; it was all of that. It sounded as if the effort of conversing with real, living persons was too much for her, as if our coming had disturbed the crystalline peace in which she dwelt.

Callina, accustomed to this—or so I suppose—murmured, "You see all things, Mother Ashara. You know what we have to face."

A flicker of emotion passed over the peaceful face, and she seemed to *solidify,* to become less translucent and more real. "Not even I can see all things. I have no power, now, outside this place."

Callina murmured, "Yet aid us with your wisdom, Mother."

"I will do what I must," she said, remotely. She gestured. There was a transparent bench at her feet—glass or crystal; I had not seen it before, and I wondered why. Maybe it had not been there or maybe she had conjured it there; nothing would have surprised me now. "Sit there and tell me."

She gestured at my matrix. "Give it to me, and let me see—"

Now, remembering, telling, I wonder whether any of this happened or whether it was some bizarre dream concealing reality. A telepath, even an Arilinn-trained telepath, simply does not do what I did then; without even thinking of protest, I slipped the leather thong on which my matrix was tied over my head with my good hand, fumbled a little with the silken wrappings, and handed it to her, without the slightest thought of resisting. I simply put it into her hand.

And this is the first law of a telepath; nobody touches a keyed matrix, except your own Keeper, and then only after a long period of attunement, of matching resonances. But I sat there at the feet of the ancient sorceress, and laid the matrix in her hand without stopping to think, and although something in me was tensed against incredible agony . . . I remembered when Kadarin had stripped me of my matrix, and how I had gone into convulsions. . . . nothing happened; the matrix might have been safely around my neck.

And I sat there peacefully and watched it.

Deep within the almost-invisible blue of the matrix were fires, strange lights . . . I saw the glow of fire, and the great raging shimmer . . . *Sharra!* Not the Form of Fire which had terrified us in Council, but the Goddess herself, raging in flame—Ashara waved her hand and it disappeared. She said, "Yes, that matrix I know of old . . . and yours has been in contact with it, am I right?"

I bowed my head and said, "You have seen."

"What can we do? Is there any way to defend against—"

She waved Callina to silence. "Even I cannot alter the laws of energy and mechanics," she said. Looking around the room, I was not so sure. As if she had heard my thoughts, she said, "I wish you knew less science of the Terrans, Lew."

"Why?"

"Because now you look for causes, explanations, the fallacy that every event must have a preceding cause . . . matrix mechanics is the first of the non-causal sciences," she said, seeming to pick up that Terran technical phrase out of the air or from my mind. "Your very search for structure, cause and reality produces the cause you seek, but it is not the real cause . . . does any of this make sense to you?"

"Not very much," I confessed. I had been trained to think of a matrix as a machine, a simple but effective machine to amplify psi impulses and the electrical energy of the brain and mind.

"But that leaves no place for such things as Sharra," Ashara said. "Sharra is a very real Goddess. . . . No, don't shake your head. Perhaps you could call Sharra a demon, though She is no more a demon than Aldones is a God. . . . They are entities, and not of this ordinary three-dimensional world you inhabit. Your mind would find it easier to think of them as Gods and Demons, and of your matrix, and the Sharra matrix, as talismans for summoning those demons, or banishing them. . . . They are entities from another world, and the matrix is the gateway that brings them here," she said. "You know that, or you knew it once, when you managed to close the gateway for a time. And for such a summoning Sharra will always have Her sacrifice; so she had your hand, and Marjorie gave up her life. . . ."

"Don't!" I shuddered.

"But there is a better weapon of banishing," Ashara said. "What says the legend . . ."

Callina whispered, "Sharra was bound in chains by the

son of Hastur, who was the Son of Aldones who was the Son of Light. . . ."

"Rubbish," I said boldly. "Superstition!"

"You think so?" Ashara seemed to realize she was still holding my matrix; she handed it carelessly back to me and I fumbled it into the silken wrappings and into its leather bag, put it back around my neck. "What of the shadow-sword?"

That too was legend; Linnell had sung it tonight, of the time when Hastur walked on the shores of the lake, and loved the Blessed Cassilda. The legend told of the jealousy of Alar, who had forged in his magical forge a shadow-sword, meant to banish, not to slay. Pierced with this sword, Hastur must return to his realms of light . . . but the legend recounted how Camilla, the damned, had taken the place of Cassilda in Hastur's arms, and so received the shadow-blade in her heart, and passed away forever into those realms. . . .

I said, hesitating, "The Sharra matrix is concealed in the hilt of a sword . . . tradition, because it is a weapon, no more. . . ."

Ashara asked, "What do you think would happen to anyone who was slain with such a sword as that?"

I did not know. It had never occurred to me that the Sword of Sharra could be used as a sword, though I had hauled the damnable thing around half the Galaxy with me. It was simply the case the forge-folk had made to conceal the matrix of Sharra. But I found I did not like thinking of what would happen to anyone run through by a sword possessed and dominated by Sharra's matrix.

"So," she said, "you are beginning to understand. Your forefathers knew much of those swords. Have you heard of the Sword of Aldones?"

Some old legend . . . yes. "It lies hidden among the holy things at Hali," I said, "spelled so that none of Comyn blood may come near, to be drawn only when the end of Comyn is near; and the drawing of that sword shall be the end of our world. . . ."

"The legend has changed, yes," said Ashara, with something which, in a face more solid, more human, might have been a smile. "I suppose you know more of sciences than of legend. . . . Tell me, what is Cherilly's Law?"

It was the first law of matrix mechanics; it stated that nothing was unique in space and time except a matrix; that every item in the universe existed with one and only one *exact* duplicate, except for a matrix; a matrix was the only thing which was wholly unique, and therefore any attempt to duplicate a matrix would destroy it, and the attempted duplicate.

"The Sword of Aldones is the weapon against Sharra," said Ashara. But I knew enough of the holy things at Hali to know that if the Sword of Aldones was concealed there, it might as well be in another Galaxy; and I said so.

There are things like that on Darkover; they can't be destroyed, but they are so dangerous that even the Comyn, or a Keeper, can't be trusted with them; and all the ingenuity of the great minds of the Ages of Chaos had been bent to concealing them so that they cannot endanger others.

The *rhu fead,* the holy Chapel at Hali . . . all that remained of Hali Tower, which had burned to the ground during the Ages of Chaos . . . was such a concealment. The Chapel itself was guarded like the Veil at Arilinn; no one not of Comyn blood may penetrate the Veil. It is so spelled and guarded with matrixes and other traps that if any outsider, not of the true Comyn blood, should step inside, his mind would be stripped bare; by the time he or she got inside, he would be an idiot without enough directive force to know or remember why he had come there.

But inside the Chapel, the Comyn of a thousand years ago had put them out of our reach forever. They are guarded in the opposite fashion. An outsider could have picked them up freely; but the outsider couldn't get into the Chapel at all. No one of Comyn blood could so much as lay a hand on them without instant death.

I said, "Every unscrupulous tyrant in a thousand years of Comyn has been trying to figure that one out."

"But none of them has had a Keeper on their side," said Ashara. Callina asked, "A Terran?"

"Not one reared on Darkover," Ashara said. "An alien, perhaps who knew nothing of the forces here. His mind would be locked and sealed against any forces here, so that he wouldn't even know they were there. He would pass them, guarded by ignorance."

"Wonderful," I said with sarcastic emphasis. "All I have

to do is go thirty or forty light-years to a planet out there, force or persuade someone there to come back with me to this planet, without telling him anything about it so he won't know what he ought to be afraid of, then figure a way to get him inside the Chapel without being fried to idiocy, and hope he'll hand over the Sword of Aldones when he gets it into his enthusiastic little hand!"

Ashara's colorless eyes held a flicker of scorn, and suddenly I felt ashamed of my sarcasm.

"Have you been in the matrix laboratory here? Have you seen the screen?"

I remembered, and suddenly knew what it was; one of the almost-legendary psychokinetic transmitters . . . *instantaneously, through space, perhaps through time* . . .

"That hasn't been done for hundreds of years!"

"I know what Callina can do," said Ashara with her strange smile. "And I shall be with you . . ."

She stood up, extended her hands to us both. She touched mine; she felt cold as a corpse, as the surface of a jewel. . . . Her voice was low, and for a moment it seemed almost menacing.

"Callina . . ."

Callina shrank away from the touch and somehow, though her face was molded in the impassive stillness of a Keeper, it seemed to me that she was weeping. "No!"

"Callina—" the low voice was soft, inexorable. Slowly, Callina held out her hands, let herself touch, join hands with us. . . .

The room vanished. We drifted, fathomless, in blueness, measureless space; blank emptiness like starless space, great bare chasms of nothingness. In Arilinn I had been taught to leave my body behind, go into the overworld of reality where the body is not, where we exist only as thoughts making form of the nothingness of the universe, but this was no region of the overworld I had ever known. I drifted, bodiless, in tingling mist. Then the emptiness between stars was charged with a spark, a flare of force, a stream of life, charging me; I could feel myself as a network of live nerves, lacework of living force. I clenched again the hand that had been cut from me, felt every nerve and sinew in it.

Then, suddenly in the emptiness, a face sketched itself on my mind.

I cannot describe that face, though I know, now, what it was. I saw it three times in all. There are no human words to describe it; it was beautiful beyond imagining, but it was terrible past all conception. It was not even evil, not as men in this life know evil; it was not human enough for that. It was—damnable. Only a fraction of a second it burned behind my eyes, but I knew I had looked straight in at the gates of hell.

I struggled back to reality. I was again in Ashara's blue-ice room; had I ever left it? Callina's hands were still clasped in mine, but Ashara was gone. The glass throne was empty, and as I looked on it the throne, too, was gone, vanished into the mirrored shimmer of the room. Had she ever been there at all? I felt giddy and disoriented, but Callina sagged against me, and I caught her, and the feel of her fainting body in my arms brought me back sternly to reality. The touch of her soft robes, of the end of her hair against my hand, seemed to touch some living nerve in me. I clasped her against me, burying my face against her shoulder. She smelled warm and sweet, with a subtle fragrance, not perfume or scent or cosmetic, just the soft scent of her skin, and it dizzied me; I wanted to go on holding her, but she opened her eyes and swiftly was aware again, holding herself upright and away from me. I bent my head. I dared not touch her, and would not against her will, but for that dizzying moment I wanted her more than I had ever wanted any woman living. Was it only that she was Keeper and so forbidden to me? I stood upright again, cold and aching, my face icy where it had lain against her heart; but I had control of myself again. She seemed unaware, immune to the torrent of feeling that raged in me. Of course, she was a Keeper, she had been taught to move beyond all this, immune to passion. . . .

"Callina," I said, "cousin, forgive me."

The faintest flicker of a smile moved on her face. "Never mind, Lew. I wish—" She left the rest unspoken, but I realized she was not quite so insulated from my own torment as I had believed.

"I am no more than human," she said, and again the faint feather-touch to my wrist, the touch of a Keeper, reassured me. It was like a promise, but we drew apart, knowing that there must remain a barrier between us.

"Where is Ashara?" I asked.

Once again the flicker of a troubled smile on her face. "You had better not ask me," she murmured. "You would never believe the answer."

I frowned, and again the uncanny resemblance troubled me, the stillness of Ashara in Callina's quiet face—I could only guess at the bond between the Keepers. Abruptly, Callina moved toward some invisible door and we were outside, on the stone landing, solid, and I wondered if the blue-ice room had ever existed, or if the whole thing had been some kind of bizarre dream.

A dream, for there I was whole and I had two hands. . . .

Something had happened. But I did not know what it could have been.

We returned another way to the Tower, and Callina led me through the relay chamber, into the room filled with the strange and mysterious artifacts of the Ages of Chaos. It was warm, and I pulled off my cloak and let the heat soak into my chilled body and aching arm, while Callina moved softly around the laboratory, adjusting specially modulated dampers, and finally gestured to the wide, shimmering glass panel, whose depths made me think of the blue-ice room of Ashara. I stared, frowning, into the cloudy depths. Sorcery? Unknown laws, non-causal sciences? They mingled and were one. The Gift I had borne in my blood, the freak thing in my heredity that made me Comyn, telepath, *laranzu,* matrix technician. . . . for such things as this I had been bred and trained; why should I fear them? Yet I was afraid, and Callina knew it.

I was trained at Arilinn, oldest and most powerful of the Towers, and had heard something—not much—about screens like this. It was a duplicator—it transmitted a desired pattern; it captured images and the realities behind them—no; it's impossible to explain, I didn't—and don't—know enough about the screens. Including how they were operated; but I supposed Callina knew and I was just there to strengthen her with the strength of the Alton Gift, to lend her power as—the thought sent ice through my veins—I had lent power for the raising of Sharra. Well, that was fair enough; power for power, reparation for betrayal. Still I was uneasy; I had allowed Kadarin to use me for the raising of Sharra without knowing enough about the dangers, and here I was repeating the same mistake. The difference was that I trusted to Callina. But even that frightened me; there had been a time when I had trusted Kadarin, too, called him friend, sworn brother, *bredu.*

Again I stopped myself. I had to trust Callina; there was no other way. I went and stood before the screen.

Augmented by the screen, I could search, with telepathic forces augmented hundredfold, thousandfold, for such a one as we wanted. Of all the millions and billions of worlds in space and time, somewhere there was a mind such as we wanted, with a certain awareness—and a certain *lack* of awareness. With the screen we could attune that mind's vibrations to *this* particular place in time and space; here, now, between the two poles of the screen. The space annihilated by the matrix, we could shift the—well, we call them *energons,* which is as good a name as any—shift the energons of that particular mind and the body behind it, and bring them *here.* My mind played with words like matter-transmitter, hyperspace, dimension-travel; but those were only words. The screen was the reality.

I dropped into one of the chairs before the screen, fiddling with a calibration which would allow me to match resonances between myself and Callina—more accurately, between her matrix and mine. I said, not looking up, "You'll have to cut out the monitor screen, Callina," and she nodded.

"There's a bypass relay through Arilinn." She touched controls and the monitor surface, a glassy screen—large, but half the size of the giant screen before me—blinked fitfully and went dark, shunting every monitored matrix on Darkover out of this relay. A grill crackled, sent out a tiny staccato signal; Callina listened attentively to no sound that I could hear—the message was not audible, and I was too preoccupied to merge into the relays. Callina listened for a moment, then spoke—aloud, perhaps as a courtesy to me, perhaps to focus her own thoughts for the relay.

"Yes, I know, Maruca, but we have cut out the main circuits here in Thendara; you'll have to monitor from there." Again the listening silence, then she rapped out, "Put up a third-level barrier around Thendara! That is a direct order from Comyn; observe and comply!" She turned away, sighing.

"That girl is the *noisiest* telepath on the planet! Now everyone with a scrap of telepathy on the whole planet will know something is going on in Thendara tonight!"

We had had no choice; I said so. She took her own place before the screen, and I blanked my mind against it, ready for whatever she should demand of me. What sort of alien would suit us? But without volition, at least on my part, a pattern shaped itself on the screen. I saw the dim symbols in the moment before my optic nerve overloaded and I went out; then I was blind and deaf in that instant of overload which is always terrifying, however familiar it may become.

Gradually, without external senses, I found orientation within the screen. My mind, extended through astronomical distances, traversed in fractional seconds whole galaxies and parsecs of subjective spacetime. Vague touches of consciousness, fragments of thought, emotions that floated like shadows—the flotsam of the mental universe.

Then before I felt contact, I saw the white-hot flare in the screen. Somewhere another mind had fitted into the pattern which we had cast out like a net, and when we found the fitting intelligence it had been captured.

I swung out, bodiless, divided into a billion subjective fragments, extended over a vast gulf of spacetime. If anything happened, I would never get back to my body now, but would drift on the spacetime curve forever.

With infinite caution I poured myself into the alien mind. There was a short, terrible struggle. It was embedded-enlaced in mine. The world was a holocaust of molten-glass fire and color. The air writhed. The glow on the screen was a shadow, then solid, then a clearing darkness. . . .

"Now!" I did not speak, simply flung the command at Callina, then light tore at my eyes, there was a ripping shock tearing at my brain, the floor seemed to rock and Callina was flung, reeling, into my arms as the energons seared the air and my brain.

Half stunned, but conscious, I saw that the screen was blank, the alien mind torn free of mine.

And in a crumpled heap on the floor, where she had fallen at the base of the screen, lay a slight, dark-haired woman.

* * *

I realized after a moment that I was still holding Callina in my arms; I let her go at the very instant that she moved to free herself of me. She knelt beside the strange woman, and I followed her.

"She's not dead?"

"Of course not." With the instincts of the Arilinn-trained, Callina was already feeling for a pulse, though her own was still thready and irregular. "But that—transition—nearly killed us, and we knew what to expect. What do you think it must have been like for her?"

Soft brown hair, falling across her face, hid her features. I brushed it gently back, and stopped, my hand still touching her cheek, in bewilderment.

"Linnell—" I whispered.

"No," said Callina, "She sleeps in her own room . . ." but her voice faltered as she looked down at the girl. Then I knew who it must be; the young nurse I had seen on the dreadful night in the Terran hospital in Vainwal. Even knowing, as I did, what had happened, I thought my mind would give way. That transition had taken its toll of me too and I had to take a moment to quiet my own pulses and breathing.

"Avarra be merciful," Callina whispered. "What have we done?"

Of course, I thought. *Of course.* Linnell was near to us both; sister, foster-sister. We had spoken with her just tonight. The pattern was at hand. Yet I still wondered, why Linnell, why not duplicate myself, or Callina? . . .

I tried to put it into simple words, more for myself than Callina.

"Cherilly's Law. Everything in the universe—you, me, that chair, the drinking fountain in Port Chicago spaceport—everything exists in one, and only one, exact duplicate. Nothing is unique except for a matrix; even atoms have minute differences in the orbit of their electrons . . . there are equations to calculate the number of possible variations, but I'm not enough of a mathematician to calculate them. Jeff could probably reel them all off to you."

"So this is . . . Linnell's identical twin . . . ?"

"More alike than that; only once in a million times or so would a twin be the duplicate under Cherilly's Law. This is her *real* twin; same fingerprints, same retinal patterns and brainwave patterns, same betagraphs and blood type. She won't be much like Linnell in personality, probably, because the duplicates of Linnell's *environment* are duplicated all over the Galaxy." I pointed to the small scar beside her chin; turned over the limp wrist where the mark of Comyn was embedded in the flesh. "Probably a birthmark," I said, "but it's identical with Linnell's Seal, see? Flesh and blood are identical; same blood type, and even her chromosomes, if you could monitor that deeply, would be identical with Linnell's."

Callina stared and stared. "She can live in this—this alien environment, then?"

"If she's identical," I said. "Her lungs breathe the same ratio of oxygen in the air as ours do, and her internal organs are adjusted to the same gravity."

"Can you carry her?" Callina asked. "She'll get a dreadful shock if she wakes up in this place."

I grinned humorlessly. "She'll get one anyhow." But I managed to scoop her up one-handed; she was frail and light, like Linnell. Callina went ahead of me, pulled back curtains, showed me where to lay her down on a couch in a small bare room—I supposed the young men and women who worked in the relays sometimes took a nap here instead of returning to their own rooms. I covered her, for it was cold.

"I wonder where she comes from?" Callina murmured.

"From a world with about the same gravity as Darkover, which narrows it a little," I evaded. I could not remember the nurse's name, some barbaric Terran syllables. I wondered if she would recognize me. I should explain it all to Callina. But her face was lined with exhaustion, making her look gaunt, twice her age. "Let's leave her to sleep off the shock—and get some sleep ourselves."

We went down to the foot of the Tower. Callina stood in the doorway with me, her hands lightly resting in mine. She looked haggard, worn, but lovely to me after the shared danger, the intimacy created by matrix work, a closeness greater than family, greater than that of lovers. . . . I bent and kissed her, but she turned her head so that my kiss fell only on a mouthful of soft, fine, sweet-scented hair. I bowed my own head and did not press her. She was right. It would have been insanity; we were both exhausted.

She murmured, as if finished a sentence I had started "... and I must go and see if Linnell is really all right ..."

So she, too, had shared that sense of portent, of doom? I put her gently away, and went out of the Tower, but I did not go to my rooms to sleep as I meant to do. Instead I paced in the courtyard, like a trapped animal, battling unendurable thoughts, until the red sun came up and Festival dawned in Thendara.

CHAPTER NINE

The morning of Festival dawned red and misty; Regis Hastur, restless, watched the sun come up, and asked his body-servant to arrange for flowers to be sent to his sister Javanne.

I should send gifts, too, to the mothers of my children. . . .

It was simple enough to arrange that baskets of fruits and flowers should be sent, but he felt profoundly depressed and, paradoxically, lonely.

There is no reason I should be lonely. Grandfather would be only too happy to arrange a marriage for me, and I could choose any woman in Thendara for wife, and have as many concubines as a Dry-Towner, and no one could criticize me, not even if I chose to keep a male favorite or two on the side.

I suppose, when it comes to that, I am alone because I would rather be alone, and responsible to no one . . .

. . . except the whole damned population of the Domains! I cannot call my life my own . . . and I will not marry so that they will approve of me!

There was only one person in Thendara, he reflected, whom he really wished to send a gift; and because of custom, he could not do that. He would not degrade what was between Danilo and himself by the pretense that it was the more conventional tie. He sat at his high window, looking out over the city, pondering yesterday's end to the Council, frightened because he had done what he had done, manifested the Form of Fire before them all. Somehow, without training more than the barest minimum, so that he could use his *laran* without becoming ill, he had acquired a new Gift he did not know he had, nor did he know what to do with it. He knew so little of the Hastur Gift and he suspected that his grandfather knew little more.

If only Kennard had still been alive, he would have gone to the kindly kinsman he had learned to call "Uncle" and set his puzzlement before him. Kennard had spent years in Arilinn and knew everything that was known about the

Comyn powers. But Kennard was dead, under a faraway alien sun, and Lew seemed to know little more than himself. Moreover, Lew had his own troubles.

At this point he was summoned to breakfast with his grandfather. For a moment he considered sending a message that he was not hungry—he had made a point with his grandfather and was not inclined to give way on it—but then he remembered that it was, after all, Festival, and kinsmen should put aside their quarrels for the day. In any case he would have to confront his grandfather at the great ball tonight; he might as well meet him in private first.

Danvan Hastur bowed to his grandson, then embraced him and as Regis took a seat before the laden table, he noticed that his grandfather had ordered all his favorite delicacies. He supposed this was as near to an apology as he would ever have from the old man. There was coffee from the Terran Zone, in itself a great luxury, and various honey cakes and fruits, as well as the more traditional fare of porridge and nut breads. As he helped himself, Danvan Hastur said, "I ordered a basket of fruits and candies sent to Javanne in your name."

"You might have trusted me to remember, sir," said Regis, smiling, "but with that brood of children, the sweets won't go to waste."

But thinking of Javanne set him to remembering again the eerie power he had somehow acquired over Javanne's matrix when it had been possessed by Sharra. . . . He did not understand and there was no one to ask. Should he go and demand the audience with Ashara which Callina had denied him? *Lew's matrix was overshadowed by Sharra; perhaps I would have power over that too. . . .*

But he feared to try and fail. And then he remembered that there was another matrix, and one within his own reach, which had been overshadowed by Sharra; though at a greater distance than Lew's; Lew had been in the very heart of Sharra's flames . . . Rafe Scott was concealed in the Terran Zone, and Regis didn't blame him. But did Rafe even know that Beltran was here, threatening all of them? Yes, he would pay a call upon Rafe this morning.

He declined another cup of coffee . . . although he was grateful for the gesture his grandfather had made, he did not really like it . . . and pushed his chair back, just as the servant announced:

"Lord Danilo, Warden of Ardais."

Hastur greeted Danilo with affable courtesy, and invited him to join them at the table; Regis knew that his grandfather was underlining a conceded point. But Danilo, bowing to them both, said, "I am here with a message from Lord Ardais, sir. Beltran of Aldaran has brought his honor guard within the city walls and has invited you to witness his formal giving up of Terran weapons into the hands of his promised wife, Lady Aillard."

"Send a messenger to tell him I will be there within a few moments," said Hastur, rising. "Regis, will you join me?"

"Please excuse me, Grandfather, I have an errand elsewhere," Regis said, and though his grandfather did not look pleased, he did not question Regis.

"I'll leave you two alone, then," he said, and withdrew. Regis discovered his appetite had returned; he poured himself the coffee he had refused and some for Danilo too, and passed the platter of honey cakes. Danilo took one, and said, sipping curiously at the coffee, "This is a Terran luxury, no? If Lord Dyan has his way, there will be no more of this . . ."

"I can well do without it," Regis said. He took a handful of candied blackfruit and offered it silently to Danilo; Danilo, accepting the sweetmeats, smiled at him and said, "No, and I have no Festival gift for you, either. . . . I am not Dyan, to send presents to his favorites as I would do to my sister if I had one."

We do not need to gift one another. . . .

Still, it is a sign I wish I might show . . .

Regis said aloud, breaking the moment of intimacy that was more intense than any physical caress, "I must go to the Terran Zone, Dani; I must see if Captain Scott knows what is going on . . ."

"I will go with you, if you wish," Danilo offered.

"Thank you, but there is no need to anger your foster-father," Regis said, "and if you go there against his will, he will take it as defiance. Keep the peace, Dani; there are enough quarrels within Comyn, we need no more." He put his honey-cake aside, suddenly losing his appetite again. "Grandfather will be angry enough that I am not there to witness the Aldaran men giving up their Terran weapons. But Beltran will never love me, no matter what I do, and I would as soon not be there to see this—" he searched for a word, considered and rejected "farce," then shrugged.

"Dyan may trust Beltran; I will not," he said, and left.

Some time after, he gave his name and business to the Spaceforce guard, black-leathered, at the gates of the Terran Zone. The Spaceforce man stared, as well he might—one of the powerful Hasturs here with no more escort than a single Guardsman? But he used his communicator, and after a moment said, "The Legate will see you in his office, Lord Hastur."

Regis was not *Lord Hastur*—that was his grandfather's title—but there was no use expecting Spaceforce men to know proper courtesy and protocol. Lawton, in the Legate's office, rising to greet him, used his proper address and got his title right, even saying it with the proper inflection, which was not all that easy for a Terran. But then, of course, Lawton was half Darkovan.

"You honor me, Lord Regis," Lawton said, "but I hadn't expected to see you here. I suspect I'll be at the ball in Comyn Castle tonight—the Regent sent me a formal invitation."

"It's Rafe Scott I came to see," Regis said, "but I didn't want to do it behind your back and be accused of spying, or worse."

Lawton waved that aside.

"Would you rather see him here? Or in his own quarters?"

"In his quarters, I think."

"I'll send someone to show you the way," Lawton said. "But first, a question. Do you know the man they call Kadarin by sight?"

"I think I'd know him if I saw him." Regis remembered the picture he had seen in Lew's mind, the day the Alton townhouse had burned.

"What kind of chance would we have of finding him, if we sent Spaceforce into the Old Town? Is there anyone there who would try and hide him from justice?"

"He's wanted by the Guardsmen there too," Regis said. "It's fairly certain that he was responsible for a fire and explosion with contraband explosives . . ." Briefly, he outlined to Lawton what he had seen.

"Spaceforce could find him faster than your guards," the Terran Legate suggested. Regis shook his head.

"I'm sure they could," he said, "but, believe me, I wouldn't advise sending them."

"There ought to be a treaty that we could at least look for a wanted criminal," Lawton said grimly. "As it is, once he sets foot in the Old Town he's safe from our men—and if he somehow sneaks into the Trade City, safe from your Guardsmen. I'd like to know why we can't have that much cooperation at least."

So would I, sir. If I were in charge, you'd have it. But I'm not, and Grandfather doesn't feel that way. Regis realized suddenly that he was ashamed of his grandfather's views. They had indeed sworn to a certain amount of cooperation with the Terrans, many times over the past years; more especially after the epidemic in which the Terran Medic division had sent an expert to assist them. But now Kennard, who had started this kind of cooperation, was dead, and it seemed the informal alliance was falling apart; Regis wished Lawton had enough *laran* so that he need not explain all this, through the slow and clumsy medium of words.

He said, fumbling, "It's—it's not a good time to ask for that, Mr. Lawton. It would take a lot of arranging. We'll deal with Kadarin if we find him, and I assume you will if you catch him here. But this is not the time to ask for formal cooperation between the Guard and Spaceforce. The important thing is to catch that man Kadarin and deal with him—not argue about whose jurisdiction he should be under."

Lawton struck the desk before him with an angry fist. "And while we argue about it, he's laughing at both of us," he said. "Listen here. A few days ago, the Orphanage in the Trade City was broken into, and a child's room was entered. No child was hurt, no one was kidnapped, but the children in that dormitory had a dreadful fright, and they described the man to Spaceforce—and it seems likely that Kadarin was the one. We don't know what he was doing there, but he managed to escape again, and he's probably hiding out in the Old Town. And now I've heard that Beltran of Aldaran has brought an army down to Thendara—"

This was Comyn business; Regis had no wish to argue it

with a Terran, however friendly. He said somewhat stiffly, "Even as we stand here, sir, Lord Aldaran is making a solemn oath to observe Compact, and giving up all his Terran weapons. I know that old Kermiac of Aldaran was a Terran ally, but I believe Beltran feels otherwise."

"But it was Beltran, not Kermiac, who managed to burn the spaceport at Caer Donn, and half of the town with it," Lawton said. "How do we know that Beltran hasn't brought his men here to join Kadarin, and try some such trick on the Thendara spaceport? I tell you, we have to find Kadarin before that gets out of hand again. You probably don't realize that the Empire has sovereign authority over all its colonies where there's a threat to a spaceport; they're not under local authority at all, but under the interplanetary authority of the Senate. You people have no Senate representation, but you *are* a Terran colony and I *do* have the authority to send Spaceforce in—"

This sounds like what Lerrys was saying. Regis said, "If you ever want good relations with Comyn Council, Lawton, I wouldn't advise it. Spaceforce quartered in the Old Town would be looked upon as. . . ."

As an act of war. Darkover, with swords and the Guardsmen, to fight the interplanetary majesty of the Empire?

"Why do you think I am telling you this?" Lawton asked, with a touch of impatience, and Regis wondered if indeed the man had read his thoughts. "We *have* to find Kadarin! We could arrest Beltran and call him in for questioning. I have the authority to fill your whole damned city with Terran Intelligence and Spaceforce so that Kadarin would have as much chance as a lighted match on a glacier!" He sounded angry. "I need some cooperation or I'll have to do *exactly* that; one of my jobs is to see that Thendara doesn't go the way of Caer Donn!"

"The agreement whereby you respect the local government—"

"But if the local government is harboring a dangerous criminal, I'll have to override your precious Council! Don't you understand? *This is an Empire planet!* We've given you a lot of leeway; it's Empire policy to let local governments have their head, as long as they don't damage interplanetary matters. But among other things, I am responsible for the safety of the Spaceport!"

Regis said angrily, "Are you accusing us of harboring Kadarin? We have a price on his life too."

"You have been remarkably ineffective in finding him," Lawton said. "I'm under pressure too, Regis; I'm trying to hold out against my superiors, who can't imagine why I'm humoring your Council this way with Kadarin at large, and—" he hesitated, "Sharra."

So you too know what Sharra's flames can do. . . .

Lawton sounded angry. "I'm doing my best, Lord Regis, but my back's to the wall. I'm under just as much pressure as you are. If you want us to stay on our side of the wall, find us Kadarin, and turn him over to us, and we'll hold off. Otherwise—I won't have a choice. If I refuse to handle it, they'll simply transfer me out, and someone else will do it—someone without half the stake I have in keeping this world peaceful." He drew a long breath. "Sorry; I didn't mean to imply that any of this was your fault, or even that you could do anything about it. But if you have any influence with anyone in the Council, you'd better tell them about it. I'll send someone to show you the way to Captain Scott's quarters."

Rafe's voice said a careless "Come in," as Regis knocked; as he entered, Rafe started up from his chair. "Regis!" Then he broke off. "Forgive me. Lord Hastur—"

"Regis will do, Rafe," Regis said. After all, they had been boys together. "And forget that formal little speech about why am I honoring your house." A grin flickered on Rafe's face, and he gestured Regis to a seat. Regis took it, looking about him curiously; in his many visits to the Terran Zone he had never before been inside a private dwelling, but only in public places. To him the furniture seemed coarse, ill-made and badly arranged, comfortless. Of course, these were the bachelor quarters of an unmarried man, without servants or much that was permanent.

"May I offer you refreshment, Regis? Wine? A fruit drink?"

"It's too early for wine," Regis said, but realized that he was thirsty from all the talking he had been doing with the Legate. Rafe went to a console, touched controls; a cup of some white smooth artificial material materialized and a stream of pale-gold liquid trickled into it. Rafe handed him the cup, materialized and filled another for himself. He came back and took a seat.

Regis said, sipping at the cool, tart liquid, "I have seen what happened to your matrix. I—" suddenly he did not have the faintest idea how he was going to say this.

"I have discovered—almost by accident—" he fumbled, "that I have some—some curious power over—not over Sharra, just over—matrixes which have been—contaminated—by Sharra. Will you let me try it with yours?"

Rafe made a wry face, "I came here so that I could forget about that," he said. "It seems strange to hear talk of matrixes *here.*" He gestured to the bare plastic room.

"You may not be as safe as you think," Regis warned him soberly, "Kadarin has been seen in the Terran Zone."

"Where?" Rafe demanded. When Regis told him, he leaned back in his chair, white as death. "I know what he wanted. I must see Lew—" and stopped dead. He fumbled for the matrix round his neck; unwrapped it. He held it out quietly on the palm of his hand. Regis looked fixedly at it, and saw it begin to flame and glow with that frightening evocation, the Form of Fire in both their minds, the reek and terror of a city in flames . . .

He tried to summon memory of what he had done with Javanne's matrix; found himself, after a brief struggle, wresting the Form of Fire slowly into a shadow, to nothing, a shred. . . .

The matrix stared, blue and innocent, back at them. Rafe drew a noisy breath, color coming slowly into his face again.

"How did you do that?" he demanded.

That was, Regis thought with detachment, an excellent question. It was a pity he did not have an equally excellent answer. "I don't know. It may have something to do with the Hastur Gift—whatever that is. I suggest you try to use it."

Rafe looked scared. "I haven't been able to—even to try—since—" but he did take the crystal between his hands. After a moment a cold globe of light appeared over his joined hands, floated slowly about the room, vanished. He sighed, again. "It seems to be—free—"

Now, perhaps, I can face Lew and do that . . .

Rafe's eyes widened as he looked at Regis. He whispered, "Son of Hastur—" and bowed, an archaic gesture, bending almost to the ground.

Regis said impatiently, "Never mind that! What is it that you know about Kadarin?"

"I can't tell you now." Rafe seemed to be struggling between that archaic reverence and a perfectly ordinary exasperation. "I swear I can't; it's something I have to tell Lew first. It—" he hesitated. "It wouldn't be honorable or right. Do you command me to tell you, Lord Hastur?"

"Of course not," said Regis, scowling, "but I wish you'd tell me what you're talking about."

"I can't. I have to go—" he stopped and sighed. Then he said, "Beltran is in the city. I do not want to encounter him. May I come to Comyn Castle? I promise, I will explain everything then. It is a—" again the hesitation. "A family matter. Will you ask Lew Alton to meet me in his quarters in the Castle? He—he may not want to see me. I was part of that—part of the Sharra rebellion. But I was his brother's friend, too. Ask him, for Marius's sake, if he will speak with me."

"I'll ask him," Regis said, but he felt more puzzled than ever.

When he left the Terran Zone, the Guardsman at his heels drew diffidently level with him and said, "May I ask you a question, Lord Regis?"

"Ask," Regis said, again annoyed at the archaic deference. *I was a cadet under this man; he was an experienced officer when I was still putting the chin-strap on the cinch-ring! Why should he have to ask permission to speak to me?*

"Sir, what's going on in the city? They called all the Guards out for some kind of ceremony—"

Abruptly, Regis remembered; his errand in the Terran Zone had kept him away, and yet this might be called one of the most important days in the history of the Domains. The Seventh Domain of Aldaran was about to be restored with full ceremony to Comyn, and in token of that Beltran was to swear to Compact . . . he should have been there. Not that he trusted Beltran to observe any oath one moment longer than it was to his advantage to do so!

He said, "We'll go to the city wall; at least you'll see part of it from there."

"Thank you, my lord," the Guard said deferentially.

Inside the city wall there were stairs, so that they could

walk atop the broad wall, past posted guards, each of whom saluted Regis as he passed. Spread out below them, he could see the men in Aldaran's so-called Honor Guard. *There must be hundreds of them,* he thought, *it is really an army, enough army to storm the walls of Thendara . . . he left nothing to our good will.*

In a little knot at the head of them, he could see Beltran, and a number of brightly clad cloaked figures; Comyn lords, come to witness this ceremony. Without realizing he was doing it, Regis enhanced his sight with *laran,* and suddenly it was as if he stood within a few feet of his grandfather, spare and upright in the blue and silver ceremonial cloak of the Hasturs. Edric of Serrais was there too, and Lord Dyan of Ardais, and Prince Derik, and Merryl; and Danilo at Dyan's side, the two dressed identically in the ceremonials of Ardais; and Merryl in the gray and crimson of Aillards, attending Callina, who stood slightly apart from them, enfolded in her gray cloudy wrap, her face partially veiled as befitted a Comyn lady among strangers.

One by one Beltran's men were coming up, laying down their Terran blasters before Lady Callina, kneeling and pronouncing the brief formula dating back to the days of King Carolin of Hali, when the Compact had been devised; that no man should bear a weapon beyond the arm's reach of him who wielded it, so that any man who would kill must dare his own death. . . . Callina looked cold and cross.

"Can't we go a bit nearer, sir? I can't see or hear 'em," the Guardsman asked.

Regis replied, "Go, if you like; I can see well enough from here." His voice was absentminded; he himself was down there, a few steps from Callina. He could sense her inner raging; she was only a pawn in this, and like Regis, she was at the mercy of Comyn Council, without power to rebel even as effectively as Regis could do.

Regis had protested once, long ago, that the path was carved deep for a Comyn son, a path he must walk whether he wished or no . . . stronger yet were the forces binding Comyn daughters. He must have thought this more strongly than he realized, for he saw Callina turn her head a little and look, puzzled, at the spot where Regis felt himself to be and, not seeing him, frown a little, but he followed her thoughts: *Ashara would protect me, but her price is too high . . . I do not want to be her pawn . . .*

The ceremony seemed endless; no doubt Beltran had structured it that way, so that the Comyn witnesses might witness his strength. There was a high heap of Terran weapons, blasters and nerve guns, at Callina's feet. What in Aldones's name, does Beltran think we are going to do with them? Hand them over to the Terrans? For all we know, he might have as many more in Aldaran itself!

Beltran has made a demonstration of strength. He hopes to impress us. Now we need some counter-demonstration, so that he need not go away thinking that he has done what we had not the power to make him do . . .

His eyes met the eyes of Dyan Ardais. Dyan turned, looking up at the distant spot on the wall where Regis stood. Regis did, without thinking about it, something he had never done before and did not consciously know how to do; he dropped into rapport with Dyan, sensing the man's strength and his exasperation at the way this put Beltran into a position of power.

Strengthen me, Dyan, for what I must do! He felt Dyan's thoughts, surprise at the sudden contact, an emotion of which Dyan was not quite consciously aware . . . *su serva Dom, a veis ordenes emprézi* . . . in the inflection with which he would have put himself at Regis's orders, now and forever, in life and death at the disposal of a Hastur . . . once, on the fire-lines during his first year as an officer in the Guards, he had been sent with Dyan into the fire lines when forest-fire raged in the Venza hills behind Thendara, and once he had looked up and found himself working at Dyan's side, strained to the uttermost, shared effort in every nerve and muscle. It was very like being back to back, swords out, each guarding the other's back like paxman and sworn lord . . . he felt Dyan's strength backing his as he *reached out* blindly with his telepathic force. . . .

GET BACK! It was a cry of warning, telepathic and not vocal, but everyone in the crowd experienced it, edged backward. The great heap of weapons began to glow, reddened, turned white-hot. . . .

They vanished, vaporized; there was a great sickening stench for a moment, then that too was gone. Callina was staring, pale as death, at the empty blackened hole in the ground where they had been. Regis felt Dyan's touch almost like a kinsman's embrace; then they fell apart again. . . .

He was alone, staring from his isolated watch-post on the wall at the empty space where the great heap of weapons had been. He heard his grandfather's voice, seizing this opportunity as if he himself had been responsible:

"Kneel now, Beltran of Aldaran, and swear Compact to your assembled equals," he said, using the word *Comyn.* Still somewhat dazed at the destruction which had overshadowed his dramatic gesture of giving up his weapons, Beltran knelt and spoke the ritual words.

"And now," he said, coming up to Callina and bending to kiss her fingertips, "I claim my promised wife."

She was rigid, conceding only the cold tips of her fingers, but she said, in a voice only half audible, "I will handfast myself to you tonight. I so swear." Regis could not see her now, he was too far away, but he knew she was cold with rage, and he did not blame her at all.

And then he caught another stray thought he hardly recognized.

I do not need these weapons, for there is a better one at my command than anything the Terrans have made. . . .

Was that Dyan? He did not recognize the touch. Nor would he recognize Beltran's; when he had been imprisoned in Castle Aldaran he had been a boy, without *laran,* unwakened, and he would not have recognized Beltran's mental "voice."

But a cold and icy shudder went over him, as he knew just what weapon was meant. Was Beltran really mad enough to think of using—*that?*

And if I have power over Sharra, is it I that must face it?

He had a certain amount of power over the Form of Fire, at least when it manifested itself within a matrix. *But neither Rafe nor Javanne had been fully inside Sharra.* He did not think he could free Lew's matrix as he had freed theirs. Lew had been closely sealed to Sharra . . . and Regis cringed away from that thought.

But he must risk it . . . but first he should give Rafe's message. A brief, swift searching told him Lew was nowhere in the crowd at his feet, and he realized that something was happening to his *laran* for which he had not in the least been prepared: he was using it almost carelessly, without effort.

Is this, then, the Hastur Gift?

Forcibly he put that thought, that fear, aside, and went in search of Lew Alton. By the time he found him, Rafe would be there, and he sensed that Lew would not want to confront Rafe Scott unprepared.

Nor was Regis prepared for seeing Lew as he saw him when first old Andres ushered him into the Alton apartments. It did not seem, for a moment, that it was Lew at all, it did not seem that it was a person at all, just a swirling mass of forces, a presence of anger, a touch of a familiar voice . . . *Kennard? But he is dead* . . . and a swift awareness of the terrifying Form of Fire. Regis blinked and somehow managed to bring Lew's physical presence into focus, to bring the new and terrifying dimensions of his own *laran* under control. What was happening to him? He never used *laran* like this, he rarely used it at all . . . but now, giving it even the slightest mental lease seemed to mean that it would fly like a hawk, free, unwilling to return to being hooded. . . . He forced it down, forced himself to *see* Lew instead of simply touching him. But the touch came anyhow, and through the texture of it he recognized something he had felt when he linked with Dyan. Quite simply he found himself saying aloud, "But of course; he was your father's cousin, and close kin to the Altons. Lew, didn't you know that Dyan had the Alton Gift?"

Of course, this is how he could force rapport on Danilo, this is how he makes his will known and enforces it . . .

But this is misuse . . . he uses it thus, to force his will . . . and this is the gravest crime for one with laran. . . .

He was never trained in its use. . . . He was sent from the Tower. . . . The Alton Gift can kill, and they turned him loose, untrained, not knowing his own power . . .

Perhaps like mine, wakening late and suddenly growing as mine has grown, like growing out of my clothes when I was a lad, I am not strong enough nor big enough to contain this monstrous thing which is the Hastur Gift . . .

With main force Regis shut off the flow and said shakily aloud, "Lew, can you put a damper on? I'm not—not used to this."

Lew nodded, went quickly to a control, and after a moment Regis felt the soothing vibration, blurring the patterns. He was again alone, in control of his own mind. Exhausted, he dropped in a chair.

Dyan is not to blame. The Council did not do their duty by him, but turned him loose, his Gift untrained, unchanneled . . .

As with mine! But again Regis stopped the flow of thought; thinking, in dismay and outrage, that the damper should have done that. Before they could speak, the door opened and Rafe came in, unannounced.

Lew's face darkened; but Rafe said "Cousin—" in such a pleading way that Lew gave him an uneasy smile. He said, "Come in, Rafe. None of this is your fault; you're a victim too."

"It's taken me all this time to get up courage enough to tell you this," said Rafe, "but you have to know. Something the Legate said this morning meant that I didn't dare wait any longer. I want you to come with me, Lew. There's something you must see."

"Can't you tell me what it is?" Lew asked.

Rafe hesitated and said, "I would rather say this to you alone—" with an uneasy glance at Regis.

Lew's voice was brusque. "Whatever you have to say; I've no secrets from Regis."

Regis thought, *I don't deserve such confidence.* But he slammed his mind shut, wanting no more of the telepathic leakage he suddenly seemed unable to shut out of his mind.

"There was no woman here to take charge," said Rafe. "I went to your foster-sister. She agreed to take charge of her."

"Of whom, in God's name?" Lew demanded, then his mind quickly leaped to conclusions.

"This alleged child who's been gossiped about in the Guards?"

Rafe nodded and led the way. It was not Linnell, however, who faced them, but Callina.

"I knew," she said in a low voice. "Ashara told me . . . there are not many female children in the Domains who might be trained as I have been trained, and I think—I think Ashara wants her . . ." and she stopped, her words choking off. She gestured to an inner room. "She is there . . . she was afraid in a strange place and I made her sleep . . ."

In a small cot, a little girl, five or six years old, lay sleeping. Her hair was copper-red, freshly minted; scattered across her face, which was triangular, scattered with pale gold freckles. She murmured drowsily, still fast asleep.

Regis felt it run through Lew, like a powerful electric shock.

I have seen her before . . . a dream, a vision, a precognitive dream . . . she is mine! Not my father's, not my dead brother's, mine . . . my blood knows . . .

Regis felt his amazement and recognition. He said in a low voice, "Yes; it is like that." When first he had looked upon the face of his newborn *nedestro* son there had been a moment of recognition, absolute knowledge, *this is my own son, born of my own seed* . . . there had never been any question in his mind; he had not needed the monitoring to tell him this was his own true child.

"But who was her mother?" Lew asked. "Oh, there were a few women in my life, but why did she never tell me?" He broke off as the little girl opened her eyes . . .

Golden eyes; amber; a strange color, a color he had never seen before, never but once. . . . Regis heard the hoarse gasping cry Lew could not keep back.

"No!" he cried. "It can't be! Marjorie died . . . she died . . . died, and our child with her. . . . Merciful Evanda, am I going mad?"

Rafe's eyes, so like the eyes Lew remembered, turned compassionately on them both. "Not Marjorie, Lew. This is Thyra's child. Thyra was her mother."

"But—but no, it can't be," Lew said, gasping, "I never—never once touched her—I would not have touched that hellcat's fingertips—"

"I'm not quite sure what happened," Rafe said. "I was very young, and Thyra—didn't tell me everything. But there was a time, at Aldaran, when you were drugged . . . and not aware of what you were doing . . ."

Lew buried his face in his hand, and Regis, unable to shut out anything, felt the full, terrifying flow of his thoughts.

Ah Gods, merciful Evanda, I thought that was all a dream . . . burning, burning with rage and lust. . . . Marjorie in my arms, but turning, in the mad way dreams do, to Thyra even as I kissed her. . . . Kadarin had done this to me . . . and I remember Thyra weeping in my dream, crying as she had not done even when her father died. . . . It was not her choice either, Thyra was Kadarin's pawn too. . . .

"She was born a few seasons after Caer Donn burned," Rafe said. "Something happened to Thyra when this child was born; I think she went mad for a little while. . . . I do not remember; I was very young, and I had been ill for a long time after the—the burning. I thought, of course, that it was Kadarin's child, he and Thyra had been together so long . . ."

And Regis followed Rafe's thoughts too, a frightening picture of a woman maddened to raving, turning on the child she had not wanted to bear, conceived by a shameful trick . . . with a man drugged and unaware. A child who had had to be removed to safety from time to time. . . .

The little girl was awake now, sitting up, looking at them all curiously with those wide, improbable amber eyes. She looked at Rafe and smiled, evidently recognizing him. Then she looked at Lew, and Regis could feel it, like a blow, her shock at the sight of the ragged, ugly scars. Lew was scowling. *Well, I don't blame him—to find out, that way, that he had been drugged, used* . . . Regis had seen Thyra only once or twice, and that briefly, but he had somehow, even then, sensed the tension of anger and desire between Thyra and Lew. *And they had been together, sealed to Sharra* . . .

The little girl sat up, tense as a small scared animal. Regis could feel again Lew's shock at the sudden, frightening resemblance to Marjorie.

Then Lew said, his rough voice muted, "Don't be scared, *chiya.* I'm not a pretty sight, but believe me, I don't eat little girls."

The little girl smiled. Her small face was charming, pointed in a small triangle. A tooth had come out of the middle of her smile.

"They said you were my father."

"Oh, God, I suppose so," Lew said. *Suppose so. I know I am, damn it.* He was wide open now, and Regis could not shut out his thoughts. Lew sat down uneasily on the edge of the cot. "What do they call you, *chiy'lla?*"

"Marja," she said shyly. "I mean—*Marguerida.* Marguerida Kadarin." She lisped the name in the soft mountain dialect. *Marjorie's name!* "But I just be Marja." She knelt upright, facing him. "What happen to your other hand?"

Regis had seen enough of Javanne's children—and his own—to know how direct they were; but Lew was disconcerted by her straightforwardness. He blinked and said, "It was hurt and they had to cut it off."

Her amber eyes were enormous. Regis could feel her thinking this over. "I'm sorry—" and then she said, trying the word out on her tongue, "Father." She reached up and patted his scarred cheek with her small hand. Lew swallowed hard and caught her against him, his head bent; but Regis could feel that he was shaken, close to tears, and again could not shut out Lew's thoughts.

I saw this child once, even before Marjorie and I were lovers, saw her in a vision, and thought it meant that Marjorie would bear my child, that all would be well with us. . . . I foresaw; but I did not foresee that Marjorie would have been dead for years before ever this daughter of mine and I should meet. . . .

"Where were you brought up, Marja?"

"In a big house with lots of other little boys and girls," she said, "*They're* orphans, but I'm something else. It's a bad word that Matron says I must never, *never* say, but I'll whisper it to you."

"Don't," Lew said. He could guess; Regis remembered that there were still those who had called him bastard, even after he was acknowledged Heir to Alton. He had her snuggled on his lap now, in the curve of his arm.

If I had known, I would have come back—come back sooner. Somehow, somehow I would have managed to make amends to Thyra for what I did not remember doing . . .

Before Regis's questioning look, Lew raised his head. He said doggedly, "I was drugged with aphrosone. It's vicious stuff; you live a normal life—but you forget from minute to minute what is happening, remember nothing but symbolic dreams. . . . I've heard that if you tell a psychiatrist what you remember of the dreams under the drug, he will be able to help you remember what really happened. I didn't want to know—" and his voice stuck in his throat.

That must have been after they escaped from Aldaran, Regis thought; *Marjorie and Lew escaped together, and Ka-*

darin dragged them back, and drugged him, forcing him to serve as the pole of power for Sharra. . . . No wonder he did not want to remember.

"It doesn't matter," Lew said, reading Regis's thoughts, and his arm went around the child, so fiercely that she whimpered in protest. "She's mine anyhow."

He looks ugly but he's nice, I'm glad he's my father. . . .

They all stared at her in astonishment; she had reached out and touched their minds. Regis thought, *but children never have the Gift. . . .*

"Thyra was half *chieri,* they said," Lew said quietly. "Obviously, Marja *does* have it. It's not common, though it's not unknown. Your Gift waked early, didn't it, Rafe—nine or ten?"

Rafe nodded. He said "I remember our—foster-father Lord Aldaran—telling us about our mother. She was daughter to one of the forest-folk. And Thyra—" he hesitated, not wanting to say it.

"Go ahead," said Lew, "whatever it is."

"You did not know . . . Thyra. She was . . . like the *chieri. Emmasca;* no one was sure whether she was boy or girl. I can remember her like that, when I was very small, but only a little. Then Kadarin came—and very soon after, she began to wear women's clothing and think of herself as a woman . . . that was when we began to call her Thyra; before that, she had another name . . . you did not know that she was as old as Beltran, that she was past her twentieth year when Marjorie was born."

Lew shook his head, shocked. Regis picked up the thought, *I believed she was three or four years older than Marjorie, no more* . . . and a welter of images, resentment and desire, Thyra playing her harp, looking up at Lew in passionate wrath, Thyra's face suddenly, dreamlike, melting into Marjorie's . . . Marjorie, saying gently; "You were a little in love with Thyra, weren't you, Lew?"

Lew set the child down. "I'll have to find a nurse for her; there's no woman in my apartments to look after her." He stooped down and kissed the small rosy cheek. "Stay here with my kinswoman Linnell, little daughter."

She caught at his hand and asked shakily, "Am I going to live with you now?"

"You are," Lew said firmly, and gestured to Rafe and

Regis to leave the room with him. Regis said, with a note of warning, "They are going to use her to depose you . . ."

"I'm damned sure they'll try," Lew said grimly, "A nice, peaceful puppet, pliant in Hastur hands—no, I don't mean *you,* Regis, but the old man, and Dyan, and that precious kinsman of mine, Gabriel—the Council never did trust the male adult Altons too much, did they? So they exile me to Armida, or to a Tower, and bring this youngster up in the way they think she should go." His face looked strained and he clenched his good hand so tightly that Regis was glad he was not the object of Lew's wrath.

"Let them try," he said, and his hand twitched as if he had it around the neck of some one, "Just let them try, damn them! She's mine—and if they think they can take her away from me again, they are welcome to try!"

Regis and Rafe exchanged glances of mingled relief and dismay. Regis had hoped that something, somehow, would awaken Lew out of his deadly apathy, make him care for some one and something again. Now it seemed as if something had done just that. Well, they had raised the wind—but there might be hell to pay before this was over!

CHAPTER TEN

(Lew Alton's narrative)

The day was darkening toward twilight. Looking out over the city, I could see the streets beginning to fill with the laughing, masked, flower-tossing crowds of Festival Night. I would be expected to appear for the Alton Domain at the great ball in the Comyn Castle; it was simply part of being what I was, and although they had not made any overt move to depose me from my place as Head of the Domain, I intended to give them no chance to say I was neglecting any part of my duty. Now, among other things, I must somehow arrange proper care for Marja. Andres would guard her with his life, if he knew she were mine, but a child that age needed a woman to look after her, to dress her and bathe her and make sure she had proper playthings and companionship. Regis offered to place her in Javanne's care; his sister had twin daughters who were about her age. I thanked him but refused; Javanne Hastur has never liked me, and Javanne's husband, Gabriel Lanart-Hastur, was one of the main contenders for the Domain. The last thing I wanted was to place this child in his keeping.

I thought regretfully of Dio. I had been too quick to dissolve our marriage. She had wanted my child, and even though our son had died, perhaps she would have allowed this one to fill the place left vacant . . . but no; that would be asking too much, that she should love another woman's child as her own. When I thought of her, the old suffering and resentment surfaced. In any case, if she were here, I could consult her about the proper way to raise a girl child. . . . I wondered how Callina would feel about it. And then I remembered that Callina had sworn to marry Beltran.

Over my dead body, I vowed silently, left Marja in Andres's care (he said that he knew a decent woman, the wife of one of my father's paxmen, who would come to care for her, if I took her home to Armida) and went to seek out Callina.

She looked weary and harried.

"The girl's awake," she said. "She was hysterical when she wakened; I had to give her a sedative. She's calmed down a little, but of course she doesn't speak the language, and she's frightened in a strange place. Lew, what are we going to do now?"

"I won't know till I see her. Where is she?"

So much had happened in the intervening hours that I had all but forgotten Ashara's plan, the woman who had been brought through the Screen. She had been moved to a spacious room in the Aillard apartments; when we came in she was lying across the bed, her face buried in the covers, and she looked as if she had been crying; but it was a tearless and defiant face she raised to me. She was still Linnell's double; even more so, having been decently dressed in clothing I supposed—correctly—to be some of Linnell's own.

"Please tell me the truth," she said steadily, as I came in. "Am I mad and locked up somewhere?" She spoke one of the dialects I knew perfectly well . . . of course; I had talked with her at length, that night on Vainwal when my son had been born, and died. And even as this crossed my mind I saw the memory reflected in her face.

"But I remember you!" she cried out, "The man with one hand—the one who had that—that—that terribly deformed—" My face must have done something I didn't know about, because she stopped. "Where am I? Why have you kidnapped me and brought me here?"

I said quietly, "You needn't be afraid." I remembered saying the same thing to Marja; she had been afraid of me too. But I could not reassure her with the same words that had comforted a five-year-old child. "Allow me to introduce myself. Lewis-Kennard Montray-Lanart, *z'par servu. . . .*"

"I know who you are," she said steadily. "What I don't know is how I got here. A red sun—"

"If you'll be calm, I'll explain everything," I said. "I am sorry, I cannot remember your name—"

"Kathie Marshall," she said.

"Terranan?"

"Yes. But I know we're not on Terra, nor on Vainwal," she said, and her voice trembled; but she made no display of fear. I said, "The *Terranan* call this Cottman's Star. We call it Darkover. We brought you here because we need your help—"

"You must be crazy," she said. "How could I help you? And if I could, what makes you think I would, after you've kidnapped me?"

That was, I supposed, a fair question. I reached out to try to touch her mind; if she could not understand our language, at least this might reassure her that we meant no harm.

Callina said, "You were brought here because you were twinned in mind with my sister Linnell—"

She backed away. "Twinned minds? That's ridiculous! Do you think I believe in that kind of thing?"

"If you do not," said Callina quietly, "how is it that suddenly you can understand what I am saying?"

"Why, you're speaking Terran . . . no!" she said, and I saw the terror rise in her mind again. "Why, what language am I speaking—?"

It was reasonable that if she was Linnell's Cherillys double, she would have *laran* potential; at least she could understand us now. Callina said, "We hoped we could persuade you to help us; but there will be no compulsion and certainly no force."

"Where am I, then?"

"In the Comyn Castle in Thendara."

"But that's halfway across the Galaxy . . ." she whispered, and turned frantically to stare out the window, at the red light of the declining sun. I saw her white hands clench on a fold of curtain. "A red sun—" she whispered, "Oh, I have nightmares like this when I can't wake up . . ." She was so deathly white I feared she would collapse; Callina put an arm around her, and this time Kathie did not pull away.

"Try to believe us, child," Callina said. "You are here, on Darkover. We brought you here."

"And who are you?"

"Callina Aillard. Keeper of Comyn Council."

"I've heard about the Keepers," Kathie said, then, shakily, "This whole thing is crazy! You *can't* take a Terran citizen and pull her halfway across the Galaxy like this! My—my father will tear the planet apart looking for me—" She covered her face with her hands. "I—I want to go home!"

I wished that we had never started this whole thing. I was remembering the aureole of doom, fate, death which I had seen around Linnell . . . merciful Evanda, was it only last night? I wondered if this had endangered Linnell in some way; what happened when Cherillys duplicates met one another? There was not even a legend to guide me. There was an old legend from the Kilghard Hills, about a mountain chief, or a bandit lord—in those days, I supposed, it would be hard to distinguish between them—who had located his duplicate so that he could command his army by being in two places at once; but I couldn't remember any more than that, and I had no idea what had happened to the duplicate once his day was done. Possibly the bandit chief let his duplicate be hanged for his own crimes. In any case, I was sure he came to a bad end.

Would this woman's presence endanger Linnell? There was one precaution I could take; I could put a protective barrier around her mind, so that she would keep her invulnerability, her complete unawareness of these Darkovan forces. I hoped that in touching her mind, to give her knowledge of the language, I had not already breached that unawareness; at least I would make sure no one else did so. In effect, I meant to put a barrier around her mind so that any attempt to make telepathic contact with Kathie, or dominate her mind, would be immediately shunted, through a sort of bypass circuit built into the barrier, to me.

There was no sense in trying to explain what I meant to do. I would have to start by explaining the very nature of the *laran* Gifts, and since, as Linnell's exact duplicate, she had *laran* potential, when I had done explaining, she might be adapted and vulnerable to Darkovan forces. I reached out as gently as I could, and made contact.

It was an instant of screaming pain in every nerve, then it blanked out, and Kathie was sobbing compulsively.

"*What did you do?* I felt you—it was horrible—but no, that's crazy—or *I'm* crazy—what happened?"

"Why couldn't you wait till she understood?" Callina demanded. But I had done what I had to do, and I had done it now, because I wanted Kathie safely barriered before anyone saw her and guessed. But it hurt to see her cry; I had never been able to stand Linnell's tears. Callina looked up helplessly, trying to soothe the weeping girl.

"Go away. I'll handle this." And as Kathie's sobs broke out afresh, "Lew, *go away!*"

Suddenly I was angry. Why didn't Callina trust me? I bowed elaborately and said, *"Su serva, domna,"* in my coldest, most ironic voice, turned my back and went out.

And in that moment, when I left Callina in anger, I snapped the trap shut on us all.

As darkness fell, every light in the Comyn Castle began to glow; once in every journey of Darkover around its sun, the Comyn, city folk from Thendara, mountain lords with business in the lowlands, offworld consuls and ambassadors and Terrans from the Trade City, mingled together on Festival Night with a great show of cordiality. Now it involved everyone of any importance on the planet; and Festival opened with a great display of dancing in the great ball-room.

Centuries of tradition made this a masked affair, so that Comyn and commoner might mingle on equal terms. In compliance with custom I wore a narrow half mask, but had made no other attempt at disguise; though I had worn my mechanical hand, simply so that I would not be a marked man. My father, I thought wryly, would have approved. I stood at one end of the hall, talking idly with a couple of Terrans in the space service, and as soon as I decently could, I got away and went to one of the windows, looking out at the four miniature moons that had nearly floated into conjunction.

Behind me the great hall blazed with colors and costumes reflecting every corner of Darkover and much of our history. Derik wore an elaborate and gaudy costume from the Ages of Chaos, but he was not masked—one part of a prince's duty is simply to be visible to his subjects. I recognized Rafe Scott, too, in the mask and whip of a *kifirgh* duelist, complete with clawed gloves.

In the corner reserved by tradition for young girls, Linnell's spangled mask was a travesty of disguise. Her eyes were glowing with happy consciousness of all the eyes on her; as *comynara* she was known to everyone on Darkover—at least in the Domains—but she rarely saw anyone outside the narrow circle of her cousins and the few selected companions permitted to a lady of the Aillard Domain. Now, masked, she could speak to, or even dance with, complete strangers; the excitement of it was almost too much for her.

Beside her, also masked, I saw Kathie, and wondered if that was another of Callina's brilliant ideas. Well, there was no harm in it; with the bypass circuit I had put into her brain, she was safely barricaded; and there was hardly a better way of proving to her that she was not a prisoner but an honored guest. They would probably think her a minor noble woman of the Aillard clan.

Linnell laughed up at me as I approached her.

"Lew, I am teaching your cousin from Terra some of our dances. Imagine, she didn't know them."

My cousin from Terra. I supposed that was another idea of Callina's. Well, it explained the faint unfamiliarity with which she spoke Darkovan. Kathie said gently, "I wasn't taught dancing, Linnell."

"You weren't? What did you study, then? Lew, don't they dance on Terra?"

"Dancing," I said dryly, "is an integral part of all human cultures. It is a group activity passed down from the group movements of birds and anthropoids, and also a social channeling of mating behavior among all higher primates, including man. Among such quasi-human cultures as those of the *chieri* it becomes an ecstatic behavior pattern akin to drunkenness. Yes, they dance on Terra, on Megaera, Samarra, Alpha Ten, Vainwal, and in fact from one end of the Galaxy to the other. For further information, lectures on anthropology are given in the city; I'm not in the mood." I turned to Kathie in what I hoped was proper cousinly fashion. "Suppose we do it instead."

I added to Kathie as we danced, "Certainly you wouldn't know that dancing is a major study with children here; Linnell and I both learned as soon as we could walk. I had only basic instruction—after that I went to training in the martial arts—but Linnell has been studying ever since." I glanced affectionately back at Linnell, who was dancing with Regis Hastur. "I went to a dance or two on Vainwal. Are our dances so different?"

But as I talked I was studying the Terran woman carefully. Kathie had guts and brains, I realized. It took them to come here after the shock she had had, and play the part tacitly assigned to her. And Kathie had another rare quality; she seemed unaware that the arm circling her waist was unlike any other arm and hand. That's not common; even Linnell had given it a quick, furtive stare. Well, Kathie worked in hospitals, she had probably seen worse things.

With seeming irrelevance, Kathie said, "And Linnell is your cousin, your kinswoman—?"

"My foster-sister; she was brought up in my father's home. We're not blood kin, except insofar as all Comyn have common ancestry."

"She's very—well, it's as if she were *really* my twin sister; I feel as if I'd always known her, I loved her the moment I saw her. But I'm afraid of Callina. It's not that she's been unkind to me—no one could have been kinder—but she seems so remote, somehow, not quite human!"

"She's a Keeper," I said, "they are taught not to show emotions, that's all." But I wondered if that were all it was.

"Please—" Kathie touched my arm, "let's not dance; on Vainwal I'm a good enough dancer, but here I feel like a stumbling elephant!"

"You probably weren't taught as intensively." To me that was the strangest thing about Terra; the casualness with which they regarded this one talent which distinguishes man from the four-footed kind. There is a saying on Darkover; *only men laugh, only men dance, only men weep*. Women who could not dance—how could they have true beauty?

I started to return Kathie to the corner where the young women waited; and as I turned, I saw Callina enter the ballroom. And for me, the music stopped.

I have seen the black night of interstellar space flecked with a hundred million stars. Callina looked like that, in a filmy web like a scrap torn out of that sky, her dark hair netted with pale constellations. I heard drawn breaths, gasps of shock everywhere.

"How beautiful she is," breathed Kathie, "but what does the costume represent? I've never seen one like it. . . ."

"I've no idea," I said, but I lied. The tale was told in the *Ballad of Hastur and Cassilda,* the most ancient legend of the Comyn; Camilla, slain by the shadow-sword in the place of her bright sister, so that she passed away into the realms of darkness under the shadow of Avarra, Dark Lady of birth and death . . . I had no idea why a woman on the eve of her bridal, even in the case of so unappealing a marriage as this, should choose to come in such a dress. I wondered what would happen when Beltran of Aldaran caught the significance of that? A more direct insult would be hard to devise, unless she had come in the dress of the public hangman!

I excused myself quickly from Kathie and went in the direction of Callina. I agreed that this marriage was a sickening farce, but she had no right to embarrass her family like this. But Merryl reached her first, and I caught the tail end of his lecture.

"A pretty piece of spite—embarrass us all before our guests, when Beltran has made so generous a gesture—"

"He may keep his generosity as far as I am concerned," Callina said. "Brother, I will not look or act a lie. This dress pleases me; it is perfectly suited to the way I have been treated all my life by Comyn!" Her laugh was musical and bitter. "Beltran would endure more insult than this, for *laran*-right in Comyn Council! Wait and see!"

"Do you think I am going to dance with you while you are wearing that—" his voice failed him; he was crimson with wrath. Callina said, "As for that, you may please yourself. I am willing to behave in a civilized manner. If you are not, it is your loss." She turned to me and said, almost a command, "Lord Alton will dance with me." She held out her arms, and I moved into them; but this boldness was unlike her, and put me ill at ease. Callina was a Keeper; always, in public, she had been timid, self-effacing, overwhelmingly shy and modest. This new Callina, drawing all eyes with a shocking costume, startled me. And what would Linnell think?

"I'm sorry about Linnell," said Callina, "but the dress pleases my mood. And—it is becoming, is it not?"

It was, but the coquetry with which she glanced up at me, shocked and startled me; it was as if a painted statue had come to life and begun flirting with me. Well, she had asked me. "You're too damned beautiful," I said, hoarsely, then drew her into a recess and crushed my mouth down on hers, hard and savagely. "Callina, Callina, you're not going through this crazy farce of a marriage, are you?"

For a moment she was passive, startled, then went rigid, bending back and pushing me frantically away, "No! Don't!"

I let my arms drop and stood looking at her, slow fury heating my face. "That's not the way you acted last night—nor just now! What is it that you want anyhow, Callina?"

She bent her head. She said bitterly, as if from a long way off, "Does it matter what I want? Who has ever asked me? I am only a pawn in the game, to be moved about as they choose!"

I took her hand in mine, and she did not pull it away. I said urgently, "Callina, you *don't* have to do this! Beltran is disarmed, no longer a threat—"

"Would you have me forsworn?"

"Forsworn or dead rather than married to him," I said, rage building in me. "You don't know what he is!"

She said, "I have given my word. I—" she looked up at me and suddenly her face crumpled into weeping. "Can't you spare me this?"

"Did you ever think that there are things you might have spared me?" I demanded. "So be it, Callina; I wish Beltran joy of his bride!" I turned my back on her, disregarding her stifled cry, and strode away.

I don't know where I thought I was going. Anywhere, out of there. A telepath is never at ease in crowds, and I have trouble coping with them. I know that a path cleared for me through the dancers; then, quite unexpectedly, a voice said, "Lew!" and I stopped cold, staring down at Dio.

She was wearing a soft green gown, trimmed with white; her hair waved softly around her face, and she had done nothing to disguise the golden-brown freckles that covered her cheeks. She looked rosy and healthy, not the white, wasted, hysterical woman I had last seen in the hospital on Vainwal. She waited a minute, then said, as she had said the first time we came face to face, "Aren't you going to ask me to dance, *Dom* Lewis?"

I blinked at her. I must have looked a great gawk, staring with my mouth open.

"I didn't know you were in Thendara!"

"Why shouldn't I be?" she retorted. "Do you think I am

an invalid? Where else would I be, at Council season? Yet you have not even paid me a courtesy call, nor sent flowers on the morning of Festival! Are you so angry because I failed you?"

A dancing couple reeled within a half-step of us, and a strange woman said irritably, "Must you block the dancing floor? If you are not dancing, at least get out of the way of those who are!"

I took Dio's elbow, not too gently, and steered her out on the sidelines. "I am sorry—I did not know you wanted flowers from me. I did not know you were in Thendara." Suddenly all my bitterness overflowed. "I do not yet know the courtesies of dealing with a wife who abandoned me!"

"*I* abandoned—" she broke off and stared at me. She said, evidently trying to steady her voice. "I abandoned *you?* I thought you divorced me because I could not give you a healthy son—"

"Who told you that?" I demanded, grasping her shoulders until she winced; I loosened my grip, but went on urgently, "I went back to the hospital! They told me you had left, with your brothers—"

Gradually the color left her face, till the freckles stood out dark against her white skin. She said, "Lerrys bundled me onto the ship before I could walk. . . . He had to carry me. He told me that as the Head of a Domain, you could not marry a woman who could not give you an Heir—"

"Zandru send him scorpion whips!" I swore. "He came to me, just after I came here—he threatened to kill me—said you had been through enough—Dio, I swear I thought it was what you wanted—"

Her eyes were beginning to overflow and I saw her bite her lip; Dio could never bear to cry where anyone could see her. She put out a hand to me, then drew it back and said, "I come here to Festival—hoping to see you—and I find you in Callina's arms!" She turned her back on me, and started to move away; I held her back with a hand on her shoulder.

"Lerrys has made enough mischief," I said. "We'll have this out with him, and we'll do it now! Is he here, that damned mischief-maker?"

"How dare you speak that way of my brother?" Dio demanded inconsistently. "He was doing what he thought was best for me! At that point I was hysterical, I never wanted to see you again—"

"And I was complying with your wishes," I said, drawing a deep breath. "Dio, what's the use of all this? It's done. I did what I thought you wanted—"

"And I come here to find you and see if it was what *you* wanted," Dio flung at me, "and I find you already consoling yourself with that damned frozen stick of a Keeper! I hope she strikes you with lightning when you touch her—you deserve it!"

"Don't talk that way about Callina—" I said sharply.

"She is sworn Keeper; what does she want with my husband?"

"You made it very clear that I was *not* your husband—"

"Then why was it I who was served with notice of a divorce? What a fool I will look—" Again she looked as if she were going to cry. I put my arm around her, trying to comfort her, but she pulled herself angrily away. "If that's what you want, you are welcome to it! You and Callina—"

I said, "Don't be a fool, Dio! Callina will be handfasted to Beltran within the hour! I couldn't stop her—"

"I've no doubt you tried," Dio retorted. "I saw you!"

I sighed. Dio was determined to make a scene. I still thought we should settle this in private, but I was on guard, too. She had made me feel like a fool, not the other way around; and she had had every right to leave me after the suffering I had put her through; but I did not want to be reminded again of the tragedy, I was still too raw about it. "Dio, this is neither the time nor the place—"

"Can you think of a better?" She was furious; I didn't blame her. If Lerrys had been there, I think I would have killed him. So she had not left me, after all, of her own free will. Yet, as I looked at her angry face, I realized that there was no way to go back where we had left off.

Others were looking at us curiously. I was not surprised; I, at least, must have been broadcasting my emotions—which were largely confusion—all through the ballroom. I said, "We had better dance," and touched her arm. It was not a couple-dance and I was grateful; I did not want quite that much intimacy, not now, not here, not with all that lay between us. I moved into the outer ring of men, and Dio let Linnell move to her side and draw her into the circle.

Strange, I thought, that Linnell, my closest kinswoman, did not know of our brief marriage nor the disastrous way in which it had ended. It was not, after all, the sort of story to tell a young woman on the verge of her own marriage. I saw how she looked at Derik as she pulled him into the set. Then the music began and I gave myself up to it, as the figure of the dance swept Dio toward me, with a formal bow, and away again. At last, as the dance ended, we faced one another again and bowed. I saw Derik slide his arm through Linnell's, and was left with Dio again.

I said formally, "May I bring you some refreshment?"

Her eyes glinted tears. "Must you be so formal? Is this nothing but a game to you?"

I shook my head, tucked my hand under her arm and led her toward the buffet. Her head hardly came up to my shoulder. I had forgotten what a little thing she was; I always remembered her as being taller. Perhaps it was the way she carried herself, proud and independent, perhaps it was only that on Vainwal, like many women, she had worn high-heeled shoes, and here she had reverted to the low soft sandals that women wore in the Domains. The pale green of her gown made her hair shine reddish gold.

Our separation need not be final. Dio as Lady Alton, and we could live at Armida . . . and for a moment I was overcome with a flood of homesickness for the hills of my home, the long shadows at twilight, the way the sun lowered over the line of tall trees behind the Great House . . . I could have this still, I could have it with Dio. . . .

The long refreshment tables were laden with every kind of delicacy one could imagine. I dipped her up a cup of some sweet red fruit drink; tasting it, discovered it had been heavily laced with some strong and colorless spirit, for a single glass made me dizzy. Dio, watching as I drank, set hers down untasted and said, "I don't want to get drunk here tonight. There's something—I don't know what it is. I'm frightened."

I took that seriously. Dio's instincts were good; and she was one of the hypersensitive Ridenows. Nevertheless, I said, "What's wrong? Is it only that there are Terrans and off-worlders here tonight?" Lawton was there, with several functionaries from the Terran HQ, and it suddenly occurred to me to wonder if Kathie would see the Terran uniforms, appeal to them for protection, accuse us of kidnapping or worse. Most Terrans knew nothing of matrix technology, and some of them were ready to believe anything about it. And I was quite sure that what Callina and I had done was now against some law or other.

Dio was lightly in rapport with me, and she turned to say with asperity, "Can't you get Callina out of your mind for a minute, even when you are talking with me?"

I could hardly believe this; Dio was jealous? "Do you care, *preciosa?*"

"I shouldn't, but I do," she said, raising her face to me, suddenly serious. "I think I wouldn't mind . . . if she wanted you . . . but I don't want to see you hurt. I don't think you know everything about Callina."

"And of course, you do?"

She said, "It was I who should have gone to the Comyn Tower, to be trained as—as Ashara's surrogate. I did not want to be nothing more than—than a pawn for Ashara. I had known one of the—one of her other under-Keepers. And so I made certain that I was—" she hesitated, colored a little—"disqualified."

I understood that. There is now no reason why a Keeper must be a sworn virgin, set apart, consecrated, near-worshipped. For good reasons, they remain celibate while they are functioning as Keeper in a circle; but not in the old, superstitious, ritualistic way. There had been a time when a woman chosen as Keeper entered upon a lifelong sentence of alienation, chastity, separation; not now. Yet, for some reason or another, Ashara chose her under-Keepers from those who were trained as virgins; and Dio's way was as good as any to avoid that sentence.

I understood, suddenly, why Callina had rebuffed me. The marriage with Beltran was to be empty ceremonial, politically arranged; Callina had no intention of giving up her role as Keeper in Ashara's place. I should have been complimented—she was well aware that I would not accept that kind of separation. She was *not* indifferent to me; and she had let me know it. And for that reason she dared not let me come near.

Folly, folly twice over, then, to love the forbidden. Yet the thought that she might fall into Beltran's keeping frightened me. Would he really be content with a formal arrangement, where he had the name of consort, and no other privileges? Callina was a beautiful woman, and Beltran was not indifferent. . . .

"Lew, you are as far away from me as if you were on Vainwal again," Dio said irritably, and took the glass of fruit juice I had dipped up for her. I watched her, wondering what would come next. I was a fool for thinking, even for a moment, of Callina, who was forbidden to me, who had put herself beyond my reach . . . Keeper or no, Beltran's wife would be forbidden; I was sworn Comyn and they had conferred Comyn immunity upon him. That was a fact, one I could neither climb over nor go round. And this business with Dio loomed between me and any life I might make for myself. I recognized, with a surge of humiliation, it was not for me to say, I will have this woman or that; it was, rather, which of them would have me. I seemed to have no choice in the matter, and in any case I was no prize for a woman. *Mutilated, damned, haunted* . . . I forced down the sickening surge of self-pity, and looked up at Dio.

"I must pay my respects to my foster-sister; will you join me?"

She shrugged, saying, "Why not?" and followed me. A nagging unease, half telepathic, beat at me. I saw Callina, dancing with Beltran, and stubbornly looked away. If that was her choice, so be it. Viciously, I hoped he'd try to kiss her. Lerrys, Dyan? If they were here, they were in costume and unrecognizable. Half the Terran colony could be here tonight, and I would not know.

But Linnell was dancing with someone I did not recognize, and I turned to where Merryl Aillard and Derik were chatting idly in a corner. Derik looked flushed, and his voice was thick and unsteady. "Ev'n, Lew."

"Derik, have you seen Regis Hastur? What's his costume?"

"D'know," Derik said thickly, "I'm Derik, tha's all I know. Have 'nough trouble 'memberin' that. You try it sometime."

"A fine spectacle," I muttered, "Derik, I wish you would remember who you are! Merryl, can't you get him out of here and sober him up a little? Derik, do you realize what a show you are giving the Terrans and our kinfolk?"

"I think—forget y'self," he mumbled, "Not your affair wha' I do—ain't drunk anyhow . . ."

"Linnell should be very proud of you," I snapped. "Merryl, go and drag him under a cold shower or something, can't you?"

"L'nell's mad at me," Derik spoke in tones of intimate self-pity. "Won' even dansh . . ."

"Who would?" I muttered, standing on both feet so I would not kick him. It was bad enough to need a Regency in times like these, but when the heir-presumptive to the crown makes a drunken spectacle of himself before half of Thendara, that was worse. I resolved to hunt up Hastur, who had authority I didn't, and influence with Derik—at least I hoped so. Merryl did, but he was no help. I scanned the riot of costumes, looking for Danvan Hastur, or even Regis. Or perhaps I could find Linnell, who might be able to persuade or shame him into leaving the room and sobering up.

One costume suddenly caught my eye. I had seen such harlequins in old books on Terra; parti-colored, a lean beaked cap over a masked face, lean and somehow horrible. Not in itself, for the costume was no worse than grotesque, but a sort of atmosphere—I told myself not to imagine things.

"No, I don't like him either," said Regis quietly at my side. "And I don't like the atmosphere of this room—or this night."

I said, "I keep thinking I have seen him before." I did not know what I was going to say until I heard myself saying it. "I feel—I feel as if all hell was going to break loose!"

Regis nodded gravely. He said, "You have some of the Aldaran Gift, don't you? Foresight . . ." he saw Dio was still at my elbow and bowed to her. "Greetings, *vai domna.* You are Lerrys's sister, are you not?"

I looked again at the harlequin-masked man. I felt I should know him, that somehow his name was on the very tip of my tongue. At the same time I felt a curious twisting fear; why could I not remember, not recognize him?

But before I could force myself further, the dome lights were switched off. Immediately the room was flooded with streaming moonlight. There was a soft "A-ahh—" from the thronged guests as through the clearing transparency of the dome, the four moons floated high, in full conjunction, one above the other; the pale violet face of Liriel, sea-green Idriel, the peacock shimmer of Kyrrdis, and the pale pearl of Mormallor. I felt a faint touch on my arm and looked down at Dio.

This is not how I had imagined we would return home together . . . for a moment I was not sure whether it was her thought or mine. Couples were moving onto the floor for the moonlight dance which was traditionally a dance for pledged couples; I saw Linnell approaching Derik—drunk or no, she would consider herself bound and obligated for this. I was unable, suddenly, to resist the old tie, the old attraction; I drew Dio into my arms and we moved onto the floor. Over her shoulder I saw that Regis was standing alone at the edge of the dance floor, his face cold and detached, in spite of the women who made a point of standing conveniently near in case he should choose one of them. Dio felt warm and familiar in my arms. Was this what I had wanted all along? I found that I resented that smile which took so much for granted. Yet the rhythm of the music pounded in my blood. I had forgotten this—the sense of being altogether in key with one another, resonating to the same music, like a single body moving to the sound, and as she had done once before, she reached out, almost without volition, and the mind-touch came between us, a locking closer than any physical intimacy . . . closeness, home, fulfillment. As the final chord of music rang in the night, I caught her close and kissed her, hard.

The silence was anticlimax. Dio slid from my arms, and I felt cold and alone again. The lights, coming on again under the dome, caught her looking up at me with a strange smile.

"So, I have had that much of you," she said softly. "Was it never any more than that, Lew—that I was a woman, and you were alone and—in need? Was it never more than that?"

"I don't know, Dio. I swear I don't know," I said wearily. "Can't we leave it for now, and settle it sometime when—when half of Thendara isn't watching us?"

She said, unexpected, her face very grave, "I don't think we will be given that much time. I'm frightened, Lew.

Something is very wrong. On the surface, everything's as it's always been, but there's something—something that shouldn't be here, and I don't know what—"

Dio had the sensitive Ridenow gift; I trusted her instincts. But what could I do? Certainly nothing could be done here, no one would dare strike at any of us before the City and the assembled guests. Still, Regis had said very much the same thing, and I was myself uneasy.

As I threaded my way through the crowd, in search of Linnell or Callina, I saw again the stranger in the harlequin costume. Whom did I know who was tall and rangy, like that, why did he strike me as strange, over-familiar? He was too tall to be Lerrys, yet it seemed the hostility which beat out toward me from him was very much like what I had sensed in Lerrys when he warned me to stay away from Dio.

(And Dio was at my side. Would Lerrys make good his threats, here and now?)

Again I moved through the crowd. I had spoken to Regis and forgotten to speak to him about Derik—there was too much on my mind, it seemed I had been moving aimlessly back and forth through this wretched yammering crowd all night, and my barriers were beginning to loosen; I would not be able to endure the mental jangle of it much longer. A few cadets were crowding near the long banquet tables, greedily attacking the heaped delicacies there, delighted at the change from barracks food. Among them I recognized both of Javanne's sons, Rafael and the older Gabriel. I supposed one of them would still consider himself my Heir. . . .

I have no son, I shall never have a son; but I have a daughter and I shall fight for her right to hold Armida after me . . . and then I was seized with a sickening sense of futility. Would there be anything to hold, after Beltran took his place in Comyn Council and destroyed us all? Would it not be better to take Marja—and Dio if she would come—and go back to Terra, or Vainwal, or out to one of the worlds at the far edge of the Empire where we could build a new life for ourselves?

I'm not a fighter. I can fight if I must, and my father tried his best, from the day I was big enough to clasp my hands around the hilt of a sword, to make certain that I would be good at it, and I had learned because I had had no choice. But I have never enjoyed it, despite his efforts to make me excel in arms-play, in unarmed combat, as a soldier.

Damn him, even his last words had been of battle . . . I could hear them now, surging inside me as if they were being spoken now, not in memory: Return to Darkover, fight for your brother's rights and your own . . .

and he had thrust me into this seething hell . . .

"How you are scowling, Lew," Linnell said in pretty reproof. "This is supposed to be a celebration!"

I tried to move my face into something like a sociable smile. Sometimes I would rather be in the ninth and coldest of Zandru's hells than in a crowd where I have to be sociable, and this was one of those times, but I was not going to spoil Linnell's enjoyment. I said, "Sorry, this ugly mug of mine is bad enough, I suppose, without making it worse."

"You're not ugly to me, foster-brother," she said, in the intimate mode that made it an endearment. "If I wish your face were unmarred it is only a way of wishing you hadn't suffered so much. The flowers you sent me were beautiful," she added. "See, I am wearing some of them on my gown."

I smiled a little ruefully and said, "You must thank Andres; he selected them. They suit you, though." I thought Linnell herself was rather like a flower, rosy and bright, smiling up at me. "I saw you dancing with Derik; I hope you told that wretch Merryl to take him away and sober him up!"

"Oh, but he isn't drunk, Lew," she said seriously, laying a hand on my wrist. "It's only his bad luck that he should have one of these spells on Festival Night. . . . He gets like this sometimes, and when he was younger, they used to keep him in bed and out of sight—he doesn't drink at all, because it makes him so much worse, he never even touches wine with dinner. I was angry with him because he took one drink—some fruit drink which had been doctored with strong *firi*, and he wouldn't offend Merryl by refusing it. . . ."

"That was a mean trick; I had some of it myself," I said. "Now I wonder just who did that, in such a way that Derik would get some?" I had a few suspicions. Lerrys, for instance, would be glad to see our presumptive king, poor thing that he was, making more of a fool of himself than usual.

"Oh, surely, it was an accident, Lew," Linnell said, shocked. "No one would do a thing like that on purpose, would they? It does taste very good, I hardly knew there was anything in it; I might easily have drunk more than one glass, and of course, poor Derik, he's not familiar enough with drink to know that something which tasted only of fruits would make him so much worse—"

So someone who had a vested interest in proving Derik thoroughly incompetent had made sure he had some harmless-tasting drink which would emphasize his various impediments and confuse him worse than ever. Merryl? Merryl was supposedly his friend. Lerrys? He might do anything which would throw us into the arms of the Terran Empire, and he had the kind of devious mind which would enjoy a dirty trick like that. I wondered how, in that family, Dio had turned out so forthright and straightforward.

I said, "Well, he certainly appeared drunk, and I'm afraid most people would think it of him!"

"When we are married," she said, smiling gently, "I will make certain no one can lead him into such things. Derik is not always a fool, Lew. No, he is not brilliant, certainly he will always need someone like Regis—or you, Lew—to guide him in matters of policy. But he knows he is not very bright, and he will let himself be guided. And I will make certain that it is not Merryl who guides him, either."

Linnell might sound and look like a delicate, flowerlike, fragile young girl, but behind all that there was strong common sense and practicality, too. I said, "It's a pity you are not Head of the Domain, sister; they would never have been able to marry you off to Beltran." I turned and saw Kathie, who had been dancing with Rafe Scott, and hoped she had had sense enough not to say anything to him. And beyond her was the harlequin who had so deeply disturbed me . . . damn it, *who was he?*

"Lew, who is Kathie really? When I'm near her I feel terribly strange. It's not so much that she *looks* like me—it's as if she were a part of myself, I know what she's going to do before she does it . . . I know, for instance, that she's going to turn—there, you see? And she's coming this way . . . and then I feel, it's a kind of pain, as if I had to touch her, embrace her. I can't keep away from her! But when I actually do touch her, I have to pull away, I can't endure it. . . ." Linnell was twisting her hands nervously, ready to burst into hysterical tears or laughter, and Linnell wasn't a girl to fret over trifles. If it affected her like this, it was something serious. What *did* happen, I wondered, when Cherillys doubles came face to face?

Well, I was about to see, whatever it was. As Kathie ended the dance she moved toward Linnell, and almost without discernible volition, Linnell began to move in her direction. Was Kathie working some malicious mental trick on my little cousin? But no, Kathie had no awareness of Darkovan powers, and even if she had potential for *laran,* nothing could get through that block I'd put around her mind.

Linnell touched Kathie's hand, almost shyly; in immediate response, Kathie put an arm around Linnell's waist, and they walked enlaced for a minute or two; then with a sudden nervous movement, Linnell drew herself free and came to me.

"There is Callina," she said.

The Keeper, aloof in her starry draperies, threaded her way through the maze of dancers seeking new partners, moving toward the refreshment tables.

"Where have you been, Callina?" Linnell demanded. She looked at the dress with sorrowful puzzlement, but Callina made no attempt to justify or explain herself. I reached out to touch her mind; but I felt only the strange, cold, stony presence which I had felt once or twice near Callina, a door locked and slammed, cold and guarded.

"Oh, Derik drew me off to listen to some long drunken tale—I thought you told me he never drinks, Linnie? He never did get it all told . . . the wine conquered him at last. May he never fall to a worse enemy. I ordered Merryl to find his body-servant and have him carried to his rooms, so you'll have to find someone else to dance with for the midnight dance, darling." She looked indifferently around the room. "I suppose I'll be dancing with Beltran; Hastur is signaling to me. Probably he intends to begin the ceremony now."

"Am I to come with you then?"

Callina said, still with that icy indifference, "I will not

give this farce any of the trappings of a wedding, Linnie. Nor will I drag any of my kinsmen into it . . . why do you think I made sure Merryl was well out of the way?"

"Oh, Callina—" Linnell said, reaching for her, but she moved away, leaving Linnell with her arms outstretched, hurt and bewildered.

"Don't pity me, Linnie," she said tensely, "I—won't have it." I was sure that what she meant was, *I can't bear it.*

I don't know what I would have said or done at that moment, if she had turned to me; but she drew herself apart from us; her eyes brooded, blue ice like Ashara's, past me into silence. Bitter and helpless, I watched her move away through the crowds in that dress that was a reminder of death, doom, shadows.

I should have guessed everything, then, when she left us without a word or a touch, silent and remote as Ashara's self, making a lonely island of her tragedy and shutting us all away from her. I watched Beltran, at Hastur's side, advance to greet her, and saw that she gave him only a formal bow and not an embrace; listened as the bracelets were locked on their wrists.

"Parted in flesh, may you never be so in spirit; may you be forever one," Hastur said, and all over the room, wives reached for husbands, and lover for lover, to exchange the ritual kiss. Callina was Beltran's consort, the marriage a legal fact, from the moment Hastur released her hand. I did not turn to see if Dio was near me. The truth of the matter is, I had, at that moment, forgotten her existence, I was so caught up into Callina's anguish.

The next dance after a handfasting was always, by tradition, a dance for married or pledged couples. Callina, with the privilege of the bride, led Beltran onto the dance floor; but they moved with nothing touching but their fingertips. I saw Javanne and Gabriel move, smiling, onto the floor; the Regent bowed to an elderly dowager, one of Callina's distant kinswomen, and they moved into the sedate measure.

"Regis," Linnell said gaily, "are you going to disappoint every unwedded woman in the Domains again tonight?"

"Better disappoint them now than later, kinswoman," said Regis, smiling. "And I notice you are not dancing—where is our royal cousin?"

"He is ill—someone gave him some punch which had more to it than he knew," Linnell said, "and Merryl has taken him away, so I have neither kinsman nor lover to dance with me tonight—unless you would like to dance, Lew? You're more my brother than Merryl ever was," she added with a touch of annoyance.

"Forgive me, Linnie, I would rather not," I said, and wondered if I was still a little drunk; I felt uneasy, almost nauseated. Was it only the general unease of a telepath when the crowds are surrounding him too closely?

"Look, even Dyan is dancing with the widow of the old arms-master," Linnell said, "and Dio with Lerrys—look, isn't he a marvelous dancer?" I followed her look, saw the brother and sister dancing, closely gathered in each other's arms like lovers rather than sister and brother, and for a moment I wanted to storm across the floor in outrage, remind Lerrys that Dio was *mine* . . . but I felt unable to move. If I tried to dance surely I would fall down, but I had drunk only a very little of that same heavily spiked fruit drink.

Regis said, bowing to Linnell, "I will dance with you as Derik's surrogate, if you wish for it, cousin. It seems I am Derik's heir—may his reign be long," he added, with a wry smile.

"No, I would rather not," she said, a hand on his arm, "but you may stay and talk with me for this dance . . . Lew, do you know the man there in the harlequin costume? Who is the woman with him?

For a moment I could not see the harlequin I had noticed before; then I saw him, dancing with a tall woman with dark-copper hair, wonderful thick curls that cascaded halfway down her back. The whirling movement of the dance suddenly turned them toward me, and—although the woman was masked—suddenly I knew her, knew them both, even behind the hideous harlequin mask.

Thyra! No mask could have concealed her from me . . . for a moment it seemed that the matrix at my throat burned as with Sharra's very fire. I stood shocked, unable to move, watching my sworn enemy, and wondering with desperate unease what brought them here, into the very heart of Thendara, with a price on Kadarin's head and the death sentence from Terran and Comyn at once! I gripped the dagger at my waist with my good hand, wishing I had not encumbered myself with the artificial one. Kadarin and Thyra, boldly dancing together here at the Comyn masked ball. . . .

But now at the conclusion of this dance, all masks were coming off; I tore mine away, using the mechanical hand; the other was firmly gripped on my dagger. Did he think that I would not attack him here because it was in the middle of a ball?

And now I saw that Regis had recognized him too. I took a single step; Regis caught urgently at my arm.

"Steady, Lew," he muttered. "It's what he wants you to do, come after him without thinking. . . ."

The matrix at my throat was suddenly alive with flame, and a voice whispered, called in my mind.

. . . *I am here! I am here . . . all your rage, all the fury of frustrated lust, let it turn on them to serve me, burning, burning . . .*

Sharra! The voice of Sharra, whispering like a frantic ghost in my mind, the fury of all my frustration, leaping up to betray me . . . Thyra's eyes, burning into mine, the red flame of her hair seeming to blaze up around her! And suddenly it flared all around her, as Thyra seemed to grow taller, to rise and tower above us into the heights of the ballroom, as I saw Kadarin's long fine hand, the hand of a *chieri,* flash and draw the sword, *that* sword. . . .

It called to me. I had dragged it unwilling through half a Galaxy because I could not leave it behind, and now it summoned me, summoned me . . . half-aware, I slid my dagger back into its sheath; my place was at Kadarin's side, lending strength to the Goddess, pouring all my own rage and terror and frustration through it . . . my hand went to the matrix at my throat. I saw some woman whose name I could not remember staring at me with widening blue eyes. . . . I heard her whisper a name I no longer associated with myself, but she was nothing to me, and a young man with the face of a mortal enemy . . . Hastur, he was Hastur . . . the mortal enemy, the first to strike! I felt his hand gripping at my arm and thrust him away with uncanny strength, so that his knees buckled and he spread to the floor; and all this time that pattern of hate and fear, mingled love and loathing, beat in my mind. . . . I took a step, then another, toward where the Goddess flamed above me.

I must return . . . return to Sharra, return to the immortal who rose in flame above me forever, burn myself in the purging fire . . . she was there, Marjorie, calling me from within the flames of Sharra, those compelling amber eyes, the cascade of red hair wildly tossing sparks and flame and the smell of burning, as I burned for her with lust and terror . . .

The one I knew to be my mortal enemy was gripping me now with both hands as I fought my way, step by step, through the cries of the yammering crowd, to where Sharra burned . . .

"No, damn it, Lew," he gasped, "You're not going, if I have to kill you first and give you a clean death . . ." and he struck at me with the dagger, tearing a line of blood across my good arm. The pain made me waver, come to myself a little, know what was happening.

"Regis—help me," I heard myself whisper.

"Your matrix! Let me—" Before I could stop him, he snatched out his own dagger, cut the string which held my matrix round my neck; I tensed, in anticipation of agony unendurable . . . *once Kadarin had ripped it away and I had gone into convulsions* . . . but even through the leather bag and the silks I felt the touch. . . .

The form of Sharra wavered, sank . . . I did not know what Regis was doing, but strand by strand, it seemed that the gripping call of Sharra lessened in my mind. I heard it still, a soft insidious voice whispering in my mind . . .

Return to me, return, take vengeance on all these who have scorned and despised you . . . return, return . . .

. . . to Darkover and fight for your brother's rights and your own . . . but now it was my father's voice; I had never thought I would be glad to hear that haunting voice in my mind, but now it recalled me wholly to myself, like a plunge into an icy stream. Then that too quieted, and I stood looking at Kadarin and Thyra where they stood together, the Sharra sword in Kadarin's hand, Thyra's hair still tossing with the last sparks of the dying flame.

Gabriel broke away from Javanne; made a quick step toward Kadarin, his sword in hand. Perhaps all he saw was the invasion by a wanted man; I never knew whether the Form of Fire had been real or whether anyone but myself had seen it. Kadarin whirled, shoving Thyra before him, as

Gabriel shouted for the Guard and the young cadets started flocking toward him from everywhere in the room. I drew my dagger again and started for him too, then stood paralyzed. . . .

The air seemed full of cold shimmering light. Kadarin and Thyra stood frozen, too, and I saw Kathie caught between them.

They did not physically touch her, but something shook her like the grip of some invisible thing with claws; tossed her aside and caught at Linnell. She was in their grip as if she had been bound, hand and foot. I think she screamed, but the very idea of sound had died in the thickening darkness around Kadarin and Thyra. Linnell sagged, held up hideously on empty air; then fell, striking the floor with a crushing impact, as if something had shaken her and then dropped her. I fought toward her, shouting soundless curses, but I could not move, could not really see.

Kathie flung herself down by Linnell. I think she was the only person capable of free movement in that hall. As she caught up Linnell in her arms I saw that the tortured face had gone smooth and free of horror; a moment Linnell lay quiet, soothed, then she struggled with a bone-wrenching spasm, and slackened, a loose, limp small thing with her head lolling on her twin's breast.

And above her the monstrous Form of Fire grew again for a moment, Kadarin's face and Thyra's blazing out from the center . . . then it all swam away and for a moment that cold and damnable mask I had seen in Ashara's Tower blazed out and swam before my eyes . . .

. . . and then it was gone. Only a little stirring in the air, and Kadarin and Thyra were gone, too; the lights blazed back and I heard Kathie scream, and heard the cries of the crowd as I elbowed my way savagely to Linnell's side.

She was dead, of course. I knew that even before I laid my hand over Kathie's in a vain attempt to feel any pulse of life. She was lying, a tumbled, pathetic little heap across Kathie's lap. Behind her, blackened and charred panels showed where warp and distortion had faded and Kadarin and Thyra were gone. Callina thrust her way through the crowd, and bent over Linnell. Around me I heard the sound of the Festival throng subsiding. Gabriel sent out the Guard that had gathered, in an attempt that I knew would be vain—Kadarin had not gone out of the castle in any recognizable way and searching the grounds would do no good, even if the Terran Legate joined his forces to ours for the man they both wanted. The other people in the crowd were wedging in around us, and I heard that horrible sound of horror and curiosity which runs through a crowd when tragedy strikes. Hastur said something, •and people began silently leaving the ballroom. I thought, *this is the first time in hundreds of years that this Festival has been interrupted.*

Regis was still standing like one of the pillars of the Castle, his face pale, his hand still gripping his matrix. *The Hastur Gift.* We did not know what it was; but we had seen its power now for the second time.

Callina had not shed a tear. She was leaning on my arm, so numbed with shock that there was not even grief in her eyes; she only looked dazed. My main worry was now to get her away from the inquisitive remnant of the crowd. It was strange that I did not once think of Beltran, even though the marriage-bracelet was still locked on her wrist.

Her lips moved.

"So this was what Ashara intended . . ." she whispered.

She collapsed and went limp in my arms.

BOOK THREE

The Hastur Gift

CHAPTER ONE

After Lew carried Callina from the ballroom, Regis Hastur's first thought was of his grandfather. He hurried toward the place where he had last seen Lord Hastur watching the dancers; he found him there, pale and shaken, but uninjured.

"Linnell is dead—" Regis said, and Danvan Hastur put a hand to his heart. He said, gasping, "What of the prince, what of Derik?" He tried to rise, but fell back, and Regis said "Keep still, sir—I'll see to it." He beckoned to Danilo, who broke into a run across the floor.

"Stay here," he said, "See that no one harms the Lord Hastur—"

Danilo opened his mouth to protest; didn't. He said *"A veis ordenes . . ."* and Regis shoved through the crowd, noticing Gabriel moving in on Beltran, who stood motionless, his mouth hanging open.

"Lord Aldaran," said Gabriel Lanart-Hastur, "I will have your sword, if you please."

"I? I have done nothing—"

"None the less," Gabriel said, evenly, "you were once among those who sought to bring Sharra among us. Your sword, sir." Half a dozen guards, with swords at the ready, moved in on him, and Beltran drew a long breath, looking from guard to guard and evidently calculating his chances; then he shrugged and handed his sword, hilt first, to Gabriel.

"Take him to the Aldaran quarters," said Gabriel, "and make certain that he does not leave them for any reason whatever, nor on any pretext, until the Regent has spoken with him and satisfied himself of his innocence. Make sure that he has no—" he hesitated, "unauthorized visitors."

The Prince. I must see what has happened to Derik. Even though he was not in the ballroom, if his shields were down—where, in the name of all the Gods, did Merryl take him?

Regis hurried up the stairs, racing through the long corridors, hallways. In the Elhalyn suite lights were blazing, and he heard a high shrill wailing. He knew, then, that he had come too late. In the main room, Derik was lying half on, half off a divan; Merryl, beside him, was flung across his body as if he had tried, at the last moment, to shield his friend and lord from some unseen menace. He was sobbing; but Derik was motionless and when Regis touched him, already cold. The wailing came from an old woman who had been Derik's nurse when he was little, and had cared for her sickly charge ever since. Regis looked down sorrowfully at the young man's body.

Merryl stood up, trying to check his tears. He said, "I don't know—suddenly he cried out as if he were fighting something away, and fell like this . . ."

"Was it you, Merryl, who thought it funny to make the prince drunk tonight?"

"Drunk?" Merryl looked up at him in bewilderment. "He was not drunk—he had nothing but some drink made of mixed fruits, so sweet that I could not touch it! He was not—" then comprehension rushed over his face and he stared, only beginning to realize the truth. "Then that was why—*Dom* Regis, did someone meddle with that drink out of malice?"

"Their malice was worse than they knew," Regis said grimly, wondering afresh who had played that cruel trick. Lerrys, perhaps, hoping Derik would make a drunken spectacle of himself before Comyn and Terran guests—to re-emphasize that the Domain of Elhalyn was in incompetent hands? If so, he had overreached himself and done murder. Not that Lerrys would have dirtied his hands in doing it himself, but a judicious bribe to one of the dozens of waiters and serving-folk, and it would be done. "If Derik's shields had been halfway normal, he would have fought, and perhaps conquered, as I did, and Lew—"

Merryl was weeping now, unashamed. Regis had always believed that Merryl had hung around and flattered the prince for his own advantage; now he realized that the youngster had genuinely cared for the prince. And Regis must break more evil news to him.

"I am sorry to have to tell you this—Linnell is dead, too."

"Little Linnie?" Merryl wiped his eyes, but he looked stunned and grieved. "It doesn't seem possible. They were both so happy tonight—what happened, Regis?"

Regis found he could hardly speak the name. "The Castle was invaded. Someone tried to summon—" he forced his lips to pronounce the name but it came out only a whisper of horror; the Form of Fire was too new in his mind. "Sharra."

Merryl said, his voice hard and venomous, "This is the doing of that Alton bastard! I swear I will kill him!"

"You'll do no such thing," Regis said. "The—invaders—Kadarin and his crew—were trying to lure Lew back to them, and he fought and was—was wounded." Again he remembered the blood streaming down Lew's arm from the wound he himself had given him; but he had no regrets. Something like that had been necessary to bring Lew to himself, to gather his forces so that he might resist Sharra. *I seem to have some power over the Form of Fire. But without Lew I could do nothing.*

"Merryl, I must go and tell my grandfather about Prince Derik. You can do nothing more for him now, lad," he added compassionately, and it did not seem at all strange to call Merryl "lad," though Merryl was only a year or two younger than himself, "You should go to your sisters."

"I am not Head of the Domain," said Merryl, "They will have no use for me." . . . abruptly awe swept over his face and he knelt.

"Prince Derik is dead. May your reign be long, Prince Regis of Hastur and Elhalyn!"

"Zandru's hells!" Regis whispered. So swiftly had everything happened that he had not even realized; what he had always feared had come upon him. Derik had died, young and childless, and he himself, Regis, was nearest the throne. All the implications struck him dumb; he was now superior in rank even to his grandfather, for there was now no reason for a Regency. *I am Lord of the Comyn. I, Regis Hastur.*

He covered his face with his hands. It was simply too much to take in, and suddenly he realized that the battle with Sharra had left him drained and exhausted, far more than he realized. He thought he would fall to the ground; his knees would not hold him upright. *And I am not yet accustomed to the* laran *I used this night. I used it to free Lew from Sharra, not knowing how or why. 'Lord of Light! Where will this end?*

He said, faltering, searching for words, "Go and—and seek for Lord Hastur, Merryl; I must tell him of Derik's death—" and some part of him wanted to hide, to run away like a child, for once his grandfather knew this, the process would be inexorable, would roll over him and crush him like one of the great earth-moving machines he had seen on the Terran spaceport. *I to rule the Comyn?*

"Let me cover him first," said Merryl. He looked down again at the dead body of the prince; bent and kissed him on the forehead, then took off his own cloak and laid it gently over Derik, covering his face; tucked it around him as if he were comforting a little child who slept. He said, his voice unsteady, "There was more to Derik than most people ever knew," and Regis thought Derik could have had a worse epitaph.

So many deaths! Lord of Light, where will this end? Marius Alton. Linnell. Derik. Will Sharra reach out and destroy all that is left of the Comyn?

Merryl said, "I am at your orders, my prince," and went.

By the time the red sun rose over Comyn Castle on that morning after Festival, Derik and Linnell lay side by side in the Chapel of Comyn Castle, together in death as in their lives; Danvan Hastur had locked on their arms the copper marriage bracelets, the *catenas* they would have worn in just a few days more. Regis felt a poignant sorrow; they were both so young, and they would have been King and Queen of the Comyn. It would have been more just to give Derik the crown he had been denied so long.

I do not want it. But I have never been asked what I want.

The death of Derik, and the accession of Regis to the crown, had been proclaimed in Thendara, but the coronation itself would not take place for some time, and Regis was glad for that. He needed some time to assimilate what had happened.

I am Lord of the Comyn—whatever that may mean in these days of destruction!

"You must name Councillors," his grandfather had told him; almost the first thing he said, and Regis's first thought had been: *I wish Kennard were alive.*

Danvan Hastur was not a powerful telepath, but he had picked *that* up, He said gently, "So do I, my boy, but somehow you must manage without him. The strongest man within the Comyn is Lord Ardais, and he has always been your friend; he was your cadet-master in the Guards. If you are wise, lad, you will make certain that he is named as one of your first advisers."

Yes, Regis thought. *I suppose Dyan is my friend. I would rather have him friend than enemy, at least.* He said something like this to Danilo when they were alone, adding "I hope you will not mind—being paxman to a prince, Dani?"

Ten days ago Danilo would have passed this off with a flippant joke. Now he only looked at Regis seriously and said, "You know that I will do all I can for you. Only I wish this hadn't happened. I know you don't want it."

"I asked grandfather to take charge of the state funeral for Derik and—and Linnell," Regis said somberly. "It's my business to see to the living. I don't suppose Gabriel and his men have been able to find Kadarin—or Spaceforce, either?"

"No; but there's rioting in the city, Regis, because Spaceforce has come over on the Darkovan side, searching," said Danilo. "If you don't order them out, there's going to be a civil war."

"The important thing is to find Kadarin," Regis protested, but Danilo shook his head. "The important thing, just now, is peace in Thendara, Regis, and you know it as well as I do. Tell Lawton to call off his dogs, or Gabriel isn't going to be able to hold the Guards back. If they've made Thendara too hot to hold Kadarin for a few tendays, so much the better—if he can't poke his nose out into the marketplace without a guardsman or Spaceforce man grabbing him, then we don't have to worry about him. But we have to get those Terrans out of the Old Town, or, I tell you, there's going to be war!"

Regis said with a sigh, "It seems to me that we ought to be able to work together, Terran and Darkovan, against a common enemy, as we did over the Trailmen's fever, last time there was an epidemic. A few Spaceforce men looking for a hunted criminal aren't hurting anyone in Thendara—"

"But they're *there,*" Danilo argued, "and the people of Thendara don't want them there!"

It still seemed to Regis that the highest priority just now was to catch Kadarin and eliminate the threat that he would try and raise Sharra again. Just the same, he knew that what Danilo said was true.

"I suppose I ought to make it a personal request to the Legate," he said wearily, "but I have to stay here and settle things among the Comyn. Grandfather—" he broke off, but he knew Danilo followed the words he could not bring himself to say.

Grandfather has aged overnight; I have always known he was very old, but until that Festival Night he had never shown his age.

"Perhaps," Dani said quietly, "he has borne this burden all these years because he knew Derik could not rule in his place if he gave up the Regency—but now he trusts you to guard the Comyn in his place."

Regis bowed his head as if this new burden had been piled physically on him, like a heavy weight. *I have known all along that this day would come; I have wished that my grandfather did not treat me like a child; and now when he does not, I am afraid to be a grown man in command of myself and others.* It was now his decision to make. He said, "Send a message to the Legate, asking him as a personal favor to me—emphasize that, Dani, as a *personal favor to me*—to withdraw uniformed Spaceforce men from the Old Town, and restrict them to the Trade City. Or better; write it and I'll sign it, and have it sent by the most prestigious escort you can find."

Danilo said, with a wavering grin, "We never thought it would come to this when we were together in Nevarsin and I learned to write a better hand than you. Now you can keep me on hand as your private secretary."

Regis knew what Danilo was trying to say without putting it into words. As Heir to Hastur he had been visible enough, always in the public eye. But he had done his duty to ensure heirs to the Hastur Domain, and for the rest he had told himself, fiercely, *I am not the only lover of men in the Domains!* But now, as Prince of the Comyn, he would be even more the public representative of the Comyn. Centuries ago, the Hastur-kin had separated the Hastur Domains of Hastur and Elhalyn, allotting to the Elhalyn all the ceremonial and public duties with the crown.

"A crown on a stick, that's what they want," he said grimly. "Something they can hang up in the marketplace and bow down to!" He thought, but did not say, that the Domains had effectively been without a King all during the two-and-twenty years of the Regency, ever since the infant Prince Derik was left fatherless, and the Domains had been none the worse for that lack.

"We had better make sure that there are any Domains to rule over," he said, when the message had been written, "Derik may not have been the only one to die. And whom shall we send with this message?"

"Lerrys?" Danilo suggested. "He knows the Legate personally—"

Regis shook his head. "Lerrys is too much a Terran sympathizer—I'm not sure he'd deliver the message at all," he said. "Lerrys's view is that the Terrans have every right to be here since we are a Terran colony. Merryl?"

"Couldn't trust him to keep his temper," Danilo replied promptly.

Regis said hesitantly, "I would send Lew Alton; but he was wounded Festival Night—"

And he is personally concerned in this business of Sharra. . . . "I wonder, Danilo; if I asked Lord Ardais to go—"

"I think he would be pleased to carry such a message to the Legate," Danilo said, "for he knows what it will do to the city, having uniformed Spaceforce about, and he is always eager to keep the people calm."

"I won't order him to do it," said Regis. "I know he does not like to go among Terrans, but he may be willing to go if I ask it personally as Lord Elhalyn. . . ."

And again the tragedy struck him; Derik was older than he was himself, yet Derik had died without so much as a *nedestro* son to carry on his name. He had loved Linnell and had waited for their marriage, so that Linnell might bear his Heir; and now they were both dead.

And I have never cared so much for any woman. So I have two sons and a daughter, since I had no hesitation in using a woman for that purpose. Gods! What irony!

Yet I shall not share my throne with any woman, at least not for a time, nor until I find one with whom I am content also to share my life.

"I will go and ask Dyan myself," he said, glancing at the climbing sun, and suddenly aware that he had had no sleep and that he was weary. "He should still be sleeping, but for this he will not mind being wakened."

But in the Ardais quarters there were only servants, and one of them told Danilo that Lord Ardais had gone out early.

"Do you know where he is?"

"Zandru's hells, sir, no! Do you think the Lord Ardais tells his comings and goings to the likes of *me?*"

"Damn! Now I'll have to hunt all through the Castle for him," Regis said, wondering whether Dyan had gone to the Guard hall to see if he, an experienced officer, could be of some help to Gabriel, or whether he had left the ballroom earlier on some private errand and was still abed somewhere with a new favorite. If so, he might not know anything of the destruction that had raged in the Comyn!

Had it been only the day before that he had discussed this very possibility—sending Spaceforce into the Old Town of Thendara to find Kadarin? He had advised against it then; but Lawton had that authority, and now Kadarin had appeared actually within the Comyn Castle, to try and lure Lew Alton back to them . . . had he any right to keep Lawton from finding this man who was wanted for murder, and other crimes, by both Terran and Darkovan?

"Gabriel may know," he said, "and there are guardsmen at the doors of the Aldaran suite; they may be able to tell us where Gabriel is—in the Guard Hall, or out hunting for our wanted man!"

The suite of rooms allotted in Comyn Castle to the Aldarans had stood empty ever since Regis could remember; it was in a wing of the Castle which Regis had never knowingly entered before. Two big Guardsmen stood outside the door which was bolted shut on the outside. They saluted Regis, and he greeted them politely.

"Darren, Ruyven—I have to speak with my brother-in-law. Do you know if *Dom* Gabriel is in the Guard Hall, or if he's gone into the city? I have to locate Lord Ardais—"

"Oh, I can tell you where the Lord Ardais is, sir," the Guardsman Ruyven said. "He's in there, talking to Lord Aldaran."

Regis frowned and said, "I heard Captain Lanart-Hastur

give orders that no one should be allowed to speak with Aldaran—"

"I didn't hear him say that, sir, I only came on at dawn," Ruyven said, "and anyhow—" he looked down at his boots, but Regis know perfectly well what the man was thinking; was he supposed to give orders to a Lord of Comyn, and, moreover, one who had been his own superior officer for many years? Regis said, "Never mind, then, Ruyven, but you'll have to let us in to see him, too."

When Regis was small, he had been curious about the locked, empty Aldaran apartments. As the Guardsman let him in, he noticed that a dank and empty smell still clung about the walls and the embroidered hangings with the Aldaran double-headed eagle. They found Beltran in the main presence-chamber; someone had brought him some breakfast and he was eating porridge and nut-bread from a tray on his lap. Dyan sat at ease in a nearby chair, drinking something hot from a mug.

He looked up curiously at the younger men, but Beltran grinned widely. Regis had forgotten how much alike he and Lew really were, even through Lew's scars.

"Well, Regis," he said, "at last we are even; you came as kinsman to my castle and I imprisoned you—and now I come as kinsman to yours, and you imprison me. I suppose it's only fair you should have your day."

It was like Beltran, Regis supposed, to put him immediately on the defensive. He said stiffly, "A word with you, if you please, Lord Ardais." He was not going to discuss Comyn business with Beltran present.

"Lord Aldaran is party to Comyn business," Dyan reminded them.

"Not this," Regis said coldly. "Are you aware, Lord Dyan, that Prince Derik died during the night?"

"Good riddance," said Dyan.

"Kinsman!" Danilo protested, and Dyan turned fiercely on him.

"Zandru's hells, must you be such a hypocrite? We all know that Derik was a weakling, about as fit to rule as my three-year-old son! Now, perhaps, there will be some force in the Comyn, and we can talk to these Terrans as they deserve!"

Regis said stiffly, "It will be my business now to talk with the Terrans, Lord Dyan. It was for that I came here—I wish you to act as my embassy to them, with a message—"

Dyan interrupted, "There is only one message I will bear to the Terrans, Lord Regis, and you as a Hastur know what that message will be: *get out!* Off our world, off our planet, and take your Empire along with you!"

Lord of Light! It is worse than I thought! Dyan went on fiercely, "We made a good start, you and I, Regis, when we destroyed the Terran weapons! Now let us have the courage to follow up that message with a stronger one, aimed directly at Thendara!"

Does he truly believe that I destroyed Beltran's weapons as a message to the Terrans? Regis said, "Lord Dyan, this is not the place to discuss long-range Comyn policy. At the moment, the Legate has sent Spaceforce into the city; I have written a formal request that they be withdrawn, so that the Guards may do their own work in looking for a wanted criminal—and murderer, or are you not aware that Kadarin's attack last night cost us Prince Derik and Linnell, and came close to destroying Lord Alton?"

"That would be a smaller loss than any," said Dyan coldly. "With Derik gone, we have a chance at a show of strength. Your grandfather has played both sides too long, Regis, and the Altons have tried to back him up. Now it is time to make it very clear to the Terrans where we stand, and now we have Beltran on our side, with a stronger message than any. . . ."

Regis realized that he should have known this all along. He said, in a whisper—he could not make his voice work—"Kinsman, are you seriously advocating the use of *Sharra* against the Terrans?"

"Not advocating; stating a fact," Dyan said. "Those who do not join with us—" he looked up, gave Regis a hard, unequivocal stare, "are traitors to Comyn, and should, for the sake of our whole world, for the survival of Darkover, be silenced! Zandru's hells, Regis, don't you realize this is the only chance for Darkover to survive without becoming what they call us—just another Terran colony?"

"The existence of the Comyn," Regis said quietly, trying not to show the horror he felt, "is based upon the Compact. Sharra when used as a weapon is in defiance of Compact—"

"And while we go on observing the forever-be-damned Compact," said Dyan fiercely, "they surround us, they will bury us! We are like rabbithorns before a pack of wolves—and you sit here peacefully saying 'B-a-a-a' while the wolves open their jaws! Do you really think that we can fight the Empire with our swords and a scant six dozen Guardsmen?"

"Why do you assume that we need to fight the Empire?"

"Regis, I cannot believe that you, a Hastur, are saying this! Are you going to hand us meekly over to the Terrans?"

"Of course not," said Regis, "but there has not been a real war on Darkover for generations. My father died in an illegal war with Terran weapons—"

"Isn't that reason enough to get them right off our world?"

Regis drew a long breath, clenching his fists to keep quiet and not shout out his defiance. He wondered if Dyan was mad, or if he really believed all this. Dyan looked at him and his face softened somewhat. He said, "You have had no sleep; and a lot has happened in this one night. This is neither the time nor the place to discuss what we must do about the Terrans. Have you had anything to eat since last night?" Regis shook his head, and Beltran said, "Sit down and join us at breakfast, won't you? We can discuss politics later. Rogan—" he beckoned his servant, "plates for Lord Hastur and Lord Danilo." And before they knew what had happened, they were seated around the breakfast table, being served porridge and broiled rabbithorn. Regis did not feel hungry, but he knew enough of matrix mechanics to know that last night's battle with Sharra had left him drained and exhausted. He ate hungrily, while Beltran, putting hostility aside, became the gracious host.

When the Terrans are gone, then we can enforce Compact again without their vicious example. . . .

But if we seriously use Sharra against them, then we must stand, not against the Terrans who are here, but against the whole Terran Empire and all their multitudes of worlds . . .

And Sharra is not to be tamed thus, it will turn on those who use it, and destroy . . .

Beltran said aloud, "I don't wish my cousin of Alton any harm. I would like to make peace with him. His Gift is necessary to the use of Sharra, and he is Tower-trained; he is the safety factor for the use of Sharra, his control and strength. Can you arrange for me to put this to him, Regis?"

"I think it would be no use," said Regis quietly. "I think he would rather die."

"That," said Dyan harshly, "would be *his* choice, not ours! But if he chooses to stand with the Terrans, then he must take the consequences—"

"No," said Beltran. "I think he is the only living man who holds the Alton Gift."

"No," Dyan said, "there is an Alton child. Lew's daughter." Beltran waved that away. "A girl child. It's a man we need, with Alton strength."

So I must keep that secret. Dyan, untrained, does not know the nature of his own Gift. He knows he does not have the Ardais Gift . . . he adopted Danilo because he found the Ardais Gift had passed to Dani through one of Dyan's father's nedestro daughters. But he does not know, and he must never know, his own Alton Gift. . . . Regis looked helplessly at Dyan, only now fully aware of what Dyan had always meant to him. He knew Dyan's cruelty, and yet he had never been able to blame him altogether, knowing what powerful forces drove Dyan; knowing Dyan a haunted man, and a desperately unhappy one.

Dyan is myself, myself as I might all too easily have been. How can I condemn him? But I cannot let him destroy the Domains in loosing this mad business of a Holy War on the Terrans, even if I must kill him—

Last night, forced by bitter necessity, I struck at Lew, who is more than friend, more than brother to me. Now it seems that I must condemn Dyan, who is no more than what I might have been, to a madman's death. What right have I to do all this?

He set down his fork, feeling that Beltran's hospitality would choke him. He held himself tightly barriered lest either of the older men pick up even a hint of his thoughts. "Forgive me, *vai dom'yn,* I have business elsewhere. Danilo, attend me," he said, rising, and turned away. "We will speak of this at the proper time, Lord Dyan."

I must see what is left of the Comyn after last night. Perhaps there is nothing left for me to rule!

CHAPTER TWO

(Lew Alton's narrative)

The sullen red of another day was dying when I woke; my head throbbed with the half-healed wound Kadarin had given me, and my arm was afire with the long slash from Regis's dagger. I lay and wondered for a moment if the whole thing had been a delirious nightmare born of concussion. Then Andres came in, and the deep lines of grief in his face told me it was real. He had loved Linnell, too. He came and scowled at me, taking off the bandage on my head and inspecting the stitches, then looked at the wound in the arm.

"I suppose you are the only man on Darkover who can go to a Festival Night ball and come home with something like this," he grumbled. "What sort of fight was it?"

So he had heard only that Linnell was dead—not of the monstrous visitation of Sharra. The cut hurt, but it was no more than a flesh wound. I'd have trouble using the arm for a while, but I held no resentment; Regis had done the only thing he could, releasing me from the call of Sharra. I said, "It was an accident, he didn't mean to hurt me," and let him think what he liked. "Get me something to eat and some clothes. I have to find out what's happening—"

"You look as if you needed a tenday in bed," Andres said crossly. Then his very real concern for me surfaced in a harsh, "Lad, I've lost two of you! Don't send yourself after Marius and Linnell! What's going on that you can't wait until tomorrow for it?"

I yielded and lay quiet. Somewhere out there Sharra raged, I supposed . . . but I would know if they came into the Comyn Castle (was I altogether freed? I did not dare look at my matrix to see) and there was nothing to be gained by going out and looking for trouble. I watched Andres grumbling around the room, a soothing sound I remembered from boyhood. When Marius or I had raced our horses at too breakneck a pace and tumbled off, breaking a finger or a collarbone on the way down, he had grumbled in exactly the same way.

Marius and I had never had the boyhood squabbles and fistfights of most brothers I knew; there had been too many years between us. By the time he was out of pinafores and able to assert himself, I was already grown and into the cadet corps. I had only begun to know what kind of man my brother was, and then he was gone from me, the furthest distance of all. I had dragged him, too, into the inexorable fates pursuing me. But at least he had had a clean death, a bullet through the brain, not the death in fire that waited for me.

For now that Kadarin was loose with the Sharra sword, I knew how I would die, and made up my mind to it. Ashara's plan, and the help of Regis Hastur's new and astonishing Gift, which seemed somehow to hold power over Sharra, might destroy the Sharra matrix; but I knew perfectly well that I would go with it into destruction.

Well, that was what had awaited me for all these years, bringing me back to Darkover at the appointed time, to the death appointed, which I should have shared with Marjorie.

We had planned our death. . . . I remembered that morning in Castle Aldaran when, hostages to the destruction Sharra was sowing in the country round, showering on the Terran spaceport in Caer Donn, I had been allowed to waken from the drugs that had kept me, passive prisoner, chained to the destruction and feeding power into Sharra. I never knew why I had been allowed to come free of the drugs; certainly it had not been any lingering tenderness on Kadarin's part for either of us. But Marjorie and I had been prepared to die . . . knew we must die in closing the gateway into this world that was Sharra. And so she and I, together, had smashed the gateway . . .

But then I, using all the power of that matrix, had taken her, and the Sword, and flung us through space bodily—the Terrans called it teleportation, and I had never done it before or since—to Arilinn; where Marjorie had died from her terrible burns, and I . . .

. . . I had survived, or some part of me had survived, and all these years had despised myself because I had not followed her to death. Now I knew why I had been spared:

Kadarin and Thyra still lived, and somehow they would have recovered the matrix and ravaged Darkover again with its fire. This time there would be no respite; and when Sharra was destroyed, none of us would be left alive. And so I must set my affairs in order.

I called Andres back to me, and said, "Where is the little girl?"

"Rella—that's the cook's helper—looked after her today, and put her to bed in the room Marius had when he was a little tyke," Andres said.

"If I live, I may be able to take her to Armida," I said, "but if anything should happen to me—no, foster-father, listen; nothing's certain in this life. Now that my father and brother are gone—you have served us all faithfully for a quarter of a century. If something should happen to me, would you leave Darkover?"

"I don't know. I never thought about it," the old man said. "I came here with *Dom* Kennard when we were young men, and it's been a good life; but I think I might go back to Terra in the end." He added, with a mirthless grin, "I've wondered what it would be like, to be under my own blue sky again, and have a moon like a moon ought to be, not those little things." He pointed out the window at the paling face of Idriel, greenish like a gem through water.

"Bring me something to write on." When he complied, I scribbled with my good hand, folded the paper and sealed it.

"I can't leave Armida to you," I said. "I suppose Gabriel will have it after me; it's in the Alton Domain. I would if I could, believe me. But if you take this to the Terran Legate in the Trade City, this will take you to Terra, and I'd rather you would foster Marja yourself than turn her over to Gabriel's wife." *Domna* Javanne Hastur has never liked me; no doubt she would do her best by Gabriel's kinsman, but it would be a cold and dutiful best; and Andres, at least, would care for my daughter for my father's sake and Linnell's if not for mine. "My mother—and my father after her—owned some land there; it had better go to you, then."

He blinked and I saw tears filling his eyes, but all he said was, "God forbid I should ever have to use it, *vai dom.*

But I'll do my best for the little girl if anything happens. You know I'd guard her with my life."

I said soberly, "You might have to." I did not know why, but I was filled suddenly with icy shivers; my blood ran cold in my veins, and for a moment, even in the dying light which turned the whole room crimson, it seemed that blood lay over the stones around me. *Is this then the place of my death?* Only a moment, and it was gone. Andres went to the window, drew the curtains with a bang.

"The bloody sun!" he said, and it sounded like a curse. Then he tucked the paper I had given him, without looking at it, into a pocket, and went away.

That was settled. Now there was only Sharra to face. Well, it must come when it would. Tomorrow Kathie and I would ride to Hali, and the plan I had made, for finding the Sword of Aldones and using this last weapon against Sharra, would either succeed or it would fail. Either way, I would probably not see another sunset. My head was afire with the stitches in my forehead. Scars to match those Kadarin had made on my face . . . well, there's an old saying that the dead in heaven is too happy to care what happens to his corpse, be it beautiful or ugly, and the dead in hell has too much else to worry about! As for me, I had never believed in either heaven or hell; death was no more than endless nothingness and darkness.

Yet it seemed I could hear again my father's last cry, directly to my mind. . . . *Return to Darkover and fight for your rights and your brother's! This is my last command* . . . and then, past that, as the life was leaving him, that last cry of joy and tenderness:

Yllana! Beloved—!

Had he, at the last moment, seen something beyond this life, had my half-remembered mother been waiting for him at that last gateway? The *cristoforos* believe something like that, I know; Marjorie had believed. Would Marjorie be waiting for me beyond Sharra's fire? I could not, dared not, let myself think so. And if it were so—I let myself smile, a sour little smile—what would we do when Dio turned up there? But she had already loosed her claim on me . . . if love were the criterion, perhaps she would seek Lerrys beyond the gates of death. And what of those husbands or wives given in marriage who hated their spouses, married out of duty or family ties or political expediency, so that married life was a kind of hell and death a merciful release, would any sane or just God demand that they be tied together in some endless afterlife as well? I dismissed all this as mad rubbish and tried, through the fierce pain in my head and the fiery throbbing of my wounded arm, to compose myself for sleep.

The last red light dimmed, faded and was gone. A chink of the curtains showed me pallid greenish moonlight, lying like ice across my bed; it looked cool, it would cool my fever . . . there was a step and a rustle and soft whisper.

"Lew, are you asleep?"

"Who's there?"

The dim light picked out a gleam of fair hair, and Dio, her face as pale as the pallid moon, looked down at me. She turned and pulled the curtains open where Andres had closed them, letting the moonlight flood the room and the waning moons peep over her shoulder.

The chill of the moonlight seemed to cool my feverish face. I even wondered, incuriously, if I had fallen asleep and was dreaming she was there, she seemed so quiet, so muted. Her eyes were swollen and flushed with tears.

"Lew, your face is so hot . . ." she murmured, and after a minute she came and laid something cold and refreshing on my brow. "Do you mean they left you alone here like this?"

"I'm all right," I said. "Dio, what's happened?"

"Lerrys is gone," she whispered, "gone to the Terrans, he has taken ship and swears he will never return . . . he tried to get me to come with him, he . . . he tried to force me, but this time I would not go . . . he said it was death to stay here, with the things that were coming for the Comyn . . ."

"You should have gone with him," I said dully. I could not protect Dio now, nor care for her, with Sharra raging and Kadarin prowling like a wild beast, Thyra at his side, ready to drag me back into that same corner of hell. . . .

"I will not go when others must stay and fight," she said. "I am not such a coward as that . . ." but she was weeping. "If he truly feels we are a part of the Empire, he should have stayed and fought for *that* . . ."

"Lerrys was never a fighter," I said. Well, neither was I,

but I had been given no choice; my life was already forfeit. But I had no comfort for Dio now. I said softly, "It is not your fight, either, Dio. You have not been dragged into this thing. You could make a life for yourself elsewhere. It's not too late."

Lerrys was one of the hypersensitive Ridenow; the Ridenow Gift had been bred into the Comyn, to sense these other-dimension horrors in the Ages of Chaos; a Gift obsolete now, when the Comyn no longer ranged through space and time as legend said they had done in the heyday of the Towers. As those who fight forest-fire keep cagebirds to tell when the poison gases and smoke are growing too dangerous for living things—because the cagebird will die of the poisons before men are aware of them—so the Ridenow served to warn Comyn less sensitive than they of the presence of forces no man could tolerate. I was not surprised that he had fled from Darkover now . . .

I only wished I could do the same!

"Dio, you shouldn't be here, at this hour—"

"Do you think I care about that?" she said, and her voice was thick with tears. "Don't send me away, Lew. I don't—I don't—I won't ask anything of you, but let me stay here with you for tonight—"

She lay beside me, her curly head against my shoulder, and I tasted salt when I kissed her. And suddenly I realized that if I had changed, Dio had changed no less. The tragedy of that thing in the hospital, which should have been our son, was her tragedy too; more hers than mine, for she had borne it in her body for months; yet I had been distraught with my own selfish grief, and left no room for her. She had come into my life when I had thought it was over forever, and given me a year of happiness, and I owed it to her to remember the happiness, not the horror and tragedy at the end.

I whispered, holding her close, "I wish it had been different. I wish I had had—more for you."

She kissed my scarred cheek, with a tenderness which somehow drew us closer than the wildest passion. "Never mind, Lew," she said softly into the darkness, "I know. Sleep, my love, you're weary and wounded."

And after a moment I felt that she was fast asleep in my arms; but I lay there, wakeful, my eyes burning with regret.

I had loved Marjorie with the first fire of an untried boy, all flame and desire; we had never known what we would have grown into, for Marjorie had had no time at all. But Dio had come to me when I was a man, grown through suffering into the capacity for real love, and I had never understood, I had let her walk away from me in the first upheaval. The shared tragedy should have drawn us closer, and I had let it drive us apart.

If only I could live, I could somehow make it up to Dio, if I only had time to let her know how much I loved her. . . .

But it is too late; I must let her go, so that she will not grieve too much for me. . . .

But for tonight I will pretend that there is something beyond morning, that she and I and Marja can find a world somewhere, and that Sharra's fire will burn out harmlessly before the mingling of the Sword of Aldones and the Hastur Gift. . . . I half-knew that I was already dreaming, but I lay holding Dio sleeping in my arms until at last, near dawn, I fell asleep too.

Red sunlight woke me, and the closing of a door somewhere in the Alton suite. Dio—had she really been there? I was not sure; but the curtains she had opened to the moonlight were open to the sun, and there was a fine red-gold hair lying on my pillow. The pain in head and wounded arm had subsided to the dullest of aches; I sat up, knowing that it was time to act.

While I dressed for riding, I considered. Surely, this day or the next, what was left of the Comyn would ride to Hali for the state funeral for Linnell—and for Derik. Perhaps it would be better to ride with them, not to attract attention, and then to slip away toward the *rhu fead* . . .

No. There was no time for that. I had loved Linnell and she had been my foster-sister, but I could not wait to speak words of tenderness and regret over her grave. I could not help her now, and either way, she had gone too far to care whether or not I was there to speak at her burying. For Linnell I could only try to ensure that the land she had loved was not ravaged by Sharra's fires. It might be that we could do something for Callina too; surely Beltran, who had been part of the original circle who had tried to raise Sharra, would die with us when we closed that gateway for the last time. And then Callina too would be freed.

I went in search of Callina, and found her in the room where I had seen Linnell playing her *rryl*, that night before we had gone to Ashara's Tower. Callina was sitting before the harp, her hands lax in her lap, so white and still that I had to speak to her twice before she heard me; and then she turned a dead face to me, a face so cold and distant, so like Ashara's, that I was shocked and horrified. I shook her, hard, and finally slapped her face; at that she came back, life and anger in her pale cheeks.

"How dare you!"

"Callina, I'm sorry—you were so far away, I couldn't make you hear me—you were in a trance—"

"Oh, no—" she gasped, her hands flying to cover her mouth in consternation, "Oh, no, it can't be. . . ." She swallowed and swallowed again, fighting tears. She said, "I felt I could not bear my grief, and it seemed to me that Ashara could give me peace, take away grief . . . grief and guilt, because if I had not—not used the screen with you, not found that—that Kathie girl, Linnell would have been alive. . . ."

"You don't know that," I said harshly. "There's no way of telling what might have happened when Kadarin drew—that sword. Kathie might have died instead of Linnell; or they might both have died. Either way, don't blame yourself. Where is Kathie?"

"I don't want to see her," Callina said shakily. "She is like—it's like seeing Linnell's ghost, and I cannot bear it—" and for a moment I thought she would go far away into the trance state again.

"There's no time for that, Callina! We don't know what Beltran, or Kadarin, may be planning," I said. "We don't have much time; things could start up again at any moment." How had I been able to sleep last night, with this hanging over us? But at least now I was strong enough for what I must do. "Where is Kathie?"

At last Callina sighed and showed me the way to where Kathie slept. She was lying on a couch, awake, half naked, scanning a set of tiles, but she started as I came in, and caught a blanket around her. "Get out! Oh—it's you again! What do you want?"

"Not what you seem to be expecting," I said dryly. "I want you to dress and ride with us. Can you ride?"

"Yes, certainly. But why—"

I rummaged behind a panel, finding some clothes I had seen Linnell wear. It suddenly outraged me that these lengths of cloth, these embroideries, should still be intact, with Linnell's perfume still in their folds, when my foster-sister lay cold in the chapel at the side of her dead lover. I flung them, almost angrily, across the couch.

"These will do for riding. Put them on." I sank down to wait for her, was recalled, by her angry stare, to memory of Terran taboos. I rose, actually reddening; how could Terran women be so immodest out of doors and so prudish within? "I forgot. Call me when you're ready."

A peculiar choked sound made me turn back. She was staring helplessly at the armful of clothing, turning the pieces this way and that. "I haven't the faintest notion how to get into these things."

"After what you were just *thinking* at me," I said stiffly, "I'm certainly not going to offer to help you."

She blushed too. "And anyway, how could I ride in a long skirt?"

"Zandru's hells, girl, what else would you wear? They are Linnell's riding-clothes; if she rode in them, you certainly can." Linnell had worn them to ride to Marius's funeral.

"I've never worn anything like this for riding, and I'm certainly not going to start now," she blazed. "If you want me to ride somewhere on a horse, you're going to have to get me some decent clothes!"

"These clothes belonged to my foster-sister; they are perfectly decent."

"Damn it, get me some *indecent* ones, then!"

I laughed. I had to. "I'll see what I can do, Kathie."

The Ridenow apartments were almost deserted this early, except for a servant mopping the stone floor, and I was glad; I had no desire to walk in upon Lord Edric. It occurred to me that Dio and I had married without the permission of her Domain Lord.

Freemate marriage cannot be dissolved after the woman has borne a child, except by mutual consent.

But that was Darkovan law. Dio and I had married by

the law of the Empire . . . why was I thinking this, as if there were still time to go back and mend what had gone astray between us? At least I would see her once more. I asked the servant if *Domna* Diotima would see me, and after a moment, Dio, in a long woolly dressing-gown, came sleepily out into the main room. Her face lighted when she saw me; but there was no time for that. I explained my predicament, and she must have read the rest in my face and manner.

"Kathie? Yes, I remember her from—from the hospital," she said, "I still have my Terran riding things, the ones I wore on Vainwal; she should be able to wear them." She giggled, then broke off. "I know it's not really funny. I just can't help it, thinking—never mind; I'll go and help her with them."

"And I'll go down and see if I can find horses for us," I said, and went down, swiftly, by an old and little-known stairway, to the Guard hall. Fortunately there was a Guardsman there who had known me when I was a cadet.

"Hjalmar, can you find horses? I must ride to Hali."

"Certainly, sir. How many horses?"

"Three," I said after a moment, "one with a lady's saddle." Kathie might ride like Dio, astride and in breeches like some Free Amazon, but Callina certainly would not. I told him where to bring them, and went back to find Kathie neatly dressed in the tunic and breeches I had seen Dio wear.

I was happy then. But I did not know it, and now it is too late—now and forever.

Some Terran poet said that—that the saddest words in any language are always too late.

The door thrust suddenly open and Regis came in. He said, "Where are you going? I'd better come with you."

I shook my head. "No. If anything happens—if we don't make it—you're the only one with any strength against Sharra."

"That is exactly why I must come with you," Regis said. "No, leave the women here—"

"Kathie at least must come," I said. "We are going to Hali, to the *rhu fead*," and added, when he still looked confused, "It's possible that Kathie may be the only person on this world who can reach the Sword of Aldones."

His eyes widened. He said, "There's something I should know . . . Grandfather told me once—no, I can't remember." His brow ridged in angry concentration. "It could be important, Lew!"

It could, indeed. The Sword of Aldones was the ultimate weapon against Sharra. And Regis seemed, of late, to have some curious power over Sharra. But whatever it was, we had no time to waste while he tried to remember.

Regis warned, "If Dyan sees you, you'll be stopped. And Beltran has a legal right—if no other—to stop Callina. How are you going to get out of the Castle?"

I led them to the Alton rooms. The Altons, generations and generations ago, had designed this part of the castle, and they had left themselves a couple of escape routes. It occurred to me to wonder why they had guarded themselves against their fellow Comyn, in those days; then I grinned with mirth. This was certainly not the first time, in the long history of the Comyn, that powerful clan had warred against clan.

It might be the last, though.

I forced my mind away from that, searching out certain elegant designs in the parquetry flooring. My father had once shown me this escape route, but he had not troubled to teach me the pattern. I frowned, tried to sound, delicately, the matrix lock that led to the secret stairway.

Fourth level, at least! I began to wonder if I would need to hunt up my old matrix mechanic's kit and perform the mental equivalent of picking the lock. I shifted my concentration, just a little . . .

. . . *Return to Darkover . . . fight for your brother's rights and your own. . . .*

My father's voice; yet for the first time I did not resent it. In that final, unknowing rapport he had forced on me, I was sure there had been some of his memories—how else could I account for the sudden, emotional way I had reacted to Dyan? Now I stood with my toes in the proper pattern, and, not stopping to think how to do it, *pushed* against something invisible.

. . . *to the second star, sidewise and through the labyrinth* . . .

My mind sought out the patterns; halfway through the flickering memory that was not mine faded into nonsense, evaporated with the sting of lemon-scent in the air, but I was deeply into the pattern now and I could unravel the final twist of the lock. Beneath me the floor tilted; I jumped, scrabbled for safety as a section of the flooring moved downward on invisible machinery, revealing a hidden stair, dark and dusty, that led away downward.

"Stay close to me," I warned, "I've never been down here before, though I saw it opened once." I gestured them downward on the dusty stair; Kathie wrinkled her nose at the musty smell, and Callina held her skirts fastidiously close to her body, but they went. Regis and Dio followed us. Behind us the square of light folded itself, disappeared.

"I wish my old great-great-whatever-great grandfather had provided a light," I fretted, "it's as dark in here as Zandru's—" I cut off the guard-room obscenity, substituted weakly "pockets." I heard Dio snicker softly and knew she had been in rapport with me.

Callina said softly, "I can make light, if you need it."

Kathie cried out in sudden fright as a green ball of pallid fire grew in Callina's palm, spread like phosphorscence over her slender six-fingered hands. I was familiar with the overlight, but it was an uncanny sight to see, as the Keeper spread out her hands, the pallid glow leading us downward. The extended fingers broke through sticky webs, and once I fancied that gleaming little eyes followed us in the darkness, but I closed my eyes and mind to them, watching for every step under my feet. We crowded so hard on Callina's heels that she had to warn us, in a soft, preoccupied voice, "Be careful not to touch me." Once Kathie slipped on the strangely sticky surfaces, fell a step or two, jarringly, before I could catch and steady her. I felt with my good hand along the wall, ignoring what might be clinging there, and once the stair jogged sharply to the right, a sharp turn; without Callina's pale light we would have stepped off into nothingness and fallen—who knows into what depths? As it was, one of us jarred a pebble loose and we heard it strike below, after a long time, very far away. We went on, and I felt my blood pounding hard in my temples. Damn it, I hoped I would never have to come down here again, I would rather face Sharra and half of Zandru's demons!

Down, and down, and endlessly down, so that I felt half the day must be passing as we threaded the staircase and the maze into which it led; but Callina led the way, with dainty fastidious steps, as if she were treading a ballroom floor.

At last the passageway ended in a solid, heavy door. The light faded from Callina's hands as she touched it, and I had to wrestle with the wooden bar which closed it. I could not draw it back one-handed, and Dio threw her weight against the bar; it creaked open, and light assaulted eyes dilated by the darkness of that godforgotten tunnel. I squinted through it and discovered that we were standing in the Street of Coppersmiths, exactly where I had told Hjalmar to bring the horses. At the corner of the street, through the small sound of many tiny hammers tapping on metal, there was a place where horses were shod and iron tools mended, and I saw Hjalmar standing there with the horses.

He recognized Callina, though she was folded in an ordinary thick dark cloak—I wondered if she had borrowed the coarse garment from one of her servants, or simply gone into the servants' quarters and taken the first one she found?

"*Vai domna*, let me assist you to mount . . ."

She ignored him, turning to me, and awkwardly, one-handed, I extended my arm to help her into the saddle. Kathie scrambled up without help, and I turned to Dio.

"Do you know where you are? How are you going to get back?"

"Not *that* way," she said fervently. "Never mind, I can find my way." She gestured at the castle, which seemed to be very high above us on the slopes of the city; we had indeed come a long way. "I still feel I ought to come with you—"

I shook my head. I would not drag Dio into this, too. She held out her arms but I pretended not to see. I could not bear farewells, not now. I said to Regis, "See that Dio gets back safely!" and turned my back on them both. I hoisted myself awkwardly into the saddle, and rode away without looking back, forcing myself to concentrate on guiding the horse's hoofs over the cobbled street.

Out of the Street of Coppersmiths; out through the city gates, unnoticed and unrecognized; and upward, on the road leading toward the pass. I looked down once, saw them both lying beneath me, Terran HQ and Comyn Castle, facing one another with the Old Town and the Trade City between them, like troops massed around two warring giants. I turned my back resolutely on them both, but I could not shut them away.

They were my heritage; both of them, not one alone, and try as I might, I could not see the coming battle as between Terran and Comyn, but Darkover against Darkover, strife between those who would loose ancient evil in our world in the service of Comyn, and those who would protect it from that evil.

I had allied myself with the ancient evil of Sharra. It mattered nothing that I had tried to close the gateway; it was I who had first summoned Sharra, misusing the *laran* which was my heritage, betraying Arilinn which had trained me in the use of that *laran.* Now I would destroy that evil, even if I destroyed myself with it.

Yet for the moment, breathing the icy wind of the high pass, the snow-laden wind that blew off the eternal glacier up there, I could forget that this might be my last ride. Kathie was shivering, and I took off my cloak and laid it over her shoulders as we rode side by side. She protested, "You'll freeze!" but I laughed and shook my head.

"No, no—you're not used to this climate; this is shirtsleeve weather to me!" I insisted, wrapping her in the folds. She clutched it round her, still shivering. I said, "We'll be through the pass soon, and it's warmer on the shores of Hali."

The red sun stood high, near the zenith; the sky was clear and cloudless, a pale and beautiful mauve-color, a perfect day for riding. I wished that there were a hawk on my saddle, that I was riding out from Arilinn, hunting birds for my supper. I looked at Callina and she smiled back at me, sharing the thought, for she made a tiny gesture as if tossing a *verrin* hawk into the air. Even Kathie, with her glossy brown curls, made me think of riding with Linnell in the Kilghard Hills when we were children. Once we had ridden all the way to Edelweiss, and been soundly beaten, when we came home after dark, by my father; only now I realized that what had seemed a fearful whipping to children twelve and nine years old, had in reality been a few half-playful cuffs around the shoulders, and that father had been laughing at us, less angry than grateful that we had escaped bandits or banshee-birds. I remembered now that he had never beaten any of us seriously. Though once he threatened, when I failed to rub down and care for a horse I had ridden, leaving the animal to a half-trained stableboy, that if I neglected to see to my mounts, next time I too should have no supper and sleep on the floor in my wet riding-clothes instead of having a hot bath and a good bed waiting.

Harsh as he had been—and there had been times when I hated him—it seemed that only now, facing my own death, was I wholly aware of how he had loved us, of how all his own plans for us had fallen into ruin. I started to say, "Linnie, do you remember," and remembered that Linnell was dead and that the girl who rode before me, clutching a cloak around her with Linnell's very gesture, was a stranger, a *Terran* stranger.

But I looked past her at Callina, and our eyes met. Callina was real, Callina was all the old days at Arilinn, Callina was the time when I had been happy and doing work I loved in the Towers. The copper bracelet on her left wrist, sign of a tie with Beltran, was a joke, an obscenity, entirely irrelevant. I let myself dream of a day when I would tear it from her wrist, fling it in Beltran's face . . .

Callina was a Keeper, never to be touched, even with a lustful thought . . . but now she was riding at my side, and she raised her face to mine, pale and smiling. And I thought; Keeper no more; the Comyn married her off to Beltran as they would dispose of a brood mare, but if she can be given to Beltran, they cannot complain if—after she is properly widowed, for while I lived Beltran would not take her as his wife—if afterward she gives herself to me.

And then . . . Armida, and the Kilghard Hills . . . and our own world waiting for us. She smiled at me, and for a moment my heart turned over inside me at that smile; then I forced myself to remember. The way out led through Sharra; and it was very doubtful that I would be alive to see the sun set. But at least Beltran, who had, like myself, been sealed to Sharra, would go with me into the darkness. But still her eyes sought mine, and against all conceivable sanity, I was happy.

Below us, now, lay the pale shores of Hali, with the long line of trees fading in the mist. Here, so the legend said, the Son of Aldones had fallen to Earth, and lay on the shores of the Lake, so that the sands were evermore mirrored and shimmering. . . . I looked on the pale glimmer of the sands of the shores, and knew that the sands were of some gleaming stone, mica or garnet, beaten into sand by the waves of a great inland sea which had washed here long before this planet spawned life. Yet the wonder remained; along these shimmering shores Hastur had lain, and here came Camilla the Damned, and the Blessed Cassilda, foremother of the Comyn, and ministered to him . . .

The shadows were lengthening; the day was far advanced, and one of the moons, great violet-shining Liriel, was just rising over the lake, waning a little from the full. We had perhaps two hours before sunset, and I discovered I did not like to think about riding back to Thendara in the darkness. Well, we would ride that colt when he was grown to bear a saddle; our task now was within the *rhu fead*, the old chapel which was the holy place of the Comyn.

It rose before us, a white, pale-gleaming pile of stone. Once there had been a Tower here; it had fallen in the Ages of Chaos, burned to the ground in those evil old days by a *laran* weapon next to which the Sharra matrix was a child's toy. We reined in the horses, near the brink of the Lake, where mist curled up whitely along the shore. The sparse pinkish grass thinned out in the sands. I kicked loose a pebble; it sank, slowly turning over and over, through the cloud-surface.

"That's not water, is it?" Kathie said, shaken. "What is it?"

I did not know. Hali was the nearest of the half-dozen cloud-lakes whose depths are not water, but some inert gas . . . it will even sustain life; once I walked for a little while in the depths of that Lake, looking at the strange creatures, neither fish nor bird, which swam, or flew, in that cloud-water. Legend said that once these Lakes had been water like any other, and that in the Ages of Chaos, some sorcerer, working with the *laran* of that day, had created them, with their peculiar gaseous structure, and the curious mutated fishbirds which flew or swam there . . . I thought that just about as likely as the ballad which tells how the tears of Camilla had fallen into the water and turned them into cloud when Hastur chose Cassilda for his consort.

This was no time for children's tales and ballads!

Kathie said in confusion, "But—but surely I have been here before—"

I shook my head. "No. You have some of my memories, that's all."

"All!" Her voice held a note of hysteria. I said, "Don't worry about it," and patted her wrist, clumsily. "Here, come this way."

Twin pillars rose before us, a twinkling rainbow glimmering like frost between them; the Veil, like the Veil at Arilinn, to keep out anyone not allied to Comyn. If Kathie's genes were identical to Linnell's, she should be able to pass this Veil—but it was not a physical test alone, but a mental one; no one without *laran* of the Comyn kind . . . and Kathie had been brought here because of her own immunity to that Comyn mental set.

"Even blocked," I said to Kathie, "it would strip your mind bare. I'll have to hold your mind completely *under* mine." I seemed to speak out of some strange inner surety, knowing precisely what I should do, and in a small corner of my mind, I wondered at myself. She shrank away from the first touch of my mind, and I warned tonelessly, "I must. The Veil is a kind of forcefield, attuned to the Comyn brain; you wouldn't survive two seconds of it."

I bent and picked her up bodily. "It won't hurt me; but don't fight me."

I made contact with her mind; swamped it, forced resistance down—somewhere at the back of my mind, I remembered how I had feared to do this to Marius. It was a form of rape, and I shrank from it; but I told myself that without this overshadowing she could not survive. . . .

The first law of a telepath is that you do not enter any unwilling mind. . . .

But she had consented; I told myself that, and without further waiting, I covered the last resistance and her mind disappeared, completely held down within my own and concealed. Then I stepped through the trembling rainbow . . .

A million little needles prickled at me, nameless force spitting me through and through like a strangely penetrating rain. . . . I was inside, through the Veil. I set Kathie down on her feet and withdrew, as gently as I could, but she slumped, nerveless, to the floor. Callina knelt, chafing her hands, and after a moment she opened her eyes.

There were doors and long passages before us, hazy as if the *rhu fead* were filled with the same gaseous cloud as was the Lake; I almost expected to see the strange fishbirds swimming there. Here and there were niches filled with things so strange I could not imagine them; behind a rainbow of colors, I saw a bier where lay a woman's body—or a wax effigy—or a corpse, I could not tell; only the long pale reddish hair; and it seemed to me that the woman's body was too realistic for any unreality, that her breast seemed to rise and fall softly as she slept; yet the rainbow shimmer was undisturbed, she had slept there or lain there in unchanging, incorruptible death for thousands of years. Behind another of the rainbows was a sword lying on a great ancient shield—but the hilt and shield glimmered with colors and I knew it was no simple weapon and that it was not what we sought. *Regis should have come with us, I thought, how will I know the Sword of Aldones when I find it?*

"I will know," said Callina quietly. "It is here."

Abruptly the passage angled, turned, and opened up into a white-vaulted chapel, with something like an altar at the far end, and above it, done in the style of the most ancient mosaics, a portrayal of the Blessed Cassilda, with a starflower in her hand. In a niche in one of the walls was another of the trembling rainbows, but as I drew near, I felt the sting of pain, and knew this was one of those protected entirely from Comyn. . . . Now was the time to see if Kathie could actually reach these guarded things. Callina put out curious hands; they jerked back of themselves. As if she had heard my thoughts—and perhaps she did—Kathie asked, "Are you still touching my mind?"

"A little."

"Get out. All the way . . ."

That made sense; if this forcefield was adjusted to repel the Comyn, then the slightest touch of my mind would endanger her. I withdrew entirely, and she began to walk swiftly toward the rainbow; passed through it.

She disappeared into a blur of darkening mist. Then a blaze of fire seared up toward the ceiling—I wanted to cry out to her not to be afraid; it was only a trick . . . an illusion. But even my voice would not carry through the forcefield against Comyn. A dim silhouette, she passed on and through the fire; perhaps she did not know it was there.

Then there was a crash of thunder that rolled through the chapel and jarred the floor as if with earthquake. Kathie darted back through the rainbow. In her hand, she held a sword.

So the Sword of Aldones was a real sword, after all, long and gleaming and deadly, and of so fine a temper that it made my own look like a child's leaden toy. In the hilt, through a thin layer of insulating silk, blue jewels gleamed and sparkled.

It was so much like the Sharra sword that I could not keep back a shudder as I looked at it. But the Sharra sword now seemed like an inferior forgery, a dull copy of the glorious thing I looked on. It was shrouded in a scabbard of fine dyed leather; words, graved in fine embroidery with copper thread, writhed across the scabbard.

"What does it say?" Kathie asked, and I bent to read the words, but they were in so ancient a dialect of casta that I could not make them out, either. Callina glanced at them, and after a moment translated.

This sword shall be drawn only when all else is ended for the children of Hastur, and then the unchained shall be bound.

Well, one way or the other, the world we had known was at an end; and Sharra unchained. But I would not venture to draw forth the sword from the scabbard. I remembered what had happened to Linnell when she was confronted with her duplicate, and I—I had been sealed to the Sharra matrix; even now I did not think I was free, not entirely.

So we had the Sword of Aldones; but I still did not know how it could be used. *The unchained shall be bound.* But how?

A tingle of power flowed, not unpleasantly, up my arm; as if the sword wished to be drawn, to leap from its scabbard . . .

"No," Callina warned, and I relaxed, letting my breath go, shoving the sword back into the leather; I had drawn it only a few inches.

"I'll take it," she said, and I sighed with relief. Callina was a Keeper; she knew how to handle strange matrixes. And while the Sharra sword was a concealment for a great and powerful matrix, the Sword of Aldones was—I sensed this without knowing how I knew—itself a matrix, and dangerous to handle. If Callina felt capable of that risk, I was not going to dispute with her about it.

"That's that," I said. "Let's get out of here."

The last light of the sun was setting as we came out of the *rhu fead.* The women went ahead of me; there was no need, now, for me to safeguard Kathie. The Veil was only to screen against those not of Comyn blood getting *into* the chapel; it had never occurred to my forefathers in the Ages of Chaos to guard against anyone getting out. I lingered, half wanting to explore the strange things here.

Then Kathie cried out; and I saw the dying sunlight glint on steel. Two figures, dark shapes against the light, blurred before my eyes; then, I recognized Kadarin, sword in hand, and at his side a woman, slender and vital as a dark flame.

She did not, now, look much like Marjorie; but even so, I knew Thyra. Kathie started back against me; I put her gently aside to face my sworn enemy.

"What do you want?"

I was playing for time. There was only one thing Kadarin could want from me now, and my blood turned to ice with the horror of that memory, and around my neck my matrix began to blaze and to pulse with fire . . .

Come to me, return to me in fire . . . and I will sweep away all your hatred and lust, all your fears and anguish in my own flame, raging unchained, burning, burning forever. . . .

"Hiding behind women again?" Kadarin taunted. "Well, give me what the Keeper carries, and perhaps I shall let you go . . . *if you can!*" He flung back his head and laughed, that strange laugh that carried echoes of a falcon's cry. He did not look like a man now, or anything human; his eyes were cold and colorless, almost metallic, and his colorless hair had grown long, flying about his head; his hands on his sword were long and thin, almost more like talons than fingers. And yet there was a strange beauty to him as he stood with his head flung back, laughing that crazy laughter. "Why don't you make it easy for yourself, Lew? You know you'll do what we want in the end. Give me that—" he pointed to the Sword of Aldones, "and I'll let the women go free, and you won't have *that* to torment yourself with . . ."

"I'll see you frozen solid in Zandru's coldest hell before that, you—" I cried out, and whipped out my dagger; I stood confronting him. There had been a time when I could probably have beaten him in swordplay; now, with one hand, and a head wound and a slash in my good arm, I didn't think I had a chance. But I might, at least, force him to kill me cleanly first.

"No, wait, Lew," said Callina quietly. "This is—Kadarin?" There was nothing in her voice but fastidious distaste, not a trace of fear. I saw a shadow of dismay on Kadarin's face, but he was not human enough, now, to react to the words. He said, in a ghastly parody on his old, urbane manner, "Robert Raymon Kadarin, *para servirti, vai domna.*"

She raised the Sword of Aldones slightly in her hand.

"Come and take it—if you can," she said, and held it out invitingly to him. I cried out, "Callina, no—" and even Thyra cried out something wordless, but Kadarin snarled, "Bluffing won't help," and lunged at her, wresting the sword from her hand. . . .

Her hand exploded in blue fire, and Kadarin went reeling back, in the blue glow; the Sword of Aldones flared with brilliance, the brightness of copper filings in flame, and flared there, lying on the ground between us, while Kadarin, stunned and half senseless, slowly dragged himself to his feet, snarling a gutter obscenity of which I understood only its foulness.

Callina said quietly, "I cannot take it now that it has touched Sharra, either. Kathie—?"

Slowly, hesitating, her hand reluctant, she knelt and stretched out her hand; slowly, frightened, as if she feared that the same blue blaze of power would knock her senseless. But her hand closed over the hilt without incident. Perhaps, to her, it was only a sword. She drew a long breath.

Thyra cried out, "Let me—"

"No, wild-bird." For an instant, I saw through the monstrous thing he had become, a hint of the man I had, once, loved as a sworn brother; the old tenderness as he drew Thyra back, holding her quiet. "You cannot touch it either—but neither can the Alton whelp, so it's a draw. Let them go; there will be a time and place—" he glared out at me again, the moment of gentleness and humanity gone.

"And nothing will protect you then; who has been touched by the flamehair, she will claim again for her own. And then the hells themselves will burn in Sharra's flame. . . ."

Gods above! Once this had been a man, and my friend! I could not even hate him now; he was not human enough for that.

He was Sharra, clothed in the body of a man who had once been human . . . and he willed it so, he had surrendered of his own will to the monstrous thing he had become! I could hardly see Thyra at his side, through the illusion of tossing flames which raged between us . . .

"No," Thyra cried out, "not now! Not now!" and the flames receded. I could see her clearly now; there had never been any fire. She came toward me, hands outstretched; only a woman, small and frail with little bones like a bird's. She was dressed like a man for riding, and her hair was the same rich copper as Marjorie's, and her eyes, clear golden-amber like Marjorie's, looked up to me in the old sweet half-mocking way; and I remembered that I had loved her, desired her . . .

She said, reaching out for a half-forgotten rapport between us, "What have you done with my daughter? Our daughter?"

Marja! For a moment it seemed I could feel the touch of sweet memory, Marjorie merging into Thyra in my arms, a living flame, the touch of the child-mind . . .

Thyra was in rapport and her face changed.

"You have her, then?"

I said quietly, "You did not want her, Thyra. It was a cruel trick played on a drugged man, and you deserve all the misery you have had from it. . . ."

But for a moment I had forgotten to watch her, forgotten that she was nothing, now, but Kadarin's pawn . . . and in that moment a stab of agony went through my shoulder and my heart felt the agony of death and I knew that Thyra's dagger had wounded me. . . .

I reeled back with the shock of it. Callina caught me in her arms; even through pain and sudden despair . . . *this was the end, and Sharra still raged, I had died too quickly, I had died* . . . I was startled at the strength with which she held me upright. Kadarin made a lunge forward, hauled Thyra bodily off me.

"No! That's not the way—we still need him—ah, what have you done, Thyra—you've killed him—"

I felt myself fainting, darkness sinking down and covering my eyes, a horrid noise battering at my eardrums—was death like this, pain and noise and blinding light? No, it was a Terran helicopter, hovering, sinking, and loud shouts, and one voice suddenly coming clear.

"Robert Raymon Kadarin, I arrest you in the name of the Empire, on charges of . . . lady, drop that knife; this is a nerve-blaster and I can drop you in your tracks. You too—put that sword down."

Through the wavering darkness before my eyes I made out the dark-uniformed forms of Spaceforce men. I should have known they would find Kadarin, one way or the other, and with Terran weapons prohibited here in the Domains. I could bring charges against them, I thought weakly, they have no right to be here. Not like this. Not with blasters outside the Trade City. I should arrest them instead of them arresting us.

Then I sank into a darkness that was like death indeed, and all I could feel was an immense regret for all I had left undone. Then even that was gone.

CHAPTER THREE

Dio watched the horses out of sight, and as they turned out of the Street of Coppersmiths, it seemed to Regis that the woman was weeping; but she shook her head, and one or two bright drops went flying. She looked at him, almost defiantly, and said, "Well, Lord Hastur?"

"I promised I would see you safely back to the Castle, *Domna,*" he said, offering his arm.

She laughed; it was like a rainbow coming out through the cloud. "I thank you, my lord. Not necessary. I've walked unguarded in worse places than this!"

"That's right, you've been offworld," Regis said, feeling again the old longing, the old envy; for all his suffering, Lew was freer than he was himself, with all the worlds of an interstellar Empire at his command. Oh, to go beyond the narrow skies of his own world, to see the stars . . . he knew now that he would never go. For better or for worse, his fate lay here, whatever it might be; an unwanted crown, the new *laran* which so weighed on him that he felt he would split asunder like a butterfly from its constricting cocoon. He was Hastur; the rest he should put aside, all his old dreams, like the brightly colored tops and balls of his childhood. He walked at Dio's side, along the Street of Coppersmiths, turning at the corner to take the road to the Comyn Castle, and heard the whispers, saw the crowd draw before him in awe and astonishment.

"Comyn . . ."

"It's the Lord Hastur himself . . . the prince . . ."

"No, for sure not, what would the likes o' he be doing here on the street and unguarded . . ."

"It's the Hastur prince, yes, I saw him on Festival Night . . ."

He could not walk down a fairly narrow and unimportant street without collecting a crowd. Lew, a marked man and disfigured, one hand sacrificed to the fires of Sharra, was still more free than himself. . . . If any man stared at Lew it was only with pity or curiosity, not this entire trust, that sense that whatever might come to Darkover, the Hasturkin would protect them and shield them.

Like my own laran, it is too much for me . . . too much for any mortal man less than a God!

He drew a fold of his cloak over the concealment of his red hair, all unshielded to the mental leakage of the crowd, wonder, astonishment, curiosity. . . . *I cannot dance with a woman or walk with one down the street but my name is linked to hers . . .*

"I'm sorry, Dio," he said, trying for lightness, "but I'm afraid they have you marked out for my Queen already; it is a pity that we must disappoint them. Now, I suppose, I will have to explain to my grandfather that I do not intend to marry you, either!"

She gave him a small wry smile. "I have no wish to be a Queen," she said, "and I fear, even if you wished to marry me, Lord Danvan would be scandalized. . . ."

I have cheapened myself with other men on Vainwal; and now I am sister to the traitor who has fled from Darkover into the Empire. . . .

He said, gently, "I did not know Lerrys was gone. But I do not blame him for running away, Dio. I wish I could." After a moment he added, "And if you are a traitor's sister, that does not make you traitor; but the more credit to you that you have remained when others have fled."

They were standing now before the gates of the Comyn Castle; he saw one of the Guardsmen stare at him, alone and unattended and with Lady Dio Ridenow, and although he was trying not to read the man's mind, he could sense the man's shock and amazement; *Lord Regis, here and without even a bodyguard, and with a woman . . .* and a secret pleasure at this morsel of gossip he could spread among his fellows. Well, everything Regis did created gossip, but he was heartily sick of it.

He crossed the courtyard, wanting to say a polite word or two to Dio and dismiss her. He had too many troubles to share them with any woman, even if there was a woman alive with whom he could share anything except a brief moment of passion or pleasure. And, abruptly, looking at Dio, he was torn by her despair.

"What is it, Dio?" he asked gently, and felt it flood through him.

He was so sure he was going to die! All he sees is his own death . . . I would have gone to death, even that, beside him, but he can only see Callina . . .

He was struck numb by the quality of her pain. No woman had ever loved him like that, none ever shown him that kind of loyalty and staunchness. . . .

He has gone to die, to hurl himself against death in finding the weapon against Sharra. . . .

Regis realized that he should have gone with Lew himself; or he should have taken his matrix, cleansed it as he had done to Rafe's. What gave him this strange power, not over Sharra, but over the Form of Fire? Kadarin was somewhere, with the Sharra matrix, and Lew might fall into his hands. . . .

He should have gone with Lew, or cleansed Lew's matrix. Or at least demanded that Callina take him to Ashara, so that the ancient Keeper of the Comyn could explain this new and monstrous Hastur Gift. *Lew at least is Tower-trained, he knows what strengths he has . . . and what weaknesses; he faces death with full knowledge, not blinded as I am by ignorance!* What was the good of being Hastur, and Lord of Comyn, if he could not even know what this new *laran* might bring him?

Dio was trying to conceal her tears. Part of him wanted to reassure her, but he had no comfort for her and in any case Dio did not want facile lies; she was one of the sensitive Ridenow and she would see through them at once. He said quietly, "It may be that we are all going to die, Dio. But if I have a chance I would rather die to keep Sharra from destroying Darkover—Terran and Comyn alike. And so would Lew, I think; and he has the right to choose his own death . . . and to make amends . . ."

"I suppose so." Beneath the understanding, she turned to him, no longer trying to conceal her tears, and somehow he realized that this was a kind of acceptance. "It's strange; I have seen so much of his—his weakness, his gentler side, I forget how strong he is. He would never run away to the Terrans because he was afraid; not even if they burned off his other hand first . . ."

"No," said Regis, suddenly feeling closer to her than to his own sister, "he wouldn't."

"You wouldn't either, would you?" she asked, smiling at him through the tears in her eyes.

He is Hastur . . . and he will stand by Comyn . . . and then, even in Dio, the curious and inevitable question: *I wonder why he has never married? Surely he could have any woman he wanted . . . surely it is not true that he is, like Lerrys, like Dyan, only a lover of men, he has had women, he has* nedestro *children. . . .*

And then, Regis felt it, a return of her own despair and pain, *our son, Lew's and mine, that frightful thing, and I rebuffed him . . . it was only because I was so sick and weak, I did not hate him or blame him, and then Lerrys took me away, before I could tell him . . . Merciful Avarra, he has suffered so much, and I hurt him again, all that horror, when I had promised that he would never have to hide himself from me . . .*

. . . and he will die still thinking I had rebuffed him because of that horror. . . .

And suddenly Regis found himself envying Lew.

How he has been loved! I have never known what it was to love a woman like that or to be loved . . . and I shall die never knowing if I am capable of that kind of love . . .

Oh, yes, there had been women. He was capable of sudden flaring passion, of taking them with pleasure, given and received; but once the flare of mutual lust had burned out, sometimes even before the woman knew herself pregnant with his child, he had been all too aware of what it was they felt for him; pleasure at his physical beauty, pride that they had attracted the attention of a Hastur, greed for the status and privilege that would be theirs if they bore a Hastur child. Any one of the five or six would gladly have married him for that status; but he had never felt for any of them anything more than that brief flaring of passion and lust; the vague distaste and even revulsion, knowing that their feeling for him was based on greed or pride.

But never this kind of disinterested love . . . will I die without ever knowing if I am capable of attracting that kind of love from a woman? No one has ever loved me thus unselfishly but Danilo, and that is different, the love of comrades, a shared companionship . . . and even that, all men seem to despise . . . a thing to be put aside with boyhood . . .

is there no more than this? Why can Lew attract this kind of love, and not I?

But with what was hanging over them, there was no time for this either. He turned to speak some word of recollection to Dio, when suddenly a shriek of wild terror surged through their minds, a wordless cry of despair and fright and utter panic, pain and fear. *A child, a child is crying in terror* . . . Regis was not sure whether it was his thought or Dio's, but all at once he knew what child it was who shrieked out in such agonized fright, and he pushed Dio before him and ran, ran like a possessed thing toward the Alton apartments.

Marja! But who would so terrify a child?

The great double doors to the Alton suite were standing ajar, swinging on one hinge. Old Andres was lying in a pool of his own blood, half over the threshold where he had been struck down.

He guarded her with his life, as he had sworn . . . Regis felt dismay; he too had been befriended and fathered by the old *coridom.* Then he realized that Andres was still moving feebly, though he was long past speech. He knelt, tears swelling up in his own eyes for the faithful old man, and Andres, with his last strength, whispered, "Dom Regis . . . lad . . ."

Regis knew that Andres did not see him; the dying eyes were already glazed, past sight. He saw only the boy of ten, Kennard's fosterling, Lew's sworn friend. And with his last strength Andres formed a picture in Regis's mind . . .

Then it was gone and there was nothing living in the room except himself. Regis stood up, stricken with pain. "*Beltran!* But how, in all of Zandru's hells, did he manage to come here, when I left him safely imprisoned . . ."

He did not even need to ask. He had left Beltran with Lord Dyan; and Dyan had agreed with Beltran that Sharra was the ultimate weapon against the Terrans . . . Lew was beyond their reach. But there remained an Alton child. . . .

There remained an Alton child; and one Gifted, even at five years old, with the *laran* of her house . . . and of her *chieri* blood. Regis felt sick; would anything human stoop to use a small child in *Sharra?* He had had reason to know that Dyan could be cruel, could be unscrupulous, but *this?*

He realized that all through this, he had been hearing

somewhere in his mind, ringing louder and wilder, the terrified shrieks of the child, the sudden flame and terror of the Form of Fire . . . and then it was gone, so suddenly that for a moment Regis was shocked, feeling that Marja must suddenly have died of terror, or been struck silent by a blow of terrifying cruelty . . .

What madness was this? Around him was the silence of death in the Alton rooms, the horrified gasps of Dio who stood on the threshold, but somewhere he was hearing a voice he knew, or was it a telepathic touch rather than a voice?

Fool, this is nothing for a girl-child! I have the strength and I am not squeamish . . . I am not one of your Tower-trained eunuchs, let me take that place rather than one you can never trust . . . and then almost laughter, silent laughter in mockery. *No, she's not dead, she is beyond your reach, that is all . . . pick on someone your own size, Beltran!*

"Lord of Light!" Regis gasped in shock, knowing what had happened. Dyan had *chosen* Sharra. Despite every warning, he had walked of his own free will into that horror which had cost Lew his hand and his sanity, which even now overpowered Regis with dread and terror . . .

Does this mean Lew is free? No, never, never, he is still bound to Sharra . . .

"Lord Hastur! Lord Regis—" a gasping servant, come in search of him, stopped in shock, staring at the dead body of the old *coridom* on the floor. "Good Gods, sir, what's happened?"

Regis said, clutching at calm and ordinary things, "This man died defending his master's—his foster-son's property and his child. He should have a funeral fit for a hero. Find someone who can see to it, can you?" He rose slowly, staring at the dead man and at the servants clustering in the doorway of the Alton suite. Then he saw the man who had come to look for him.

"Sir, the Lord Hastur—your grandsire, sir—he has ordered—" again the man, confused, shifted ground, "he has asked if you will come and attend on him . . ."

Regis sighed. He had been expecting that; what conflicting demands was his grandfather to make on him now? He saw Dio and knew she could not bear to be left out of what was happening now. Well, she had a right to know.

"Come along," he said, "Lew and I were *bredin,* once, and you have a claim on me, too."

He found his grandfather in the small presence-chamber of the Hastur apartments; Danvan Hastur said, "Aldones be thanked, I have found you!" The Terran Legate has sent a message to you personally, Regis; something about a Captain Scott and permission to authorize Terran weapons—" He looked at his grandson, and tried to speak with the old authority, but only managed a shocking parody of his old strength. "I don't know how you came to put yourself in a position where Terrans could bid you come and go, but I suppose you'll have to deal with it—"

He is old. I am the real power of Hastur now and we both know it; though he will never say so, Regis thought, and spoke to the unspoken part of his grandfather's words, whatever the actual words had been.

"Don't trouble yourself, sir; I'll go and deal with it." He suddenly felt deep compassion for the old man, who had spent so many years holding the power of the Comyn, without even *laran* to sustain him.

He has had all the troubles of a Hastur and none of the rewards, he thought, and then was startled and shocked at himself. Rewards? This monstrous *laran* which threatened, unwanted, to split him asunder, so that he walked with the terrible knowledge of a power whose forces he could not even imagine?

Gift? The Hastur curse, rather! He felt as if his very arms and legs were too big for him, as if he walked halfway between earth and sky, his feet hardly touching the ground, and all without knowing why. Desperately, he wanted Danilo at his side. But there was not even time to send a message to his paxman, and in any case, if Dyan had flung himself recklessly into the danger and terror of Sharra, Danilo was Lord Ardais, for Dyan was as good as dead, and so were they all; let Danilo stay free of this if he could. He said brusquely to the Spaceforce man who had brought the message, "I'll come at once." Dio turned to follow him and he said, "No. Stay here." He could not encumber himself with any woman now, certainly not when Danilo had been denied the privilege of attending him.

"I *will* go," she said wildly, "I am a Terran citizen; you cannot prevent me!"

It wasn't worth arguing. He signaled to the Spaceforce man to let her come, and together they clambered into the surface car. Regis had never ridden in a Terran vehicle before; he hung on breathless, as it tore through the streets, men and women and horses scattering as it roared and jolted over the cobbles; he thought irrelevantly, *we must forbid this, it is too dangerous on such old and crowded streets.* Once through the gates into the Trade City the streets were a little smoother and he hung on desperately, not wanting to show his fright before Dio who was apparently accustomed to this kind of breath-taking transport.

Through the HQ gates, the Spaceforce driver barely stopping to flash a pass of some sort at the guard, then tearing across the abnormally smooth terrain to the very gates of the skyscraper; and up in the lift, Dio doggedly keeping at his heels all the way, then into Lawton's office.

Rafe Scott, white as death, was there, and Lawton didn't waste words. He gestured, and Rafe poured it out.

"Kadarin has gone to Hali! I suddenly discovered that I was reading Thyra—I don't know why—"

Regis did. He could *feel* Sharra, through and around Rafe, a monstrous and obscene flame, unbodied, inchoate and Rafe was part of that ancient bonding.

Kadarin, bearing the Sword. Thyra. Beltran. . . .

Dyan, who had recklessly flung himself into the volcano.

And Lew, somewhere, somewhere . . . bound, sealed, doomed

"Well?" Lawton said crisply, "Will you authorize me to send a helicopter, and men properly armed with blasters, to arrest Kadarin out there? Or are you going to stick to the letter of your Compact, while they work with something which is farther outside of your Compact than a super-planetbusting bomb, let alone a blaster or two?"

Am I going to authorize . . . who does he think I am? Then, in the sudden humility of power recognized and feared, Regis knew that he could no longer avoid the responsibility. He said, "Yes. I'll authorize it." He managed to write his name, though his hand shook, on the form Lawton held out to him. Lawton spoke into some kind of communicator.

"All right; Hastur authorized it. Let the copter go."

"I want to—" *I should go with the copter. Maybe I can*

still do something for Lew . . . or his matrix if it's sealed to Sharra . . .

Lawton shook his head. "Too late. They've taken off. All you can do now is *wait.*"

They waited, while the sun sank slowly behind the mountain pass. Waited, while time wore away and dragged, and finally Regis saw the helicopter, a tiny black speck hovering over the mountain pass, coming nearer, nearer.

Dio rose and cried out, "He's hurt! I—I have to go to him—" and dashed for the lift. Lawton simultaneously answered some kind of blinking light, listened, and his face changed.

"Well," he said grimly to Regis, "I waited too long, or you did, or somebody. They've got Kadarin, yes, but it looks as if he's managed to commit another murder while everybody stood by and watched. They're going to take him down to Medic. You'd better come along."

Regis followed, through the sterile white walls of the Medical division. An elevator whined softly to a stop and Spaceforce men hauled out prisoners. Dio had eyes only for Lew, carried between two of the uniformed men. Regis could not tell whether he was alive or dead; his face was ghastly, his head lolled lifeless, and the whole front of his shirt was covered in blood.

Bredu! Regis felt shock and grief surging over him. Dio was clinging to Lew's lax hand, crying now without trying to hide it. Behind, Kadarin moved manacled between two guards. Regis barely recognized him, he was so much older, so much more haggard, as if something were consuming him from within. Thyra, too, was handcuffed. Kathie looked pale and frightened, and one of the guards was carrying Callina, who appeared to have fainted; they set her in a chair and gestured to someone to bring smelling-salts, and after a minute Callina opened her eyes; but she swayed, holding to the chair. Kathie went swiftly to her and held her up. One of the Medic personnel said something and she frowned and said, "I'm a nurse; I'll look after her. You'd better look after Mr. Montray-Alton; the woman stabbed him, and it looks as if it may have finished him—he was still alive when the helicopter landed, but that's not saying much."

But Regis looked at the long sword Kathie had let slide

to the floor; and something inside him, something in his blood, suddenly awoke and shouted inside his veins.

THIS IS MINE!

He went and picked it up; it felt warm and *right* in his hands. Callina opened her eyes, staring, a strange, cold, blue gaze.

The moment Regis had the sword in his hands, looking at the curling letters written on the scabbard, all at once he seemed to be everywhere, not just where his body was, but as if the edges of his body had spread out to encompass everything in the room. He *touched* Callina and saw her with a strange double sight, the woman he knew, the plain quiet Keeper, still and prim and gentle, and at the same time she was overlaid with something else, cold and blue and watchful, like ice, strange and cold as stone. He *touched* Dio and felt the flood of her love and concern and dread; he *touched* Kadarin and drew back, THIS IS THE ENEMY, THIS IS THE BATTLE . . . NOT YET, NOT YET! He *touched* Lew.

Pain. Cold. Silence. Fear and the consuming flame . . .

Pain. Pain at the heart, stabbing pain . . . Regis spread out into the pain, that was the only way to explain it, felt the broken torn cells, the bleeding out of the life. . . . NO! I WILL NOT HAVE IT SO! The trickling silence that was Lew was suddenly flooded with terrible pain, and then with heat and life and then Lew opened his eyes, and sat up, staring at Regis. His lips barely moved and he whispered, "What—what are you?"

And Regis heard himself say, from a great distance, "Hastur."

And the word meant nothing to him. But the gaping wound had closed, and all around him the Terran medics were standing and staring; and in his hand was this sword which seemed, now, to be more than half of himself.

And suddenly Regis was terrified and he slid the sword back into its sheath, and suddenly the world was all in one piece again and he was back in his body. He was shaking so hard that he could hardly stand.

"Lew! *Bredu*—you're alive!"

CHAPTER FOUR

(Lew Alton's narrative, concluded)

I have never remembered anything about that helicopter ride to the Terran HQ, or how I got to the Legate's office; the first awareness was of hellish pain and its sudden cessation.

"Lew! Lew, can you hear me?"

How could I help it? She was shouting right in my ear! I opened my eyes and saw Dio, her face wet with tears.

"Don't cry, love," I said, "I'm all right. That hell-cat Thyra must have stabbed me, but she seems not to have hurt me much."

But Kathie motioned Dio back when she would have bent to me, saying with professional crispness, "Just a moment; his pulse was nearly gone." She took some kind of instrument and cut away my shirt; then I heard her gasp.

Where Thyra's knife had gone in—perilously near the heart—was only a small, long-healed scar, paler and more perfectly cicatrized than the discolored scars on my face.

"I don't believe this," she protested. "I saw it, and *still* I don't believe it." She took something cold and wet and washed off the still-sticky smears of half-dried blood which still clung to the skin. I looked ruefully at the ruined shirt.

"Get him a uniform shirt, or something," said Lawton, and they brought me one, made out of paper or some similar unwoven fiber. It had a cold and rather slippery texture which I found unpleasant, but I wasn't in a position to be picky; besides, the medical smells were driving me out of my mind. I said, "Do we have to stay down here? I'm not hurt—" and only then did I see Regis, the Sword of Aldones belted around his waist, an unbelieving look of awe on his face. Later I learned what he had done; but at the moment—everything was so mad already—I simply took it for granted and was grateful that the Sword had come to the hands of the one person on this world who could handle it. I think, originally, I had supposed that Callina, or perhaps Ashara, would have to take it, as Keeper. Now I saw it in Regis's custody, and all I could think was, *oh, yes, of course, he is Hastur.*

"Where is Thyra? Did she get away?"

"Not likely," said Lawton, grimly, "She's in a cell downstairs, and there she'll stay."

"Why?" Kadarin asked. His voice was calm, and I stared, unable to believe my eyes; on the shores of Hali he had appeared to me as something very far from human; now, curiously, he looked like the man I had first known, civilized and urbane, even likable. "On what charges?"

"Attempted murder of Lew Alton here!"

"It would be hard to make a charge like that stick," Kadarin said. "Where is the alleged wound?"

Lawton stared irritably at the blood-soaked shirt which had been cut from me. He said, "We've got eyewitnesses to the attempt. Meanwhile we'll hold her for—oh, hell!—breaking and entering, trespass, carrying concealed weapons, indecent language in a public place—indecent exposure if we have to! The main thing is that we're holding her, and you too; we need to ask you some questions about a certain murder and the burning of a townhouse in Thendara . . ."

Kadarin looked directly at me. He said, "Believe what you like, Lew; I did not murder your brother. I did not know your brother by sight; I did not know who he was until afterward, when I heard in the street who it was that had been killed. To me he was simply a young Terran I did not know; and for what it is worth, it was not I who killed him but one of my men. And I am sorry; I gave no orders that anyone should be killed. You know what it was that I came for, and why I had to come."

I looked at this man and knew that I could not hate him. I too had been compelled to do things I would never have dreamed of doing, not in my right mind; and I knew what had compelled him. It was belted, now, around his waist; but through that I could see the man who had been my friend. I turned my face away. There was too much between us. I had no right to condemn him, not now, not when through my own matrix I could feel the pull, irresistible, of that unholy thing.

Return to me and live forever in undying reviving fire . . . and behind my eyelids the Form of Fire, between me and what I could see with my physical eyes. Sharra, and I was still a part of it, still damned. I took one step toward him; I do not know even now whether I meant to strike him or to join hands with him on the hilt of the Sharra matrix concealed in its sword.

Hate and love mingled, as they had mingled for my father, whose voice even now pulsed in my mind, *Return* . . . *return* . . .

Then Kadarin shrugged a little and the spell broke. He said, "If you want to throw me in a cell, that's all right with me, but it's only fair to warn you I probably won't stay there long. I have—" he touched the hilt of the Sharra sword and said lightly, "a pressing engagement elsewhere."

"Take him away," Lawton said. "Put him in maximum security, and let him see if he can talk himself out of there."

Kadarin saved them the trouble of taking him; he rose and went amiably with the guards. One of them said, "I'll have that sword first, if you please."

Kadarin said, still with that impeccable grin, "Take it, if you want it."

Watching, I wanted to cry out a warning to the Space-force men; I knew it was not a sword. One of them thrust out his hand . . . and went flying across the room; he struck his head against the wall and sank down, stunned. The other stood staring at Lawton and turning back to Kadarin; afraid and I didn't blame him.

"It's not a sword, Lawton," I said. "It's a matrix weapon."

"Is *that—?*" Lawton stared, and I nodded. There was no way, short of killing Kadarin first, that they could get it away from him; and I was not even sure that he could be killed while he wore it, not by any ordinary weapon anyhow. I did warn them, "Don't put him and Thyra in the same cell."

Not that distance would make any difference, when that sword was drawn. And would I go with them? Just the same, I was glad to have Kadarin, and the Sharra matrix, out of my sight. I started to rise, only to have the young doctor push me down again on a seat.

"You're not going anywhere, not yet!"

"Am I a prisoner, then?"

The doctor looked at Lawton, who said, scowling, "Hell no! But if you try to walk out of here, you'll fall flat on your face! Stay put and let Doctor Allison go over you, why don't you? What's the hurry?"

I tried to stand up, but for no discernible reason I found myself as weak as a newborn rabbithorn. I could not get my legs under me.

I let the young doctor go over me with his instruments. I hated hospitals, and the smell was getting to me, reviving memories of other hospitals on other worlds, memories I would rather not have to face just now; but there seemed no alternative. I noticed Kathie talking to one of the doctors and, as on Festival Night, I wondered if she would accuse us of kidnapping or worse. Well, if she did, the story was so unlikely on the face of it that probably no one would believe her; Vainwal was half a Galaxy away!

There were times when I didn't believe it myself. . . .

Before the doctor had finished listening to my heart and checking every function of my body—he even had me unstrap the mechanical hand, looked at it and asked if it was working properly—Regis had come back into the room. He looked grave and remote. At his side was Rafe Scott.

"I've seen Thyra," he said abruptly.

So had I, I thought, *and I wish I had not.* Even though her attempt to kill me had been thwarted, I found I could not bear to think of her. It was not all her fault; she was Kadarin's victim as much as I, a more willing victim, perhaps, eager for the power of Sharra. But thinking of the woman made me remember the child, and I saw Regis's face change. I was not used to this, Regis had never been so sensitive a telepath as that . . . but I was beginning to realize that this new Regis, with the sudden opening of the Hastur Gift, was a different Regis from the youngster I had known most of my life.

Regis said, "I have bad news for you, Lew; the very worst. Andres—" his voice caught, almost choking, and I knew. During those carefree years at Armida, Andres had been like a father to him, too.

My father, Marius, Linnell . . . now Andres. Now, more than ever, I was wholly alone. I was afraid to ask, but I asked anyhow.

"Marja?"

"He—defended her with his life," Regis said. "Beltran—would have taken her into Sharra; she has the Alton Gift. But Dyan . . ."

I was braced to hear that Dyan had been party to this; I was not prepared for what Regis told me next.

"Somehow—he thrust her out—*elsewhere.* I could find no trace of her, even telepathically. I do not know where he has her hidden; but somewhere, she is safe from Sharra. And Dyan—did you know he has the Alton Gift, Lew?"

In the confusion I had forgotten. But I should have known, of course. Power to force his will on another mind, even unwilling . . . and Dyan had Alton blood; he and my father had been first cousins. My father's mother was own sister to Dyan's father, and there were other kin-ties, further generations back.

Once, under terrible pressure—I had used a little-known power of the Altons, I had teleported from Aldaran to the Arilinn Tower. Dyan might, for some reason, have done this to Marja—but he could have sent her anywhere on Darkover, from Armida itself to Castle Ardais in the Hellers—or to the Spaceman's Orphanage in Thendara where she had been brought up.

When there was time, I would have to make a search for her, physical and telepathic; I did not think Dyan could hide her from me permanently, or even that he would want to. But before that, Kadarin held the Sharra matrix, and if he chose to draw it, I knew I could never trust myself again. I tried to warn Regis of this. He touched the Sword of Aldones, and he looked grim. "This is the weapon against Sharra. Since I belted it on . . . there are many things I know," he said, strangely, "things I had not learned. I have known for days that I have a strange power over Sharra, and now, with *this*—" it was as if something spoke *behind* and *through* the Regis I knew; he looked haggard and worn, years older than he was. But now and then, as I looked into his eyes, the other Regis, the youngster I knew, would peep through; and he looked frightened. I didn't blame him.

"Show me your matrix," he said.

I balked at that. Not without the presence of a Keeper. I said, "If Callina is there," and he turned to one of the doctors and asked what had happened to her.

"She was faint," said Kathie, "I took her into one of the cubicles to lie down. It must have been all the blood."

That alerted me to danger. Darkovan women don't faint at trifles, or at the sight of blood. I had to shout and create a scene, though, before they would take me to her; and I found her in one of the small cubicles, seated stone-still, her eyes withdrawn and pallid, as if she were Ashara's self, gazing at nothing in the world we could see . . .

Regis shouted at her, and so did I, but she was motionless, her eyes gazing into nowhere unfathomable distances. At last I reached out, tried to touch her mind—I felt her, very far away, some cold icy *otherness* . . . then she gasped, stared at me, and came back to herself.

"You were in trance, Callina," I told her, and she looked at us in consternation. I believe that even then, if she had taken us into her confidence, it might have been different . . . but she made light of the curious trance, saying lightly, "I was resting, no more . . . half asleep. What is it, what do you want?"

Regis said quietly, "I want to see if we can clear his matrix and free him from the . . . the Sharra one. I did it for Rafe. I think I could have done it for Beltran if he had asked me." I picked up the unspoken part of that: Beltran was still eager to use Sharra, he had regarded it as the ultimate weapon against subjection to the Terrans . . . blackmail to get them off our world forever.

And Dyan, wrong-headed and desperately anxious for power the weakening Comyn Council would not yield to him, had followed him into subjection to Sharra. . . . I could feel Regis's grief and sorrow at that, and suddenly for a moment I saw Dyan through Regis's eyes; *the older kinsman, handsome, worldly, whom the younger Regis had liked and admired . . . then feared, with still the extreme fascination that was closely akin to love . . . the only kinsman who had wholly accepted him.* I had seen Dyan only cruel, threatening, harsh; a martinet, a man eager for power and using it in brutally unsubtle ways; a man sadistically misusing his power over cadets and younger kinsmen. This other side of Dyan was one I had never seen, and it gave me pause. Had I, after all, misjudged the man?

No; or else even his love of power would never have misled him into the attempt to gain that ultimate perversion of the Comyn powers: *Sharra's fire* . . . I had been burned by that fire, and Dyan had seen the scars. But in his supreme arrogance, he thought he could succeed where I had failed, make Sharra serve him; be master, rather than slave to Sharra's fire . . . and Dyan was not even Tower-trained?

"All the more reason, Lew, that you must be freed," Regis argued. After a moment I slipped the leather thong off over my head and fumbled one-handed to unwrap the silks. Finally I let it roll out into my palm, seeing the crimson blaze overlaying the blue interior shimmer of the matrix. . . .

Callina focused her attention on me, matching resonances, until she could take it into her hand; the trained touch of a Keeper, and not overwhelmingly painful. Then I felt something like a tug-o-war in my mind, the call, restimulated, of Sharra, *Return, return and live in the life of my fires* . . . and through it I felt Marjorie . . . or was it Thyra? *In my embrace you shall burn forever in passion undiminished* . . .

I felt Regis, through this, as if he were somehow reaching into my very brain, though I knew it was only my matrix he was touching, disentangling it thread by thread . . . but the more he worked on it, the stronger grew the redoubled call, the pulse of Sharra beating in my brain, till I stood burning in agony. . . .

The door was flung open and Dio was in the room, rushing to me, physically flinging Callina aside. "What do you think you are doing to him?" she raged.

The flames diminished and died; Regis caught at some piece of furniture, staggering, hardly able to stand erect.

"How much do you think he can stand? Hasn't he been through enough?"

I collapsed gratefully into a chair. I said, "They were only—"

"Only stirring up what's better left alone," Dio stormed. "I could feel it all the way up to the eighth floor above here . . . I could feel them *cutting* at you . . ." and she ran her hands over me as if she had expected to see me physically covered in blood.

"It's all right, Dio," I said, knowing my voice was hardly more than an exhausted mumble. "I was trained to—to endure it—"

"What makes you think you're able to endure it now?" she demanded angrily, and Regis said, in despair, "If Kadarin draws the Sharra sword . . ."

"If he does," Dio said, "he will have to fight; but can't you let him get together enough strength to fight it?"

I did not know. Rafe had never been farther than the outer layer of the circle we had formed around Sharra; I had been at its very heart, controlling the force and flow of the power of Sharra. I was doomed, and I knew it. I knew what Callina and Regis had been trying to do, and I was grateful, but for me it was too late.

My eyes rested on Callina, and I saw everything around me with a new clarity. She was everything of the past to me; Arilinn, and my own past; Marjorie had died in her arms, and then I had found in her the first forgetfulness I had known. Kinswoman, Keeper, all the past . . . and I ached with regret that I would not live to take her with me to Armida, to reclaim my own past and my own world. But it was not to be. A darker love would claim me, the wildfire of Sharra surging in my veins, the dark bond to Thyra who had made herself Keeper of that monstrous circle of Sharra, fire and lust and endless burning torture and flame . . . Callina might call me to her, but it was too late, now and forever too late. Dio spoke to me, but I had gone back to a time before she had come into my life, and I hardly remembered her name.

What were we doing here within these white walls?

Someone came into the room. I did not recognize the man although from the way he spoke to me I knew that he was someone I was supposed to know. One of the accursed Terrans, those who would die in the flames of Sharra when the time was ripe. His words were mere sounds without sense and I did not understand them.

"That woman Thyra! We had her in one of our strongest cells, and she's gone—just like that, she's gone out of a maxmimum security cell! Did you witch her out of there somehow?"

Fool, to think any cell could hold the priestess and Keeper of Sharra the Fire-born. . . .

Space reeled around me; there was a slamming thunderclap and I stood braced on the cobblestone of the forecourt of the Comyn Castle, my feet spanning the enlaced symbols there . . . and I knew Kadarin had unsheathed the Sword. Kadarin stood there, his pale hair moving in an invisible wind, his hands on Thyra's shoulders, his metallic eyes cold with menace, and Thyra . . .

Thyra! Flames rose upward from her copper hair, sparks trembled at the tips of her fingers. In her hands she held naked the Sharra Sword, cold flames racing from hilt to tip. Thyra! My mistress, my love—what was I doing here, far from her? She raised one hand and beckoned, and I began nervelessly to move forward, without being conscious of the motion. She was smiling as I knelt at her feet on the stone, feeling all my strength going out to her, and to that fire that flowed and flamed in her hands . . .

Then the flame flared blue and wild to the heights of the castle, and I knew Regis had unsheathed the Sword of Aldones. They were there, there physically, standing across from me, Regis and Callina, and she *reached* for me, enfolding me in the cold blue of Ashara's icy limbo, and then we were not in the Castle courtyard at all, but in the gray spaces of the overworld . . . far below I could see our bodies like tiny toys from a great height, but the only reality in the world was those two swords, crimson with flame and cold ice-blue, crossed and straining at one another, and I. . . .

I was a puppet, a mote of power in the astral world, something stretched to breaking between them . . . Callina's voice, reminding me of Arilinn and all of my past, Thyra's crooning call, enticing, seductive, with memories of lust and fire and power . . . I was torn, torn between them as I felt myself a link between the two circles, Regis and Callina with the Sword of Aldones, Thyra and Kadarin, each pulling at me fiercely to make a third, to lend my power. . . .

And then there was another strength in the linked circles . . . something cold and arrogant and brutal, the harsh touch as of my father's own strength, the Alton Gift which had opened my own to power, but this was not my father's touch. . . . *Dyan! And he had always disliked me . . . and I was at his mercy . . .*

I did not mind dying, but not like this. . . . Again in my mind was the final cry of my father's voice, and we were so deeply enlaced that I could see Dyan look past me at Regis with infinite warmth and regret that in the end they should have been on opposite sides. *I wanted to stand at your side when you were King over all of Darkover, my gallant Hastur cousin . . .* and then, through me, I could feel Dyan's touch on the memory of my father's destroying call, the last thought in his dying mind . . .

And Dyan, in a moment of anguish and grief:

Kennard! My first, my only friend . . . my cousin, my kinsman, bredu *. . . and there is no other, now, living, who bears your blood, and if I strike now I shall have killed you past death or any immortality . . .* and then a final, careless thought, almost laughter, *this son of yours was never fit for this kind of power . . .*

And abruptly I was free, free of Sharra, thrust entirely away, and in that moment of freedom I was locked into the closing rapport of Regis and Callina, the sealed circle of power . . .

The fire-form reared high, higher, the size of the castle, the size of the mountain, with a scorching darkness at its heart . . . but from Regis, risen now to giant-size, blazing cold lightning struck at the heart of Sharra as he held the Sword of Aldones, poised to strike . . .

Sharra was bound in chains by the Son of Hastur who was the Son of Light . . .

And clothed in his cloak of living light Aldones came!

Now there was nothing to see, no human form, only fire lapping higher and higher, the spark of the Sharra matrix blazing out from the center of that darkness, and the core of brilliance through the veils clothing the figure of the God, like Regis in form, but Regis looming high, higher, not one of the Hastur-kin but the God himself . . .

Two identical matrixes cannot exist in one time and space; and once before, so the legend said, Sharra had been chained by the Son of Aldones, who was the Son of Light. . . .

I cannot explain the legend, even now, although I saw it. I had felt the daemon-touch of Sharra. Infinite good is as terrifying, in its own way, as infinite evil. It was not Regis and Kadarin fighting with identically forged swords, one a copy of the other. It was not even matrix battling against space-twisting matrix, though that was nearer the truth. Something tangible and very real fought behind each sword, something that was not on this plane of reality at all, and could manifest itself and maintain a foothold in this dimension only through the swords. Lightnings streamed between them, wrapped in the rainbow aura that was Regis and Hastur, coiling into the licking flames at the heart of which Thyra glowed like a burning coal.

And then for an instant I felt that last bright arrogance reach out, Dyan shining across the space, his hawk-face keen and curious. For an instant then I think the linkage broke and the swords were only swords, and for a split second we stood in the courtyard of the Castle again and the cobbles were unsteady under my feet. And in that moment I know that he could have reached out and killed either of us. . . .

And for a moment Thyra stood before me, only a woman again, although the Form of Fire still licked around her, and the smell of burning beat on the air, and her throat was naked to my knife . . .

I had sworn their death in vengeance for my hand. But in that moment I could remember only that there had been a time when she stood before me, only a frightened girl, terrified by her own growing powers. If the Gods themselves had put a dagger into my hand at that moment I could not have struck her down, and for a moment it seemed as if a great question vibrated in the overworld, and in this world and through all the universes of my mind; *Will you have the Love of Power or the Power of Love?*

And everything in me surged toward Kadarin, whom I had once loved as a brother, and to the young and beautiful Thyra whom I, as much as Kadarin, had destroyed. I have never been able to explain this, but I knew in that one searing moment of testing that I would die in Sharra's fire myself rather than hurt either of them any further than they had already been hurt. Everything in me cried out an enormous and final *No!*

And then we were battling again in the gray limbo of the overworld, and the two swords crossed and blazed like interlaced lightnings . . .

Then the flames sank and died, and a great darkness blazed at the heart of the Sharra matrix. I saw a blaze of endless fire, and the searing flame strike inward, and then a great vortex seemed to open inwards, into a great whirling nothingness. Into that nothingness were swept away Kadarin and Thyra, two tiny, disappearing figures, whirled away and apart . . . and a great wordless cry of pain and despair and at the last instant, so faint that I never knew whether I heard it or not, a split-second cry of joy and rediscovery which made me hear again in my mind my father's last cry . . .

"Beloved—!"

Silence and nothingness, and darkness . . . and the great and damnable Face that I had seen in Ashara's overworld of blue ice . . .

And then I was standing in the gray light of dawn on the cobblestones in Comyn Castle, facing Regis, only a shrinking, hesitant young man again, with the Sword of Aldones half-raised in his hand, and Callina pale as death beside him. There was no sign anywhere of Kadarin or Thyra, but sprawled on the cobbles before us, broken and dying, Dyan Ardais lay, his body blackened as if with fire. The Sword of Sharra lay broken in his hand. There were no jewels in the hilt of the sword now; they lay charred and ugly, burnt pebbles which, even as the first rays of the sun touched them, evaporated into pale gouts of rising smoke, and were gone forever . . . as Sharra's power was gone forever from this world.

Regis sheathed the Sword of Aldones and knelt beside Dyan, weeping without shame. Dyan opened pain-filled eyes, and I saw recognition in them for a moment, and pain beyond the point where it ceases to have meaning. But if Regis had hoped for a word, he was disappointed; Dyan's eyes glinted up at him in a moment, then fell back and stared at something which was not in this world. But for the first time since I had known him, he looked content and at peace.

If he had been willing to kill us all, Sharra would have triumphed . . . I knelt, too, beside his body, conceding his hero's death, as Regis laid his own cloak over Dyan's body. He still held the Sword of Aldones, but from that, too, all glow and power had faded; the blade was blackened all along its length as if with the strange fire in which it had been quenched. After a moment Regis laid the Sword of Aldones on Dyan's breast, as a fallen hero's sword is laid to be buried with him. None of us protested. Then Regis rose, and the rays of the rising sun touched his hair . . . snow white.

It was over; and beyond hope I was free, and alive . . . beyond countless, measureless havoc, I had come free. I turned to Callina, and at last, knowing we were free, caught her for the first time in my arms and pressed her lips hungrily to mine.

And all desire died in my heart and mind as I looked down into the chill eyes of Ashara.

I should have known, all along.

Only a moment and she was Callina again, clinging to me and crying, but I had seen. I let her go, in horror . . . and as my arms released her, Callina crumpled very slowly to the pavement and lay there unmoving, beside Dyan.

I knelt again, turning her over, catching her up in my arms, uncaring; but she was still, unmoving, already cold. And now I knew. . . .

Generations ago, a powerful Keeper, of the Hastur line, had held all the power of the Comyn . . . and as she grew older, had been reluctant to set aside her power; and so she had concentrated power in the Aillard line, and many of those women had been her under-Keepers, giving their own powers to Ashara, so that Ashara, whose flesh had failed and who lived now within the matrix, went abroad in the body and personality, like a garment, of her newest Keeper . . . and of these, my young kinswoman had been the last. I had wondered why I could never touch her mind, nor come near, except now and again for a moment. . . .

And again the terrifying question from the overworld seemed to beat in my heart; *the Love of Power or the Power of Love?*

I will swear to my dying day that Callina had loved me. . . .

Otherwise, would that ancient Hastur sorceress have risked the end of her undying mind and all her power, to risk all for my freedom from Sharra's bondage? Regis and I, alone, could never have faced that last undying blaze of Sharra's fire. But with Callina recklessly throwing all of Ashara's powers into the fray, through the body of the young Hastur who was her far kinsman, so that the strength of the first Hastur, whoever and whatever He was, manifested itself through the Sword of Aldones . . . so that Regis took on the majesty and power of the Son of Light, even as the one who held Sharra took on the Form of Fire . . .

Dyan, too, in the end, had not been able to strike with Sharra to wipe out his kin. All his life he had fought for the honor of the Comyn, though in strange ways, and in the end he had acted first to protect my daughter, then to protect me, and finally he could not strike down Regis . . .

The Love of Power or the Power of Love? I wonder if that question had beat in his mind, too, during the final moments of that battle?

Somewhere above me in the castle, I heard a sound, not with my physical ears, but in the recesses of my mind; cleared now from the searing presence of Sharra, I was conscious of it all through me; the sound of a child crying, a telepath child, alone, hungry, frightened, wailing for her mother who was dead and the father she half feared, half loved. And I knew where she was. I saw Regis, his shoulders bowed beneath his new and terrible burden, his hair incredibly turned white in that all-consuming battle, and saw him turn wearily toward the Castle. Had his grandfather survived that battle which must have rung in the minds of all the Comyn?

Yes; Danilo went to him and cared for him, lent him strength . . .

Regis heard the crying too, and turned to me, with a weary smile.

"Go and look after your daughter, Lew; she needs you, and—" unbelievably he smiled again, "she's old enough to have the Gift but not old enough to hold it within reasonable bounds. Unless you go and comfort her, she'll drive everyone in the Castle—everyone in the City—mad with her wailing!"

And I went in and ran unerringly up the stairs to the one place where Dyan had known I would not search for Marja and where she would be safely concealed; the Ridenow apartments which Lerrys and Dio had shared. And as I burst in through the great outer doors, hurrying to the empty room, I saw Dio holding Marja on her lap, but she could not silence her wailing and struggling until I bent over them and clasped them both in my arms.

Marja stopped crying and turned to me, the telepathic shrieking suddenly quieted, only soft hiccuping sobs remaining as she clung to me, sobbing. "Father! Father! I was so scared, and you didn't come and you didn't come and I was all alone, all alone and there was a fire, and I cried and cried and nobody heard me except this strange lady came and tried to pick me up . . ."

I quieted the hysterical outburst, pulling her to me.

"It's all right, *chiya,*" I crooned, holding her in one arm and Dio in the other. "It's all right, Father's here—" I could not give Dio a child of her own. but this child of my own blood had somehow survived out of all the holocaust that had raged in the Comyn . . . and never again would I mock at the power of love which had saved us both. I had wanted to die; but I was alive, and miraculously, beyond all, I was glad to be alive and life was good to me.

Laughing, I set Marja down, drawing Dio into my arms again. Never once did she ask a question about Callina. Perhaps she knew, perhaps she had been a part of all that great battle which, even now, I was beginning to doubt—had it ever happened except in my own mind? I never knew.

"We have just time," I said, "to file a stop on that Terran divorce action. I think it hasn't been ten days yet—or have I lost track of the time?"

She laughed, a wavering smile. "Ten days? No, not quite."

Marja interrupted us, setting up her telepathic demand again. *I'm hungry! And scared! Stop kissing her and hold me!*

Dio drew her close between us. "We'll get you a big breakfast right away, *chiya,*" she said softly, "and then someone will have to try teaching you the elementary manners of living in a telepathic family. If you are going to do that every time I kiss your father—or anything else, little daughter—I am afraid that I will start making noises like a wicked stepmother from the old fairy tales! So you will have to learn some manners, first thing!"

Incredibly, that made all three of us laugh. And then we went back to the Terran Zone to withdraw an unnecessary divorce decree. Somewhere along the way—I forget just where—we stopped and ate fresh hot bread and porridge at a cookstall, and everyone who looked at us took it for granted that I was out for an early breakfast with my wife and daughter. And I found I liked the feeling. I no longer felt them staring only at my scars.

If Dio had not accepted Marja . . . but she was not that kind of person. She had wanted my child, and now I had put my child in her care. The hurt would never leave her, for that pitiful monstrosity which should have been our son; but Dio never lived in the past. And now we had all the future before us.

Marja held on to my hand and Dio's as we went into the Terran Zone. I looked back, just once, at the Comyn Castle which lay behind us.

I knew I would never go back.

But I did go back, just once more. It was only a few days later, but Marja had already begun to call Dio "Mother."

EPILOGUE

"Crowned King? King of *what?*" Regis said, shaking his head gently at his grandfather. "Sir, with all respect, the Comyn effectively do not exist. Lew Alton survives, but he does not wish to remain at Armida—and I cannot see any reason why he should. The Ridenow have already bowed to the inevitable, and applied for their status as Terran citizens. Dyan is dead—and his son is a child three years old. The Lady of Aillard is dead, and so is her sister; no one remains among the Aillard but Merryl . . . and his twin sister, who is the mother of Dyan's son. The Elhalyn are gone . . . do you still think we must treat the Terrans as enemies, sir? I think it is time to accept that we are what they say—one of their lost colonies—and apply for protected status, to keep our world as it should be . . . immune to being overrun by Empire technology, but still part of the Empire."

Danvan Hastur bowed his head. He said, "I knew it would come to this in the end. What is it that you want to do, Regis?"

With that new and terrible sensitivity, Regis knew what his grandfather was feeling, and so his voice was very gentle as he spoke to the old man.

"I have asked Lawton to come and see you, sir. Remember he is blood kin to the Ardais and to the Syrtis, sir; he might have been among the Comyn."

Dan Lawton came into the room, and to Regis's surprise he bowed deeply and knelt before Danvan Hastur.

"Z'par servu, vai dom," he said quietly.

"What mockery is this?" demanded Hastur.

"Sir, no mockery," said Lawton without rising. "I am here to serve you in any way I can, Lord Hastur, to be certain that your ancient ways will not suffer."

"I thought we were now no more than a Terran colony . . ."

"I do not think you understand what it is to be an Empire world, *vai dom,*" said Lawton quietly. "It means that you have the right to define what Darkover will become; you who inhabit Darkover alone. You may share or not share your own fields of learning—though I hope we will be allowed to know something of matrix technology, so that nothing like this Sharra episode may ever arise again without our knowledge. You and you alone—you people of Darkover, I mean, not you personally, with all respect, sir—may determine how many Terrans and on what terms may be employed here or may settle here. And because your interests must be protected in the Federation of worlds that is the Empire, you have the right to appoint, or to elect, a representative in the Empire's Senate."

"A fine thought," said Danvan Hastur wearily, "but who is left that we could trust, after all the deaths in the Comyn? Do you think I am going to appoint that scamp Lerrys Ridenow, just because he knows Empire ways?"

"I would gladly serve you myself," said Lawton, "because I love my home world—it is my home world as well as yours, Lord Hastur, even though I have chosen to live as a Terran; I too was born beneath the Bloody Sun, and there is Comyn blood in my veins. But I think my task is here, so that there may be a Darkovan voice in the Terran Trade City. Regis has found a candidate, however."

He gestured to the door, and Lew Alton came in.

His scarred face looked calm now, without the tension and torment which had inhabited it for so long; Regis, looking at him, thought: *here is a man who has laid his ghosts. Would that I could lay mine!* Within him the memory blurred, *a time when he had been more than human, reaching from the center of the world to the sky, wielding monstrous power* . . . and now he was no more than human again and he felt small, powerless, shut up inside a single mind and skull . . .

"A man who knows Darkover and Terra alike," said Regis quietly, "Lewis-Kennard Montray-Alton of Armida, first Representative to the Imperial Senate from Cottman Four, known as Darkover." And Lew came and bowed before Lord Hastur.

"By your leave, sir, I am going out on the ship which takes to the stars at sunset, with my wife and daughter. I will gladly serve for a term, after which you will be able to educate the people of Darkover to choose their own representatives. . ."

Danvan Hastur held out his hand. He said, "I would gladly have seen your father in this post, *Dom* Lewis. The people of Darkover—and I myself—have cause to be grateful to the Altons."

Lew bowed and said, "I hope I may serve you well," and Hastur said, "All the Gods bless you and speed you on your way."

Regis left his grandfather talking with Lawton—he was sure a time would come when they would like and respect one another, if not yet—and went out into the anteroom with Lew. He took him into a kinsman's embrace. "Will you come back when your term is over, Lew? We need you on Darkover—"

A momentary look of pain crossed Lew's face, but he said, "I don't think so. Out there—on the edge of the Empire—there are new worlds. I—I can't look back."

There have been too many deaths here. . . .

Regis wanted to cry out, "Why should you go into exile again?" But he swallowed hard and bent his head, then raised it, after a moment, and said, "So be it, *bredu.* And wherever you go, the Gods go with you. *Adelandeyo.*"

He knew he would never see Lew again, and his whole heart went after him as he went out of the room. *The Empire is his, and a thousand million worlds beyond worlds.*

But my duty lies here. I am—Hastur.

And that was enough. Almost.

As the red sun was setting behind the high pass, Regis stood with Danilo on a balcony overlooking the Terran Zone, watching as the great Terran ship skylifted, bound outward to the stars. *Where I can never go. And he takes with him the last of my dreams of freedom, and of power. . . .*

Do I want the Love of Power or the Power of Love?

And suddenly he knew that he did not really envy Lew. No woman had ever loved him as Lew had been loved, no. But Dyan had left, in his death, a shining legacy of another kind of love; something he had heard, and only half remembered from his years in St. Valentine-of-the-Snows, returned suddenly to his mind.

"Dani, what is that thing the *cristoforos* say . . . greater love hath none. . . ."

Danilo returned, in the most ancient dialect of *casta*, the one they had spoken at the monastery:

"Greater love no man knoweth than he who will lay down his life for his fellow."

Dyan had laid his life down for them all, and in his death, Regis had come to a new understanding; love was love, no matter whence it came or in what form. Some day he might love a woman in this way; but if that day never came, he would accept the love that was his without shame or regret.

"I will not be King," he said, "I am Hastur; that is enough." An echo stirred in his mind, a memory that would never wholly surface.

Who are you?

Hastur . . . it was gone, like a stilled ripple in the Lake. He said, "I'm going to need a lot of—a lot of help, Dani."

And Danilo said, still in the most ancient dialect of Nevarsin, "Regis Hastur, I am your paxman, even to life or death."

Regis wiped his face . . . the evening fog was condensing into the first drops of rain, but it felt hot on his eyes. "Come," he said, "my grandfather must not be left too long alone, and we must take counsel how to educate our sons—Mikhail, and Dyan's little son. We can't stand here all night."

They turned and went side by side into the Castle. The last light faded from the sky, and the great ship, outward bound into the Empire, was only a star among a hundred thousand other stars.